1001 Dark Nights
Bundle 8

1001 Dark Nights Bundle 8
ISBN 978-1-945920-27-1

1001 Dark Nights Bundle 8

Six Novellas
By
Christopher Rice
Melissa Foster
Rebecca Zanetti
Liliana Hart
Jennifer Lyon
Riley Hart

1001 Dark Nights

EVIL EYE

CONCEPTS

Sign up for the 1001 Dark Nights Newsletter
and be entered to win a Tiffany Key necklace.

There's a contest every month!

Go to www.1001DarkNights.com to subscribe.

As a bonus, all subscribers will receive a free
1001 Dark Nights story
The First Night
by Lexi Blake & M.J. Rose

Table of Contents

One Thousand and One Dark Nights

Once upon a time, in the future…

*I was a student fascinated with stories and learning.
I studied philosophy, poetry, history, the occult, and
the art and science of love and magic. I had a vast
library at my father's home and collected thousands
of volumes of fantastic tales.*

*I learned all about ancient races and bygone
times. About myths and legends and dreams of all
people through the millennium. And the more I read
the stronger my imagination grew until I discovered
that I was able to travel into the stories… to actually
become part of them.*

*I wish I could say that I listened to my teacher
and respected my gift, as I ought to have. If I had, I
would not be telling you this tale now.
But I was foolhardy and confused, showing off
with bravery.*

*One afternoon, curious about the myth of the
Arabian Nights, I traveled back to ancient Persia to
see for myself if it was true that every day Shahryar
(Persian: شهریار, "king") married a new virgin, and then
sent yesterday's wife to be beheaded. It was written
and I had read, that by the time he met Scheherazade,
the vizier's daughter, he'd killed one thousand
women.*

*Something went wrong with my efforts. I arrived
in the midst of the story and somehow exchanged
places with Scheherazade – a phenomena that had
never occurred before and that still to this day, I
cannot explain.*

Now I am trapped in that ancient past. I have taken on Scheherazade's life and the only way I can protect myself and stay alive is to do what she did to protect herself and stay alive.

Every night the King calls for me and listens as I spin tales. And when the evening ends and dawn breaks, I stop at a point that leaves him breathless and yearning for more. And so the King spares my life for one more day, so that he might hear the rest of my dark tale.

As soon as I finish a story... I begin a new one... like the one that you, dear reader, have before you now.

KISS THE FLAME
A Desire Exchange Novella
By Christopher Rice

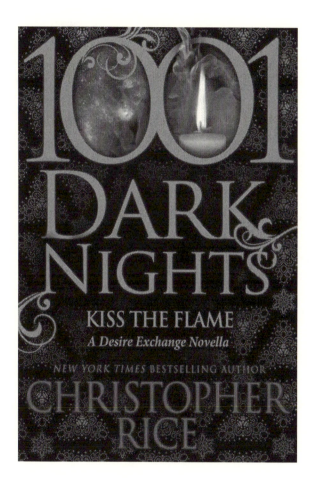

Acknowledgments

I feel like I've found a new family at 1,001 Dark Nights. I can't thank my fellow series authors enough for all they've done to welcome me into the world of romance. After years of publishing dark thrillers, it was time to try something different, something new. Something with a happier ending, and Liz Berry, M.J. Rose, and Jillian Stein not only made that possible, but rewarding.

Kimberly and "Shy Pam", you ladies are the best. Kasi, you're a great copyeditor and Asha, you're one of the best cover designers at work today. Period.

A big thank you to K.P. Simmons and Inkslinger P.R. as well.

Thanks also to my crew at The Dinner Party Show, in particular my best friend and co-host Eric Shaw Quinn, for making it possible to meet my writing deadlines while also producing a weekly live Internet radio broadcast. Ben Scuglia provided additional copyediting for which I'm very grateful.

A big thank you to everyone at The Montelone Hotel in New Orleans for making it such a special place to stay every time I visit. I hope you're happy with how you're portrayed in these pages. And I hope Lilliane figures out a way to conceal her identity so she can keep reserving a room there for many books to come. In fact, let me get to work on that one right now.

The Candlemaker

We see ghosts every day; we just don't realize it.

The woman a few feet behind you on the street corner, for instance, the one who doesn't quite belong. Maybe she gazes at you with too much interest and seems unaffected by the commotion surrounding you both. When you turn to look at her a second time, she vanishes, leaving you to wonder if she was a trick of your imagination or if she merged so quickly with the crowd of pedestrians surging through the intersection you just lost track of her.

This is how we see ghosts—often and without our knowledge.

They don't appear to us in states of dismemberment or disarray, leering at us like horror movie ghouls. They are not tricksters, not demons. Rather, they have been chosen by forces beyond our comprehension to remain among the living. But to qualify for this privilege, they must possess an undeniable respect, an undeniable *love,* for human beings. Only then will the spirit world see fit to grant them a particular purpose that justifies their continued visits to our mortal plane.

For years now people in the French Quarter have caught glimpses of a handsome, elegantly dressed man who takes long walks in the rain, his silk vests and perfectly pressed slacks bone-dry underneath the purple bloom of his umbrella. But glimpses are all they get. If someone's curious look turns into a lingering stare, if their expression becomes suspicious, this man employs the favored trick of all ghosts; he halts the clock of human experience and quickens his steps until he's found a comfortable distance between himself and his suspicious observer. Then he releases his grip on what we ordinary mortals call seconds and minutes.

The same can be said for those who walk past his tiny shop in the middle of the day, its plate glass windows filled with shelves holding rows of fat candles in burnt umber glass containers. At first glance, they assume the place is closed because the items inside are so expensive, potential customers must make an appointment to gain admittance. But this ludicrous proposition— how expensive can a candle be, really?—doesn't hold them for more than a few steps. When they turn to get a second look, the store and its contents have vanished without a trace, leaving them convinced their passing glimpse of purple wax was just a trick of the mind.

But the shop's tiny front door does open for a select few. To these people, a wood plank, hand-painted sign appears over the entrance, bearing the outline of a small gold flame, and the shop's name, *Feu du Coeur*. They are drawn through the shop's entrance by a smell so overpowering it brings tears of gratitude to their eyes or a lustful quickening to their pulse. For them, the light within looks inviting and warm, and the man waiting for them inside, the same man who takes long walks in the rain under his purple umbrella, offers them not only his name, Bastian Drake, but a chance to change their lives forever.

1

LANEY

Before college, Laney didn't believe men like Michael Brouchard existed, men who look brawny enough to play for the NFL but spend their days leading passionate discussions of paintings like *The Kiss* by Gustav Klimt. Men who don't trip over the pronunciation of words like *mélange* and *rococo*, who combine their fierce intelligence with artfully tousled dark hair and thick-framed glasses that make them look like Clark Kent. Men with strong, veiny, muscular forearms dusted with light tufts of hair. Forearms they keep exposed by rolling the sleeves of their plaid shirts up just far enough to offer teasing glimpses to their admiring students, glimpses that leave those students, students like Laney Foley, wondering what it would feel like to have those powerful hands slide up their thighs, grasping, kneading, before their owner leans in all professor-like and asks if he can—

"Miss Foley?"

"Sure," Laney grunts.

"*Sure?*"

"I mean...yes..."

A ripple of laughter spreads through the tiny classroom. Laney's cheeks flame. There are only ten other students in her discussion section for Foundations of Western Art II, but she's convinced they're all peering into her mind and tittering over the dirty thoughts she's been having about their TA.

The Kiss fills the pull-screen across the room, a patchwork of gold and other bright colors framing the placid facial expression of a beautiful young woman held in her lover's firm, upright embrace. Its image is cast by the digital projector sitting a few feet from where Michael has been pacing for most of class. Something about all that glittering eroticism in the same small classroom as her handsome young professor has sent her on a fantasy spiral and now she can barely recover.

He's not a professor, she reminds herself. *Not technically. He's a grad student. A teaching assistant. Just a few years older than me.* The real reason for the slight age difference between them is not something Laney wants to share with her classmates. Most of them drive cars with monthly notes three times her parent's mortgage. God forbid she get branded the girl from Lafourche Parish who had to bust her hump in community college for two years before she could land a scholarship good enough to cover the cost of tuition here.

"In 1894, Gustav Klimt was commissioned to create three paintings to decorate the ceiling of the Great Hall at the University of Vienna," her teacher says. "I asked you what year those paintings were destroyed."

"1945," Laney says.

"Meeeaaaaaah," erupts the Hollister-clad frat boy a few desks away. It's the guy's best vocal impersonation of a wrong answer buzzer from a game show, and he inflicts it on them all at least twice a class. In high school, Jake Briffel was probably the kid who spent most of his time shoving smaller kids into lockers. Now he brandishes the one weapon a bully can still get away with using once they reach college—his mouth. So far, all of Laney's discussion sections have offered up some version of a Jake Briffel, and she's been pretty good at ignoring most of them.

"Listen to the question, genius," Jake says. "Klimt got the commission in eighteen ninety-four. You really think they would have waited a whole decade to deploy his art?"

Ugh, Laney thinks. *Why'd he have to make it so easy? I totally could have ignored him if he hadn't made it so—*

"Actually," Laney says. "His question was when were the

paintings *destroyed*, not *deployed*. Because we're talking about art. Not soldiers. You probably got confused because the paintings were destroyed by the Nazis when they retreated from Vienna. Which happened in 1945. As I just said."

Jake's anger radiates like the heat of a small fire. She could care less. She's too stricken by the expression on her teacher's face.

Maybe Michael Brouchard is proud of her. It's probably the most she's said in class this whole year. But do you moisten your bottom lip with the tip of your tongue and then bite it gently and pretty much look like you're about to spread someone across your desk just 'cause you're feeling proud of them?

"Thanks, scholarship," Jake snarls. "I'm sure your Nazi history will go over big with the other lunch ladies at the caff." He caps off this insult with a contorted facial expression meant to imply that *lunch ladies* are by their very nature mentally challenged.

She should laugh it off. But the twofold insult—the reference to both her scholarship and her work study hours—catches her so off guard she finds herself blinking madly, suddenly terrified that she might be on the verge of stunned tears, as if Jake's words had the force of a literal slap.

How did he find out about her scholarship? Silly of her to think somebody wouldn't eventually. Most colleges are like small towns, she figures, just another place where a secret can only be kept for a day. Why should Chamberland University be any different? And it hasn't been the easiest—slinging meatloaf and spoonfuls of brown rice for the few freshman stuck on meal plan. But it's a job like any other, and God knows, she's had worse jobs. Graveyard shift at a gas station on the West Bank; busser at a French Quarter nightclub where she was too young to serve drinks but old enough to have her ass grabbed by an endless stream of conventioneers. But Briffel's cruel joke has her suddenly convinced everyone in school's been laughing at her under their breath as they carry their trays to their tables. *Look at the sophomore who's three years older than the other sophomores. The one whose mother used to shuck oysters for a living before she keeled over dead at thirty-one. The one who stays up late mixing cheap drug store moisturizers together 'till she's got a recipe as potent as whatever top brand moisturizer the other girls here are using to look like runway models at eight in the frickin' morning.*

She stops blinking. Her vision clears, thank God, leaving her with strained breaths and a rushing sound in her ears.

When she looks up, she finds herself staring into her teacher's eyes. She's never found anger beautiful before, but that's the only word she can think of to describe the rage that's hardened Michael Brouchard's features into statuesque angles. He's been studying her, taking in the physical signs of how deeply Briffel's comment wounded her, and when he shifts his focus from her to Briffel, Laney hears the sound of a gun cocking somewhere in her mind.

"Mr. Briffel," Michael says. "Since we're all speaking so freely now apparently, allow me to take this moment to tell you how impressed I am with the speed at which you Google the answers to most of my questions on your phone underneath your desk. However, I'm a bit concerned that even those assignments for which you are given adequate time to prepare are also reading like you just Googled a bunch of crap on your phone under your desk. So with that in mind, I have the following suggestion. If you would like to place your focus on those classmates of yours who are working *a lot* harder than you are, perhaps you should take what you see there as motivation for something other than an inappropriate comment which could result in a reduction of your grade."

"You can't do that," Briffel whines. "You can't reduce my grade just 'cause I made a *joke.*"

"Try me," Michael Brouchard says. It's not quite a growl, but it's close enough to one that Laney can almost smell fur.

Michael rests both fists on the front edge of Jake Briffel's desk. The frat boy stares up at him slack-jawed, too frightened to come up with his next move or even a passable response.

Laney wouldn't be surprised to see a wet spot in the dude's pants.

Lord knows, there's about to be one in hers, although of a different origin.

Briffel's been a jerk from day one, but he's never been quite this mean to anyone in class before now. Maybe that's the only reason their teacher went after him with such focused, passionate anger. But when Michael turns away from Briffel's desk, his eyes meet hers for a telling instant. Just long enough to tell her he's got her back. Just long enough to suggest his thoughts about her might be as full of passion and abandon as the thoughts she's been having about him.

Laney's no stranger to lust. She is, however, a stranger to gorgeous, intelligent men leaping to her defense. The combination of the two not only makes her head spin, it makes the memory of Briffel's cruel joke feel as distant as China.

"Laney?"

Michael's call halts her steps and sends gooseflesh racing up her back. It sounds like he's only a few feet away, which means he must have rushed out of class with most of the other students in order to catch up with her. Two urges battle for control of her legs—the urge to run like hell, and the urge to fall to her knees on the sidewalk in a gesture of total worship as he approaches.

"Too much?" Michael asks once he's a few feet away.

He's winded, she realizes. *He* did *run to catch up with me.* The thought of him giving the brush-off to other students as he slipped from the classroom in pursuit makes her feel both giddy and guilty.

It's a crisp fall day in New Orleans, just cool enough for a light, hooded sweater like the one he clearly slid on in a hurry given how unevenly it sits across his shoulders. Sunlight bounces off the tinted windows of The Jillian Stein Arts Center behind him, making the trees that surround the building look like they're on fire. It lances the oak branches overhead, a shaft of it falling across his right eye, causing the hazel iris to shimmer in a way that makes her gasp.

She'd never thought of a man as being *beautiful* before she met Michael. Plenty of guys she'd met were hot, handsome, or *ruggedly handsome*, that special third category she used to define edgy, unconventional sex appeal. But something about his combination of hard angles and lingering, thoughtful expressions, of determined masculinity matched with a gentle, careful demeanor—beautiful is the only word she can think of to describe those contradictions and the effect they have on her pulse. And it's the only word she can literally think as he stares into her eyes, waiting for a response to his cryptic question.

"I'm sorry," she finally says. "Too much? What do you mean?"

"Some students, they don't like it when…you know, a teacher kind of steps up to bat for them. It makes them feel—"

"Nice?" she says before she can stop herself.

At first, it looks like her answer has made him wince. But after another second or two, it's clear Michael is fighting a smile so strong it looks ready to conquer his face. But he's fighting it, that's for sure. Because the fact that he made her feel *nice* pleases him, and it pleases him a little more than a teacher should be pleased by his student.

"Or nice," he finally says.

"I appreciated it. Honestly."

"Well, you know, Jake is such a jerk and—wow. I shouldn't be saying that. Sorry. I shouldn't be talking about another student that way. I shouldn't…"

And suddenly he's lost his grip on his words and his eyes are roaming her body as if he's thinking all sorts of things about it he shouldn't. And she can feel Michael, the guy who's only three years older than she is, fighting with Mr. Brouchard, the guy who's supposed to be her teacher, the guy who's probably signed some sort of contract that says he won't do any of the things he's thinking about doing to her right now with any student ever.

"You make me say things I shouldn't, Laney Foley."

"Make you?"

"Sorry. That's not exactly fair, I guess."

"You apologize a lot when we're not in class, Mr. Brouchard."

"Yeah, well, whatever I did to make you call me Mr. Brouchard, I apologize."

"You're right. Jake is a jerk."

"Still, I shouldn't have said it…"

"The thing in class?"

"No. Just now. When I called him a jerk. The thing in class? If you're good with it, I'm good with it. Because to be honest, that was the only thing that mattered to me. That you were good with it."

"I'm very good with it," she says. It feels like she spoke in almost a whisper, but Michael nods like he's heard her clearly.

"A couple weeks into semester, you went quiet. I wasn't sure what happened. But I missed you. I missed your contributions, I mean, and today, when you spoke up again, I was so happy, I wasn't about to let Jake Briffel scare you into hiding again."

"Hiding?" She hates the defensive tone in her voice. "I've got perfect attendance. For the discussions and the lectures."

"There are lots of ways to hide."

"Still…"

"I didn't mean to offend you."

"No, it's just… I'm not like a lot of the students here, Michael."

"Yeah, I know. You're better than most of them."

"Well, no, I just meant that—thank you, by the way, for saying that—but what I meant was when I first got here I was kind of…Well, I was kind of a bitch."

"Not in class, you weren't," he says.

"Everywhere else I was. I guess because I'm one of the *lunch ladies*. I was expecting people to reject me right off so I thought I'd beat them to the punch by speaking my mind even when they didn't really ask me to."

"What's wrong with speaking your mind?"

"Well, for instance, if I gave you my honest opinion of that sweater and you didn't ask for it…"

Startled, Michael lifts his right arm and examines the heather-gray material of the sweater's sleeve. "You don't like this sweater?"

"No. It's great. I was just using it as an example. But if I really didn't like it, and I just told you I didn't like it even if you hadn't asked me if I'd liked it or not, well, then, you know…that would kinda be, you know, like how I was when I first started…" The last time she felt this stupid and nervous she'd been stumbling through a toast at her friend Tiffany's wedding, a toast Tiffany had asked her to give at the last minute because no one in Tiffany's family was willing to salute her marriage to a groom who was fifteen years older than her and had shown up to the ceremony in a tuxedo-painted T-shirt and khaki shorts with the bulge of his flask visible in the back pocket. Her face feels like it's turned into sandpaper, her throat like she's breathing through a straw, and all this is distracting her from the fact that Michael Brouchard is pulling his sweater off, sleeve by sleeve, reaching up and adjusting the collar of his shirt, making sure the top button is still undone, before looping the sweater over the top of his satchel. Once he's done, he gives Laney a warm smile.

"Is that better?" he asks.

A patch of hard chest is visible now. And then there's that thick, muscular neck, and those forearms, those forearms of total sexual destruction, forearms she'd love to leave handprints on in her efforts to pull him deeper inside of her. The only thing that would make the scene better would be if he were gently sliding a chocolate covered cherry in between her lips and asking if he could rub her feet.

"Better," she says.

"Good," he says, with a smile that almost knocks her on her ass. Has he ever smiled that way with her in class? Has he ever smiled that way with *anyone* in class?

"So this *I'm not allowed to speak my mind* trip you're on," he says. "I'm feeling like these words aren't entirely yours," Michael says.

"My friend Cat kinda contributed."

"I see…"

"Do you?"

"I feel like I'm seeing more of you today than I ever have."

"Yeah, well, it's the first time we've ever talked outside of class. Really earning your paycheck with that deduction, aren't you professor?"

"Okay. A little bite there. I can see what Cat's talking about."

"Oh, that's nothing, Mister Brouchard."

"Michael…"

"Sorry. Michael."

"It's the Rose Scholarship, isn't it?" he asks suddenly, as if he's nervous to put the question so bluntly.

"I'm sorry?"

"The scholarship you're on. It's the Rose Scholarship."

"You've been researching me?"

"Yes," he says. "Yes, I have." Not sort of. Not kind of. He didn't attach qualifiers to it. He didn't apologize for it, either. He simply said, yes, he's been researching her just like she's been researching him; hunting down his Facebook profile to find out how old he was, Googling his full name to find out where he did his undergraduate work—LSU—and if he was also born in New Orleans—he was, and if like her, he had to fight and claw for just about everything good in his life, or if like most of the other students here, privileges galore had been handed to him on a silver platter by several assistants. She hasn't been able to find an answer to the last question, and she wonders if this is the best way to do it. By actually talking to him, rather than tapping keys on her computer late at night while building a fantasy life for him. For *both* of them.

"Yes," she says. "It's the Elizabeth Rose Scholarship."

"Full ride, but you lose it the minute your GPA drops under a three point six."

"That's the one," she answers.

"That scholarship's got something like six hundred applicants every year. That's pretty damn impressive, Miss Foley. Nothing to be ashamed of."

"Who said I was ashamed?"

"Briffel implied you should be. I'm here to say he's wrong. Dead wrong. And a jerk. But like I said, I'm not supposed to call him that."

"And if I'm not supposed to call you Mister Brouchard, then you shouldn't call me Miss Foley."

"My apologies, Laney."

"No more apologies either. You know, unless you do something really shitty."

"Can I buy you a drink?" he asks. It's the first time he's broken eye contact with her since they started this conversation. "A not-shitty drink."

"Like a *drink*-drink?"

"Yes. You're twenty-three, right? I'm sorry…if you're sober, I didn't mean to…"

Yep. He's totally been Googling me. Or Facebooking me. Or whatever I've been doing to him.

"No. I'm not sober. It's just…"

"Or if there's another way you'd like to celebrate."

"Celebrate what?"

"The fact that you got the Rose Scholarship."

"C'mon. It's not like it's the *Rhodes* Scholarship."

"Now you're starting to sound like Jake Briffel."

"Lord. Kill me now."

"Not a chance. All right, fine, so I guess I missed the big blowout you had when you found out you got the scholarship and that's it? No more celebrations for you?"

"There wasn't a blowout. There wasn't *anything*, really."

"Really?"

"No. When I got the news, I made the mistake of telling my dad."

"The *mistake*?"

"He thinks college is a waste of time. And he thought the time I spent trying to get into a good one was also a waste of time. So mostly he looks at me and just sees…a waste of time."

It's one thing to make this kind of joke with someone like her friend Cat. Sarcasm is their preferred means of communication, after all. But Michael's been so gentle and kind, stating the cold hard fact of her family situation plainly feels like she's showing him an open wound.

"I have a feeling you're a lot more than that," Michael says softly.

"Than a waste of time?" she asks.

"I can't imagine referring to someone of your accomplishments and intelligence as a…waste of time," Michael says. She can feel the pulse of protective anger moving through her teacher as he struggles with these final words, as potent and shiver-inducing as when he stared down that loudmouth Jake Briffel. And because Michael is a polite and intelligent man, she realizes this is his most diplomatic way of calling her father a jackass. Which is exactly what her father is.

"He got over it. Eventually. The way he gets over everything."

"And how's that?"

"He never talks about it again."

"That's rough."

Oh, honey, she almost says. *That's nothing. Let me tell you about the three times I got held up when I was working at the gas station. Or my best friend from high school who dropped out junior year because she got pregnant and ended up turning tricks for six months after she had the kid and before I dragged her into the first rehab that would take her family's crappy health care plan.* But that's the kind of speech Old Laney would have launched into at the drop of a hat, laying it on too thick and too soon so her classmates would know from the get-go she wasn't like them; so she could spare herself the pain of future rejection once they found out where she'd come from.

New Laney lays low. New Laney flies under the radar, blends in as much as she can even though she can't afford the outfits required to do it.

She didn't come to Chamberland University to make friends. She's here because she wants options, the option to be something other than a gas station attendant or a lunch lady. Maybe it *was* her fault she'd never found a way to say that to her father without making him feel bad about his own life. But that's just the way it is. For now, anyway. Until she can get a job good enough that her dad can finally retire. Maybe then he can finally take the time he needs to grieve the loss of her mother, a task he's been putting off for years. But until that blessed time comes, she doesn't want to spend the next three years completely alone as she builds a better life for herself, and while she's got no plans to pledge a sorority any time soon, maybe if she follows Cat's instructions, she'll have less trouble finding study partners.

"It was my fault," she says, because it sounds like something New Laney should say. Humble, meek, obedient. Not angry.

Not wounded. Not poor.

"How's that?" Michael asks.

"He'd just worked a double offshore and I shouldn't have—you know, I shouldn't have expected him to be excited for me when he already told me he wouldn't be. I just thought that when the actual news came in, maybe he'd..."

"So what you're saying is you never had a party or a dinner or any kind of celebration at all?"

For some reason, this admission shames her, even though it shouldn't. Even though she wasn't the one who stormed out of the house in a rage because she'd dared to speculate about more than one possible future for herself. But there's no judgment in Michael's voice. There isn't any in his expression either.

"No," she finally says. "Never."

"All right, then. I'll pick you up at seven."

"What?"

"Eight's better? Maybe six thirty?"

"Seven's fine, but what do you—I mean, what are we doing?"

"Where do you live?"

"I'm in Berry Hall on East Campus."

"Great. I'll be outside at seven."

He's walking away quickly.

She calls after him, and when he stops and turns, she can see the eagerness and the fear in his expression, both of which he was trying to hide with a rapid-fire invitation and a hasty escape. A dozen different versions of a rejection gather in her mind. *You're my teacher, I can't. It's not appropriate. You're way too hot. I can't be trusted alone with you.*

"Why don't I meet you there?" she says.

There's a flicker of disappointment in his expression, but his furrowed brow is soon joined by a cocky grin. "But you don't know where we're going," he says.

"Right. That's why you have to tell me."

Don't ask me why. Please don't ask me why I'm afraid to get in a car alone with you. New Laney isn't supposed to tell those kinds of stories anymore.

"Do you know where Perry's is? In the Quarter?"

Everyone knows where Perry's is. It's one of the most famous restaurants in town. All she can manage is a nod.

"See you there at seven, Miss Foley."

His sudden reversion to the use of her last name stabs her in the gut. Is it because she just refused his offer of a ride? Is he rounding down their plans from date to friendly dinner?

A friendly dinner at *Perry's?* Fat chance. A candlelit courtyard, a bubbling fountain, those weathered, fern-dappled French Quarter walls rising on all sides of them. She's seen pictures of the place online and in magazines and it practically oozes romance. If he'd wanted a friendly dinner, there were plenty of diners near campus where they could meet.

"What should I wear?" she calls after him.

"Whatever you like to celebrate in," he says, and then he's disappeared into a crowd of students heading toward the nearby parking lot, and she doesn't manage a deep breath until several minutes after she can't see him anymore.

2

"Either you get some teacher dick tonight or I quit being friends with you."

"Cat! *Honestly!*"

They're heading away from campus and in the direction of the French Quarter when Laney's best friend powers down the driver's side window of her BMW. A brisk wind rips through the leather-upholstered car, blowing Cat Burke's platinum blonde hair back from one side of her angelic face and carrying with it the clatter of the lumbering St. Charles Avenue streetcars they're flying past at Laney doesn't-want-to-know-how-many miles an hour.

Cat drives like she consumes Diet Coke—relentlessly and without regard for her well-being, and Laney knows full well her best friend isn't willing to hear anyone's opinion about either compulsion, including Laney's. But she's startled Cat waited this long to open her window. She usually drives with it down, just like a smoker would. Only Cat isn't a smoker. To Laney's knowledge Cat's never smoked at all, except maybe the occasional joint at a party, after which she usually complains of nausea and heads straight back to her dorm room to take a three-hour nap covered in Funyuns dust. The way Laney figures it, keeping the window open while she drives is one of Cat's many desperate methods for regulating her own body temperature, which always seems to run several degrees above normal, another side effect of being one of the most hyperactive people Laney has ever met.

Cat Burke is always hot. Cat Burke is always full of opinions. Cat Burke always has a plan, usually a plan for someone else. Usually whoever is trapped in her car with her, and usually that person is Laney. And the reason it's taken Cat this long to lower her window is because she's convinced the lecture she's been giving Laney is super-important.

"Cat. Honey. Let's get something clear. You're picking me up tonight even if I don't sleep with him."

"Nope. You'll get a cab. This is an ultimatum, Sister Mary Laney Foley. Like one of those thrillers you love to read when you're in a crappy mood. I'm calling it *The Laney Ultimatum*. Starring Laney, Professor Forearms, and his headboard. See, I know big words too."

"*Forearms* is not a big word."

"I meant *ultimatum*, smart ass!"

"Right, and I get that you *think* it's an ultimatum, Cat. And I think it's sweet that you think you can give me ultimatums. But if you don't pick me up tonight when I call you, I'm going to start a rumor that you're a serial killer. And I'm going to start it on the *WWL Eyewitness News*. Got it?"

"Whatever, Miss Independent," Cat fires back. "You took my ultimatum about the dress, didn't you?"

"I added a jacket."

"After I told you to!" Cat barked.

"You told me to go sleeveless and I refused."

"You're covering up too much 'cause you're trying to pretend like you don't want to sleep with him!"

"I'm trying not to freeze to death!"

"It's sixty-five degrees outside!" Cat whined. "Whatever! For the last time, I am *not* picking you up tonight. And the reason I'm not picking you up tonight is because you are going home with this man the minute he even hints that he wants you to. And you know why?" Cat bends toward her over the gearshift, growling like an angry lion. "Because he's *hhhhhhawwwwwwwwwwwt*. With five h's and ten w's."

"And you're being shallow," Laney hissed back, "with twenty s's and eleven o's."

"Oh, don't you get all high and mighty on me. You've been

mooning over this guy for months."

"Yeah, and *mooning* isn't necessarily the best basis for a good relationship."

"I'm not talking about *that* kind of mooning!"

"I know what kind of mooning you're talking about. Stop interrupting me! What I'm saying is that *mooning* is something you do over One Direction or Five Seconds of—"

"Oh, so now you're saying you wouldn't go out on a date with One Direction? That's just crazy talk!"

"*The whole band?*"Laney snapped. "Are you nuts? You think I'm just going to lie back and let them take turns?"

"I guess that sounds better in the fanfic version," Cat muttered.

"What kind of fanfic are you reading?"

"Leave me alone. Tumblr doesn't do it for me."

"Cat, let's just agree that you and I have different value systems in this area, okay?"

"Oh, kiss my butt, Laney Foley. Kiss my *butt* with your value systems!"

"I don't even know what that means."

"You have been making goo-goo eyes at Michael Brouchard for the whole semester and now he finally got the message and suddenly you're a nun? Oh, and by the way, the guy's not only *hot* but he likes to talk about the kinda stuff you like to talk about and—"

"And what kind of *stuff* is that?"

"Oh, you know," Cat answers, talking under her breath and out of one corner of her mouth. "Art and books. And—more art."

"Why are we friends?"

"'Cause I don't put up with your b.s., girlfriend. Day one, I saw right through your whole routine."

"I don't have a routine," Laney groans, even though she does. Or she did, and she knows Cat's right.

"Hi, I'm Laney," Cat's impersonation captures the quiet tone Laney often drops into her voice because it softens the harsh Cajun accent she inherited from her mother. "And I can never enjoy life or have any fun because I have to work harder than you because my parents didn't buy me a car—"

"They *didn't* buy me a car. They have *never* bought me a car, and they never will buy me a car, Miss BMW, because they can barely afford to buy themselves a car."

"Be that as it may!" Cat responds with the grand dismissiveness of an inconvenienced monarch. "You still act like you have to work harder than me—"

"I *do* have to work harder than you," Laney says. "If my GPA drops below a three point six, I don't get to go to school here anymore. If you get a C, your father sends you consolation roses."

"*Be* that as it *may*," Cat responds with a careful and menacing enunciation that tells Laney's she's on the verge of pointing out one too many hard facts about their vastly different backgrounds. "When you're not working, it's your responsibility to actually enjoy your life. And that does not include staying in your dorm room all night reading sad books about gnomes."

"There are no *gnomes* in *Lord of the Rings*."

"Still!"

"And the trilogy has a happy ending, by the way."

"Says you."

"And you know, there are some people who consider Tolkien to be one of the greatest novelists of all time."

"And if he could get you to go outside once in a while, I'd feel the same."

"Seriously. Why are we friends?"

"'Cause I'm one of the only people you couldn't scare away when you got here," Cat says. There's more truth to that statement than Laney would like. "So don't you scare him away tonight just because he makes you have feelings you can't control. That's all I'm saying, okay?"

Despite the degree to which the woman frays her nerves, Laney adores Cat Burke. Her new best friend shares the loud, brassy no-time-for-bullshit quality of some of Laney's favorite cousins, and her dad on a good day, and that's the real reason they became friends right off the bat. Most of the other girls at school were too busy finding eight hundred different ways to avoid expressing a real feeling that might endanger their chances of landing a rich husband. But Laney's favorite thing about Cat by far is her tendency to cap off an elaborate diatribe with the expression, *That's all I'm saying, okay?*

They ride in silence for a few minutes, a silence punctuated by Cat's desperate slurps from her Diet Coke.

"This is a risk," Laney finally says. "This is a really big risk, Cat."

"Most good things are, honey."

"Still."

"Still what?"

"He's..."

"Three years older than you. That's all. Who cares what the rule book says?"

"I care what my scholarship says," Laney says. She's staring out the window at the passing parade of Greek Revival mansions, houses she used to dream of living in as a child, never once believing she'd someday have the chance to attend college in the same neighborhood.

"You're really afraid he's going to drop your grade if you have one bad date?" Cat asks softly, as if she can sense the thoughts running through Laney's head won't be dispelled by a smart remark or a sarcastic ultimatum.

"No," Laney says. "No, of course not. I'm afraid we're gonna have one really good date. *Really* good. And then another really good date. And then another. And then something will..."

"Something will what?" Cat asks. The bite and the fight have both gone out of her voice.

"Something will go wrong. I don't know. He'll lose interest. Or maybe I will. Maybe he'll turn out to..."

Maybe he'll pin me to the passenger seat by throwing one strong arm across my chest like Bobby Dautrieve did, start snarling at me about how I'm a bitch and a tease cause all I wanted to do was kiss, and who the hell did I think I was trying to get myself into a good school when really I'd never do better than a good-looking guy like him. And maybe then, I won't have my father's switchblade like I did with Bobby, won't have the wherewithal to drive it down in between his legs, close enough to snag the fabric of his jeans on the blade, but not his flesh. Won't have the time to get away like I did with Bobby, 'cause he wasn't sure if he'd been stabbed or not so he just decided to scream his head off while I ran fast enough to beat the band.

"Laney?" Cat's voice cuts through the scary flashback strobing through Laney's mind.

"Maybe he'll turn out to be horrible and then I'll feel like I'm stuck with him 'til the semester's over. Just so he won't punish me."

"He won't punish you, Laney."

"You don't know that. *I* don't know that. *He* probably doesn't even know that. Jerks never think they're jerks."

"Exactly. Bad men don't wear uniforms. But the good ones don't either. That's why you gotta see what they've got under their clothes to find out who they *really* are. You know what I'm saying?"

"I know you're talking about sex. Again."

"No, I'm using sex to point out what Professor Forearms would probably call a *universal truth*."

"Now that is a pretty big word. Or term, excuse me."

"Uh-huh. Whatever. Point is, if you're going to find out who someone is, you actually have to get to know them. And sometimes that means taking a risk."

"I know that. But this is a *big* risk, Cat."

"Right. And maybe that means it'll be a big reward."

"You know, you act like you're this big sex bomb, but it's not like you're hopping into beds all over campus or anything."

"Laney, I'm not talking about the size of his junk. I'm talking about *life*."

"Life?"

"Yeah. *Life.* You can't live life in your head or in books. And you can't live it in fear either."

"I know. I just—"

"Just *nothing.* You deserve something better than fending off drunken frat boys. For one, you're older than most of them, and for two, you don't have much in common with any of them. *This* guy might be just right for you."

"This *teacher,*" she says. "This teacher might be just right for me."

"Whatever. If he does anything remotely shitty I'll totally lie to everyone and say he put his hands all over me and tried to trade grades for sex."

"You're not one of his students."

"Who cares? I'll get one of his actual students to do it. I'm real persuasive with Jell-O shots."

The image of Cat and one of Laney's stumbling, inebriated classmates trying to recount a badly rehearsed and bogus tale of sexual harassment to a school administrator reduces Laney to tears of laughter.

"Or you could just agree to pick me up tonight," Laney says. "That would make things a lot easier. For now, at least."

"Oh, of course, I will. You don't really think I'm going to leave you stranded down there if it doesn't go well?"

"I don't know. You can be pretty stubborn, Cat."

"Takes one to know one," Cat says. "No, seriously. I'll pick you up if you need me to. That said, a real gentleman would drive you home even if he ain't gettin' any. Info like that is all part of the discovery process."

"Yeah, well, I don't get in cars with guys on the first date."

"Yet another thing you're gonna have to get over."

Laney ponders telling Cat the story of Bobby Dautrieve and her father's switchblade, but she's in no mood to let any of her horrible past dating experiences out of the little boxes she keeps them in, not when she's poised to have a night so magical it could make them all seem like hazy, distant memories.

"One thing at a time, Cat," Laney answers, before she realizes she's squeezing her clasped hands in between her knees tightly enough to cause pain in the heels of both palms. "One thing at a time."

3

Laney has walked past Perry's countless times during French Quarter bar crawls, gazing covetously into its lantern-lit courtyard. She's always assumed the only way she'd be able to score a meal there would be if a friend of hers landed a job as a bartender. But now, here she is, giving Michael's last name to the restaurant's handsome maître d', following him under a soaring wrought iron archway that feels like the gateway to a royal palace.

Most of the restaurant is contained inside a restored, two-story carriage house that sits at the back of an expansive, planter-filled courtyard. The house has a long, narrow balcony traveling the length of its second floor, and at one corner of it, Michael stands behind his empty chair next to a candlelit table for two. Laney's got at least another minute of following the host through the rings of cast iron tables that surround the courtyard's gurgling stone fountain before she reaches him, but her teacher has already greeted her arrival like a perfect gentleman.

Once inside, Laney mounts the rickety wooden steps leading to the second floor, her heart hammering the whole time. Her outfit is a fail, she's suddenly sure of it. She should have listened to Cat. And she's frantically re-dressing Michael in her mind, making him less imposing, less dashing, less desirable. But when she steps out onto the balcony, he looks even better than he did from below. His brown corduroy blazer has leather elbow patches, and the top three buttons of his dark blue dress shirt are undone. When she's within a few feet of the table, she catches a whiff of his cologne, an intoxicating scent that makes her think of backyard campfires and vanilla ice cream. Then she sees the Mylar balloons tied to the back of her empty chair, stamped with celebratory expressions written in various bright colors: CONGRATULATIONS! AMAZING! GOOD WORK!

Michael Brouchard has staged the congratulatory dinner she never had, the one her father effectively canceled a year before when he stormed out of the house in a rage. As if the balloons weren't enough, there's a bottle of champagne chilling in an ice bucket next to the table. Laney hesitates behind her empty chair, grasping the back of it with one sweaty hand. She reads the champagne bottle's label in the flickering candlelight. It's Veuve Clicquot, the vintage, her first year of high school.

They've only had one conversation that's lasted longer than a few minutes, and already Michael has filled a gap in her life. Not only that, he recognized it was there in the first place, that it was pulling at the fabric of her self-worth more than she wanted to admit. She knew tonight would be full of seductive risks, but didn't expect to start here, with an overwhelming sense of having been seen and heard and valued.

He gestures to her empty chair, waits for her to take her seat before taking his own. Only once she's seated does she realize Michael had extended his hand toward hers and she'd been too distracted by the balloons and the champagne to notice. Now there's no going back to rectify her rudeness without sounding like a sputtering idiot. The host, who has stood by politely throughout her hesitation, hands her a menu and departs. She's folding her napkin across her lap when she sees a large envelope resting against the edge of her plate, as large as a wedding invite. Her name is written on the outside in precise, draftsman-like handwriting. Just her first name. Not her last name. And not *Miss Foley*, which they both agreed he wouldn't call her anymore.

Laney.

Her hands shake as she tears open the envelope, as she unfolds the piece of heavy sketch paper inside of it. The breath goes out of her when she finds herself staring down at the amazingly detailed pencil sketch of—*me. That's me. That's me holding a rose in one hand while more rose petals shower down all sides of me. Roses for the Rose Scholarship. Oh, my God. He drew* me.

The card seems to waver suddenly. She's blinking back tears.

She can't remember the last time anyone has been this thoughtful, this kind. She's never thought of herself as a victim of abuse. But what do you call an entire lifetime of having your own intelligence, your own competence used against you, an entire lifetime of everyone from your parents to your friends thinking they don't really have to show up for you because you do such a good job of showing up for yourself?

Sometimes you don't know you've got a shell around your heart until it cracks.

Get it together, Laney. Get it—

"Laney…are you all right?" Michael asks.

A sane and reasonable answer is right on the tip of her tongue.

And then she snorts.

Her hand flies to her nose to prevent a messy disaster, but there's no hiding the tears now. And Michael's expression goes from slightly wounded—maybe he thought she was about to laugh at all his beautiful gestures—to outright concern.

"Wow," Michael mutters. "I better cancel the violinist."

"Michael…"

"I know. I said I was just going to buy you a drink and I kinda—"

"Michael, I can't. This is …"

"This is what?"

"You're my teacher," she whispers.

Even in the candlelight, she can see his cheeks reddening. The last thing she wanted to do was embarrass him, and God knows the last thing she wanted to do was cry.

"Has nobody ever done anything nice for you, Laney?"

She goes rigid, feels herself reaching for the same kind of smart comeback she'd use if Cat hit her with the same accusatory question.

"This isn't just nice," she says.

"Good," he says, staring into her eyes, "because I didn't do it just to be *nice*."

The lust in his tone brings a flush of heat to the sides of her neck, to the spot between her shoulder blades that always gets tingly when he looks at her, to the insides of her thighs. It paints gooseflesh down her arms. And by the time she's done savoring this light suggestion of his desire for her, her tears have dried and her throat feels clear again.

"The card was too much," he says quickly. "I'm sorry."

"No, it wasn't," she responds. "Please. Don't be sorry."

"No. Maybe I should have drawn something else. Something that had meaning, but wasn't...you know, *you*. It's just... Well, when I got home this afternoon, I was trying to remember the artists you liked so I could use something from one of their works. But I kept remembering the way you looked when we said good-bye and I—"

"You drew it this *afternoon?*" she asks, dumbfounded, waving the card in the air next to her. She knew he was a scholar, but she didn't know he was also an artist himself.

"Yeah, I know. Too much."

"It's not too much," she says, taking care to fold up the card, return it to its envelope and slide it into her purse. It's the least she can do after treating it like a handkerchief.

"Is it a *little* too much?" he asks.

He makes a small space between the thumb and index finger on his right hand, and that's when she can see from his cocked eyebrow and the slight dimple in his chin, that he's being a *little* sarcastic. He doesn't regret a thing he's done, despite how they've done her in. The balloons, the champagne, the card; he wouldn't take any of them back for an instant.

"It isn't too much," she says.

"I know," he says quietly.

"But it's dangerous."

"Dangerous," he says, as if it's the first time he's heard the word.

"That thing I said earlier. About you being my teacher. That's still true."

"I know," he says. "And I like that you keep pointing that out."

"Why?"

"Because it means you want me as much as I want you," he says.

"How do you figure that?"

"People don't point out barriers unless they want to overcome them."

"Yeah, and that can be a dangerous thing," she counters.

"If it's not done right, maybe."

"Anyway we do it might be dangerous, Michael."

"What kind of man do you think I am?" he asks with a mischievous smile, far more mischievous than any he's given her, or anyone, for that matter, in class.

"I don't know. *Yet.*"

"Well, that's why we're here, then," he says. "This is why dates were invented. Even if they start off kinda weird."

"So this is a date?" she asks.

"Please tell me you didn't think otherwise."

She laughs against her will, and he bites his bottom lip gently at the sound of it, his eyes brightening and the angel's press under his nose becoming more pronounced as he suppressed a grin.

"Okay," she says. "It's a date."

"Good. How else would I get to hear you say the word *dangerous* over and over again like it's a dessert you've been craving all day?"

"You didn't really hire a violinist, did you?"

"No."

"Good, you know, 'cause all of this is…good enough. It's *way* good enough."

"I hired a mariachi band for later. You know, to walk us down Bourbon Street."

As she barks with laughter, she feels her hand start a quick trip toward her blushing neck. She wills it to her lap, closes her left hand over it.

"Brass bands are so overdone, you know?" he says.

"Uh-huh."

He hasn't opened the champagne bottle yet. She's not about to ask him too, not after her mini-breakdown. But she could really use a glass or two or three or four.

Just then, the handsome waiter appears and rattles off a bunch of specials she doesn't hear because she's too busy watching Michael watch the waiter with an intense set to his jaw. It's like he's using the waiter's arrival to catch his breath after the tension and awkwardness of the last few minutes. And just this slight evidence of emotional strain on his face calms her slightly. But only slightly.

Despite his handsomeness, and despite his heartwarming gifts and the effort—and cash—he put into them, she can't stop seeing him as a luxury she can't afford. And she fears that no matter what he says, no matter what he does, nothing will stop the march of anxiety and doubt across her mind.

Maybe it never stops, she thinks suddenly, in a voice so clear it seems almost divine. *Maybe the doubts and the fears never go away. Maybe you just take the risk anyway and see what happens because what happens might be wonderful. And maybe the risk is easier to take once he embraces you, once his breath is against your neck.*

She's gotten so lost in thought she's startled to find them alone again.

"Hear anything you like?" he asks.

"To be honest, I wasn't really paying attention."

"Me neither."

"What? Seriously? You looked like you were hanging on his every word."

"I wasn't."

"You had me fooled."

"Good, I guess. I mean, I didn't ask you here to *fool* you. But hey, if we ever play poker."

Don't make a joke about strip poker. Please don't make a creepy joke about strip poker.

After a few minutes of Michael not making a joke about strip poker, Laney finally becomes convinced he's not going to make a joke about strip poker.

"Strip poker!" Michael barks.

When she realizes he read her mind throughout their long silence, she rocks forward, hands to her mouth, to keep her laughter from seizing control of her entire body.

Michael is undeterred; he makes *ooga-boogah* motions with both hands in the air in front of him. "*Stripping…nudity reference…first date…awwwwwkward,*" he continues like he's narrating the trailer for a 1950's horror film.

"Stop," she begs in-between gasps.

"*Awkwaaaaard,*" he adds one last time, in a softer version of his full-throated Vincent Price impersonation. He punctuates it with two fluttery hand motions, then he sits back in his chair, bright-eyed and beaming because his joke hit home.

It takes her a while to get her breath back. She's run such a gamut of emotions in such a short time, she feels exhausted to the point of near delirium. She wishes she could bottle this moment, this easy, if a little breathless, smile they're sharing now. At the very least, she wants to fix it in place and keep the rest of the date somewhere in its vicinity. God knows, they've already wandered far from the evening she'd scripted for them both before she arrived; polite flirting followed by a gentle give-and-take of not-too-personal personal details, all of it building up to the reveal, on both of their parts, of some sort of personal trauma in their respective pasts. (This final act, she had hoped, would be accompanied by copious amounts of booze.)

But he's sidelined her by giving her something she didn't realize had been taken from her, some celebration of the fact she landed an impossible-to-get scholarship. As a result, she's made known the depth of her attraction to him against her will. Now that he's read her mind as well—*strip poker!*—and made her laugh until she thought she was going to pass out, what choice do they have left except for total candor, total honesty?

"We could always wait," Laney says.

"For what? I wasn't exactly planning to throw you across the table right here if that's what you—"

"Until the end of the semester. Until you weren't my teacher anymore."

"So you want to call it a night and try this again in a couple months?" he asks with a wry smile.

"Well, not right now I don't want to call it a night. I mean, I'm kinda hungry."

"Oh, well, good. 'Cause we're at a restaurant."

"I can see that. A restaurant with balloons."

"*I* brought those balloons. The best the restaurant could do was a candle in a piece of bread pudding. That would never do."

"Let's see the night through. If that's okay."

"This night can end however you want it to, Laney Foley."

"Thank you, Michael Brouchard."

"In fact, I'll even let you take that champagne bottle home with you if you'd like. That way you won't be unfairly influenced by a spirit you can't contain. Get it. Spirit. 'Cause it's alcohol?"

"The strip poker thing was funnier."

"Yeah, well, they can't all be winners."

"You're a winner. That's all that counts."

He cocks his head to one side, lifts his glass to toast her. He doesn't milk every compliment she gives him for all it's worth, doesn't press her to elaborate or clarify, and she likes that. So many of the men in her life, including her father, have demanded constant validation from her while pretending never to need it, and sometimes the contradiction makes her head spin. But not with Michael. Not so far, at least.

"I thought about it, you know," Michael says quietly.

"Thought about what?" she asks, startled by the sudden seriousness of his tone.

"Waiting until the semester was over."

"Why didn't you?" she asks.

"I tried waiting once. It didn't go so well."

"What do you mean?"

Michael grips his water glass, brings it to his mouth and takes a thirsty gulp. His eyes have left hers for the first time since the waiter arrived. She can't tell if the memory he's about to impart wounds him to this day, or if he's simply embarrassed by what he's about to reveal.

"I met her my junior year at LSU. She had a boyfriend and I didn't want to do anything to screw up anybody's relationship, so I kept my mouth shut. Then they had some kind of fight or falling out. I couldn't really tell and I thought if I asked too many questions, it would make it obvious that I was into her. So I kept my mouth shut and just tired to be a *good guy friend* and all that. And little by little, I managed to find out she and the guy had separated. He was going off to med school in Houston and she didn't want to leave Louisiana. Anyway, the point is it took me weeks to get all the info because I was all about flying below the radar. Playing it super-safe. I didn't want it getting back to her that I was asking around just in case she and the boyfriend were still serious. Finally I worked up the nerve to ask her out, but a couple weeks turned out to be too long."

"She got back together with the guy?"

"No," he answers, staring down into his water glass, working his jaw slightly as if a piece of gum were stuck to the back of his teeth. "She was listening to her iPod and she stepped off the curb before the light changed and a truck hit her. She died instantly."

"Oh my God," Laney says. It's more of a sharp exhalation than a statement.

"So that's why when a woman walks into my life who has everything you do, I don't wait."

Or you tell her this story, which sounds too good to be true. Or just bad enough that it's too bad to be—

—shut up, Laney. He's looking you in the eye, for Christ's sake. Liars don't look people straight in the eye.

"What was her name?"

"Brooke."

Yeah—and her last name, Nicholas Sparks?

—Shut up, Laney!

"I'm so sorry, Michael."

"Listen, I didn't tell the story to get a Purple Heart. Honestly, was she the love of my life? I have no idea. But that's the point. I have no idea because I never stepped up to bat. I wasted too much time waiting for the moment to be perfect. I don't want to make the same mistake with you, Laney."

The waiter arrives. Laney isn't remotely ready to order, but she pops open the menu and pretends to study its contents. She can't think of a better way to hide her suspicion the story Michael just shared with her isn't true.

Or maybe only half-true, which would be just as lame.

"Ready?" Michael asks.

"I'll be ready by the time you've ordered," she mutters.

She's not, but she orders anyway. Something not too expensive, something that won't leave her bloated and sleepy.

Once the waiter departs, she bends forward, as if she's about to take Michael into confidence. "Bathroom," she whispers, and then gestures to her face, which she assumes is still tear-splotched.

He smiles and nods.

It's a single bathroom, thank God, and when she throws the lock, her first deep breath in hours fills her lungs. Relief, that's what she's feeling, relief that she might be about to catch Michael in a lie, that she might be on the verge of freeing herself from this whole reckless mess.

If she were able to afford a smartphone of her own, she wouldn't have to stoop to calling Cat. But she can't afford one, so calling Cat it is.

Here goes, she thinks.

Cat answers. "What are you doing?"

"Where are you?"

"Answering questions with questions. Not a good sign."

"I need your help," Laney says.

"Don't tell me he's being weird. Ugh. Is he being weird? I can meet you out front. I'm at CC's."

"Wait, seriously? You're a few blocks away?"

"Yeah," Cat answers.

"What happened to not picking me up if I didn't go home with him?"

"I was *joking*. You really think I'd leave you down here without a car?"

"That's actually really sweet."

As sweet as expensive champagne, balloons and a custom-made hand-drawn card. But she hadn't done the best at accepting those gifts either.

"Laney, *why* are you calling?"

"Do you have wifi?"

"Uhm, yeah. How do you think I'm passing the time?"

"Google something for me."

"Okay. I'm ready," Cat says, without bothering to ask for an explanation.

"Brooke. LSU. Truck. Accident. Killed Instantly."

"What kind of date is this?" Cat asks.

"You're looking for news articles or an obituary from about two or three years ago."

"Oh my God. You're fact-checking your date! Seriously? You're having me *fact-check* your date?"

"If I had a smart phone, I'd do it myself. Now start Googling."

Silence falls on the other end, followed by the click of laptop keys, followed by a few grunts here and there as Cat scans the search results.

"Here it is," Cat finally says. "A news story from three years ago." She quickly skims through the story, "*Baton Rouge Police have announced that alcohol did not play a factor in the accident that killed a Louisiana State University junior three days ago. Twenty-one-year-old art history major Brooke Daniels was struck and killed by a cold storage truck at three in the afternoon while walking home from class. The driver did not flee the scene and has been cooperating with authorities since the accident. The announcement from Baton Rouge P.D. seems to confirm witness reports that Daniels was listening to music on her iPod and appeared distracted when she stepped into the intersection before the light changed...* Do I have to keep reading?"

"No," Laney says. "He was telling the truth."

"So you *were* fact-checking him? Honestly. Laney, no one's going to be able to fall in love with this guy *for* you. Go back to the table!"

Cat hangs up.

Now that it's gone, she's embarrassed by the sense of relief that filled her when she thought Michael might turn out to be a liar. Would it really have been a comfort to know he was just like a dozen other scam artists and players she'd managed to expose before things got serious?

Christ, was she already *that* bitter?

Bitter.

That's probably the least of what Michael would think of her if he knew she hadn't believed his story.

Did he get a whiff of her suspicions? Did she leave the table too quickly?

There's a sparkling champagne flute sitting next to her empty plate, and when she takes her seat again, he gives her a smile as warm as the one he gave her when she first sat down.

"I thought the whole cork-popping thing wouldn't have been appropriate given we kind of started off awkwardly," he says, lifting his glass. "But we can still do this part."

She returns his toast and takes a hearty slug of champagne. Hearty enough to cause Michael's eyes to widen while he takes a polite, restrained sip from his own glass. He sets his glass down with a thud that sounds final. Laney sees the strain behind his smile.

"You didn't believe me, did you?" he asks.

"How'd you know?"

"Your face looks exactly the same. You didn't splash water on it or anything."

CIA, here I come.

"No," she answers. "I didn't believe you."

"And now you do?"

"Yes. I did some research."

"Wow. That's one hell of a bathroom they got here."

"I'm sorry."

Michael stares down into his champagne glass. *Strike two,* she thinks. *One more strike and you're—*

"So I guess a lot of guys have lied to you on first dates before," he says with a lack of anger that surprises her.

"Yes, but still…"

"Okay. Let me just say a few things."

"I'm listening," she answers, trying not to sound too relieved that she's temporarily off the hook for explaining her suspicions.

"You need to learn that *cannot* is not two words."

"What?"

"Also, I encourage you to get a copy of *The Elements of Style* by Strunk and White and read the section on paragraphs, because sometimes you cram what should be about three paragraphs into one and it can make your papers confusing."

"You're talking about my classwork? Right now?"

"Yes."

"I wasn't aware it was a class in composition."

"If you didn't have any talent for analyzing and discussing art, I wouldn't be worried about your composition. But you do, so I am. Also, I know you're a bigger fan of periods like Baroque and Rococo, but you're going to have to stop leaving out *all* Renaissance painters when we do comparison assignments. Because whether or not their work appeals to you on a personal level, we can't just ignore the entire Renaissance when we survey trends in Western Art that started in the Middle Ages."

"I see…"

"Do you?"

"Yeah, you're attacking me because I didn't believe your story."

"No, Laney. I'm proving to you that no matter what happens between us, I'll still be able to do my job. At the end of the semester, you'll get the grade you deserve, based on the work you've done in class. Not based on whether you let me do the things to your body I've wanted to do now for months."

What things? Tell me now. All of them. Each and every one. Tell me what you want to do to my—

"I have a copy of Strunk and White," she says, downing a shot of champagne.

"As we all should."

"It doesn't exactly make for sexy bedtime reading."

"You don't strike me as the type who reads a lot of romance novels."

"*You* strike me as the type who does. For strategy."

"A woman who can't handle criticism. I can handle that."

"*Excuse me?*"

Michael bows his head and holds up his palms in a gesture of defeat.

"That was shitty," he says. "I'm sorry."

The sincerity of his apology dissolves the anger that's been blocking her own. "I'm sorry I didn't believe your story."

"I'm sorry so many guys have lied to you in the past."

Before either of them can be sorry for anything else, like the weather, perhaps, or the fact that humankind has yet to invent a flying car, the waiter brings their food. Once he departs, she realizes this is the moment when she should tell a story of her own, a revelation that could make up for her suspicions of his own, something that balances the scales, make her as vulnerable as he made himself.

I'm already vulnerable, she thinks. And there it is, that hard knot of resistance that won't seem to fade no matter what she does. No matter what *he* does.

"I read a romance novel once," she finally says.

"*Pride and Prejudice?*"

"No! It was contemporary. I can't remember the name. It was *sweet.*"

"You say that like it's a bad thing."

"Contemporary?" she asks, teasing him.

"No," he answers with a smile. "Sweet."

"Sweet's all right, I guess."

"But you're not a fan of happily ever after?"

"Sure. If, you know, it's *earned.*"

"Earned? How?" he asks, eyes wide as he takes a large bite of food, a sign that he won't be rushing to fill the silence if she doesn't answer because he'll be too busy chewing.

"I don't know yet."

He chews and chews and *chews.*

"Want to learn?" he asks.

"I'll answer after you swallow that bite."

He makes a show of swallowing his bite.

"Well…want to?"

"We'll see," she says.

He shoots her a wicked grin, and when he attacks his plate again with a fork and a knife, she imagines it's with the same force and passion he'd like to unleash on her body.

This night can end however you'd like it to, Laney Foley.

Isn't that how he put it?

She hopes he's a man of his word because the only thing she's sure of is the night's not over yet.

4

LILLIANE

Lilliane Williams isn't afraid to walk the French Quarter alone at night, even in a black leather dress that flatters her curves, even while carrying a jeweled leather suitcase so shiny and ornate it could make the steeliest pickpocket salivate with desire. She doesn't hesitate to cut through back alleys. She takes her time strolling lonely, shadowy side streets. Her primary concern isn't assault; it's encountering someone who might realize she hasn't aged a day in fifty-six years.

But if she were to run into someone from her old life, her life before she wandered into that strange candle shop in April of 1959, that person would probably assume she was a distant relative of Lilliane Williams. Maybe even a reincarnated version. But not the same woman who worked as a housekeeper for a wealthy white family in the Garden District for several years, the same Lilliane Williams whose disappearance wasn't even reported by the local papers because back then the local papers didn't report on the disappearances of black people.

When she's several feet from the opening of an alley, Lilliane senses the low, quick approach of a stalking human predator, hears something behind her that could either be the cock of a gun or the click of a switchblade. As soon as the man grabs for the suitcase, she wills him headfirst into the nearest stone wall. But whatever drugs are coursing through his system have made him impervious to solid concrete and oblivious to her show of supernatural strength.

He whirls, gun raised.

"Lord! *Really?*" she says with a groan.

"Give it to me, bitch, or I'll fucking put a bullet in you. Swear to God."

"If you insist," Lilliane answers brightly.

She sets the suitcase down on the pavement in front of her. Then, just as the thief goes for the handle, she stretches her arms out on either side of her and rises twenty feet straight up into the air, tendrils of gold dust spraying from her open palms like two small bursts of heavenly rocket exhaust. Her miraculous self-propulsion flattens the flaps of her leather dress around her legs with a sound like giant wings beating the air. Perhaps it's reckless to perform this trick right here, right now; just beyond the neon-lit mouth of the alley is a parade of tourists. But this display of power is working its intended effect on her would-be attacker.

The shower of gold dust coats the suitcase, causing the guy to recoil in horror, and the sight of her rising into the air literally knocks him onto his ass. When Lilliane sees his gun spinning across the pavement away from him, she allows herself to sink back down to earth, but not before landing one swift kick to the young man's jaw.

"Run along now, little boy. I've got a date."

Reeking of fresh urine, he does as instructed.

Lilliane picks up the suitcase and continues on her way.

A date? Not really.

More like a regular delivery. Sure, it sounds dry, far too mechanical to describe the miraculous contents of the suitcase she's once again carrying confidently in one hand. But while the man scheduled to appear to her in twenty minutes' time is most certainly handsome, there's very little between them she'd be willing to call affection. So she shouldn't call it a date, just as she shouldn't call Bastian Drake a *man*.

What an absurd name, she thinks. She's fairly sure it's not even his real one. But over the years Bastian, or whoever he is, has remained as closely guarded with the details of his own history as he was on that summer afternoon in 1959 when they met for the first time. Despite all their fights, he's never once revealed what his life was like before he took that ridiculous name, before he became the candlemaker, before he became a… Silly that even now her mind trips over the exact word for him, as if just thinking it to herself amounts to some kind of confession.

Ghost. Bastian is a ghost.

Her plight is easier to manage when she's angry, and there are other descriptions of him she prefers because they allow her to remain in a state of barely controlled, but energizing rage.

Captor, owner, overseer, warlock. If he had told me that day what his candle could really do. If he had told me what the consequences would be if I didn't—

A few steps into Jackson Square, she slams into a pedestrian, some drunken little white boy whose wide eyes fill immediately with lustful admiration at the sight of the gorgeous, full-figured black woman in the form-fitting leather dress. She can't lie to herself; she appreciates the attention, feels a deep, growling urge to take him to the nearest alley, strip him of his clothes, place her hands against his blushing, sweating cheeks and stare right into his soul. But she has made a commitment to use her powers in only the most secret and structured way, and only on the willing. That's why she built The Desire Exchange. And performing a radiance on a fresh-faced college boy in the middle of the French Quarter on a Friday night is far more reckless than the aerial routine she just pulled on her would-be mugger.

Those eyes, though. That sweet boyish face…

The skinny little blonde who suddenly hooks the guy under one armpit must be his girlfriend. How else to explain her sudden possessiveness and the dagger-glare she gives Lilliane as she drags Lilliane's not-so-secret admirer off into the crowd?

As she watches the not-so-happy couple disappear, sadness blooms inside of Lilliane like ink meeting water. Sadness tinged with grief. Maybe they're truly in love. Maybe later that night they will fight and scream and cry and then tearfully make up, their feelings for each other renewing, strengthening before exploding into a crescendo of fiery make-up sex. These things have all been lost to Lilliane, thanks to Bastian Drake.

Well, not the sex. She can manage the sex just fine. Better than ever, in fact. It's amazing how skilled you can become in the bedroom when you have all the time in the world to study the act of lovemaking and you suffer none of the costs of aging.

But all the feelings humans tangle throughout the bedroom and beyond, all the emotions humans call *love*, those are gone now. They've been gone for decades.

Lilliane pauses to catch her breath, to flush the poison of grief and regret from her system. She studies the tarot card readers, the street musicians, and the knots of drunken tourists. The brightly lit facade of St. Louis Cathedral rises overhead.

She loves the French Quarter. Unlike many of her fellow radiants, she doesn't leave the compound very often, but when she does, it's to come here. She doesn't have to work to blend in because in the French Quarter, all you have to do to blend in is dance with the chaos. Still, what must the people all around her assume she must be? A cocktail waitress, a street performer, or God forbid, a stripper?

If they find her outfit strange, they'd find the real explanation for it even stranger. The leather dress is perfectly weighted to provide just enough drag to keep her on target when she takes to the air. Radiants can't fly; they leap, and if they don't posses the muscle-strength, or if they haven't weighted themselves down properly, a leap can turn into something that looks like a zigzagging balloon after the air's been let out of it.

Suitcase in hand, Lilliane heads down Pirate's Alley and into a long pool of shadows that rises up the cathedral's side wall. She gives a quick glance in both directions. Confident she's alone, she rises skyward until she's crested one of the flat areas of the roof that sits on either side of the cathedral's spire.

"Beautiful, isn't it?" These words are the first sounds Bastian makes as he materializes on the roof of St. Louis Cathedral. No doubt he's referring to the expansive view. Lilliane studies the vast shadowed square below.

At night, the high wrought iron gates, which usually grant admittance to the center of Jackson Square, are closed, leaving the proud statue of Andrew Jackson astride his horse alone in a sea of shadows. Outside the fence, the tarot card readers and street musicians she stood among only seconds before look like small, animated dolls. And just beyond the stream of traffic on Decatur Street, a cargo ship as tall as a high-rise office building glides past the city on the inky black waters of the Mississippi River.

"And to think, most will never see it," Bastian says.

"See what?"

"The *view*, darling. It's not like there's a viewing platform up here."

"Don't attempt to mollify me with talk of my powers," Lilliane says quietly. "I'm not in the mood, Bastian."

"*Mollify* you?" he asks, sounding genuinely hurt. "What a curious word."

She hands him the suitcase with enough force to knock a normal man back on his heels. But he is not a normal man. *At what point are you allowed to stop referring to a ghost as a* man?

Bastian is suddenly silent as he hefts the suitcase. He goes about his usual routine; caressing the handle slowly, carefully running his fingers along the array of inset jewels along the top. To a curious onlooker he would look like some kind of leather fetishist. The truth is far stranger. Bastian cannot slip through the cracks in human time carrying any object he hasn't handled for at least ten minutes. It's one of the few rules of his existence he's shared with her.

"Yes, it's lighter than usual," she says after the silence between them becomes uncomfortable. She had expected him to mention it first.

"And your mood?"

"Normally, I bring you six jars. This time I've got two. You'll make do, I'm sure."

"Your *mood*, Lilliane. What's troubling you this evening?"

"I normally seem pleasant during our little visits?"

"Perhaps not," Bastian answers, nonplussed as always. "But you rarely say anything as specific as *I'm in a bad mood*. So I thought I might take a chance and ask."

"I didn't say I was in a *bad* mood. I said I wasn't in the mood to be distracted with talk of my abilities."

"Distracted from what?"

"None of your business."

"I see."

She could leap from the roof in an instant, ending this awkward little exchange. Bastian would have to stay right where he was. Unlike her, he doesn't have the power to leap tall buildings in a single bound, and unlike him, she doesn't have the power to simply vanish at will. But Bastian won't go anywhere until he's made enough physical contact with the suitcase to spirit it away. Away to wherever it is he goes; she knows better than to ask him exactly where.

"There was a boy," she says. "Down there somewhere."

"A boy?"

"A college kid. In the square, just now. He gave me a look. A look that made me remember things. Things I miss."

"I see."

"Somehow I doubt that," she says quietly.

"And someday, sooner than he thinks, that boy will be a man. Paunchy and middle-aged and stewing in regret over the roads not taken, and you will still be Lilliane. Youthful and powerful and capable of bringing a person's innermost desires to life."

"I tired of these conversations years ago."

"*Two* jars," he says.

"Managerial difficulties. Don't trouble yourself."

"Consider me troubled. I helped you build The Desire Exchange, Lilliane. And I did it so you'd have a sense of purpose."

"You did it to keep me busy," she answers.

"There's a difference?"

"You thought it would make me less angry."

"What happened, Lilliane?"

"We were infiltrated."

"*Infiltrated?* By what?"

"Humans," she answers. "Ordinary, desperate, fear-ridden, beautiful, mortal humans. Humans with fake identities and guns."

"I take it no one was hurt?"

"Well, you would have been able to sense it, right?" she asks. He has the ability to appear to any of them whenever he'd like, but beyond that, he's never disclosed how much of a real psychic connection exists between him and his bastard stepchildren. Can he sense their losses? Their rages? The glittering unfurling of the powers they unleash inside of The Desire Exchange?

He doesn't take the bait. But he doesn't vanish either. And he's had long enough to make his necessary mark on the suitcase.

"One of our radiants—his father sent people looking for him," she finally offers.

"I see," Bastian says quietly.

"Ryan Benoit. You remember Ryan Benoit, don't you?" This accusatory question hits its target; Bastian lowers his gaze. Did he also flinch? She can't be sure.

"Of course I remember, Ryan," he says quietly. "I remember all of you."

Radiants. He still has trouble with this word, given he didn't come up with it. So she decides to hit him with another word he's sure to find far more troubling.

"Your children, you mean," she says.

To this, Bastian betrays no response. He's never been able to refer to them as his offspring or anything of the sort; never been willing to claim them as family. No matter how kind he is to her, Lilliane is sure he regards her and the other radiants as nothing more than unfortunate accidents, the necessary downside of his incredible magic.

"Anyway," Lilliane says, satisfied to have struck two blows in a row, "it was a bit of a mess, but it's all worked out now."

"You're sure your secret's safe? Despite this incident?"

"We provided their ringleader with the same service we provide all of our clientele. She was quite happy with the result."

Lilliane cocks her head in the direction of the suitcase. Bastian pops it open.

Inside are six cushioned slots just large enough for the jars she brings him on a regular basis. Four of the slots are empty. But the golden radiance swirling within the two glass jars she did bring is strong enough to illuminate Bastian's face, an illumination that fills his hollow eyes, turning his pupils and sclera into vague gold outlines and not much else.

"Alexandra Vance," Lilliane says, tapping one jar. "Emily Blaine," she continues, tapping the one next to it.

"It doesn't matter," Bastian says quietly.

"*What* doesn't matter?"

"Their names. Who they came from. One batch is as good as the next. In the end, it's all the same energy. The bravery to face your heart's true desires. Once I add it to the candles, it finds who it needs to find."

"I see. And what about *my* candle, Bastian? The candle you sold me. Did it find who it needed to find?"

For a second, she thinks he's about to vanish just to avoid answering this question. But he's staring past her into the night sky, head cocked like a dog's at the sound of a whistle. She follows the direction of his gaze and sees three Mylar balloons rising into the night sky over Jackson Square; they're stamped with congratulatory expressions in bright letters:

CONGRATULATIONS! AMAZING! GOOD WORK!

Bastian doesn't normally respond to an environmental intrusion in this quick and reflexive way. Something about these balloons means something to him. And when his entire being flickers, it seems to startle him as much as it does her. He looks down at his chest, checks the security of his grip on the suitcase's handle.

"Bastian," she asks quietly.

"It seems my services are soon to be required," he says meekly.

And then he's gone.

It's the first time she hasn't seen him disappear of his own accord.

Summoned, she finally thinks. *He was summoned. And he couldn't control it. He had no choice.* The sight of the man she holds responsible for her interminable fate rendered so suddenly powerless leaves her speechless. It almost makes her anger vanish as quickly as Bastian just did.

Almost.

6

LANEY

"So…." Michael says.

"So," Laney answers. Her phone buzzes in her pocket.

It's a text message from Cat.

Status update?

A horse drawn carriage clatters past them. In a high, barking voice, the driver recounts the history of the house and courtyard in which Perry's resides while Laney and Michael stand in front of the restaurant's entrance like awkward teenagers, the carriage passengers gawking at them like they're artifacts themselves. The Mylar balloons bob in the air just above Laney's head, the end of their strings tied around her right wrist. When the carriage finally moves on, they're left with boisterous knots of tourists filing past them in the direction of Bourbon Street, folks who don't have to worry about being awake for work or class in the morning, folks eager to burn the midnight oil in a city where the bars never close.

"Late for another date?" Michael asks.

Laney realizes she's been rudely staring at the phone in her hand.

"Yeah, I've got like seven tonight. Clients mostly."

"*Clients?*" Michael asks, barely able to contain his laughter.

"Yeah. I'm real popular with the rest of the faculty too."

"Oh!" he barks. "You went there. You totally went there."

"It's a friend of mine," Laney says. "She's checking up on me."

"Okay," Michael says. "Write her back. Tell her we got off to kind of a shaky start, and then after that, we played it safe for the rest of the meal and talked about stuff like our favorite TV shows from childhood and the weather. And now we're standing outside the restaurant and we're both thinking that while this would probably be the *safest* moment to call it a night, we've both had a little champagne, and we just had a ten minute discussion about whether or not an adult can use those baby wipes on himself on a regular basis without being called OCD. And so we're both afraid that if we end the date now, we're not going to make another one because every time we think of the other person we're going to see a toilet or a baby's butt or something."

"It sounds like you've had a lot more champagne than I have," she says.

"It *sounds* that way, but it's not technically true."

"This is true. Still, it's a little long for a text message."

"Well, what does she want to know?"

"Status update."

"Well, tell her it's going well. Tell her the story about Brooke isn't something I make up just to get into my student's pants."

"I thought we were past that."

"We are. Sort of. Anyway, don't tell her all that. Just tell her that we're both a little tipsy and we're going to take a walk through the Quarter to try to sober up. Which will be cool. 'Cause we'll be the first people in history who have ever tried to sober up in the French Quarter. *And—*"

"You have become a man of many words tonight, Michael Brouchard."

"*Become?* I lead a discussion section, Laney."

"True. What should I tell her for real?"

"Tell her we're going to be on crowded, well-lit streets the whole time if she'd like to follow us from twenty paces."

"Oh, I don't think she's going to follow us."

"She kind of already is. Isn't that her right there?"

Laney follows the direction of Michael's pointing finger and finds Cat waving at them from across the street as drunken tourists weave to avoid her. Her laptop and purse are slung over one shoulder.

"Cat Burke, right?" Michael says. "I taught her last year. We called her Cat Nap. One guess why."

"Hi, Mister Brouchard!" Cat calls from across the street.

"It's Michael, Cat. Just Michael. I'm a grad student. I don't teach high school."

"Uh-huh," Cat answers, then she sees Laney's glare and her smile fades. "CC's closed!"

"Okay," Laney answers.

"Uhm...I'm gonna go to Café du Monde. Maybe get some coffee."

"Sounds like a plan," Laney says. "You go have some coffee."

"Oh, I see!" Cat calls back. "Now you can't wait to get rid of me."

"Or you could just stop talking," Laney replies.

"*Bye!*"

They watch Cat hurry off down the crowded sidewalk. When Laney turns to face Michael, he gives her a crooked grin, his barely contained laughter causing the nostrils on his Roman nose to flare.

"I didn't ask her to do that," she says.

"Do what?"

"Wait around like that."

"She's protective of you. I'd say that's a point in her favor."

"Earlier she said she wouldn't come and get me if I didn't promise to have sex with you tonight."

"*Another* reason I'm a Cat Nap fan!"

"Let's walk, mister," she says, taking his hand in hers quickly, casually, before any of them can consider it a moment or a turning point. And suddenly they're walking hand-in-hand down the sidewalk toward Jackson Square as if they've done it their whole lives.

"I have an idea," Michael says.

"Shoot."

"I saw it on a TV show," he says.

"Which one?" she asks.

"Not saying."

"*What?*" she cries.

"No, seriously. You'll think I'm a giant nerd."

"Whatever. I didn't meet you tailgating. You're my teacher."

"Fine. It's from a *Doctor Who* Christmas special."

"Oh, wow. That is nerdy."

"It's a *great* show!" Michael whines.

"I've never seen it."

"Then don't judge. Please. I'm feeling really judged right now."

"I'm just teasing."

"I feel so vulnerable," he says in a meek, small voice. "Is this how women feel all the time?"

"Keep it up with the sexist jokes and the last you'll feel of me will be my hand coming out of yours."

"I'm not a nerd," he whines.

"Yes, you are. And it's kind of what makes you sexy."

"Good. 'Cause where I come from, nerds weren't considered sexy."

"Well, where I come from, there weren't any nerds. Just crystal meth dealers. And in my book, sexy men have teeth and they don't think the wires in their house are talking to them."

"Yikes."

"Yeah. So what was this…uhm, *Doctor Who*-related idea you wanted to run by me? Time travel?"

"You *have* seen the show!" Michael cries.

"Maybe one episode. I don't know. I mean, I haven't seen all the Christmas specials like you have. Nerd."

"Never mind," he mutters. "It's a stupid idea."

"Oh, my God. Don't do a baby voice. Now I feel terrible."

"Okay. It goes like this. We ask each other a series of questions. But the person answering can only answer with one word."

"What about the person asking the questions?" Laney asks.

"The question can be as long as you want. But the answer can only be—"

"One word!" Laney finishes for him.

"That's right."

"Got it. Who goes first?"

A gang of drunken frat boys are heading straight for them, and for a second, she fears they're going to have to separate to let them pass. But when she starts to pull her hand free from Michael's, he tightens his grip and at the last minute, the frat boys realize they're up against an iron wall. They part on either side of the determined couple while Laney savors Michael's resolute grip, the raw evidence of his determination not to let her go over something trivial and inconvenient.

"You first," Michael says. "We'll do five-and-five."

"I get to ask five questions, then you ask five?"

"Yep."

"Okay—"

"Also, no follow-up questions," he adds.

"Wait. What do you mean?"

"I mean an answer can only be one word. If you want clarification, you have to ask another completely different question."

"All right. Let's start before you make any more rules," Laney says.

"And no yes-or-no questions."

"*Oh my God!*"

"It'll make sense once we start playing. Trust me."

"*If* we start playing."

"I'm done making up rules. I promise. Hit me."

"Okay," she says. "What will you be doing with your life in five years?"

There's a few seconds of silence between them, punctuated by sounds of their footfalls and the balloons rubbing together in the air behind her.

"Loving," he says.

Her heart races and her breath catches and the restraints of the game become instantly clear and make her dizzy. *Loving who? Loving what? Loving how? Loving...her?* But follow-up questions aren't allowed. Leading yes-or-no questions are also out.

"Where do you see yourself living?" she asks.

He starts to answer, then stops himself, probably because he was about to break one of his own rules.

"Italy," he says. He grunts in his throat and purses his lips. She wonders if the answer's more specific than he liked, but rules are rules, after all.

"What's the one thing you can't do without?" she asks him.

"Food," he answers.

"What's the one thing you can't do without aside from food, water, and shelter?"

"Follow-up question," he says with a low growl.

"I'm allowed one each round."

"That's a new rule."

"That's right," she answers. "It's my rule."

He grunts.

"Love," he says.

One question left. This round, anyway.

"What was the first thing you thought when you saw me?" she asks.

"Finally," he answers.

His simple, elegant answer knocks the wind out of her. Can he feel her come close to losing her footing? They're paces away from Jackson Square, and he hasn't missed a step.

"My turn," he says. They're passing through the deep shadows under a townhouse's second floor balcony, but she can hear the hint of a smile in his restrained tone.

"Ready," she says, even though she feels anything but.

But by the time they've entered Jackson Square, he still hasn't asked her a question, which leaves her wondering if he's done with this game. If his final, dizzying answer was all the pretext he needs to take her face in his hands and—

"What's your biggest fear?"

"Failure," she answers without a second thought.

And as the word just hangs there, suddenly the limitations of the game infuriate her. She's aching to give a more specific answer. To tell him what *kind* of failure she means. But refusing to give into this urge forces her to question it, and suddenly all her qualifications, her desire to specify and narrow it down to *one kind* of failure seem full of duplicity. She's always wanted to do everything perfectly; that's the long and short of it. When people tell her there's no perfect way to do anything, she usually blocks out their words with a plastic smile and a series of nods.

They're walking along one side of the cast-iron fence girding the center of the square and hung with cityscape paintings and caricature sketches by the street artists who have set up shop along the flagstones. She can already smell the horses lined up along Decatur Street. But Michael's grip feels lackluster all of a sudden. When she glances down at their hands, she sees he's holding her hand just as tightly as he was before. It's her own thoughts and fears that have made him feel suddenly faraway. Maybe that's another point of the game—to give the most honest and authentic answer, and then force yourself to remain present in your own skin.

"What do you want most in the world?" he asks.

"Security," she says.

She sucks in a deep breath, tightens her grip on his hand.

"Is this hard for you?" he asks.

"No yes-or-no questions."

"Sorry. Give me a sec."

A second passes. Then another second passes. Then another...

"If you could live anywhere in the world, where would you live?" he asks.

"Italy," she answers.

His hand jerks in hers. He makes a low throaty grunt that sounds satisfied.

When they reach Dumaine Street, he pulls her to their right and suddenly they're walking past a long row of horse-drawn carriages sitting idly at the foot of the square. They're also walking away from the bright lights and green awnings of Café du Monde across the street, where Cat currently waits for her somewhere amidst the crowd of camera-toting tourists with shirtfronts dusted by the powdered sugar that's slipped off their beignets with every bite.

Two more questions in this round.

He's sure taking his sweet time coming up with them.

"What's the one thing you can't live without?" he asks.

There's no rule against asking a question that's been asked of you, so she decides to answer.

"Truth," she says.

Not love, she realizes. *He said love and you didn't say love. And maybe that's okay. Maybe you don't have to have exactly the same answers for him to...* She doesn't want to finish that sentence. But she does anyway. In her head. About a dozen different times. *For him to want you, kiss you, need you,* love *you.*

"Describe your family in one word," he says.

"Distant," she answers.

They're heading back in the direction of St. Louis Cathedral, and for some reason this side of the square is quieter. Maybe because the shadows offered by the oak branches overhead are longer and darker.

"Your turn," he says quietly.

"If you could be anything in the world right now besides a teacher, what would it be?"

"Artist," he answers.

"If you could be any animal in the world, which one would you be?"

"Eagle," he answers.

"Really?"

"No follow-ups. You've got three more."

Her heart races. Her face feels hot.

"If you could do one thing to me right now, what would it be?" she asks.

The cold metal of one of the fence posts presses up against her back, and that's when she realizes he's taken her into his embrace. His hands, his powerful, kneading hands, grip her waist, making the loose fabric of her dress feel as insubstantial as a blush of humidity. He brings their mouths and bodies together with the hunger of a hundred class sessions, a hundred long looks, a hundred fevered daydreams. As soon as she tastes him for the first time, she realizes the real question isn't whether or not the passion between them is wrong or right, but how long would they be able to resist it?

She grips the back of his head, slides her fingers to the back of his thick, powerful neck. There's that smell, his smell. Maybe it's his cologne, or maybe it's some intermingling of scents that are more purely, naturally *him*. Vanilla, campfires, and something musky. Only when she feels his palm grip the underside of her thigh does she realize she's about to wrap her right leg around his waist, that her dress is sliding up her leg and if she doesn't lower it soon she'll be exposing herself right in the middle of Jackson Square.

Their lips part. He cups her face in his hands. She slides her leg back to the ground, slowly so as not to send the false message that his touch is repulsive; she just can't risk exposing herself to passersby.

"You have two more questions," he growls.

"Will you wait?" she asks.

"For?"

"One word answers only. Remember?"

"Yeah, and no yes-or-no questions either, remember? You still want to play this game?"

"It was your game, professor."

"And you were being a very good bad little student."

"Will you wait, Michael?"

"I already said I would."

"Michael..." Her hands find his face, and somehow this touch feels more forbidden and electrifying than their passionate kiss, just allowing her fingers to gently rest against the hard angles of his face she's studied day after day in class. To feel the heat of him in this gentle and unhurried way.

"Laney," he says, in a gentle imitation of her own breathless voice.

"Even if I make you wait forever?"

"Is that your plan?" he asks quietly. But he's taken his hands away from her flaming cheeks, and suddenly it seems awkward to continue touching his face when he's just released her own, and just like that, with just one slightly disjointed question, there's a foot of distance between that feels like a mile. "To make me wait forever?" he asks.

A minute goes by before she realizes she hasn't answered, hasn't said anything to assuage his fears. She's been so damn focused on her own. The slight distance between them is enough to allow every muscle in her body to knot with tension, a tension so uniform and persistent there's no mistaking it for what it truly is—resistance.

When he takes her hands in his again, he's not preparing for another passionate embrace. It feels like he's comforting her.

"So I guess this is where this night ends?" he asks.

"I need—I mean, I just need…"

Deep breath. Deep breath. If she could just get one more deep breath. The sensations throughout her body feel like a terrible moment of self-realization; passion and panic sit side-by-side within her fundamental being, and she's going to have to learn how to separate them.

"Cat's waiting for you at Café du Monde, right? You want me to walk you over there?"

"No. I'm fine."

She is so obviously and clearly *not* fine that this response renders Michael silent.

A panic attack. Is that what's happening? Is she literally having a panic attack because the most beautiful, amazing man she's ever met has just promised to take her fears away? She's become that woman she used to sneer at in movies, the one who can't accept a gift from the universe, the one so full of fear and anxiety she can't take a chance on anything. How can that be? That's not Laney Foley. Laney clawed her way out of a neighborhood of people who thought she was personally insulting them by reading books. She worked three jobs at once to put herself through community college, applied for every scholarship she could. Aren't *those* the parts of life that are supposed to terrify people, paralyze people? Not the possibility of being loved by an amazing man.

But for her, passion could be dangerous, couldn't it? This kind of a passion in particular.

A teacher's passion.

She hasn't read the fine print of her scholarship agreement, because she doesn't want to read the goddamn fine print on her scholarship agreement, thank you very much. She's been so damn focused on the idea of Michael punishing her with a bad grade if things didn't work out, she hasn't stopped to consider whether her own scholarship involves a real consequence for going to bed with someone responsible for her grade. Even if it were only an allegation, brought by him, or anyone, or a jerk like Jake Briffel, what would happen if she were accused of trading sex for grades to maintain her status in the university's most exclusive and competitive scholarship?

Now there are black spots crowding her vision, darker and more menacing than the shadows all around him. It feels like she's breathing through a straw. And her arms, shoulders and neck are tingling. Not sensual, anticipatory tingles. This is oxygen deprivation as a result of hyperventilation. This is anxiety and fear run amuck in her veins.

Yep. Definitely a panic attack.

"I'll be fine," she says, pulling away from the fence and from him.

"Laney?"

"Just. Please. I need a …"

Her feet finish the sentence for her.

She's already broken into a run when she realizes that's exactly what she's doing. Running. She is literally running away from the man of her dreams, away from the sound of his voice calling out to her, his struggle over whether or not to chase her evident in his pained sounding cry. Only once she's left Jackson Square in her dust does she realize what the slight tug on her right wrist meant as she took off. She snagged the balloon's strings on the fence as she ran, releasing them into the night sky.

7

He's right behind me, Laney thinks. But when she turns, she finds herself on a shadowy, side street with blurry, disjointed memories of how she got here. And Michael is nowhere to be seen.

She remembers racing across Bourbon Street, darting through thick crowds, dodging a mounted policeman whose horse expelled hot breath on one side of her face in a terrible burst. She ran with the conviction that each pounding step would drive the breath back into her lungs, flush the ice-cold prickles from her skin. To some degree it's worked. She's gasping now instead of wheezing. But she's also alone and too close to Rampart Street, the Quarter's northern boundary.

Silly of her to think Michael would have been able to keep up, not without drawing the attention of cops on Bourbon. That's how fast she was running, and if he'd run that fast to keep up, what would we have looked like? Even in flats, her near-sprint has left her feet throbbing with pain.

Still, why did she stop right *here?* Why was she suddenly overcome by the sense that he was just a few feet away??

I can smell him, she realizes. *I can smell him as strongly as if I were still in his arms. Vanilla and campfires and some kind of spice I can't name.*

Several second-floor balconies cover the depth of the sidewalk, their filigree ironwork dappling the street with scatters of shadows. A strange glow emanates from the windows of the tiny shop across the street. The glow is just faint enough for her to make out the wood-plank sign hanging over the open door and the gold outline of a tiny candle flame. The shelves inside the front window are lined with uniform candles, each one so large she could hold one in both hands, one hand on each side of the glass, and her fingers wouldn't touch.

A candle shop open at this hour, this far from the main drag?

But it's the source of the smell, Michael's smell. It has to be. Just to be sure, she pulls a piece of her dress close to her nose. Maybe his cologne rubbed off on her during their embrace and she's coated with the stuff. But her dress smells more like dinner than the man of her dreams. When she lifts her head again, when she gazes across the street at the quaint little candle shop bathed in a gold light that feels otherworldly, a tide of it hits her again.

With each step she takes toward the shop, she feels as if she's slipped further out of her own body.

It's only the second day of class and he's asked them to meet him at the sculpture garden at the New Orleans Museum of Art in City Park. He's telling them how art is something that's present in their everyday lives, not just something you visit in museums or study in books. The bright sculptures shining in the sunlight all around them are proof of that. And that's when she realizes he's not like any other man she's ever known, as she gazes up at him, sitting cross-legged on the grass with the other students as he speaks. Handsome and brilliant and full of passion for something besides football. That was when she first caught his particular smell and it felt like he had unzipped her soul without touching her. And the moment had been so intoxicating, so powerful, she'd shoved it down and repressed it, and now it's coming back to her unfiltered, uncensored, overpowering and raw.

She knocks on the doorway's frame. There's no answer.

The shop before her is tiny, but too beautiful and immaculate to have been carelessly abandoned at this late hour. Instead of a register or counter, there's a small desk tucked in one corner beneath a row of ribbon wheels attached to the wall above. A large black table with a round marble top takes up the center of the tiny space. The table's curvilinear supports make her think of snakes, if you made snakes rounded and elegant and lined their bodies with tiny flecks of ivory.

The source of the smell is sitting on a metal tray, a few

inches from a vase exploding with yellow flowers she doesn't recognize. It's a candle just like the ones lining the shelves in the front window, only this one is lit. And the smell coming from it is *Michael*.

"Good evening," a male voice says.

She cries out, startled. The man suddenly standing a few feet away only smiles. She can't decide if he's handsome or just pretty. His outfit looks so formal and out-of-date she wonders if he's some kind of tour guide. Most of the tour groups she's spotted that evening were led by women dressed like vampires, but maybe there's a Jazz Age walking tour of the Quarter she's never heard of. Because with his purple silk vest, his linen tailored slacks, and his slicked-back, side-parted hair, the Jazz Age is exactly where this man seems to belong.

"What is this?" she asks, pointing to the candle. She hasn't just asked. She's barked it. At the sound of her tense, frightened anger, the shopkeeper doesn't flinch or recoil. Instead, he gives her a placating smile, as if her harsh question were an enticement to learn more about her.

"It's a candle," he says.

"I know it's a candle. But what's the smell. I mean, what's it made of?"

"Would you like to sit down, miss?"

"No. I don't want to sit down. I want you to tell me what's in this candle. *Please*."

She can hear the strain in her voice, the losing battle against tears.

"The human brain is a mysterious thing," the man says. "Smells trigger memory, mostly, and so I would suggest that the individual ingredients are irrelevant. Irrelevant to the experience you're having right now."

"Irrelevant?"

"Forgive me, I don't mean to dismiss your feelings. I suggest that their source might be somewhat larger than what's contained in that candle."

"Yeah, but..."

This is insane. Is she really about to explain Michael's aroma to this strange man?

"I was with a man earlier and he…"

"He was what?"

"He smelled like this candle. Just like it. Look, I'm sorry. I don't mean to sound so crazy."

"In the Quarter, at this hour, you'd have to work rather hard to seem like the crazy ones."

She laughs in spite of herself.

"Right. But still…I just, I really need you to tell me what's in it. Can you just tell me…?" *Because I'm suddenly afraid that this smell is all I'll ever be able to have of him, the only piece of Michael I might be able to keep.*

"This man," the candlemaker asks. "Did he upset you?"

"Did he *upset* me?" The strain in her voice turns into a stammer. She tries to wipe tears but it feels like she's missing each one. "No. No, he didn't upset me. He did everything perfectly. He did everything right. But he's…"

"He's what?"

"It's not possible," she says. "He's my teacher."

"Oh, I see. So he's considerably older than you?"

"Three years. Not that old."

"And he'll be your teacher for the rest of your natural life, of course."

"He's not big on waiting."

"So he's refused to wait?"

"No. He hasn't *refused* to wait. It's just that—"

"What? What has he done that's upset you so?"

"Nothing. He hasn't done anything to upset me, other than be exactly what I want."

"The miserable bastard," the candlemaker whispers with a smile.

His smile is disarming and Laney finds herself laughing through her tears.

"Can you please just tell me what's in this candle so I'll stop losing my mind?"

"You think that'll do it, do you?"

"Easy, fella. We just met."

"I see. Well, it's a proprietary blend, designed to stimulate certain areas of the brain which ignite passion."

"Are you serious? Is that what's on your marketing materials?"

The candlemaker gestures to a notecard taped to one side the candle's glass container. "No. It's much simpler actually," she says.

Laney lifts the notecard's flap and reads the calligraphy within.

Light this flame at the scene of your greatest passion and your heart's desire will be yours.

"I'm Bastian," the man says. "Bastian Drake."

He extends his hand. She takes it gently in her own, sees the skin on his fingers is remarkably smooth. The guy looks like he must be in his twenties, but he talks like he's from a bygone era.

"Laney," she answers. "Laney Foley."

"Take it," he says.

"Excuse me?"

"The candle. Take it. It's yours."

"I can't afford it."

"You can because it's a gift."

"Seriously?"

"I am."

"You'll get in trouble."

"With who? I own this place."

"Seriously."

"My stars, you aren't very good at accepting gifts, are you?"

"In my experience they come with *rules.*"

"Rules? Like don't fall in love with your teacher? A rule that I'm sure has *never* been broken before."

"I'm on a scholarship. A good one. If I do anything to screw it up—"

"Then what?"

"Then I'm back on the West Bank busting my ass to find a job while my family tells me over and over again how I was an idiot to try for something better. How I don't really love them because I want a different life for myself."

"I see. But if you follow the *rules*, everything will be perfect, right?"

"If I keep my scholarship, I've got a shot."

"And even if you waited until this man was no longer your teacher, you still think it would endanger your scholarship."

"People might talk."

"I see. So it's not just your scholarship. You're also afraid of what people will think."

"You know what I mean."

"I do. I do know what you mean. Fear doesn't come from our circumstances. It comes from within. And that means we can change our circumstances and fix what we think is the problem, and the fear will still be there, waiting to be dealt with."

"And how do you deal with it?"

"You stop living in a dozen different imaginary futures and you start living in today."

"Oh, everyone says that like it's so easy."

"No, actually. Everyone says it because it's something we all need to do a better job of, and we need to do a better job of it because it's incredibly difficult."

Thanks, Yoda. But she's glad she doesn't say it because it would be intolerably rude given how nice this man is being. But she wouldn't be Laney Foley if she didn't have some sort of comeback.

"I got where I am today by focusing on the *future*," she says.

"Indeed, and wherever it is you are today, Miss Foley, it seems like a very painful place."

His response has silenced her and this seems to please him. He picks up the lit candle in both hands. She waits for him to blow it out, but instead he pinches the flame itself between two impossibly smooth fingers, then he moves to his tiny desk. When he begins packaging it for her in a brightly colored paper bag complete with tissue paper and an elaborate clover of turquoise and purple ribbon, her mouth opens to protest. Even though his back is turned, he must have heard her sharp intake of breath because he says, "Not another word."

"You're a strange man, Mister Drake."

"Of this," he says, turning, a disarming smile on his youthful face, "I am most certainly aware, Miss Foley."

When she takes the bag from his hand, she glimpses some sort of pulse of gold light in both of his eyes, probably a trick thrown by a pair of passing headlights outside. But for there to be passing headlights, you would need to have a passing car, and the street outside is utterly silent. Something has just happened right behind her, however, because just then Bastian's smile fades and his gaze cuts to the shop's entrance.

The beautiful, full-figured woman standing in the doorway wears a black leather dress several shades lighter than her own skin. Her fixed, stony expression is impossible for Laney to read. Her first guess is that she's a jealous wife or girlfriend who has mistaken their exchange for flirtation. But this has less to do with the woman's rigid posture and intent gaze and more to do with Bastian's apparent shock at seeing her on his doorstep.

"Good evening," the woman says.

Then Laney remembers she's a tear-splotched, disheveled mess who just ran clear across the French Quarter in the throes of a panic attack. Maybe that's why the woman's studying her with something that looks vaguely like disdain.

"Hi," Laney says quietly. Then to Bastian, whose gaze is still fixated on their visitor, she says, "Thank you, Mister Drake."

"Bastian," he answers, his reflexive politeness still in effect even as he refuses to take his eyes off the beautiful black woman a few feet away.

"Thank you, Bastian."

At the last possible second, the woman steps aside and allows Laney to leave the shop. But a few paces from the entrance, Laney feels eyes on the back of her neck. She turns, sees the woman is staring after her with that same haunting, unreadable expression on her face.

8

LILLIANE

"What's her name?" Lilliane asks, as she watches the young woman hurry off into the night.

"Lilliane, don't—"

"What's her name, Bastian?"

When she started searching, Lilliane assumed there was very little chance she'd actually find the shop. It rarely materializes in the same place twice and she's fairly sure it vanishes as soon as Bastian delivers his special gift to his latest victim. So the shock of seeing it all again—the round black marble-topped table, the vase of strange yellow flowers, the ribbon wheels above the tiny, makeshift desk, all of it looking exactly as it did on that long-ago afternoon— has left her stunned.

Nothing, however, could have prepared her for the act of witnessing an exchange just like the one that changed the very fabric of her being decades before. It was one thing to know they'd been happening every so often over the past fifty-six years, but seeing one unfold right before her eyes has filled her with a strange blend of sadness and anger for which she has no name. Part of her is terrified the woman will meet a fate similar to her own, the other is filled with bitter jealousy over the prospect that she will not.

"Laney," Bastian says. "Laney Foley."

"Do you know their names before you appear to them? Is

that how it works?"

He doesn't answer. He just stands there in the middle of his rapidly assembled stage-set of a shop like a perfectly put-together street performer. "Did you know my name, Bastian?"

"No."

"I see. Well, I'm going to keep an eye on her." Lilliane descends several steps until she can spot the girl's shrinking silhouette blending with the bright smear of lights of Bourbon Street. "I'll make sure she makes the right decision."

"It's possible your intervention will be of no use."

"Well, if you've taught me anything, Bastian, it's that anything's possible."

"Lilliane, don't let your anger guide you."

"Don't speak to me of my anger!"

She whirls to face him, finds herself staring at the grimy front door to an abandoned store. Just a few inches from her nose, a dusty FOR LEASE signs tilts to one side against the filthy glass.

Bastian is gone. The candles are gone. It's no use arguing with a being who can stop time.

Fair enough. She's got work to do.

9

LANEY

Laney isn't surprised to wake up in her dorm room alone. Her roommate, Perfect Skinny Kelley, as Cat calls her, is carrying on two love affairs at the same time: one with her boyfriend, the other with her boyfriend's off-campus apartment.

Thanks to both of her roommate's lovers, Laney didn't have to endure any complaints about the overpowering scent of Bastian Drake's candle when she got home the night before, and this morning there's no one around to tease her for printing out Michael's late night e-mail and reading it over and over and again until her eyelids grew heavy and she fell asleep on the paper like a child cuddling a stuffed animal.

Berry Hall is one of the older dorms on campus, a blocky ten-story high-rise with crappy AC made bearable by huge, easily opened windows that allow her to fill the room with a nice cool breeze. Did she leave one of them open last night? Her alarm clock isn't set to go off for another forty minutes, but she is jerked awake with such force it's like the damn thing is already squealing right next to her head. Maybe a sound from outside is to blame. But when she reaches behind the Pottery Barn curtains and feels for the window handles, she finds them both shut tight.

The first item on her morning agenda is three cups of coffee from the Kelley's Keurig—Kelley has charitably allowed her four a day—and a good hour-and-a-half of work on her Geology paper before hauling it across campus to her lecture for History of the Americas II. That was the plan she made at the beginning of the week anyway, before she had a date with her teacher, before she suffered her first full-on panic attack.

Maybe it was the intensity of her dreams that awakened her, dreams of Michael's lips, fingers, eyes, and tongue, or maybe she'd finally had enough of the puddle of drool in between her cheek and the paper on which she printed out Michael's e-mail.

Or maybe it's frickin' Maybelline for all she cares.

The only thing she feels like doing now is reading his e-mail for the seven-hundredth time.

So I realized after I lost track of you that I don't actually have your phone number, which meant I couldn't call. There's a fine line between chasing and stalking and I don't want to cross it, which means I wasn't going to track you down at your dorm. I know that's what the guy in a movie would have done. But honestly, that's a reason to call campus security, right? (Also, I think I had too much to eat because it was clear after I chased you for half a block I was never going to be able to catch up with you without barfing. I thought the only thing worse than catching up with you if you didn't want to be caught would be catching up with you covered in barf. Agree?) I will say, aside from being an excellent student, you're an incredible runner, Miss Foley. So here's my phone number. (It's right here. See? 555-7639.) If you're done with me, you can throw it away and everything will go back to normal. Promise. If heartbroken is your idea of normal. : (Don't worry. I'm a big boy, I'll get over it. But if this is my last chance to say this, here goes. You are an amazing woman who isn't giving herself enough credit for how remarkable she is. It would be amazing if you gave me the opportunity to tell you that every day (or every other day, or maybe every other three days until we hit the six month mark. Whatever Cat decides is "healthy.") But if you're not able to give me the chance, please print out that sentence and keep it on a card in your wallet and read it when things are getting you down. In fact, I'll type it over with a space and a fun font so it looks better when you take it out and read it on a crappy day. Like this:

You are an amazing woman who isn't giving herself enough credit for how remarkable she is.— M.B.

> *Yours In Comic Sans,*
> *Michael*

P.S. I was tempted to put my phone number right next to the quote above so you'd never forget it. I think professional artists call that branding.

If only he could have been a jerk about the whole thing.

If only he could have been defensive and angry and hurt, all things some childish part of her probably wanted from him as soon as she took off the night before.

But, no. Even in the face of her crazy, he's humble and self-effacing and attuned to appropriate boundaries and intelligent and charming as ever.

Her laptop—Cat's old laptop computer that Cat gave to her at the beginning of the year when she upgraded her own—chimes at the arrival of a new e-mail.

When she sees the message isn't from Michael, her heart drops a little. Then she sees it's from the office manager for the undergraduate art history program and her heart drops more than a little.

Please call the office immediately regarding your discussion section for Foundations of Western Art II.

As she listens to the phone ring, her breaths are short and

shallow. And by the time the woman on the other end answers, Laney is stammering a greeting and clearing her throat at the same time.

"This is Laney Foley," she finally manages. "I have, uhm, an e-mail from you guys about my discussion section."

"Right, right, right," the woman says quickly while tapping keys on her computer. Whoever she is, her caffeine levels are at peak, while Laney is still struggling to open both eyes. "Let me get this up here on my screen. Give me a second."

"Sure," Laney says.

He lost it. I didn't write him back last night and he lost it and now he's going to punish me. The e-mail was bullshit and now the axe is going to——-

"Yeah, here we go," the woman says. "He says you two talked about some sort of scheduling problem that's started to come up for you on Wednesdays. Does that sound familiar?"

"Uh-huh," she grunts.

No. Oh, my God. What's happening?

"And so he thought it would be best if the department moved you to a different discussion section. So I went ahead and checked your schedule and it looks like you've got an opening on Friday, and it just so happens we've got another discussion section we could move you into then. But it's with a different T.A. Kimberly Stockton."

"Is that allowed? Moving me into a class with a different teacher?"

"Yes. It's just a discussion section. They follow the same syllabus."

"Sure. Right. Yeah."

What the hell are you doing, Michael?

"Your final grade will be an average of the grades Michael gave you in his Wednesday class, and what you receive from Kimberly in the Friday class."

"So Michael won't give me my final grade. Kimberly will."

"Kimberly will be grading your final three assignments and at the end of the semester, those will be averaged with the grades you've already received from Michael. Does that make sense?"

"Yeah. Yeah it does."

What he said to her the night before? He couldn't take away her fears if she didn't give him the chance. Well, that was bunk. He'd just removed one of her biggest fears with a single e-mail to his department.

Then why am I still so goddamn afraid?

Laney pretends to listen as the woman explains how it will take a few days for the system to reflect the schedule change, but that next Friday she should report to Kimberly's class and here's the name of the classroom where Kimberly Stockton's discussion section meets and—blah blah blah.

Instead, she hears her pulse pounding in her ears, bringing with it the terrible realization that it's just like Bastian Drake said to her the night before. The fear is still there. The fear comes from within her, not from Michael, not from the art history department, not from the Rose Scholarship.

I'm not good enough.

There it is. A voice clear as a bell, a voice that sounds like her mother, her father, and all of her cousins rolled into one, a voice that speaks to her so clearly and with words that sound so carefully chosen, how could she *not* listen to it? How could she not heed its angry, hurtful advice?

You can go to as nice a school as you want, little girl, but it won't change the fact that you are poor white trash putting on airs and he's gonna smell this on you every day while you smell vanilla and campfires, and then he's gonna drop you like a cold, hard stone.

Is she still on the campus health plan? What are the names of the antidepressants she's heard other students talk about, the ones that actually work? Phrases like "anxiety disorder" and "panic syndrome" are dancing together in her brain now, as she tries to come up with any possible solution to this relentless, mental assault. If she didn't have a class in a few hours and a paper due next week, she'd probably head for the nearest bar. But instead she claws her hands through her hair and tilts her head forward and draws a deep breath through her nose.

And without meaning to, she inhales the scent of the candle at the foot of her bed.

The sunlight bounces off the chrome sculpture nearby, fills his eyes briefly before he blinks and smiles and continues with his passionate lecture. And she's so hypnotized by his beauty, she's stopped nervously picking at the grass next to her. And when he sees her looking up at him, he locks eyes with her and smiles, smiles longer than any teacher should at a student.

"What the fuck *are* you candle?" she hears herself saying.

Laney unties the bow so she can part the bag's handles, then she removes enough of the tissue paper to pull the candle free. She sets it on her bed and stares at it as if it's a kitten about to take its first steps. Wide veins of purple and brown are threaded through the wax. Twelve hours later and the scent has the same effect of delivering her straight to the sculpture garden outside the New Orleans Museum of Art, to the moment when her heart first opened to Michael.

She figured the notecard taped to the side was just for display and expected Bastian to remove it before packaging up the candle. But he left it right where it was when she wandered into his shop.

Light this flame at the scene of your greatest passion and your heart's desire will be yours.

She doesn't believe in magic or spells or voodoo. She *does* believe in following advice, and a lot of the advice Bastian gave her last night sounded good. No, *wise*. Experienced. So why not follow the flowery, romantic instruction printed on this card?

Sure, it sounds like the making of some silly little spell, something her crazy aunts might do for a sick relative or a friend who'd been cheated on. But sometimes stuff like that could have a placebo effect. And right now, she would try anything to silence these viciously critical voices running riot in her head.

Anything.

It takes all that self-control she's got, but she waits until after her lecture to text him. She's moved into the shady overhang of one of the older buildings fringing the Quad, far from the other students lounging on the grass during an unseasonably warm afternoon.

Looks like you're not my teacher anymore.

Just seven words, but they took fifteen minutes to write.

Cat's got one of those thought bubble logos that tells you if the other person has started typing in response to your text.

Laney's old school cell phone has no such feature, and people often marvel at how fast she can fire off text messages using a regular telephone keypad.

So Laney waits. And waits. And waits. And then feels stupid for waiting because she sure as hell took her sweet time texting him back and maybe he's teaching or—

I hope you're not upset.

Three minutes. Not a bad response time for a guy who was walked out on—make that *run* out on—the night before. And then another one follows right on its digital heels.

Kimberly's a good egg. Just don't say anything negative about cubism. She's kind of obsessed.

Noted, Laney responds.

So the next time we go out to dinner it won't be as teacher and student. It'll just be a date with a guy who's crazy about you.

The breath leaves her. She rests her head against the stone column next to her.

If there's going to be a next time...

Then, just as she lifts her fingers to type, he responds again.

Maybe there's another barrier you need me to remove. Just say the word.

Before she can think twice, she starts tapping keys.

I'm not the biggest fan of my history teacher. Can you rub him out for me?

Too jokey, too soon?

Sorry. Assassinations are a third date thing.

Laney explodes with tension-releasing laughter, so high and barking it draws the attention of a guitar player strumming for adoring freshman a few yards away.

Why are you so perfect? she types.

I'm not, he responds. *I just try to be when I meet someone worth trying for.*

She's about to respond when she feels a strange prickling on the side of her face. Her index finger hovers over the keypad. She looks up, tries to find the source of this strange feeling.

The guitar player's gone back to performing for his adoring fans. But further away, across the Quad...

It can't be.

It's the woman from last night, the one Bastian Drake was startled to find standing in the entrance to his tiny shop. The one who wouldn't smile or introduce herself, who studied Laney with a cold, unreadable look. She's too far away for Laney to read her facial expression now, but she stands just as proudly. Her outfit is more casual, a cream-colored sleeveless peasant dress that billows around her generous frame. Some sort of jeweled headband sits on her dark hair like a glittering tiara.

Right now, she is more afraid of leaving Michael in the lurch then some jealous stalker girlfriend.

I would very much like to have dinner again.

An instant response. He must have been waiting on pins and needle for her text.

Is tonight too soon?

There goes her breath, and here comes her pulse.

She remembers the panic that threatened her just that morning, an attack that promised to be as powerful as the one she'd suffered the night before in Michael's arms. Then she remembers what ended it.

Light this flame at the scene of your greatest passion and your heart's desire will be yours.

It's not too soon, she types.

But first I need to do a magic spell a strange man in the French Quarter gave me because I think it might prevent me from having another panic attack when you kiss me.

K. Teaching right now so I'll get back to you about a plan ;)

The knowledge that he took time out from an actual class to send her all those texts makes her giddy. And this reminds her that he's no longer her teacher, no longer responsible for her grade, which makes her even giddier. Then she remembers her audience across the Quad. But when she looks up, the woman is gone. Maybe she imagined her. Given her mental state over the past twelve hours, she wouldn't be all that surprised.

All right, Mister Drake. Let's see if your candle's all it's cracked up to be.

She actually considered carrying the candle around in her

backpack for the rest of the day. That way she could head straight to the sculpture garden after class and be done with this nonsense. But the overpowering scent would have earned her far too many angry looks as it washed over the library and then the lecture hall, that's for sure. So she's got no choice but to head back to her dorm room, praying under her breath that Kelley didn't come home earlier than expected and throw the thing out because she hated the smell. God knows, Cat bitched to high heaven when Laney had stepped into her car with it the night before. And it hadn't been the scent of vanilla and campfires that had earned Cat's ire either.

"Why would anyone make a candle that smells like a dirty fish tank?" Cat asked.

A special recipe intended to stimulate the centers of the brain that promote passion.

Isn't that what Bastian Drake had told her? That or something similarly dramatic. But if the candle smelled so different to Cat's nose than to Laney's, maybe that gave some truth to Bastian's self-promoting ridiculousness.

"Laney Foley."

She didn't imagine it. The beautiful black woman from the night before is standing a few feet away, just steps from the entrance to Laney's dorm.

"I need to speak with you," the woman says. "It's important."

"Listen, I don't know what you think was happening last night. But he just gave me a candle. That's all. I've never seen him before and I'll probably never see him again. He seemed nice, but apparently he's not all that nice if you think he's— anyway. Just a candle. That's all. I promise."

"It is *not* just a candle," the woman answers.

"Ma'am, please. I've had kind of a rough day and I just…I don't mean to be rude, I just *really* don't need any more drama right now."

"If you don't want any *drama* in your life, then *don't* light that candle."

If the woman really thinks Laney slept with her man, where's her self-righteous outrage? She seems conflicted. Like there's more she wants to say, but can't.

"What is it?" Laney asks. "A bomb?"

"No."

"Poison? *Drugs?*

"Is there somewhere we can talk?"

"I'll throw it away. How does that sound? As soon as I get upstairs, I'll throw it in the trash. And we're done, and it's all good."

"No. We're not *all good.*"

"Okay. I've said my piece and I'm done, so I'm gonna go. Take care and please don't follow me or else I'll call campus security. Have a nice afternoon."

And with that, she starts for the entrance to her dorm. In what feels like one motion, Laney slides her keycard through the reader, steps inside the foyer and pulls the glass door shut behind her with both hands. When she turns, the woman's nowhere to be seen. Just a loose smattering of students on the distant lawn. She should still call someone, campus security maybe? File some kind of stalking report. If that's even a thing.

The elevator's on the tenth floor and she doesn't feel like waiting for it so she bounds up the fire staircase to her room on the seventh. The door is open a crack which must mean Kelley's home. Laney pulls the knob, already scripting a speech for Kelley about how they should all be on the lookout for a strange woman who just stopped her outside and probably thinks she banged her weird, Jazz Age-obsessed boyfriend.

As soon as Laney steps into her dorm room, the woman in question turns from the open window as if she's been waiting patiently for several minutes. A scream reaches the bottom of Laney's throat. The woman raises one index finger and quietly says, "Please don't scream, Laney. Everything will be all right if you just listen to me."

"*What the fuck?*"

"Is the language necessary?" her visitor asks.

"Yes. What the *fuck?*"

"I guess it's preferable to screaming."

"Which you asked me not to do. And which I'm not doing. So I repeat. What the fuck?"

"What's the question exactly?" her visitor asks.

"The *question* is *what the fuck?*"

"I'm not really sure how to respond," the woman answers. "Perhaps my name will do. I'm Lilliane. And once you've calmed down a little, I'll show you something else that will also make you curse a lot. I can't wait, honestly."

Lilliane extends her hand. Laney refuses to take it, refuses to move an inch from where her feet are planted just inside the doorway to her dorm room.

"We're on the seventh floor," Laney says. "How did you—?"

"What the fuck?" Lilliane finishes for her.

"Yeah."

"Laney Foley, we can do this one of two ways. I can show you a variety of things I'm capable of, none of which you will ever be able to explain in any rational or scientific way. And a great many of which will reduce you to a sputtering wreck in the corner of your room. *Or* I can show you only those things that you will eventually be able to dismiss and discount once I'm on my way. Option two, I can assure you, will allow you to lead a far more balanced and normal life. And believe it or not, despite the manner in which I have entered it, my objective is for you to lead a balanced and normal life from here on out."

"There's nothing normal about jumping seven stories through an open window."

"It wasn't open. But yes, you're right. There's nothing normal about it. Just as there is nothing normal about this candle."

The candle in question is still on Laney's desk, right next to her open laptop, easily within Lilliane's reach, but the older woman refuses to touch it. Instead, she studies it as if it were a dead rat.

"Have you calmed down a bit or do you need to curse some more?" Lilliane asks.

"I'm done cursing. For now."

"Good. Then read the webpage I've opened on your computer."

At her desk, Laney tilts the monitor back until the sun isn't whiting out the screen. When she hits the right angle, she finds herself staring down at a black and white photograph of Lilliane. Her hair is different, and the posed, black-and-white photo looks like it's from another era, but it's definitely the same woman. The site is called *FORGOTTEN INJUSTICE*, its title framed by ghostly human profiles with no facial features. Laney scans the captions above and below Lilliane's picture, then clicks on some of the links in the header to make sure the site is legit. On another page, she comes across a recent *Times Picayune* article praising the site's mission, which is to document old, unsolved missing persons cases within the black community local newspapers refused to report on at the time. The woman standing right behind her is one of those cases. And she hasn't aged a day since she went missing.

And there it is, Laney thinks. One day, you're walking along and then suddenly something totally inexplicable drops right down in the middle of your life. Either you lose your mind or this extraordinary thing—a woman who hasn't aged a day in fifty-six years, for instance—becomes as undeniable as gravity. After all, wasn't there a time in all of our lives when complete sentences sounded to us like magic because we couldn't yet speak one ourselves? How was this any different? How is the woman and what she might be capable of any different to Laney's everyday life than a complete sentence is to an infant?

"This is you," Laney hears herself say.

"Yes."

"This is you in nineteen fifty-nine."

"That is me, four months before I met Bastian Drake."

"I see." *No, I don't.*

"Do you need to curse again?"

"Maybe."

"It doesn't offend me. It's a sign that you're not focused and I would like you to be able to retain everything I'm about to say to you."

"Okay. *Fuck.* There, I said it. It's out of my system."

Laney sinks down into her desk chair. It occurs to her, too late, that Lilliane now stands between her and her only exit. But there's nothing menacing in the woman's expression. She looks sheepish, and after a few seconds, she manages an indulgent smile.

"He's a ghost," Lilliane finally says.

"A ghost? Bastian Drake is a ghost?"

"Yes. Last night you had an extended conversation with and accepted a gift from a ghost. Just as in April of nineteen fifty-nine I wandered into a strange little candle shop in the French Quarter I'd never seen before and had an extended conversation with *and* accepted a gift from a ghost."

"Am I dead right now?" Laney asks.

"No. Focus. What did it smell like?"

"Bastian?"

"The candle."

"Vanilla. Vanilla and campfires."

"And I take it the man for whom you have deep feelings smells exactly the same way?"

"Yes," Laney whispers.

Lilliane smiles distantly, nostalgically, and for a second Laney thinks her visitor is blinking back tears. But none come. Maybe this woman, this *being*, isn't capable of making them.

"Mine was pears and cinnamon," Lilliane says. "Pears and cinnamon," she adds, her voice a hoarse whisper.

"Are you a ghost too?" Laney asks.

"No. Changed, yes. But not a ghost."

"Changed by what? By Bastian?"

"Close. By his candle. By *that* candle," she says, pointing to the one next to Laney's elbow. "His shop. It never appears in the same place twice, you see. And it only appears to someone like you, someone struggling with what they want and how they want it. *Bastian* only appears to someone like you, I should say, and he only gives a candle to someone suffering under the same struggle."

"And you were suffering?" Laney asks, and then forces herself to gulp before she says, "In nineteen fifty-nine?"

Lilliane closes her eyes, shakes her head as if shrugging off the memory.

"He'll tell you that most of the time his magic, the magic in that candle, only does good. That once lit, the flame releases a force that allows a person's true passion to become their everyday life. And how can that be a bad thing?"

"And what would *you* tell me about his magic?"

"That there is a risk to it," Lilliane says. "A risk he doesn't disclose. I would tell you there are some people in whom fear runs so deep, in whom resistance is so strong, the flame's energy isn't strong enough to overpower them."

"Wait a minute," Laney says. "Just tell me, if I were to light this candle right now, what would happen? What would I see?"

"You would see something that would either make you scream bloody murder or fall down on your knees in prayer. Or possibly both. And then, shortly thereafter, you would have the most intense orgasm of your entire life. Then you would regain consciousness covered in a kind of gold residue which you wouldn't be able to wipe off or shower away, and you would go to the man you currently desire with absolute surrender and abandon and a total absence of fear."

Neither one of them speaks for several minutes. Outside, a bird chirps madly. Is it trying to warn her the woman she's talking to just flew seven stories up the side of Berry Hall?

"And you *don't* want me to light this candle?" Laney finally asks.

"What I've just described is one possible scenario. There are two. If you're one of the obstinate ones, like I was, if your mind is strong enough to talk yourself out of your desire, even when that desire is amplified by the flame's energy, things will go very differently."

"Okay…"

"Are you a stubborn person, Laney Foley? Are you full of reasons why it will never work with the man you can't chase from your thoughts and your heart?"

Her answer is in the speed with which her eyes drop to the pockmarked linoleum floor between them.

"I see," Lilliane whispers. "It's a good thing I warned you then."

"And what happens to the stubborn ones?" Laney asks. "What happened to you?"

"We call ourselves Radiants. It's far better than what he used to call us."

"Bastian?"

"Yes. *The Refused.* That was his nickname for us in the beginning. Because we had refused his gift, you see."

"How?"

"The flame's energy is drawn from those who have lived out their deepest sexual desires. That's what fuels his candles. The life force of desire, if you will. Bastian used to collect this force himself. I'm not exactly sure how. There's much he won't tell me. Now I collect it for him, at a place I run called The Desire Exchange."

Amazing that the name of a silly urban legend seems like the only *real* thing in this entire conversation. Maybe because it's familiar.

"I always thought that place was a joke," Laney says.

"Everyone does. It's how we stay exclusive."

"You run it?"

"Yes. It's where I've managed to put some of my abilities to use. To *good* use, that is. I was the first, you see. The first person to refuse his gift."

"But, Lilliane, what does that mean, to refuse his gift? I don't understand."

"It means that for twenty-four hours after you light the candle, twenty-four hours after you see spirits emerge from it and you're bathed in an energy that fills you with a desire like you have never known, even then, you *still* don't go to the person you desire with all your heart. You don't complete the connection the flame is driving you to make. And so, the flame's energy never reaches its final destination. It becomes trapped within you and as a result you are forever changed."

"How?"

Lilliane looks into Laney's eyes for the first time in several minutes, and while she's yet to shed a tear, the pain is so raw and evident it's hard for Laney to hold the woman's gaze. But it would be too rude to look away.

"I don't want to say," Lilliane says.

"Why?"

"Because it will sound better than it is. And I don't wish my life for you. For anyone."

"Don't I have the right to make a choice?" Laney asks. "Isn't that why you came? So that I could know the risk?"

"I've stayed out of Bastian's affairs until now. But I wasn't prepared for how I'd feel when I saw it all again. When I saw you standing there just like me. The shop exactly like it was all those years ago, just on a different street."

"You think I'll want to be like you if you tell me what you are?"

"Perhaps."

"If all you wanted was to keep me from lighting this candle, why didn't you just jump back out the window with it before I got upstairs?"

"I don't know," she answers. It sounds almost petulant.

"Of course you do. You waited. You waited to tell me all of this. So don't just give me half your story. Please."

The woman takes a seat on Laney's bed, her posture as casual as a friend who just dropped by for a chat and Diet Coke. The forced nature of this gesture chills Laney to the bone.

"I don't age, as you can see from that picture. I don't sleep, because I don't need to. I don't eat. And I don't fly, exactly. But I leap, which is sort of like flying but you can't let the mind wander for very long." Then, as if she's just rattled off the items on a grocery list, she smooths her dress over her thighs and offers Laney a weak smile.

"Is that all?" Laney asks in a hoarse, strained voice.

"No," Lilliane says primly. "If I suck in a little bit of your breath, I have the power to make your deepest sexual fantasy materialize in your immediate physical area for an extended period of time. To do this, I literally dematerialize."

"Dematerialize?"

"I cease to exist as an individual being on this physical plane. I become your fantasy. All of it. The room, the props, the players. It's another fun perk of the energy that's been trapped in me for fifty-six years."

"I see."

"No, you don't. And it's my hope that you never will."

"Because you think if you just tell me about this stuff and don't show any of it to me, I'll be able to pretend like none of this ever happened once you leave."

"Once I leave *with* the candle. Yes."

"You can't just wipe my memory or something?"

"No. I cannot."

"Good, I guess," Laney says. "So the energy in this candle, you collect it for him even though you know the risk, even though it turned you into something amazing you don't want to be?"

Lilliane averts her eyes. "There was no one else like me in the beginning. Bastian was all I had. And even he wasn't sure what had happened to me. We figured it out together as best we could. And then a few years later, there was another. And another. And we saw the trend. By then, I'd become comfortable with my new abilities so I took over some of his operations. I thought it would allow me to control him. But there's no controlling him. He can't even control himself."

"How come?"

Lilliane meets Laney's stare again. "He's a servant to forces he doesn't fully understand. But if you must know, I help people at The Desire Exchange. They leave enlightened, not *transformed*. And by God, I help far more people than he appears to on the streets of the French Quarter. That's for sure. It's good work I do."

"And ten bucks says it's got something to do with your other power. The one where you..." Laney can't even bring herself to repeat the words Lilliane just used. *Dematerialize?* Become a fantasy? It's all nuts! "So is that all?" Laney asks.

"All of what?"

"All of how you've been changed."

"No," Lilliane says, shaking her head, staring into Laney's eyes again with a piercing look that threatens to break Laney's heart. And then the piercing look is joined by a dazzling gold radiance that fills both of the woman's eye sockets, a radiance that rides the swell of emotion within Lilliane. It's a full-fledged display of something Laney only glimpsed in Bastian's eyes the night before. Then it's gone and Lilliane once again stares back at her with beautiful, but very human brown eyes, filled with pain, but not with otherworldly golden light.

"I can feel lust," Lilliane says, her voice almost a whisper. "I can feel raw sexual attraction to another person. But I have no desire to commit to them. To anyone. I have never again had the experience of looking at a man and believing that anything would be possible if he just took me in his arms.

"True love, Laney Foley, is wanting the world for someone even when they won't do what you tell them to, even when they don't want you back. True love is the ability to make yourself absolutely vulnerable to someone despite the risks. In fact, when you're truly in love, the only real risk is that you won't do justice to that love. It's a hard thing to define, true love. I'll give you that. But you can define it when it's gone. Oh, my heavens, how you can define it when it's gone. Believe me. *That* is how I have *also* been changed, Laney Foley. And I do not wish the same for you or anyone."

"How do you know, Lilliane? How do you know it's been removed from you completely?"

"I went to him," she whispers. "After several days, after I realized that simply lighting a candle given to me by a strange white man in the French Quarter had changed my fundamental being, I went to the man I smelled every time I lifted that candle to my nose. I went to the man who had once filled my dreams and made my heart flutter every time he came near. And when I looked at him I felt nothing. It was as if I was staring upon sandpaper and dust. I could take to the sky but my heart had been emptied."

"Maybe you were just angry," Laney says. "You'd had a traumatic experience. You probably—"

"I know your intentions are good, Miss Foley, but I've had decades to sort through this. Literally decades. This is my story, I'm sorry to say. The same is true for the other Radiants."

"How many are there?" Laney asks.

"Twenty-three," she answers. "And when I saw you in that shop last night, I was not willing to add another to our ranks."

For a while, neither one of them speaks. A dull pounding of bass echoes down the hall. It's that hushed period of early evening when most classes are finished and students have retreated to their dorm rooms before venturing out to dinner.

Did a part of her innately sense Bastian Drake's shop had some kind of magic to it? The same part of her that might assume a strange, distant sound in a creaky old house could possibly be a ghost. And did she really not care or pause to consider the idea because Bastian *seemed* totally sincere about her well-being?

Is it easier to believe in guardian angels or demons? She's not entirely sure. But she's willing to bet it's the former. Which one is Bastian Drake?

"So," Laney finally says, her voice sounding reedy and distant. "If I light the candle, I'll either be forced to have sex with the man I'm falling for, or I'll freak out and run, and then I'll be turned into an immortal who can never fall in love again. Both options sound like rape, if you ask me."

"You don't have to have sex with him to complete the connection. You simply have to tell him the truth that's in your heart. Whether or not you use your entire body to do it is up to you."

"But that's not what happened to you?"

"As I said, once the other Radiants started to come in, we collected their experiences, identified the trends. Some of them went to the object of their desire right after they lit the flame and had quite a time in between the sheets. But they ran like hell as soon as orgasms were achieved. They never told the person how they truly felt. That's the key."

"That and you have to stay with them for twenty-four hours?" Laney asks.

"No. For a sleep."

"I'm sorry. A what?"

"You have to share yourself with them either physically or verbally and then sleep beside them for a night. Which might have something to do with why Radiants never sleep again."

"And if you stay the night, you stay with them forever?"

"Oh, no. You stay with them for as long as it's meant to last. The flame offers an opportunity to finally act, not a guarantee that it will last forever once you do."

"None of this is fair," Laney mutters.

"Oh, Laney Foley. Find me a world that's fair and I will take you in my arms and fly us to it. The supernatural universe contains as many quirks and rules as quantum physics."

"Yeah, I'm getting that. Provided, you know, you're not nuts."

"This man of yours," Lilliane says. "The one who smells of campfires and vanilla. What's his name?"

"Michael?"

"Is he resisting what exists between you?"

"God, no," Laney answers. "He couldn't be resisting any less."

"Good. Then he'll be safe no matter what you decide."

"What do you mean?"

"Some Radiants start out as the objects of desire for those who light the flame, only they resist it too, because it's terrifying. The energy comes to them and they know nothing of the candle in the first place so—"

"Get it out of here," Laney says. She's on her feet before she realizes she's made the decision to stand. Her back is to her desk, and the candle and the laptop with its screen filled with the vintage photograph of Lilliane. "Take it. Please. Just get it out of here."

"Are you sure?"

"Well, aren't you happy? Isn't this what you wanted?"

"I wanted you to be able to make a choice based on all the infor—"

"I've made it. Take it. Please."

"Very well," Lilliane whispers.

Facing her roommate's side of the room, Laney studies the Keurig coffee maker and the perfectly made bed and all the photographs of Perfect Skinny Kelley and her perfect family on a variety of beach vacations, hoping these ordinary objects will return to her to a sane and normal world. But even as she tries not to, she's listening intently to the small scraping sounds of Lilliane lifting the candle up off the desk.

"There's something else that I want," Lilliane finally says.

"Lilliane, I don't mean to be rude, but I don't think I can handle any—"

"Go to him," Lilliane says. "Go to him and tell him the truth that's in your heart. You don't need magic or a ghost to help you do it. Find the courage within yourself and go to him as soon as you can. If I am proof of anything, it's that all the time in the world can't bring back certain moments, certain opportunities."

Laney turns to face the woman just as she starts for the door.

"Lilliane!"

Startled, Lilliane turns in the doorway.

"What if he's not happy that I didn't light the candle? Could he appear to me again?"

"That won't happen," Lilliane says with utter confidence.

"How are you so sure?"

"Because I'll make sure it won't."

"Thank you," Laney whispers.

Lilliane nods and starts to leave again.

"And Lilliane?"

The woman stops, but she doesn't return Laney's stare.

"I don't believe you," Laney says before she can think twice.

"Which part?"

"I don't believe you can never fall in love again. I think it's still in you somewhere. Maybe it's just a matter of time."

"And what makes you think that?"

"What you did today was too kind and selfless for me to believe your heart is empty."

Lilliane looks up, giving Laney an answer to her earlier question. Yes, Radiants can cry.

"Thank you, Laney," Lilliane says. "And I wish you and Michael the very best."

With a polite nod that belies her tears, Lilliane departs with the candle in one hand, carrying the scent of Bastian Drake's frightening magic away down the hall.

11

Thirty minutes after Lilliane exited Laney's dorm room, in the traditional, non-flying manner, Laney has walked most of the distance to the restaurant where Michael waited. He sent the address by text while she and Lilliane were discussing ghosts, magic candles, and *dematerialization.*

Lilliane was right about one thing. In no time at all, Laney has started to discount some of the more impossible suggestions of the woman's visit. She's decided the website had to have been a fake, for sure. You could do amazing things with Photoshop, like forge an entire *Times Picayune* article. Or make a photograph you took yesterday afternoon look fifty-six years old.

That flying up the side of a seven-story building, though? See, that *one's harder to—*

They're all members of a cult. That's it. A cult that makes strange drugged candles that sometimes poison people, and Lilliane's crazy tale of flame energy was designed to cover up their criminal enterprise. Laney has a hunch that a good cover story doesn't sound completely and utterly wacko, and also doesn't take almost an hour to tell. But who knows? Maybe Lilliane thought Laney was some paranoid stoner who went for psychic readings every other week and would totally buy into a nutso story of spirits and ghosts and haunted candles and—

Yeah, and then there's the part where she just appeared in your room. On the seventh *floor. Without using the elevator or the stairs. Which meant she had to fly, or leap, or whatever she said she does, up the side of the—*

Michael spots her through the restaurant's glass front door. He's sitting by himself at the mostly empty bar. The place is homey and brightly lit, surrounded by sleepy residential blocks, the exact opposite of the rowdy elegance that surrounded them the night before. The quieter surroundings give her a sense of elation. Laney wonders if she's coming to accept that only moments before she was visited by something, by *someone*, truly extraordinary. If only half of what Lilliane said was true, perhaps anything is possible. It seems the world is more limitless than Laney previously thought. She wants to savor this feeling while it lasts, this sense that the prison of rules and risks Laney has lived in for most of her life was just a sandcastle waiting to crumble under the force of a gentle tide.

Is this how she would have felt if she'd actually lit that damn candle? Fearless and elated?

If she hadn't left her dorm in a daze, she might have remembered to bring her umbrella. Only a light roll or two of thunder interrupted the walk there, but suddenly there's a crack loud enough to make her jump.

A small tinkling bell heralds her arrival when she opens the restaurant's front door. There's no host, just a waitress making friendly conversation with the customers at one of her tables, so no one stops her as she walks toward the empty barstool next to Michael. His smile could melt ice, but the rest of him is poised and rigid. *Tense.* He probably figures a big hug isn't the best move given the last time they saw each other she was running like hell in the opposite direction.

"They have a dessert here that is literally a scoop of ice cream on top of a doughnut," he says without preamble.

"Seriously?"

"I am *so* serious. We didn't have dessert last night, so I figured it would give us something to do."

"Something to do?"

"Yeah, while we wait for the moment of truth."

"What do you mean?"

"Well, I'm not your teacher anymore, so if you just don't like me I guess now's the time to say it so we can part as friends. But I recommend waiting until you've had just a little of this doughnut because it is truly one of the best things on the—"

"Michael Brouchard, I've wanted you from the moment I laid eyes on you."

He looks like the wind's been knocked out of him. Was she really that coy? Did he really have that much doubt about how she felt for him?

She wants to break eye contact so she can hold on to the courage she needs to speak the truth of her heart, but there's no looking away from the suddenly vulnerable expression on his face.

"I knew it the first time I saw you," she continues, "the first time I heard you speak, the first time you shared your heart with your class. I knew I'd never met a man like you and I would never meet a man like you again. And the way I felt for you in that moment scared me so bad I did everything I could to deny it. And I waited. I waited each day for you to screw up and give me some sign you weren't really the man I wanted you to be. And every day I sat there and gazed up into your beautiful eyes, I realized that sometimes—*sometimes* a fantasy comes true. All my life I've wanted to feel for someone the way I feel about you. I just had no idea I'd be so goddamn scared when those feelings finally showed up.

"I tried to rehearse this on the walk over. But all I did was come up with a million ways to tell you how I might screw this up if we *try*. A million ways to tell you I'm less than perfect. Because there's a part of me that thinks if I just lay it out on the table now, you'll be able to forgive me if I run again."

"I've already forgiven you," he says.

"I know. But I don't want to sound like this big victim or an angry poor girl with a shell around her heart. And I don't want to plan my escape. And now I know that's a good thing, that I'm afraid, afraid of the way I feel for you. It's a good thing because it means it's real. It means I'm going to give you something I've never given anyone before."

He pales.

"I'm not a virgin," Laney says quickly. "That's not what I'm talking about."

"Okay," Michael says quietly, sounding relieved. Laney

pauses. Michael watches her intently and simply waits.

"I'm giving you my trust," she tells him.

"Trust."

"Yeah. It's not something I give out easily. If you haven't noticed."

She grabs for the nearest napkin. As she uses it to wipe at her tears, she feels Michael gently take her other hand in his.

There's a crack of thunder loud enough to make everyone in the restaurant jump. Outside, a deluge begins, instantly rattling the huge plate glass windows.

"I've noticed," Michael whispers. He brings her fingers to his lips and kisses them gently. "I just figured that would make me feel honored once I finally earned it."

She laughs, which brings more tears to her eyes. As they clear, she feels a stab of embarrassment or shame.

"So you're not a fan of virgins?"

"I'm not looking for a conquest, Laney. There are no notches on my belt."

"That's 'cause you mostly wear braided belts."

"I get a lot of crap for that."

"Not from me. I think they're classy. But mostly I like that you can't leave notches in them. It speaks to your character."

"Does it?" he asks with a broad smile. "Well, I'm glad you noticed."

"Were you just listening? There's almost nothing about you I haven't noticed."

"Likewise. But the point is, I'm looking for a partner, Laney. I'm not looking for a woman who only lets me sketch her one time."

"Good to know," she says, lacing her fingers through his until the two of them are officially and indisputably holding hands.

Thunder cracks, followed by a flash of lightning. Everyone in the restaurant jumps again except for them. They're too busy staring into each other's eyes.

"Do I really need to write in shorter paragraphs?" Laney asks.

"What do I care? I'm not your teacher anymore." He makes

his eyebrows dance up and down and gives her an evil grin.

"No, but seriously, the stuff you said last night—"

"Was a lot of *bull*," he says. "I was just trying to prove that I could be objective if I had to stay your teacher."

"Could you?"

"Could I have stayed your teacher?"

"Could you have been objective?" she asks.

"Probably not."

"Well," Laney says, lifting his fingers to her lips, and giving them a gentle kiss. "It's a good thing you're not my teacher anymore."

"I'll say," he whispers.

She gives his fingers another kiss. Just this simple, tender act causes her pulse to quicken.

"I know you don't believe it yet, but you belong here, Laney," he says quietly.

"At this school or with you?"

"Both."

The lightning and thunder return. This time the flash is so bright, for a few seconds it covers up the fact that the power has gone out. The customers inside the restaurant groan as total darkness descends.

"Well," Michael says, gripping her hand and sliding off his stool. "Looks like we're gonna have to find another place for desert."

"Where's that?"

"We'll figure it out."

Michael didn't bring an umbrella either, so he takes off his leather jacket and holds it over their heads as he guides her in the direction of his car. It's one of those relentless New Orleans storms, the kind that usually blows through on summer afternoons and are twice as frightening when they appear at night, with their fat, pelting drops and sudden gusts of wind. The power is out on the entire street which turns the cars alongside them into vague, dripping shadows. She has no idea which belongs to Michael. When he stops suddenly next to a stubby, bright-orange box with tires, she almost loses her footing.

Once he shuts the door after her, once she's sealed inside the little box, she starts laughing.

"It's a Kia Soul!" she cries as he slides behind the wheel.

"Are you making fun of my car?"

"No. I'm so happy."

"Why? It's not that great, really. And it's used. My friend's loaning it to me until I can afford to get something else 'cause even he hates it."

"Yeah, but it's a Kia Soul. Don't you understand?"

"No!"

He turns the key in the ignition. The first squeal doesn't sound promising.

"All my friends, hell, make that everyone around me, have all this expensive crap all the time. Cat's got a brand new BMW. My roommate's got this Keurig coffee maker and she acts like it's a charity project to let me have four a day. Meanwhile, I can't even afford a smartphone. But *you*. You, Michael Brouchard, drive a crappy *used* Kia Soul, and that is a beautiful, beautiful thing."

"And it won't start," he says.

"Seriously?"

"Seriously," he says. He turns the key again. Nothing happens.

"Oh."

"We could go back inside the restaurant," he offers.

"We could."

"Or we could stay here," he says.

"What would we do if we stayed here?"

Before they have time to speculate, he's curved an arm around her upper back and brought their bodies as close together as he can over the gear shift, close enough for his mouth to find hers, for his free hand to cup the side of her face gently, then her chin, holding her in place so he can direct and focus the force of his kiss.

He is panting when he breaks, lips still inches from hers. "I guess we could stay here and make out like teenagers."

"Or discuss some extra credit," she whispers.

"I'm not your teacher anymore, Miss Foley."

At these words, her waist suddenly feels molten, liquid, a reminder that not only is she free from the risk of damaging her academic standing, *he's* the one who set her free. He's the one who made the effort to switch her to a different class. He didn't lecture her or condescend to her or tell her that her fears were meaningless. Instead, he figured out what they were and did his best to make them disappear.

"Oh, yeah," she says, cupping his chin in her hand. "Then get in the backseat with me and prove it."

Even in the rainy darkness, she can see his eyes widen at this brazen request. She can feel the shudder of lust that moves through his body before she releases the back of his neck. She kicks the door open, blinks against the blast of rain, then she's in the backseat only to find he's beaten her there, which makes her laugh.

"Are you sure?" he asks.

"I wouldn't have said it if I wasn't."

He resumes their previous pose, only without the gearshift between them. Arm curved around her upper back, lips together in another determined kiss.

When he breaks, his left hand is kneading the inside of her thigh with a steady rhythm and a firm pressure that bathes her entire body with heat.

"And how exactly do you want me to prove that I'm not your teacher anymore?" he rasps, lips inches from her own.

Deftly, as if it were nothing, he unsnaps the button on her jeans, begins tracing gentle patterns along the newly exposed skin just above the hem of her panties.

"Why don't you start by doing two of the things you always wanted to do to me in class?" she asks in between breaths.

"Just two?" he asks, gently taking her earlobe between his teeth, suckling it briefly, but loud enough to make a slight smack when he releases it.

"All right, before we come up with how many things I'm gonna let you do right here, you can give me a ballpark figure for all the dirty, no-good things you've wanted to do to me since the semester started."

"Should I leave out the things that are only legal in other countries?"

"Let's leave out other countries altogether."

"Well, it's not that I spent the semester wanting to do specific things to you…"— his fingers dip below her panty line, grazing her folds but avoiding her clit—"It's that I wanted to make you respond certain ways. For instance,"—his fingers start a return trip and this time he's narrowed the space between them so she'll know what's coming—"I wanted to see the expression on your face while I gave you absolute"— his fingers arrive at her clit—"total pleasure."

First he grazes it on both sides, then he circles it several times with his index finger before shifting to the pointer finger and back again. The knowledge that he's intently studying her every move while he tests, probes and massages the seat of her bliss causes the pleasure to intensify to such a point that her breaths stutter. He lifts his fingers to his mouth, savors the taste of her, and goes back to work without stopping his intense study of her every writhe and gasp.

"Do I look like you expected me to?" she asks in between gasps. "While you…"

"Oh, no. You look far more beautiful than I even thought possible." His tongue travels the nape of her neck, as another finger joins the first two in their intensifying assault on her clit. "And you taste better than I could have dreamed."

The rhythm of his tongue against her neck is exploratory and eager; the rhythm of his fingers on her clit is determined and confident. The combination of the two makes her dizzy. His husky whisper is in her ear.

"This is what I'd like to draw. *This*. Right here. *You*. The way you look when I do my hardest to make you moan, to make you come. You, right now, under my touch. You're art in the making, Laney Foley."

The rain veils the windows, and the blacked-out street offers no stray illumination strong enough to pierce the veil. But she still feels deliciously exposed. Wedged together in the cramped backseat, at first their pose seemed forced and awkward. But now, Michael's half embrace feels all-consuming.

His choice to keep one arm curved around her upper back doesn't just steady her as jolts of pleasure shoot through her, it reminds her that he isn't clawing at her in a desperate bid to secure his own release. He has devoted himself utterly and entirely to her pleasure, and that alone deserves some kind of reward.

When she moves to free him, he starts to dazzle her clit with three dancing fingers, as if he's trying to incapacitate her with pleasure before she has a chance to release his cock. Maybe he relishes the power and the control. But she's determined, and when she finally closes her hand around it, he groans against her neck.

"Laney," he moans, all pretense of student-teacher role-play gone. Her name issues from him on another shuddering groan as her hand slides the considerable length of his erect cock. "*Laney…*"

"This is one of the things *I've* wanted to do all semester," she whispers.

Just one? She expects him to ask. But he's past the point of dirty talk. Instead, he lifts the fingers he's been probing her with to his lips again, sucks her juices from his fingertips, teeth clenching, breath leaving him in a hiss at the raw taste of her.

"Laney…" He groans again.

She's amazed and delighted that a backseat make-out session could blossom into this flowering of desire. She's dizzy over the realization that simply by pleasuring her, Michael brought himself so close to release that the head of his cock is flame-hot and throbbing in her grip. And this thought brings her to the edge of bliss as well. The sight of her, every facial expression during this delicious assault, tasting her on his fingertips—all of these things have stripped quick words and any trace of restraint from the man of her dreams. She feels like a goddess of infinite power.

"Laney," he cries. There's an almost desperate tone to his voice. Someone outside of the car might have been able to hear him, she isn't sure. The rain is still drumming against the roof and windows, but his fingers are still working a frenzied rhythm against her clit, which turns all of her worries about the outside world into something as light and easily lifted as a wedding veil.

When she's confident he's within seconds of release, she says, "Michael?"

He stares into her eyes, but he's too breathless to answer with words.

"This is what I want to see," she whispers.

He tries to kiss her, but his orgasm rips through him before his lips can make it to hers. For a few seconds his mouth is a silent O, until the rapid-fire groans tear from him like desire's gunfire. To witness his orgasm from this close, their noses inches apart, his hot gasps bathing her lips, causes her scalp to tighten and that special spot in between her shoulder blades to tingle. Her hand is slick with his cum and her strokes have spread it down the length of his shaft.

Michael collapses against one side of her body, breathing against her neck. She figures he's spent. His fingers have stopped their blessed work on her pussy. He's now caressing her mound in lazy, inattentive circles with the heel of his palm, too exhausted to probe it but still to hungry to let it go.

But then suddenly, he's shifting beside her. Sitting up, moving around, moving *her.* Before she realizes quite what's happening, he's pulled off her jeans, spread her down the length of the seat, her upper back resting against the door as his sweaty palms spread her thighs. Even spent and covered in his own cum, he's still devoted to her pleasure. She's just spotted the crown of his head through the shadows above her waist when his teeth graze her clit and he applies a sucking pressure with both lips that makes her feet feel like they're about to float free from her body.

She's close to the edge, feels the promise of a thundering orgasm building like approaching storm clouds. But she can feel resistance too, and with it, the sudden fear that she's separating from her body, that her fear is taking over again. He's working frenzied magic on her sex, but she needs more than his fingers and his tongue. She needs *him.*

"Up," she manages.

"What?" he gasps. His wide eyes stare up her prone body, his jaw slathered in her juices.

"With me," she manages, gasping. "Up here with me—*be* with me."

He gets the message. Michael slides up the backseat, lips suddenly within inches of hers, arm curving under her back, his weight and his power blanketing her suddenly, making her feel both prone, exposed but also protected, all in the same delirious moment. She can tell he's hesitant to give her a taste of her most secret parts, so she grabs his chin and brings their mouths together, and he takes this as a signal to drive the heel of his palm gently against her nub, before the tips of his middle two fingers take up a slow, steady, measured walk atop her throbbing clit.

Exposed, but protected. Probed, but held. These combinations make the specifics of their location—crammed in the backseat of a stranded car on a darkened street in a rainstorm—seem like vague abstractions. Suddenly anything beyond the feel of his fingers against her, the taste of his tongue and the low breathy growls as he seeks to drive her over the edge of bliss cease to exist. Suddenly there is only him. And that's when her pure pleasure takes the form of a scream that could be mistaken for terror by someone who hadn't just discovered what every inch of her tasted like. She expects him to close a hand over her mouth, to muffle her cries. But instead, he grinds his nose against the nape of her neck and laughs encouragingly, gently and with a sound of such rich satisfaction she wishes she could bottle it and save it forever.

When her sense of times returns, she's still shuddering.

"I can't move," Michael finally says. He's still right where he landed as her orgasm tore through her, on top of her and pinning her to the seat, his lips pressed to the nape of her neck.

"Me either," she says.

"I don't want to move."

"Me either."

"Let's not move."

"Sounds like a plan," she says, stroking the back of his neck. "Or maybe just to the side. A little bit. So I can breathe again."

"Sure," he says, following her instruction.

It works. When they were lying in a cramped tangle, bathed

in the afterglow of their frenzied climax, she couldn't have cared less about breathing normally. All that mattered was the weight of him and his determination not to let her go, and she wouldn't have said anything to disrupt it. But if they're going to talk, oxygen is key.

Neither one of them has pulled up their underwear or buttoned their jeans, and as they lie together across the backseat, their exposed privates rest against each other, still pulsing heat.

"What are we going to do about your car?" Laney asks.

"Wait until the rain stops and see if someone from the restaurant will give us a jump," he says. "I'm not in any rush, are you?"

"Hell, no. We've waited this long."

"I probably shouldn't say this now, but I would have waited longer if you'd asked me to."

"And that's why I didn't want to make you wait another day," she answers.

"So what happened?" Michael asks her.

The rain hasn't let up in the slightest and the power in the surrounding neighborhood isn't back on. But they've managed to arrange themselves in a comfortable, intimate tangle in the Kia's cramped backseat, and right now, Laney wouldn't trade these cramped quarters for a beach lounger in the south of France.

"I mean, I know I give good e-mail, but it wasn't *that* good," he says. "Or was it? I feel like something else happened, something that made you change your mind. Or your heart."

A change of heart. That's one way of putting it.

Too bad she can't think of any normal, everyday terms to describes Lilliane's visit. Michael seems to feel these thoughts moving through her and props himself up, smoothing her hair away from her face.

"Was it not being your teacher anymore that did it?" he asks.

"Sort of."

"Sort of?" he asks. "Seriously. What happened?"

The same resistance that knotted itself through her muscles the night before when he kissed her in Jackson Square returns.

But this time she feels justified. If she tells him anything about Bastian or Lilliane, he'll think she's a lunatic. But another voice joins the chorus of fear in her head, and this one sounds more steady and clear. What happened today *happened*, the voice tells her. There's no way around it, and if she doesn't tell Michael about it, it's as good as keeping a secret. And is that really how she wants to cap off a night of total honesty and total bliss?

There will always be a reason not to tell her truth. There will always be a reason not to bare her heart. There will always be the fear that she is too poor, too angry, too blunt, too smart for her own good. Fear, she has learned, will latch on to any self-doubt or insecurity you have in its quest to keep your life small. Fear tells you it's protecting your heart when it's really just starving it to death.

"Laney?" Michael asks into the sudden, growing silence between them.

"Do you believe in ghosts?"

She can sense a smart remark on the tip of his tongue. But the seriousness in her tone takes a second to wash over him. He grunts before answering. "I'm—well, I guess I'm willing to believe in a lot of things, if someone gives me proof, yeah."

"Okay. A few things first."

"Sure."

"First I need to say I'm not on any drugs, legal or illegal. I have no history of mental illness, although I'm probably a good candidate for anxiety disorder."

"Many of us are," Michael says gently.

Michael sits up suddenly, then gently pulls her to a seated position next to him and begins tugging her jeans up partway. She does the rest of the work of covering herself, allowing him to do the same for himself. Then, just when she thinks she's going to have to tell this story with the two of them awkwardly sitting side by side in the backseat, he leans against the door next to him and invites her to wilt into his body, a small gesture that makes what she's about to do feel much easier.

"Okay," she continues, "and I want you to know, I'm just telling you what I saw and what I heard. I still don't know what any of it means."

"You can tell me whatever you need to tell me, Laney," he says.

And she does. Starting with the moment she ran from him the night before, she takes Michael through her visit to Bastian Drake's shop, describing the candle, its smell—*his* smell—the notecard and her strange but inspiring conversation with Bastian. Next, she describes Lilliane's visit, complete with its stalkery opening act, doing her best to leave nothing out, which isn't easy. Every now and then she has to circle back to fill in some detail of Lilliane's crazy story she left out the first time. All the while, Michael remains silent, listening to her intently as rain drums the roof.

By the time she's finished, the afterglow of their first shared orgasm is gone.

She prepares herself for an interrogation spiced with accusations.

"You're safe?" he asks, but it takes her a second or two to realize it's a question. "This woman, Lilliane. Whoever she is, she assured you that you're safe from whoever these people are, right?"

"I love that that's your first question."

"Of course it is," he says, and kisses her forehead. "Why wouldn't it be?"

"Well, you could have gone with, *Are you fucking nuts?*"

"Someone else could have gone with that. Not me."

"Someone like my father, you mean?"

"That's not my place to say. Yet."

"You did just go down on me, remember?"

"Like I'd ever forget, Miss Foley," he whispers, tracing the edge of her chin gently with one finger, as gently as he traced patterns along the bare flesh of her stomach before he explored her pussy for the first time. It's true that she'd asked him not to call her Miss Foley. But that was a different time, a different time only twenty-four hours in the past, but it still felt like a dark and remote period of her life—a *before* time when the fear that he'd never taste the most intimate parts of her dogged her every step. Now that he's not her teacher anymore, any role-play to the effect will send gooseflesh up the insides of her thighs.

"Let me guess," she says. "Your parents are perfect. Your mom sends you baked goods and your dad welcomes you home with a box of cigars and man talk around the fireplace."

"My parents are perfect at sending checks and asking me when I'm going to get some sense and apply to law school. But I'm not complaining. The checks are big, but I put as much of them as I can in savings. As for the *man talk* around the fireplace, ever since my father retired three years ago, they've spent a grand total of five minutes in the continental United States. I think it's better that way."

"Do they come home for holidays at least?" Laney asks.

"Nope."

"Not even Christmas?"

"Not even Flag Day," he says with an arch smile that does little to hide his bitterness. "It's better that way. Trust me."

"Why?"

"Because then I only have to justify the meaning of the creative arts to my students."

"How'd you turn out so civilized?"

The question throws him. He studies her through the darkness, brushes her hair again from the side of her face. "*They're* civilized, I guess," he finally says, sounding distant, as if he's still measuring his answer.

"Sorry," Laney says, taking his hand. She brings his fingers to her lips so she can kiss them gently. "How'd you turn out so—warm, generous, and attentive? So selfless."

Each new term of praise causes his smile to brighten. Either that or each of the tiny kisses she's landed on his fingertips traveled a direct line to his soul. "Sometimes," he says quietly, "the best way to make up for what we weren't given is to give it to someone else."

"Well," Laney says. "I don't do one-way relationships, so expect plenty of it in return."

"Count on it," he whispers, kissing her forehead. "So you've told me what you saw, and I believe every word, but what do *you* think it means?"

"I think there's no logical explanation for how she got up to my room so fast," she says.

"There's not a fire stairway or anything?"

"There's only one and I was on it," Laney says.

"Another entrance maybe?"

"There's the key card entrance, which I went through, and then the fire stairway, which I was on. Now it has an exit door that only opens to the outside, but even if someone propped it open, I was on those stairs the whole time. I would have seen her. And after I walked away from her outside the dorm, she just vanished. She would have had to get between me and one of those doors and she didn't... I mean, the rest of it could just be some crazy woman's rambling. But that part—I just can't get past that part, Michael."

"The things she said, though. Did you believe her?"

"There were moments. There were moments when I believed because she clearly believed it."

"Wow," he says softly.

"I'm sorry, Michael."

"Why are you sorry?"

"This crazy story. This doesn't make for the best start. For us."

He shifts slightly until he can take her face in his hands.

"Are you out of your mind?" he asks in a whisper.

"That's what I was afraid you would say."

"No no no. That's not it."

"Well, then what? I'm so confused."

"If there was even a moment when you believed the things Lilliane said to you today, that means you chose me over the chance to live forever, the chance to be as beautiful as you are now for all time. Tell me, Laney. How could I ask for a better start than that?"

When their lips meet, she takes his face in her hands, enjoys once again the thrill of being able to touch him in such an intimate way. Even though just she's felt the heft of his cock and the heat of his seed. She lays her fingers gently against the hard ridges of his cheekbones and jawline while their kiss seals them together. It still feels as tender and powerful as it did the night before.

12

LILLIANE

Alone on a bench across from St. Louis Cathedral, Lilliane watches the rain collect atop the candle's round bed of wax, marveling at how the deepening pool inside the glass container makes the candle look like a pathetic, ordinary thing. The thunderstorm has cleared Jackson Square of its street musicians and artists. She has set the candle just outside the shelter offered by her umbrella.

It wasn't easy to leave the comfort and warmth of her hotel suite in this storm, but she didn't want to risk Bastian appearing to her at her hotel for the first time. The Montelone has been her safe space for years. But if ever there was a night for Bastian to break decorum and cross a boundary unannounced, it was tonight, on the eve of her thwarting his efforts directly for the first time since they met decades before.

The sudden ghostly silence that fills Jackson Square doesn't surprise her in the slightest. Lilliane has seen Bastian stop time before but the sight this time is impressive. Frozen raindrops surround her, each one suspended perfectly in place. The security lights along the rooflines of the Cabildo and the Presbytere, which seemed to waver only seconds before in the wind and rain, now pierce the air around her, as substantial as ivory tusks. Where their beams hit the frozen raindrops, they carve stained-glass patterns of light and dark through the air itself.

In contrast to the drama of this dramatic, frozen tableaux, Bastian's approaching footsteps are quiet, almost polite. They're the only two people for blocks who can see each other right now. Still, she refuses to look at him as he closes his purple umbrella and rests it against the edge of her bench. She does the same with her own umbrella as he hefts the candle from the bench in both hands.

A sound like a snake's hiss draws her full attention at last.

What was once Bastian's gift for Laney Foley is now dark sand passing through the gaps between his pale, smooth fingers, dark sand laced with just the slightest hints of gold radiance, which flicker and die as it floats through the air, turning to dust, vanishing altogether before it can reach the flagstones at Bastian's feet.

"Never seen that before," Lilliane says.

"Neither have I," Bastian responds.

"Well, there's plenty more where that came from. I've kept you well stocked."

"What will it matter if you try to stop me every time?"

"Oh, Bastian. There's no stopping you."

"You did today."

"Who knows? Maybe today was a one-time thing. Or maybe I'll try again. Depending on my mood."

"Until—?"

"Until what?"

"Is this a game you're going to play with me now?" he asks.

"Are you suggesting I'm trying to blackmail some answers out of you?" Lilliane asks.

"Your words, not mine."

"I see."

"I could just abandon you," he says.

"Could you, really?" she asks. "*Could* you just abandon me, Bastian?"

He doesn't answer.

"That's what I thought," she says. "You have no control over what you do. I saw it last night on the roof of the cathedral. You were pulled away from me by a force you barely understand."

She realizes he is the closest to anger she's ever seen him, and this satisfies her deeply. His eyes are ablaze with the gold radiance they must both work to conceal from ordinary humans in moments of anger and passion.

"Twelve-hundred people," he says.

"Excuse me?"

"Twelve-hundred. That's how many I've visited since this journey began. That's how many I have helped. There are only twenty-three of you, Lilliane."

"Yes, but we live forever with the knowledge of what you've done."

"With what you *failed* to do."

"You liar!" she roars. She's on her feet before she can stop herself, her voice echoing queerly through a square emptied of time and wind. "I was *not* some little college girl with doubt and mixed feelings. He was my boss's son and he was *white*. We could have been lynched, Bastian. What would your *candle* have done for us then?"

"We'll never know," he answers.

"You smug bastard. Sitting in judgment of me when we know nothing of what you really are! You act like a guardian angel, but this is your punishment, isn't it? You and your little shop. You've been sentenced to appear, again and again, at the beck and call of—you don't even *know* what, do you? What I want to know is *why*? What secret are you hiding? What did you do when you were alive to earn this punishment?"

"You have had fifty-six years to be rid of your anger, Lilliane," he growls. "And yet here it is again. Maybe this is all *your* punishment."

"What is your name, Bastian?"

"Good evening, Lilliane."

"What is your *real* name?"

"If there are consequences for what you've done, we shall experience them together, I am sure."

"What is your name?"

In an instant, she is soaked. The rain slams to the flagstones around her. The lights along the roofline overhead take on their indistinct, wavering quality. Time is returned to its normal course and flow. Bastian is gone.

The candle is gone too, reduced to handfuls of vanishing dust in a moment somewhere between the seconds of ordinary mortal time.

Small victories, Lilliane thinks. *Small victories.*

13

LANEY

From the moment she met him, Laney pictured Michael living in a brightly painted shotgun house somewhere near campus, with a small front yard full of strange modern sculptures and a Golden Retriever he'd named after a famous painter. In reality, his tiny studio apartment is in a large, red brick building in the Warehouse District, and there's no trace of a pet. And there are no sculptures, unless you count the elaborate cast-iron frame of his king-sized bed, its posts shaped like obelisks with small, four-sided glass lanterns on top. As she scrapes her muddy shoes on the welcome mat, Michael pulls a box of matches from the nightstand drawer and starts lighting the stubby candles inside each lantern.

The power's working just fine, but he's not turning on any of the lights. Maybe it's a nod to Lilliane's crazy story. Or maybe he's just trying to rush her into bed so he can do all the things to her body they didn't have room for in the Kia's cramped back seat. It didn't take more than fifteen minutes for the temperature inside the stranded car to become stifling, but the rain was still coming down in sheets, so a jump was out of the question. The cab driver was friendly and Laney couldn't help but wonder if the poor guy smelled the scent of sex wafting off his two passengers. Worse, had he been able to detect Laney's struggle not to paw at Michael's cock through his soaked jeans? Now that she has Michael all to herself again, the idea of more delayed gratification feels as delicious as his bed looks.

"A friend of mine's a sculptor," he says. "She made this for me. They're modeled after the lamp posts that light the entrance to St. Peter's Square in Rome."

"Italy," Laney says. But what she's really thinking is, *a woman made this bed for you? This whole bed? Who? I'll have Cat investigate. And kill her.* "You love Italy."

"You remembered," he says with a smile.

Don't ask what kind of lady friend would make him a huge, elaborate bedframe out of cast iron. Artists are different. Maybe they make huge expensive things for one another without expecting sex in return.

"Janine," Michael says suddenly.

"Excuse me?"

"She made the bed. Janine. That's her name. And this summer she married her girlfriend in Provincetown."

"So that would mean her girlfriend is now her wife," Laney says.

"Very smart, Miss Foley."

"You're gonna have to stop calling me that, Professor Brouchard."

"Not when it almost makes you come every time I do."

"You know how to make me come for real now. Who cares about making me *almost* come?"

Before he can finish his lustful growl, and before he can close the distance between them, she says, "So is Italy your first real love?"

"You could say that," he says. He curves his arms around her from behind, nuzzles his lips against her neck, allows her to study the bed before them, maybe so she can imagine all the pleasures he'll provide once they're both tangled in its chocolate-colored sheets. Safe from the rain. Safe from the fallout of a teacher-student relationship that might have damaged them both.

"Sophomore year of high school my parents took me on a summer trip to Rome, Florence, and Venice," Michael says, his voice dreamily trailing off. "Let's just say there was my life before I saw the ceiling of the Sistine Chapel and there was my life after. That was the day art became the only way of trying to make sense of the world that held any logic to me. And the whole time, my parents thought I was just weeping because I was exhausted from jet lag."

It feels like this is just Michael talking, not Michael the teacher. He never offered her classmates access to his teenage self, a privileged high school student with a heart so open he wept at his first up-close glimpse of Michelangelo's most famous work even though he was raised by two people with hundred dollar bills and ice water flowing through their veins. For now, this Michael is just for her.

"Want to know what else makes me smart?" Laney asks.

"There's plenty that makes you smart."

"Well, thank you for saying so, but right now I'm smart enough to know you haven't turned on any of the lights, which means there's something in this apartment you don't want me to see."

"Or," he says, kissing her neck softly. "I'm just trying to get in your pants again. I mean, last time I had to cut off power to a whole neighborhood before you let me taste that sweet beautiful little pussy you've got between your legs."

She's not sure if it's the sudden burst of dirty talk or the fact that he delivered it in the same gentle tone of voice with which he told the story of his high school trip to Rome that causes her breath to leave her. His hands slide down her waist. When he cups her thighs, she slips quickly from his embrace, makes a beeline for the side of the apartment he's deliberately left in shadow.

There's a few seconds of fumbling before she finds the switch on a gooseneck lamp. With one flick of her wrist she's illuminated a cramped but orderly art studio. The lamp's bulb is so bright she has to blink for a few seconds to get her bearings.

Two easels flank a drafting table serviced by a high stool. On one of the easels sits the beginnings of an oil painting that looks like a landscape. It could be an abstract; she's not sure. Most of the space is dedicated to larger versions of pencil sketches like the one he gave her the night before. If this were one of those scary movies her friends in high school always wanted her to sneak into, all the drawings on display would be of her. And there would be too many of them and they would all have been drawn from photographs of her he snapped in secret. And the character who played her in the movie would be sort of getting the message that her new lover was a psycho while the girls in the back row of the theatre screamed that very message at the top of their lungs.

But this isn't a horror movie, so she's not the subject of the drawings on display here in Michael's apartment. They are, however, just as detailed and beautiful as the one he presented her with the night before—French Quarter street scenes, images of the riverfront, various angles on the Chamberland University campus. In fact, there's only one or two human figures in any of them, mostly shadowy, distant pedestrians, and that makes the portrait Michael drew of her seem all the more special.

"So is this your secret?" she asks. "You're an actual artist and not just someone who studies them?"

"My secret is that I'm just as happy teaching art as I am making it. Which is a very rare thing indeed. And to be honest, it's not really a secret. A blessing, perhaps."

"So you really *were* just trying to rush me into bed?" she asks.

He's embracing her from behind again, his every touch making her remember the mad, yet focused flicker of his tongue across her clit. At the sight of the dry paintbrushes sitting bristles-up inside an old coffee can, a plan occurs to her.

"Maybe I just thought you'd be a little kinder on my work if you saw it after I made love to you," Michael whispers.

"*Love*, huh?"

"I said I was going to *make* love. I didn't say you'd *fall* in love with me." He gives her a light nip on her earlobe. "Yet."

She clasps his erection through his rain soaked jeans.

"That is *so* inappropriate, Mister Brouchard," she says, tone full of mock indignation.

"Why? I'm not your teacher anymore, *Miss* Foley."

"But you were," she rasps, palming his length as he flickers his tongue against the nape of her neck. "You *were* my teacher, see? And you made me want you more and more every day I came to class. You kept rolling up the sleeves of your shirts so I could see these forearms." She clutches both for effect, as if she were about to pull them free of her waist. She does nothing of the kind. "Some people would call that an abuse of power, Professor Brouchard. Toying with your students like that."

"If you were in my head, *Miss* Foley, seeing the things I saw every time you walked into my classroom, listening to my heart race when you sat down in your desk, you'd know who really had the power." He gives the front of her jeans a hard tug, just hard enough to send a brief shockwave of pleasure through her aching folds.

"Still," she gasps, "some people would say it was wrong. The way you felt about me. The way I feel about you."

"Oh, yeah," he growls into her ear. She hasn't yet heard his voice drop to quite this timbre of raw lust. The sound of it has her soaked. "Should I force those *people* to sit in the corner and watch while I turn your writhing body into a work of art, while I fuck you until you can barely speak? Then those *people* can decide whether or not I did a good enough job of teaching Miss Laney Foley about art."

This isn't just dirty talk. This is delicious, riotously *filthy* talk, and it's threatening to drive her to the bed right then and there.

The plan. The plan. Don't forget your plan!

If it works, she'll have Cat to thank. Who else?

Cat was the one who pulled that silly article from the pages of *Cosmo* a few weeks ago, the one with the picture of the happy couple in bed, smiling as they studied crude pencil sketches of a man and a woman's body. *Your Lover's Special Spots*, it was titled. As Cat read her the article, Laney mocked the idea of drawing circles on some silly sketch just so you could let your lover know where you wanted them to lick you and pinch you and kiss you and probe you. But secretly, behind the sarcasm, she'd longed to have a man do it. And now she had him. But they weren't going to draw on some stupid sketch. She has a much better canvas in mind.

Michael's hard, hungry kiss makes her feet feel like they're leaving the floor. She breaks suddenly, takes a step back and lifts a single admonishing finger into the sudden space between them.

"Not so fast, Professor," she says.

His eyebrows arch. His half-smile is indulgent, but there's a flicker of real fear in it, which is exactly what she was hoping for.

"The power deferential between a teacher and a student can be very, very damaging to intimate relationships like the one you seem *determined* to have with me."

"Is that so?" he asks.

"It *is* so," she says, brushing past him. "It is most certainly so, *Mister* Brouchard. Just ask one of the counselors at the Student Health Center. They even have pamphlets on the subject."

"And I take it you've read every—"

"I'm not *finished*," she snaps. For now, she is the teacher and he is the student. What better way to vent all the stress and pressure of their previously bottled up attractions for one another? Well, there's probably five or six or maybe even eight better ways. But they'll get to those soon enough.

"There are, however, certain *steps* we can take to try to correct that difference," she explains in her best schoolmarm tone. "Make the playing field a little more even, if you will."

"Oh, I will," he says under his breath.

"Focus, Professor."

"I am, believe me," he says. "I'm very focused on you, Miss Foley."

"Good. Then take off your clothes. All of them."

There's a mischievous glint in his eyes, but his body's gone rigid. He might like the idea of this script she's started to write for them, but he also loves being in control. Loves it so much that stripping down in front of her while she sits on his bed a safe distance away, her arms crossed over her chest, has caused his desire to short-circuit for a few seconds.

Slowly, carefully, he unbuckles his belt and unbuttons his jeans. He's taking his sweet time. She figures it's his best attempt to appear calm and indulgent. But she can practically taste his nervousness; she loves the flavor of it as much as she loves the sight of his muscular chest as he peels back the wet flaps of his dress shirt, of his powerful hair-dusted thighs as he tugs his jeans down his legs.

His chest rises and falls with breaths quick and shallow enough to suggest fear. He'd probably like nothing more than to cross the room and tear her clothes from her body, if only to make them equals. But that's not on the syllabus. Not yet.

"Turn around and put your hands on the edge of the table," she says. "Both of them."

He complies. When he realizes he's turned his naked body squarely into the harsh light of the drafting table's lamp, he squints and takes a deep breath to steady himself. But his cock is rising and throbbing. If it's fear he's feeling, in another few seconds, his fear will have him hard as a rock.

When she reaches past him for one of the paintbrushes in the coffee can, he flinches. That's when she's realizes he's kept his eyes closed and her sudden movement has startled him.

"Relax, teach," she whispers. "Everyone's got something to learn."

She sinks to her knees on the floor, sets the brush to one side; she'll need it in a minute if all goes according to plan. But in the meantime, all she needs are her own hands. And her fingers.

"Wh—what are you going to—?"

"No matter what I do," she interrupts him, "keep both hands on the edge of the table and both feet on the floor. The second you let go or step off the floor, we're back to square one."

"And what's square one?"

She hears the slap of her hand against the hard flesh of his ass before she realizes what she's done. She just spanked him. Well, she didn't spank him. She just slapped her former teacher on his bare ass. He lets out a short, startled grunt. She's just as startled as he is. Startled by how quickly and easily she's taken control, by how much the sight of him, in his tall, muscled, nervous glory has filled her with energy and hunger. She feels like she could run a mile without breaking a sweat. It's like her body—no, her *soul*—has taken control of her actions and found the perfect way to exorcise the frightened little girl who ran from him the night before.

Lilliane was right. Crazy, perhaps. But right. She didn't need

Bastian Drake's candle at all.

"Square one," she says carefully, her voice shaky with excitement. "Is whatever I say it is."

"You are a bad, bad girl, Laney Foley," he whispers.

"And bad teachers like bad girls," she whispers back. "Both hands on the table."

She starts with just the tips of her fingers, traces swirling patterns over the arches of his bare feet around his hairy ankles, up the sides of his legs. She's memorizing the location of each spot that makes him wince, jerk or shift his weight from one foot to the other. Kneeling on the floor beside him, she monitors the two-handed grip he maintains on the edge of his drafting table as her own fingers slide up the insides of his thighs. He releases a desperate moan when she hops to her feet and he realizes she's skipping his cock and balls. Instead, she allows her fingers to travel the hard ridges of his muscular back.

So far, his most sensitive spots have been the undersides of his biceps and the very back of his neck, so she lingers there, teasing him, testing him, watching his grip on the drafting table turn white-knuckled. Then she sinks to her knees again.

He's mine now. My schedule, my pace, my touch. No rules, no risks, no consequences. Mine.

When her fingers travel the underside of his balls, Michael has to throw his head back and choke out several moans to keep from breaking the rules. So she lingers there too. Back and forth. Back and forth...

"Laney—Jesus. You h-have to—*Laney*."

"Nice job so far," she answers, pulling her hand away. "Now it's time for stage two."

Surrendering to just her fingers has rendered him a sweaty, gasping mess. And while her original intent was solely to learn the most sensitive parts on his body, she realizes this ritual has erased the power deferential between them, whatever the hell *that* is. He was right. She really did read it in a pamphlet. With each inch of his body her fingers have traveled, she's claimed more of her right to desire him as much as he's desired her. Hell, she's claiming her very right to desire, her right to feel lust, to give into it now and then without first jamming it through the ringer of every doubt and fear she can come up with.

The paintbrush is as soft as it looks. The bristles give easily as she drags them gently across Michael's flesh. His struggle now is more intense. He whispers her name every few seconds. She can't tell if they're encouragements or pleas. Either one is more than fine. Then he gasps her name; he groans and growls her name. But he doesn't lift either foot off the floor, he doesn't release his grip on the table even as she paints the underside of his balls with the brush's soft bristles.

He shudders from the assault, teeth gritted, gripping the table's edge, leaning forward far enough that the balls of his feet come up off the floor before he drives them back down again.

Is this an infraction? She thinks not. He's doing so well. He's working so hard. *For her.*

As she squeezes herself into the few inches of space in between him and the desk, she keeps up her soft, silky tease of his balls. Despite being on her knees, she feels as if the power is all hers. Michael looks down at her through squinted eyes, his nostrils flaring, his grunts throaty and pained with desire delayed, frustrated, and enflamed.

"Excellent work, Michael," she whispers. For the first time, she drags the bristles up the length of his jerking shaft.

"Am I, Miss Foley?" he gasps. "Am I doing a good job?"

"Yes," she whispers. She grips the base of his shaft in one hand and sets the brush aside. "You've done a very good job." The tip of his glistening cock is inches from her lips now. The heady, masculine smell of him fills her nostrils.

"Time for stage three," she says.

She's never been this aroused with a man's cock in her mouth before. Blowjobs are usually drudgery or just plain work, something she gives out to dateable guys she's sure will lose interest if she doesn't let them past second base. The idea of feeling this genuinely connected to another man while his cock is down her throat has always seemed like a ridiculous abstraction, something from a romance novel she would never admit to reading. Despite his curses and his pleas, Michael still hasn't let go of the drafting table right behind her. He's still following her rules.

"Laney," he cries.

He's asking her for permission. She's not quite sure for what, but when his cock jerks in the hand she's using to assist her lips, she gets an idea. He's close. He must be. And he's using her name as a warning. If she's not careful, he'll unleash his seed inside of her in another few seconds. Her sudden hunger for it makes her head spin. She's never let someone cum in her mouth before. But she wants him to. She really wants him to. But it's too soon. Worse, it's unsafe in ways that have nothing to do with domination and control. But tell that to her sudden hunger for every part of him, a hunger that makes recklessness feel like strength.

"Laney," he cries.

She pulls him from her mouth. "Do it," she says before she can think twice. "Do it now."

He doesn't come.

He releases the table instead, twines his fingers through her hair, grips the back of her head in one hand, smoothes her tangled bangs back from her forehead with the other. He's staring down at her, studying her with parted lips as she works him over. He didn't want permission to come down her throat. He wanted permission to be released from the rules of her game. Permission to touch, to hold, to caress, to gaze and study.

Suddenly she's on her feet and they're moving toward the bed. He's undressing her with swift precision and an absence of frenzy, each movement governed by the total focus wrought by absolute desire.

By the time he sends her backward down onto the bed, she's naked, the silky comforter kissing her thighs and back as he bears down on her, reaching for the nightstand drawer, tearing the condom wrapper open with his teeth. She's seen so many erections flag during this pivotal step in the process; given the guys they belonged to that wasn't always such a bad thing. But Michael is so hard his cock won't stop jerking long enough for him to slide the condom on. So they both sit there for a few seconds, their rasping breaths fighting with the sounds of the rain pelting the windows. The sight of him sitting on his bent knees, shadows painting the slope of his upper back, steadying his cock with one hand while sliding the condom on with the other makes her lips ache. He's blocking the desk lamp now so she can't tell if her thighs are actually shaking, but it feels like they are. It feels like she's shaking down to her bones as she feels herself opening for him before he even touches her pussy.

"Michael," she whispers.

Gently, he pushes her back into the pillows, his lips inches from hers. He stares into her eyes and he licks the tips of his fingers, holds her gaze while he swirls his moistened fingers around her right nipple. "Yes, Laney."

"Fuck me."

It's not a challenge. It's not a dare. It's not a porn-star snarl. She's never given permission in this simple and direct way before in her life. It's always been, *Yes, I'm ready*, or worse, *Sure, go ahead*. What she's just given him is more than permission. This is beyond simple consent. This is a promise, an offering to match his raw desire with her own.

At first, she thinks he's hesitating because he's still staring into her eyes. Then she feels him pressing against her moist entrance and she realizes he wants, once more, to watch every wave of pleasure ripple through her expression. He wants to turn her into a work of art by fucking her. She's so hot, wet, and open, he smiles and lets out a small, satisfied laugh of surprise. She realizes how much she's given her body over to him when she feels her ankles meet against the small of his back.

"Need you," she gasps. *"Need you, Michael."*

These words make her feel more vulnerable than anything else she's done all night, or all week.

"Need me, want me," he growls. "Take your pick. I'm yours."

He finds her clit with one hand, rubs circles around it while keeping his thrusts varied in a rhythm she can't predict. The knowledge that she's on her back beneath him seems more philosophical than real. She feels boneless suddenly, and that can only mean one thing. She's astonished her orgasm snuck up on her this quickly. She feels as if she's been filled by it an instant. That's never happened to her before. There have always been false starts, sputtering engines. Waves of pleasure that seemed to break just short of the shore. But now Michael fucks her hard and deep, and she feels like she's about to fly apart. This is the moment when another guy would desperately jackhammer into some porn film imitation of a female orgasm. But Michael's learned enough about her body to know it's the combination of his cock's suddenly steady thrusts and the way he's circling her clit with his fingers that have done her in.

She starts by trying to say his name, but this vain attempt turns into a series of cries that have too many emotions swirling through them to be defined. Somewhere in the midst of her bliss, he's pulled free of her. He's suckling her clit while stroking himself at the same time, making her feel worshiped and serviced even amidst her near-delirium. She places her hands gently against his shoulders to let him know she can't take any more, that her body's fully spent. That's when he rises up onto his haunches, brings their mouths together. She grips the back of his neck but at the same instant she fears her nails have dug into his skin, he yanks the condom off, and comes all over her stomach, his seed hot and copious.

He crumples against her as his barking groans turn into delighted laughter.

And for a while there's only the sound of the rain and the gentle feel of his fingers smoothing back her bangs. This is going to be his thing, she can tell. Brushing her hair back from her forehead. And the fact that he's going to have a *thing* that involves her hair makes his expansive bed's embrace feel all the more safe.

"Now you have to lie with me for a night," he says. "Isn't that how it works?"

"How what works?" she asks.

"If you'd used the candle, I mean. Isn't that how the story went?"

"I think it was just a story."

"Maybe, maybe not."

"It doesn't matter," she says.

"Why?"

"Because the only thing I need is—" His embrace tightens even as her words suddenly leave her.

How could her old fears return in this moment, after the amazing night they've shared? Hadn't she done enough to chase her fears away forever?

Maybe that wasn't how this worked. Maybe there was no one thing or one act that could make your fears go away forever. The best you could do was to wake up each day and make a resolution to ignore fear's invitations to false comfort and illusory safety—its invitation to say less, risk less, to love less, to be less. It was a daily decision, being willing to fall in love, and now it was hers to make. That's why she rolled over and took Michael Brouchard's face in her hands, staring into his expectant gaze as she finished the sentence that had lodged in her throat only seconds before.

"The only thing I need is you, Michael Brouchard."

14

LILLIANE

"What's a pretty lady like you doing crying in the rain?" The doorman had watched her approach and pulled open the door when she was a few steps from the entrance to the Hotel Montelone.

Jerry is Lilliane's favorite doorman, probably because his constant flirting makes her feel young in spirit as well as body.

"Who says I'm crying?" Lilliane says, trying to effect her brightest tone.

"You's missing a skip in your step, that's all."

"The rain makes everybody look like they're crying, baby."

He holds open the door as she closes her umbrella, then together they step into the chandelier-lit, marble-floored lobby with its proud grandfather clock and huge, colorful bouquets on every surface. The Carousel Bar is packed as always, spilling a constant stream of drunken laughter onto the short set of carpeted steps just inside the hotel's entrance.

"Not good for you to be walking alone out in this kinda rain, Miss Davis," Jerry says, taking her arm and leading her up the steps, even though there are only a few of them and they're more than easily managed by a woman of any age.

She's been using this alias at the Montelone for almost twenty years now, and soon she'll have to come up with another or start avoiding the hotel altogether. She doesn't run this kind of risk at the other businesses in New Orleans she's fond of; she'll typically frequent them for five years or so before hanging back and waiting for management and most of the staff to get replaced. But here she's gone with baggier dresses, hats with veils and bigger sunglasses. Eventually, even those will fail to do the trick and some of the hotel's long-term staff members will start to wonder why one of their regular guests hasn't aged a day in years. But tonight, just the thought of saying good-bye to the Montelone, even if it's only for a little while, is more than she can bear.

"Well, Jerry, maybe next time you'll have to escort me on my walk."

"That would be an honor, Miss Davis. If I'm not working, that is."

"I'm a guest here, am I not? Are tending to my needs not considered part of your job?"

"Miss Davis. Meeting any of your needs would be my utmost priority. Even if I didn't work at the Montelone."

"You dawg," she whispers, slapping him lightly on the shoulder. His broad, toothy grin has as much charm as desire in it.

"Front desk has something for you, ma'am," he says.

"What is it?"

"I don't know. But it's been here a while. They forgot to give it to you when you checked in."

"Thank you, Jerry."

As she crosses the lobby, she wonders if this is some new trick of Bastian's. Maybe he feels guilty for her abandoning her in the rain. But for that to be the case, he'd have to feel suddenly guilty for fifty-six years of abandoning her whenever she posed a question he couldn't or wouldn't answer. The front desk clerk sees her coming, smiles, reaches under the desk and hands her a tiny envelope with her first initial written on the outside. Like so many of the new hires, the clerk has a thick European accent Lilliane can't quite place.

"Who left this?" Lilliane asks, trying to sound casual.

"I'm not sure, madam. I wasn't on duty at the time. But I do know that it was weeks ago and we informed her that you were not in residence at the time."

"*Her*. Did you tell her I would return?"

"I'm sure we didn't. That would be strictly against policy. But according to my manager, she didn't need us to. She was confident that you would be back eventually and insisted that we give it to you the minute you returned."

"I see. Thank you."

It's not in the same cursive as the notes attached to the candles in Bastian's shop, but it looks vaguely familiar.

There are only twenty-three people who know she stays here on a regular basis—twenty-four if you count a ghost named Bastian Drake—and all of them could get in touch with her by phone. No need to send a mysterious handwritten note and wait weeks for it to be delivered.

In the past, she's used the hotel for numerous meetings related to The Desire Exchange, so it's possible an old client is trying to track her down. But former clients are all provided with her contact information as well as phone numbers for several of the other Radiants who oversee applications. The Desire Exchange subsists off the referrals. If former clients had to jump through a dozen hoops to make them, The Exchange's profit margins would shrink considerably.

Lilliane knows she should wait until she's comfortably ensconced in her suite. But the Desire Exchange's recent infiltration by a determined young woman and her Navy SEAL lover has her more than a little on edge when it comes to messages from strangers.

As the elevator rises, she tears open the envelope. Her eyes dart immediately to the unfamiliar phone number written across the bottom of the card inside. The penmanship is another story. At first, it seems only vaguely familiar. Then, recognition; she hasn't laid eyes on the person responsible for these pen strokes in at least five years.

When she finally looks up from the message written on the card, she realizes the strangers getting onto the elevator are coming from a floor above her own. She's missed her stop entirely and now she's hurrying to shove the card where no one else can see its short, blunt message:

**THERE'S A WAY OUT, LILLIANE.
THERE'S A WAY FOR US TO LOVE AGAIN.
CALL ME. PLEASE.**

* * * *

Also from 1001 Dark Nights and Christopher Rice, discover The Flame, The Surrender Gate, and Dance of Desire.

About Christopher Rice

New York Times bestselling author Christopher Rice's first foray into erotic romance, *THE FLAME*, earned accolades from some of the genre's most beloved authors. "Sensual, passionate and intelligent," wrote Lexi Blake, "it's everything an erotic romance should be." J. Kenner called it "absolutely delicious," Cherise Sinclair hailed it as "beautifully lyrical" and Lorelei James announced, "I look forward to reading more!"*KISS THE FLAME:* A Desire Exchange Novella will be available this November from 1,001 DARK NIGHTS. Before his erotic romance debut, Christopher published four *New York Times* bestselling thrillers before the age of 30, received a Lambda Literary Award and was declared one of People Magazine's Sexiest Men Alive. His supernatural thriller, *THE HEAVENS RISE*, was a nominated for a Bram Stoker Award. Together with his best friend, *New York Times* bestselling author Eric Shaw Quinn, Christopher co-hosts and executive produces THE DINNER PARTY SHOW WITH CHRISTOPHER RICE & ERIC SHAW QUINN which debuts a new episode every Sunday evening at 8 PM ET/ 5 PM PT at TheDinnerPartyShow.com.

Also from Christopher Rice

Thrillers
A DENSITY OF SOULS
THE SNOW GARDEN
LIGHT BEFORE DAY
BLIND FALL
THE MOONLIT EARTH

Supernatural Thrillers
THE HEAVENS RISE
THE VINES

Paranormal Romance
THE FLAME: A Desire Exchange Novella
THE SURRENDER GATE: A Desire Exchange Novel
DANCE OF DESIRE

Dance of Desire
By Christopher Rice
Now Available

From *New York Times* bestselling author Christopher Rice, comes a steamy, emotional tale of forbidden romance between a woman struggling to get her life on its feet and the gorgeous cowboy her father kept her from marrying years before. The first contemporary romance from Christopher Rice is written with the author's trademark humor and heart, and introduces readers to a beautiful town in the Texas Hill Country called Chapel Springs.

* * * *

"It's a terrible idea," he says.

"Why did she tell you?"

"Because she wants me to stop you."

"That's not true. I talked to her this afternoon and she told me she wanted me to go."

"Well, she must have changed her mind," he says.

"Well, I haven't changed mine."

"A sex club?" he bellows. "What are you? Crazy?"

"Since when are you so full of judgment, cowboy? I've never seen you in church!"

"And I've never seen you in a sex club!"

"Have you been to that many? Who knows? I could have a whole secret life you don't even know about."

"I know who you are, Amber. I know *how* you are."

"And what does that mean?"

"Amber, you stayed a virgin until you were nineteen. That puts you in the, like, one percentile of girls in our high school."

"How do you know that? I never told you that!"

"I had my sources."

"You were keeping tabs on my virginity? That's rich. I thought you were too busy starting fistfights outside the Valley View Mall so you didn't have to feel anything."

"And you were too busy tending to my wounds 'cause it

gave you an excuse to look at my chest."

"Get out of my house!"

"Amber—"

"Get out!"

He bows his head. A lesser man would ignore her request, but he knows he's bound by it.

"I shouldn't have said that," Caleb whispers. "I'm sorry."

He turns to leave.

"You know, I forgave you a lot because you lost a lot. But don't you pretend for one second that you joined our family with a smile and a thank you and that was that. Those first few years, it was like living with a tornado. You were *impossible!* An you were nothing like the guy I'd..."

He turns away from the front door. "The guy you'd what?"

"All I'm saying is that even if I'd wanted to..."

"Wanted to what?"

He's closing the distance between them. Her head wants to run from him. Her soul wants to run to him. Her body's forced to split the difference. She's got no choice but to stand there while he advances on her, nostrils flaring, blue eyes blazing.

"Tell me why you really don't want me to go," she hears herself whisper. "Tell me why you—"

He takes her in his arms and rocks them into the wall, so suddenly she expects her head to knock against the wood, but one of his powerful hands cushions the back of her skull just in time.

His lips meet the nape of her neck, grazing, testing. It's hesitant, the kiss he gives her there, as if he's afraid she's an apparition that will vanish if he tries to take a real taste.

He gathers the hem of her shirt into his fist, knuckles grazing the skin of her stomach. She's trying to speak but the only thing coming out of her are stuttering gasps. She's been rendered wordless by the feel of the forbidden, by the weight of the forbidden, by the power of the forbidden.

It's the first time they've touched since that night on the boat dock, if you don't include the light dabs of hydrogen peroxide she'd apply to the wounds he got fighting, usually while they sat together in the kitchen, her parents watching over them nervously. Twelve years living under the same roof and they never shared so much as a hug after that night, nothing that might risk the feel of his skin against her own.

And now this.

Now the intoxicating blend of the cologne he wore as a teenager mingling with the musky aroma of his belt and boots. Now the knowledge that he'd asked after her virginity years before, that the thought of her lying with another man had filled him with protective, jealous rage then just as it does now.

She feels boneless and moist. One of those feelings isn't an illusion.

If this is what it feels like to be bad, she thinks, *no wonder so many people get addicted.*

"Tell me," she whispers. "Tell me why you really don't want me to go."

"I am," he growls.

He presses their foreheads together, takes the sides of her face in both of his large, powerful hands. It's torture, this position. It's deliberate, she's sure. It keeps her from lifting her mouth to his. Keeps her from looking straight into his eyes. He's fighting it, still. Just as she's fought it for years.

She parts her lips, inviting him to kiss her.

"Please," he groans. "Just, please *don't* go."

"Caleb…" She reaches for his face.

DARING HER LOVE

A Bradens Novella
By Melissa Foster

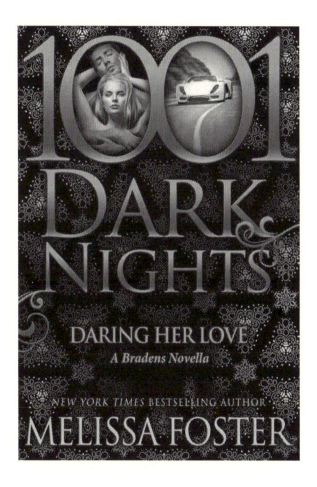

Acknowledgments

It was such a pleasure to work with Liz Berry and MJ Rose, two talented women who inspire me on a daily basis. I'm proud to be part of the 1001 Dark Nights team, and I hope my readers love the rest of the authors as much as I enjoy reading them. If you enjoyed reading about Eric and Kat, I hope you'll check out Hugh and Brianna's story, along with the rest of the mouthwatering Bradens and Love in Bloom family.

Writing a book is never a solo operation. I'd like to thank Brandi Bradley Glover for offering up her husband's name. I hope I did him justice. I'm indebted to my fabulous Filthy Fosterette Street Team, and all the wonderful readers and friends who follow me on social media and reach out via email. Keep your notes coming! I love hearing from you, and often take inspiration from stories you graciously share.

Many thanks to my amazing editorial team, Kristen Weber and Penina Lopez, and my meticulous proofreaders, Marlene Engle, Juliette Hill, Lynn Mullan, and Jenna Bagnini.

Not a day goes by that I'm not thankful for my own hunky hero and research partner, Les. Love you more than chocolate cupcakes, babe. Here's to real-life romance!

Dear Readers,

In DARING HER LOVE you'll meet Eric James and Kat Martin, along with a few of our hot, wealthy, and wickedly naughty Bradens. The Bradens are just one of the families in my award-winning contemporary romance series, Love in Bloom. The Love in Bloom family includes several subseries: Snow Sisters, The Bradens, The Remingtons, Seaside Summers, and The Ryders. For a checklist, family tree, and publication schedule, please visit my website www.MelissaFoster.com and be sure to sign up for my newsletter so you never miss a release. www.MelissaFoster.com/Newsletter.

Happy reading!
Melissa

Chapter One

IT WAS HIS eyes. Definitely his eyes. They were the type of eyes that said things Kat Martin had spent a lifetime spotting—and the last year avoiding—at Old Town Tavern, the bar where she worked in Richmond, Virginia. She could spot a player a mile away, from the expensive suit to the open-necked dress shirt, showing just enough skin and a smattering of chest hair to make a girl's insides quiver. And boy did this man show it well. Her insides were doing some kind of crazy *sex-me-up* dance. Even from across the crowded airport bar, the intensity of the insanely sexy man's seductive gaze beckoned her, goading her into doing naughty things she had no business doing at this point in her life.

Kat had spent enough years sowing her wild oats. Ever since her best friend, Brianna, had been swept off her feet by professional race car driver Hugh Braden, Kat had longed for more. Watching her friend fall blissfully in love with a man who treated Bree and her daughter, Layla, like they were the very heart and soul of his being, Kat had become pickier about men and the treatment she'd accept. And she had to admit, she was a little lonelier because of it. Finding a tough alpha male who was also loving, monogamous, and romantic was like searching for a tick in the woods.

Oh boy. Mr. Fuck Me Eyes was on the move, and *holy hell*, this man didn't move; he prowled. Slow, determined steps, clearly meant to amp up Kat's pulse—*Damn, you do it so well*—were intensified by eyes radiating power, sex, and sinful promises. Promises that a year ago Kat would have been aching to explore, but now she was looking for Mr. Right, not Mr. Goodbar.

Sweet Jesus, he had that tousled, just-been-fucked hair thing going on, too, and the perfect amount of scruff covering a not-quite-chiseled chin, which, unfairly, only made him hotter. And his mouth. *Well, fuck me sideways.* Kat had a thing for mouths and all the pleasures they could give. This guy had two sweet bows over a full lower lip, the kind she'd love to sink her teeth into. She hadn't had these types of thoughts about a guy in so long that she had to wonder what she'd done to deserve this temptation. She'd already missed her flight because of a storm. Did she really need to spend her evening fending off Adonis himself? He probably had an anaconda in his pants, too. Wouldn't that just top it all off?

He placed a hand on the back of her chair, and the temperature in the room spiked. Lowering himself to the seat beside her and smelling like heaven on legs, he looked at her like he'd already staked his claim. Kat knew guys like him were about notches on belts and conquering prey, and she was done being prey. She was looking for a bird who would stay in the nest, not a cuckoo flying over it.

She chanced a glance at him, instantly regretting it. His features were well defined and disarmingly youthful, like he'd grown into a man but the rebellious teenager in him refused to completely grow up. A trait Kat knew and loved so much, it caused her mouth to go dry.

He motioned to the bartender. "Bourbon sour, please."

The drink of bad boys. "Of course." *Shit.* She didn't mean to say it out loud, and from the way his lips quirked up, he obviously knew exactly why she did. She tried to ignore the musky scent permeating her senses, tipped her head back, and gulped down her martini. That'd calm her nerves.

The bartender placed his drink before him.

"Thank you. Can you please get this beautiful lady another of whatever she's having, too? It seems I've driven her to drink by ordering a bourbon sour." His eyes narrowed just a hair and filled with wickedness that revealed his true cocky colors, and hell if it didn't turn her on even more.

This was not the way to find Mr. Right.

She didn't even try to pretend he'd misread her comment. This guy was too sharp for her to play innocent. "Thank you. A lemon-drop martini, please."

"My pleasure." He leaned in closer, his knee brushing hers. "I'm Eric."

His amber eyes were even more alluring up close, a daunting haze of yellow and brown looking at her as if he was thinking about all the things he'd like to do to her and gauging her reaction closely. She shifted in her chair.

"Kat," she managed.

Eric paid for their drinks and lifted his glass. "To bourbon sours and lemon-drop martinis." His voice was rich and confident, with an undercurrent of strength and desire. "And whatever else will be."

Holy. Crap. She could imagine a lot of *whatever else*, and that was a problem. She should get up and walk out right now. Save herself an hour of innuendos that would only leave her wondering why she wasted her time. This wasn't a stay-in-the-coop type of guy. Hell no. This was a sneak-into-the-coop, take-his-fill, and get-the-hell-out sly fox. She knocked back her drink, relishing the sweetness as it slid down her throat.

He leaned in even closer. "I don't bite," he said.

If Kat had learned one thing working at the tavern, it was that there was only one way to handle a guy like this, and that was to beat him at his own game.

"That's a shame," she said with a smirk that had slayed many men. She hadn't played this way in a long time, and reveled in the excitement tickling up her spine.

Eric slid his leg between hers, brushing her inner thigh and causing her dress to inch up, which he followed with his very large, very hot hand. Deliciously lewd thoughts simmered inside her, coalescing with heat prickling her in all the best places.

He leaned in so close she could see sparks of lust in his eyes. "Darlin', I'll bite, nip, suck, lick, and anything else your gorgeous body desires. I'll turn you on in ways you never knew possible." He hovered there, his cheek a fraction of an inch from hers, his warm breath caressing her ear, and his searing heat seeping into her skin.

Kat. Couldn't. Breathe.

She loved men, and she loved hot sex, but she'd never find Mr. Right if she was playing around with Mr. Wrong. This was supposed to be her big starting-over weekend. She'd officially quit her job and was heading to Colorado so Brianna, a photographer, could take pictures for her website and portfolio. But Lord did he smell good, and the way those promises slid from his tongue made her believe…

Maybe one last goodbye to the old me…

His fingertips slid beneath the edge of her dress, causing her breathing to hitch in her throat and her hand to cover his, stopping it from moving any farther north. If her brain was short-circuiting over his voice and his hand on her leg, what would happen if that luscious mouth of his touched her skin? She needed to break this spell, but it had been a long time since she'd been this turned on—and the idea of turning off the lust coiling deep in her belly was not nearly as enticing as the man before her.

If I do this, I'll regret it seven seconds after we're done.

He leaned back just enough for his face to come into focus, and her resolve slipped away like silk off skin.

"Or," he said, his gaze penetrating and controlling, "I can be gentle, tender, and make it last all night."

Yes, please.

Kat needed to get ahold of herself. "Awfully confident for a guy who's only said a handful of words to me."

A coy, smoky smile curved his lips, bringing as much heat as his hand tightening around her thigh. "I'm a man who knows what I want, and I know how to pleasure a woman. And you"— he lifted his hand from her leg, leaving a wanting ache low in her belly, as he traced the edge of her jaw with his finger—"look like someone I once knew, which makes me a little bawdy."

She didn't know what to make of that comment, but his gaze was too distracting for her to think. His brows knitted together, and even the amber rims of his eyes seemed to darken. God he was beautiful, in an unforgettable kind of way. Kat swallowed past the lust threatening to drown her, and forced words from her lungs.

"Excuse me for a moment. I need"—*room to breathe*—"to visit the ladies' room."

"Of course." His hand sank to her thigh again, then dragged down to her knee as he sat back casually, as if he hadn't just set her world on fire.

Kat stood on legs way too wobbly, and as she shimmied her dress down her thighs, he rose beside her. *The perfect gentleman. Oh, he is good.* Why had she thought it was a smart idea to wear the slinky dress Brianna had sent her? She should have worn jeans or sweats. Something that wouldn't have gotten her into this position. And why was he standing so close, sending incendiary thoughts about what he'd feel like lying above her, with those muscular thighs pressing down on her?

"Don't get lost now," he said as she took a step away.

She felt his eyes on her as she walked down a long, dimly lit hallway to the ladies' room and fumbled for her cell phone. She called Brianna, silently hoping Brianna would tell her to run.

"Hey, did you get on a flight?" Brianna asked.

"I'm about to get on something if you don't stop me," she said, nearly breathless.

"What? Kat, are you okay?"

"No. Yes. Fuck. Bree, I don't know." She paced the bathroom floor, her heels echoing off the tile.

"Okay, slow down. What's going on? It's okay if you can't get a flight. Hugh has a friend coming out from Virginia at some point. I'm not sure when because of the storm, but he can probably come save you from whatever's going on."

"Save me? Yeah, that'd be great if he can get here in the next thirty seconds, because I'm flirting with danger, and danger has never looked so good."

Brianna laughed. "Wait. Are we talking about a guy? You're at an *airport*—remember, Kat?"

"No shit. The old Kat is rearing her ugly head. I need reinforcements. It's been a year, Bree. *A year* since I've felt this turned on, but I know I shouldn't even consider this—"

"I'm not sure which *this* you're talking about, but if you feel that turned on, go for it."

She pictured Brianna's thinly manicured brows arching with mischief, and she shook the image away. "Who are you? Please put my best friend on the phone, because she'd never tell me to get it on with a guy in an airport."

"Kat, when I met Hugh, you pushed me past my comfort zone, remember? You told me to live a little. You've been good for so long, and you haven't met Mr. Right yet. What if it takes another ten years? I've learned a lot being your friend, and I say, take your own advice. Go for it. Just this once, then move on."

She considered that, eyeing herself in the mirror. Could she be the old Kat for a night and be the new Kat tomorrow? She pushed her blond hair off one shoulder and admired the way her dress clung to her narrow hips and waist, accentuating her breasts. She imagined Eric's hands on her, and her insides shuddered. *Shuddered!* It had been way too long. "He is delicious, Bree. Like he walked off Hollywood Boulevard and right into the airport. But I don't know."

"Does he seem safe?"

"Not by sexual standards. Not by a long shot." Goose bumps chased up her limbs at the thought of being bad, very, very bad.

"If you don't do it, will you make me crazy wishing you had?"

"Yeah, probably." Brianna knew her so well.

"Do him and forget him. You'll be here by tomorrow and he'll be wherever he's going, and you can go right back to finding the right guy. *And* you won't drive me crazy."

Kat sighed. "Bree, you're the best friend ever. But this change has been good for me. I like who I've become over the past year, and I don't want to go back to being less discerning."

"Oh please. You've always liked who you were, and so has everyone else. Please tell me what you need from me, because my incredibly sexy husband is waiting for me in the bedroom. We finally got Christian to sleep, and now Mama wants to play." Bree had worked so hard, and given up so much, to raise Layla. Knowing she now had a baby boy, too, and a husband who adored her, delighted Kat—and made her long for the same.

"I wanted you to talk me out of it," Kat admitted.

"Okay. Don't do it. He's wrong for you. He's a player. He's…Wait. I don't even know him."

"Bree!"

"Okay, okay. Don't do it. He probably has a disease, or he's a freak, or he—"

Kat laughed. "Stop. It's not working. I still want him."

"You're impossible." Bree giggled, and Kat heard the low murmur of Hugh's voice. Jealousy slithered through her. Talk about luck. Hugh looked like Patrick Dempsey and practically *defined* romance. Kat used to make fun of the twelve-year abstinence plan Bree had sworn to for the sake of her daughter. After all, how many women in their midtwenties gave up sex and dating? But it had paid off for her threefold. She was so in love with her husband that it had driven Kat to reevaluate her own lifestyle and choices. Being more discerning with men hadn't brought her Mr. Right yet, but that didn't mean she was giving up.

Kat ended the call with Bree and took another look in the mirror. Inhaling a deep breath, she was still unsure of what she was going to do. Who knew how long it would be before she caught a flight, and she already had a nice little buzz going. Maybe she should just enjoy the chase and not satisfy the throbbing ache between her legs.

She shoved her phone back in her purse on the way out of the ladies' room, stopping cold at the sight of the tall, dark, and infinitely sensual man stepping into her personal space and squashing any hesitations she might have had.

THE HALLWAY WAS dark, Kat was hot, and although Eric hadn't been looking to get laid tonight, that had changed the minute he'd first spotted Kat across the bar. Something in the tilt of her head, the way her honey-blond hair fell in front of her eyes, reminded him of a girl whom he'd tucked away in his memory long ago but hadn't ever been able to forget. A bright light in his otherwise dark past. He'd been unable to look away, riveted by the haunting familiarity and her striking beauty. And now, as he stepped in closer, settling his hands on her supple curves, he saw that up close she was even more riveting.

There was no denying the heated look in her eyes she was desperately trying to ignore, or the heat pulsing between them as he tightened his grip on her hips and breathed in her feminine scent.

"What…?" She narrowed her gorgeous blue eyes, and it was there, in her eyes, where he felt himself getting lost.

"Not *what*, darlin'." He pulled her against him, pressing his hard length against her hips, as he did what he'd been aching to do since he'd sat down beside her. He slid a hand to the nape of her neck. Her skin was just as smooth as he'd imagined. Her reaction, a quick inhalation, the pulse point in her neck vibrating, was exactly what he'd counted on. "*Where*."

He gauged her reaction carefully, not wanting to scare her off. Judging by the sensual vibes radiating from her, he knew that would be hard to do. Her lips parted as he lowered his mouth to hers, hovering a breath away.

"Tell me no, and I'll walk away." He searched her eyes, and as a sweet sigh of surrender left her lips, he nearly took his cue and slanted his lips over hers. But Eric had too much at stake to go into this blindly. Consent went a long way in keeping his wallet away from money-hungry vultures. Most women didn't follow the Capital Series Grand Prix races, but those who did would see him with dollar signs in their eyes. "Words, darlin'. Give me the okay, or send me away."

Her brows pulled together as her hand slid between his legs and cupped his balls. "Clear enough?"

Their mouths crashed together, tongues tangling for control as she stroked him through his pants, and he backed her up against the wall with a *thud*. Fuck. He didn't mean to be so rough, but there was no calming the beast within. Holy fuck, it'd been a while since he'd kissed such a luscious, forgiving mouth. He could only imagine what it would feel like around his cock. Acutely aware of their less-than-private surroundings, he kicked open the men's room door and tugged her inside. They slammed against the door, kissing and pawing, as he hiked up her dress, needing more of her, and shoved his hand inside her lace panties. She was hot and so damn wet he couldn't stifle a groan as he dipped his fingers into her heat and settled his teeth on her neck.

She palmed his cock, rubbing him through his pants as he stroked over her swollen clit. A stream of sexy sounds sailed from her lips, and he sealed his mouth over hers again. Her hand fell away, and he gripped her wrist and held it above her head.

"Come for me, darlin'. Come on my hand, then my mouth, then my cock."

Their mouths came together again in a hot mess of a kiss, filled with greed. She strained against the hand that held her wrist as she gave in to her release, crying out into his mouth as her body pulsed around his fingers. He brought her down slowly, running his tongue over the swell of her lower lip, loving the flush of her skin, her breathlessness, the way her body went soft against him as he dropped to his knees, pushed her panties aside, and buried his tongue in her velvety heat.

She spread her legs wider and fisted her hands in his hair. "Yes. So good. Harder. Oh, yes…"

She tasted sweet and hot and so damn good. He took her clit between his teeth, flicking it with his tongue and earning another cry of pleasure as a second climax gripped her. He stayed on his knees, gripping her hips, laving her swollen sex, until the last shudder of pleasure rolled through her. Then he was on his feet, taking her in another punishing kiss as he blindly fished a condom from his wallet, tore his pants down, and sheathed himself. His hands clutched her hips as her eyes came open.

"I don't usually do this," she claimed.

He searched her eyes, and somewhere behind the lust he saw the honesty in her words, and that chipped away at the ice around his heart.

"That either makes me a hell of a lucky guy, or a dick for corrupting you."

Her lips curved into a smile as she slipped out of her panties and tucked them into his jacket pocket. "Let's go with lucky. If your performance sucks, then we'll go with the latter." She dragged her tongue over his lower lip, then sank her teeth into it.

He tasted blood, which sent heat searing straight to his

groin. Who was this potently feminine woman with an undercurrent of devilish vixen who played him as well as he played her? He'd never been so turned on in his life. He tucked his hand beneath her knee and hiked it up to his hip.

"What I wouldn't give for an hour alone with you in a bedroom. Buckle up, darlin', because you're in for a wild ride."

He drove into her in one hard thrust, causing them both to gasp a breath. Then their hands and bodies took over. She grasped his biceps as he pounded into her and claimed her luscious mouth in another mind-numbing kiss. Gripping her ass, he lifted her from her feet. Her legs wound naturally around him, squeezing him so tightly, it brought him to the brink of release.

"Fuuuuck, that's good," he said through gritted teeth.

"Been a…" She dug her nails into his arms. "Long time."

Her head tipped back with a needy moan as her climax claimed her. The sound of her ragged breathing and the sight of her surrendering to him so completely had him giving in to his own intense release.

Her chin fell to her chest with a heavy breath. "Damn, you're totally not a dick."

He laughed. "And you're fucking beautiful." Holding her tightly with one arm, he slid his other hand to the nape of her neck again, brushing his thumb over the delicate hairs there. "What time is your flight? Let's have another drink."

Her eyes turned serious, and she wiggled out of his hands, shimmying her dress down over her hips. "I, um. This was fun, but…" She slipped on her heels, which must have fallen off during their tryst.

"But?" A sense of urgency gripped him. He wanted to know more about her, to spend more time with her. He could count on one hand the number of times he'd wanted to know more about a woman. He didn't know what the hell had come over him, but his gut was clenching at the thought of her walking out of that door.

She nibbled on her lower lip for a moment, her eyes rolling over him, and then she squared her shoulders and said, "This was fun, but now I intend to forget it."

Chapter Two

HOLY SHIT. HOLY shit. Holy shit. Kat hurried away from the lounge and ducked into the first ladies' room she saw. One look in the mirror confirmed what her body, still vibrating from head to toe, was telling her—that was fucking incredible. She was still catching her breath as she pulled her comb from her purse to try to tame her well-fucked look. She pressed a palm to the counter, needing the stability while her legs regained their strength. What was she thinking? She'd gone a year without amazing sex, and now? Now it was like she'd had a taste of fine chocolate and she had to walk away from it. Walk away! She'd never been good at leaving sweets behind. Even when she hid a bag of M&M's from herself she knew she might as well put a spring on her ass, because every time she sat down, she popped back up for more. And now…she wanted more.

She lifted her eyes to the mirror again. Her face was flushed, her lips swollen from the intensity of their wicked kisses, and down below? She didn't think she'd ever stop humming down there. Lordy, Lordy that man was hung like no other, and damn did he know how to use all those gloriously hard inches.

She snagged paper towels from the dispenser and cleaned herself up while she tried to calm her racing heart. Her body was still trembling ten minutes later, as his words rolled through her mind. *Come for me, darlin'. Come on my hand, then my mouth, then my cock.*

Check. Check. Double check.

How had she gone so long without feeling the temptation of a real man? Who was she kidding? She'd never felt anything like the power behind Eric...Eric? *Ohmygod.* She didn't even know his last name.

I'm a slut.

A tramp.

A two-bit hookup in an airport bar.

She couldn't suppress the smile on her lips. He was *so* worth it! She dug out her cell phone, in need of a little pep talk from Bree, and realized she'd missed several texts from her. Kat scrolled through them, smiling and finally calming down as she read three identical texts, each repeating their secret pep talk, a line from *The Help.*

You is kind. You is smart. You is important.

You is kind. You is smart. You is important.

You is kind. You is smart. You is important.

The last text read, *1, 2, 3, click your heels and forget. Poof! You're a good girl again. Love you!*

"No doubt about it, Brianna, you are the very best friend in the world," Kat said aloud before sending Bree a thank-you text.

She left the bathroom feeling edgy and a little dazed, her body still reeling from their encounter. An hour later she was finally seated on a flight to Colorado. The man beside her smelled like cigarettes and looked like he'd slept in his clothes. She closed her eyes and rested her head back, thinking of Eric. She could still feel his fingers pressing into her ass, the coarse hair at the base of his cock against her sensitive skin, and the way his eyes bored through her. Her cheeks heated as his naughty words came back to her again.

As the plane lifted into the air, she reveled in the weightless feeling, but it was the slow burn in her belly as she revisited the feel of Eric's tongue taking her to the edge of ecstasy that had her squirming in her seat. God, she must be losing her mind. She could smell his cologne all around her.

A heavy hand landed on her thigh, and her eyes flew open as she pushed it away—and her chest constricted at the devilish grin smiling back at her. *Eric.*

"Hey there, darlin'."

"Eric? What are you doing here?" Her heart was beating a mile a minute. Could he tell that she'd been fantasizing about them? That the mere sight of him had her twitching in places that had no business twitching?

"I offered the kind gentleman who was sitting here a little something to exchange seats with me."

"You paid him off so you could sit here? But—" *Ohmygod.* How would she forget about him now?

"Don't you worry yourself over him. I'm sure he's happy as a clam sitting in first class."

"First class?" *You gave up first class to sit with me?*

"Some say it's the only way to travel." His eyes rolled over her, lingering on her mouth before dropping to her breasts, making her body go ten types of crazy. "I think they've got it all wrong. I've got the best seat on the plane."

Her mind was spinning. "You're going to Denver?"

"Weston, actually, but Denver's the closest airport."

"Weston?" No way! That was where she was going.

"Yes. I've got business there. Where are you headed?"

"Weston." Her stomach dipped, but her engine was revving again with the possibilities of what this could mean.

No. No. No.

She needed to nip these thoughts in the bud. No good could come from a guy who'd banged her in an airport bathroom.

"Vacation, work, or family?" he asked.

She shook her head, unable to clear her thoughts enough to answer. She didn't want to talk about her plans. She needed him to know exactly where she stood. The sooner he returned to first class and sent the smelly guy back to his rightful seat, the sooner she could forget what she'd done. Although, she had a feeling that forgetting Eric was not going to be easy. If it was even possible.

"Eric, I'm not sure what you're thinking, but"—she lowered her voice to a whisper—"I'm not looking for another hookup. I shouldn't have done what we did. I'm really not that person anymore."

"Anymore?" He arched a brow and lowered his voice. "We can visit that later. For now, I think I got the message pretty clearly when you said you intended to forget what happened between us." He placed a possessive hand on her thigh and said, "But I don't intend to let you."

She was too shocked to respond, and embarrassingly, totally turned on by his aggressive behavior.

"You see, Kat, I like you. I like the fire in your eyes, the strength in your convictions." He pressed his lips to her ear and said in a gravelly voice that made her insides melt, "I love the taste of you and the way you look when you lose control."

Heat stroked over her. He lifted one shoulder in a casual shrug, his lips curving up in a sinful smile that made her wish his hand would inch up her thigh again. Holy fuck. Those eyes of his must be hypnotizing her. How on earth would she make it through a long flight sitting beside him? She glanced at his hand, currently possessing her thigh, and placed her hand over his, trying to lift it from her leg.

He laced their fingers together, still smiling, but with a clear challenge in his eyes as he said, "Tell me to leave and I'll go back to my seat."

She could barely think past the blood rushing through her ears and the fire heating up her veins at his audacity, which should have turned her off but was totally turning her on. He was controlling, but thoughtfully so, giving her an easy out with every step. Allowing her to be in control of her decisions. *Sort of.* Was there a woman alive who could resist his charms? She didn't even know his last name, and she found herself relaxing her hand as he turned his so they were palm to palm, and laced their fingers again.

"What's your last name?" she asked.

"James. Eric James. You?" His gaze never wavered as he waited for her answer.

"Martin."

"Kat Martin," he said under his breath, as if he were memorizing it or weighing the feel of it on his tongue. He raised their joined hands and pressed a kiss to the back of hers. "Tell me, Kat, what turns you on besides dirty talk and a hard cock?"

She bristled.

"I struck a nerve. So dirty talk is only okay in quiet conversations or intimate moments. Duly noted. My deepest apologies."

Kat was seriously considering getting up and walking away, when he leaned in closer and said, "That tells me what you said is true. You're not a typical hookup girl."

"I think I made that clear," she said sternly.

"Verbally. Yet you're still here, holding my hand, and that flush on your cheeks isn't caused by the altitude. I know it's caused by me, because a girl who was interested in hooking up with any willing and able man wouldn't have flinched at what I said." His piercing gaze made her pulse ratchet up another notch—or ten.

"You have a strange way of getting to the heart of matters," she said, taking her hand back from his, and—confusingly—she missed his touch.

"I think I'm pretty direct. Besides, there's nothing more beautiful than the spark of confidence in your eyes right now." He lowered his voice again. "And knowing that while your eyes are holding my gaze, you're asking yourself, what do I want? Should I walk away? Do I want to hold his hand again? Does he want to hold mine?"

Her mouth went dry at his uncanny ability to rattle *and* excite her at once.

"You're intrigued, turned on, and maybe a little scared. But not by me, because I'm hardly someone who's dangerous in that way, but rather, you're scared by the feelings I evoke in you. Should you walk away? Only if you want to truly forget what you felt back there. I know I don't want to forget one second of it. I was more alive when I was touching you, tasting you, fucking you, than I've ever been."

She'd never been spoken to in such vulgar terms, and she might go straight to hell for this, but she loved every single word he said.

When she finally responded, her voice was shaky but audible. "I wondered what other talents your mouth was capable of."

His head tipped back with a nearly silent laugh, and then he pinned her with a piercing stare. "I'm good at a lot of things, like being honest. I've never met a less forgettable woman than you, Kat. I want to know everything about you. What you feel like when you're dancing close to me, what makes your eyes light up in the mornings, and what you sound like as you fall asleep. What you're into—in and out of the bedroom. But mostly, right this second, I want to know how your hand feels in mine again." He turned his hand palm up and held it out to her.

His smile warmed, became less sexual, and somehow, he was already becoming familiar. She gazed at his hand, and as she lowered her palm to his, that felt familiar, too.

AIRPORT HOOKUPS WEREN'T new for Eric, just as hookups anywhere else on the planet weren't, but the sense of loss he'd felt when Kat had walked out of the bathroom had struck him numb. It didn't make any sense. She hadn't done any one thing, said any one thing that was remarkably significant, but she'd made his entire being hum. From his thoughts to his heartbeat to the fire racing through his veins, Kat electrified him. And then there was the sense that he somehow already knew her, and it lingered like a web in a tree, almost invisible, yet undeniably present.

The minute he'd seen her walk on the plane, his heart had tumbled in his chest, and that, too, was new. He wasn't about to take the chance of never seeing her again, not when she'd already turned his mind, and his body, inside out. As a professional race car driver, Eric James was used to making snap decisions that his life depended on. When he set his sights on something, he didn't back down. Hell, backing down wasn't even in his vocabulary. But usually those decisions happened on the racetrack. Never before had he felt possessive of a woman— and certainly not after just meeting her. But the possessive, and some might say, obsessive, traits that made him a world-champion racer were riding the surface of his skin and gnawing at the pit in his gut—the gut that produced instincts he trusted with his life.

He knew he was testing Kat's boundaries, but in addition to knowing what he wanted, he knew himself too well to play games with either of their emotions. She needed to know the real him, not the guy the rest of the world saw in magazines and on television. He rarely let anyone inside the walls he'd constructed around himself, but he was so drawn to her, he instinctively knew he had to go in no holds barred or not at all.

The churning in his gut calmed when she set her hand in his.

Kat blinked up at him, and the confusion in her eyes pulled all his strings. Even the ones he never knew he had.

"I don't know why I'm holding your hand. You're a dirty-talking guy I barely know. You paid someone off so you could sit beside me, and for all I know, you're a crazy-ass stalker."

He laughed. "All of that is true. For all you know I am a crazy-ass stalker, and yet..." He held up their hands.

"I'm *so* not this person," she whispered harshly.

"I have on good authority that you *are* Kat Martin."

"Yes, but not the woman"—she leaned in closer—"who has sex in a bathroom and then does this." She lifted their hands.

"Then tell me who you are."

She sighed and rolled her eyes, looking so fucking adorable he had to fight the urge to kiss her again. He had no idea what compelled him to hold her hand, except that he had wanted desperately to be closer to her, to keep their connection, and he was thrilled that she allowed him to.

"I'm a waitress slash bartender slash"—she paused, as if debating whether to continue, and then added, "going to see her best friend, and I'm totally uninterested in talking about myself." She turned a scrutinizing gaze on him. "Who are *you?*"

"This is where I run into trouble." He was always wary of revealing what he did for a living, because no matter what, it always changed the way people treated him. They were either in awe of his celebrity, or immediately wrote him off as a pompous ass.

"Let me guess: You're married, on a business trip, wife and kids are at home." She tried to pull her hand away, and he tightened his hold.

"First of all, you couldn't be further from the truth. I've never been married, am not in a committed relationship, and I have no children that I know of."

"That's reassuring," she said with another eye roll.

"Hey, all I can give you is the truth."

"Okay, then tell me who you are. No games, no lines, just lay it out there."

The truth came easier than he'd imagined. "Eric James. Capital Series Grand Prix racer." The airplane rumbled and bumped, knocking them both forward. Eric put an arm out in front of Kat to keep her from jolting forward. Her eyes were wide and fearful. "It's okay. Just a little turbulence." He took both her hands in his and reassured her. "Just a few bumps from the storm. You're okay."

She nodded, but he could tell she was still frightened.

"You don't fly much, do you?"

She shook her head.

He gathered her as close as he could while strapped into their seats. "It's okay. Focus on our conversation. Ask me anything you want to know, Kat. Look at me. Focus on me."

The fear in her eyes nearly did him in. He wanted to press his lips to hers and kiss away the fright. Instead, he kissed her forehead. "I've got you. You're safe. Talk to me, Kat."

"Are you really a race car driver?" Her voice was thin, shaky.

"Yes. I really am."

"As in the Grand Prix racing series that Hugh Braden has won a bunch of times?"

"You follow racing?" He loved driving—the speed, the freedom, the risk—and would be thrilled if she followed the series, but she didn't look like a racing groupie.

"No, but I follow Hugh. His wife is my best friend."

"You know Brianna?" The plane jostled again, and she sucked in a sharp breath. He lifted the arm of the chair to bring her in closer, then stroked his hands down her back. "It's okay. Tell me how you know Brianna."

"We worked together at the tavern where she met Hugh."

"Oh, shit. You're *that* Kat?" Hugh had told him a little

about Brianna's best friend over the years. He knew how close she and Brianna were and that she was godmother to Brianna's daughter, Layla. Hugh had said Kat was spunky, and that as a single mother, Brianna had relied heavily on her.

"Is that bad?" She raised her brows, and he couldn't resist tucking her hair behind her ear so he could see her eyes more clearly.

"No, darlin'. Hugh speaks very highly of you. I had no idea you were *that* Kat."

"I love Brianna. She's the strongest woman I know, and such a good mother." Her eyes warmed and her voice turned thoughtful. "Hugh is so good to her."

"Hugh's a good man, and he loves her and the kids to the ends of the earth. He's a lucky man."

"Because she loves him?"

"Because they love each other, and he has a family." *Something I never really had until I met Hugh.* He thought about his friend and the way Hugh's father, Hal Braden, had always treated Eric like a son, and Hugh's five siblings treated him like family, too. His heart ached at the thought of his biological family. He'd left home at sixteen to escape the nightmare of two heroin-addicted parents, and despite the fact that they'd since gotten clean, they still didn't have a warm relationship. He pushed past the familiar thickening in his throat and turned his attention back to the incredibly sweet and beautiful woman beside him.

"Tell me about your family, Kat. Are you close?"

"I'm close to my parents and my younger brother, and Bree's mom is like a second mother to me. We're really close, too." She smiled and added, "And Hugh's father, well, he treats everyone like they're his children."

"Hal Braden is an amazing man, that's for sure. His love has pulled me through more times than I'd like to admit." He realized what he was about to reveal and changed the subject. "So you and I are both headed to the Braden ranch?"

"You're staying there?" Her eyes were wide, but it was the excitement in her eyes he couldn't miss, and damn did he like it.

"Yes, I am." *I'm a lucky bastard.*

"Oh, no. We can't. You and I…"

"Relax. It's not like I'm going to take you on their kitchen floor."

"Oh, God," she said in a whisper. She separated their hands, lowered the arm of the seat between them, and held up her palm, staving him off. "Stay there. Just…stay there."

He was amused by her sudden nervousness. "Whatever you say."

"God, Eric. I had no idea you knew them, much less were staying with them. What we did was supposed to be a one-time thing. A last fling; then I'd go back to looking for Mr. Right, and—"

"Whoa. What?" He cocked a brow.

She covered her mouth and closed her eyes for a beat. When she opened them, the worry was replaced with humor. "Looking for Mr. Right."

"You're looking for a *husband?*" A trickle of worry skittered through him.

"No. Yes. I don't know. Not exactly *looking*, just…trying not to attract the wrong type of guys."

He scoffed. He was totally the wrong type of guy, and yet he couldn't imagine walking away from her.

"What? Is it wrong to want to be adored? To want romance? With flowers and wine and sweet words that make my stomach flutter?" She sighed dreamily. "I used to live like tomorrow may never come, you know, less discriminatory with the guys I dated, staying out until all hours. And do you know where that got me? Not far, that's for sure. I had tons of great sex, but great sex doesn't equate to true love, and in my case, it equated to a lot of lonely nights *after* the great sex." She shrugged, smiling like she was amused by her life. "Ten years of working the same job, several years of night classes for a business degree that I've never used, and wondering why my life wasn't going where I wanted it to, and then Brianna met Hugh and everything changed."

She could have been reciting the soundtrack to his life.

"I took stock in my life and what I wanted out of it, and a year ago I told my boss, Mack, whom I adore, that I wanted *more*, and he totally got it. I mean, where was I going as a bartender and a waitress? I confessed my dreams, poured my heart out to him, because really, he is so much more than a boss. He's always been like an older brother I could tell anything to. I admitted that I wanted to do something to help others, something exciting, breathing life into the dreams of others. And trust me, I know how stupid that sounds, but Mack connected me with his friend Shea Steele, a public relations rep to the rich and famous, and she's been mentoring me in PR day in and day out. I've probably got more diverse experience than half the PR reps out there. It's been a wild and crazy ride, but I've always tried to face my fears, and this was just one of a few that I hadn't conquered. My dream of owning my own business."

"So, this trip?"

"This trip is about breaking free. Starting over. I quit my job, and I'm going for it." She leaned in close and whispered, "Like our hookup. My last bite of cake before my big diet."

He smiled, but inside he felt the burn of longing. He didn't want to be a last bite of cake. He wanted to be the whole celebration.

"So, you're going into PR for the rich and famous?" he asked.

"No. No offense to you, but I feel like celebrities don't really need the type of PR help I want to give. I mean, so much exposure comes from just *being* rich and famous. I want to help the little guys, and I don't care if that means earning peanuts, or not gaining exposure for my business as quickly as I might if I helped bigger names. I want to focus on nonprofits, companies and people who are doing good in the world in bigger ways. This trip is about getting ready to dive in feetfirst. Brianna is taking pictures for my website and brochures, which is fitting, considering it was Brianna and Hugh who gave me the inspiration to do all of this. I was there the day they met, and looking back? It was nothing short of magical that the two of them would meet so randomly. And even though they met at the tavern, I couldn't imagine it happening twice, and I worried that it was also putting me in a bad place to meet the kind of person I would like to be with in the future. Someone stable and loving, and interested in the world around them, not just the next good lay."

She held his gaze for a long time, and he wondered if she was thinking that he belonged in that group of people, too. He wanted to tell her that it was Hugh's relationship with Bree, and the way it had sated Hugh so completely, that had Eric carousing less with random women and focusing on fleshing out the things that were important to him, like creating a scholarship for his foundation, the Foundation for Whole Families, that helped families affected by drug use. The foundation gave him fulfillment vastly different from what racing or women ever could.

But he held his tongue, because surely these coincidences would seem far-fetched to Kat, and perhaps even contrived. Neither definition entered his mind, but the word *fate* certainly did.

"Now," she finally said, "I'm ready for everything. A fulfilling career and hopefully, a loving, stable relationship. Maybe I don't deserve that, but I want it."

She made him want that, too.

"I already have contracts with four nonprofit clients Shea sent my way. They were too small for her, but perfect for me. So, to answer your question, I'm not really looking for a husband, but I'm definitely trying not to attract the wrong kind of guys anymore." She leaned her head back against the seat and laughed. "I'm not very good at that, am I?"

"On the contrary. I think you're very good at not finding the wrong type of guys." Eric took her hand in his again. "Maybe it's your definition of *wrong* that's off."

Chapter Three

WESTON, COLORADO, WAS a small ranch town, markedly different from the fast-paced city life Kat was used to. Here, dressing up meant a nice pair of Levi's and shinin' your boots, and she loved it. She'd been to Hal Braden's ranch a number of times, but the breathtaking view of rolling hills and green pastures never failed to fill her with a peaceful feeling, which shockingly overrode the nervous energy of riding in the rental car in close proximity to Eric. Small talk had come surprisingly easy, even if most of it was laced with flirty comments and naughty innuendos. The more time Kat spent with Eric, the more she liked him. But she couldn't ignore the warning bells going off in her head. The man was a definite player, and she was over that part of her life.

It was well after midnight when they finally pulled down Hal's dark driveway.

As they stepped from the car, Eric pointed to the horses in the pasture. "Do you ride?"

"No, but it's on my list of fears to conquer."

"How's that going for you? Conquering your fears?"

Kat watched her handsome driver with interest as he rounded the car and grabbed his bags from the trunk. He'd asked her several personal questions on the drive over, like what she did with her time now that Brianna was gone and how her best friend traveling so much affected their relationship. Most guys wouldn't give a hoot about such things, or even think to ask. She liked that about him. He wasn't as self-centered as she'd originally pegged him.

"Okay," she finally answered. "I've got a few left to overcome."

"Like?"

"Gosh, I don't know. Like flying, maybe, as you saw."

"You did great on the plane tonight."

She rolled her eyes. "I can do better. And my other fears are sort of silly. I know you'll laugh, but I used to be afraid of driving fast."

He arched a brow.

"Don't worry. I totally love driving fast now. Of course, fast in Richmond means sixty-five miles per hour. Nothing like the high speeds you and Hugh drive." She reached for her bag, and he touched her hand.

"I've got it."

"It's okay. I can take it." She didn't want to lead him on, but there was no denying the heat between them, which had only gotten stronger on the drive over.

"Don't worry, you don't have to sleep with me for me to carry your bag." His lips quirked up, and before she could respond, he added, "But you'll want to, and who am I to try to dissuade you?"

Hell, yeah, she wanted to—but she couldn't go there. Not at the Braden ranch and not with a man who'd already proved that he could easily turn her world upside down—and would then move on.

"Eric, I'm not sleeping with you again." *No matter how much I want to.*

He closed the trunk, and with moonlight shining down on his gorgeous face and his eyes boring into her, he stepped closer and said, "If the airport was all we'll ever have, then how about one final kiss?"

"A kiss?" She was already salivating at the thought.

"One kiss." He stepped closer, causing their thighs to

brush, and she felt the heat of him from her head to her toes and in all the best places in between. "Then that's it. A send-off, if you will."

"A send-off." This guy was trouble with a capital *T*. She'd like to get him off, not send him off.

The darkening of his eyes told her that he didn't miss the breathlessness she felt. He ran his fingers through her hair, settling his warm palm over the nape of her neck and sending a now slightly familiar rush of anticipation through her.

"Tell me no," he said in a rich voice, "and I'll back off."

No, was on the tip of her tongue, but it got lost somewhere between *please* and *kiss me now*. She clutched the waist of his pants, unsure of her voice, and hoped he'd take it as confirmation that she wanted the kiss just as much as he did.

"Kat," he whispered against her lips. "You're not going to be able to forget me. I won't let you."

He sealed his lips over hers, and their bodies bumped, causing the bag he had slung over his shoulder to slide down his arm and crash against their hips. They both smiled for a blink of an eye, and then his mouth was claiming hers again, pulling her in to his taste, his scent, the slick slide of his tongue over hers. She tried to hold on to her thoughts—*make it a short kiss, a short farewell*—but his hand sank to her ass, pressing her against his formidable erection, and her thoughts spun away. No man had ever tasted so good, tested her resolve so aggressively.

When their lips finally parted, she kept her eyes closed, reveling in the electric currents coursing through her body, the stinging of her lips, the ache of desire in her loins. His fingers brushed through her hair, and she heard him exhale a soulful breath as his forehead touched hers. She opened her eyes and found him looking at her in a way he hadn't before. His gaze was tender, a little confused, and intense with something more than desire. She wanted to take a picture and disappear into that look for hours.

"Who are you, Kat Martin?" he whispered. "You feel so familiar, like I've known you forever."

The porch light turned on, and neither of them moved. She wasn't sure they even breathed. The sound of the front door opening broke through her foggy brain. She forced herself to swallow the thick taste of desire and take a step back. But their eyes held, and she had a strange feeling that she'd left a piece of herself with him.

ERIC COULDN'T SHAKE the feeling that he'd met Kat before. He searched her eyes, looking for some sense of recognition beyond the obvious, but he sensed he was alone in his recognition. The relief was bittersweet. She stirred memories of his troubled youth, memories that he usually kept buried so deep that no one could unearth them. Only these memories were laced with something pleasurable. Fleeting feelings of happiness that broke through his treacherous upbringing.

Kat touched her lips, as if she could hold in the heat of their kiss, but it was the lingering look of desire in her eyes that told him there was no way in hell she was going to forget their kiss. He knew he couldn't. How could he when she was so sweet, so sexy, and sparked such good feelings inside him?

He slung her bag over his shoulder and stepped in close as Hugh and Brianna descended the porch steps. Kat was nibbling on her lower lip again, watching their friends approach, and he could read the worry filling her eyes. He touched her hand, prepared to reassure her that he wasn't going to say anything to Hugh and Brianna, when her eyes narrowed.

"That never happened," she said harshly before pasting a smile on her lips and hurrying into Brianna's open arms.

"I can't believe you're here!" Brianna hugged her. "And I'm so glad you met Eric. How did you guys hook up?"

Kat's smile fell flat, a beat that Hugh obviously didn't miss as he shot a quizzical look at Eric.

"We met in the rental car line," he explained quickly, "and decided to save a few bucks." Kat's relieved sigh was a nod of approval.

"I'm so glad. Come on. The kids and Hal are asleep, of course, but I'll get you settled in your room." Brianna and Kat headed for the house.

Both men were well over six feet, and they stood eye to eye.

The coy look in Hugh's dark eyes wasn't lost on Eric as he embraced his friend.

"Good to see you, Hugh."

"It's been a while. How was your trip?" Hugh closed the trunk of the car, and they headed down the gravel path toward the front door.

"Great. No issues other than the delays."

They'd known each other since their early racing days, when they'd shared everything from secrets to women. But love had changed Hugh, and even now, a few years and a baby later, Eric could see the fulfilled look in his friend's eyes.

"Want to talk about the vibe you two are giving off?" Hugh asked.

Hugh had been too good of a friend to Eric for him to lie to him, but he also had the unexpected urge to protect Kat's privacy.

"She's a gorgeous woman. I'm a good-looking guy. We're gonna have some kind of vibe." Easy enough and not a lie.

"There is truth in that statement, my friend." They climbed the porch steps, and Hugh touched Eric's arm before opening the door. "Eric, how are you really? Anything new on the parental front?"

Nothing like starting with the hardest subject. "I'm well, and no. Nothing new. They live their simple, and thankfully sober, lives, and I live mine. I'm glad to be here, though, Hugh. Nothing beats a weekend at Hal's." Eric had gotten a job at the racetrack when he was fifteen, and a mechanic had taken him under his wing. At sixteen, he'd moved out. Eric had thought about reaching out to his parents many times those first few years, but it had been too painful seeing the people who were supposed to care for him being unwilling to care for themselves. And later, when they'd finally cleaned up their lives, they were still disinterested in him. To this day, their interaction was minimal.

Hugh searched his friend's eyes, and Eric wondered what he saw there. The longing for a childhood he'd never have, unresolved anger toward his parents, or the longing for a woman who had somehow infiltrated the walls he'd built around himself and who'd overtaken his thoughts in the space of a few hours.

"Well, bro," Hugh said. "You're here now. Let's get you settled in."

Settling in wasn't something Eric had ever been good at, but between the Bradens' welcoming arms and the knowledge that Kat was inside, he wanted to try.

Chapter Four

AFTER A SLEEPLESS night of beating herself up for what she'd done with Eric, Kat decided to forgive herself. After all, she was only human, and Eric James was some kind of sexual god. Any woman would have given in to his sweet seduction.

Now if she could only stop thinking about him.

That wasn't likely to happen anytime soon. She'd spent the entire night reliving their last kiss, playing over the sound of his voice when he'd said he felt like he'd known her forever. She couldn't deny feeling a thread of familiarity when they'd kissed in the driveway, but she'd assumed it was because they'd been kissing in the airport and those kisses were still fresh on her mind. As was the rest of what they'd done.

It was almost six o'clock Saturday morning, and Kat was sitting on the back patio, listening to the sounds of the ranch coming to life. She'd always been an early riser, and with the time difference between Virginia and Colorado, her body thought it was eight o'clock. The sun peeked over the mountains, sending ribbons of pink across the sky, and not for the first time, she wondered what it would be like to live someplace like this, away from the noises and smells of the city and surrounded by family. Hal's sons Treat and Rex owned the neighboring properties to the ranch. She knew Treat and his family were away at one of the many resorts he owned. She'd seen Rex, a burly cowboy with linebacker shoulders and long, ink-black hair topped with an ever-present Stetson, down by the barn when she'd come outside. Rex ran his father's ranch, and it seemed to Kat that he worked from dawn to dusk.

"You look a million miles away," Eric said as he came through the patio doors, looking devastatingly handsome in a pair of jeans and a white T-shirt that stretched tight over his muscular chest and biceps. His voice still carried the grogginess of sleep, and his hair was standing on end, as if he'd just rolled out of bed. She wondered if that was his daily look, *sexily rumpled*.

He sat in the chair beside her, and she noticed his feet were bare, and for whatever reason, it upped his sexy factor even more. She loved a man who was confident and comfortable in his own skin, and Eric was the epitome of both. She smiled, taking in the warmth in his eyes and the absence of the intensity she'd seen last night.

"Just thinking about what it would be like to live here," she answered.

He handed her his coffee mug. "Sip?"

"Sure. Thanks." She closed her eyes, savoring the warm liquid. "You take cream and sugar, too. That's convenient."

"I'm sure we have a lot in common," he said as she set the mug in his hand. He raised his index finger and placed it over hers, holding her hand gently in place.

Her pulse quickened. Guys hit on her all the time at the bar and she never paid them any mind. But something about Eric made her entire body take notice, and most curiously, her heart warmed when he was near.

He smiled and released her finger. Even without his touch, their threaded connection remained, and she tried again to remind herself that he was a one-night stand, not a potential boyfriend.

"I have a place in upstate New York like this, in the Silver Mountains. I don't have horses like Hal does, but I've got about a hundred acres of wooded mountain property with a stream that runs through it. It's nice. Quiet."

"Sounds beautiful. Do you spend a lot of time there?"

He sipped his coffee and shook his head. "Between my race schedule and my charity efforts, I don't get as much time there as I'd like."

She wondered how much of his time was spent chasing women, too, and it bothered her that she cared.

"I figured you'd be tired after our late night. I expected to be alone for the sunrise." He took another sip of his coffee and gazed out over the mountain.

"You came out specifically to watch the sunrise?"

He nodded. "I always do when I'm here. There's nothing more beautiful than a Colorado sunrise." He brushed her hair from her shoulder. "Except, it appears I was wrong. You're far more beautiful than the sunrise."

She laughed. "There you go again, showing me all your mouthy talents."

"You haven't even begun to see how talented my mouth can be." He rubbed his scruffy chin. "But that wasn't a line, even though it sounded like one. I'm sorry if I came across too strong, or managed to turn you off in some way, but I'm not going to deny how attracted to you I am."

She felt her cheeks heat up and shifted her eyes away. He turned her chin, so she had no choice but to look at him.

"Are you embarrassed by my honesty or turned off by it?" His gaze was serious, his words sincere, and she felt her heart warming again.

"Do you always say what you're thinking?"

"Yes. My filter is set rather low." He smiled and handed her his mug again, which she gladly took. She needed caffeine for this conversation. "Do you always avoid answering questions that make you uncomfortable?"

"Do you like to make me uncomfortable?" She couldn't stop herself from playing along. He was different from any man she'd ever met, and as much as his directness repeatedly caught her off guard, she was completely drawn to it, to him.

"That's a loaded question." He turned in his chair, bringing his leg between hers. His hand came to rest on her knee, but his heated gaze never wavered. "I might be purposely trying to push your buttons, but it's only because I find you incredibly attractive and interesting." He leaned in close, sucking all the air from her lungs. "Were you able to forget our kiss?"

Her lips tingled with the reminder.

"Tell me something, Kat. Do you remember every man's kisses like you remember mine?"

Hell no.

"Do you still feel my lips on yours? The press of our mouths, the slicking of my tongue over yours? Do you still taste me the way I still taste you?" His thumb stroked slow circles on her knee, making it hard for her to think. "Last night when you were in bed, did you close your eyes and remember the feel of me filling you up the way I remembered the tight hold your body had on me?"

He paused, and she didn't know if it was for effect or because he saw that she was no longer breathing. Either way, she was thankful, because her body was so tightly wound that he nearly had her coming apart with nothing more than words— and that damn thumb of his, which was sending pinpricks of desire racing up her thigh.

He lifted his hand from her leg, leaving a wave of cold air behind, and he cupped her cheek, brushing that talented thumb over her lower lip. She could barely breathe as he leaned in even closer.

Kiss me.

"All night I thought about what it would be like to wake up with you in my arms. To kiss you good morning and feel your body soft and warm against mine. I want to kiss you, Kat. One kiss."

She didn't think before the whisper left her lips. "Kiss me."

He pressed his lips to hers lightly, warm and sweet. Her insides quivered at the tenderness of this unobtrusive kiss, the delicious feel of his mouth touching hers. When he pulled away without deepening the kiss, she had a burning desire for more, and that's when her brain began kicking into gear again. She shook her head, trying to ward off the dreamy intimacy he'd suffused her with. What was she doing?

"Last night was supposed to be our last kiss," she reminded him.

He smiled. "Did you want it to be?"

She pushed to her feet, feeling agitated and annoyed at the

way her body thrummed from his touch. She was frustratingly turned on. *No*, she didn't want that to be their last kiss, but she didn't want a weekend fling, either. He was watching her as she paced the patio, and that annoyed her even more, because she knew he sensed her frustration and was just letting her pace it off. That should piss her off, but it was another goddamn turn-on, the way he was so in tune with everything about her. She'd never met a man who looked that closely into her feelings or her actions.

"You're messing with my head," she finally admitted.

He set the coffee mug on the ground beside his chair and stood, taking her gently into his arms. "Then tell me not to, Kat. Tell me to leave you alone once and for all." His words were rough, challenging, belying the way he embraced her. His grip on her hips tightened. She loved his strength and had thought all night about how hard he'd thrust into her, reliving the intensity of their sex for hours upon hours.

He rocked his hips against hers, and her breath left her lungs in a rush.

"You're all about hookups," she said, pushing at his chest, and wanting to keep him close at the same time. "It's too easy to get swept up in you," she finally managed.

"How do you know I'm about hookups?" His gaze was unyielding.

"You picked me up in the airport bar," she reminded him.

"One could say you picked me up." He smiled, but it didn't dampen the heat in his eyes.

She fisted her hands in his shirt, unsure if she was holding him close or keeping him at bay. "You followed me to the bathroom."

"You wanted me to."

"I did not. *You* kissed *me*!"

"That's not how I remember it. I remember asking you to send me away, the same way I just did, and you grabbed my cock."

Oh shit. He was right.

"The truth is, I *have* always enjoyed fast women. You read me right, darlin'. No doubt about that."

Aha! See!

"But that's not why I approached you in the bar. You looked familiar, not fast. Yes, you were sexy and gorgeous with a killer body and eyes that make my cock take notice, but you felt familiar. You felt different, right, in a way other women don't. And when I tasted you…"

Her knees weakened as his lips brushed against hers.

"There was no going back. There is no going back. You feel it too, Kat. I know you do."

"I…" *Do not say it. Do not tell him you want him.* "I don't want to be a hookup."

His eyes narrowed, and his voice filled with desire. "What do you want to be?"

How the hell should I know? A girlfriend? A date? A lover? She was a woman who conquered her fears and took life by the horns, but she couldn't come up with an answer to save her life. All she knew was that she wanted to be *something* to him, which was probably a very bad idea.

"When you're ready to tell me what you want, let me know." He released her, leaving her weak and confused as he picked up the coffee cup and headed for the door. He reached for the handle, and she swallowed to keep her heart from climbing out of her throat.

"I want what you can never be," she finally managed.

He stopped with his hand midreach. His chin dropped, as if in defeat. He turned slowly, and the determination in his eyes was unmistakable. She swallowed hard at her misinterpretation of his actions as he closed the distance between them.

"How can you possibly know what I can and cannot be?" His tone was so dark and serious that it momentarily numbed her.

"You said you were all about fast women."

"No. I said I have always *enjoyed* fast women."

"What is it with you and *words*?" She crossed her arms, a barrier between his heat and her heart.

"Words are clear. If you use them well, they leave no room for misinterpretation." His gaze softened. "I have always *enjoyed* fast women. Past tense. That's a true fact. But for whatever reason, I find myself completely and utterly captivated by you. I want to know everything about you, what fears you want to conquer, what emotions you're hiding. I want to explore and enjoy you, Kat. Present tense." He paused, and the silence pulsed and swelled between them. "So tell me, Kat. What is it that you want?"

The door to the patio slid open and Layla ran out, barreling into Kat. "Auntie Kat!"

Kat tore her eyes from Eric's, relieved at the interruption. If they'd been alone for one more second, God only knew what answer she would have given him. The man was so intense, and everything he said was so impassioned, she was surprised the sparks between them didn't ignite.

"Hey, sweetie!" She hugged Layla, eyeing Eric over her head and still floundering for an answer. "Look how tall you've grown, and your hair has gotten so long. You are gorgeous, just like your mom, but you look twelve, not ten."

Layla giggled. "I've missed you so much. Mom's giving Christian a bath and Daddy is making breakfast." She was the spitting image of her mother, with cocoa-colored eyes, shiny dark hair, and a sparkling smile. She turned to Eric and wrapped her arms around his waist. "Uncle Eric, I've missed you, too."

As Eric scooped Layla into his arms and kissed her cheek, the tension Kat had felt only moments ago disappeared. "I've missed you, too, kiddo."

"Daddy said to tell you to stop bothering Auntie Kat and to go inside and help him cook breakfast."

He set Layla down on the patio, but his focus never left the little girl. "Then I'd better go help. Your father is a mess in the kitchen."

"No, he's not," Layla said with a laugh. "He loves to cook."

Eric crouched beside her and whispered something in her ear that made Layla giggle. She looked up at Kat and nodded. Kat wondered what the heck he was whispering, but she wasn't about to ask. Eric reached behind Layla's ear, and when he opened his hand, there was a gold charm bracelet in his palm.

Layla gasped as he hooked the bracelet around her slender wrist and rose to his feet, then bowed dramatically. "I bid you farewell, my beautiful ladies."

After he walked inside, Layla held her wrist up for Kat to admire the pretty bracelet with the heart charm dangling from it.

"That's beautiful, Layla. Does Uncle Eric bring you gifts often?"

"Uh-huh. Sometimes he sends them in the mail with a card. He sends them to Christian, too." She blinked up at Kat with mischief dancing in her eyes, and Kat felt her heart squeeze at Eric being so thoughtful. "He said soon you were going to call him Prince Eric."

Kat's jaw fell open. She remembered when Hugh and Brianna had first met, right before Layla's sixth birthday, when Layla was going through a major princess phase. She'd called Hugh *Prince Hugh*. What in the hell would make Eric say such a thing to a little girl who obviously adored him? It was one thing to mess with her feelings, but a little girl's?

She didn't know how to respond, and she really didn't know what to make of the man who was so sweet with Layla, fully engaged, warm, and loving, while he oozed sexuality and possessiveness with Kat. How would she make it through the weekend when every time they were close he nearly brought her to her knees with desire?

Chapter Five

ERIC SPENT THE afternoon catching up with Hugh and discussing the setup of the foundation scholarship while futilely trying not to think of Kat. She and Brianna had been chatting and laughing and carrying on with the kids just outside the open window, drawing his attention at every sound of her sweet voice. Kat's laugh was so carefree and full of life, and it tweaked his heart at every turn with a whisper of familiarity.

"Dude, you're fading out on me here," Hugh said.

"I was just thinking about something."

"You mean someone?" Hugh lifted his chin toward the window.

"There's something so familiar about her. I feel like I know her, Hugh. It's weird as shit and a little unsettling."

"Unsettling in a bad way? Because as I mentioned last night, the vibes you two give off are not at all unsettling." He pushed from the table and retrieved two bottles of beer from the fridge, giving one to Eric.

"Thanks." He opened the bottle and took a swig, then sat back and crossed his ankle over his knee. "I feel like I know her. She reminds me of this girl I knew as a kid."

"Hey, stranger things have happened," Hugh said. "Ask her. Maybe it's her."

No way was he asking Kat if she went to Camp Kachimonte. He'd snuck into the camp the summer he'd turned nine, when he'd needed a reprieve from his stoned parents—and, embarrassingly, when he'd needed to eat. His parents weren't big on providing for him as much as feeding their drug habits. Hugh knew about his parents, but what he didn't know was that Eric had snuck into the camp cafeteria most afternoons that summer. He didn't have many distinct memories of those afternoons, as most of them blended together in a jumble of fear and shame, but three instances stuck out in his mind. Once when he'd stopped a big kid from picking on a younger boy, and a little doe-eyed, blond girl who couldn't have been more than five or six years old had told him that he was the bravest boy she knew. The second time was when that same little girl had dropped her ice cream sandwich in the dirt and he'd snuck into the kitchen after it was closed to get her a new one. She'd told him that he was the kindest boy she knew. Those things shouldn't mean much to a nine-year-old boy, but Eric hadn't received many accolades when he was growing up, and he'd held on to those little golden nuggets of praise and used them to pull himself through the harshest of days.

"No. There's no way it's her, and it was a long time ago. She reminds me of her, that's all."

He thought about the third, most powerful memory, the one he revisited most often. Not for the praise, but for the look in the little girl's eyes when she'd said the words that to this day he still struggled with. He'd been swimming in the lake a good distance away from the kids from the camp when he'd seen the little girl flailing in the water. He'd been caught a few weeks earlier sneaking into the camp, and when the police had brought him home, his stoned father had taken the belt to him. He knew what was waiting for him if he got caught again, but when he'd seen the little girl go under, he didn't hesitate to save her. He dragged her up to the beach and turned her on her side, the way he'd seen the lifeguards teaching the older kids during one of their safety lessons. She'd spewed water, coughing and gagging, and when she'd finally sat up, her tear-soaked eyes had widened and she'd pressed two tiny palms to his cheeks. He could still feel the pressure of them on his skin. *You saved me. You're my real-life hero*, she'd said before pressing her lips to his. She was a little girl, and there was nothing sexual about the kiss. It was a frantic, relieved expression of gratitude, but when the counselor saw them, his eyes had blazed with fury and a chase had ensued. Thank God Eric was a fast runner. He'd scaled the fence and taken off like a bat out of hell. He'd had lots of practice running in those early years—and he'd spent every day since trying to escape his past.

HAL BRADEN CAME through the patio door and scooped little Christian into his arms, pressing his lips to the squirming boy's forehead. He was a formidable man at six foot six. Even at almost seventy, he had a commanding presence, with shoulders that filled a doorframe, a barrel chest, and a deep, gravelly voice that rivaled Clint Eastwood's. He was a man made of love and loyalty, having raised six children by himself after losing his young wife to cancer, and Kat loved him dearly. He'd not only embraced Brianna and Layla like they were his own flesh and blood, but he'd welcomed her into their tight-knit family, too.

Layla ran from the table where they'd been sitting and hugged him. Holding Christian in one arm, he leaned down and kissed her head. "How're my favorite girls?"

"We're about ready to do our photo shoot," Brianna said. Today they were taking candid photos and headshots of Kat for her promotional materials and website. She could still hardly believe her business was coming to fruition.

"Are you ready to go see Uncle Rex and Auntie Jade?" Hal asked.

"Yes! Yes! Uncle Rexy said I can ride his new horse!" Layla ran to Brianna and hugged her goodbye.

"Take your riding boots, Layla, and tell Auntie Jade I said not to pump you full of chocolate this time."

"Aw, Mom. Auntie Jade says you can't rule me when I'm there. I'll go get my boots." She ran for the door, and Hal laughed.

"You might as well give that up, darlin'. Jade's got a bun in the oven, and she's bubbling over with mama love. Let her spoil the child a little." Hal settled a hand on Brianna's shoulder and kissed her head the same way he'd kissed Layla's.

"Well, paybacks will be fun, I suppose," Brianna said. "I'll sugar up her little muffin baby and then give him or her back buzzing with energy."

"That's what family's for. Love 'em up the best you can. No harm in that." Hal turned his dark eyes on Kat and spread his large hand on her shoulder. "How about you, darlin'? You have a beau on the horizon?"

His use of *darlin'* touched her heart, and she realized it was the same endearment Eric used for her. She wondered how much time Eric had spent with Hal over the years.

As if on cue, Hugh and Eric sauntered outside. They were both gorgeous men, but heck if Eric didn't make her weak in the knees even though she was sitting down. He was still barefoot, with a beer in one hand and a crooked smile hovering somewhere between scorching and volcanic. Was she the only one who felt his potent masculinity like a vibrator set on high?

"Not at the moment, Hal," she finally answered as Eric took the seat beside her, bringing a heat wave with him.

Hal's knowing eyes shifted between the two of them. "Uh-huh. Well, don't you worry, darlin'. Your heart'll lead the way."

"Pop, are you preaching love again?" Hugh put an arm around his father's shoulder and kissed his son's pudgy cheek.

"Preaching truth, son. Preaching truth. I'm taking the kids over to Rex's now so y'all can get on with your evening."

"Thanks, Dad. You sure you don't want to go to dinner with us after Bree and Kat wrap up their photo shoot?"

"I'm going to hang around here in case Rex and Jade need me to take over. Christian here loves his grandpappy something fierce, right, Christian?" Hal kissed the little boy's cheek, and Christian giggled. "You kids have a good time." Hal patted Hugh on the back and smiled at the others as he said, "I love y'all, though."

The open affection Hal lavished on them tugged on Kat's heartstrings and reminded her why she wasn't interested in being a weekend hookup, not even for mega-hot, ultra-orgasmic Eric. She wanted more for herself.

"Bree," Hugh said with a hopeful smile, "it would be great to have some professional shots for the announcement of the foundation's scholarship next month. We were thinking that in addition to the pictures you'll take at the foundation picnic tomorrow, maybe you could take a few shots of us today?"

"Sure. We should take those at the track, though, right? With you guys in full race attire?" Bree asked.

Kat pictured Eric in the jumpsuit she'd seen racers wear.

She loved a man in uniform. Cringing inwardly, she realized how superficial that was, a little too reminiscent of her past, and again she reminded herself that she was supposed to be taking charge of her future, not hooking up for a weekend.

"That would probably be best," Eric said. "Kat, I hope you'll be joining us at the picnic tomorrow."

Kat's stomach flipped at the prospect of spending more time with Eric. So much for her resolve to remain distant. She'd go anywhere he asked. Twice.

"Oh my gosh," Bree said. "I forgot to mention it. I'm so sorry, Kat."

"I'd love to go. It'll be a great experience to watch your PR people in action. Thanks for the invitation. I guess I'll go change and fix my makeup for the pictures." Kat stood, and Eric rose beside her.

He smiled as he pulled her chair out for her to step around. "Kat, is it okay with you if we tag along? I don't want to take over your shoot, or make you uncomfortable by being there."

Little did he know that he made her the best type of uncomfortable by doing hardly more than breathing. She knew that his being there when she was having her picture taken would be distracting, but this was take-charge Kat. She was facing her fears and she was not going to run from this one—fear of falling for a player who could make her body sizzle with nothing more than a glance.

"Thanks for asking, but I'm fine with it. It'll be fun."

The wicked glint in his eyes stayed with her long after she walked inside, and she knew her attraction to him was too intense to be ignored.

Chapter Six

DOWNTOWN WESTON HAD been built to replicate an old Western town, complete with old-fashioned storefronts and hitches to tie up horses, although Kat imagined those were just for show. She couldn't imagine anyone riding a horse into town for business. It was late enough in the afternoon that the streets weren't crowded but still early enough that Brianna and Hugh were garnering attention from people walking by while they set up the photography equipment. Bree smiled and answered their questions easily, as if this were what she'd done every day of her life. Kat knew better. Becoming a professional photographer had been a lifelong dream for Brianna, and although she'd worked with a well-known photographer in Richmond and she was talented beyond belief, it wasn't until she and Hugh had come together that she'd allowed herself to indulge in the activity she loved most as something more than a hobby.

Kat tried to calm her nerves by looking herself over one last time in the full-length mirror Brianna had brought with them. She'd had no idea that taking pictures would be such a production. They'd had to take two cars to allow for all of Bree's equipment. Kat assumed they'd find a few locations in town and then maybe take a couple of candid shots with the mountains in the background. She'd thought the whole photo shoot might take an hour, but Hugh and Brianna were setting up big white umbrellas and plugging lights and fans into generators. It looked like a movie set, and it had Kat's nerves going all sorts of crazy.

The longer she looked over her cap-sleeved navy blue dress, the more she worried that the neckline was too low or the dress was too tight. She caught sight of Brianna and Hugh in the mirror, wondering if she should ask Brianna if she should change since they'd brought several outfits for the photo shoot. Hugh touched Brianna each time he walked past. He leaned in close and whispered something that made Brianna blush and turn toward him. When Hugh wrapped an arm around Brianna and lowered his lips to hers, Kat shifted her eyes away from their reflection and caught Eric's.

He wore a pair of faded jeans and a black T-shirt. She knew now that the just-been-fucked hair was his natural style, and like every time she saw him, her stomach fluttered and flipped. He was standing a few feet behind her with a serious, assessing look in his eyes that made her worry over her outfit again.

She glanced over her shoulder, trying to see the back of her dress to make sure she hadn't gotten dirt on it. "Do I have something on me, or does this dress just look bad?"

"You could wear rags and you'd still be the most beautiful woman around." His smile was warm and sincere. A flash of the gentleman had come out to play.

"Thank you," she said, relieved by both the warmth and the compliment. "You looked deep in thought."

"Did I? I'm just thinking about the scholarship fund for the foundation. I'm excited to get it launched." His eyes turned serious again.

This was a side of him she hadn't yet encountered. "You mentioned a foundation and scholarship earlier. What type of foundation is it?"

"It's called the Foundation for Whole Families. We help children of drug-addicted parents and reunite families whose lives have been shattered by drugs." His brows drew together. "There are so many children who need help. Many are barely making it from day to day; they're in need of food and general caretaking. These kids need to know that someone cares about them."

The passion in his tone and the intensity of his gaze

coalesced, bringing him into a whole new light in Kat's eyes. This was not the all-about-sex player she'd met in the bar. This was a man clearly affected by the plight of those he was helping, and that touched her deeply.

"Our efforts are focused on the safety and future of the children, of course, but the goal isn't to simply remove them from their unsafe environments. We provide counseling for the entire family, treatment when necessary, and ensure that the children have a safe place to stay while their parents are in treatment, or for some, while their parents are in jail. But that's just the beginning. These children need to have a chance at a future, not just the tools to get there, and that's where the scholarship comes in."

"You're giving them hope for a better life. And you said *we*. Are you on the board for the foundation?"

A humble smile reached his eyes. "I'm actually the founder. The picnic we're going to tomorrow is for the foundation. I give a lot of my time to the foundation, and to the kids."

She wondered how many more layers were hidden beneath his bold facade. This side of him was so unexpected. She wanted to know more, not just about the foundation, but also about Eric and what made him tick.

"I knew we were going to a picnic for charity, but I had no idea it was for your foundation."

"The picnic not only enables us to do fundraising, but to visit with families we've helped and thank our donors. It's one of my favorite events." He ran a hand through his hair, and a contented look filled his eyes. "There's no better feeling than knowing a kid—a family—has a chance at being whole and having a future."

Boy had she misjudged him. Her stomach clenched at the assumption she'd made that he was interested only in a piece of ass. She noticed that Hugh and Bree were finished setting up, and she didn't want to hold them up, but she felt bad for judging Eric so unfairly, and apologizing to a man who was doing so much for others couldn't wait. Not one single second.

"Eric, I think I owe you an apology. I know I've been a little off-putting, and I'm sorry. I misjudged you, and I had no right to judge you in the first place. I hope you can forgive me."

He stepped in closer, and the earth shifted beneath her. The vortex that was Eric James sucked her right in. Her heartbeat quickened, her breathing went shallow, and the familiar sparks that she'd come to expect when they were together sizzled and popped. How he went from one extreme to the other so seamlessly intrigued her even more.

"Darlin'." His gaze moved slowly over her face, returning to her eyes with all the heat that was missing when he was discussing work, along with a new flicker of unexpected tenderness. "Don't apologize for being cautious. You're making a big change in your life, one that takes insurmountable courage and determination. The last thing you need is to fall for the wrong guy."

She swallowed past her fear of the answer and asked, "Are you the wrong guy, Eric?"

"Only you can make that determination. I told you where I stand. Have you given any thought to what it is that you want, Kat?"

His words from this morning sailed through her head. *I find myself completely and utterly captivated by you. I want to explore and enjoy you, Kat. Present tense.* She was completely enamored with him, from his aggressive sexuality to his intelligence and passion to help others. But Kat wasn't naive, and he'd made his intentions clear. *Present tense.* Not future tense. Not that she expected him to think past today after having just met her, but for her own sanity, she needed to acknowledge what she was considering. *A weekend hookup.*

In the space of a breath, she decided that she was probably overthinking the situation. They were visiting friends, and staying at Hugh's father's house, so there weren't going to be many chances to be alone anyway. It wasn't like they were going to have wild sex on Hal's kitchen table—although her tightening nipples seemed to love that idea. The most she and Eric could do was sneak a few kisses, and she knew by the vibrations thrumming through her that a few kisses would never be enough.

He touched her arm, bringing her mind back to the

moment.

"I think I'd like to get to know you better," she said.

He smiled, and just as it reached his eyes, it turned sinful.

She quickly added, "But I respect Hal and our friends, and I'd never want to jeopardize our friendship over a tryst, so we should just keep that in mind."

He leaned in close and said, "I can promise you that I will try to remain discreet, but honestly, Kat, I've never been as drawn to a woman as I am to you, and there may be times when that attraction surpasses even my most valiant efforts to keep it concealed."

THE SWEET AND sultry look in Kat's eyes sent Eric's stomach tumbling, but the tilt of her chin when she turned at the sound of Brianna calling her name sent a shock of recognition through him. It was the same wave of familiarity he'd had from the moment he'd first seen her. Only now that faint familiarity mingled with what he intimately knew about Kat—the feel of her body pulsing with need and wet with desire, the claw of her nails against his skin, the strength of her inner muscles when she was in the throes of ecstasy, and the sound of his name as she cried out in pleasure. *Aroused* didn't begin to describe the feelings building inside him. It wasn't just the desire to have her naked beneath him, to run his hands and mouth over every inch of her flesh. He wanted to know more about the woman who was strong enough to walk away from everything she'd known for ten years and start anew. The woman who said she faced her fears and didn't fawn over him because of his celebrity.

He watched her join Brianna, her eyes sliding to him every few seconds. The late-afternoon sun danced off her blue eyes as she let Brianna guide her into position, and she adjusted her stance and posed for the camera. A rosy blush spread across her cheeks as Brianna called out commands as if Kat were a model. She could have been, with that silky blond hair and a body that could—was—stopping traffic. Determination filled Kat's eyes, as if she'd decided that this was just another fear she had to overcome, and he wondered if he, too, was one of her fears.

Hugh came to his side, watching Bree with the same intensity that Eric was watching Kat.

"You okay? Do you mind waiting while she does the shoot?" Hugh asked.

Eric was still stuck on the idea of being one of Kat's fears. He didn't know if it was because he was around Hugh and Brianna, who radiated *commitment*, or if it was Kat herself, but he swore then and there that he wasn't going to allow himself to be slated as *that* guy.

"'Course not. What could be better than watching a beautiful woman pose for the camera?"

"Watching a beautiful woman take her picture," Hugh said, eyeing Brianna.

They both laughed.

"You're a lucky guy, but I'm not telling you anything you don't already know. How's Brianna holding up with Christian and the race schedule?" Their schedule was grueling for a single man, and Eric had wondered how the racers' wives held up with children to care for while they were on the road. Layla was already six when she and Bree had begun traveling with Hugh, but a baby took all sorts of preparation, not to mention that it couldn't be easy getting a baby to sleep in unfamiliar surroundings.

"You know Brianna. She loves our kids and she loves me. Even if it were too difficult, she'd never admit to it. But I'm ready to slow down. I'm cutting my schedule back even further next season. I want Layla to have more stability, and I don't want to be racing around the country without my family." When Hugh and Brianna had first married, Hugh had cut his schedule way back, and he'd made no secret of wanting more for his family than life on the road.

"That's a huge step, but it's not unexpected."

"It's time," Hugh said at the same moment Brianna took Kat's hand and led her farther down the sidewalk, breaking their spell. "Think about how crazy our schedule is. This is the one weekend we've had off in months, and we had to coordinate seeing our friends and family on the exact same weekend—at my *father's* house of all places." Hugh patted Eric on the back. "I've won enough races to last a lifetime, but there's never enough time to spend with my family."

Eric imagined that if he'd grown up with a father like Hal and five siblings who all looked out for one another, he'd crave that settled-down feeling, too. He watched Kat come out of an office building, where she must have changed her clothes. She looked hot in a pair of jeans and a low-cut white blouse, the perfect blend of sexy and professional. Brianna fiddled with Kat's hair, and they both laughed. Kat's eyes shifted toward Eric, and her lips curved up in a sweet smile that erased all of Eric's thoughts with the exception of one. He didn't want this weekend to end.

Chapter Seven

"ARE WE GOING to pretend that the sexual tension between you and Eric isn't thick enough to cut with a knife?" Bree asked as she parked at the racetrack.

"If I say yes, will you believe me?" Kat had already filled Bree in on their airport sexcapade, and she knew it didn't matter what she told Bree; her bestie would see right through to the truth. And it was the truth that worried her. She couldn't stop thinking about him, wondering about all sorts of things, not just the incredible sex.

"Not likely." Bree cut the engine and turned a serious gaze to Kat. "He's a good guy, Kat. When he's with us, he's so great with the kids, and he's done amazing things with his foundation."

"Yeah, I get that impression."

"But…he's not exactly good boyfriend material, and with all the changes you're making in your life, I think you need to know that."

"Really, Bree? A guy who fucked me in an airport bathroom isn't good boyfriend material?" Kat laughed. "I'm not so sure I'm good girlfriend material, either, despite the changes I've made."

Brianna opened her car door. "How can you say that?"

"Because. Yes, I've been more careful about the guys I've

dated, and I've upended my life to follow my dream, but…" She pressed her lips together, steeling her resolve to be honest with her friend, and with herself. "Don't you think there's a reason I had sex with him at the airport?"

"Of course. You're making all these changes and needed to relieve some stress, and he's hot and sexy. I mean, other than Hugh, he's the best definition of *heartthrob* I've ever seen. And if you tell Hugh I said that, I'll totally deny it."

They both laughed, but in her mind, she wasn't laughing at her own confession, which was vying for release. Kat clutched the door handle.

"Bree, I've been lonely. Bored, even."

"But you have all this exciting stuff going on. How can you possibly be bored?"

Kat leveled a serious stare on her best friend, waiting for her meaning to come through. Bree hadn't enjoyed her sexuality after Layla was born until she'd met Hugh. She hadn't had the same freedoms, explored the darker sides of her passions like Kat had. *Finally*, Bree's eyes widened with understanding.

"Oh, you mean…" Her cheeks pinked up, which made Kat laugh because, even though she knew Bree had an amazing sex life with Hugh, her friend was still the sweet, shy girl she'd always known.

"Yup." She sighed.

"But, Kat, what does that mean? That you can never have a monogamous relationship because you like doing it with strangers?" The concern in Bree's eyes and her worried tone made Kat cringe.

"I don't know," she admitted. "I don't think I like sex with strangers, per se. I just…" She tried to figure out how to explain what she'd felt at the airport—and every time she'd seen Eric since they'd met. "When I first saw Eric in the bar, I could tell he was a player. You know I can spot them a mile away, and I was ready to turn him away. But the minute he spoke, my insides turned to mush. I swear that man sprinkles gasoline with every word, and his smile is all the fire he needs to ignite the flames. Bree, I know I shouldn't admit this, but I wanted him more than I've ever wanted a man in my life."

"But just him? I mean, does that happen with other guys? You said you haven't been hooking up with guys for a long time. You've been dating, but I don't think that's what you're talking about with Eric."

They got out of the car, and Kat spotted Eric and Hugh coming out of the clubhouse wearing their racing suits and carrying their helmets. They were looking at each other, smiling as they talked. Kat's pulse ratcheted up about fifty notches, and when Eric turned those amber eyes on her, her breath hitched in her throat. She reached for Bree's arm, steadying herself as desire weakened her knees *again.*

"It's just him," she managed. "Definitely just him." Whatever else Bree said didn't register as three women, wearing skimpy skirts and barely there tops, ran from the other side of the parking lot, flipping their hair and touching Hugh and Eric in a way that made Kat's blood boil. Kat wasn't usually a jealous person, but there was no denying the claws of jealousy piercing her skin or the fierce determination in every step as she closed the distance between them, determined to rip the girls to shreds.

"Kat!" Bree grabbed her arm, holding her back. "They're groupies. It's all part of it."

"Doesn't that bother you?" Kat snapped. She was breathing hard, tugging her arm from Bree's grip.

"It used to, but Hugh knows how to handle it."

Kat broke free as Eric's eyes locked on her again. She stopped cold a few feet away from him as he signed autographs, watching her the whole time. What was she doing? He wasn't her boyfriend. Jesus, he wasn't even her date! She had no business being jealous, but that didn't stop anger from curling inside her like a snake preparing to strike. She spun around and stomped back to the car with Bree on her heels. Kat pressed her palms to the hood of the car and let her chin drop to her chest.

"Holy crap. What is wrong with me?"

Bree leaned her butt on the car beside her, smiling like she had just unearthed all Kat's secrets. "I think you just might be monogamy material after all."

"That's great, Bree. Just what I need. One-sided monogamy."

"I hear it's all the rage these days," Bree teased as the men approached.

Kat sensed Eric's presence before she turned and saw the intense look in his eyes. Hugh and Bree retrieved the equipment from the backseat while Kat tried to remember how to function like a normal person instead of a jealous groupie.

"That look you gave me back there was definitely a turn-on," he said quietly enough that only she could hear him.

"It was the look of insanity." *Like the torrent going on inside me right now.*

His eyes narrowed as he rubbed the back of his neck and stepped in closer. "If I didn't know better, I'd think it was jealousy."

Kat circled the car to help carry the equipment. "Don't flatter yourself." She hoisted a bag toward her shoulder, and Eric intercepted it, pinning her in place with a dark stare.

"I thought you wanted to get to know me better. Shouldn't I be flattered by your look of *insanity*?"

She closed the car door, and they headed across the parking lot toward the track. The girls who had fawned over Eric and Hugh had joined a group of people by the clubhouse. Kat tried to ignore the *insanity* prickling her nerves.

"Don't you get enough of an ego boost from being fawned over by strangers?" She knew it was a bitchy thing to say, but she was powerless to stop the attitude from flying in his face like a big red flag. He stopped walking and gripped her arm—hard. The wicked look in his eyes told her that he didn't see it as a red flag at all.

"I said I was interested in enjoying *you*, Kat. That means *you*, not some girls who want an autograph." The hint of anger in his voice had her stepping back, and him stepping forward. "I'm a public figure. I get hit on all the time."

"Good for you." She walked toward the track where Hugh and Bree were setting up the equipment, and he gripped her arm again, more gently this time, keeping her beside him.

"Yes, good for me." The words were cold, but his eyes were warm. "I can get as much ass as I want, whenever I want. I can also risk disease or bad press, right? That's real attractive. Let's not forget the shame that follows a good hookup." His tone turned thoughtful, and Kat swore she saw a shadow of hurt wash over his face. "We both know that shame, don't we?"

She knew that shame, and she hated it almost as much as she hated that she'd made him feel bad for just being the celebrity he was. "Yes," she said quietly.

"For the first time in my life, I didn't feel that shame, Kat. Not for one second after being with you." He paused, and she wondered if it was so she could let his words sink in or for him to gather his thoughts as his eyes searched hers. "I know we just met, but I feel something between us that's more powerful than I've ever felt before. I want a chance to explore that with you."

He slid his hand to the nape of her neck and stepped in closer, bringing their lips a whisper apart. He didn't seem to care who saw them, and she didn't care either, because being this close to Eric, feeling his heat embrace her, seeing the desire in his eyes, consumed her. She desperately wanted to press her lips to his, to tell him she was sorry.

She opened her mouth to apologize, and before she could say a word, he said, "I'll never lie to you and pretend that there wasn't a time when those types of girls turned my head. But right here, right now, there's only you and me. And until we decide otherwise—until *you and I* make that decision together—you don't have to worry about what I'm doing with any other woman."

He stared at her for a long stretch, long enough that his words sank into her heart and filled her with hope.

THE SECOND ERIC had seen jealousy flash in Kat's eyes, he'd known that he never wanted to make her feel that awful emotion again. And he was going to do everything within his power to ensure she never had a reason to feel that way. After signing autographs for the women, he'd asked Hugh if he'd mind if he asked Kat out, and thankfully—*God, thankfully*—he didn't.

Eric didn't waste a second as he gazed into Kat's eyes. "Go out with me tonight. Just the two of us."

Her eyes shifted to their friends. "But we're visiting Bree

and Hugh."

"I asked Hugh if he minded, and he doesn't. I'd be happy to ask Bree, too, if you want. And I know I'm asking you to take time away from your best friend, but if you give me tonight, Kat, I'll fly you back to see Bree whenever you want. One night, that's all I'm asking." *Although I want so much more.*

She opened her mouth to speak, and he pressed his lips to hers. He didn't need to hear her say she didn't want a fling, because he didn't either. She kissed him tentatively at first, but as he slicked his tongue over the seam of her lips, she opened up to him, meeting his passion with her own. Her body melted against him, and when he deepened the kiss, her arms wound around his neck. This was what he'd dreamed of all night and longed for all day. The taste of her desire, the total release when she gave herself up to their kisses, the feel of their bodies fighting for more.

The sound of girls giggling pulled him from the heat of the moment, and he remembered they were in a parking lot surrounded by strangers and leaving Hugh and Bree waiting.

He reluctantly ended the kiss, keeping her so close he could hear every breath she took. "Say yes, Kat."

Her eyes were smoky, her skin was flushed, and her answer came in a whisper. "Yes."

"Yes," he repeated, because he felt like he might burst with gratitude and needed a release before he gathered her in his arms to kiss her again.

"You don't know a thing about discretion, do you?" she asked quietly as her eyes darted around the parking lot, finally landing on Bree and Hugh, who were smiling and whispering, with their eyes locked on Kat and Eric.

"I know a hell of a lot about discretion, but I don't want to be discreet with you." He offered her his hand, and when she slid her fingers between his, relief swept over him. He lifted their interlocked hands and kissed the back of hers.

"But didn't we just talk about this? Not that I'm complaining, but..." Her smile told him that she was totally on the same page with him.

"I thought that was about having sex in Hal's house, which

is something I'd never do unless you were officially mine in the world's eyes." Eric stopped in his tracks as his mind became laser focused. That was exactly what he wanted, for the sassy blonde who wasn't afraid to call him on his shit or act on her emotions to be *his* in the eyes of the world.

Chapter Eight

"I HAVEN'T BEEN this nervous about a date in years." Kat set her hairbrush on the sink and turned to Brianna. "Are you sure you don't mind that we're going out? I feel bad about going out with Eric when I'm supposed to be visiting with you."

"Oh, please. Do you really think I'd complain about having a night to go to bed early with my incredibly hot husband? Go, have fun." Brianna fluffed the back of Kat's hair and looked at her reflection in the mirror. "You look gorgeous. Those jeans fit perfectly, and only you could wear a shirt that tight and show that much cleavage without looking slutty."

Kat bumped her with her shoulder. "Shut up."

"That man will not be able to stop kissing you tonight. After that kiss at the track, I can't even begin to imagine how you've thought of anything since."

"He is an incredible kisser, but I still feel guilty about going out. It's not even like this can lead anywhere. I'll probably never see him again after this weekend, and I'm missing out on time with you and Hugh and the kids."

"Trust me, you'll see enough of us tomorrow at the picnic, and you'll be glad you had the reprieve from the kids. And as far as seeing him again goes, Eric has houses all over, including Richmond. If you two want to see each other, you'll find a way." Brianna's brows knitted together. "I've never seen you this nervous. What's really going on?"

They went into the bedroom, and Kat slipped her feet into a pair of boots. "He told me not to wear heels. What do you think that means?"

"It means you're not going flamenco dancing *and* that you're avoiding the question."

"Fine, but you're going to think I'm crazy because we both know he's had a *busy* social calendar and nothing can come of this. But…I'm really attracted to him, and not in just a sexual way. Sometimes when he looks at me, I feel like he's looking inside me, like he can see all the things I'm trying to hide. I feel like so much hinges on this date, and I know that's insane." The word tripped the memory of the scene in the parking lot, when jealousy had consumed her, and she knew her feelings for Eric were already bigger than she was letting herself admit.

Bree looped her arm in Kat's and they headed toward the stairs. "After being a single mother for six years, prepared to be one for twelve more, and then meeting Hugh when I least expected it, nothing seems insane to me."

"So you don't think I'm making a huge mistake? Going backward from the progress I've made toward being more responsible where men are concerned?"

They stopped near the top of the staircase, and Bree smiled at Kat. "I never thought you needed to change in the first place. That was all in *your* head. I thought you were perfect, and happy, the way you were." She looked down the stairs, and Kat's gaze followed.

Eric stood at the bottom of the staircase holding a bouquet of red roses in one arm. His dirty-blond hair was still damp, and he wore a pair of dark, low-slung jeans and cowboy boots, and looked hotter than sin. His black button-down shirt was open at the top, revealing the same patch of chest hair that had Kat's heart racing when she'd first seen him in the airport. His cheeks were clean-shaven, giving him a completely different edge than the scruff had. His eyes were dark and serious, taking a slow stroll over every inch of her as she descended the stairs. By the time she joined him she felt naked under the heat of his gaze. His spicy, earthy scent swallowed her whole as he leaned in and kissed her cheek.

"You look beautiful, darlin'."

She'd never tire of hearing him call her darlin'.

He handed her the flowers. "These are for you."

"You didn't have to get me flowers." She wondered when he'd even had time to pick them up.

"A little birdie told me that you like romance."

"I'll put those in a vase for you," Brianna offered.

Kat had been so swept up in him that she'd forgotten anyone else was there. "Thank you." She handed Brianna the flowers, and that's when she saw Hugh across the room. He was holding Christian and had a wide smile on his lips. Layla and Hal were there, too, and the approval in Hal's dark eyes was inescapable.

"Are you guys sure you don't mind if we go out?" Kat asked, feeling fairly embarrassed by the depth of emotion in Eric's eyes, which she was sure everyone else could see just as clearly.

"Who are we to stand in the way of young hearts?" Hal crossed the room and put a hand on Eric's shoulder while Kat's embarrassment etched into her skin.

"Dad said that Eric might be your Prince Charming, like he was Mom's," Layla said as she reached for Hugh's hand.

Kat drank in Eric's appreciative gaze, his tender, confident smile, and even though she knew the appropriate reaction would probably be to feel guilty for going out and letting a child believe that something could actually come of this date, she couldn't help hoping that maybe Hugh was right.

Chapter Nine

FROM THE FIRST moment Eric saw Kat standing at the top of the stairs, looking beautiful in a pair of jeans and a tight shirt that showed off every lush curve, he'd wanted to take her in his arms and never let her go. He'd thought about her all day, and after that amazing kiss they'd shared in the parking lot, he hadn't been able to stop thinking about kissing her again and again, but he'd promised himself he'd take it slow tonight. This date wasn't about getting her into bed. It was about getting to know her and letting her know he wanted more than a quick hookup.

He closed the door behind them and reached for Kat's hand as they descended the porch steps and he led her toward the yard.

"Where are we going?" Kat asked as they crossed the grassy lawn to the large barn at the foot of the hill.

Eric pulled open the doors, and the scent of leather, hay, and manure assaulted them. He drew in a deep breath. "Smell that? That's the scent of stability, family, and strength."

"Because of Hal?" she asked as they walked into the barn.

"Because of all of the Bradens. Their love knows no boundaries, and it's always been a source of strength for me." He walked to the stall of an old red mare named Hope. Hope pressed her muzzle into his sternum, and he petted her wide jaw.

"How're you doing, Hope?" he said to the horse. "Are you ready to give us a ride?"

"Wait, what?" Kat's eyes widened. "I don't ride."

He took her hand in his. "Not yet, but with me and Hope, you'll do fine. That is, if you trust me to help you conquer your fear of riding."

"I don't know," she said, nervously stepping back.

He pulled her in close and gazed deeply into her eyes. "Do you think I'd let you get hurt? Trust me, Kat. I'll be right there with you, holding you. I'll make sure you're safe." He turned to Hope, who *neigh*ed and nodded her big head, as if confirming his idea was a good one. "I want to take you someplace special, and horseback is the only way to get there."

"But…" She trapped her lower lip between her teeth, looking so damn cute he had to press his hands to her cheeks and kiss her.

"I'll make you a deal. If we get up on the horse and you're too scared, we'll end this part of our date and go into town."

She hooked her finger into the waist of his jeans. "You really won't let me fall?"

"Never."

"What if Hope takes off running and you can't stop her?" The worry in her eyes was palpable.

He gathered her in his arms. "That won't happen. Hope knows how to take care of her riders, and I know how to take care of you. Trust me?"

She swallowed hard and nodded.

He slid his hand to the nape of her neck and gazed into her blue eyes. God, he loved her eyes, and the way her neck fit perfectly into the curve of his hand.

"I've never met anyone like you, Kat. You're as strong as you are vulnerable. I want to do dirty things to you and protect you at the same time."

"Your filter is slipping again." A rosy blush colored her cheeks.

"Yeah, that tends to happen around you." He led Hope out of the barn.

"Where are we going, anyway?" She petted Hope's side, and he could see her fingers were trembling a little.

"Let me help you up, and then I'll tell you." He hoisted her onto the horse, and she held on to Hope's neck for dear life. A low laugh escaped Eric's lungs, earning him a scowl from Kat. "I'm not laughing at you. It was just a loud smile at how cute you are."

He grabbed a leather backpack he'd packed earlier and shrugged it on, then mounted Hope behind Kat. "Normally I'd have you sit behind me, but I don't want you to feel unsafe, and besides, this way I can put my arms around you." He circled her waist with one arm and hugged her close, then pressed his lips to her cheek. "And you can learn how to manage the reins. Okay?"

"Yeah. I think so."

"You sound a little nervous."

"Uh-huh. Go, before I change my mind."

He laughed and showed her how to hold the reins. "Okay. Put your hands on either side lightly so you can feel how I do this. You're lucky. Hope practically has the entire mountain memorized, so she's the perfect host for your first lesson."

Kat leaned her head back against his chest and slid her hands along his forearms. "You're the perfect host for my first lesson."

Eric's heart swelled in his chest. He pressed a kiss to her cheek and reveled in how right the moment felt. How right Kat felt, pressed up against him, putting her faith in him to take care of her.

Rex had long ago cleared the trail so that Jade could ride without worrying about her horse running over felled trees or large rocks, and he'd installed solar lights along the path for evening rides.

"This trail runs all the way to the river," Eric explained as they entered the forest. The last rays of sunlight peeked through the trees, illuminating the dirt trail.

"When the sun goes down, won't Hope have a hard time seeing?"

"When it gets a little darker, the solar lights that Rex installed will come on." He pointed out lights attached to the trees. "Safety first, remember?"

They rode up the mountain, serenaded by the sounds of the breeze rustling through the trees and skittering along the ground.

Eric felt Kat's body relax against him. He hated not being able to see her face, but he was learning to take his cues from her body language and from changes in her breathing.

"Feeling more at ease?"

"Yes, thank you. Hope is so gentle, and you make me feel safe."

"Thank you. Hope is a doll. Hal bought her for his wife, Adriana, when she first got sick. He swears he can communicate with Adriana through the horse." He had never understood how a man could love a woman so much that he refused to let her go, even after death, and he'd never been one to believe in love at first sight, but every minute he spent with Kat made him question those beliefs.

"Hal's heart belongs to Adriana," Kat said. "He probably sees her in everything and everyone he loves, don't you think?"

"Maybe so. Can you hold the reins for a minute?"

"Sure, but what if I do something wrong?" She pressed her back to his chest, like she needed the contact and reassurance.

"You won't. Just hold them gently. Don't tug in one direction or another." He released the reins and wound his arms around her waist. "I just needed a minute to be closer to you." He rested his cheek against hers. "Don't you love being out here, without the noise of the city or commitments nagging at you?"

A happy sigh escaped Kat's lips as Hope followed the trail around a wide bend. The smell of damp earth and chillier air enveloped them as the river came into view.

"I've always loved it here," Kat said. "But I like it even more being here with you."

"Me too. I think you'd like my property in Sweetwater. I'll have to take you there sometime. We can skinny-dip in the lake." He felt her bristle against him.

"I don't do deep water."

Eric tightened his hold around her middle, thinking of the little girl from his past. "Just another thing we can overcome together."

As the sun set, the lights on the trees came to life, illuminating the trail down to the river. He held tightly to Kat as they descended the mountainous slope, and when they reached level ground, Eric helped Kat off of Hope.

"How'd you do?" He brushed her hair away from her face so he could see her eyes and felt himself getting lost in the emotions he saw there.

"That was remarkably romantic. I never knew riding a horse could be romantic, but that was…" She sighed a contented, dreamy sigh that tugged at his heart. "Wonderful."

He touched his forehead to hers and breathed her in. "I'm so glad. And there's more romance where that came from." He kissed her softly, loving the sweet sound of appreciation she made.

Together they unpacked the backpack and spread a blanket out on the ground. Kat took out the sandwiches he'd made while she was getting ready for their date.

"When did you have time to make these?"

"Right after I picked up your flowers." He smiled, watching her move to Hope's side. She looked thoughtfully at the horse.

"Don't we have to tie her to a tree or something?" She petted Hope.

"Any other horse, maybe, but not Hope. She never takes off. I swear sometimes I think Hal is right about her ability to understand humans." He removed a bottle of wine and two plastic wineglasses from the backpack.

"You thought of everything," she said as she came to his side.

Eric held up one finger as he took candles out of the side pockets of the backpack. "Now all we need are candleholders." He scanned the ground and found two big, flat rocks and placed them by the edge of the blanket. He set the wide-based candles on them and pulled a lighter from his pocket. "Feel free to lavish me with praise now," he said as he lit them.

She rolled her eyes, and he tugged her against him, making her laugh. He loved her laugh. Hell, there was no denying how much he loved everything about her. She was sassy and sharp, and the way she looked at him made his stomach go all sorts of funky, in a very good way. It occurred to him that he should probably be freaked out by how quickly he'd become taken with her, especially since he'd felt himself falling for her from the moment he first set eyes on her. But freaking out wasn't anywhere near his radar screen. He wanted to bring her deeper into his life, to drive full speed ahead into the feelings she stirred in him.

He pressed his lips to hers, and they sank down to the blanket side by side. He handed her a sandwich and poured the wine. "To our first date."

"So, this is how a race car driver woos a woman? I was expecting fast cars and faster hands." She leaned back on her palm and shifted onto her hip, looking radiant in the evening light. Her lips were curved up in a smile, and her baby blues hovered between shy and seductive—a look that was not only hard to resist but also seemed to come straight from her heart. It was probably the most honest look he'd seen on anyone in a very long time.

"You've already experienced my fast hands, and you know I love fast cars." He sipped his wine, enjoying the way she was waiting to hear what else he had to say. She was so different from the women he usually dated, none of whom would enjoy a meandering horse ride to a river. He wanted to enjoy every second with her and not rush through any part of their date.

"I don't usually *woo* women, but I think you know that by now." He stretched out beside her. "I want to woo you, Kat. I want to get to know you and let you see the real me, which I can assure you, will also include fast hands and fast cars."

"The real you? Tell me about the real you." She finished her wine and set her glass aside.

Eric thought about her question as they ate, and when they finished, he slipped off his boots, then rolled up the bottom of his jeans. "The real me wants you barefoot, please."

She smiled and did as he asked. "I'm game."

He rose to his feet and reached for her hand. With their jeans rolled up to midcalf, he led her along the water's edge.

"Are you avoiding my question?" she asked.

"No. Just thinking about it. I don't often think about who I am with any real significance, and I don't want to give you a glib answer—a race car driver, an adrenaline junkie. I guess over the past few months I've been learning more about who I want to be, so who I am is changing."

"For the better?" she asked.

He stopped to pick up a rock and tossed it into the water. "I'd like to think so. The growth of the foundation is part of that." He drew her in close and kissed her. "Maybe you're part of that, too."

"YOU MAKE THIS seem so easy and so right," Kat said, gazing up at him with appreciation.

"Should it be difficult?" He picked up another rock and studied it for a moment.

"Complicated, maybe? I don't know. Usually when I go out on a date it doesn't feel like this. It's more...*questionable.* There's nothing questionable about how I feel when I'm with you. I *want* to be with you, and I can sense that you want to be with me, too." She watched his lips curve into a smile as he tossed the rock into the water and reached for her hand again. Even though she'd been surprised by his kiss at the racetrack, she loved that he was openly affectionate. Something as simple as holding his hand made her feel special.

"Tell me about your foundation. How did you choose what type of families to help when there are so many families in need?"

"Experience," he said, and that one word, spoken with a modicum of heaviness, made her wonder if he'd had drug issues in the past.

"Personal experience?" she asked carefully.

He sank down to a boulder and pulled her down beside him. "This isn't something I usually talk about, but since we seem to be breaking all the rules..."

"I didn't mean to pry," she said quickly.

"You're not prying, and if there's a chance you'll go out with me again, which I hope you will, then I want you to know the real me, like I said." He squeezed her hand, but his eyes searched the river, as if he might find some answers there.

He turned to face her, and the way he took her hand between his underscored the importance of what he was about to reveal. Kat readied herself for a confession of drug use, which was something she wasn't sure she could deal with.

"I didn't have what you'd call an ideal childhood. My father was a stonemason, and he hurt his back when I was three or four. My mom was a stay-at-home mother, but after my father hurt his back and was put on disability, she took a job at a grocery store. My father was left to care for me while she worked, and between his pain and my being a rambunctious little boy…"

His voice was laden with sadness, and when he shrugged like it was no big deal, Kat knew he was just trying to act strong.

"I'm sorry. Was he abusive?"

"Not often. He went from pain pills to heavier drugs. Heroin mostly, and my mom eventually quit her job to care for me, but somehow she got tied up in the drugs, too. I don't really know how or why, but by the time I was six or seven, they were both a mess."

Her heart cracked wide open at the thought of Eric as a little boy, having to deal with that situation. "Did you have any other family members who could take care of you?"

He shook his head, and in the next breath he squared his shoulders, lifted his chin, and strengthened his tone. "No other family members, but I took care of myself. I learned to stay out of their way, to sense when they were high, or when they were in a bad place *needing* to get high."

Kat couldn't imagine living like that, and at such a young age. She wrapped her arms around him, wanting to comfort him and wishing she could make all the hurt she saw in his eyes disappear. At first he didn't embrace her back, but she pressed her cheek to his chest, listening to the steady beat of his heart, and a few seconds later his arms came around her and he breathed deeply. She felt tension seep from his body, and she was thankful he trusted her enough to open up to her.

"I'm sorry you went through such a hard childhood." She pulled back and pressed her hands to his cheeks, holding his gaze. "Look how far you've come. You're a real-life hero, helping other families."

Eric's brows knitted together. "Say that again."

"Look how far you've—"

"No, the hero part," he said quickly, searching her eyes.

"You're a real-life hero?"

"That's how I know you, Kat." He scrubbed his hand down his face. "Holy shit. You're Kay. You were at Camp Kachimonte. You were my bright light the summer I turned nine."

Her chest constricted, and now she was the one searching his eyes. "How did you know I went there? I didn't become Kat until I was a teenager and wanted a cool name. I went to camp the summer I was six."

"I was there. That was a particularly difficult summer with my parents." The muscles in Eric's jaw jumped a few times. He rubbed the back of his neck, as if the conversation had caused a knot there. And when he finally spoke again, it was with a heavy tone. "We rarely had food in the house, and I spent most of my time outdoors, keeping a low profile to stay out of their way. But that summer I snuck into the camp." He caressed her cheek and said just above a whisper, "And I met you. I knew you looked familiar when I first saw you in the airport, but I thought I was imagining it."

"I don't understand." She had only a few fleeting memories from that summer, none of which included Eric.

"I met you that summer. You dropped an ice cream sandwich, and I snuck into the kitchen and got you a new one. And I stopped a bully from beating up a kid. You told me I was the bravest boy you knew."

Kat smiled, but she had no memory of those incidents. "I must have been too young to remember."

"Do you know why you're afraid of deep water?" He pulled her up to her feet and walked to the water's edge, kicking water up and speaking fast. "I wasn't supposed to be there. I'd already gotten caught sneaking in once, and the punishment was pretty harsh, but I saw that you were in trouble, flailing in the water, and no one was helping you. I couldn't let you drown. I dove in and dragged you to shore. You were so scared. God, I've thought about this a lot over the years. Your words pulled me through some of my darkest nights. You grabbed my face, the way you just did, and you said, *You saved me. You're my real-life hero.*"

Kat's heart thundered against her ribs as memories came rushing back. "I remember now. You ran away."

He nodded. "The counselor came after me. After you said that to me, you pressed your lips to mine. You were so little, so scared. It was like relief was flooding out of you. I think the counselor thought I was doing something wrong, because you were crying, but I couldn't stick around to explain and chance being brought home by the police again."

"I called after you. I think I said, *Boy, come back!*" She remembered now. Eric's wide eyes had stared back at her, and then he was gone. "You must have been so scared."

"Only of what waited at home if the police had brought me to the door again. I can't believe it's really you. It's surreal. Like you've been there all the time, just waiting for me to find you."

She smiled at that. "Do you know how slim the chances are that we'd meet again after all these years? Or that you'd even remember something like that? Like me?" She took a moment to digest it all before saying, "I think I've just seen your sentimental side, and I really, really like it. What happened next?" They held hands as they walked back toward the blanket.

"I don't know. The years blur together in a shameful nightmare of making it through each day. Lots of scary nights, fights, days where my parents were too drugged out to speak to me. At fifteen I got a job working at the track, and a mechanic there took me under his wing. I eventually moved out of my parents' house, and they eventually got clean."

"And that's why you help families that have been affected by drugs." She understood so much about him now and admired him even more for what he'd been through.

"Yes, and believe me, the irony of the fact that I've spent my life moving as fast as I can, and that it probably has something to do with escaping my past, is not lost on me."

"That doesn't matter. What matters is that you were strong enough to not only stay safe and sane, but you've taken your painful past and turned it into a way to help others. I think that's the most admirable thing a person can do." She went up on her toes and pressed her lips to his. "You really are a true-life hero. And I'm lucky enough to have found you twice in one lifetime."

He touched his forehead to hers. "I'm the lucky one, sweetheart. You brightened my summer then, and you've turned me upside down over the past two days. You make me want things I've never wanted before. I can't believe how much I feel for you already, or how happy I am when I'm with you."

"Thank you for trusting me enough to share your secrets with me."

He breathed deeply again, as if a great weight had been lifted from his chest. "Thank you for not judging me for my past."

"Judging you? We can't pick our parents."

"Even so, thank you."

She eyed the river. "You inspire me. Since you're helping me overcome my horseback riding fear, would you be willing to help me overcome my fear of deep water? It's one fear I haven't been able to conquer yet."

"I'll help you with anything, anytime. But are you sure you want to swim here?"

She was already stripping down to her underwear, and he was drinking her in with a lascivious stare. "Scared?"

"Hell, no. But if you're going to walk around in that skimpy silk and lace, I can promise you that you should be scared. Very, very scared."

"Oh gosh." She feigned wide-eyed innocence. "Then I'd better take them off." She turned her back to him and slipped her bra straps down her arms.

"Kat." His voice was thick with desire.

She glanced over her shoulder as she wriggled out of her panties, giggling when he stepped from his boxer briefs, fully erect, every muscle pulled taut as she crooked her finger.

"I need my big, strong hero to help me into the deep water."

Chapter Ten

ERIC THOUGHT HE must have died and gone to heaven. Kat stood in waist-deep water, her skin shimmering in the moonlight as she clutched his hand. She wasn't the least bit shy about her body, and he loved that about her. Just like he loved so many other things about her. The strength of her convictions, the courage she had to take control of her life. She was warm and understanding, and excruciatingly sexy. It was killing him to keep his hands to himself, when what he really wanted was to take her in his arms and make love to her.

"I think this is more an effort in overcoming my desires than conquering your fears," Eric said. "This is some kind of test you're giving me, and I'm going to fail. Big-time."

Kat giggled. "You'd better not fail. I'm counting on you to help me overcome my fear. I can't remember ever being in water deeper than this."

He pulled her in tight against him and felt her trembling. "At least not since that time at camp, huh, baby?" He kissed her temple. "Are you nervous or cold?"

"Both." She wrapped her arm around his waist.

"You're killing me. Do you have any idea what it's like to see your bare breasts in the moonlight, with that sweet, trusting smile on your lips that makes me feel like a total letch for wanting to touch you?"

She stepped in front of him and pressed her naked body to

his, and he scooped her up into his arms and carried her deeper into the water. She squealed, but it wasn't a frightened squeal. It was a delightful, playful sound that filled him with happiness. She clung to him so tightly that he sensed her delight was turning to fear as they sank chest deep. He tightened his grip and said, "I've got you, sweetheart."

"Don't drop me. Don't let me go," she pleaded.

"Never." He guided her legs around his waist, and she narrowed her eyes. "I'm not trying anything. I just want to get a better grip on you."

"Uh-huh." She tightened her legs around him. "Hey, careful with that water snake poking its head where it shouldn't."

He laughed. "If you put a den by a bear, you can't complain when he takes shelter." He'd never do anything she didn't want to, but he realized that this playful banter was a great distraction. He took a step into deeper water, submerging their bodies up to their necks. She dug her nails into his skin.

"Wait." She drew in a deep breath.

He stopped walking and reassured her. "I've got you. I won't let anything happen to you. I promise. Talk to me, Kat. What scares you most about the water?"

"Drowning," she snapped.

"Look at me." When he had her full attention, he asked, "Were you ever taught to swim?"

She nodded. "I know how. My father made me learn that summer when I almost drowned, but even though I knew how, it never helped waylay my fears."

"Okay, then staying afloat is completely within your control."

Her legs tightened around his waist, pressing against his erection.

"Keep doing that and I won't be responsible for what happens." He smiled to let her know he was kidding. "I've got you. We're just going to stay right here for a few minutes, neck-deep. When you're comfortable, just loosen your grip a little. Trust yourself. Trust your ability to save yourself."

"That might take a while."

"I've got all night," he assured her.

"I'm talking months." She looked from side to side, and her gaze softened. "The river's really pretty, actually. It looks like the moonlight is dancing off the ripples."

"Yes, it's almost as pretty as you." He ran a hand down her back and patted her butt.

"Flirt."

"Truth teller." He pressed his lips to hers. "I can't believe I'm going to ask you this, because there is no better position than this one right here—unless of course you'd agree to sink down about eight inches."

Her eyes widened. "*Tsk!* I'd smack you if I weren't afraid of falling under."

"Damn. Thought I could trick you into loosening your grip. Focus on me, and I want you to untangle your legs from around me and let them hang in the water. I'll hold you. I promise."

"No." She clenched her jaw.

"Fierce belligerence. That's a total turn-on." He pressed his hips forward, and she gasped.

"Hey!" Her eyes filled with mischief. "You're supposed to be helping me overcome my fear of deep water."

"It's not my fault you're sexy as hell and even hotter when you're mad. Now, drop your legs and trust me to keep you safe, or I'll carry you out of this water and you'll definitely have an active snake on your hands."

She laughed, and he breathed a sigh of relief.

"I have faith in you, Kat. You can do this."

She rolled her eyes and slowly unwound her legs. "Don't let go."

"I would never." He held her around her waist. Her arms were wrapped around his neck, and their mouths were at the perfect height for him to seal his lips over hers. He kissed her sensuously, relishing the slick feel of her body against his, the easing of her hold around his neck, and the melting of the tension from her body.

"You're doing so well," he said against her lips. "Keep kissing me, and you'll be able to tread water in no time."

She giggled as he took her in another kiss, this one turning up the heat by about a zillion degrees. His hand slid to the bottom of her spine, pressing her body to his as he took a step into deeper water.

She drew back quickly, and he leaned forward, capturing her mouth in another kiss.

"You're tricking me," she snapped.

"No, Kat. I'm opening the door so you can see that you're really in control of everything. You're holding yourself up." He ran his hands lightly over her ribs. "When you're ready, let go, and I'll hold you until you feel comfortable."

"Let go?" Her eyes skidded to the water.

"Kick your feet and move your arms, and I'll hold you right here." He gripped her ribs. "You won't go under. I promise."

She nodded, and he could see her readying herself for her moment of truth, swallowing hard, gritting her teeth, then licking those delicious lips of hers.

"I'm so proud of you right now. You can do this."

She slid her arms down his shoulders and over his biceps, gripping them tightly.

"It's okay. You can hold me. Kick your feet. That's a girl. Now use your arms to tread water. I will not let go until you tell me to."

Her arms slid into the water, and she treaded water beautifully.

"How do you feel?"

"Like a child." She smiled.

"Trust me, you look nothing like a child." He blew her a kiss. "Do you feel buoyant? Want to try on your own?"

"I remember how, even though the last time I swam was so long ago. I'm just scared. I always tried to conquer this fear, but I never made it. I've never been able to force myself to go into deep water. There are only a few things I'm still trying to overcome, but this one scares the daylights out of me. But with you, I *want* to try harder. I want to overcome it."

"Like I said, I can stand here all night. Take your time."

Kat treaded water, her eyes never leaving his, and a few minutes later she said, "I'm ready."

"Okay." He took his hands away, keeping them open in the water so he could grab her if need be.

"Ohmygod. I'm doing it. Eric!" She squealed as she treaded water. "This is amazing. It's fun. It's freeing!"

"God, you're beautiful." He stayed close as she swam around, never putting her head underwater, but keeping herself afloat with a sidestroke and breaststroke.

"I'm doing it. I'm not going under."

"You're capable of anything, Kat. There's nothing you can't do."

She swam over to him and wrapped her arms and legs around him. "There is one thing I can't do."

"I don't believe that for a second."

She sealed her lips over his in a mind-numbing kiss. "I can't carry you out of the water and have my way with you."

He scooped her up into his arms again and carried her from the water, their bodies dripping wet, their lips locked in a searing-hot kiss. He laid her on the blanket and reached for his wallet. A minute later he was sheathed and perched above her, silently noting the burgeoning emotions filling his chest.

As he came down over her and their bodies joined together, she reached up and touched his cheek.

"What have you done to me, Eric James?"

"Whatever it is, it's not enough. One night is not enough. Nothing will ever be enough. I feel like I've been waiting for you all my life. Promise me one more night, Kat."

"Just one?"

He lowered his lips to hers, and beneath the moon and the stars, as Hope stood sentinel, their bodies fell into sync, and Eric found the only thing that had ever felt like *home*—and she was right there in his arms.

Chapter Eleven

BY SEVEN THIRTY the next morning the Braden house was bursting with energy. Christian was stuffing Cheerios into his little pudgy cheeks, and Layla was in full waitress mode. Her bangs were pinned up on top of her head in a pretty barrette, bringing her wide smile into full focus. She was obviously pleased to have a big-girl responsibility as she placed a plate of pancakes in front of Hal.

"Would you like butter, Poppy?" Layla asked.

Hal wrapped a thick arm around her and pressed a kiss to her temple. "No, thank you, sweet girl. These look delicious just as they are."

A proud smile passed between Kat and Brianna. Kat had grown up in Richmond, and when Brianna had first interviewed for the job at Old Town Tavern, she and Kat had immediately hit it off. Kat had been part of Brianna's life since before Layla was born, and she could hardly believe how many years had passed. Layla was obviously flourishing as part of the Braden family.

Eric walked into the kitchen, freshly showered, with hair that looked towel dried and oh so sexy. His eyes immediately found Kat, and his lips curved up in a sinful smile that made her heart race. Every second they'd been together last night had brought them closer to each other and taught her more about herself. She could hardly believe that she'd blocked out the episode at the camp when she was younger, but now her fear of deep water made total sense. Eric had been so thoughtful with her last night when they'd taken Hope down to the river. He had an innate ability to be seductive and careful at the same time, and that brought out the good girl and the bad girl in Kat. The combination had surprised her, after she'd tried for so long to be discerning and to act more responsibly. What she'd learned last night was that she was happier just being herself. She didn't need to be with strangers. She simply hadn't found the right man, one who brought out the naughty and the nice aspects of her personality the way Eric did. Going skinny-dipping with him was the biggest thrill, and the most intimate moment, she'd ever shared with a man. Maybe she should be embarrassed by her brazenness in initiating the striptease, but she wasn't. Not one single bit. How could she be when her heart felt so full? And now, as she watched Eric press a kiss to Christian's cheek and swoop Layla into his arms as she walked toward the kitchen, making her giggle like crazy, she found herself picturing Eric as a father.

"Are you cooking this morning?" Eric asked Layla, bringing Kat's mind back to the moment.

Shocked at where her mind had traveled, she tried to distract herself from her thoughts by taking a sip of orange juice. It didn't help.

Layla giggled again. "No. I'm serving. Do you like my outfit for the picnic? Auntie Riley made it." Riley was engaged to Hugh's brother Josh. The two of them were fashion designers in New York City.

Eric set her on her feet and twirled her around with a low whistle. "You are going to be the belle of the picnic."

Kat loved that he gave Layla his full attention, and obviously Layla did, too, because she hugged him again before rushing off to serve another plate.

"What can I do to help?" Eric asked.

Hugh walked into the room behind him and patted him on the back. "Why don't you take that seat next to Kat. I've got this." Hugh touched Hal's shoulder. "Hi, Pop. More coffee?"

"No, thank you, son."

The front door opened, and Rex's deep voice echoed through the house. "I smell pancakes." He had an arm draped around his very pregnant wife, Jade, and his cowboy boots *clunked* across the hardwood floor as they joined them at the table.

"Pop." Rex patted Hal on the shoulder. "How's it going, Kat?"

"Wonderful. How are you?" Kat asked.

"Mighty fine. Thanks for asking." Rex swept Christian out of his high chair, making the little boy squeal with delight and kick his feet. He tucked the boy against his burly chest as he pulled out a chair for Jade. "Sit down, babe. I'll grab your food."

"I've got it, Uncle Rex." Layla set a plate in front of Jade.

"Well, aren't you the perfect hostess?" Rex bent to kiss her. Layla beamed at his praise. He sat beside Jade, bouncing Christian on his knee.

"You're anxious for your own baby, aren't you?" Kat asked as Eric sat beside her and draped an arm over her shoulder. She glanced at him, surprised by, and reveling in, his display of affection.

"That I am." Rex leaned over and kissed Jade's cheek, then pressed his large hand to her belly.

"Rexy has been ready for this baby since the day he asked me to marry him." Jade leaned forward to kiss Christian, who was busy trying to get his fingers into Rex's mouth. "You should probably put him back in his high chair before he thinks it's playtime instead of breakfast time."

"How about you, Kat? Do you want children?" Eric asked, surprising the hell out of her.

"Yes. I definitely want children one day. I love kids," she answered with her heart in her throat.

Beneath the table he placed his bare foot on top of hers as he said, "So do I."

"Whoa," Hugh said as he came into the room and set platters of pancakes and eggs on the table. "What the heck happened on your date last night?"

"Did Hope treat you well?" Rex asked.

Brianna carried a tray of fruit to the table, and Hugh pulled out a seat for her. She had her eyes locked on Kat. Kat had been bursting at the seams this morning, and she'd already shared the details of their incredible date with Bree.

"Hope was quite a lady," Eric said, setting a warm gaze on Kat. "She made it easy for Kat to relax into the ride."

Was she the only one who heard that double entendre? She hoped so.

"Hope has a way of making people comfortable." Hal's eyes traveled around the table.

"Yes," Kat said. "Thank you for letting us take her out. And the lights on the trail were so romantic."

Jade smiled up at Rex. "That's my Rexy for you. Always full of romance."

"Safety first, romance second," Rex corrected her.

Jade rolled her eyes. "What is it with men? Can't they just admit that romance is what drives them?"

"Hey, don't lump us all together." Hugh draped an arm over Bree's shoulder. "I'm totally a romantic at heart. I just didn't know it until I met Bree and Layla." He winked at Layla.

Eric placed a possessive hand on Kat's shoulder, and she tried to keep from grinning like a lovesick fool. From the smiles on Bree's and Jade's faces, she'd failed miserably.

"It takes a special woman to bring out the romance in a man," Eric said casually, as if he hadn't just sent her whole world spinning.

Hal set his napkin on his lap and said, "You're all full of hogwash. Your hearts are driving your cart, not your heads." He shook his head. "One day y'all will understand the power of love. You can't dissuade it, you can't escape it, and you sure as hell can't rule how or when it presents itself."

Kat didn't care if it was wishful thinking or a rationalization on her part, but she clung to Hal's words and felt better about her heart summersaulting in her chest after she'd known Eric for only two short days.

BY TWO O'CLOCK Weston County Park was packed, and the fundraising event for the Foundation for Whole Families was in full swing. These types of events brought the foundation to life for Eric. He loved seeing the families they'd helped to reunite and enjoyed meeting some of their generous donors. When he'd first started the foundation, there'd been a part of him that had played out the scenario of a foundation such as this coming into his life as a youth, causing him to imagine reliving that part of his life differently. But he'd quickly nixed those painful dreams, knowing the impossibility of such a thing. Instead, he used those hopes to help grow the foundation, poured his passion and desire for a better childhood into every family they helped. Watching some of those families flourish made it all worthwhile.

He watched as Emily Braden, Hugh's cousin, approached with her fiancée, Dae Bray, a demolition expert. Emily was an architect and an expert in the passive-house movement, and she'd been at Eric for a while to build green with his next outpatient center. He'd been meaning to contact her about his plan to build in Trusty, Colorado, the neighboring town to where Emily and Dae lived.

"I heard some smart-mouthed race car driver just bought the five-acre commercial lot a block off Main Street in Trusty." Emily brushed her long dark hair from her shoulders and hugged Eric. "How's it going, smart-mouth?"

"A pleasure to see you, too, Em." He embraced her, then opened his arms to Dae. "How's it going, man? I see being engaged hasn't made her any less feisty."

Dae pulled Emily into his arms. "That's my girl."

"I've been meaning to call you about checking out passive structures for the new Trusty Outpatient Center." Eric noticed Hugh heading their way.

"Now you're talking my language," Emily said. "It's not like I haven't been drawing them up for the past three years, waiting with bated breath for you to get off your ass. I'll email you Monday with some ideas."

"Who's the smart-mouth?" Eric teased.

Hugh joined them and greeted his cousin and Dae with open arms. "It's a regular reunion."

"We're just passing through." Emily pointed to the baseball fields, where two softball games were just beginning, one for older kids and one for adults. Emily pointed to the Wiffle ball field, and as she headed for the softball game, said, "But you boys should join that game."

Eric laughed and waved as they walked away, his eyes skirting the property, seeking the woman who had so quickly touched his heart. He found her across the grassy field, carrying Christian and holding Layla's hand as Brianna talked with another woman a few feet away. He could watch her all day long, and she looked so natural with the baby in her arms while chatting with Layla that it did funky things to his stomach again. He watched them walk over to a clown who was doing magic for a group of families. She pressed her lips to Christian's cheek, then said something as she pointed to the clown. Damn, the emotions she incited in him had his whole body going warm and made his mind jump ahead to something he'd never imagined settling down enough to have. *Family.*

He shifted his eyes away, the unfamiliar urges telling him that he was somehow falling for Kat after only a few days. He tried to focus on the people walking by, on Hugh's voice as he talked about the picnic. Hell, on anything but the little voice in his head saying, *She's the one. The only one.*

He focused on the table with the raffle prize baskets, thinking about how few donations they'd received the first year. Now the table overflowed with donations. The Denver Broncos donated baskets of football paraphernalia, and dozens of local businesses donated goods, from jewelry baskets, books, and leather goods to lotions and hardware. The generosity of the community was endless.

"We did well, basing the event here," Eric said to Hugh. It had been Hugh's idea to make Weston the home base for the fundraiser each year, and since Eric hadn't had the benefit of a close-knit community growing up, he was happy to become part of Hugh's.

"Weston cares, that's for sure." Hugh pointed to Kat and Brianna. Kat was holding Christian and tickling his stomach. "Looks like Kat's taken to my boy."

Eric's heart warmed again at the sight of her loving up Christian. "I can't believe you've kept Kat a secret from me for so long."

"Shit. You haven't wanted a girlfriend. Ever. To be honest, I was completely floored this morning when I saw you two at breakfast, but Bree wasn't. She said she knew the minute she saw you two together yesterday morning that you were meant to be together. Something about vibes." Hugh cleared his throat, as if to say, *Told you so.*

Eric had never been more excited to see a woman than he was this morning. He'd slept fitfully, wishing Kat were in his arms and wondering if she'd been thinking of him, too. It had taken all of his restraint not to walk down the hall and knock on her bedroom door. When he'd finally seen her, he'd had to fight the urge to take her in his arms and kiss her good morning. But after only one date, he knew that was presumptuous, regardless of how intimate they'd been, how close he felt to her, or the fact that she'd already promised she'd go out with him again tonight. Relationships weren't something he had experience in, and he was taking his cues from her.

"I've always said that your wife's a smart woman," Eric said. "Kat and I connected on every level from the moment we met, and even so, this is all so new to me that I was a goddamn nervous wreck this morning. I was worried that she'd changed her mind. That she'd look at my history with women and decide I wasn't worth the risk."

Hugh slung an arm over his shoulder. "Dude, you're an amazing man. You must know that. Any woman would be lucky to be with you."

"This isn't about being lucky to be with me. I know my downfalls. You and I both know that I've never been a settling-down type of guy, but ever since I began thinking about the future, I've felt different. And Kat…Holy hell, Hugh. Kat? She's the most intense, passionate, intelligent woman I've ever met. I finally understand how you fell for Brianna so quickly."

"And Layla, man. I fell for them both. I love Layla like she's my own flesh and blood." Hugh gazed lovingly at his family a few feet away and took a few steps in their direction.

"I know you do. I have to tell you, I meant what I said this morning. I'm thinking more and more about settling down and having a family. And Kat just might be the oil in my gears. I was thrilled when she didn't shy away from me during breakfast." Kat looked up, and their eyes caught. His heart skipped in his chest, and the ability to walk and talk at the same time suddenly eluded him. He stood stock-still and said, "I'm the lucky one, man. If she'll have me, I'll make sure she never regrets it."

Before taking the few final steps to Kat, he said, "I think your father was spot-on about the heart leading this cart. I could no sooner walk away from Kat than I could walk away from racing."

Chapter Twelve

ERIC HELD UP a burlap sack, smiling at Kat and ignoring the smirk Hugh was giving them while he and Layla stepped into their own potato sack. Rex and Brianna and about a dozen other couples were also preparing for the big race, while Jade, who was too pregnant to take part, stood off to the side with Christian, cheering them on.

"Wanna jump in the sack with me?" Eric asked Kat.

"Heck yeah, I do." Kat held on to his arm, loving the feel of his hard muscles and the heated glint in his eyes. She lowered her voice and said, "Bragging rights. I can say I got the head of the foundation in the sack."

His head tipped back with a hearty laugh. "Darlin', you can have all the bragging rights you want where I'm concerned." He pressed a kiss to her lips, and she nearly melted on the spot.

She'd spent the entire day in awe of the way he handled himself. The man hobnobbed with wealthy donors and heads of corporations with the same zeal as he scooped babies into his arms and tossed a ball with teenagers. He gave his full attention to the adults and children in equal measure, which endeared him to Kat even more. Eric's presence was as stable and commanding as a towering tree. Kat imagined that he'd have been just as debonair in a dark suit and tie as he was in his jeans. And now, as he draped an arm around her, grinning like a fool, he also looked like an eager kid ready to win a race—and the whole combination of hot, sexy, and playful made her swoon a little more.

The race started with a roaring cheer from the crowd, and Kat promptly tripped on a lump of grass and lost her footing. Eric caught her before she face-planted into the dirt and pulled her against him.

"You okay, graceful girl?"

She laughed. "Nice. Let's win this race!"

With his strong arm around her waist, they found their groove, quickly catching up to Rex and Brianna. Rex reached out and grabbed ahold of their potato sack.

"Going somewhere?" His Stetson was perched high on his head, and the challenge in his dark eyes made Kat burst out laughing and nearly tumble to the ground again.

Eric's grip on her waist saved her. He shot Rex a competitive stare, and Rex was now laughing, too. "We're only going one place, my friend. Ahead of you." He glanced at Hugh and Layla and said to Kat, "Let's let Layla beat us."

She fell a little harder for him that very second and knew she was steps away from tumbling head over heels from not only the ground but for Eric, too.

Eric kept an eye on Layla, holding them back until she crossed the finish line. Layla was so excited, she jumped into Hugh's arms, squealing with delight. Then she ran to Eric and Kat and hugged them both.

"You guys were so good. I'm sorry you didn't beat us, but you still did really well!" She turned to Rex and Brianna and threw her arms around Bree's neck. "We beat you, Mom! Dad and I beat you!"

Kat swore she saw longing in Eric's eyes as he watched the scene unfold.

"You sure did," Brianna said to her exuberant daughter. "You were amazing!"

"Yeah, but you were still great!" Layla hugged her again before racing back to Hugh and hugging him again.

Brianna's gaze caught on Kat's, and the dampness in her eyes nearly pulled tears from Kat's. She knew how much it meant to Brianna for Layla to adore Hugh the way she did. She felt Eric's arm circle her shoulder, and she leaned in to him.

"God, I love that little girl," she said wistfully.

"I have a feeling you'll have your own little girl who is just as wonderful one day." Eric hugged her close, and when she gave him a quizzical look, he said, "What? You're a woman who wants children. I'm just sayin'…"

She didn't know what surprised her more—the fact that the man she'd pegged as a player was holding her in front of so many important people and talking to her about a future, or the fact that she could actually imagine a future with him after knowing him for just forty-eight hours.

Chapter Thirteen

ERIC WAS STILL riding high from the afternoon when he and Kat left the ranch for their date later that evening. They'd been inseparable after the potato sack race, and by the time they'd returned to the ranch after the picnic, they'd felt like a couple. He hadn't hesitated to keep Kat in his arms as they visited with Hope, even though Hal was there chatting up the old mare—and thankfully, not only had Kat been receptive, but she'd reciprocated his affections in earnest.

He parked the car at the racetrack and cut the engine.

"What are we doing here?" Kat peered into the darkness.

"You'll see." He came around the car and opened her door, pulling her in close as she stepped from the car. "You said you liked to drive fast, and you really can't do that safely on the roads, but here…"

"I am not driving a race car," she said adamantly.

"No? Well, then, come with me, but first…" He lowered his lips to hers, giving in to the urge that had consumed him for far too long. Her lips were warm and sweet, and when he slicked his tongue over hers, she made the sound of surrender that he'd heard in his dreams, and it nearly sent him into full-on *take* mode. It took all of his focus to draw far enough back to speak.

"I love kissing you," he said against her lips, then pressed his mouth to hers again. "I never want to stop."

He had a burning desire, an aching need, for another kiss,

and as he sealed his lips over hers, his tongue plundering her mouth, his resolve to take things slow frayed with every sexy moan that escaped her lips. His hand moved over her hip to the curve of her ass. God, he loved her ass. It was firm and round, and he couldn't wait to see it bare beneath him. He was hard as steel, and every move she made brought him closer to losing all control and letting his hands wander to all the soft, dark places he craved.

Fuck. This was anything but slow. But holy hell did she feel good, taste good.

With a groan, he tore his lips from hers. "Kat, I want to make love to you more than I've ever wanted any woman in my life, but…"

She pressed her hands flat on his chest, breathing hard. "We're so bad for each other. Sorry."

"No, darlin'. We're perfect for each other, and this is all on me. I can't resist you." He lifted her chin so he could press his lips to hers again, lightly this time. "I want to give you a night you'll never forget, and as much as I want that to include so much pleasure that you never want to touch another man, I promised myself that I'd be a gentleman."

Her eyes darkened, as she said with a soft laugh, "Well, that's a stupid promise."

"If I take you to bed, I'm a player. If I'm a gentleman, I'm stupid. You're going to be the death of me."

She dragged her finger down the center of his chest. "But what a fun death it will be."

With another groan, he took her hand and led her toward the track.

"Fast cars and fast men go hand in hand, don't they?" she asked as he unlocked the gate.

"It takes a certain mentality to want to push limits to the extreme and risk your life every time you're on a track, and that need for danger probably does play out in several other parts of our lives." When their feet hit the pavement, the lights came on, illuminating the empty track and the bleachers beyond. Eric's pulse kicked up at the spectacular sight. It happened every damn time, whether he was racing or not. The thrill of the race and his incessant need for speed sent a burst of adrenaline through him.

"Wow, how did you get them to let us come in all alone?" Her eyes were wide as she looked around the track, finally landing on his silver Jaguar XJ220. "And holy cow, whose car is *that*?"

He took out his cell phone and sent off a quick text thanking his buddy Clay for taking care of the arrangements for tonight and sticking around to handle the lights. "Celebrity has its benefits, and I rarely pull strings, but tonight"—he took her hand and led her to his car—"is special." He loved the look of awe in her eyes, but not because he needed the ego stroke. He loved seeing Kat happy, knowing *she* was being treated special, like she deserved to be. He wasn't kidding that he wanted to make this night unforgettable for her, and if that meant that he had to pull a few strings, her smile made it all worth it.

He opened the door to the Jag and motioned for her to climb in. "This is your night, darlin'. Take her for a ride."

Kat took a step back and shook her head. "Oh no. I can't drive a car that costs more than I've earned in my entire life."

"You have no idea how adorable you are, do you?" He placed his hands on her hips and tipped her chin up with his finger. "It's a car, Kat. Not an airplane."

She shook her head. "I can't."

"You can. I thought you were all about conquering your fears."

"I am, but—"

He pulled her in close. "Okay, then, I'll take you for a spin first, and then you can drive." He helped her into the passenger seat, loving the way her fingers played over the rich leather seats. "You look like you belong in this car," he said as he hooked her seat belt. He couldn't resist kissing her again before settling into the driver's seat.

The car roared to life, and he gave her hand a gentle squeeze, then kissed her knuckles. "Hang on tight, Kitty Kat, because you're in for the ride of your life."

"Don't crash," she said as she clutched the edge of the seat.

"No chance of that when I have such precious cargo." He leaned across the seat and kissed her again, because really, it was torture not to.

THE NIGHT WAS cool, but Kat's entire body was on fire. She couldn't believe Eric had made these special arrangements for her, and she wondered how he'd gotten his car here when he'd rented one at the airport. But those questions went out the window the minute he took off around the track, leaving her heart in the dust.

"Holy crap! This is so fast!" She couldn't stop from yelling. There was too much fear, too much elation, rushing through her. Everything outside her window was a blur. She'd never been more frightened in her life, but Eric was the picture of calm, confident, and badass race car driver. His eyes were focused on the track, his chin was set tight, and his hands gripped the steering wheel with the strength of a hurricane and the grace of a new father.

"This is nothing. I'm just getting warmed up." He winked without taking his eyes off the road ahead. "I'd hold your hand, but safety first at this speed."

"How fast is *this speed*?"

"Not very. One forty."

Ohmygod!

"Relax, darlin'. I have a little experience with driving fast." He kicked up the speed, and Kat felt her whole body push back into the seat.

"Close your eyes," he said. "Feel the rush."

She closed her eyes, focusing on her heart slamming against her ribs. She wasn't sure if it was the speed or purely Eric.

"Inhale deeply and blow it out slowly."

She did, and then she did it again.

"That's it, darlin'."

"I can't even feel any bumps in the road!" With her eyes still closed, it was the most incredible experience in the world, turning her trust over to him and really letting go of all control. "It's like we're aboveground, floating. But more intense, like a roller coaster without all the peaks and valleys." She unfurled her fingers from around the edge of the seat and laid them in her lap. Her limbs prickled with adrenaline, but the fear began to slip away.

"One day I'll take you out in one of my convertibles, and then you'll really feel the rush. There's nothing like the gust of wind blowing by. It's rejuvenating."

She felt his energy, his confidence, and when she opened her eyes, she saw that he had a big smile on his face, which calmed more of her anxiety. He was usually darkly intense, and now all that intensity was layered in light. "Wow, you *really* love this."

"There are few things I love more than driving fast. Look straight ahead, not at what's passing by. Feel the energy of the track, feel the control, the power beneath you."

She tried to focus on everything he said, but her eyes kept darting back to him. Energy, power, and control radiated off of him, not the car, and it drew her further in to him.

He slowed as they drove the long stretch of track leading to where they'd first begun, and when he came to a stop, Kat's heart was still racing. She was breathing hard, but it wasn't fear that had her pulse skyrocketing; it was seeing the elation on Eric's face, sensing the thrill he took from the ride. When he reached for her hand, she realized she was gripping her thighs. He took both of her hands in his and placed them between his own.

"Are you ready to take a spin?"

"I'm scared shitless, but I want to do it. I mean, I'm used to driving fast, but this is a whole new level of fast." She trapped her lower lip between her teeth with the confession and placed his hand over her heart. "Feel that?"

"The thrill of the ride." He leaned across the console and placed a kiss where his hand had been, sending shivers of lust rippling through her.

When he came around to her side of the car and helped her out, her legs were shaking.

"You're trembling." He pulled her flush against him and rubbed his hand down her back. "That's totally normal. Don't let it worry you."

"I won't go that fast, but you'll be with me, right?" She felt his heart beating harder than he let on.

"Of course. I'll be right there with you every step of the way."

"Your heartbeat is going so fast, but you seem so calm."

He pressed a tender kiss to her forehead. He was as strong as he was gentle, and she loved getting to know all of his complexities.

"My whole life has been about moving fast." His eyes turned serious, and a look of something darker, deeper, washed over his face and quickly disappeared, as if he was used to doing that, too, locking away parts of himself. "Let's get you started."

He helped her into the driver's seat and buckled her in, tugging the belt to test it out before letting go.

"Uh-oh." She covered her mouth with the realization that she couldn't drive the car. "This is a manual transmission. I can't drive it."

He laughed. "You've never driven a stick?"

She shook her head. "I feel so stupid. I was so caught up in the excitement that I didn't even realize you'd been shifting gears."

"Well, then, it looks like you're in for a driving lesson." He closed the door and went around to the passenger seat. "Do you know the mechanics of driving a manual transmission?"

"Sure. Push the clutch, shift, use my right foot for the gas."

His lips quirked up in that sexy way he had. "Awesome. Go for it."

"Wait. What? Can't I ruin the clutch or something? I've seriously never done this before, and this car must have cost a small fortune."

"Darlin', I have a small fortune, and you're not going to ruin the clutch. Let's give it a try."

"I like when you call me *darlin',*" she admitted, trying to distract herself from being nervous.

"That's good, because I like calling you *darlin'.*" His eyes darkened.

"Do you call all your women that?" *Oh shit. Word vomit*...Her nerves definitely had the best of her.

He shifted his eyes away, and when he turned back, they

were serious. "It's not like I have a harem of women that I keep around for the hell of it."

"That's not what I meant. I'm sorry. I'm just nervous and not thinking before I speak."

"Kat, I've been with plenty of women, and I have no idea what I did or didn't call them, but I can tell you that I've never felt with anyone what I feel when I'm with you. *Darlin'* comes naturally when I'm with you, but if it makes you uncomfortable, I can call you something else."

Now she felt stupid for asking. "I'm sorry. Please don't change. I do truly love it when you call me that. It makes me go all gooey inside. It was a silly question."

"Gooey, huh? Why does that turn me on?" He leaned across the console. "It wasn't a silly question at all. It was real, and I like real. Believe me. I have a million questions I want to ask about the men you've been with, but the answers would only torture me, so I'm pretending you've never been with another man, and for now, that's working mighty well."

She laughed. "I'll try that."

He tipped her chin up again with his finger—she loved when he did that because he was giving her his full attention, and she knew he wanted her to give him hers, which meant that whatever he was going to say was important. "You just continue being yourself. I'll answer all of your questions honestly." He kissed her softly, then settled back into the passenger seat.

"Any more questions before we get started?"

"Just one." She paused for a moment before asking, afraid of how the answer might feel. "Have you ever done this before for a woman? Taken her to the track after it was closed and let her drive your car?"

His intense gaze never wavered from hers. "Not once. I've never let a woman drive any of my cars. Hell, I've never let anyone but my team drive them."

"Then why me?"

He stared at her for a long moment, and when he finally spoke, he began with a knitting of his brows and a smile. "I told you there was something about you that makes me want to be closer to you. I feel like you're part of me. Like you have always been part of me. I know it's crazy, but crazy has never felt so right."

She exhaled a breath she hadn't realized she was holding. "The camp."

He settled a hand on hers. "Have I scared you off yet with my directness?"

"Not even a little. I've felt like you were familiar, too, and after last night, I can't stop thinking about you. About us."

"I think that's the best thing I've ever heard. Now let's see if we can make you a race car driver."

"Okay." She smiled at the excited glint in his eyes. "But here's the thing. If I *do* ruin your car, you've been duly warned. All my worldly belongings would not be able to pay for whatever I might break. Of that I'm one hundred percent certain."

"I'm sure you can pay me back in more interesting ways." His face spread into a devilish grin as he placed his hand on her thigh.

"Gosh, you do know how to keep a girl on her toes."

"On your toes is not at all where I'd like to keep you."

How was she supposed to concentrate with *that* on her mind?

"Shall we?" He nodded to the track. "Some people like to get comfortable while the car is off, pretending to gas up and change gears, but I'm all for feeling your way through things. Why don't you start her up and let her roll."

"Start her up. Let her roll. Got it." Her heart was racing from his innuendos. She tried to focus on shifting the car into first, and it jolted forward and stalled.

"That's okay. Try it again."

"I'm sorry. I suck at this."

"No, you don't," he said with a comforting smile. "You're learning, and learning to do anything can take time. Stop thinking about getting in my pants and think about driving."

She laughed. "Oh, that'll help."

"You know you want me." The heat in his tone made her cheeks flush. "I'll tell you what. If you can get us around this track safely, I'll think about giving you a shot at the old bod."

She glared at him. "Like you wouldn't if I couldn't drive?"

He shrugged with a too-fucking-sexy smile. "Let's not find out. Focus on the road and drive this baby so we can get to the fun stuff."

She eased into first gear, then second. "Maybe I don't want fun stuff."

"Not likely," he said as she shifted into gear. "Look at you. You're made for this kind of driving. Keep it up, darlin', and I might just let you drive my Ducati."

"I don't know what that is, but if it's slang for your penis, you ain't seen nothing yet." She flashed what she knew was her best flirty, smug grin, while watching the road, and took the speed up to seventy-five. "This is awesome!"

He chuckled. "You're incredibly sexy when you're driving. How does it feel?"

"Amazing."

"Give me real feelings, Kat. You're too smart for cliché answers, and I want you to really experience the thrill of the ride. Focus on how it makes you feel inside. Tell me what *you* feel."

She loved the way he challenged her, and she loved that he cared enough to ask for her real feelings. Feeling more confident with his words, she kicked up the speed to eighty. "It feels dangerous and exciting, like you."

"I feel dangerous and exciting?"

"Definitely, and I wish the windows were down and I could feel the world racing by."

"Loosen your hands on the wheel just a little. While it's important to be in control, it's also important not to forget that you're in control. Part of that is recognizing the power it takes to manage the vehicle and where that power comes from. If you're too tight, your reflexes will be slower."

She loosened her grip a tiny bit, the ache of her death grip easing around her knuckles. "That does feel better. It's like you have experience with this driving stuff," she teased.

"Feel the power, Kat. Feel it everywhere. When you get out of the car, you'll realize your entire body—back, legs, feet, hands, neck—were all tightly wound. Allow yourself to ease up just enough to remain in control of the car without the fear. Become one with the energy. Let it sink into you but not take you over. You control it."

She focused on each muscle and realized that he was right. Her body was like one big bundle of nerves. "Amazing. Wait..." She wanted to dig deeper, to give him more. "Once I got past the dizzy, anxious feeling, it's like a feeling of euphoria. It feels unreal, like I'm infused with a sense of freedom and power. I totally get the allure of driving fast."

"My fearless wonder."

She loved hearing the possessiveness in his voice.

"Are you ready to conquer more fears?"

"More? Should I pull over?"

"It's up to you. This is your night. Take her around as many times as you'd like. I could watch you drive all night long." He lowered his voice and said, "But there are other, more pleasurable things I'd like to do, too."

That was too enticing to pass up. She could only imagine what *more pleasurable things* would mean with a man like Eric.

Chapter Fourteen

"I CAN'T BELIEVE you trusted me to drive that luxurious car. Thank you so much. That was more fun than any date I've ever been on."

She had no idea of the night he had in store for her. "Is that it? Our whole date?"

"No, I just meant so far, it's been amaz—more exhilarating than any other date. Ever."

He pulled her in close. "You can say 'amazing,' Kat." He brushed her hair from her shoulder, feeling her heartbeat quicken against his and loving the way she clung to him. "I just want to be sure that when you're in the moment of doing the things you want to experience, you allow yourself to fully engage, on every level. Using every sense. Most people float through life on the surface, and it's a richer experience if you allow yourself to take it apart layer by layer."

"Layer by layer," she said just above a whisper. "Now I'm thinking about using all of those senses in a different way."

"Oh, we will. Like now, holding you in my arms. Your perfume fills my lungs, and I can taste, just from memory, your mouth on mine. The rapid beat of the pulse at the base of your neck underscores the feel of your heart beating fast and hard against mine. The press of your fingers on my back sends signals through my body, arousing all of my senses." He pressed his lips to hers, taking a tender taste of what he hoped was yet to come.

"Let yourself go to fully experience every aspect of everything you do."

He lowered his lips to her neck and kissed her just below her ear. "The fear," he whispered, then kissed the hollow of her neck. "The anticipation." He pressed his cheek to hers, tightening his hold on her, letting her feel the effect she had on him. "The allure of the unknown."

He felt her holding her breath and whispered, "Breathe, Kat. Let yourself feel."

As he sealed his lips over hers in another, hotter kiss, it took every bit of his strength not to let his desire take over. He wanted everything with her, but mostly, tonight, he wanted her trust and for her to experience new and exciting things in life to help her understand how special she was. When their lips parted, they gazed into each other's eyes, passion burning between them.

"You gave me one more night, and I intend to take advantage of every second of it." He took her hand in his and led her out of the gates to the emergency-landing field behind the track, where his helicopter was waiting.

She stopped cold at the sight of it. "A helicopter?"

"Just to get us to dinner."

"Dinner?" She tightened her grip on his hand. "I don't like to fly in planes. What makes you think I'll get in that whirling death machine?"

He smiled, sensing her strength beneath her fear. "You have complete control over what we do. If you say no, we'll take the rental car to a restaurant. But if you trust me, I think you'll see there's no fear you can't overcome."

"But…it's night, and we're in the mountains."

He pulled her in close again. "Both true facts. And the place we're going to eat is on top of a mountain a few minutes away. This is a quicker means of travel and an easier way to face your fears. It's all about the experience."

"Are you trying to woo me with your money? Because I don't care about money." She crossed her arms.

"As much as that accusation stings, I understand why it might look that way. But the answer is no. I'm trying to *woo* you into seeing that you and I are made of the same stuff. I know all about fears, Kat. I know about running from them and overcoming them." He paused, letting the truth of his confession sink in.

"I want to be the one to help you overcome yours, all of them. Kat, as far as I know, I have one more night to show you who I am. Not who the media sees, or who people think I am. I debated taking you to a low-key restaurant with champagne and dancing with the rest of Weston, Colorado. There is some allure in that. I get it. But that wouldn't show you a damn thing about me. It would only prove that I know how to play the dating game, and with you, this doesn't feel like a game. It feels real."

He let out a breath and rubbed the back of his neck, trying to figure out how to explain what was going on inside him. But it was all so new that he had no idea where to begin.

She eyed the helicopter. "You really feel safe in that?"

"Always. Safety is my number one concern. And I hired my pilot tonight so that I could make sure you felt safe, too. I could have piloted it myself, but I want to be right there beside you in case you need me."

Her gaze softened. "You did?"

"Yes. I'm not trying to impress you, or buy your affection, Kat. If I were, I'd have hired a limo to take us to the most expensive restaurant, bought the most expensive bottle of wine, and given you cheesy lines. I could have any number of women, just like you could have any number of men—which I'm totally *not* thinking about. And before you ask, I've never taken any woman up in my helicopter before." He looked deeply into her eyes, hoping she'd see the sincerity in them.

"The truth is, I want you to fall for me for who I am inside. And a big part of who I am happens to be a guy who desperately wants to help you overcome your fears so you can enjoy life the way I do."

She sighed, as if she liked hearing that. "Thank you for thinking of me like that. That means a lot to me."

"Hopefully one day *I* will mean a lot to you, too."

KAT COULDN'T BELIEVE she was even considering getting into the helicopter. But with Eric's arms around her, and the protective way he looked at her, like he'd never let anything hurt her, along with what he said about experiencing life, she wanted to do this. And surprisingly, not just for herself, but for him, too. She saw in his eyes the same conviction she'd seen when he was talking about helping families through his foundation, and she loved knowing that it brought him pleasure to help her.

"You can say no, Kat, but if you give it a chance, you might enjoy it. It's like driving fast, only a hundred times better, and I'll be right there, holding you every step of the way. Not that you'll need it. You're stronger than you think."

She inhaled a deep breath, gathering her courage. "You have to know that I'm scared shitless again."

"The choice is yours, and I won't be disappointed either way." He caressed her cheek and softened his tone. "But you were scared shitless to drive the stick shift and you made that car your bitch."

Laughing, she pressed her cheek to his chest and said, "Fine. But if we crash, it's on your shoulders."

Kat was sure her heart would explode as she climbed into the helicopter, and she was thankful that Eric stayed close to her, helping her buckle into the plush leather seats and slipping a headset over her ears.

"We can hear each other through these, and they'll help keep out the rest of the noise." He took her hand in his and settled into the seat beside her. "I'm so proud of you."

"You might not be when I'm crying like a baby and clawing to get out of this thing midair."

He pointed to the emergency-equipment locker. "No worries. We have parachutes, and I know how to skydive."

"Is there anything you don't know how to do?" She had a feeling there wasn't. She could practically see the gears behind those intense eyes of his churning before he finally answered.

"Maybe. I've never had a steady girlfriend, but I'm learning. I think day one is going pretty well so far." He must have seen the surprise in her eyes, because he quickly added, "Don't look so shocked. You said you're trying to attract the right type of guy, and I want to be that guy. You've got your fears and I've got mine, but together we can accomplish anything."

Before Kat could respond, the pilot asked Eric if they were ready and he gave him a thumbs-up. The headphones helped with the sounds of the chopper blades, but the feel of the vibrations and the way her stomach dropped as the helicopter lifted off made her wish she'd stayed on the ground.

Eric put an arm around her shoulders and brought her in close. "I've got you, Kat. It's a little like being in an elevator."

His voice in her ears was soothing, and his grip on her was strong and possessive, which made her feel much more comfortable.

"Can you hear me okay?" he asked.

She nodded.

"I'm going to talk you through this. Is your stomach okay? Do you feel sick at all?"

She shook her head. "It's a little like floating, but roller coasterish, too."

"Yes. You'll get used to it as we move forward. If you get scared, squeeze my hand, okay?"

She nodded, but in her head she envisioned scrambling into his lap as the helicopter seemed to rise straight up, and she felt herself being pushed down into the seat. She squeezed his hand, and he tightened his arm around her shoulders as the helicopter moved forward.

"Better?"

"Yes," she finally managed. His touch calmed her, and the way he was watching her so intently, as if he could and would fix any discomfort she might have—which she was realizing he probably could—made her feel completely safe.

"Look out at the lights of the city." He pointed out the window, then quickly returned his hand to hers.

Kat's chest felt full and tight, as the tail end of fear slipped away. "I've never seen anything so spectacular. We're so much lower than the airplane was."

"We're going there." He pointed over the mountains, and a few minutes later, a circle of green lights came into view. "That's the helipad where we'll land."

"What's up here?" The lights of the city fell away behind them, and there were only the lights of the helipad and a few others in the distance.

"Dinner," he said casually, as if everyone in the world took a helicopter to the top of a mountain for dinner. "How do you feel?"

"Exhilarated. A little anxious, but not enough to stop me from doing it again, and lucky." She gazed into his eyes and said, "Really, really lucky that you wanted to do this for me. I also feel spoiled rotten and like I owe you big-time after this."

"Darlin', you don't owe me a damn thing, and don't you ever let a man make you feel like you owe him anything. Ever. I do things because I want to, not to get something in return."

The vehemence in his voice surprised her. The helicopter touched down, and Eric helped Kat out and hurried her away from the blades, shrouding her body with his as they dashed outside the circle of lights.

"Are you okay?" He searched her eyes, and his gaze rolled down her body, making her shiver.

"Perfect."

"What do you feel?"

She loved that he asked for more. Most guys would be happy with a one-word answer. She was still reeling from the excitement of the ride, but she tried to get her brain to function clearly. "I feel a sense of power again. Like facing my fear made me even stronger."

"That's the beauty of the mind. Fear is all up here." He tapped his head. "If you can capture that fear and put it into perspective, then you realize it's not something that has to control you or limit you."

"That's what I realized with my job, but I hadn't put that idea into play with my other fears."

"Unfortunately, I had to learn it at a very young age. I recognized fierceness in you the first time our eyes connected at the bar," he said as he pressed his hand to her cheek. "I need to speak to the pilot for a moment. Promise me you won't come any closer to the helicopter than this. The blades are dangerous."

"I promise." She'd promise him anything. He was so caring

and thoughtful, and yet, unlike other men, his tenderness was bordered by a sexual undercurrent like she'd never felt before. And she sensed that the honesty about his past wasn't coming easily, but earnestly.

"I'm so happy you were courageous enough to do this." He pressed his lips to hers. "I'll be right back."

She watched him talking with the pilot, glancing back at her every few seconds, attentive and protective. She'd never dated a guy who was so in tune to everything about her or who cared enough to try to be. She looked around the deserted mountaintop and wondered what he had in store for them next, because there was no restaurant anywhere in sight.

The pilot climbed back into the helicopter, and Eric jogged over to Kat. With his body between her and the gusting wind, he guided her farther away from the helicopter as it kicked up dust and dirt and lifted into the sky.

"He's leaving us here? Are we going mountain climbing next?" she hollered over the sound of the blades as they carried the chopper away.

He laughed. "Would you be willing?"

"You look way too serious. No, not at night I wouldn't, but during the day I might." She loved that he tugged her in tight against him again. She fit there perfectly, and he smelled heavenly.

With the helicopter gone, he smiled at her and brushed her hair from in front of her eyes. "No hiking tonight, I promise." He led her away from the lights of the helipad to a black Land Rover she hadn't seen parked by the edge of the woods—and apparently, the edge of a road as well.

"You're like James Bond, with cars and helicopters popping up whenever you need them." She climbed into the passenger seat, enjoying his deep laugh as he settled into the driver's side.

"James Bond, huh? That's one I haven't heard before." He started the car, and the headlights illuminated a road that disappeared beneath an umbrella of trees. "We're on our way to Falling Grace. Have you been there?"

"No, but it sounds either very creepy or quite romantic."

He reached for her hand. "I assure you, there's nothing

creepy about it."

A few minutes later they pulled up in front of Falling Grace, a chateau-style restaurant built near the edge of a cliff. Candles flickered in every window, and brilliant white lights lit up the woods on the periphery of the property, giving the evening a magical feel. In-ground lights illuminated a stone walkway that snaked through gardens with a fountain on one side and ornate sculptures on the other.

Kat looked down at her jeans, then at the expensive cars parked all around them. "I'm not sure I'm dressed for this."

"Darlin', clothes do not make someone appropriate for a restaurant. You're just as gorgeous in your jeans as you were in your dress and your suit." He pressed his hand to the small of her back, bringing her body flush against his again.

She would never, ever tire of this closeness.

His eyes moved from hers to her mouth, then back up again, stealing her worries about her clothing one brain cell at a time.

"We're both wearing jeans. The way I see it, we can lose the clothes altogether and go in naked, or take our chances."

His smile was contagious, and his sense of humor only made him even more attractive. "Nothing ever rattles you, does it?"

"Life's too short to get too rattled over things that don't matter. Clothes are meaningless." He took her hand and led her toward the entrance.

"I really do like the way you think. Have you always been this confident, or did that come with your success?" She noticed the way his eyes flashed serious for a second, then just as quickly brightened again. He did that a lot, momentary deep thinking.

"That, my darlin', is a great question." He held the restaurant door open without answering, making Kat wonder about the sore spot she'd just touched.

A pretty brunette greeted them with a pleasant smile. "Good evening. Welcome to Falling Grace. Do you have a reservation?"

"Yes," Eric answered. "Two for James, please."

The hostess's eyes widened, as if recognition suddenly

dawned on her. "Yes, of course, Mr. James. Your table is ready. Please, follow me."

Eric's hand never left Kat's back as they followed the hostess through the dimly lit restaurant, past tables full of important-looking people dressed to the nines, with regal voices and assessing eyes. They passed through double doors at the rear of the restaurant, and to Kat's surprise, they were led to an open elevator. A handsome gentleman dressed in a dark suit greeted them.

"Mr. James. Ma'am." He moved to the side as they stepped inside.

Kat looked at Eric, hoping for a clue as to where they were going. His easy smile wasn't giving anything away. He pressed his hand to her waist, and she moved happily against his side. They stood behind their host, and Eric's hand slid to the curve of her butt. She glanced up at him, and he arched a brow. God, she loved this rakish side of him.

The elevator doors opened and the gentleman stepped out and led them down a hallway lit by candles. It was chillier than the restaurant, and Kat realized that they were surrounded by stone. The ceiling, walls, and floor were all hard rock. The hall opened up to a single room, carved into the side of the mountain. A glass wall overlooked a spectacular waterfall. Colorful lights beamed from the mountainside into the cascading water, providing the most magnificent, magical view she could ever imagine. She reached for Eric's arm to steady herself.

"Eric," she whispered, full of awe.

"Yes?" He smiled, and she couldn't find her voice.

The gentleman pulled out a chair for Kat. She sat, and before she could thank him, Eric did.

"I'll retrieve your drinks," the man said before leaving them alone, and Kat finally breathed.

"I don't think they minded our attire," Eric said, settling in beside her. "I hope you don't mind, but I ordered you a lemon-drop martini. I figured we could start over."

"Start over?"

He reached for her hand. "I hope to be with you long past tonight, and the story you tell your friends should be a bit more romantic than picking each other up in an airport lounge."

Her heart skipped a beat. "That's really thoughtful."

"And a little selfish, I'm afraid. I'm sure you have guy friends, and I don't want them picturing you doing naughty things with me in the men's bathroom."

She laughed. "I'd never tell anyone that."

He arched a brow. "I have a feeling Brianna knows."

She nibbled on her lower lip, and he used his free hand to draw her closer by the nape of her neck.

"That's okay, darlin'. I was kidding. I just want you to have a story you're proud to tell, not one that makes you wonder if you made a mistake."

"Thank you." She leaned forward and pressed her lips to his.

He deepened the kiss, sliding his knee between her legs and moving closer. The press of his lips sent a rush of heat through her. She'd been dying to kiss him all evening, and now, with the crashing of the waterfall just beyond the glass and shadows dancing in their private candlelit room, she took her fill. His tongue swept over every dip of her mouth, over her teeth, and then he pulled back and slicked it over her lower lip, leaving her breathing hard and moving hungrily in for more. She wound her arms around his neck, and their mouths came together hard and fast. His hands slid to her hips, holding her there, burning right through her clothing. She wanted to move from her chair to straddle his lap and let their bodies decide where to go next, but the sound of footsteps brought her mind back to reality, and she moved away with a whimper of loss.

His hand slid from her hip, down her forearm, and his fingers laced with hers, as if he, too, couldn't stand losing the connection.

She was acutely aware of the heat consuming them, and she was sure that when their waiter returned with their drinks and set them on their table, he felt it, too.

"Would you like a few minutes to consider the menu?" he asked.

"Yes, please. We'll ring for you when we're ready." Eric nodded toward a button near the doorway that Kat had somehow missed. She wondered how he knew what it was for and realized he'd probably been there before.

She told herself it didn't matter. He was with her now, and that was all that was important.

"As you wish, sir." With a nod, the waiter retreated again.

"Where were we?" With both hands, he reached for her hips and pulled her onto his lap. He gathered her hair over one shoulder and kissed her cheek. "You're incredibly hard to resist. I truly had the best of intentions for tonight's date, so don't try to get into my pants."

"*Tsk!* You are infuriatingly sexy, and funny, and—"

His mouth covered hers hungrily, and his hands tangled in her hair, holding her as he devoured her. His lips were hard, like the rest of him, as he kissed and nipped and sucked her lower lip into his mouth before taking her in another greedy kiss.

She pressed her chest to his, and then his hands were on her back, traveling down her sides, and finally—*Lord, finally*—he caressed her breasts. Her head tipped back with the sheer pleasure of his touch. His teeth dragged over her collarbone, and his tongue made a hot path between her breasts.

"God, I want to taste you," he said between kisses. He cupped her cheeks in his hands and searched her eyes. "I suck at good intentions with you, Kat. I can't help it. When I'm alone with you, you obliterate my rational thoughts. "

"Stop talking," she said as she pressed her lips to his.

His thumbs brushed over her nipples, bringing them both to tight peaks. They ached for more. *She* ached for more, as she writhed against his erection. His lips were demanding; then they softened, in a stretch of slow, drugging kisses that drew a moan from her lungs.

"Kat," he said against her lips. "Open your eyes, darlin'. Let me see you."

She blinked, only then realizing how lost in him she'd become, how hard she was breathing.

"Hi." He tucked her hair behind her ear.

"Hi."

"I'd like nothing more than to lay you on that table and make love to you. To watch your beautiful eyes as you give in to your pleasure."

Her breath left her lungs in a rush.

"You're so fucking sexy, you kill me." His lips tipped up, and he touched his forehead to hers. "I want to touch you, Kat. Tell me no, and I'll back off. Tell me yes, and I'll make you come before dinner." He pressed his cheek to hers and said, "And after, many times over."

Chapter Fifteen

HE WAS SCREWING this up, he was sure of it, but Eric was powerless to stop touching Kat. He needed to feel her shudder against him, and he could see by the flush of her skin and the darkening of her eyes that she was wound just as tightly as he was.

He'd called ahead to request the private room, but his intentions had been to talk, not to make out. But with Kat, he was lucky he'd made it as long as he had. Everything about her, from the way she watched him to the feel of her hand in his, turned him on, and he knew he'd never get enough of her.

Her eyes never left his. "Okay," she said with a tremble in her voice.

"Kat." Her name came off his lips seconds before he took her in another mind-blowing kiss.

"Come with me, sweetheart." He brought her to her feet and kissed her again, deep and slow, savoring the feel of her pressed against him as he unbuttoned her jeans and slid his hand inside her panties. "Oh, baby, you're so ready for me."

He sealed his lips over hers as he teased her with his hand and deepened the kiss again. He dipped his fingers inside her, earning a needy moan. He backed her up against the wall. Aware of the harshness of the cold stone, he was careful not to push her back too far as he made love to her mouth and brushed his thumb over her clit, earning another heady moan.

"Love those sounds. So sexy." He sealed his teeth over her neck as he pressed his fingers in deep, using his thumb to bring her clit to attention, while seeking the spot that would send her over the edge.

Her head tipped back, and he slid his other hand beneath her shirt, squeezing her nipple as he recaptured her mouth in a rough kiss. Electric currents seared through him as she went up on her toes, gripping his biceps so hard he was sure he would bruise.

"I want my mouth on you, darlin'," he said in a heated breath.

He sucked her tongue into his mouth, but even that wasn't enough. He wanted to drop to his knees and feast on her sweetness, but she was so close to coming, her breathing was hitched. He lifted her shirt and tore down her bra, exposing a perfect rosy nipple. With a moan of his own at the gorgeous sight, he took her breast in his mouth, grazing his teeth over the taut peak.

"Oh God," she cried. "Eric…Yes…God…"

He sucked harder and quickened his efforts down below. Her legs trembled, and she fisted her hands in his hair, holding his mouth to her. He used his teeth, sensing her greed for more.

"Yes. Yes. Oh God." She sucked in a sharp breath as she shattered against his hand. Hot and wet, her sex pulsed tight around his fingers.

He brought his mouth to hers again, bringing her down slowly. His fingers remained inside her until the last of her climax shuddered through her. He gathered her into his arms and held her until her breathing calmed and her body melted against him. And in that moment of intimacy, he was so damn sure that she was the only woman for him that he nearly told her so.

She gazed up at him, and the sensual look in her eyes nearly laid him flat. "What about you?" she asked so fucking sweetly that he nearly came undone.

"I can wait."

"But—" She reached between his legs, rubbing his throbbing cock.

"My release is a bit messier than yours." He kissed her again. "Anticipation will heighten the pleasure. It'll be worth the wait." He helped her right her pants and walked her to the ladies' room they'd passed on the way in. "I'll wait for you here. Take your time."

After she went into the bathroom, he turned to the wall and pressed his fist against it, trying to regain control of his emotions.

The bathroom door opened, and she reached a hand out, snagged his shirt, and tugged him inside. Before he could get a word out, she was unzipping his pants and tugging them down.

"Kat, we don't have to—"

She sealed her lips over his, cupping his balls and making him groan.

"Fuuuck." He fisted his hand in her hair and held their mouths together.

She pushed from his chest. "Shush," she said with a finger over his lips and a challenging gaze. "It's my turn to play."

She dropped to her knees, looking like his darkest fantasy come true, and licked his shaft, base to tip, lingering over the wide crown before taking him in deep.

"Holy fuck." He pressed his palms to the walls to keep from grabbing her head and guiding her as he fucked her insanely talented mouth.

She cupped his balls again, sliding her finger over the sensitive skin behind them as she worked him with her other hand and her wicked mouth. She squeezed his sac and his hips kicked forward. It was useless. He couldn't hold back. He tangled his hands in her hair as he rocked his hips. Holy hell, she was going to make him come fast if she kept up this pace. He closed his eyes against the tingling heat crawling up his spine.

"Kat," he growled. "Stop, Kat. I'm gonna come."

She released his throbbing cock and licked her lips. "Less mess this way." She took him in deep again, holding his gaze and driving him out of his fucking mind.

"You don't have to," he said through gritted teeth. But fuck, did she feel good. Her mouth was a treasure trove of pleasure, hot and wet and oh so willing. Seeing her lips stretched around his cock was the most erotic thing he'd ever witnessed, and when she pulled back and ran her tongue over the sensitive glans and lapped up the glistening bead, he nearly lost it right then and there.

"I want to taste you," she said, then she took him in deep again, and holy fuck, she ran her finger between his cheeks, shredding the last of his control. He came hard, groaning through his clenched teeth, and she swallowed every last drop.

His chin tipped forward with a hiss, and he lifted her to her feet as she licked her shiny, swollen lips. "You're unfuckingbelievable."

He sealed his lips over hers, tasting himself and not caring. Her desire for him turned him on even more. He was hard again in seconds, aching for more of her, to feel her wrapped tightly around him. He reached for the button on her jeans, but she was already pulling them down. He tore off his boots, pushed from his own pants, kicking them to the side, and helped Kat with hers.

"Condom," she said quickly.

He snagged one from his wallet and tore it open with his teeth, sheathing himself quickly. He lifted her easily and lowered her onto his hard shaft. They both groaned with their intense coupling.

"What is it with us and bathrooms?" He pressed his lips to hers as he thrust into her hard and deliciously deep.

"Some people like hotels. I think we're sexier." She used his shoulders for leverage as he clutched her hips, and they moved together in a fast, even rhythm.

"*You're* fucking sexy. But I'm going to get you in a bed eventually."

"I can't wait." She lowered her lips to his, and he pressed her back to the wall so he could drive in deeper. "Wait," she said against his lips.

She shifted from his arms and placed her hands on the wall, bending over slightly at the waist. When she looked over her shoulder and her hair fell over her eye, Eric nearly lost it.

She crooked her finger. "Take me harder."

He wrapped his arm around her waist from behind and

drove into her. "Fuck. I'm not going to last like this." He used his other hand to stroke over her clit, and she was right there with him on the brink of release. He could feel it in her trembling limbs, in the tightness between her legs. He sank his teeth into the curve of her shoulder, and her hips bucked, her inner muscles clenched around him, and he followed her over the edge, chasing his own intense release.

He rested his cheek against Kat's back, lost in a fog of lust and greed and fucking love. It was right there on his tongue. Three fucking words he never thought he'd feel, much less want to say. But he swallowed them down, holding her tightly until they were both breathing normally again. Then he turned her in his arms and kissed her sweetly.

"I WANT MORE than this with you, Kat."

His gaze bored right through her. His words wrapped around her frantically beating heart and squeezed. She was afraid to admit she wanted that, too.

"I mean it. I want to talk with you, get to know you even better, and spend more time with you. I want to love you properly, in a real bed, and preferably, wake up with you in my arms." He pressed his lips to hers. "I've never wanted that before."

She wanted desperately to believe him, but she wasn't naive, and she was afraid to believe he really meant that he wanted more, as in a future. "We've got this weekend. Let's focus on that."

His brows drew together. "Focus on that? You don't want more?"

"I do. More than you could ever know, but I'm not going to fool myself into thinking that a guy like you can be satisfied with a girl like me."

He ran his hand through his hair as he tugged on his jeans. "Seriously? I knew we shouldn't have fooled around. A guy like me?"

Frustration rolled off of him as she pushed her legs into her jeans and zipped them up. She touched his arm, and he bristled.

"All I meant was that I don't want you to feel like you have to make promises you can't keep. I'm a big girl, Eric. I know you've got women galore, and you have a whole life out there that doesn't include some bartender slash waitress turned PR girl from Richmond, Virginia." She held his gaze, and when he offered his hands to her, she took them willingly.

He gathered her close, and his serious tone softened. "Kat, I'm not that guy. I don't make promises I can't keep. Hell, I don't make promises. Period." He searched her eyes, and she wondered if he could see how she was hanging on to his every word and her hopeful heart was hanging by a thread.

"Except to you, Kat. I want more with you, and I'm prepared to make you promises that I will most definitely keep." He ran his fingers through her hair. "I want my life to include a bartender slash waitress turned PR girl from Richmond, Virginia."

She could hardly breathe, her heart was so full.

"Say you want that, too, Kat. Say you feel what I feel. Tell me that you feel like the pieces of your life have finally come together." He caressed her cheek, making the thickening in her throat even worse. "You've always been a part of me, and I never want that to change."

She heard the honesty in his voice, saw the pleading in his gaze. God, how could she have fallen so hard so fast? "I want it, Eric. I want it all. I'm just scared."

"Me too." He pressed his lips to hers. "But not of us. I'm scared of walking out of this bathroom and never feeling what I feel again. I'm scared of not seeing you for another twenty years."

She gulped in air to ensure she was still breathing. "I'm right there with you. But where do we go from here?"

His smile was relieved and sexy and so full of love she pressed herself closer to him, wanting to be sure he saw the same thing in her eyes as she did in his.

"I think we start with dinner," he said as he pressed his lips to hers. "And then maybe dessert. And then, hopefully, we'll fall into forever."

—The End—

* * * *

SIGN UP for MELISSA'S NEWSLETTER to stay up to date with new releases, giveaways, and events

NEWSLETTER:
http://www.melissafoster.com/newsletter

CONNECT WITH MELISSA

FACEBOOK:
https://www.facebook.com/MelissaFosterAuthor
TWITTER:
https://www.facebook.com/MelissaFosterAuthor
WEBSITE: http://www.melissafoster.com/
STREET   TEAM:
http://www.facebook.com/groups/melissafosterfans

About Melissa Foster

Melissa Foster is a *New York Times* and *USA Today* bestselling and award-winning author. Her books have been recommended by *USA Today's* book blog, *Hagerstown* magazine, *The Patriot*, and several other print venues. She is the founder of the World Literary Café, and when she's not writing, Melissa helps authors navigate the publishing industry through her author training programs on Fostering Success. Melissa has painted and donated several murals to the Hospital for Sick Children in Washington, DC.

Visit Melissa on her website or chat with her on social media. Melissa enjoys discussing her books with book clubs and reader groups and welcomes an invitation to your event.

Melissa Foster's Book List

AFTER DARK SERIES
WILD BOYS
Logan
Heath
Jackson
Cooper

Love in Bloom books may be read as stand-alones. For more enjoyment, read them in series order. Characters from each series carry forward to the next.
Full LOVE IN BLOOM SERIES order

SNOW SISTERS
Sisters in Love
Sisters in Bloom
Sisters in White

THE BRADENS (Weston, CO)
Lovers at Heart
Destined for Love
Friendship on Fire
Sea of Love
Bursting with Love
Hearts at Play

THE BRADENS (Trusty, CO)
Taken by Love
Fated for Love
Romancing My Love
Flirting with Love
Dreaming of Love
Crashing into Love

BRADEN WORLD NOVELLAS
Promise My Love

THE BRADENS (Peaceful Harbor, MD)
Healed by Love
Surrender My Love
(More Coming Soon)

THE REMINGTONS
Game of Love
Stroke of Love
Flames of Love
Slope of Love
Read, Write, Love

SEASIDE SUMMERS
Seaside Dreams
Seaside Hearts
Seaside Sunsets
Seaside Secrets
Seaside Nights

THE RYDERS
Seized by Love

Please enjoy this sneak peek of
Hugh Braden and Brianna Heart's story,
HEARTS AT PLAY, The Bradens

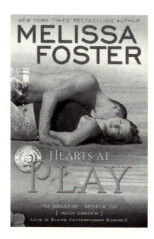

KAT BURST THROUGH the stockroom doors of Old Town Tavern, nearly plowing into Brianna.

"Jeez, Kat. What the hell?" Brianna Heart had been working since noon, and she had another two hours to go before her ten-hour shift was over. She didn't have the energy for Kat's drama. Not tonight, when she still had to muster the energy to pick up Layla, her five-year-old daughter, from her mother's house, get her to bed, and then make invitations for Layla's birthday party.

"Patrick Dempsey is here. I saw him. He's sitting at a table in the bar. Oh my God—he is even hotter in person." Kat flipped her long blond hair over her shoulder and tapped her finger on her lip. "I wonder if he's looking for a date."

"Kat." Brianna shook her head. "You're crazy. You always think you see famous people. Not a lot of famous people are clamoring to get into Richmond, Virginia."

"Bree, I'm telling you. I think I need to change my underwear." She looked at Brianna and furrowed her perfectly manicured brows. "Oh, honey. Here. Let me help you with your hair. You could be the prettiest bartender slash waitress out there and you know it. Well, besides me, of course." She began fluffing Bree's straight, shoulder-length brown hair.

Brianna shook her head. "Please. If it is Patrick Dempsey, I'll be the last person he's looking at." She wiped her hands on the little towel she kept looped over her belt at all times—because she didn't have time to breathe, much less go searching for something to dry her hands on.

"Oh, come on, Bree. Don't you want to get out of this place? What better way than with a famous sugar daddy?" Kat looked at her reflection in the glass and flipped her long blond hair over her shoulder again.

"*Ugh*. No, thank you. The last thing Layla needs is that kind of lifestyle, and the last thing I need is to stand in the stockroom talking about fictitious people. I love you, Kat, but I gotta get out there." She patted her back pocket. "I need the tips. Layla's birthday is coming up."

"I can't believe she's going to be six. Gosh, that went quick. What does she want?"

"A puppy, a kitten, a bigger bedroom." Brianna sighed. "But I think I'm gonna get her a winter jacket. Kill two birds with one stone." She winked as she headed out of the stockroom and up to the bar. A quick scan told her that Patrick Dempsey was definitely not there. She snagged the empty glasses from the bar and wiped it down.

Mack Greenley, the manager of the bar, sidled up to Brianna. She'd worked for Mack for the past five and a half years, and though she was twenty-eight and he was only thirty-eight, he'd taken her under his wing as if she were his daughter.

"Booth." Mack was a big man with a mass of brown hair and a thick, powerful neck.

"Got it." Bree wiped her hands on the towel, grabbed an order pad, and went to the only occupied booth in the small bar. It was Thursday night at seven o'clock. Another half hour and the bar would be packed for Major League Baseball playoffs. Brianna focused on her order pad, thinking about Layla's birthday and wishing she could afford the time or money to get her a pet, like she wanted. But as a single mother, she couldn't balance working fifty hours each week with taking care of Layla *and* a pet. It was just too much. She pushed the thought away and feigned a smile.

"Hi, I'm Brianna…Bree. What can I get you?"

The guy in the booth lifted his head in her direction, and Brianna's breath caught in her throat. She felt her jaw go slack. The man's thick, windblown dark hair looked as if someone had just run their hands through it. *While kissing his glorious lips and feeling that sexy five-o'clock shadow on their cheek. Jesus, he does look like Patrick Dempsey…on steroids.*

"A sidecar and a glass of water, please," he said.

Brianna couldn't move. She couldn't breathe. She couldn't even close her damn mouth. *Shit. Shit. Shit. Shit.*

He cocked his head. "Are you okay?"

Are you kidding me? Does your voice have to be so damn smooth and rich? That's so unfair. She cleared her throat. "Yeah, sorry. Long day. One sidecar coming up." She cursed at herself all the way back to the bar.

Kat grabbed her arm and pulled her toward the sink, their backs to way-sexier-than-Patrick-Dempsey steroid guy. "I told you," she whispered. "Jesus, you're lucky. What are you gonna do?"

Brianna looked over her shoulder at the handsome man. *Trouble.* That's what she saw. She'd known men like him before. Hell, that's how she ended up with Layla.

"Nothing. He wants a sidecar. You take it to him." Brianna handed her the pad and went to help the woman she and Kat called Red—a slutty redhead who spent every Thursday night trolling the bar for men.

Brianna focused on making Red her cosmo. The din of the customers fell away. Her mind circled back to the Patrick Dempsey look-alike's voice. It was so…so…different from any other man's voice. He didn't speak as if he were rushed, and he looked at her eyes instead of her breasts, which was also different from most of the male customers at the tavern. She started when Kat touched her shoulder.

"Bree, come on. You do it. I can't take him from you. He's probably a big tipper. Look at that jacket."

Brianna glanced at the brown leather jacket hanging on the end of the booth. "It's okay. You go. I'm good." She handed Red a cosmo.

"Do you know who that is?" Red lifted her glass toward the handsome man.

Bree shrugged. "No idea." *But I'm sure he'll take you home.*

"I think that's my date," Red said.

Isn't every man? Brianna watched Kat bring him his drink. Her crimson lips spread with a flash of her sexiest smile. Brianna knew Kat's next move. The hair flip. Then she'd touch his shoulder and…She watched Kat throw her head back in an exaggerated laugh. Brianna sighed and turned away. *He's probably an ass.* She'd made it this long without a man dragging her through emotional hell; she wasn't going to cave now. She pulled her shoulders back and rotated just in time to see Red sliding into the seat across from him.

—End of sneak peek—

TEASED
A Dark Protectors Novella
By Rebecca Zanetti

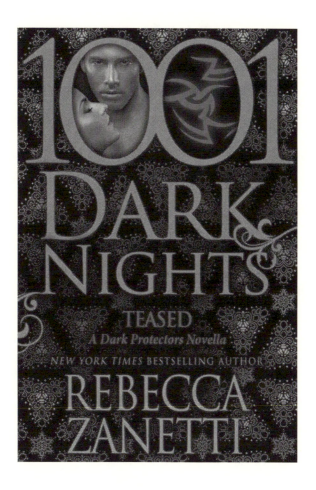

Acknowledgments

I am truly thrilled to be included with the amazing authors in the 1001 Dark Nights group! Liz Berry combined a love of reading and a brilliance for business in this exciting venture, and I'm excited to be part of the fun. I'm also honored to call her a friend, and I can't thank her enough for the good talks, ingenious ideas, and phenomenal work. Thank you also to MJ Rose, Kimberly Guidroz, and Pam Jamison for their dedication and awesome insights. A huge shout-out goes to Jillian Stein, the most amazing social media manager in the world, and the woman who has greatly reduced my stress level. Thanks also to Asha Hossain, who creates absolutely fantastic book covers.

Next I need to thank Alicia Condon and Kensington Publishing for helping me create and grow the Dark Protector world and fan base, as well as for being so supportive with my branching out a little with the series. My next shout-out goes to Caitlin Blasdell and Liza Dawson, my insightful and very hard working agents, whom I appreciate so much.

As always, a big and heartfelt thank you goes to Big Tone, my own six-and-a-half feet tall grumpy badass Alpha male. The man takes care of things, even during a recent unexpected natural disaster, and I can't express how secure this makes me. Thanks also to Gabe and Karly, our terrific kids, who definitely keep things interesting, and who I love dearly.

Finally, thank you to Rebecca's Rebels, my Facebook street team, who have been so generous with their time and friendship. And last, but not least, thank you to all of my readers who spend time with my characters.

~ RAZ

Chapter One

Chalton Reese stepped smoothly around several women wearing Christmas garlands in lieu of clothing, ignoring their outstretched pamphlets. New York winter was setting in, and the wind was attacking the garlands, revealing way too much flesh. Street vendors hawked theater tickets to his left, and fluffy creatures from children books mingled to the right, trying to get tourists to pay for photographs.

Massive blinking billboards showing holiday sales bombarded him from all sides in a sensory overload that slapped him with an instant migraine.

He hadn't been in Times Square for nearly six decades, and that wasn't long enough. Not even close.

Yet the woman he followed hummed quietly beneath her breath, winding through the throng, a definite hop in her step. She had to be truly crazy to enjoy the crowd milling around.

He barely tolerated crazy, and he hated crowds. What he wouldn't give to be in his secluded computer control room deep in the Idaho mountains. But no. When the king of the Realm ordered a vampire on a mission, a vamp went on a mission. Even if that guy hadn't been on a mission in a century.

He hadn't been away from his computers for decades. Like most vampires, he employed logic and order...and couldn't for the life of him figure out why Dage had sent him on this mission. But the king always had reasons, and he usually kept them close to his vest.

Chalton stepped over a pile of what appeared to be chilidogs and hastened his step to keep the woman in sight. Olivia Roberts. A no-nonsense name with just a bit of softness. Unlike the woman. She was *all* soft and curves. Deep brown hair, light green eyes, and a figure that could literally stop a trolley cart.

He'd always liked curvy, and the beauty in front of him was overflowing with curves. Once again, he frowned, and a hot dog vendor jumped out of his way, fear sizzling from him. Chalton shook his head and tried to force his face into harmless lines. The last mission he'd been on had involved firing from a distance. Most of his missions had included guns, shooting, and death. But he'd given up the life of an assassin to become a computer geek.

Yet here he was in bone-chilling cold, surrounded by cement and glass, chasing a woman who filled out her blue parka like he'd drawn her on a notepad. Perfectly.

She clip-clopped on surprisingly high-heeled boots down a cross street, easily winding between people and stepping too close to moving vehicles. He calmly followed her, pleased to be finally getting somewhere. After watching her for two days just write news articles in her apartment, he'd started to wonder if she'd ever meet her mysterious source in person. He needed to find out who was feeding her information.

A dark van pulled up next to her, its windows blackened out. The side door slid open.

Hell. Chalton burst into a run.

A man wearing a ski mask reached out, yanked her inside, and shut the door before she could let out a scream. The van jerked to the right, horn honking, inching through the traffic.

Chalton reached it and grabbed for the door handle. Metal scratched his palm and cut deep. Bugger. It was locked. The rusty metal ripped away from the door, and he threw it to the ground.

The van veered away from him, hopped the opposite curb, and careened down the sidewalk. Bystanders yelled and jumped out of the way, spraying snow. A display of holiday T-shirts flew up in the air and crashed down in the middle of the street. The van continued on, horn blaring. Chalton jumped over a downed bicycle and ran after the careening vehicle, measuring the distance between it and the four-way stop up ahead along with the probability of an accident if the driver ran a red light.

He calculated the timing of the street light signals, catching view of a yellow light up ahead. Yep. It'd be red soon, and the van would run it. The woman probably wasn't wearing a seatbelt. The van was older and weighed around six thousand pounds. It'd withstand an accident, but without a seatbelt, Olivia might get injured. He couldn't let her get injured before he discovered her source.

Besides, after keeping an eye on her for a few days, he felt an odd sense of responsibility for her. The pretty brunette wouldn't become harmed on his watch.

The van scraped against a brick building and sparks flew. People scrambled out of the way, throwing purses and shopping bags, dodging into the street. Horns blared, and vehicles screeched to stops.

He kept his heart rate slow and his mind sharp, maneuvering around frantic people while keeping pace with the van. Two cabs collided in front of the van, careening through ice, no doubt trying to get out of the way. The driver of the van hit the brakes, but it was going too fast and impacted the yellow taxis with a loud crunch of metal on metal.

One taxi driver jumped out of his cab, swearing loudly and rounding his car.

Chalton ran in front of the guy and grabbed for the van driver's front door. Locked. The window was shaded so heavily he couldn't see in, but the hair on the back of his neck rose. It wasn't the first time he'd been in the cross hairs of a gun.

A muffled scream came from inside. Olivia.

He jumped up on the hood of the van, ignoring the hiss of steam coming from the engine. The front window was dark but not as dark as the sides. A shorter man sat in the driver's seat with a SIG pointed straight at Chalton.

* * * *

Panic threatened to consume her, so she struck out. Olivia struggled against her captor and yanked off his ski mask, her nails scraping down his face.

"Bitch," he yelped, slapping her across the cheek.

Pain exploded beneath her cheekbone. Her ears rang and she scrambled away from him. Sirens sounded in the distance, giving her hope. She leaned to the side to see the driver of the van pointing a gun out the front windshield.

A man crouched on the hood, gaze on the gun.

She shivered.

No fear showed on the guy's hard-cut face. No emotion whatsoever. Black eyes seemed merely curious as he and the driver played some weird game of chicken. But she could almost feel the driver's stress and could definitely smell his body odor.

"Um, there's nowhere to go," she whispered as the trill of sirens came closer.

The guy in the backseat reached over and grabbed her hair, pulling back her head. Pain lanced down her scalp, and she hissed. "What do you want with me?" she muttered.

"Who's your source?" the driver asked.

She blinked. Her source? Chills cascaded down her back. "I don't know."

The hand in her hair yanked, and she cried out, her eyes watering from the pain.

The man outside the car switched his gaze to her, and she felt the impact of those eyes through her entire body. He lifted an eyebrow.

What the hell? He had a gun pointed at him, there was pandemonium all around, and he seemed mildly interested. Who was the bystander? Was he some undercover cop?

"Shoot him," the guy holding her ordered.

Her eyes widened, and she opened her mouth to yell a warning. Before she could get out a sound, the guy on the hood punched through the glass. Shards sprayed along with red. Blood.

She screamed and tried to duck away from flying glass.

The punch was so powerful the guy kept coming, one hand swiping the gun out of the way and the other snaking around the driver's neck. The driver screamed and wrapped both hands around the guy's arm, flopping like a beached fish.

Olivia yanked her head free, turned, and plowed her fist into the other guy's nose. Cartilage crunched. He howled and grabbed his face, fury darkening his eyes. She scrambled back, reaching for the door handle and kicking out. Her boot tip caught the guy under the chin, throwing back his head.

Her fingers scrambled along the handle and she jerked, sliding the door open and falling backward. Her arms flailing, she managed to kick her kidnapper once again as he lunged for her before her ass hit the pavement. Water from a puddle splashed over her legs.

Pain vibrated up her spine.

Her mind fuzzing and her heart beating so fast her throat clogged, she scampered to her feet and stumbled away from the van. The guy she'd kicked shoved free just in time for the blond guy to finish with the driver, grab the doorjamb, and swing his legs around. Both knees clamped onto the guy's neck and twisted, throwing him to land on the snow covered pavement.

Olivia stilled, her gaze meeting her savior's as he landed on his feet, facing her.

Except he didn't look like a savior. Standing next to the van, his size became apparent. Well over six-feet tall, muscled and tight, with blond hair tied at the nape, he looked like an avenging...what? Not an angel. Definitely not an angel. He wore black slacks and an expensive looking button-down shirt with the sleeves rolled up. One arm dripped blood from deep scratches, and he didn't seem to notice.

The crowd milled around, some passing by, some glancing into the van.

But nobody existed except for the man. His face was an intriguing blend of hard angles: prominent jawline, slashes for cheekbones, high brows. Handsome in a too-sharp-to-be-real look. But those eyes...intelligent and knowing.

She swallowed. There was no doubt he was allowing her to look her fill. Waiting and...*allowing*.

What in the world?

She breathed out, trying to slow her heart rate. Then her

brain kicked back into gear, so she turned on a heel and ran.

She tripped over a dog that scurried beneath a cart peddling roasting chestnuts. Run. She had to run. Sirens came from too far away, and she knew, somehow she just knew, that the blond guy wouldn't let her talk to the cops.

Her initial assessment about him was wrong because he couldn't be a cop. Not once had he identified himself, and he didn't seem to have a badge or a gun. In fact, a cop probably wouldn't have knocked out both men without at least trying to gain their cooperation.

The blond didn't care about cooperation.

She hurried across the street to the now moving throng of shoppers, her instincts humming. Keeping her balance, she turned slightly to look behind her. Panic rippled through her instantly.

He stalked her, calmly, easily winding through the mass of people. No tension showed on his face or in his movements. He could be out for a nice stroll through the neighborhood.

Except for his eyes. Focus, intense and absolute, lived in those dark orbs. He tracked her, keeping pace, not seeming to notice that people naturally got out of his way.

Or maybe he did notice and just didn't care.

She turned back around, her shoulders hunched. Escape. Where the hell could she go?

Pushing past a group of teenagers holding shopping bags, she edged in front of them to block her from behind. Then she dodged into a large department store and headed for the back, past all the holiday dishes.

She'd learned early on in life to listen to her instincts, and right now, they were screeching at her to get away from the man.

So she loped into a jog, careful not to trip in her favorite boots, and turned up the escalator, the toes of her shoes touching down briefly on each step. Reaching the top, she hustled through the lingerie department and ran smack into a saleswoman. Bras of every color went flying.

"Oh my. I'm so sorry." Olivia reached out to steady the girl, who appeared to be around nineteen.

The girl laughed and shoved back bright purple hair. "Are

you all right?"

"No." Olivia glanced around and took several deep breaths. She should probably call the police now that she was safe.

A hand banded around her elbow in instant heat. "She had a scare outside and needs some water." The voice was smooth, cultured, and commanding.

The salesgirl blinked and stepped back, her eyes widening right before her smile followed suit. "Hello." She coughed and then pushed out her boobs under a nice silk shirt that matched her hair. "I'll, ah, get water." Turning on a sparkly wedge, she stepped over abandoned bras to head through a doorway behind the cash register.

Olivia slowly turned around and then tilted her head back...way back. The blond stared down. "Who are you?" she hissed.

"Let's go." He pulled her toward the aisle, having rolled down his shirt sleeves. Probably to cover the blood.

"No." She jerked back, not surprised when his hold didn't relent. "Release me, or I'll start screaming." That sounded like a good idea anyway. She sucked in air.

The world spun.

Somehow, she ended up with her back against a brick column and her front plastered against an impossibly hard male body. Panic engulfed her, and she opened her mouth to scream.

His mouth planted against hers, driving all sound back down her throat. A warm palm cradled her head, her whole head, and held her in place. She stilled. Completely.

Her eyes widened just as his narrowed.

Heat spread from him, all but surrounding her. The look in his eyes captured her attention as it quickly spread from determined to something...else. Something hungry.

Not once in her life had she been called dainty, but with his large frame blocking her, she felt small. Feminine. And somehow, from the interest in his eyes, powerful.

"Get your mouth off mine," she murmured against his very warm lips, her body shocked into holding still.

One of his eyebrows, much darker than his hair, arched. "Are you going to scream?" he whispered right back, the movement of his mouth against hers sending irresponsible tingles down her torso.

"Probably." Yeah. She kind of liked her lips moving against his.

He grinned. Right against her mouth, he smiled, and the tingles turned to tidal waves.

What was *wrong* with her?

She blinked.

He growled low. *Growled.*

She trembled, and some of it might have been from fear.

He levered back, his face still only an inch from hers. "Turn on that sexy heel and come with me now, or I will toss you over my shoulder and we go. Either way...we go."

She leaned back into the brick, studying his face. No humor...no give. He meant every word. While she wanted to be a badass warrior, she'd already seen him move and fight. She wouldn't win. And now she had the young salesgirl to worry about. Would he hurt her?

Olivia couldn't take the risk. "Fine." The second she was outside, she'd make a break for it. No matter how tough the guy, a good kick to the nards would take him out. Probably.

He slid his hand down her shoulder and clasped her elbow, setting her slightly in front of him and propelling her toward the down escalator. She allowed him to maneuver her but kept her shoulders back and her head up. They rode down, and tension vibrated down her back.

She tried to look agreeable as they wound through the store and exited outside to the gray and snow-falling day.

Then she turned and shot her knee up as fast as she could.

Chapter Two

Chalton shifted his hips in order to deflect the female's knee and yet allow her to keep her balance. Her pretty emerald eyes had given more than ample warning of the strike coming.

She huffed and set her leg back down.

"You done?" he asked mildly.

A wild, very wild, flush worked its way up over her neck, chin, and high cheekbones. "Not even close."

Damn, he liked that spirit. Liked it a whole lot. "That's unfortunate." He glanced around at the mass of bodies rushing past them living lives he truly didn't care about. "Olivia, we need to talk."

She tried to step back, and he grasped her hand to keep her from being swept away. "How do you know my name?" All color drained from her pretty face.

He cocked his head to the side. "I've been following you for two days."

Her pointed chin lifted. "I haven't gone anywhere for two days."

"I know. It's been very boring." But now she was in his hands, and he could finish his mission. Although threatening her to keep quiet and stop writing about his people didn't seem so clear-cut now that he'd had his mouth on hers. On her very heated, soft, feminine mouth. His gaze dropped on its own volition to those plump lips.

She cleared her throat. "Stop looking at me like that."

He lifted his head. "Like what?"

She licked her lips, and he groaned out loud. "What do you want, buddy?"

He grinned. "Chalton. My name."

"Chalton." She rolled the sound around on her tongue.

Now he fucking loved his name. "Yeah."

"Russian?"

"A long time ago." About three centuries, to be exact.

"You don't have an accent." Suspicion darkened her eyes to the color of a green sapphire he'd seen once in a royal crown.

"Я хочу, чтобы лишить вас голым."

"Hmm." Her shoulders settled, as she no doubt found some measure of safety with people all around them. "What did you say?"

He couldn't repeat what he said since it involved getting her naked and was no doubt very inappropriate. "I wished you a good day."

"Right. What do you want?" Clearly, she didn't believe a word he said.

"To talk." He glanced around. "Away from the crowds and the cold wind."

"Ah." She nodded, the wind lifting her hair. "In your spaceship or lair? You wanna wear my skin as a suit, do you?"

He laughed, unable to help himself.

She blinked again. "Murderous kidnappers shouldn't have such nice laughs," she murmured and then stilled.

Did the woman say everything that was in her head? While the idea should irritate him, instead he found an intriguing charm in the idea. Creative people were often the most interesting, now weren't they? "I have no plans to murder you."

"That's a relief," she snapped, trying to pull her hand free.

He kept it, quite liking it where it was in his. Then he settled. Energy cascaded around her, filtering through the air. "Ah, hell." Enhanced. The most beautiful woman he'd held in eons was enhanced and thus a possible vampire mate. Was she psychic? Empathic? Human females with special gifts were probably linked to the witches and were possible mates to immortals like him. "The king had better not be matchmaking," he muttered, losing his smile.

Olivia lifted a finely arched eyebrow. "The king? What king?"

Now he was blurting out his thoughts. "Forget it. We need privacy for a talk as well as to protect your safety. Any idea who the men in the van were?" They were human, but he hadn't had a chance to interrogate them before she'd bolted into the store, and now it was too late. The cops had arrived and were questioning people down the street.

He knew the second she caught sight of the police because her body stiffened and drew in air. "Don't do it," he said, leaning into her.

She gasped, and her head shot up, those green eyes narrowing. "Kiss me again, and you'll lose a lip."

He grinned. "Damn, you're feisty." Then he lowered his head to within an inch of hers, letting intent and focus show. "And that wasn't a kiss."

She swallowed and glanced down at his mouth before looking back up. Pink colored beneath the smooth skin on her face, and she cleared her throat. Her scent of wild flowers wafted around and tempted him far more than he liked, as did the curiosity in those stunning eyes. "Back away," she whispered.

"Promise you'll come with me and not scream." He tried to smooth his face into reassuring lines. "You have my word I won't harm you."

She snorted. "Right." Her shoulders drooping, she glanced around. "I appreciate you rescuing me from the guys in the van, but I don't know you. Or trust you."

He nodded. "I understand, but you're probably still in danger. Let's get out of here."

She shook her head. "I'll make you a deal. There's a café across the street. We can go in, have a cup, and talk. Make your case and explain why you rescued me from the van, who you are, and what you want from me." She turned back to him. "Or I start screaming my bloody head off and kicking like you've never seen a woman kick."

His groin tightened. Right there, in the middle of the sidewalk, just like a teenager...he got hard. Spunk and brains had always done him in with women, and this one had both in spades. The cops were getting closer, and there was a good chance the men in the van had friends also looking for the female. "Fine." He kept ahold of her to lead the way across the street, winding through barely moving vehicles.

Her skin was soft and her hand small. Somehow, it felt just right in his.

He shook his head. There wasn't time for this. Even as his body rioted, he could feel danger stalking near. Energy popped in the air, and his breath quickened.

Just as he reached the coffee shop door, a ping next to him threw up concrete.

Shit. Somebody had shot at them. He pivoted and shoved Olivia in front of him, propelling her to the side of the building. Covering her with his body, he glanced around the corner.

Sunlight glinted off a riflescope atop the brick building across the street. The gunman was crouched down, barely visible behind the sniper's rifle. He'd only taken one shot, and the passersby hadn't even noticed.

"What?" Olivia gasped, her back to the building.

"Sniper across the way." He looked down at her fashion boots, quickly calculating escape routes. "Can you run in those things?"

"Sniper?" She tried to lean around him and look, but he planted a hand on her upper chest and shoved her back. "You're freakin crazy."

He squinted up at the steel-structured building across from his current one-way street. If there was one killer, there might be two, and Olivia was vulnerable on the street. No movement showed across the way, but his instincts kept humming.

Going with his gut, he grabbed the door of a cab driving by and yanked it open. The driver hit his brakes, scattering slush. Chalton shoved Olivia inside before him. He sat and slammed the door.

The cab driver, a swarthy man wearing a spotted tie decorated with Rudolph, glared. "Get out. Light isn't on."

Chalton drew out several hundred-dollar bills from his pocket to hand over the seat. "Drive. Now."

The guy snatched the cash and turned to hit the gas pedal.

Olivia recovered and scooted for the other side, reaching for the door handle.

Chalton clasped her arm and dragged her into his side, giving her a warning squeeze. When she stiffened, glancing at the driver, he leaned in to whisper, "The driver can't take me, and you'll put him in definite danger if you ask for help."

She exhaled slowly, thoughts scattering across her pretty face.

"Drive faster, and I'll tip you well," Chalton spoke louder, keeping his gaze on Olivia. Who was trying to shoot her? While he'd read all of her news reports detailing the missing proprietary information from the labs his people had used to generate a cure for a virus that had attacked vampire mates, he hadn't spent any time reading her other works. "What are you involved in?" he growled.

She shivered and clasped her hands in her lap. "Bite me," she whispered back.

Hell, he'd love to bite her. A pretty woman should never say such a thing to a hungry vampire.

He leaned over her to look out her window, and she gasped, edging back in the seat. The figure on top of the building ran in pace with the taxi, rifle in hand, easily keeping up. He wore all black—including a mask. Yet there was something familiar in the way he moved.

Chalton frowned. Who the hell was that?

They needed to cross an intersection. No way could the sniper leap across the street.

Apparently the shooter realized the same thing, because he ran ahead. Probably to set up for a shot.

"At the corner, turn left suddenly," Chalton ordered the driver. "It'll be worth a thousand." He hoped he had that much in his pocket.

Olivia turned wide eyes on him. "You are batshit crazy, you know that?"

The driver shrugged and kept to the left, honking his horn several times to keep folks moving.

Bullets sprayed the side of the taxi.

"What the hell?" the driver bellowed.

Chalton yanked Olivia across his body to the other side, blocking her. She landed with a muffled *oof.*

"Oh my God. They are shooting at us," she yelled.

"Yes." Chalton glanced ahead.

She frantically patted his sides. "Shoot back."

He frowned. "I don't have a gun."

"Why the hell not?" she yelled.

"Don't like them." Not anymore. He didn't need guns. Finally, they reached the intersection. "Turn. Now."

Tires screeched as the driver turned. Chalton grabbed the back of Olivia's head and pushed her toward the floor. "Get down." Depending on the angle, the shooter might be able to make a shot through the back window.

The driver edged down in his seat, barreling through traffic. The stench of fear filled the car.

Chalton ducked down and took a good look. With his eyesight, he could make out the serial number on the rifle as well as the height of the shooter. The guy stood up, watching the cab, his gun aimed harmlessly at his feet. He stood several inches over six-feet tall, with a well-muscled form. Smooth and graceful even with such bulk.

He yanked the mask off, revealing a cap of dark hair and familiar, mocking dark eyes. Then he smiled—slow and dangerous.

Everything in Chalton stilled. His head jerked back. "Son of a bitch."

Olivia glanced up from her perch on the floor. "What? Do you know the guy?"

"Yeah." A rock settled hard in his gut. "He's my older brother."

Chapter Three

Olivia planted both hands on the torn leather seat and pulled herself up. Fear tasted like acid in her throat, and an unwelcomed heat filled her lungs as a prelude to a possible panic attack. "Your brother just shot at us?"

"Apparently." Chalton eyed the festive storefronts now speeding by. "Stop at the next light and let us out," he ordered the driver.

Olivia edged toward her door that led to the busy street.

The driver, muttering beneath his breath, yanked the car to the curb. "Get out of here." He turned furious eyes toward the back seat. "I'm calling the cops."

Chalton handed over what looked like a wad of cash. "No cops." Without waiting for an answer, he clamped a hand around Olivia's arm and hastened her across the seat and out his door.

The cabbie sped off.

Olivia glanced at the top of nearby buildings. "Tell me you only have one brother."

"Two." Chalton rubbed the back of his neck. "We need cover." Keeping her arm, he led her across the sidewalk to a specialty cigar shop, quickly texting something on a type of smartphone she'd never seen before.

Olivia's ears rang and her temples began to pound. She glanced around the shop for another exit, but a glass cabinet blocked the entire rear of the store. One proprietor assisted two elderly gentlemen near the wall. No help there.

Chalton kept his gaze out the window at the people hurrying by.

"What is your plan?" Olivia asked, trying to wriggle out of his grasp.

"Hold on," he said, not moving.

The strong scent of pipe tobacco wafted around, reminding her of her grandfather, who lived in Washington state near a forest. That's where she could go for a while until things calmed down. All she had to do was escape Chalton and get on the road. Then she could figure out who wanted her dead.

His hold remained secure around her hand, easily keeping her captive. She reached for his restraining hand with her free one and dug in her nails.

He slowly turned his head and focused on her. "What?"

"Let. Go."

"No." He turned back to the window.

She dug in, making sure to draw blood. Her fingertips suddenly burned. "What the heck?"

"Move now." He opened the door and tugged her outside to where a dark town car had maneuvered to the curb. Yanking open the door, he pivoted and pushed her inside before following.

Coolness surrounded her along with the scent of expensive leather. Chalton sighed and relaxed back into the seat. Then he reached into a side cupboard for two bottled waters, handing her one.

She took the water, her heart racing. A dark partition remained up between the back and front. "Who is up there?" she asked.

"Hired driver." Chalton opened his water and tipped his head back to drink.

She rapped her knuckles against the partition and then winced. "Hey, buddy? This is kidnapping, and you're an accomplice."

"Hired driver paid really well," Chalton said smoothly.

She whirled on him, her temper finally catching up to the fear of the day. "What do you want from me?"

His dark eyes narrowed. "I want to know who your source

is, where your research materials are, and where the latest article for *Life and Science* is."

"For what story?" She kept her chin up. After working for the magazine for nearly five years, she knew how to protect a source. More importantly, the only way to save her friend's life was to find the subjects of her article.

He smiled without an ounce of humor. "You know what story. The one about the laboratory in Oregon researching genetic mutations that hints at something...new."

New? Yeah. That was one way of putting it. The research hinted that there were other species walking around on earth who had more chromosomal pairs than humans. Something more...than human. Something that would certainly have a way to save Ronni from dying way too young. "I don't know what you're talking about."

He exhaled and stretched out long, very long, legs. "Sure you do. Your first two articles in the series detailed missing researchers from Oregon along with hints about their missing research, all leading up to an article coming next week with a big reveal. I'm assuming the big reveal is the actual research into chromosomal pairs, into extra ones belonging to an imaginary species, and you're being duped."

"Oh yeah?" She put her hands on her hips and pivoted in the seat to face him. "If I'm being duped, then why are people trying to either kidnap or shoot me?" She was on to the find of the century, and she needed to get back on track to meet her source for the evidence. "Let me out of this car, and I won't press charges."

"Do I look like I'm worried about charges?"

No. Not at all. He looked like some badass vigilante in tailored clothing. All muscle, intelligence, and...maleness. So damn *male* he could define the word. "You should be worried," she countered, her stomach dropping. The guy couldn't care less. She'd seen his face. She knew his name. "You're going to kill me," she whispered, her heart clenching. "Or try to," she added quickly.

He tossed his empty water bottle into a trash receptacle near the door. "I've saved your life twice. If I wanted you dead, you'd be dead."

A chill crawled down her back. "But you need the information you mentioned." Then would he kill her? Or try to?

He leaned toward her, bringing heat. "Listen, Livy. I will not kill you. I promise."

Livy? Only her grandpop called her that, and hearing the nickname from Chalton's handsome lips gave her odd tingles she really had to banish. She pressed her lips together. "Have you killed anybody before?

"Yes."

She knew it. Of course he had. The guy was definitely a soldier from the way he moved. "In times of war?"

"Yes."

Hope unfurled inside her. "In other times?"

"We're usually at war." He shrugged. "Where's your research?"

She slowly twisted the lid open on her bottle. "At my apartment on my computer." If she could just get home, she could break free. No way did he know her neighborhood as well as she did.

"No it isn't. The only stuff on your computer is recipes, Christmas card lists, music, games, and videos. No work." He rubbed his strong jaw.

She frowned. "How do you know what's on my computer?"

"I hacked it."

Hacked it? He'd freakin hacked it? "How dare you."

He rolled his eyes. "I'm guessing you have a laptop somewhere, one with the WIFI disabled, that you use for writing. It isn't in your apartment, and you haven't gone anywhere the last two days. Where is it?"

She blinked, her throat closing. Her hand shook, but she tipped the water bottle to her mouth and drank, allowing the liquid to soothe. Finally, she drew in a deep breath. "How do you know the laptop isn't in my apartment?"

"I searched your place while you were sleeping last night." He grinned. "Love the yellow panty set with the day of the week sewn in, by the way."

She gasped.

"And," he continued, "you really shouldn't hide your grandmother's jewelry beneath the kitchen sink in an old coffee can. It's way too easy to find there."

Oh God. He'd actually been in her apartment while she'd slept. Vulnerability slammed into her chest. "You dick," she murmured.

He nodded. "If I wanted to harm you, I could have already."

Yeah, but he hadn't found the information he'd wanted, now had he? Just how deadly would he become if he got his hands on her laptop and research materials? She shuddered. "So, let me get this straight. You're a good fighter, you're drop-dead quiet at night, and you know how to hack a computer."

"I'm complex," he drawled. "The research?"

As far as she could tell, the research, or the secrecy of it, was the only thing keeping her alive. "I'm not telling you." Unfortunately, she didn't exactly possess the important documents proving the existence of this super species since her meeting had been thwarted by the guys in the van. "Why is your brother trying to kill me?" Her eyes widened. "Or was he just after you?"

"I'm thinking he was shooting toward you," Chalton said.

"Toward?"

"Yeah. If my brother wanted a bullet to impact either one of us, we'd be bleeding right now. So my thought is that he was after you, saw me, and fired for fun."

Her eyes widened. "Your brother fired at us for fun?"

"You'd have to know him." Chalton rubbed his chin. "I haven't talked to him in a long time, but—"

"Why not?"

"Huh?"

"Why haven't you talked to your brother?" she asked.

His eyes sobered. "Long story and family stuff. But if Jared is after you, it has to be connected to the Oregon lab stories."

"Why? What does your brother do besides shoot at people from rooftops?" She had to figure a way out of the car when it slowed down.

"He's for hire—a bit of a vigilante. Anybody could've hired

him." Chalton shook his head. "This doesn't make sense. Who is your source for the Oregon lab series of stories?"

She clamped her mouth shut.

His chin lowered. "Listen. I don't want to scare you, and I don't want to hurt you. But I have a job to do, and I need to get a name from you."

Her mind spun. "So it's true. It's all true." Sure, she had the proof, or she would have it soon. But somehow, she'd still held doubts. "There's a species out there, or at the very least a human mutation that has created beings with more chromosomal pairs than twenty-three." More than human.

"Don't be silly." He reached out and clasped her chin with his thumb and forefinger. "My employer wants the information from the Oregon research labs because it is proprietary and could lead to drugs that'll wipe out dangerous diseases. There's no ultra-human, and you have to know that."

But the documents were clear, and she trusted Helen, her source. The woman was brilliant and knew what she was talking about. "This can't be about a simple drug."

"It's about many drugs, which means millions, if not billions, of dollars." He released her. "Give me the information, and I'll make sure you're protected. You need that."

She would be fine if she could just put some distance between herself and anybody trying to kidnap her, including Chalton. When she obtained the rest of the proof, she could finish her article and the truth would be out there, so there'd be no reason to harm her. Plus, then she could find the people who could save Ronni's heart from quitting for good. A thirty-year-old woman who'd been afflicted by an odd virus that had attacked her heart, Ronni had been Olivia's best friend since preschool. "Obviously you've read the two published articles, and you know a third is coming, so I'm not going to lie to you," Olivia said.

"Good."

"But I've already turned in the third article to my editor, and it runs next Wednesday. So it's too late." She lifted her hands.

"No you haven't," Chalton countered. "I hacked all the computers at the magazine as well as your editor's two computers at home. The guy plays way too much Zombie Bagus IV, by the way."

Her mouth dropped open. "You did not hack the magazine. We have top of the line firewalls."

"Took me almost five minutes, but I was eating a bagel at the time." He leaned in. "Maria Ortiz has pictures of her grandbabies all over her computer. Todd Jones has an affinity for sports cars, and Frank Softos likes pictures of naked softball players. Shall I go on about more of your colleagues?"

"God no." She sat back. How had he hacked the system so easily? "Who are you?"

He leaned into her space, all intent. "I'm a guy who gets the job done, no matter the job. Work with me, Livy. It's your only option."

Man, she must really be on to something with the story. Just how far did the knowledge go? The lab was a private lab, but it did have governmental funding. Was the government doing experiments? "Are you a soldier?"

"Not anymore."

She blinked. "What does that mean?"

"I used to be a soldier, a long time ago, and now I work with computers. Primarily." He glanced out the window. "I'm having men fetch your things from your apartment, including the jewelry. Is there anything you want me to make sure they pack?"

She sat back, her ears burning. "You're doing what?"

He lifted an eyebrow. "I'm taking you to a safe house and figured you'd want your things with you. On the way we need to acquire your research materials and laptop."

Oh, absolutely not. "My neighbors will report me missing, as will friends and coworkers." So would her grandfather after a few days, since they spoke at least once a week.

"I sent emails to your boss from your computer, and I left notes on your neighbors' doors in your handwriting saying you're taking a vacation. As for your grandfather, he won a two-week fishing trip in Alaska but had to leave immediately." Chalton pointed to her small purse. "There should be a message from him."

She could only gape. "Who are you?"

"I told you."

No, he really hadn't. "All I know is that you were a soldier, are probably in your early thirties, and now work as a computer hacking mercenary for hire. And you have two brothers you haven't spoken to in a while. Brothers who shoot at you."

He shrugged. "What else is there to know? Except you need to cooperate with me for your own safety, which obviously is in doubt."

"I'll be fine once I publish the next article." She spoke evenly, hoping he was truly rational.

"That will never happen." He lifted a shoulder. "Honest. You need to understand that we will take out the entire building housing the magazine in order to prevent that from happening. The whole block if we need to do so."

She studied him. Dead serious. Not an ounce of doubt showed on his hard-cut face. "You mean that."

"I truly do." He brushed a wayward hair off her forehead. "We'd try desperately to limit casualties, probably by calling in some sort of deadly gas leak and forcing an evacuation, but I can't guarantee nobody would be hurt."

The sheer calmness of his statement convinced her. "You people are zealots."

"No."

"Crazy, greedy bastards?" Heat roared into her face, burning her cheeks.

"Not really." He leaned back and stretched out again. "Look at us as folks trying to do the right thing and protect a bunch of people. From diseases and, ah, such."

Her focus narrowed. "What are you not telling me?"

He smiled, full of charm this time. "Nothing. I assure you."

Yeah, right. "I'm not telling you where my laptop is." There was no reason to deny its existence to him, considering it was obvious she'd written the articles somewhere and had the supporting documents beforehand.

"I won't make you talk." His long fingers tapped a rhythm on the leather armrest. "But you have to understand that I'll go through every aspect of your life, every friend, every acquaintance, as well as your financials, until I find the location of your hidey-hole."

She bit back a growl. "You'll never find it."

"We'll see."

The car took a sharp left and drove onto the freeway. "Where are we going?" she asked.

"The airport."

Her head jerked back. "What? Why?"

"I didn't say the safe house was in New York, now did I?"

Chapter Four

Chalton stepped from the car and held out a hand for Olivia. She completely ignored him and charged out by herself, stepping to the side and glaring at the private jet waiting on the tarmac.

"Kidnapping and transporting across state lines will land your butt in federal prison for a long time, jackwad." She pressed her hands to her curvy hips. "You could still stop this train of disaster before it ruins your life."

Those green eyes lasered into him, and his cock sprang to life. That spirit combined with obvious intelligence just turned him the hell on. "Thanks but no."

She hissed and looked around the quiet and remote hangar at the private part of the airport. "Where is everybody?"

"The pilots are in the plane and waiting. Other than that, we're the only ones close enough to hear if you start screaming. So don't." A part of him, one he didn't much like, wished she'd start fighting again just so he could put his hands on her. He wouldn't hurt her, but man, he'd like to kiss her for real. "Please embark."

Now she crossed her arms. "Screw you."

"Is that an invitation?" Ah, hell. He shouldn't have said that.

Color burst across her face, and she swung out her arms. "No. And if you think I'm meekly going to get on that plane bound for psycho-ville, you're fucking crazy." Her eyes sizzled, and even her lips turned an enticing rosy shade of red.

"God, you're beautiful," he murmured.

Somehow that made her even madder. "You are such a dick. Guys like you don't find girls like me beautiful." Spitting fire, she glared up at him.

He leaned into her, loving the way her eyes widened in awareness. "Guys like me?"

"Yes." She slapped both hands against his chest and shoved, snarling when he didn't move an inch. "Guys who spend hours in the gym, probably only eat protein, look like action movie stars, and probably date models who weigh three pounds."

He frowned. "What's wrong with protein?"

"Nothing," she shouted.

Somehow he'd made her so angry she'd stopped making any sense. "Your beauty isn't exactly a matter of opinion, darlin'. You're stunning."

"Stop playing with me," she almost growled.

"I haven't started playing with you, and when I do, you'll fucking know it," he shot back, rapidly losing a temper he never lost.

That apparently did it, because she levered back and kicked him square in the ankle. Pain ricocheted up his shin. Before he could respond, she pivoted and punched him right in the mouth.

"That's it." He ducked a shoulder into her stomach and lifted, easily tossing her over his shoulder.

She landed with a soft *oomph* and stilled. Then the air must've filled her lungs. "You goddamn sonuvabitch loser fuckwad hacker dickhead," she screamed, kicking out and punching his ribs with small fists.

The woman had quite a temper, now didn't she?

He turned and headed toward the plane. If she was his, he'd tuck his fingers in very inappropriate places to stop her tirade and hold her in place. As it was, he had to just wrap an arm around her legs to protect his front and allow the blows to the back to continue. "Man, you're feisty," he said.

Her response ran together so quickly he couldn't make out individual words, but he was fairly certain a death threat was in there somewhere.

He carried her right up the stairs to the plane, ducked, and dropped her ass on a leather sofa. Before she could strike out, he manacled her wrist and zip-tied it to the arm of the couch.

"What the hell?" She looked up, eyes round.

He sighed. "I can't have you jumping out, now can I?" Ignoring her furious struggles with the tie, he strode down the aisle to rap on the door and then lean in. Charlie, a feline shifter, was piloting along with a vampire copilot. "Take her to the drop, and wait for me there. Please radio for a second plane."

Charlie grinned at the swearing coming from the back. "Man, she can string words together."

Chalton nodded. "Wait until she really gets going." He shut the door and headed back toward the furious woman. "The plane ride won't be long, and the copilot will come out and cut your binding after reaching cruising altitude."

She stopped swearing and looked up at him, her eyes the green of fury. "You're not coming with me?"

His chest warmed. Even though she was pissed, did she want him with her? "I have something else to do here, but then I'll meet you. I promise."

Her glare turned even darker. "I hope you get hit by a bus."

All right, so she didn't want him with her. "I'll try." Indulging himself and knowing she'd probably bite him, he leaned down and pressed his mouth against hers. When she didn't bite, he moved, finally kissing her.

Fire lanced through him and landed in his gut. She kept still and then slowly, tentatively kissed him back. He kept the pressure light and gentle, when all he really wanted to do was push her back and go as deep as they both could take it.

Finally, he lifted his head. Her eyes had softened to the color of a spring meadow, and her lips pursed in a thoughtful O.

She leaned toward him, her gaze on his. "I'm probably going to kill you," she whispered, temper still in her tone.

He grinned. The woman had made him smile more in the last several hours than he had in many years. "Thanks for the fair warning. Here's one back. Every time you swear at me, every time you physically attack me, and definitely every time you try to kill me...I'm going to kiss you until you stop."

Her lip curled. "Then I'll just have to succeed with the kill."

Smart and spirited. "I look forward to it." Whistling, he turned on his heel and exited the plane.

A ruckus sounded from inside, and he turned just as Charlie leaned out to shut the door. "She kicked me," Charlie complained, rubbing his shin.

"She does that." Chalton chuckled and slid inside the car. It was time for a family reunion.

* * * *

Igor's smelled the same. Leather, pipe smoke, tobacco, and varnish. Different vodkas took up the shelves, and men sat around in booths or at the bar drinking. No dart boards, no pool tables, no video games. It was a bar, and bars were for drinking.

Chalton made his way to a booth at the back, not surprised to find his brother waiting. "You shot at me," he said mildly, pressing into the booth.

"I didn't hit you," Jared returned, pushing a shot of vodka from the home world his way. "I almost hit you in the leg just for fun, but I thought it might freak out the woman too much."

Chalton took the drink and downed it, enjoying the warmth spreading right to his gut. It had been over a hundred years since he'd drank with his brother, yet the moment felt like home. Was it home? He should've tried to mend fences before now, but he had struggled for so long to find himself again that he hadn't reached out. Then it became odd to reach out. "Who hired you?"

"Right to business, is it?" His brother's dark eyes glimmered in the dim light. He'd cut his long dark hair shorter so it just reached his nape, and he'd filled out even more in the century or so they'd been apart. "Your hair is long."

"Yours is shorter than normal." Even though they sat only a couple of feet from each other, the chasm felt much bigger. Grand Canyon big. Chalton reached for the bottle to pour two more shots, wanting so badly to return to normal. "No longer trying to be a pirate?"

Jared sighed. "The high seas aren't what they used to be, unfortunately."

Chalton shook his head. "I'm sure you've found many ways to rob people without a ship and dangerous weather." For years, his oldest brother had been a feared pirate on the open seas, even after the seas were somewhat tamed. Truth be told, Chalton had always liked that part of Jared. Admired it, even. "Now you're taking contracts for innocent women?"

"As are you," Jared returned, reaching for his glass. "Please tell me you're not playing the conscious here...we both know your former occupation."

"I was a soldier," Chalton said, defensiveness rising up in him.

"An assassin for the Realm," Jared said softly.

This time the liquid didn't burn quite as much. "I did my job, and I had a purpose."

Jared drank down the shot. "Being a pirate had a purpose, too. Damn, I miss those days."

Even without the long hair, Jared looked dangerous enough to be a pirate. Square jaw, broad shoulders, fighting shape. But beyond that, a wildness lived in him and always had. He'd never tried to force Chalton into his escapades, somehow understanding Chalton's need for something more than adventure.

"Those days will come back somehow and someday," Chalton said. Maybe with hovercraft or something goofy like that.

"I hope so."

"Was that Theo with you when you tried to shoot me?" Chalton asked. Had both of his brothers held him in a scope on the same day?

"Nope. Haven't talked to him since the last day I talked to you." Jared poured more vodka.

What a shitty day that was. They buried their father, had an immeasurable amount of alcohol, and had ended up battering each other bloody, saying things that never should've been said. Things none of them probably even meant. "So you haven't seen him in a century, either?"

"Nope." Jared glanced sideways. "You haven't talked to him?"

"No." Chalton scratched his neck. "I, ah, am sorry about the fight. It wasn't any of our faults that our father died."

Jared gazed at the smooth wooden table. "I should've been with him when he sought out Peter Libscombe."

"We both should've, but he didn't let us know." Instead, when their father went to challenge Peter Libscombe over a land dispute dealing with several mountain ranges, he'd taken his brother. "Uncle Jack should've called us."

"Maybe. Neither one of us would've asked for help, either." Jared kicked back in the booth. "Uncle Jack killed Peter Libscombe and survived that battle but died in the Kurjan war."

Chalton blinked. "Hell, that's true." His mother had let him know, but he'd been in the middle of planning Realm strategy during the war and hadn't reached out to his brothers...yet again. "That makes you the patriarch of the family." He chuckled, unable to help himself.

"Sounds all official and grown up, right?" Jared shook his head. "Mom's on me to find a mate and give her grandkids."

"Well, you are four centuries old." That was still young as far as Chalton was concerned.

"You're three." Jared played idly with his shot glass.

Yeah, and he had a job to do. "Were you hired to kill Olivia, Jared?"

"No." Jared poured more drinks. "I was hired to capture her and get her to give up her source for the story about vampires existing. The gun was because I knew somebody was following her but didn't know it was you or the humans in the van."

"Who hired you?"

"Private group out of Monaco. Wealthy group of vampires with a small power base. Don't align with the Realm but don't oppose your people, either. They just want the magazine articles stopped before humans start believing it."

Chalton nodded. All immortal species vowed to keep their existence a secret. If humans knew immortality was possible, they'd never stop trying to obtain it. War with humans would be disastrous because humans would lose. Vampires were male only, and since so many human females eventually became vampire mates, the risk in losing too many of them was unacceptable. Enhanced human females, those with extra gifts like psychic or empathic abilities, could mate a vampire, shifter, demon, or witch.

He cleared his throat. "I've locked the woman down and will discover and take care of her source."

Jared eyed him. "Oh, will you?"

"Yes."

"She's a looker, isn't she?"

Chalton leaned back. "She's stunning." He twirled his glass in his hands. "And enhanced."

Jared's eyebrows shot up. "Enhanced? You thinking of settling down?"

"No." But if he were, it'd be with a sexy, curvy, brilliant smartass of a woman. Like Olivia. "Not anytime soon."

"Me either." Jared tipped over the empty vodka bottle. "So you're not claiming the woman."

"No." Heat spiraled through Chalton, and his focus narrowed. "Are you?"

"No." Jared grinned. "We're at a standstill then."

Chalton's shoulders went back. "I don't see how. I have the woman."

"Where is she?"

Now he chuckled. "I'm not telling."

"Well, then. I guess I'll have to change your mind." Faster than ever, Jared shot out the first punch.

Chalton's cheek exploded in pain, and his head jerked back. Anticipation roared through him, and he plowed a fist into his brother's nose.

It was on.

Chapter Five

Two hours. Two whole hours. Olivia had sat in the chilly private airplane hangar, cuffed to a metal chair, for two hours. The pilots were in an office, doing a bunch of stuff with maps and ignoring her.

She'd kill them.

Once she got free, and she would, she'd end them. Somehow. Okay, she didn't know how, but she'd come up with a plan. Or run. Yeah, that was it. She'd just run and call the police. Much better plan.

A loud whir echoed, and the massive hangar door opened. A jet, this one a little smaller than the one that had flown her there, rolled in. The engines cut, the door opened, and Chalton jogged down the stairs.

She gasped. Cuts and bruises marred his skin, while rips showed throughout his bloody clothing. "What happened to you?"

"Family reunion." He reached her in long strides. "Charlie?" he called out.

The pilot with reddish-blond hair stepped out of the office and lobbed a small key toward Chalton. "Have fun."

Olivia should've kicked him a few more times. She hissed, and he quickly dodged back inside the office.

"Easy," Chalton said, unlocking her cuffs. "We're in a quiet part of the very private airport, and nobody else is around. I have a car right outside, and you can choose to walk or go over my shoulder again." Then he stepped back and crossed his arms.

She leaned to look around him at two men transferring items quickly from the plane to outside. Hey. That was her suitcase. "You brought my belongings."

"Yes. I had them collected while I dealt with my brother. He won't harass you again." Chalton fingered a bruise under his left eye.

She jumped to her feet. "Oh my God. You killed your brother."

Chalton blinked, studied her, and then threw back his head and laughed. Finally, he coughed. "I did not kill Jared. We got in a fight, I knocked him out, and then I came here. He has no clue where you are, so he'll back off now. So long as our missions are the same, which they are."

She planted both hands on her hips. "Meaning making my articles disappear."

"Yes." He towered over her without even meaning to do so. "Walk or ride, baby. Make a decision because night is falling, and I'd like to get cleaned up."

It was beyond tempting to kick him again and fight, but she wouldn't win. And everybody else around there worked for him and certainly wouldn't jump in on her behalf. Even so, pride mattered. She just couldn't help it. She leaped up, punched him in the gut, turned, and ran around him.

Well, she tried to run around him.

He halted her with one arm banded around her forearm. "Jesus, Livy." Jerking her around, he ducked, and once again she found herself face down over his shoulder.

How did he do that? It wasn't like she was a hundred pound yoga instructor. Yet the guy slid into motion, easily striding across the hangar for the outside like she wasn't flopping over his shoulder like a flounder. "Let me go," she ground out, trying not to shake out her aching fist. His stomach was harder than a boulder she'd tripped over at the lake last summer.

Cool air brushed across her legs as they exited the hangar, the world tilted, and she found herself in the front seat of a dark SUV. Chalton leaned over her, his handsome face within an inch of hers, snow dotting his hair. "Do I need to tie you to the seat?"

Heat and male...so damn much heat and male. Her gaze dropped to his lips, and swear to God, everything inside her turned mushy. How could this be happening? No way, no way, was she attracted to a kidnapper. "Stockholm syndrome," she murmured.

He smiled, those gorgeous lips moving. "Keep telling yourself that."

Her gaze slashed up to his to see those dark eyes sparkling with humor and so much more. Desire? Want? Heat? She drew herself up—finally. "I am not attracted to you."

"Liar." A very slight dimple winked in his left cheek. "You really do blurt out the first thing in your head, don't you?"

Unfortunately. "I'm a little off, so give me a break." Geez. It wasn't every day a girl got shot at, kidnapped, and kissed in a way that only happened in romance novels.

"Livy, you're not afraid of me, and you know it. Instincts and all that." Smoother than glass, he reached around and secured her seatbelt around her.

She crossed her arms. Truth be told, she wasn't feeling afraid of him. He had saved her, and if he'd wanted her dead, he wouldn't have transported her a couple hours away in a very nice jet. Even so, being kidnapped had to involve some danger, right? "You and I are not on the same side." It was all she could think of to say.

He leaned back, his lips still curved. "Maybe not today, but if I've learned anything in my long life, it's that alliances shift quicker than an eye blinks."

His long life. Right. "What are you? Maybe thirty...two?"

He laughed. "You have to be getting hungry. I'll feed you the second we get to the ranch." Without waiting for an answer, he shut the door and crossed to jump into the driver's seat. The Jeep ignited with a low hum, and they sped out of the deserted tarmac.

She glanced around for some type of weapon, her mind spinning. Soon fields lined the way...and then cornfields? "Are you kidding me? Where are we?"

"Iowa." His hands rested easily on the steering wheel, in perfect control. "We have a safe house here."

"Who are 'we'?"

He shrugged. "Doesn't matter."

The hell it didn't. Night began to fall, turning the leaves of the fields ominous and so dark. Freaky, *monsters are inside here*, dark. She shivered.

He glanced her way. "What?"

"Cornfields. Creepy. Big monsters."

"Quite the imagination you have there. I obviously have been neglecting this place too much since the stalks are still up, even without corn. Why don't you write fiction instead of pseudo-facts?"

She chose to ignore the *pseudo* part. "I like facts and telling a story. Informing people instead of just entertaining them." Although someday she would like to pen a novel—maybe a journalistic thriller or something like that. "You can't tell me the snowy cornfields at night aren't a little freaky."

"Not a bit." He rolled his neck.

Figured. The guy didn't seem scared of much.

A farmhouse in the middle of an Iowa corn farm? "Who in the world are you?" she muttered, staring uneasily out the window.

"Somebody trying to save your life," he said just as quietly.

"I don't need you to save my life." Once she'd published the last article, the truth would be out there, so she'd be perfectly safe. "Why don't you just tell me the truth? How much do you know about the species with thirty chromosomal pairs?"

"Doesn't exist."

Right. The thought was unimaginable, but what if? Plants had fewer chromosomal pairs, while humans had twenty-three. What would a species with thirty pairs be like? Would they be immortal? Her mind had been calculating possibilities since Helen had reached out with the information, and she figured the species would be airborne. Made sense. "We both know the people who hired you have something more to protect than just drug patents."

"Really?" He turned his full focus on her. "How do we know that?"

Heat climbed into her face, and she tried to banish it. The

guy looked deep into her, as if he knew. But no way could he know her odd ability—nobody knew about it. "Instinct."

"Right." He turned back to the quiet country road. "Now who isn't telling the truth?"

Her mouth dropped open, and she shut it quickly. He was just being sarcastic. No way could he know something about her she couldn't even explain. "I bet the species can fly." Made sense that they'd be a combination of God's creatures, and the ability to fly would be a step up from human abilities.

Chalton snorted. "Ridiculous."

She rounded on him. "How long do you plan to keep me in Iowa?" If she didn't escape, and she surely would, somebody would report her missing at some point.

He rubbed what looked like a granite-hard jaw. "I'm keeping you here until you give me the identity of your source and the location of all supporting documents. Then I just need you to sign a nondisclosure agreement, and I'll go on my way."

Something, and she wasn't sure what, sounded off in the statement. "What aren't you telling me?"

He sighed. "Nothing."

Lie. It was her gift, one she didn't understand. She could tell, almost always, when somebody was lying to her. And Chalton had been lying to her from the first second he'd opened his mouth. Such a sexy man shouldn't be a liar. "Are your orders to kill me?"

His head jerked back. "Of course not."

Truth. Interesting. "What if I don't sign the nondisclosure agreement?"

He growled low and didn't answer.

Yep. That's what she'd thought. "I guess it makes sense," she said thoughtfully.

"What?"

"That the extra-chromosomal species would kill to keep their secret. I mean, if humans knew about them, they'd be hunted and studied. We all want to be immortal." Yet she wasn't going to give up her story, because no doubt an advanced species would be able to cure human diseases. It was time they shared such knowledge. "Do you know any of them?" she asked.

He exhaled heavily and shook his head. "You are crazy, you know that?"

"I am not." For goodness sakes. She'd listened to Helen detail the science perfectly, she'd done her research, and then she'd read the proof in black and white. "I saw the studies and the results."

"Yet somehow the rest of the world hasn't?"

She nodded. "Yes. I saw copies of research from a couple of labs that no longer even exist. The labs themselves have been destroyed."

"Somebody is lying to you," he murmured. "This is about drugs and patents. Not a new species on earth."

Interesting. She couldn't detect a lie, but she wasn't getting a feeling of truth, either. So he might believe his story but have doubts, or he might be a phenomenal liar. Earlier she could tell, so now he might be shielding his lie better. Either way, intrigue kept her studying him. "You know what I think?"

"God, no."

She bit back a snarl. "I think you know the truth and that you work for this species that's immortal."

"I think you're nuts." He glanced her way. "Beautiful and spunky...but insane."

Warmth flushed through her followed by a welcomed temper. "If you take me back to the airport, or to a commercial airport, I won't turn you in to the FBI. I promise."

He grinned and swerved down a barely there driveway. "No."

Alone in the middle of nowhere with a sexy soldier hacker who might have kill orders on her? There had to be a way for her to get to safety. She studied the tall stalks flying by outside, snowy leaves glimmering in the moonlight. If she jumped out of the vehicle, she could surely hide in there, but what then?

"I wouldn't."

She jerked back toward him. "Excuse me?"

"The cornfields are dangerous at night. Creatures and all of that." Amusement deepened his voice.

"Jerk," she said, eying his fit form. "Why don't you have a gun?"

Tension emanated from him, filling the Jeep. "Don't like them and don't need them."

She narrowed her gaze. "Interesting. Was there a time you did use guns?"

"Yes, and that's all I'm saying about guns." He leaned forward to squint out of the front windshield at the moon. "We'll be at the farmhouse in about five minutes."

Good. Then she'd come up with a plan to get home. Hopefully Helen hadn't been scared off and would arrange to meet with the final proof again.

Chalton stilled.

Her heart rate rose out of instinct. "What?" she whispered.

He drew in air, his head not moving, his eyes roaming. "Shhh."

She pushed back in her seat, looking outside. Nothing out of the ordinary.

Chalton drew a phone from his back pocket, hit a button, and held it to his ear. "Dage? I think I might have a problem."

Dage? Who was Dage? And what problem? Olivia swallowed, her breath heated. What was out there?

Suddenly, lights rammed into focus behind them.

"Shit." Chalton muttered. "How far is backup?" he said to the mysterious Dage. Then, "Not good. Get the word out as soon as possible."

Olivia grabbed the dash and half-turned to see a lifted truck rapidly gaining on them. "Who is that?"

"Don't know." Chalton pressed the gas pedal, and the Jeep lurched forward.

A truck suddenly blocked the way ahead, and he slammed on the brakes. The vehicle skidded and then stopped. With a snap of his wrist, he flipped off the headlights.

Three men strode out of the cornfield to stand in front of the truck.

The vehicle behind the Jeep stopped, with the lights still glaring through the back window.

A lump settled in Olivia's stomach, and her hands shook. "Friends of yours?" She squinted through the front, trying to see better. The men looked...odd. Even in the soft moonlight, they looked incredibly tall and pale. Two had really dark hair with what appeared to be red tips, and the other man had red hair with dark tips. Some type of cult?

"Stay here." Chalton jumped from the Jeep and slammed the door. "You're trespassing, assholes."

The guy in the middle moved forward just a foot, spraying slush. "We don't want a problem with the Realm. Just give us the journalist, and we'll go."

"You take her and you have a definite problem with the Realm," Chalton said evenly, his stance widening.

What the heck was the Realm? Olivia moved to open the door, but Chalton shook his head, still facing the men. She stilled. Should she get out of the Jeep and help him? Or maybe she should let him deal with the men using the threat of the Realm, whatever that meant.

"Who's her source for the articles?" the tall guy asked.

"We've taken care of the source," Chalton responded. "Now leave. You can't afford another war right now, and you know it."

War? What war?

"We had her first, and we're taking her to headquarters," the guy said as his buddies fanned out.

Had her first? Did these guys work with the ones in the van?

"Thought you stopped hiring jobs out," Chalton said.

"It was daylight. No choice," the guy said. "Now hand her over."

So the guys in the van worked for these guys? Why couldn't they go out in daylight? Olivia quickly released her seatbelt.

"I've called for backup," Chalton said. "Leave now."

"No." With a battle cry that echoed over the cornfields, the lead guy charged Chalton.

Chapter Six

Chalton pivoted and tossed the Kurjan over the Jeep. The soldier's elbows hit as he bounced to the other side. Holy hell. It was three to one, and that wasn't counting the force in the truck behind the Jeep.

How had the Kurjans tracked him to his safe house? He held his hands out to the men now angling toward each side of him. They'd worn dark clothing instead of uniforms, no doubt wanting to blend in as much as a Kurjan could. "Listen, guys. We want the story quashed as badly as you do, and I'll make sure it happens. Time to leave." If they didn't listen to reason, he was screwed. Backup was at least an hour away.

"No." The guy to the left drew out a green gun.

A laser-shooting gun that could take down an immortal. "That's not necessary." Chalton shifted his feet so he could attack.

"Sure, it is." The soldier pointed it at Chalton's head. "Olivia Roberts? Get out of the vehicle."

The door opened behind Chalton, and he could hear Olivia dropping out of the Jeep. She maneuvered up by his side, her heels sinking into the snow with soft plops. "If you don't mind, I think I'll remain with Chalton."

The soldier brandishing the weapon straightened. "Chalton? Reese?"

Damn it. Chalton partially moved in front of Olivia. A bullet from the green gun could easily kill her. "Nope. Not me."

The soldier he'd thrown over the Jeep crossed around the

other side, blood covering half of his face. "This changes everything. I say we kill him."

"We're at peace, dumbass," Chalton drawled, his mind skidding into attack mode. If they killed him, they'd take Olivia, and she wouldn't last minutes before they figured out she was enhanced. The Kurjans had no problem forcing enhanced human females to mate with them. They were male only, just like vampires. "So time to go."

The leader smiled, revealing sharp canines that glowed yellow in the night. "We're not at peace, not really. We're just all regrouping. So you dying won't have much of an effect."

"Yes. Let's kill him." The guy with the gun took aim.

Olivia shoved in front of him, her hands waving. "No, no, no. Okay. Let's stop this." Then she stopped moving. "What's wrong with your teeth?"

Chalton grabbed her arm and pushed her behind him again.

She peered around his side. "Are your eyes...purple?" Her voice rose on the last. "Oh my goodness. Can you fly?"

The Kurjan frowned. "No." Then he pulled the trigger.

The laser impacted Chalton in the right shoulder, quickly forming a bullet and lodging in his flesh. He stumbled back and Olivia braced him with both hands. Pain exploded throughout his chest. "Get in the Jeep and drive through the cornfield," he grunted, keeping her covered.

"No," she whispered back, sliding out from behind him. "Don't kill him, and I'll come with you."

The Kurjan chuckled. "How about I kill him and you come with me?"

Stalk leaves rustled next to him, and a large body stepped out from the darkness. "I don't think so, asshole." Green lasers fired quickly, impacting both soldiers in front of Chalton.

"Theo?" Chalton said, shaking his head. What was his younger brother doing there?

The Kurjan to his left moved. Chalton drew the knife from his boot, dropped and rolled, slicing both Achilles tendons. The Kurjan screamed, fangs dropping, and fell to the ground.

Chalton levered up and punched the soldier several times in the face, hard as possible, until the guy passed out.

Grunting, Chalton shoved to his feet and turned, surveying the area. "There are—"

More bullets pierced his back, and he fell forward, rolling and trying to stand back up. Theo calmly aimed over him, impacting another Kurjan in the face, firing until the guy went down. "Came from the truck behind you." Theo craned his neck. "Looks like he was alone."

The bullets firmed inside Chalton, and he tried to remain standing and keep control. But pain ripped through him, and he growled, his fangs dropping low.

Olivia's eyes widened and she screamed, backing away against the Jeep.

Tingles detonated behind Chalton's eyes, and he could feel them change from black to a sizzling gold.

Olivia gasped and pressed her hand to her chest.

He smiled, blood gurgling out of his mouth. "Guess you were right. We do exist." Then he pitched face first toward the freezing snow, darkness slamming through him.

* * * *

Fear tasted like copper in her mouth. Olivia leaned against the Jeep, her chest heaving, her brain misfiring. Fangs. Chalton had actual fangs, as had the pale-faced guy. Her knees shook, and she tried to lock them in place.

On the ground, Chalton breathed heavily, out cold.

Run. She had to run.

Theo sighed. He had Chalton's size and dark eyes, but his hair was a shaggy brown around his collar. "There's nowhere to go," Theo murmured, tucking his gun in the back of his waistband.

Not true. If she could make it to the truck behind the Jeep, she could steal it.

"Listen, Olivia." Theo strode forward and grasped Chalton beneath the armpits. "The guys on the ground are Kurjans, and they'll torture you in ways you can't even imagine if they capture you. More backup is surely on the way, and if you take their truck, they will get you. Come with me and you'll be safe." He ducked and tugged Chalton up and over his shoulder in a fireman's carry, grunting with the effort.

She swallowed. "Ku-Kurjans?" The fangs could only mean one thing.

"Yep. Enemy of most vampires." Theo turned to stride toward a slight opening in the snowy cornfield. "I can't carry my brother and force you to come with me, so it's your choice. Kurjans or vampires? Up to you."

Vampires. Freakin vampires. And brother? So this was the younger brother. "Chalton is a vampire, and he's your brother," she said slowly, her brain just not working right. Shock? Yep. That was it. She was totally in shock.

"Yes. We're vampires, we won't hurt you, and we can't make you one of us. Everything you think you know is just silly legend. Pretty much." He crossed into the field. "Come or not," he called back.

She glanced frantically around. The Kurjan Chalton had punched was beginning to stir. Was backup really coming? How could there be real vampires? Advanced species, sure. But legends were correct?

The guy on the ground groaned.

Her feet launched into motion before her brain could even make a decision, running after Theo. She had to get away from the Kurjans, and now, more than ever, she had to know more about the species. Vampires. The only way to follow the story and stay safe, for the time being, was to run after Chalton.

Leaves slapped her, but she caught up to Theo. "So he won't die from the bullets?"

"No. He's strong enough to push them out of his body within an hour, probably." Theo didn't turn around.

A relief she probably shouldn't be feeling washed through her.

Her heels sank into moist earth, and small rocks tried to trip her up, but she scrambled after Theo, her heart thundering. How could it be true? Vampires. Real vampires. She'd been kissed by one.

Theo's face was longer and a bit leaner...but no less handsome than Chalton's. He moved with predatory grace as well. Maybe it was a genetic thing.

The smell of dirt and plants filtered around her, and the wind whistled somewhere in the distance. Strong moonlight allowed her to see the path, and when Theo took a sharp turn, she followed, stopping with a gasp at seeing a dark helicopter waiting quietly.

Theo turned and grinned. "I was going to make a bunch of crop circles to mess with Chalton but didn't have time." He shifted his weight, slightly jostling his brother. "Would you please look through your purse and pockets for a tracker? The Kurjans found you somehow."

She blinked and rummaged through her purse. "There's no way they could've gotten a track—" Her fingers brushed a smooth metal disk the size of a small battery, and she drew it out. "Well, hell." One of the guys in the van must've shoved it in there. Smart bastards.

"Throw it," Theo said.

She nodded and chucked it over several bare stalks. Life had gotten way too weird.

Theo reached forward and opened the back of the helicopter. "Get in."

She inched across uneven ground. Was this a good idea? Probably not. But waiting for more of the pale monsters seemed like a worse idea. So she lumbered inside and scooted to the far end on the plush leather seat.

Theo hefted Chalton in, allowing his head to drop onto Olivia's lap.

She gasped and then settled back. Chalton had to weigh over two hundred pounds of solid muscle, and yet his brother had just carried him without losing breath. Vampires must be wicked strong.

The door banged shut, and within a minute, Theo was in the pilot's seat starting the engines.

Quiet. The interior remained quiet. She frowned. "I've toured many areas in different helicopters, and we've always had to use headsets to talk. Why, or rather how, is it so quiet in here?"

"Technology. We have our own," Theo responded, lifting

back on what looked like a small steering wheel.

Exactly. That was why she had to expose the species...to gain that technology and save Ronni. "I bet your scientific knowledge is impressive," she muttered.

The copter rose smoothly into the air. "We like to think so."

"Um, where are we going?" she asked.

He didn't even bother to shrug.

Chalton stirred, and his eyelids flipped open. "Olivia." Said as a statement, not even a hint of a question.

"You're a vampire," she said, looking down at his angled face.

He lifted an eyebrow. "Humph." Wincing, he reached for the hem of his shirt and began to tug the material up.

"What are you doing?" she asked.

"Need room," he grunted.

Geez. She reached down and helped him, drawing the bloody material over his head.

He settled back down with a satisfied sigh. "Thanks."

Moonlight cascaded in from the front, and instruments glowed around, illuminating the space well enough for her to see several bullet holes in his torso. His ripped, predatory, hard as a rock chest. As she watched, a bullet spit out near his right rib cage to clatter to the ground. The hole slowly closed.

"Holy crap," she whispered.

He turned his head to the front. "Theo? We have a problem."

Theo glanced over his shoulder. "One beyond the Kurjans?"

"Yes. What the hell are you doing here?" Chalton remained in place, his head rather heavy on Olivia's thighs.

Theo turned the wheel a bit. "I was hired to find Olivia and put an end to the articles she's writing about a species that has extra chromosomal pairs. Figured the Realm would have you on it since you're the computer hacker, so I, ah, traced your movements and was planning to take the woman at your vacation home in the middle of corn."

So it was actually Chalton's place? Weird. A vampire growing corn. Olivia frowned. "Wait a minute. Add in Jared, and that's quite a coincidence, right?"

"No," Chalton said grimly, shoving up to sit next to her. "That can't be."

"What are you talking about?" Theo asked.

"Jared was also hired to get her," Chalton said.

Theo looked over his shoulder, his face hardening. "Well, hell. All three of us on the same case? You're right. No coincidence."

"Call Jared and have him meet us at Benny's," Chalton said. "Nobody can trace the place to us, and we'll have time to figure out who wants us all on the same case in the same place. What common enemy do we have?"

"Just Peter Libscombe's kids, Petey and Saul," Theo said.

Tension wound through the luxurious craft, heavy and dark. Olivia shivered.

Theo reached forward and typed something with one hand into an odd machine in the dash. "Sent the message, and I let him know we're being set up."

"Who is Peter Libscombe?" Olivia asked.

"Enemy as long as we can remember. Peter killed our father; our uncle killed him and then died in battle recently. Peter had two sons, although I didn't think they'd want to continue to fight," Chalton muttered as another bullet pinged out of his sternum.

Theo shook his head. "Saul is in South America on a peace mission. He'd never try to harm anybody. But Petey…"

Chalton nodded. "Petey is a chip off his old man's crazy block. Was a missionary for hire during the war because he just liked killing. But I didn't think he'd try to take all of us on."

Theo rubbed the back of his neck. "I've had a watch on both of them, and Petey disappeared about five years ago. I thought he'd probably died in the war, but now I'm thinking he's been laying low and planning."

"Agreed," Chalton said. "He's two hundred years old and loves killing. Avenging his father would be fun for him and not honorable. Just fun."

Olivia shivered. "Are Petey and Saul vampires?"

"No. Shifters," Chalton said.

"Shifters?" she yelped. "Shifters exist? I mean, people who shift into animals? Like birds?"

Chalton leaned his head back, shutting his eyes. "Shifters exist and can become canine, feline, or multis, which turn into anything of same size. Except multis don't seem to exist any longer and have evolved into different species of bears."

Holy crap on a double cracker. "Can you guys cure organ failure?" She held her breath.

"Why?" Chalton opened his eyes and focused on her.

She shrugged. "Just asking."

"Is that your motivation for these crazy articles? Your friend, Ronni?" he asked quietly.

Her head jerked back. "How do you know about Ronni?"

"I know everything about you. It's my job," he said simply. "As much as I'd like to help you and your friend, we are unable to cure human diseases."

How was that even possible? "I don't believe you."

"It's true." He rubbed the now closed bullet wound. "We haven't been much interested in science until recently, when we had to begin researching and ultimately curing a virus that harms us. We haven't meddled with human issues."

Issues. "You must have some knowledge that we don't. Or at the very least, equipment we lack. Look at this helicopter. And your phone. And your bullets." How dumb did he think she was?

He nodded. "The schematics for any equipment the queen felt would help humans has already been leaked."

"The queen?" she asked.

"Yes. Our queen was a human geneticist before mating the king, a vampire. Now she's immortal." Chalton wiped blood off his flat stomach.

"He changed her into a vampire?" Olivia whispered, her heart dropping.

Chalton grinned. "No. You can't be changed into a vampire. You could mate a vampire, and thus your chromosomal pairs would increase to immortality, but you wouldn't become a vampire."

Theo snorted. "Can you imagine? Now that's crazy."

"Definitely. Most legends are weird, especially the *have to suck blood* ones. We only take blood in cases of sex or war," Chalton continued.

Sex? She cleared her throat. "But I saw you...in the sun."

"Yeah. False urban legend," Charlton said. "Although, the Kurjans can't go into the sun, so maybe the legend is kind of a cross between vampires and Kurjans." He cleared his throat. "Theo, you're full of shit. No way did you go to all this trouble, waiting for me in Iowa, on the off chance I'd been assigned to find Olivia, so tell me the truth."

Theo turned the craft to the left. "Don't get mad."

"You asshole," Chalton said without much heat.

Olivia glanced at him and lifted her eyebrows.

He rolled his eyes. "How? I have firewalls that I even invented."

Theo grinned over his shoulder. "They were really good, too."

Ah. Olivia bit back a smile. "He hacked your computers."

Chalton shook his head. "Yeah, but you don't realize what a big deal that is."

"How so?"

Theo snorted. "Chalton is the best of the best. And I hacked him." Pure brotherly pride echoed in his voice.

Chalton jabbed two fingers in a hole near his sternum and yanked out a bullet to throw at his brother's head. "I'm glad you've kept up your computer skills. Come work with the Realm."

Theo hunched forward. "Only if Jared does. We're all in or we should be all out."

"Aren't you loyal, considering since you haven't spoken to Jared in a century?" Chalton muttered.

"Eh." Theo lifted a large shoulder. "A century isn't that long, considering we live forever. We've all been busy. I figured we'd all end up working together again at some point. So we should all be in...or all out. Don't you think?"

Chalton frowned. "It's not that simple."

"Yes, it really is." Theo clicked some levers on the dash. "Let's fight about that once we figure out who's trying to draw the three of us out at once."

"Good plan," Chalton said, leaning his head back and reaching for Olivia.

She blinked as he wrapped his huge hand around hers. Warmth and an odd feeling of safety filtered through her. She didn't know him, she sure as heck didn't understand him, but somehow, that simple touch calmed her as nothing else could have.

Of course, that just gave her one more thing to worry about. How would a vampire react to blackmail? She, unfortunately, was probably going to find out.

Chapter Seven

After Theo had landed the helicopter on the roof, Chalton led a subdued Olivia down the stairwell to the penthouse suite of one of the legendary apartment buildings in New York. How many laws had he broken by letting her know that vampires, Kurjans, and shifters existed? Probably enough to get them both killed.

Treason had become an unfortunate byproduct of his current mission. "That's why I stick to the control room," he muttered.

"What?" she asked, stumbling into him.

"Nothing." He also didn't like the silence coming from his younger brother, who took up the rear. It was almost as if Chalton could feel the guy thinking things through. Man, he'd missed his brother. Why hadn't he reached out before now? Fighting a war seemed like a lame excuse. He had to make things right.

They reached the vestibule, and Chalton punched in a code near the door.

"Where are we?" Olivia whispered as they entered the grand foyer of an opulent penthouse.

"Our great-uncle Benny's New York home," Chalton said, drawing her inside.

She glanced down at the sparkling fifties-style marble. "You have the code?"

"Sure." Chalton pressed a button near the door, and heavy drapes swung open across the living room to reveal the New York skyline. "He's in Europe this time of year, so his place is open for anybody needing to camp out." Chalton waited until Theo had entered and shut the door, leaning back against it, after assisting her out of her jacket. "Talk," he ordered.

Theo flushed. "Well, none of this makes sense."

"Who hired you?" Chalton released Olivia's hand, and she moved past him and headed straight for the floor to ceiling windows and incredible snow-filled view. "Time to talk, Theo."

He nodded. "That's just it. I was hired by, well, mom."

Chalton stilled, the hair on the back of his neck rising. "Excuse me?"

Theo shrugged. "Mom is involved in a group investing heavily in different enterprises, and some of those are pharmaceutical facilities the Realm has used to research and manufacture the virus that formerly impacted vampire mates. Their stock has risen, mainly because of byproduct research, so mom's making a killing."

Chalton rocked back on his heels. "So she and her group hired you to track down Olivia? And do what? Kill her?"

Theo snorted. "Of course not. I'm supposed to bribe her to let the story go."

Chalton frowned, his mind spinning. "Was it mom's idea for you to go after Olivia?"

Theo frowned, his eyes sizzling. "No. Well, I don't think so. It seems like she mentioned one of her partners suggesting we tamp down on the articles talking about possible immortals."

Chalton nodded. "Okay. Go get mom, and get all the information you can. In fact, bring her here, just in case she's in danger from whomever is trying to get us all involved in this. Find out who told her to hire you." He reached for his phone and called Jared, having kept tabs of his brother's location and contact information through the years. "Where are you?" he asked when his brother snapped a greeting.

"On my way to have a little discussion with the group that hired me. Somebody is setting us up, and I'm starting with them."

Chalton nodded. "Good plan. Theo is getting mom and bringing her to Benny's. Apparently somebody got to her, too…and that's how he was hired."

"Fuck. I'll call you when I get answers." Jared clicked off.

Chalton shoved his phone in his pocket. "He gets more charming every year."

"Look who's talking." Theo opened the door. "I'll be back with mom. Bye, Olivia." He swept outside, and the door automatically locked behind him.

Olivia turned around, nicely framed by sparkling lights across the city. "Your family is very interesting." She glanced at the door behind him, at his bare chest, and then at a spot over his shoulder. "So."

"So." Amusement dashed through him as his body finished repairing itself. His injuries weren't bad enough for him to need somebody else's blood, but he'd truly love to bite her anyway. So far, he'd treated her with kid gloves, and now they had to come off. "I know it's been a long day, and you've had more than one shock to your system, so as soon as you give me the name of your source and the location for your research materials, you should catch some sleep while you can."

"No." Her eyes, tired as they looked, still spit sparks at him.

"No?" he asked, pushing away from the door.

She held her ground, her gaze turning very alert. "I will, however, make a deal with you."

"Is that so?" He reached her in several long strides, stopping just close enough to force her to tilt her head to meet his gaze. Intimidation was a necessary evil, and although he hated to frighten her, other enemies would do much worse. "Give me the terms of this deal."

She crossed her arms beneath her ample breasts. "Back away."

"No." His dick went hard as rock, and tension began to filter around them.

Pink climbed into her cheeks, and she licked her lips.

He bit back a groan. Why did she have to be so delectable? "What's the deal, Olivia?"

She cleared her throat, and a vein pulsed wildly in her delicate neck. "I've been thinking about the situation, and I guess I understand why you'd want to keep your existence private."

"Good."

She relaxed her arms and pushed back her hair. "I'll stop writing the articles so long as you fix my friend, Ronni."

Ah, what a sweetheart. "Who's your source?"

"My source stays protected." Her chin firmed into a stubborn, albeit very cute, rock.

"No." Regret tore through him, but he couldn't allow for emotion quite yet. "I have to know the identity of your source to figure out how they gleaned the information." While Olivia may not understand the issue, the breach in protocol merely ended with her. It had to have started somewhere else.

"Sorry. Source stays protected."

He rubbed his chin and studied her. "I want to be reasonable, but I have my orders, Livy. Give me the source, and I'll do my best to make sure he's protected throughout this."

Her nostrils flared. "You're lying."

He lifted his chin. Yeah. There was a good chance that her source was an immortal enemy that had wanted to draw out the Reese brothers, and as such, he would be beheaded for leaking such information. "How do you know?"

She shuffled her feet and broke eye contact. "Good instincts."

"Are you empathic?" he murmured.

She jerked. "No. I don't think so."

Interesting. "But you can tell a falsehood?" He'd never heard of an enhanced female being able to do so, but it could be an offshoot of empathic abilities, so it did make some sense.

"I just have good instincts."

Ah, the lies humans told themselves to avoid anything they couldn't rationalize with logic. He stepped right into her space.

"What are you doing?" she gasped, her chest rising.

He slid curly dark hair off her shoulder. "I'm facing a bit of a dilemma."

Her head lifted, although her gaze only reached his lips and stayed there. "How so?" Her voice lowered to a breathiness that licked along his cock.

"I need a shower to wipe off the blood and grime, so my choices are to bind you or have you join me." It was crazy, but he'd give his left arm for her to join him in the shower.

She half-coughed and half-laughed. "Are you hitting on me?"

His hand curled around her nape. "Yes."

Her gaze lifted to his, and her pupils widened. "That's insane," she whispered.

"I know." Hell, the woman was right. "But here's the deal. My brothers won't return for several hours, and then we'll have to move again. I want you, and you want me, so let's take the edge off so we can think." His mind hadn't been clear since he'd first sighted her two days ago, and he needed clarity. One good night, and he could get her out of his system. "What do you say?"

"I say you're crazy." She stepped back against the window. "If all I wanted was an orgasm to take the edge off, I sure as heck don't need you for that."

Humor bubbled up, and he full-on laughed. The woman was one of a kind. "Well then." His hands slowly went to unbuckle his belt, and he drew the heavy leather through the loopholes, quite enjoying the way her breath caught and her eyes widened. "Plan B it is, then."

* * * *

Every dark fantasy she'd had in her wild mind flashed through her brain. "Wh-what are you doing?" she asked, her lungs feeling way too full all of a sudden.

He grinned and continued releasing the belt.

Yeah, she was more tempted than she would like to jump his bones and just go for it. The guy was a vampire—a real, honest to goodness, vampire. Somebody with advanced genes could probably go all night, right? Probably all night and all of the next day.

She liked sex. Sure, it had been a long time since she'd tried it, and it had never been crazy fireworks time, but she'd liked being close to a man. Her last boyfriend, an accountant named Chuck, had taken a while to get going but had then been all right closer to the finish line.

Something told her Chalton didn't need any time to get going, and he'd probably be much better than all right.

Yet, she wasn't giving up Helen, her source, and so far, Chalton hadn't promised to save Ronni. Sleeping with him would be a colossal mistake, and she'd lose leverage. "What's up with the belt?" she asked again, eying the thick leather. A slow shiver wound through her body.

His grin widened. Shoot. He'd seen the shiver.

"Livy." His voice deepened to nearly guttural.

Desire unfurled in her abdomen. Then reality slammed her in the face. "Are you glamoring me?" she asked, anger rippling along her skin.

His eyebrows drew down. "Glamoring?"

"Yeah. What vampires do." She put her hands on her hips. "Making me want you."

He chuckled again. "Oh, you want me, and it's all you. There's no such thing as glamoring."

Truth. She opened her senses, and he was definitely telling the truth. "Oh." Then she focused on the belt, and her knees bunched to run around him.

Quick as a whip, he grasped her wrist. "That's a pretty blush you have there, gorgeous. What exactly are you imagining me doing with this belt?"

She stopped breathing, and her face heated to the point of pain. No way was she into all the "tie 'em up and spank 'em" rage going on right now. Yet there was something undeniably sexy about that leather in his strong, and no doubt capable, hands. "We, ah, are not on the same side here."

"We could be," he murmured. "If you keep publishing information about us, you're going to harm a lot of people. I know you don't want to hurt anybody."

No, she didn't. "All you have to do is save Ronni, and I won't publish another word. I promise."

He sighed. "We can't save human hearts, sweetheart. Hell, we can't even cure the common cold or cancer. We don't have the knowledge, either."

"There has to be something you can do."

He studied her, those dark eyes seeming to see everything. "There is one thing, but it's asking for a lot."

Her chin lifted. "What is it?"

"She's an enhanced female human, so somebody could mate her, and her chromosomal pairs would increase to near immortality, so her heart would repair itself."

"Enhanced?" Olivia asked.

"Yes. I searched her apartment when she was sleeping to see if your research was hidden there, and she definitely gives out vibrations. Strong ones. I'm guessing that's what drew you as friends, and I'm thinking she's probably psychic."

"I don't understand."

"Many human females are most likely distant cousins to the witch nation, and they have gifts beyond the norm like visions, empathic abilities, or many others, and they can mate an immortal."

"Mate?" Olivia's voice wavered on the end.

"Yes. It's forever, probably. So like I said, it's a lot to ask." He ran the leather through his hands. "Since this is my mission, I'd be on board. So if that's your final offer, it looks like it'd be me."

No! The reaction careened inside her and planted in her heart. "I assume mating means what it, well, means?"

"Yes. Sex and a good bite...and forever."

She blinked. "You said *probably* forever."

He nodded. "There was a virus that attacked vampire mates, hence all the research you found, but we cured it. The queen modified the virus, so technically the mating bond of immortals can be reversed."

"Technically?"

He shrugged. "The reversal has only worked on mates who've been widowed for centuries and not from currently living mates."

"Has anyone still living and mated tried?"

"No."

This was all so unbelievable. "Isn't there somebody else who could mate Ronni?" Not that Ronni would probably agree, anyway.

"My mission, my duty." He lifted a shoulder the size of a small mountain. "It's how it works."

Olivia kicked an imaginary pebble. "I want to save my friend, but I don't want to force you into a forever relationship with somebody you've never met." With somebody that wasn't Olivia. Geez. She had it bad for the guy.

"A lot of matings are arranged, so it's not unheard of in my culture." His gaze pierced hers and deep. "I do have one condition."

Tingles exploded throughout her abdomen. "Which is?" she croaked.

"One night with you."

Her entire body stopped moving, and her heart probably stilled for just a second. "You want to sleep with me as a condition?"

"There won't be any sleeping."

She slowly shook her head. "You're trying to blackmail me for sex?"

"It's extortion, not blackmail. And you tried to extort me first."

This was all just way too insane. "I can't sleep with you and then have you sleep with my best friend for life."

"Like I said, there won't be any sleeping. Look at it like different lifetimes…Ronni won't be here any longer if I mate her, and your friendship will be over."

Olivia blinked. "Why won't she be here?"

"My mate?" Both of his eyebrows rose. "She'll be somewhere safe at headquarters whether she likes it or not."

The possessive tone did very unnerving things throughout Olivia's body, the least of all creating a little jealousy. "I can't ask you to mate forever, even to save my friend. Besides, there has to be a cure out there. Your people must have incredible resources, and I'm sure they could find one to save a heart."

"Perhaps." Chalton rubbed his chin. "But I doubt it. The queen works brutal hours trying to cure diseases, and so far she hasn't succeeded with human ones." He dodged forward and tossed Olivia over his shoulder again.

"What are you doing?" she squawked, once again looking down at his fine ass.

"Done talking." Turning, he began to move through the living room.

Well that didn't sound good.

Chapter Eight

Chalton strode for the bedroom, a wiggly woman over his shoulder and fire in his heart. It would be his duty to mate Ronni, but every cell in his body protested vehemently.

He'd never believed in fate, and he sure as hell didn't believe in soul mates.

Yet having Olivia in the same space as him felt right. When she laughed, he could actually feel the humor, and when she seemed sad, every urge he owned pushed him to make it right.

Was she his?

If so, how could he mate her best friend? How could he mate anybody? Maybe he couldn't. There had to be something…more. In order to mate, there had to be that something that mated vampires couldn't even explain.

He didn't have the words, either…but he felt it for the woman now struggling to get off his shoulder. "Knock it off." He jostled her just enough to illustrate her precarious position.

She stilled.

He'd never drop her, but the threat was there, now wasn't it? She didn't know him well enough to understand he'd break every bone in his body before allowing her to get even a bruise. Good thing, too. The woman would certainly use that to her advantage.

He strode through the long entrance to the bedroom and dropped her onto the larger than life four-poster bed. She bounced and quickly scooted up to the headboard, her eyes wide.

And interested.

He sighed. "I also should tell you that the mating with Ronni might not work."

"Why not?"

"Because I'm interested in somebody else, and none of us really understand how or why we mate who we do. Some believe in fate."

Her hands curled into the thick bedspread. "Who are you interested in?" The tone came out accusatory and a little hurt.

He frowned. "You."

She blinked and her lips formed a slight O. "We just met."

"That doesn't seem to matter to vampires," he said wryly.

"I'm not easy," she spat out, seeming to be arguing with both of them.

He threw back his head and laughed. "Livy? I know everything about you, including past lovers. Believe me, your number is ridiculously small for somebody so gorgeous."

Her shoulders went back. "Oh yeah? What's your number?"

He lost his smile and fought the urge to shuffle his feet. "You don't want to know."

"Yeah, I do."

"Too bad. I've lived more than three hundred years, darlin', and I've had many careers...not once as a monk." Though every woman he'd ever met paled to nothing compared to the spitfire glaring at him.

His cell phone dinged, and he answered it. "Chalton."

"What the hell is going on?" Dage Kayrs growled clearly over the line.

Chalton kept Livy in his sight. "I'm not sure. This may be an attack on my family through Olivia. We're investigating. Also, the Kurjans are involved."

"Can't blame them," Dage ground out. "The first two articles more than hint at our world. Is the woman cooperating?"

"No." Chalton eyed her.

"Make her."

"Right."

Dage sighed. "Shall I talk to her?"

Temper, rare and hot, roared through Chalton. "You want

to? Sure. Give me a second." He turned and typed in several commands on his phone, illuminating the massive flat-screen television across from the bed. Dage slowly took shape.

"King Dage Kayrs, please meet journalist Olivia Roberts," Chalton said dryly.

Olivia kept her arms crossed. "So you're the vampire king."

Dage's dark hair was ruffled, and his silver eyes pissed, but he looked every inch the badass soldier he'd always been, even in a dark shirt with pressed black pants. "Rumor has it. Why won't you give us your research and source's name?"

"Because I want to protect my source and blackmail you into saving my friend," Olivia said calmly while facing one of the most dangerous beings on the entire planet.

Chalton bit back a grin as Dage stopped moving and focused carefully. "I see."

Chalton edged a little closer to Olivia in case he needed to intervene. "You've read the reports and know about Ronni Alexander," she said.

"Yes. Heart disease. We can't fix that," Dage said evenly, his gaze not leaving Olivia's.

"I could mate her," Chalton responded.

"Oh, hell no," came an explosion from off camera before Dage's mate, Emma Kayrs, shoved her way into view. "You are mating for love and no other reason."

The queen had piled her dark hair atop her head and wore her customary white lab coat over T-shirt and jeans. Her belly had slightly protruded as her second trimester had begun.

"How are you feeling, Emma?" Chalton asked softly.

"Huge, but I'm not throwing up any longer," Emma said cheerfully, her curious gaze seeking out Olivia. "There will be no arranged mating."

Olivia scooted to the edge of the bed. "You're the queen? The scientist?"

"That's me." Emma leaned into Dage's side as if she belonged just there, which she did.

The king instantly softened somehow, putting an arm around his mate.

"Good. With all of your resources, you must be able to

prevent heart failure," Olivia pressed, her concern riding the airwaves around her.

Emma frowned. "No, I'm sorry. I've been trying to mutate some of our research to cure cancer, but I haven't even been able to do that yet. The human body and diseases are so much stronger than current research." She sighed. "I'm very sorry."

Olivia sat back, her shoulders slumping. "She's telling the truth."

Emma's gaze sharpened. "Are you enhanced?"

"Apparently," Olivia muttered.

Emma glanced from Olivia to Chalton and then back again. "Well, isn't this interesting?"

Amusement glimmered in Dage's silver eyes. "Yes."

Emma pressed both hands to her hips and leaned toward the camera. "How are you even considering mating somebody else when, well, it's so obvious, Chalton."

One did not just tell the queen of the Realm to bugger off and mind her own business. "Nothing is obvious, Queen Kayrs," Chalton said gently.

She snorted. "You only call me that when you're irritated and trying to deflect."

Dage rolled his eyes. "Stop teasing Chalton. He doesn't have a sense of humor."

"Yes, he does," Olivia shot back. "He's very funny."

Emma's mouth dropped open, and Dage's cheek creased in a half-smile.

Emma turned to her mate. "Oh, this is fun."

Dage nodded and then sobered. "Seriously. How much danger are you in, and should I send backup? Talen has returned from Iceland, and he's pissy I sent you on a mission without him."

Chalton's chest warmed. He had two families—his brothers and the Realm. "Tell Talen I can handle my own mission."

"He knows that but feels left out." Dage spoke to Olivia. "Talen is my brother and our strategic planner, and he's the sensitive one around here."

Chalton chuckled. Talen was about as sensitive as a brick chimney. "Tell him to take up yoga and relax."

Dage laughed. "Talen and yoga? I'd pay a small fortune to see that." His smile slid away. "Seriously. How are you doing?"

Ah. There was the meddling, pain in the ass, too worried king that was more of a friend. "I'm fine, Dage. I haven't had to kill anybody, and the reunion with my brothers only involved a few bruises."

"Good." Dage studied him, probing deep. "It's time you made up with your brothers."

"I know." Chalton fought against the dull needle pricking his brain. The king was trying to read his mind. "Get the fuck out of my head."

Emma slapped Dage.

Dage shrugged. "Just checking. Good mental block, by the way."

"Thanks."

Olivia glanced from one to the other, looking a little dazed. "I think Chalton is fine—I mean, he was just trying to blackmail me into having sex with him."

Emma coughed, her eyes widening. "Chalton? Really?" Her gaze swung to him, and he could actually feel his face heating. "Was he successful?"

"I haven't decided," Olivia said, a smile in her voice.

Delight now filtered across Emma's face, no doubt having just found another best friend. "Olivia, we really must get together when this is all over."

"I'd like that," Olivia said.

Concern darkened Dage's eyes at the same rate it flew through Chalton's veins. "Not a good idea," Chalton muttered. Those two women together would wreak havoc.

"Agreed," Dage said thoughtfully.

Ah, hell. Now the king was going to matchmake.

Emma leaned forward to whisper, "You really should say yes. Even if it's just for one night. Sex with a vampire is truly out of this world."

Dage exhaled heavily. "Chalton? Call me with updates." With that, the screen went black.

Olivia cleared her throat.

"Who's your source? Extortion doesn't make sense any

longer," Chalton said, wanting nothing more than to get back to his regular routine at this point.

She eyed him, emotion bright in her eyes. "They can't fix Ronni."

"No."

"Well then. I guess I'll take you up on your offer."

He rocked back. "My offer?" His voice came out hoarse, and his body roared into overdrive.

"Yeah. I mean, I just discovered that life is a whole lot different than I thought, and I do like a good adventure." She stood and turned to face him, her face flush with bravery and need. "I'll take the night...without sleep."

* * * *

What in the world was she doing? She'd just agreed to have sex with a vampire. In fact, forget the guy was a vampire. She'd just agreed to get naked and horizontal with the sexiest and probably the most dangerous man she'd ever met.

They did it horizontally, right?

"Why?" he asked, tossing the belt over his shoulder and moving toward her.

The scent of man and the warmth of male washed over her. "I want to." Sometimes life was as simple as that. Plus, her curiosity had gotten her far in life, and she just couldn't turn it off. "Do we really have to have an in-depth conversation about this?" Geez. Kiss her already.

"No. Just making sure this is what you want." He lifted her against his torso, turning to stride toward the bathroom.

"You're strong," she said breathlessly, grabbing his very bare chest for balance.

He grinned. "You're a lightweight, sweetheart."

She scoffed. "Not even close." Did she really want to get naked with such male perfection? Nobody had ever called her petite. Or small. Or fit. "Wait. I'm not—"

Then his mouth was on hers.

Hot and deep, he commandeered her lips, sending her senses spiraling. She moaned low in her throat and kissed him back, or rather followed his lead.

Still kissing her, he somehow reached into the shower and flipped on the water. Slowly, keeping her pressed against his muscled body, he allowed her to slide down him until her feet settled on the smooth tile.

She broke the kiss, her mind turning to mush, her breath panting out. A sense way too sharp to be desire sliced through her, making her want him with a craving that should give her pause. But it was too late to pause.

The look in his eyes was pure lust…and it was for her. He wanted her…all of her.

Drawing courage from that look, she reached for the hem of her dress and yanked it over her head.

The sound he made, low and guttural, vibrated through her body to land between her legs. "Beautiful," he murmured, reaching out to snap the front clasp of her bra.

Her breasts sprang free, and she shrugged out of the thin cotton.

He shoved off his pants.

Whoa. Okay. Vampires were built…really, really, really built. Hard and erect, he was ready to go.

Heat breathed through her, and she glanced around as steam filled the opulent bathroom. Chandelier on the ceiling, marble everywhere, top of the line towels. "Um—"

He drew her into the shower, and she groaned from the heated steam. Shower heads came at them from every direction, and she couldn't help a small chuckle from escaping.

He grinned and tugged her under the rain-shower head, which drenched her in decadent heat. Turning her around, he reached for a dispenser and filled his palms with shampoo before rubbing it through her hair.

She closed her eyes and tilted back her head, pure pleasure rushing through her. He had great hands. Then they moved lower, down her spine, to her butt. Her eyes flashed open.

Why hadn't she started doing lunges like she'd planned last month? "Um—" She turned, surprised a little when he let her.

"Um what?" he asked, shampooing his hair, his gaze never leaving hers. The suds ran down ripped muscles, corded everywhere, perfectly defined.

"This is a bad idea," she breathed, suddenly very aware of every dimple and curve she hadn't been able to banish. Edging to the side, she began to reach for the glass shower door, ready to flee.

"Oh, there's no running, little girl," he murmured, catching her arm and planting her against the tile. "If you don't want me or like me, then you're free to go. But if you're saying things in your head that you really shouldn't say about yourself, then we're going to have a problem." He stepped right into her, so male and sure. "And you really don't want that kind of a problem with me." One knuckle lifted her chin.

She swallowed. How could a threat sound so sexy? "I can think what I want."

He chuckled. "I thought so." Slowly, definitely deliberately, he set both hands around her waist and lifted her until they were eye to eye. "Put your legs around me."

She gulped and did what he'd said.

"Good." He leaned in, his breath brushing her lips. "If you were mine, I'd make you walk around naked all the time until you actually started to enjoy it and have the confidence such a beautiful woman should have."

Well. Sweet, and definitely sexy, but come on. Normally she was just fine with her confidence level, but being naked with perfection would rock anybody for a moment or two. "I don't need you to save me, Chalton. I'm fine."

He grinned against her mouth. "We all need saving once in a while."

Sweet. She liked him sweet. She leaned in and licked along his bottom lip, tasting salt and man.

His broad chest hitched.

Yeah. Power for the girl. She'd show him confidence. Her knees clasped his hips, and she dug both hands into his thick hair, taking his mouth. He allowed her to play, letting her go deep, before taking over and kissing her so hard her head was against the tile by the time he let her breathe.

Wow.

He flipped off the water and stepped from the shower, still

carrying her like she weighed nothing. As if to prove his point, he flipped her around once before setting her on her feet.

She grabbed for his forearms to steady herself.

"Let's dry you off," he rumbled, reaching for a towel to thoroughly, very thoroughly, dry her head to toe, lingering in the good spots. Finally, she was on so much fire, she just grabbed the towel and dropped it. "Enough foreplay."

He fetched another towel, dried off faster than possible, and lunged. Within seconds, they'd cleared the bathroom and she found herself on her back on the bed with a heated vampire over her.

She reached up and smoothed back his thick hair. "You're beautiful," she whispered.

He grinned and kissed her, licking along her neck and down her jugular. She shivered. A vampire was kissing her above her freakin jugular. The erotic threat, the possibility of it, pulsed down her and between her legs.

He caressed along her skin, wandering across her collar bone.

She explored his shoulders, noting the strength, until he reached her breasts and tugged one nipple between his teeth.

Electric sparks flew straight from her breasts to her clit, and she arched against him.

"Nice," he whispered against her, flicking her nipple before wandering to nip and suck the other one.

She moved against him, her mind reeling. There was an edge to Chalton, one just starting to emerge, that gave her pause and turned her on. He'd been so reserved so far...so in control.

Could she make him lose that control?

God, did she want to?

Right now so much need coursed through her she could barely grasp a thought, much less be logical. He continued moving down her body, peppering kisses along her abdomen before reaching her core.

She planted a hand on the top of his head. "No." Too intimate. Way too intimate. This was supposed to be a wild romp for fun.

He glanced up, between her legs, and allowed his fangs to

drop low. Sharp and deadly looking, they stole her breath. He somehow smiled around them, and they retracted. "I'm going to play, and I'm going to be nice. Deny me again, and I'll use fangs."

She opened her mouth to protest, and he nipped her clit.

A mini-detonation rocked her, and she gasped, her head going back on the pillow. It felt too good.

Then he went at her. Slow and soft, fast and firm...he played her body like he'd designed it. Tension uncoiled in her abdomen, lifting her higher. So close. She was so close. "Chalton," she moaned.

He pressed two fingers inside her and sucked her clit into his mouth.

The room hazed, sheeting white. She detonated into a million pieces, flashing out, orgasming so violently her entire body clenched with the action. He prolonged the ecstasy until she fell back to the bed, limp, with a soft sigh.

Then he inched back up her, kissing everything on the way, levering right above her.

His face was all angles and firm lines, dark with desire. "Now we get serious."

Chapter Nine

Chalton fought every animalistic urge he owned to flip her onto her hands and knees and take her hard. The woman tasted like honey and heaven…and his. He'd felt her orgasm deeper than his own body, and now he wanted more. So much damn more.

She stared up at him, those pretty eyes wide, her expression bemused and a little wary.

Smart girl.

He shifted his hips between her legs, forcing them open wider. Her skin was softer than cotton candy and twice as sweet. Keeping her gaze, he began to push inside her. She was tight, even after her orgasm, so he took it slow, careful not to harm her.

She paused. "Condom?"

He grinned. "Don't work with vampires, and I can't get you pregnant unless we're mated." The instances where immortals had impregnated nonmates were too few to even consider statistically.

Her body enclosed him, taking him home. She lifted her knees, widening her thighs. Her body trembled around him in powerful aftershocks of her first orgasm of the evening. He wondered how many he could wring from her before she lost the sass and submitted.

He reached halfway and dropped down to kiss her, memorizing the shape of her lips and the taste of her mouth. He took her deep and had to shove hard to make it all the way inside her, planting himself to the hilt.

She gasped into his mouth, her body going rigid.

He lifted. "Take a moment and just relax." His heart beat like he'd run ten miles, but he had to give her time to adjust to him. He tuned in his senses, making sure the apartment was safe and no threat lingered near. Nothing felt out of the ordinary, so he focused back on Olivia.

She nodded, softening, her body releasing tension one muscle at a time that he could feel. "Man, you're huge," she said.

He barked out a laugh. How did she do that? He wasn't a guy who laughed much, and never out of the blue. Yet she brought out parts of him that had been long dead. "And you're soft. We make a perfect pair."

A small smile lifted her kissable lips. "You don't have to go with the sweet words. I'm not leaving."

He stilled and let some of his weight press her to the bed, reminding her of his strength. "I go with the truth, and with you, the truth is beyond sweet." Then he lowered his head to capture her gaze. "Knock yourself again in such a manner, and I'll fetch that belt."

Her mouth gaped, and spunk filled her eyes. "You're kidding."

"Nope." He'd never hit her with the belt, but he could think of a few ways to torture her a little with it. He hated the modern view of perfection being stick thin, and to think it had even messed with Olivia's mind a little just pissed him off. "Are we clear?" he asked evenly.

For once, she apparently decided not to push him. "Yes."

"Good." He settled his hips against hers. "Better now?" he asked, his biceps vibrating with the need to *move*.

She caressed down his flanks and over his ass, her nails slightly scraping. "Much better." She squeezed. "No mating, right?"

Sorrow, surprising in its intensity, slammed through him. Yet he forced a grin. "I promise I won't bite you." *Tonight* a small voice whispered in the back of his head. He ignored the voice and slid out of her only to push back inside.

It was like heaven and ecstasy and perfection all rolled into one devastating sensation. Her full breasts rubbed against his chest, and he could spend days just worshiping them. He leaned down to nibble on her earlobe, and her sex spasmed around his dick.

The woman was so responsive. What would she be like in full trust? As an enhanced female, she could mate an immortal who would have years to gain that trust. To see just how wild the intriguing woman could get.

"Does biting hurt?" she asked.

"Yes, but when you're caught up in the moment, it's bearable." His gums tingled with the need to let loose his fangs.

"Um, can you bite without mating?" she asked.

He nodded, trying to banish thoughts of biting her to the abyss. "Yes, we can bite without mating, but during sex it's a huge risk." He was way too attracted to her, and if he bit her during sex, there was a solid chance they'd end up mated. "I can bite you later, when I'm not inside you, to show you."

"I think I'd like that."

The woman was too curious, without a doubt. No wonder she'd become a journalist. "I could've bitten your thigh when I was playing, but I didn't want to scare you." So long as he wasn't thrusting inside her, he could bite her all she liked.

Her breath caught. "Oh." She tilted her hips to take more of him. He gave her more, adjusting his thrusts so each stroke, each delectable slide into her body, brushed him against her clit. Soon she began to tremble beneath him.

She'd thrown her head back, revealing the long line of her neck.

His fangs dropped, forcing him to concentrate on retracting them. The second they were safely out of the way, he increased the strength of his thrusts. Yeah, he'd have to go down on her again later and bite her thigh. Just the thought drew his balls up tight.

"What if I bite you?" she asked.

"Go ahead." The woman thought too much, and he was going to get her out of her head if it was the last thing he did. He reached between them, massaging a finger against her clit.

She moaned deep. "Wait. That's too much."

There it was. She didn't like being out of control any more

than he did, but enough of that. "I think it's just enough." He waited until she shook her head, until she opened her mouth to argue, and then he pinched.

She gasped, arched, and her body climaxed around him, gripping strong enough to hurt. A small scream escaped her, and she shut her eyes.

To see her let loose like that was a gift he couldn't explain.

He pumped faster, keeping control, enjoying the bite of her nails against his flanks. Every time he shoved inside her, she went into another mini-spasm around him.

Fire lanced down his spine and gripped his balls. He let himself go, coming hard. Finally, he dropped his damp forehead to hers, more than a little surprised by how immense his release had been.

She murmured something beneath him, caressing small circles against the small of his back. Offering comfort. He wanted to keep that sweetness forever with a fierceness that gave him pause.

Lifting up, he turned to the side and snuggled her into him. All woman, soft and fragrant, settled into him with a soft murmur. Without a doubt, he'd never felt like this.

She wiggled her butt to get closer.

Instant fire roared through him, making him hard all over again.

She sighed. "That was lovely."

Was? Oh, hell no. "Baby? We're just getting started," he whispered into her ear. They had all night, and he'd promised there would be no sleeping.

"Oh yeah?" she murmured sleepily. "What about that belt?"

Ah, the darlin' liked to issue a challenge, did she? "Want to be tied up?" he asked.

She chuckled, her body moving against his. "Not really. And that was wild, so how about we get some sleep and recover before round two?"

"Oh no." He wrapped an arm around her waist and dragged her lower half against his already rock-solid erection. "Forget sleep. Round two just started."

* * * *

Morning light filtered through the sheer drapes they hadn't bothered to cover the night before. Olivia flopped one leg out of the covers, her face buried in a pillow. She'd never be the same. Ever. When Chalton had said there'd be no sleeping, he'd actually meant it.

Sex with a vampire was over the top and out of this world.

Yet somehow, she figured it was more Chalton than his species. The guy was passionate, giving, and powerful. It was like he'd known her body better than she did.

With morning arriving, she should be swamped with vulnerability. But she was just too satiated, content, and relaxed to draw up any insecurities.

Besides giving her bliss all night, he'd peppered her with compliments that had the ring of truth. While she might wish she weighed a good twenty pounds less…he liked her just fine. More than fine.

His cheerful whistle echoed from the bathroom as he showered.

She blinked and shoved herself to sit, swaying just a little. Time to get back to reality. Glancing around, she spotted a phone near the bed. Who in the world still kept a landline? Uncle Benny must be quite the character. Chalton had said nobody could trace him to Benny, so the phone had to be safe to use.

In fact, she'd have to borrow it considering Chalton had thrown her phone out of the helicopter the night before so it couldn't be traced. She dialed, and Ronni picked up on the first ring. "Hello?"

"Ronni? How are you?" Olivia asked, worrying her bottom lip.

Ronni gasped. "Olly? Where are you? I mean, you said not to call the police if you went underground, but you didn't call, and I'm about two seconds away from reporting you as missing. What the—"

"I'm fine." Geez. She should've called. "I'm so sorry to worry you, but I had to chase a story, and you know how I get.

More importantly, how are you?"

"I'm fine," Ronni wheezed, obviously not fine. "Are you still writing about the weird chromosomal mix-up story?"

"Yes, and I'm totally on to something." Okay. She just couldn't go into the existence of vampires over the phone. Or the whole mating aspect. She glanced at the partially open bathroom door. Could she really force Chalton to mate Ronni? Especially since she wanted nothing more than to get him back into bed and naked for the next century or so? There had to be another way. "I'm working on a cure for you," she whispered.

Ronni sighed. "Honey, there is no cure. I'm not a candidate for a new heart, and there's nothing that'll fix this one. You have to let it go. For me."

"I'd do anything for you." Even play chicken with the king of the vampires in an elaborate extortion scheme. There had to be a vampire out there who could mate Ronni that wasn't Chalton. Then they could get unmated with the mutated virus, probably. Yeah. Good plan. "I have so much to tell you, but we should meet in person."

"When?" Ronni coughed.

"Soon." The shower cut off. "Um, I have to go. I'll call you as soon as I can." She gingerly replaced the receiver and sat up in the bed, actually taking her first good look at her surroundings. "Whoa." Original oil paintings lined the walls, gorgeous and obviously one of a kind depictions of different cities at the turn of the century. Ornate furniture was angled around in a pleasing style…homemade and top of the line. Uncle Benny had some cash.

Chalton stepped out of the bathroom wearing worn jeans and a dark T-shirt, towel rubbing his hair dry. "Benny only has jeans here, so it's casual day."

Her mouth watered. "Um, okay."

His phone buzzed, and he drew it from his pocket, sighing upon reading the face. He put it to his ear. "Hi, Dage." Within a second, he lost his smile, his face hardening to stone. "When? Great. Thanks." He clicked off and shoved the phone in his pocket. "Get dressed. We have to run."

She shoved from the bed and grasped her wrinkled dress.

"Um—"

"Now, Olivia." He dodged into the closet to grab boots and yank them on before tossing her boots at her. "Go barefoot until we're in the garage. You won't be able to run in the heels, but bring them."

She yanked the dress over her head and stumbled toward the door. "What's going on?"

Chalton took her arm and began jogging through the apartment, grabbing her coat on the way. "Dage has been monitoring all chatter in New York, and he thinks there's a strike team on the way here."

Strike team? "The Kurjans?"

"No. He's smoothed things over with the Kurjans by telling them I mated you and you're no longer a danger to our world."

Mated her? Her heart thumped. "Then who?"

"Petey and Saul, who were sons of Peter. I figured someday they'd come after us, but not through you."

She shook her head, trying to keep up. "How did they find us?"

"I don't know." He drew a gun from the back of his waist and slowly opened the outside door. "Keep your head down. There's a back exit that isn't on the plans, but we have to reach the end of the hall."

She nodded and ran barefoot after him, wishing she'd taken time for a shower. They reached the end of the hallway, and Chalton shoved a pretty watercolor painting to the side to expose a keypad. He punched in a code, and the wall opened to reveal an elevator.

He tugged her inside, and the door smoothly shut.

An explosion rocked the building.

She stumbled and fell on one knee. He helped her up, rubbing her leg. "You okay?"

"Yes," she gulped. "What was that?"

"They probably breached the front of the penthouse." Chalton angled between her and the door. "This elevator goes to a secret parking area a floor below the parking garage, and it isn't on the blueprints, so we'll be okay. But we'll need to exit the garage, so they may see us."

She nodded, her heart thundering. "I understand."

"Good." He rubbed his forehead. "I just don't get how they found us."

"I don't know, but I was on the phone with Ronni just a few minutes ago. Do you think she's in danger?" Olivia clasped her hands together.

Chalton stilled. "You were what?"

His tone of voice, low and dark, shot adrenaline through her veins. "I, ah, called Ronni when you were in the shower."

"How? I took your phone."

"Um, yeah. I used the landline."

His eyes narrowed, and a flash of green shot through the black. "You. Did. What?"

"Um." Awareness, the kind that deer no doubt felt when faced with a hungry lion, rushed through her and cramped in her stomach. How did his eyes do that? "Your eyes just turned goldish."

"Vampires have secondary eye colors that come out when we're aroused...or furious."

Yep. Probably furious. No arousal there. Olivia tried to hold her ground. "I had to check on Ronni, and I figured the phone was safe since it's a landline and you said nobody can track you to Benny."

"I told you not to reach out."

"Yeah?" Fear morphed to necessary temper so she didn't start whimpering. "Well, I don't work for you."

He moved then so suddenly she didn't see it coming, pivoting and putting her against the wall. "They traced your call."

Well, hell. "It's not my fault they have some sort of tracker on Benny's phone." Geez. How in the world was she supposed to know that?

"They don't," Chalton ground out. "They must have one on Ronni."

Panic heated Olivia's lungs. She pushed Chalton, trying to get to the door. "How could they even know about Ronni?"

"They probably didn't. But I showed up in town, grabbed you, and I'm sure they investigated everything about you at that point. I didn't see this coming."

"So it's my fault. Then I have to protect her. We're going to her place."

"Right now, we have to get out of here safely." He shoved her behind him again, not so gently this time, as the elevator continued to descend. "Then we'll have a nice discussion about your lack of obedience."

Obedience? Did he fucking just say *obedience*? She punched him square in the kidney. "Don't even think about trying it, dipshit," she said, struggling not to yell.

He turned so suddenly she could only blink, grasping her wrists and yanking her toward him. His face, usually set in such calm lines, was a hard rock of pure fury. Danger seemed tame compared to him. His eyes glowed a luminous gold, and tension of the darker kind cascaded from him. "When the door opens, you will follow me and get on the bike without another fucking word. Got it?"

Instinct ruled, and she nodded numbly.

"Good." He turned back around, the muscles in his shoulders visibly vibrating and completely blocking her view of the door.

She swallowed several times, trying to calm her rioting nerves. Oh, they were so going to talk about his ass-backward attitude. When he wasn't so angry, of course. She was brave...not stupid.

Since the first realization about vampires, she might have had a rather romantic view of them as an immortal species. There was an edge present, an animalist, definitely predatory, aspect to him that she hadn't imagined. He'd hidden that part from her until this morning.

"Sex does change things," she mumbled, donning her coat.

His shoulders went back, but otherwise he didn't twitch.

She didn't want to poke the bear, but she had to say something. "Ronni is in danger if they're watching her. I have to do something."

"Ronni was perfectly safe with them watching her until you called her. Now she's in danger," he responded, his voice unrelenting.

Well, geez. Her fist closed with the need to punch him again, but caution won out this time. She'd probably pushed the vampire as far as she wanted at the moment.

The building rocked again. How many explosives were the Libscombe family using, anyway?

The elevator hitched and then kept descending.

Chalton growled low.

Olivia shivered and fought the urge to burrow into his back for reassurance. As much danger came from the pissed off vampire as from the explosives attacking Benny's nice penthouse. She hadn't given thought that one little phone call would result in an attack.

The door opened, and Chalton sprang out, gun at ready.

A garage-sized room held several motorcycles and what looked like a golf cart without wheels. Chalton made tracks toward a supped up Harley and swung one leg over the side.

She hurried after him, grabbed his arm, and jumped on the bike, trying to tuck her dress up for some modesty. Leaning down, she shoved both boots on her feet before tucking them on the foot step thingy. "I've never ridden a motorcycle."

He handed back a helmet. "Put this on, hold on to me, go limp, and let me guide you."

She nodded and shoved the helmet over her head.

The bike came alive with a loud roar.

She wrapped her arms around Chalton's waist and leaned in, allowing herself to find some comfort in his warmth. Sure, he was angry with her, but deep down, she knew he wouldn't let anybody hurt her.

He swung the bike in a large circle and aimed down a narrow tunnel. Bricks sped by, making Olivia dizzy.

Light became apparent, and they shot out of the tunnel into an alley. Bullets instantly impacted the side of the motorcycle.

Chalton swerved and opened the throttle on the icy roads.

Olivia screamed and shut her eyes, holding on with every ounce of strength she had.

Chapter Ten

Chalton positioned the bike the best he could, trying to keep his body between Olivia and any bullets. As far as he could tell, only one enemy soldier took post across the alley. A quick glance confirmed the guy's identity as one of Petey's soldiers. Chalton had kept a dossier on Petey's forces through the years, just in case. The rest were probably covering other exits, not even sure this was an exit.

The guy fired again, and pain rippled through Chalton's leg. Blood spurted.

He opened the throttle, and the bike jumped forward. Yanking to the right, he drove up on the sidewalk, putting vehicles between the bike and the shooter. A passerby screamed and jumped out of his way.

Olivia held on tight, her helmet against his shoulder, finally doing as he'd told her. He could not believe she'd made a phone call from the penthouse.

Smoke billowed out from the top floor, and several of the windows had been blown to bits. Glass and debris still rained down. Benny was going to kill him. Literally. Benny would literally try to cut off his head. It was nearly unimaginable how much money Chalton would have to offer to keep peace in the family.

He banished all thoughts of payoff and concentrated, using split-second reflexes to keep metal between them and bullets. Taking a sharp right, he then angled into another alley, turned left, and hugged several buildings before hitting the open and icy road.

The soldiers would come after them but wouldn't be able to catch the bike.

He took back roads as much as possible, and within an hour, his body began to relax. Unlike the penthouse phone, his cellphone was encrypted and couldn't be traced. Even though it buzzed incessantly in his pocket, he ignored it to keep driving away from danger.

Finally, they reached the warehouse district, and he pulled alongside a nondescript medium-sized metal building with logos for a bread company on the side. He tapped a keypad by a door, and it swung open, so he drove the bike inside.

The bike went silent.

Empty space surrounded them, while a small apartment was set in the far corner and enclosed by cinder blocks. Olivia used him for balance and pushed off the bike, stumbling back and taking off the helmet. Her stunning mahogany hair tumbled down over her shoulders. "You've been shot. Again."

He nodded and swung off the bike, wincing when his thigh protested. Reaching in the hole, he dragged out the bullet, biting his lip to keep from swearing. "I'm fine." Crossing his arms, he took a good look at his woman. Yeah. He was done pretending otherwise. "I am not happy with you."

She rolled her eyes. "Get over yourself. I had no clue about Ronni's phone being bugged."

"Hence my order to stay low and not contact anybody," he said evenly, holding on to his patience with both rapidly tiring hands.

"Perhaps you should've explained yourself better," she said sweetly, sarcasm in every line of her scrumptious body.

"Maybe I should've explained the consequences better," he murmured.

She stepped back. "You can't blame me for your uncle's penthouse being blown up."

"Yet I do." Could she not see she'd put her life in danger? If Dage hadn't been monitoring so closely, Olivia would've been caught in the crossfire. Chalton's phone buzzed again, and he yanked it to his face. "Damn it. What?"

"Benny's blew up. You okay?" Theo asked.

"Yes. We're at safe house three. You have mom?"

"No. Can't find her." Frustration darkened Theo's tone. "She went shopping, apparently, and didn't leave any more information with the house staff."

Chalton sighed. "Meet me here, and we'll figure out the best way to find our mother."

"Fair enough. You text Jared and have him meet us. It's time we figured out who's after us…other than the Kurjans."

"The Kurjans have been appeased, for the time being anyway. I saw one of Petey's men waiting to ambush me. We definitely have the right enemy in mind." Chalton said.

"It's about time. I'm tired of waiting for the bastard to make a move," Theo said grimly, hanging up.

Chalton nodded and quickly dialed Jared. "Jared, I need a favor. Will you pick up a friend of Olivia's? She's in danger." He quickly gave the coordinates. "Thanks. See you soon." He clicked off the phone and turned to study his woman. "Jared will bring Ronni here."

"What will you tell her?" Olivia asked.

He shrugged. "Let's figure that out when she gets here." Striding forward, he took Olivia's hand and led her out of the garage space and into the small apartment. She followed without protesting, which was a nice change. He released her and pointed toward the one bedroom and bath. "You mentioned a shower. There are clothes in the closet that should fit you."

She stilled. "Whose clothes?"

Did the woman sound jealous? He bit back a grin. "My mom's. This is a safe house for in case we need one…it's equipped for all of us." Somebody, probably Jared, had updated it throughout the years. "Go, Olivia." He needed a few minutes to regain control so he stopped wanting to throttle her.

She must've sensed his mood because she headed for the bedroom, stopping at the door to turn around. "Why haven't you and your brothers talked for so long?"

He turned, surprised at the question. "Our father died, and we were each in a bad place, so we turned on each other instead of to each other." It really was as simple as that. "But a hundred years for us is like a few weeks for humans. We just haven't had time to make up."

She leaned against the doorjamb, dark circles under her pretty eyes. "What bad places?"

He breathed out slowly. "Damn, you're a curious one. I had killed too many people, in war and out, and was facing a crisis of a sort. So I put up my weapons and turned to technology, which soon became computers as they were invented." Dage had saved his soul with the offer to work for the Realm as the computer expert and no longer as an assassin, without question.

"And Jared?"

"The love of his life, or rather, who he thought was the love of his life, mated somebody else. I never liked the witch." Chalton shrugged. "Theo had lost his best friend in a battle with an enemy shifter clan out of Africa, and he was blaming himself."

The timing had sucked all around. "We screwed up and should've helped each other instead of fought." Yeah, that was on him. He was the logical one and should've reached out before now. "It'll be okay, Olivia. I promise."

She nodded, pale and wan, and turned to disappear in the bedroom.

What was he going to do? If life were perfect, he'd court her for a decade and then make her his. As it sat, he'd promised to mate her dying best friend.

She reappeared in the doorway, buck ass nude. "Chalton? Want to join me?"

His cock sprang to action with an "oh, hell yes." Yet he shook his head. "I'm seriously pissed at you, Livy. Give me some time to cool down."

She snorted. "Don't be such a dork. Our time might be limited, considering we seem to be at war on several sides with pretty scary enemies. Let's take the moment."

His gaze swept down her curvy body and then back up, lingering on her breasts. Full and firm, they all but begged for his mouth. "You asked for it." Letting the beast in him take over, he strode toward the woman made just for him.

* * * *

Olivia swallowed and backed into the room, wondering once again at her own sanity. Adrenaline from the bombing and chase had been coursing through her system, and she'd felt brave. Chalton Reese, no matter his perfection, thought she was beautiful.

It was an intoxicating feeling, and it had gone right to her head. So when she'd taken off her clothes, she'd figured…why not?

As Chalton moved toward her with the grace of any predatory animal, her question was answered. He was pissed, he was dangerous, and he was unknown. Truly, she did not know him. Not really.

Now not only had she poked the beast, she'd pretty much punched him right in the nose with the dare.

"Um—" She took another step back.

"Too late." His expression matched his words. Stony and determined…and so damn male. He reached her and threaded his fingers through her hair, tangled, and pulled her right up on her toes.

She gasped, opening her mouth, and he took full advantage. Driving his tongue in, dueling with hers, bending her back to be kissed hard. His other hand clamped on her hip and yanked her into pure male muscle.

The whimper up her throat would've embarrassed her if her mind wasn't spinning. She was naked, and he was fully clothed, swamping her with a heated vulnerability she shouldn't have liked. Yet she kissed him back, unable to move an inch, desire rushing through her stronger than hundred-year-old cognac.

He broke the kiss and lifted her easily, all but tossing her on the bed. She bounced once, and then he was on his knees on the floor, his mouth on her core, her legs over his shoulders.

She tried to sit up, to protest, but one hand flattened over her abdomen.

He glanced up, his eyes a burning gold. "Stay in place."

The spit on her tongue dried up, and she froze.

"Down," he ordered, no give on his chiseled face.

She blinked once and then lay back down, her heart beating so fast her ribs ached.

He licked her, humming with pleasure, and nipped her clit.

Sparks flew through her so hot and fast she could only gasp. Then he went at her, licking, nipping, and biting…in perfect rhythm, until she was a mass of aching nerves ready to beg.

She glanced desperately around the small bedroom. Black and white photographs of airplanes through the years covered the walls, and a heavy oriental rug sprawled across the concrete floor. He nipped her again, and she closed her eyes against the heated bliss.

"Chalton," she moaned.

He released her and turned to rub his nose against her thigh. She gyrated against him, needing much more, so close to the edge a strong breeze would carry her over.

Pain lanced through her thigh.

She partially sat up, and the hand on her abdomen pushed her back down. He'd bitten her. His tongue made quick use of closing the wound, and then landed square on her clit.

She whispered his name, fireworks flashing behind her closed eyelids. The orgasm rolled through her, pounding, stronger than any lightning strike. He prolonged the waves, using his mouth and his fingers, until she flopped back down with a low moan.

Then he stood.

She tried to form words, but nothing would come.

He ripped his shirt over his head, revealing all of that smooth, strong muscle. Then his pants hit the floor.

No way could she join him this time, but he definitely deserved an orgasm. So she widened her thighs.

Slowly, he shook his head, raw need in his dark eyes.

She frowned.

He grasped her hands and tugged her to stand. Her legs wobbled. Then he turned her around and lowered her to her hands and knees on the bed, facing the headboard. Strong hands grabbed her hips, and he thrust inside with one controlled shove.

She sucked in air and dug her nails into the dark bedspread. Holy crap he was huge. A feeling, an uncoiling, started deep inside her. How was that possible?

He flattened his hand between her shoulder blades and pushed down until her head hit the covers. She turned to the side to breathe, a powerful predator behind her.

Open and vulnerable, she could only feel.

So much heat and undeniable power. Yet she had to ask. "Is this because you're mad?"

He stopped moving, buried balls deep inside her. "Does this feel mad?" he asked.

No, it felt fucking amazing. He was so deep she wasn't sure where he ended and she began. "No, but I wanted to make sure." Her voice was muffled in the covers.

He slid out and powered back inside her. "This is for fun and because it feels good. This"—he smacked her ass and hard—"is because I was pissed."

"Ow," she howled. Then, because he'd surprised her, she laughed out loud.

He paused again. "You're laughing?" Amusement darkened his tone.

She shivered from the tenor and laughed again. "I can't help it. You surprised me, and that's how I react." And yet, she was having fun. Without question.

"Interesting." He peppered several smacks to her rear end, and she stopped laughing altogether. "Better."

Oh, he did not. Worst of all, since he was firmly implanted inside her, every smack had ricocheted sparks throughout her body. Somehow he ignited her desire again, this time into a hunger that actually hurt.

"I might have to harm you," she gasped into the bedclothes.

A slap to the center of her ass had her arching and riding the fine edge between pain and pleasure.

"So that's how to quiet you," he murmured, rubbing her heated flesh.

Her mind caught his meaning several seconds after her body had spasmed. "Hey—"

SMACK.

She arched again, taking more of him in.

He chuckled a low rumble, grasped her hips, and began

pounding with a harsh rhythm that took her completely out of reality. The slap of flesh against flesh filled the room along with their ragged breathing.

He pulled her back to meet his thrusts, controlling her, taking her places she hadn't known existed.

She broke with a low cry, the orgasm taking her over, filling her with so much pleasure she could barely breathe.

He shuddered and fell over her, his lips brushing her ear.

Slowly, he pulled out, and she felt a sense of loss way out of proportion for the moment. He turned her over, pushed her up on the bed, and sprawled over her, his elbows taking his weight.

"You okay?" he asked, pushing damp hair away from her face.

She nodded, too much emotion swamping her to allow speech. If she talked, she'd say something really stupid about love and destiny. She'd lost her mind. A couple of amazing orgasms and she'd gone crazy.

He placed a gentle kiss against her lips. "You feel it, right?"

She nodded again, wanting nothing more than to stay right there, in his arms, forever. How nuts was that?

"Me too." He kissed the corners of her mouth, her nose, her cheeks, even her eyelids.

A rumble sounded from outside.

He drew her up and off the bed, patted her still smarting ass, and pushed her toward the bathroom. "That's one of my brothers. Take a quick shower. We'll figure everything out later."

She nodded and hitched toward the bathroom, small aches and pains springing to life. He felt like hers, but what about Ronni? What would she give up to save her best friend's life? How could she ask Chalton to give up his freedom for eternity?

Chapter Eleven

Chalton dragged on the borrowed jeans, leaving them unbuttoned while padding barefoot into the vast garage space. Theo arrived on an impressive looking Ducati seconds before Jared roared in on a Harley with a pale brunette holding on for dear life behind him.

The second he killed the engine, she pushed off the bike. "You are such a complete dickhead of an asshole," she muttered.

"I told you to hold on," Jared said calmly, swinging off the bike and turning on Chalton. "Miss Temper here didn't want to come, so I had to convince her."

Ronni rounded on him, both hands on her too slender hips. "This is kidnapping, and you better believe I'm going to press charges on your ass."

Theo grinned. "What in the world did I miss?"

"You're an accessory, asshole," Ronni snarled, her Columbian accent sharpening the words.

For a feisty brunette, she really was cute. Long hair, deep brown eyes, curvy figure. Not Chalton's type, but if he remembered right, Jared had a thing for women from romantic countries. Spunky women.

Though by the thunderclouds gathering in his deep eyes, he didn't have a thing for this one.

Chalton cleared his throat. "Ronni? Olivia is through that door taking a quick shower. I'm sure she'd like to see for herself that you're all right."

Ronni gave him one of the most scalding looks he'd ever

received before lifting her head high and stomping through the room and out of sight. The apartment door slammed behind her hard enough to rattle the outside door.

"She's ill," Jared said, eyebrows raised.

"Yes. Heart problems," Chalton said.

"I could smell it on her, but she sure as shit doesn't let it slow her down," Jared muttered, rubbing his jaw. "The girl knows how to hit." Now he sounded impressed.

"Well, at least she's a fighter. I've offered to mate her to save her life," Chalton said, his gut aching.

Jared rocked back on size sixteen boots. "You smell of another female, brother. Planning a harem?"

"No." He frowned. "Things have gotten a little out of hand."

"Fuck. I leave you alone for one little century, and now you've got two women to mate. You know you can only mate one, right?" Jared drawled.

"Asshole," Chalton said without heat. "Did you find the people who hired you to track down Olivia?"

Jared growled. "No. They seem to have disappeared, but don't worry, I will find the bastards." He turned toward Theo, who was watching the exchange with barely contained amusement. "Where the hell is our mother?"

Theo sobered. "No clue. She doesn't check in with me any more than you, and she gets irritated if any of us get too overbearing."

"I called her, but she hasn't responded," Chalton muttered.

"Me too," Jared said.

Theo glanced at his phone. "She hasn't called me back, either." Then his phone buzzed, and he grinned. "There she is. She called me first." Triumph lightened his hard face as he answered the phone. "Hi, Mom." His smile disappeared, and he cut a look at his brothers. "Who the fuck is this?"

Chalton stopped breathing, his body settling into battle mode. "Record it," he mouthed, charging closer to his brother as Jared did the same.

Theo nodded and hit a button on his phone. "Let me see her." He glanced down at the phone, holding it out so they could all see their mother tied up, furious, in a chair.

Petey Libscombe came into view. The years hadn't been good to him. His hair had thinned, very rare for a shifter. "You had to know I'd be coming."

Chalton shrugged. "We figured you'd be out trying human balding cures."

Theo snorted.

Petey growled low and stepped behind their mother. "As you can see, I've taken good care of your mommy. She's at her little hidey-hole in the city, perfectly unharmed. Be here in an hour or I cut off her fucking head." The picture went dark.

Theo turned and ran toward the apartment, stopping in the small living room and connecting the phone to the huge plasma television to bring up the recording for a wider view. Their mom slowly took form on the massive screen. "Where is her hidey-hole in the city?"

Chalton shook his head.

"No clue," Jared said, his voice sounding like death on a promise.

Chalton growled. "I don't understand. How can she have a place in the city we don't know about? What does she do there?" He spoke with her several times a week, and not once had she mentioned a getaway place.

Theo ran through the video frame by frame. "Nothing here shows us where she is." He froze the screen. Their mom sat, tied and gagged, on a purple office chair. A bookshelf lined the wall behind her, stacked high with tons and tons of books. Her brownish hair curled around her shoulders, and her dark eyes shot furious sparks.

Rage threatened to cut off Chalton's ability to think, so he took several deep breaths to regain control. It was unthinkable, even in times of war, to go after females, and especially somebody's *mother*.

"I'm going to cut off his nuts and feed them to his brother," Jared said, his fingers curled into fists.

"His brother is in Morocco right now and probably not a part of this," Theo muttered.

"Don't care," Jared responded.

Olivia walked out of the bedroom wearing a cute black yoga outfit that showed off her curves to perfection, leading a bewildered looking Ronni. "I know it sounds crazy, but it's all true. There are actually people who turn into animals, although I haven't seen that happen yet. For now, it's just vampires and the weird white-faced dudes." She glanced up at the screen and stopped cold, her face going white. "What did you do?" she whispered.

Chalton frowned. "We didn't do that."

"I don't understand." She walked closer to the screen. "Why would anybody hurt Helen? Where is she? What's going on?"

Shock clipped through Chalton. He grasped Olivia's arm and flipped her around. "How do you know my mother's name?"

Olivia's mouth dropped open and then closed with a snap. "Your *mother*?"

"Yes." Oh, he so did not like where this was going. "Again, how do you know her?"

Olivia pressed a hand to her stomach. "She's my source for the story. I mean, everything I know about immortal species came from her."

* * * *

Olivia caught sight of Ronni's too pale face and drew her forward to sit on the lone leather sofa in the barren room. Telling her about immortals had been more difficult than she'd thought. Maybe the innocuous living space would help calm her friend. The television took up one wall, the bedroom entry the other, pictures of airplanes the third, and behind them was a utilitarian kitchen.

Ronni sat, her hands trembling. "Those are not vampires. Vampires don't exist."

"Chalton?" Olivia called.

He eyed them, let his fangs drop, and then growled.

Ronni gasped.

Chalton rolled his eyes and let his fangs retract. "We have bigger issues right now to deal with. Why the hell did my mother give you proprietary information?"

Olivia shrugged, her mind spinning. "I don't know. She called me up out of the blue, said she had read my articles about the North Platt labs using animals for testing, and that she had a great story for me. When we met, she gave me the first few documents about missing information."

Chalton rocked back on his heels, thoughts scattering across his face. Dark-looking thoughts. He glared at Jared. "Any ideas?"

"None I like having," Jared retorted, crossing arms that looked firmer than steel and twice as strong. "Theo?"

"Dunno." Theo shrugged.

"Considering our mother basically committed treason against, well, everybody…maybe we should figure this out," Chalton snapped.

Jared shook his head. "If the Realm finds out about this, they'll cut off her head."

"No, they won't," Chalton returned.

"Oh yeah? Why the hell not?" Jared hissed.

Chalton rose to his full height. "Because Dage Kayrs is my friend, and you don't cut off the head of your friend's mother." By the time he finished the sentence, he was yelling.

"Bullshit," Jared yelled back, stepping within punching distance.

"You have always had a hard-on for the Realm, and it's time you fucking made peace," Chalton bellowed.

Jared grabbed him by the lapels and leaned in. "I don't give a shit about the Realm and never have. So long as they stay out of my way, I'm fine."

"They've never been in your way," Chalton yelled into his brother's face, arms shooting up to break the hold. Every inch of his body wanted a brawl, and he braced to take the punch that was no doubt coming.

"Stop it right now," Olivia yelled, her voice much higher than theirs.

They both stopped, their heads swinging to look at her.

She stood and planted her hands on her hips. "Far as I can tell, the last time you got into it, you didn't speak for a hundred fucking years. So how about this time you work together, get your mom back, and act like brothers?" Her voice rose high enough at the last that Chalton winced.

"Your woman is loud," Jared said, backing up to sit next to Ronni on the sofa.

"I am not his woman," Olivia screamed, her face turning red.

Ronni cleared her throat. "It kind of seems like you are." When Olivia swung an irritated look back at her, she shrugged. "Well, it does."

"I can't be," Olivia whispered.

Ronni smiled at her and turned that smile on Chalton. "Hey, so I appreciate the offer of mating and all of that, even though I think you're all certifiable. But I am so not mating the guy my best friend loves. Sorry."

"I don't love him," Olivia snapped.

"Yes, you do," Chalton bit out. It was one thing to play hard to get or to take time to figure out feelings, but no way was she going to lie out loud to him. "It happens fast with vampires, so deal with it."

"What about Ronni?" she asked, pain slicing through her. "She'll die."

Ronni reached up and tugged Olivia down to sit. "We all die." Then she glanced around the room. "Okay, maybe not. But most of us do." She frowned and glanced sideways at Jared. "Is this possibly a trick? The whole vampire thing?"

He lifted an eyebrow and let his fangs slide out. "Feel."

She gingerly reached out and ran a finger down the wicked canine. "Feels real."

It retracted.

She leaned away from him. "You're sure you won't suck all my blood out and turn me into the undead?"

Jared rolled his eyes. "Jesus."

Chalton glanced at their helpless mother on the screen. "We have got to find her place in the city."

Olivia cleared her throat. "Um. I know where that is. It's actually my private office in the city. I gave Helen a key because she wanted a quiet place to go, and we arranged for her to leave me information there for the story. It's where my laptop and all my notes are hidden."

More tension roared through the room, and Olivia fought the very real urge to run like hell. "I can, uh, draw a diagram of the building and outlying area, if you'd like."

Chalton nodded, his eyes black orbs of pure fury. "Is there any chance our mother told you why she decided to betray the immortal world?"

Olivia cleared her throat, trying to remain calm. "Um, no. She didn't mention she was immortal."

"No reason at all for giving up the information?" Jared asked, tension cutting lines in the side of his mouth.

"She just said that she had information that had to get out there, and that the researchers behind the studies had all disappeared. She felt that the medical advancements being hidden could be an impressive help with human illnesses." Olivia smoothed her hands down the thick yoga pants.

"So she knew about Ronni," Jared drawled. "She used your motivation against you."

"I think she really wanted to help," Olivia countered.

"Did she mention us?" Theo asked, rubbing his jaw.

Olivia shook her head. "Your mom looks about forty years old, so if she'd mentioned three grown sons, it would've been a red flag, don't you think?"

"Good point," Chalton said grimly. "All right. I'll contact the Realm and get satellite imaging going for the building, while you start diagraming."

Jared pushed to his feet. "You know this is a trap, right?"

"Right." Chalton nodded. "Definite trap."

Olivia stood and then faltered. "If it's a trap, how can you go in?"

"It's our mom," Chalton said. "No choice. So let's get as prepared as possible."

Well, that was just fantastic. What could go wrong?

Chapter Twelve

Olivia ignored her extremely pissed off lover and kept flush against the building, adrenaline shooting through her veins faster than a motorcycle at full throttle. A gun lay heavy at her back beneath a buttery-soft leather jacket, and a knife scratched against her calf inside a badass leather boot.

Chalton's mom knew how to dress apparently.

Ronni, similarly armed, nudged her. "I'm thinking we're idiots for coming," she whispered.

Olivia swallowed down bile. "I know." Yet she was a journalist, and stories sometimes became dangerous. She started this one, and she'd by damn finish it.

Chalton cut her a look from across the doorway of the older brick building. He'd ordered her to stay at the warehouse, but both she and Ronni had insisted on coming. When he'd decided just to tie them up, Theo had intervened, saying that they had a right to finish this out, too.

Jared had agreed with tying them up, his gaze remaining pretty hot on Ronni.

But the satellite pictures with heat signatures illustrated that Petey was long gone from the office. The pictures showed a lot of people in the vicinity but no guns. Well, no visible guns. They could be hidden, and Petey might be nearby ready to strike.

Chalton was a different man in battle. Hard, cold, and meticulous…completely banishing the lover who'd rocked her world last night. For the first time, she could see the assassin he used to be.

No doubt he'd kill to protect his mother, but Olivia said a quick prayer that he wouldn't have to do so. What would that do to him?

He gave some weird hand signal. Jared nodded and yanked open the quiet green door, while Theo tensed behind Ronni.

Chalton went in first, Jared second, then Olivia hustled after him, trusting Theo to protect Ronni. Even now, her breathing was labored behind Olivia.

There had to be some way to save her.

Jared lifted some cool-looking scope down the hallway and gave a quick nod. Several doorways lined the way, all to small offices, all seemingly quiet since it was Sunday.

They reached the third office on the left, and Jared pointed the scope at the door. Olivia stood up on her tiptoes to see the readout, which showed the heat signature of one person tied up on a chair. A smaller person. It had to be Helen.

Jared meticulously ran the scope around to see the entire office. No heat signatures...no other people.

Olivia breathed a sigh of relief. Okay. So the trap wasn't inside.

"They'll be waiting when we leave," Chalton whispered.

Jared nodded. "I have men closing in on the area. If there's a threat, they'll find it."

"The shifters are still an hour out, but they'll be here as soon as possible," Chalton said, having called for more backup the second they'd formed a plan.

"If Petey is around here, waiting to take a shot, he's mine," Jared said.

Chalton shook his head. "Whoever has the shot can take it."

"It won't be a shot, and you've come too far to return to darkness," Jared said.

Chalton studied him but didn't answer. "Ready for go?"

Jared's face hardened even more and he nodded.

"Ready," Theo said, his voice strong and determined.

Olivia tensed, ready to jump inside and do something. Anything. Okay. Duck and cover.

Chalton kicked the door in and went in low, while Jared went in high. Theo covered Olivia and Ronni in the hall.

"Clear," Chalton called out.

Olivia ran inside just as he was gingerly removing the gag from Helen's mouth.

"Get out," Helen screamed, struggling furiously with her bindings, tears streaming down her face. "Now. Go."

The door slammed shut behind Theo, and he turned to pound on the heavy oak. An explosion rippled through the hallway outside, and ceiling tiles rained down in the office.

Chalton drew a knife from his boot to cut his mother's bindings.

Jared rushed for the window.

"Stop. It's wired," Helen hissed.

Jared slowed down and peered up and then surveyed the windowsill. "Yep. Wired from the outside."

Ronni hitched to his side and bent down to survey the outside sill. "Mercury lever. If we lift the window or even try to break the glass, the vibrations will make it blow."

Jared glanced down at her.

Ronni shrugged. "I haven't always been dying, you know."

"You work with a bomb squad?" Jared asked.

Ronni scoffed. "No. I'm a police shrink. But the job gives me access to tons of different classes, and bombs are interesting."

"Can you diffuse one?" Jared asked.

"No." Ronni blanched. "Sorry."

Helen stood and was instantly enfolded by Chalton. She shoved him. "What are you three doing here? It's a trap. You had to know it's a trap."

"Of course it's a trap," Chalton said, gingerly touching a bruise at her hairline. "Are you all right?"

She rolled her eyes. "Of course I'm fine. I'm just bait, you know." Irritation wrinkled her forehead. Then she caught sight of Olivia. "Oh no. What in the world are you doing here?" Rushing forward, she gathered Olivia in a lilac-scented hug.

"I came to help save you." Olivia returned the hug and then levered back to study the shorter woman. Since Olivia's parents had died when she'd been young, she'd enjoyed the maternal comfort provided by Helen. "So. There's quite a bit you didn't tell me."

Helen smiled, her dark eyes identical to Chalton's. "True."

"How could you lie to me and get away with it?" Olivia asked. "I can usually tell.

Helen smiled. "I've been immortal for centuries, dear. Masking a lie isn't as difficult as you'd think."

"Why, mom?" Jared asked, gently leading Ronni away from the wired window. "Why in the world would you leak proprietary information and put a bounty on your head?"

Helen shrugged. "I figured the king would send Chalton to investigate. I hired Theo, and I had friends of mine hire you to all track down Olivia."

"Why?" Chalton asked, his eyebrows drawing down.

"You boys haven't talked in over a hundred years."

Helen put both hands on her hips. "I thought that having a common goal would get you in the same place, and look! It worked."

"Is that all?" Theo asked, a smile barely lifting his lips.

"Um." Helen shuffled stunning black Manolo's. "Well, I did notice that Olivia was enhanced. As is Ronni, by the way."

Chalton groaned. "This is some elaborate matchmaking scheme?"

"Well, it was, but I admit it got out of hand. I didn't expect Petey to make a move." Helen swallowed. "It's my fault. Obviously he was watching me, and when I arranged for you all to be here at the same time, he finally made a move. I'm so sorry."

That did explain the timing. Chalton strode toward the crumpled inward door. "Let's get out of here and deal with the treason and matchmaking issues later. It sounds like the explosion completely blocked the door."

Olivia straightened and craned her neck, her gaze searching. "Something is off. I feel...something. A weird vibration."

Ronni frowned. "What do you mean?"

Olivia turned toward Helen. "Did they touch anything in the room? Leave anything?"

Helen glanced around. "I'm empathic, not psychic. I was knocked out for a little while, but I did hear them rummaging in the desk. I figured they were looking for the research I'd leaked to Olivia."

Olivia inched toward the desk and bent down to study the drawers. Gingerly, she pulled out the bottom one.

"Hell," Jared murmured, looking over her shoulder.

Olivia sucked in air. "We have a bomb, folks."

Chapter Thirteen

Chalton hurried around the desk to study the bomb. Different wires cascaded out from a compilation of material only known to the immortal world. When it blew, it'd take out the entire building.

A timer ran along the side, and he had to bend down to read it. "We have two minutes."

He levered up and glanced around the room. The outside walls were brick, the door was blocked, and the window was wired from the outside. "Everybody take cover. It has been a while, but I'll do what I can," he said evenly, trying to remain calm.

Ronni cleared her throat and stood up. "I have no clue how to diffuse a bomb." She grasped Helen's arm and drew her over to the bookshelf. "Anybody?"

"I know more than most." Chalton reached for a pair of scissors on the desk, his gaze on Olivia. "When you sense lies or truth...what is it like?"

She blinked, panic darkening her eyes. "Like?"

"Yes. Do you smell a lie? See a lie? Just sense it?"

She rapidly shook her head. "There's a subtle vibration I sense through the air."

He smiled and tried to banish all concern. "Good. That's good. Come here."

She moved without hesitation, arriving at his side and kneeling down, her gaze on the bomb. "I don't know anything about bombs."

He gripped the scissors. "Wires send out vibrations, just like people do." He leaned toward her. "I'm going to press on each wire, and I want you to listen to and catalog the sound."

She swallowed and glanced at him. "I can see patterns in books, colors, words, speech, even the air sometimes."

He frowned, wanting nothing more than to force open the door and tell her to run. "You see one here?" he asked instead.

She gulped in air and studied the bomb. "The wires. Colors and crossing." A tingling set up from her...popping the air around him. "I don't sense the bad ones."

He angled to the side, the scissors at ready. "This pink wire is an instant detonation if cut. I can tell by the way it's inserted. We have to cut all the other ones first, but I don't know the order." Careful and slow, he pressed the scissors on the wire.

She glanced up, her face pale. "Okay. That was shrill."

He hadn't heard a thing. She was amazing but obviously getting freaked out. Couldn't blame her. "Okay. Let's try the yellow one." He tried to convey confidence in his gaze.

"Not as bad," she said. "I can hear the difference."

"Good. Now blue." He went through each one, careful not to cut. Finally, they were done. "In order from barely shrill to very shrill, it goes blue, yellow, red, black, and then pink. Right?"

Tears filled her eyes. "No way will this work." She pushed back her hair, and her hand visibly shook. "The good news is that even if we blow up, you won't die, right?"

He wanted to lie to her, but she'd know it. "We can die, sweetheart. By beheading, by losing all our blood, and by being blown to bits."

She grimaced. "Oh. Guess we'd better get this right." She bent down so close she was almost nose-to-nose with the myriad of wires. Just in case this was it, she couldn't leave things unsaid. "I do love you, you know," she whispered.

"I know," he whispered back. "I realize it doesn't make sense to you, but when it happens, it happens quickly for my people. I love you, too."

She glanced up, a small smile on her face, tears in her eyes. "Guess we'd better live."

"Fucking get to it," Jared ordered from across the room

where he and Theo tried to shield Ronni and Helen.

"I'm sorry we didn't talk for so long," Chalton said. There was a chance that his crazy plan wouldn't work, and he'd end up in pieces. It was time to become a strong family again, even if it was during his last moments. "You're my brothers, and I carry you with me at all times."

Theo nodded. "Ditto, and a hundred years isn't long, really. We would've caught up."

"Yeah," Jared said with a low growl. "Without anybody committing treason."

Helen sighed. "I believe we're running out of time. I love you boys."

"You can do this. Blue wire first," Olivia said quietly.

Chalton, his hand steady, clipped the blue wire.

Olivia breathed out. "Good. Okay, good. Um, twenty seconds. Yellow wire."

He moved to cut. It seemed to help her to direct, so he let her, although he'd already memorized the order.

"The red wire."

He swallowed and then snipped the red wire, his body tensing for the explosion.

Nothing.

His chest heaved. "Fifteen seconds."

She grimaced, her gaze on the wires. "The next is the black wire, but it's underneath the pink one. You can't cut the pink."

He inched to the side and slid the scissors beneath the pink wire, holding his breath. With a slight twist of his fingers, he snapped the black wire and glanced at the timer. "Ten seconds."

She coughed. "Thank you for the last couple days. They were crazy but the best of my life."

"Ditto." He snapped the pink wire, dropping the scissors and tackling her to the ground, covering her completely.

Quiet reigned.

She looked up at him, her gaze wide.

Slowly, he turned and moved back to the bomb. It had frozen at one second. One second.

"Are we done?" Jared asked, tension riding his voice.

Chalton went limp. "Yeah. Bomb's out." He yanked Olivia

into him and covered her mouth with his, taking her deep and showing her everything he was feeling. She kissed him back, giving him the sense of coming home. Finally.

A throat clearing drew him away from her.

"We still need to get out of here," Jared snapped, heading for the bookcase and tossing books on the floor. "We'll have to go through the inner wall to the next office and so on until we can get out to the hallway."

Chalton nodded and moved to help pull the bookshelf away from the wall.

"Me first." Theo pivoted in a stunning spin-kick to demolish the drywall.

Olivia rushed for the hidden wall safe on the other side, opened it, and drew out her laptop and a stack of manila files.

Jared jumped in to assist Theo, and within minutes, they were in a small office that appeared to belong to a bunch of performing belly dancers, based on the costumes strewn around.

They had to attack another inner wall to enter a magician's office to be able to access the outer hallway. Once there, they filed out single-handedly the same way they'd arrived.

Sirens trilled in the distance.

"We need to be out of here," Chalton said, leading the way into the sunlight and around the corner. "Look natural." He glanced left and right, looking for a threat but finding nothing.

Crowds moved past them, several people stopping to gape at the smoke billowing out of the brick building from the inner hallway explosion. The smoke was secondary without any remaining fire, so hopefully nobody had been harmed. He couldn't smell any blood or sense death, so the strike had been localized well.

Chalk one up for Petey.

The crowd thickened, and he tried to maneuver between shopping bags and kids on a field trip holding museum bags. He paused near an alley, scouted the quiet row, and moved on.

A man in a hat jostled him, stepped by, and shoved Olivia into the alley.

Chalton turned in time to see a knife flash against her delicate skin. Everything in him quieted, and he shut off all emotion, even as he wanted to roar. He followed with his brothers flanking him, guns already out.

The hat fell off.

"Petey," Chalton breathed, his focus on the knife pressed against her vulnerable jugular. Her fear climbed into him, and he had to concentrate to keep from losing his mind. His entire body heated and then chilled to ice. Petey held her around the waist, knife to her throat, her back to his front.

"You took out my bomb?" Petey asked, his blue eyes flashing. Standing well over six-feet tall, the blond easily pulled Olivia deeper into the alley.

"Yes." Chalton took note of the area, looking for a place to take him down. A series of stench-riddled garbage bins lined the way, while puddles glimmered all over. "Why don't you stop hiding behind a little human?"

Petey pressed his nose to her hair and breathed deeply. "Your little human. She reeks of you."

Olivia's eyes widened, fear filling the green. Her head was back and her head was arched to avoid the sharp blade digging in. A sliver of blood rolled down her neck.

Chalton fought to keep from turning into the predator living inside him. "Only cowards hide behind women." Or kidnap mothers.

Petey shrugged. "Your people killed my father. I guess killing your mate is a fair exchange."

"She's not my mate," Chalton ground out, angling a little to the right as Jared went left. "But I will avenge her death in ways you can't even imagine right now." She *was* his mate, and his fangs tried to flash. A rumbled set through him. Everything inside him rioted at the image of her in danger. "I will kill you, Petey."

"Ah. The Realm assassin makes an appearance. Thought you went limp there," Petey spat, backing away.

"Just took a vacation." It had been way too long since he'd fired a weapon, but there was only one chance to save Olivia. "Let the girl go, and I won't kill you."

Petey smiled and let his fangs drop. "No."

Allowing instinct to take over, Chalton grabbed his weapon

and fired.

The bullet impacted Petey's wrist, going right through to his collarbone and missing Olivia by centimeters. Petey dropped the knife and yelled as blood sprayed from his injury.

Chalton leaped for him, shoving Olivia away and continuing down to the ground. Nothing existed. No thought, no feeling...only protecting his mate.

His knife was instantly in his hand from his boot, and he shoved down through Petey's throat right to the concrete. Grunting, Chalton twisted right and then left, sawing until the head rolled under a dumpster.

He growled and stood, wiping his knife on his jeans. Turning, his fangs out, blood on his face, he saw Olivia right before she pitched forward in a dead faint. Theo caught her before she could hit the dirty ground.

Slowly, reality returned to Chalton. His brothers and mom stared at him, concern bright in their eyes.

He focused on the woman he loved. To save her, he'd had to become what he'd vowed never to become again. A monster who killed.

Had he just lost her?

* * * *

Olivia settled into the plush sofa at Helen's house, her gaze on the slowly forming king on the broad plasma television. Apparently vampires rarely used texting and instead had to see each other in full color.

Ronni perched quietly on a settee, drinking an iced tea, more pale than ever. Helen was in the other room trying to keep Uncle Benny from sending troops to kill Chalton, while he and his brothers stood as a unit to face the television.

King Dage Kayrs stood as well, his hands behind his back. "Is it over?"

"Yes," Chalton said. "We have the research and have stopped the stories. The mission is concluded."

Dage frowned and studied Chalton. "Are you all right?"

"Fine, King. Stop worrying," Chalton said.

The king nodded, glancing to the sides. "It's good to see you and your brothers together." He focused on Jared. "He's been lonely without you."

"Ditto," Jared said.

"Good." The king visibly relaxed. "Your mother was matchmaking instead of committing treason, as far as I'm concerned. We'll keep her involvement out of any reports whatsoever, so this stays between us. The issue is concluded."

"No." Olivia sucked deep for courage and stood to face what could only be termed a deadly predator. "I haven't promised to stop writing the articles."

Dage's eyebrows rose. "Chalton? Your mate seems to have a different idea than you do."

"We haven't mated," Olivia said as sweetly as she could.

"We will," Chalton shot back.

"Maybe." She tried to appear calm and not scared shitless. "That's private, and we'll discuss it later." As of now, her insisting on accompanying him on the mission had resulted in his killing somebody, and a new darkness had entered his eyes. Did he resent her? He had a right. "My business is with the king."

"Is that so?" Chalton asked, his voice dangerously mild.

She shivered. "Yep. Here's the deal. You promised to save my friend, King. If you figure out how to do so, then I'll even write an article debunking the extra-chromosomal species." She could come up with something interesting that made sense and might still help human scientists. "Deal?"

The king studied her, his silver eyes nearly glowing. "Chalton? Any ideas?"

Ronni cleared her throat. "Um, hi, Vampire King. I'm not mating Chalton. Period."

Amusement flashed across Dage's face. "I could find you a lonely shifter."

Was he kidding? Olivia frowned.

"I'll mate her." Jared stepped closer to the camera.

Ronni gasped. "Ah, well, hmmm."

He turned to face her. "You want to live or not?"

"I really do," she murmured. "But the whole mating thing?

It's forever."

"Yes," he said.

Olivia shook her head. "It doesn't have to be."

"Yet it does," Jared said, his gaze not leaving Ronni's.

Dage chuckled. "Well then, problem solved. Olivia? Send me a copy of your new article as soon as it's written. Chalton? Take all the time you need with your family, but please do check in." The king clicked off without another word.

Chalton shook his head. "Olivia? Would you and Ronni please join my mother in the other room? I'd like to talk to my brothers."

Olivia nodded and tried to keep her knees from shaking.

Ronni opened her mouth to protest, and Jared shook his head. "We'll talk in a few minutes, and I'll lay out your options for you. For now, please give us a moment."

Olivia took her hand. "Let's go." If nothing else, they could probably make a break for it.

Chapter Fourteen

Chalton waited until the door closed behind Olivia. "Have you lost your damn mind?"

"Probably." Jared crossed to the bar and poured three glasses of aged Scotch. "But here's the deal. Olivia won't stop until her friend is saved, and the king will be forced to do something about it, which would just hurt you."

"We can find her somebody else to mate," Chalton muttered.

"True, but this way, our mates will be friends and maybe we'll see more of each other." Jared handed glasses to Chalton and Theo.

Chalton drew himself up short. "I'm sorry about the last century, but you sure as shit don't need to mate my mate's friend to stay in contact."

Jared took a deep swallow and hummed in pleasure. "I know, but why not? I hadn't planned on mating, so why not save Olivia's friend? We can mate, I can save her, and then we can go our separate ways."

Chalton frowned. "Do you think it'll be that easy?"

"Sure." Jared took another drink.

Man, was he clueless.

Theo snorted and shook his head. Then he sobered. "Are you all right, Chalton? I mean, with, you know."

"Killing Petey?" Chalton tipped back his head and took a deep swallow, allowing the potent brew to warm his insides. "I think so." But he'd made Olivia faint. Would she ever be able to see him as anything but the killer he was at heart? "I might have a few more nightmares, but he was threatening my mate."

Jared nodded. "You did what you had to do."

"Amen," Theo said.

Chalton grinned. It was good being with his brothers again. "You know what this all means, right?"

Theo shook his head.

"You're both part of the Realm now, whether you like it or not." Man, it'd be fun to see Dage try to meddle in Jared's life. The king couldn't help it.

Jared snorted. "Great."

Yeah, it actually was great. Chalton nodded.

Jared shuffled his feet. "I guess it wouldn't harm us to align with the Realm. Dage was pretty cool about mom committing treason."

Chalton nodded. "He's a bigger matchmaker than mom. God help us if they ever sit down to chat."

Theo coughed. "They both can stay away from my love life. I'm not mating for centuries."

"We'll see." Chalton downed the rest of his glass and turned for the doorway. "Speaking of mates, I need to set things straight with Olivia."

Theo cleared his throat. "What if she's not okay with, well, everything? She did faint."

Chalton nodded, not stopping. "I know, and she doesn't have a choice. She will be all right." He hoped that was true. The idea of losing her now hurt somewhere deeper than his body.

He steeled his shoulders, strode into the kitchen, and tossed her over his shoulder.

She gave a small eek and tried to find her balance.

He grinned. They might as well get things off to the right start. Planting his hand across her ass, he easily kept her in place.

* * * *

What in the world was happening? Once again, she was upside down over his massive shoulder. "Damn it, Chalton." She punched him in the kidney. "You have got to stop doing this."

She'd been in the middle of a discussion with Helen about real events at the turn of the century.

"No." His strides were relaxed and easy as they wound through several hallways to enter a bedroom decorated with a nautical theme. He bent over, and she ended up sitting on a bed. "We need to talk."

Her heart hurt. "Are you mad at me?"

He frowned and crossed his muscled arms. "No. Are you afraid of me?"

"No." She licked her lips. "Sorry about the whole fainting thing. I missed breakfast." And had never been held at knifepoint or seen a fight to the death.

He grinned. "You're going to mate me."

Yeah, she was. "Well. You might have to court me first, and meet my grandfather." And tell her all about his hundreds of years of life. Maybe she should write a fictional novel about his times. Yeah.

"I can do that." He leaned over her and brushed his lips against hers.

"We have plenty of time to court." What a nice, old-fashioned word.

He leaned back, his face an inch away from hers, his dark eyes blazing. "Not really. I'll give you a week, but you're wearing my bite at that point."

She breathed in. "Wait a minute."

"I will. An entire week."

It was going to take her a lot longer than a week to tame his Neanderthal tendencies. She might as well do it while being immortal. "A week it is." She smiled.

Possessiveness and promise glittered in his masculine gaze. "I love you, Olivia."

She wrapped both arms around his neck. "I love you more."

"Impossible." Then he kissed her, filling her with what could only be love and hope for the future. The very long future.

* * * *

Also from 1001 Dark Nights and Rebecca Zanetti, discover Tricked and Tangled.

About Rebecca Zanetti

Rebecca Zanetti is the author of over twenty-five dark paranormals, romantic suspense, and contemporary romances, and her books have appeared multiple times on the New York Times, USA Today, and Amazon bestseller lists. She has received a Publisher's Weekly Starred Review for Wicked Edge, Romantic Times Reviewer Choice Nominations for Forgotten Sins and Sweet Revenge, and RT Top Picks for several of her novels. She believes strongly in luck, karma, and working her butt off…and she thinks one of the best things about being an author, unlike the lawyer she used to be, is that she can let the crazy out. Her current series are: The Scorpius Syndrome, The Dark Protectors, The Realm Enforcers, The Sin Brothers, and The Lost Bastards. Find Rebecca at: www.rebeccazanetti.com

Also From Rebecca Zanetti

SCORPIUS SYNDROME SERIES
Scorpius Rising
Mercury Striking
Shadow Falling
Justice Ascending

DARK PROTECTORS
Fated
Claimed
Tempted
Hunted
Consumed
Provoked
Twisted
Shadowed
Tamed
Marked

REALM ENFORCERS
Wicked Ride
Wicked Edge
Wicked Burn
Wicked Kiss
Wicked Bite

SIN BROTHERS
Forgotten Sins
Sweet Revenge
Blind Faith
Total Surrender

MAVERICK MONTANA COWBOYS
Against the Wall
Under the Covers
Rising Assets
Over the Top

Tricked
A Dark Protectors Novella
By Rebecca Zanetti
Now Available

He Might Save Her

Former police psychologist Ronni Alexander had it all before a poison attacked her heart and gave her a death sentence. Now, on her last leg, she has an opportunity to live if she mates a vampire. A real vampire. One night of sex and a good bite, and she'd live forever with no more weaknesses. Well, except for the vampire whose dominance is over the top, and who has no clue how to deal with a modern woman who can take care of herself.

She Might Kill Him

Jared Reese, who has no intention of ever mating for anything other than convenience, agrees to help out his new sister in law by saving her friend's life with a quick tussle in bed. The plan seems so simple. They'd mate, and he move on with his life and take risks as a modern pirate should. Except after one night with Ronni, one moment of her sighing his name, and he wants more than a mating of convenience. Now all he has to do is convince Ronni she wants the same thing. Good thing he's up for a good battle.

Mercury Striking

By Rebecca Zanetti
Book #1 of The Scorpius Syndrome series
Now Available

With nothing but rumors to lead her, Lynn Harmony has trekked across a nightmare landscape to find one man—a mysterious, damaged legend who protects the weak and leads the strong. He's more than muscle and firepower—and in post-plague L.A., he's her only hope. As the one woman who could cure the disease, Lynn is the single most volatile—and vulnerable—creature in this new and ruthless world. But face to face with Jax Mercury...

Danger has never looked quite so delicious...

"Thrilling post-apocalyptic romance at its dark, sizzling best!" —Lara Adrian

"Nothing is easy or black or white in Zanetti's grim new reality, but hope is key, and I *hope* she writes faster!" —*New York Times* bestselling author Larissa Ione

* * * *

MERCURY STRIKING

In the end, there is no doubt that Mother Nature will win.
--Dr. Frank. X Harmony, *Philosophies*

CHAPTER ONE

Life on Earth is at the ever-increasing risk of being wiped out by a disaster, such as sudden global warming, nuclear war, a genetically engineered virus, or other dangers we have not yet thought of.
--Stephen Hawking

Despair hungered in the darkness, not lingering, not

languishing . . . but waiting to bite. No longer the little brother of rage, despair had taken over the night, ever present, an actor instead of an afterthought.

Lynne picked her way along the deserted twelve-lane interstate, allowing the weak light from the moon to guide her. An unnatural silence hung heavy over the barren land. Rusting carcasses of vehicles lined the sides; otherwise, the once-vibrant 405 was dead.

Her months of hiding had taught her stealth. Prey needed stealth, as did the hunter.

She was both.

The tennis shoes she'd stolen from an abandoned thrift store protected her feet from the cracked asphalt, while a breeze scented with death and decomposing vegetation lifted her hair. The smell had saturated the wind as she'd trekked across the country.

The world was littered with dead bodies and devoid of souls.

A click echoed in the darkness. About time. Predators, both human and animal, crouched in every shadow, but she'd made it closer to what used to be Los Angeles than she'd hoped.

A strobe light hit her full on, rendering sight impossible. The miracle of functioning batteries brought pain. She closed her eyes. They'd either kill her or not. Either way, no need to go blind. "I want to see Mercury." Since she'd aimed for the center of Mercury's known territory, hopefully she'd find him and not some rogue gang.

Silence. Then several more clicks. Guns of some type. They'd closed in silently, just as well trained as she'd heard. As she'd hoped.

She forced strength into her voice. "You don't want to kill me without taking me to Mercury first." Jax Mercury, to be exact. If he still lived. If not, she was screwed anyway.

"Why would we do that?" A voice from the darkness, angry and near.

She squinted, blinking until her pupils narrowed. The bright light exposed her and concealed them, weakening her knees, but she gently set her small backpack on the ground. She had to clear her throat to force out sound. "I'm Lynne Harmony."

Gasps, low and male, filled the abyss around her. "Bullshit," a voice hissed from her left.

She tilted her head toward the voice, and then slowly, so slowly they wouldn't be spooked, she unbuttoned her shirt. No catcalls, no suggestive responses followed. Shrugging her shoulders, she dropped the cotton to the ground, facing the light.

She hadn't worn a bra, but she doubted the echoing exhales of shock were from her size Bs. More likely the shimmering blue outline of her heart caught their attention. Yeah, she was a freak. Typhoid Mary in the body of a woman who'd failed. Big time. But she might be able to save the men surrounding her. "So. Jax Mercury. Now."

One man stepped closer. Gang tattoos lined his face, inked tears showing his kills. He might have been thirty, he might have been sixty. Regardless, he was dangerous, and he smelled like dust combined with body odor. A common smell in the plague-riddled world. Eyeing her chest, he quickly crossed himself. "Holy Mary, Mother of God."

"Not even close." A silent overpass loomed a few yards to the north, and her voice echoed off the concrete. The piercing light assaulted her, spinning the background thick and dark. Her temples pounded, and her hollow stomach ached. Wearily, she reached down and grabbed her shirt, shrugging it back on. She figured the "take me to your leader" line would get her shot. "Do you want to live or not?"

He met her gaze, his scarred upper lip twisting. "Yes."

It was the most sincere sound she'd heard in months. "We're running out of time." Time had deserted them long ago, but she needed to get a move on. "Please." The sound shocked her, the civility of it, a word she'd forgotten how to use. The slightest of hopes warmed that blue organ in her chest, reminding her of who she used to be. Who she'd lost.

Another figure stepped forward, this one big and silent. Deadly power vibrated in the shift of muscle as light illuminated him from behind, shrouding his features. "I didn't tell you to put your shirt back on." No emotion, no hint of humanity echoed in the deep rumble.

His lack of emotion twittered anxiety through her empty abdomen. Without missing a beat, she secured each button, keeping the movements slow and sure. "I take it you're Mercury." Regardless of name, there was no doubt the guy was in charge.

"If I am?" Soft, his voice promised death.

A promise she'd make him keep. Someday. The breeze picked up, tumbling weeds across the lonely 405 to halt against a Buick stripped to its rims. She quelled a shiver. Any weakness shown might get her killed. "You know who I am," she whispered.

"I know who you say you are." His overwhelming form blocked out the light, reminding her of her smaller size. "Take off your shirt."

Something about his command gave her pause. Before, she hadn't cared. But with him so close she could smell *male*, an awareness of her femininity brought fresh fear. Nevertheless, she again unbuttoned her shirt.

This time, her hands trembled.

Straightening her spine, she squared her shoulders and left the shirt on, the worn material gaping in front.

He waited.

She lifted her chin, trying to meet his eyes although she couldn't see them. The men around them remained silent, yet alertness carried on the oxygen. How many guns were trained on her? She wanted to tell them it would only take one. Though she'd been through hell, she'd never really learned to fight.

The wind whipped into action, lifting her long hair away from her face. Her arms tightened against her rib cage. Goose bumps rose over her skin. She was accustomed to being vulnerable, and she was used to feeling alone. But she'd learned to skirt danger.

There was no doubt the man in front of her was *all* danger.

She shivered again.

Swearing quietly, he stepped in, long, tapered fingers drawing her shirt apart. He shifted to the side, allowing light to blast her front. Neon blue glowed along her flesh.

"Jesus." He pressed his palm against her breastbone—directly above her heart.

Shock tightened her muscles, and that heart ripped into a gallop. Her nipples pebbled from the breeze. Warmth cascaded from his hand when he spread his fingers over the odd blue of her skin, easily spanning her upper chest. When was the last time someone had touched her gently?

And gentle, he was.

The contact had her looking down at his damaged hand. Faded white scars slashed across his knuckles, above the veins, past his wrist. The bizarre glow from her heart filtered through his fingers. Her entire chest was aqua from within, those veins closest to her heart, which glowed neon blue, shining strong enough to be seen through her ribs and sternum.

He exhaled softly, removing his touch.

An odd sense of loss filtered down her spine. Then surprise came as he quickly buttoned her shirt to the top.

He clasped her by the elbow. "Cut the light." His voice didn't rise, but instantly, the light was extinguished. "I'm Mercury. What do you want?"

What a question. What she wanted, nobody could provide. Yet she struggled to find the right words. Night after night, fleeing under darkness to reach him, she'd planned for this moment. But the words wouldn't come. She wanted to breathe. To rest. To hide. "Help. I need your help." The truth tumbled out too fast to stop.

He stiffened and tightened his hold. "That, darlin', you're gonna have to earn."

THE PROMISE OF SURRENDER
A MacKenzie Family Novella
By Liliana Hart

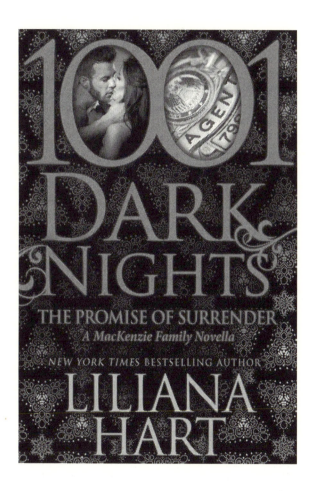

Acknowledgments

To Scott,

I'm glad I married you. Even though you jumped out of the closet and scared me.

Chapter One

She had him pegged for a cop the second he stepped out of the beat-up pickup truck.

He opened the back of the cab and pulled out a cardboard box, maybe a foot long and wide. His worn sneakers scuffed against the graveled parking lot, and even through the surveillance cameras that covered every square inch of her property, she could see the outline of his backup weapon strapped to his ankle.

"Lord, save me from rookies." Mia stopped processing her inventory to watch him out of curiosity. She'd spent the weekend at an estate sale and ended up with more boxes than she'd planned. That was usually how it went, but she had a knack for things that would sell for a profit.

The guy was tall and thin as a rail, his hair long and shaggy, and he had a partial growth of beard on his face. She could see why they'd want him for undercover work. He had the naturally too-thin build that made him able to pass for a junkie. He was just a baby, maybe a year or two out of the academy, and he had no idea the toll that working undercover would have on his life.

"Get out while you still can, boy." She shook her head sadly.

There was no warning them—the rookies. They thought working undercover was like it was on TV—sexy and dangerous—living life on the edge between good and evil. And then six months into the job they realized it wasn't so sexy, but it sure as hell was dangerous. They were lying to spouses and family and friends, living a double life, and they were doing things the soul would never be able to reconcile. All for the greater good.

His jeans and T-shirt looked like he'd gotten them straight from a thrift store and he wasn't quite comfortable in them. He was used to being pressed and polished. A silver-spoon kid. He'd probably been a patrolman, used to the uniform, and the dead giveaway was the way he kept tapping his elbow against his side, checking for his duty weapon.

He walked like a cop. And his eyes scanned the area like a cop—like he was trying to see where his backup was located just in case he needed a rescue. Surely working undercover hadn't changed that much in the last ten years. This guy was lucky to be alive if his commander was sending him out with that much green on him.

Mia wasn't the most patient of people on her best days. And today wasn't one of her best days. It was barely noon, and a variety of customers had already come into the shop. Each one had made her head pound a little harder.

She'd opened Pawn to Queen six years before with nothing but sweat, blood, and the money she'd taken in one lump sum from her pension. There'd been no rhyme or reason as to why she'd picked Surrender, Montana. Not that she wasn't familiar with the area and all the little towns that dotted the Montana landscape like pictures on a postcard. But there'd been something about Surrender that had called to her to make it home.

Even with the appeal of the rolling hills, white fences, and the shops downtown with matching black awnings and flowers placed along the wooden walkways, she knew she couldn't sully the peaceful image of the town with her shop. She'd never fooled herself into thinking her clientele was a cut above all the other pawnshop owners out there. For the most part, she was dealing with the dregs of humanity. So she'd built her shop on the outskirts of town, just outside the city limits on the other side of the hill.

Surrender was unique in that it was located at the base of several large hills, nestled like a little green jewel in the valley. Any direction visitors came from, the exits led to one main road, up and over the hill, so when they reached the top there was a crystal clear view of the little town tucked below—the *Welcome to Surrender* sign gleaming a bright and polished green at the summit.

Mia lived in a pretty little apartment above the bakery. It was painted white and had beveled windows and a spindled railing along the balcony. Smells of cinnamon rolls and fresh baked bread wafted up through the vents each morning. She was still considered an outsider, though people were friendly when she did her weekly grocery shopping or stopped to grab a bite to eat at the diner. They were friendly—but wary.

The people in Surrender came from a different era. The men were rugged and muscled from working the ranches. The denim of their jeans worn at the knees and back pockets, their boots scuffed and comfortable from use. The ranch women were as sturdy as their men, and they all worked like dogs to preserve a heritage that would go to their own children. Ranching was harsh, but it provided a good life.

The town ladies—at least that's what Mia liked to call them—were a whole different story. It was almost comical the way they scurried about from shop to shop, gossiping more than attending to errands. It was their pastime and they made no apologies about enjoying it immensely.

They'd start the day at the bakery, then take their recyclable shopping bags over to the mercantile. They'd eventually wander to the bookstore, the florist, and a little place that only sold honey and homemade candles made of beeswax, visiting with the shop owners and catching up on any news they might have missed—engagements, new babies, whose cows got loose and caused a ruckus, or who got drunk and disorderly down at Duffey's Pub the night before—all news was met with equal excitement.

There was a clothing boutique for ladies owned by Annabeth MacKenzie, but it didn't exactly cater to the kinds of things Mia liked to wear, though Annabeth was very sweet, if a little shy. Next door to Annabeth's shop was a clothing store for men that carried the hardy clothes for ranch life—Wranglers, Stetsons, and boots. There was a feed store next to that, an ice cream parlor, and the bakery occupied the corner building.

There was always some kind of ladies club meeting happening one place or another. Casserole recipes were doled out like gold bullion, and they all dressed like every day was Sunday.

Mia was a puzzlement to the women in town. She didn't talk about herself, though she was always friendly when they spoke to her. But she'd had a lot of practice avoiding invasive questions, so she smiled and turned the conversation around so she wasn't the focus.

She'd had to fill out a background check when she'd rented the little apartment, but law enforcement records didn't show on a standard check. All they knew was that her name was Mia Marie Russo and she was a thirty-four-year-old female with no family and no criminal history. And it hadn't hurt that she'd been able to pay six months rent up front.

Her landlady had been disappointed at the lack of news to carry on to her friends. It wasn't every day a single woman with a sleeve of tattoos and purple streaks in her hair moved to Surrender. And it wasn't every day that same woman built a pawnshop on the outskirts of town and carried a visible weapon everywhere she went.

Mia had built her shop just after the exit at the base of the other side of the hill, away from the pristine beauty of Surrender. She'd picked the perfect location. It was nothing but open land—no trees or hills or valleys. With the amount of cash and valuable inventory she often had on hand, it was best not to give people available hiding places.

A long, rectangular cabin with a metal roof had given her the most efficient space for the best price, and it was surrounded by a graveled parking lot. In a year or two she'd be able to afford to have it paved. She'd had bars installed on the windows for extra security and the door at the back of the cabin was solid steel and bolted tight unless she was unloading a shipment or leaving or entering the premises. Her front door was always locked and customers had to be buzzed in. She was always armed. Which she was grateful for after the customers she'd already dealt with that morning.

Her first customer of the day had been an addict trying to pawn what looked like family heirlooms. He'd probably stolen them from his own mother, as he'd seemed familiar with each piece. She'd lowballed him, hoping he'd reject the offer, but he'd taken the cash with shaky hands and a gleam in his eye that told her he was already focused on his next fix. She entered the information into the online database, put the heirlooms in an envelope, and stuck them in the safe beneath her register. Maybe someone would come in looking to get them back.

Her second customer had been a woman on the verge of a breakdown. The woman carried a baby in a sling around her chest and held a toddler by his chubby hand. Mia had listened with a pounding headache while the woman sobbed out a story of betrayal about her no-good husband. And in the end, she'd given the woman a little more than she should have for the wedding ring set. Everyone deserved a fresh start.

Her third customer had been a big brute of a man, decked out in Vaquero biker colors and 1% patches. He'd parked his Harley sideways in front of the steps that led up to the door, and she'd felt the reverberation of his footsteps as he made his way onto the porch and hit the buzzer multiple times. She debated whether or not to let him inside. It was the reason she'd had the system installed in the first place and the cameras in the lot. It was her business. Her terms.

Her gun was holstered at her waist and her right hand rested comfortably on the sawed off she kept beneath the counter. She flicked the button to release the door latch and allowed him entry. Each step he took shook the floor-to-ceiling metal shelves.

Her display counter was three sides of a big square—the fourth storeroom. Her register was centered in the middle of the square so no one could reach over the counter and take money. Her customers didn't know it, but she'd invested in bulletproof glass to protect the more expensive items she kept in the display counter.

Biker dude pressed his palms down on the glass and stared her down. She'd been stared down by worse than him, so she just stared back.

"Can I help you?" she finally asked.

"I believe you have something of mine. It's a music box. Very old. Wooden. And when you open it and wind it up you can see all the workings on the inside."

"You've lost an antique music box?" she asked skeptically.

"It was my mother's," he lied easily. "I was told it was brought here and you paid someone for it. I'll give you double what you paid."

"That's very generous of you, but the only music boxes I have are sitting on the shelf over there. You're welcome to check them out."

His jaw clenched and his smile sent chills up her spine. "Maybe you forgot you bought it," he said. "So I'm going to ask you one more time." He pressed against the counter and leaned forward until his face was inches from hers. "Go get the music box from the back."

He couldn't mistake the sound of her cocking the shotgun, and his brown eyes narrowed with malice. "Like I've already said. I haven't acquired any music boxes recently. Maybe check down the road at *Pawn and Go* in Myrna Springs."

Her voice was calm, but her heart hammered in her chest. She'd have to be fast if things went to shit. If it weren't for the bulletproof counters, she could've pulled the trigger and shot straight through. But she knew in her gut there was no way she could be fast enough to pull the shotgun out, aim, and fire. She'd let him get in too close. Her mistake, and she knew better. Civilian life had made her soft.

She stared him down with nothing but bluster, and to her surprise, he took a step back and dropped his hands down to his side.

"Why don't you keep an eye out for that music box? My brothers and I will come back for a visit soon. Real soon."

He left the shop, the door banging shut behind him, and she breathed out a sigh of relief.

"Perfect. Now I've got an entire outlaw motorcycle club to deal with. Must be my lucky day."

Mia went to the front door and made sure the latch was closed tight, and then she went into her office and unlocked the bottom drawer of her desk. Inside it sat the wooden music box she'd bought from Tina Wolfe the day before. She'd given her a hundred bucks for it and the woman had gladly taken it.

Mia wasn't one to judge—she dealt with people from all walks of life—and she knew that sometimes life dealt one shitty hand after another. That's the impression she'd gotten from Tina. She was a woman who looked like she'd ridden a hard road. Her license placed her at twenty-six, but Mia would've guessed a hard forty. A combination of the sun, alcohol, and the smoke that reeked from her clothing had aged her face considerably.

She'd ridden in on a nice Harley and she'd dressed the part. But there'd been a look of weariness on her face Mia found impossible to ignore. And when she looked a little closer, there was also an edge of fear. Tina was running from something or someone, and whatever cash she could get on her way was how she was going to survive.

So Mia had given her the cash and taken the music box. It was a nice piece. Early 1940s and in good shape. And the music still played crystal clear and she watched, fascinated, as the intricate wheels and cogs played *You Are My Sunshine*. It was a piece that caught her interest enough that she'd decided to take it home. Though now she had to wonder what there was about it that made the biker want it so badly.

She'd moved it to a safe location and grabbed a couple of the estate boxes from the storeroom, moving them to the front counter so she could start documenting the new inventory. Less than twenty minutes later, she'd looked up to see the rookie cop in her parking lot.

He buzzed her door, box in hand, and had a smirk on his face. She'd had about enough of people for the day. The easiest thing to do would be to let him keep buzzing and slip out the back for an early lunch. But he'd be back. He seemed determined.

Mia knew people. She knew how to read them and she knew how to fuck with them. It was all part of the job description—former and current. So she hit the buzzer and released the locks on the door. And then she barely glanced at him as he walked toward the counter. Just a quick look and an arched eyebrow. And then she dismissed him as nothing special and went back to the inventory she'd been cataloguing before bikers and cops had started overrunning her shop.

The box landed with a light thump next to her and he waited a few seconds in silence. His fingers drummed against the counter and he cleared his throat. She tried to hide her smile.

"What am I invisible?" he said. He wasn't from around this area judging by the accent. Maybe Chicago, if she had to guess.

He was easily summed up. Hot head. Thought he was too good for the job and God's gift to police. His badge was still shiny and new and he'd moved from the big city to Montana, where none of the departments were very big outside of the major cities. The only reason a man made that big of a change was for a woman or so he could start over. This guy didn't look like the kind of man who'd do anything for a woman, so she was guessing door number two.

He wouldn't last a month working undercover in this territory. Drugs were a huge problem, and the agents working u/c were used to the terrain—running suspects to ground across mountains and rivers—facing drug cartels one night and the outlaw motorcycle clubs the next. Manpower was short and physical characteristics determined the job more than ability—if you looked like a crackhead or a meth dealer you worked ops completely different than if you had the build of a biker.

She'd been neither. She'd always looked younger than her age and she'd ended up in various high schools across the state, looking for whoever was supplying the kids with drugs. It was a job that had been finite. She couldn't look eighteen forever.

"I'm talkin' to you, lady. Can you take a look at this? I'm in a hurry."

"Everyone looking for fast cash usually is," Mia said. "Give me a second. I'm almost done."

"You don't seem very concerned about customer service."

"You're the one trying to get cash from me. I don't have to be concerned about customer service. There are other pawnshops. You're welcome to go there."

She could practically hear his teeth grinding together and decided she might as well see what he wanted and get him out of her shop. With the clientele she usually catered to, she wasn't the only one who'd be able to sniff him out as a cop.

The sigh that escaped her lips was genuine and filled with annoyance. She dropped her pen and moved over, never looking at him directly. The inattention seemed to really bother him, so that meant he was something of a glory hound as well. It wasn't often she felt instant dislike for someone, especially another cop, but this guy rubbed her the wrong way.

"Take your stuff out of the box and set it on the counter."

He did as she asked and she crossed her arms over her chest, wincing as he jostled it with a heavy hand before setting it clumsily on the counter.

Mia had never been accused of being a bad poker player. Her life had depended on her reactions more times than she could count. But to say that she wasn't surprised would've been a lie.

A wooden music box, identical to the one she'd held in her hands only moments before, sat in front of her. She pulled a pair of latex gloves from under the counter and slipped them on before opening the top of the music box.

It was in excellent condition, and even the green felt on the inside had similar age spots to the other. She wound it up from the bottom and the cogs and wheels began turning as *You Are My Sunshine* played. She ran her fingers around the edges and all but took it apart, looking for the tiny stamp mark that authenticated it. But it didn't have one. Because it was a fake.

"It's a nice piece," she said as if she'd never seen one like it. "I'll give you ten bucks for it."

He sputtered, "Ten bucks? Are you fucking crazy? It's gotta be worth at least a hundred and fifty. It's an antique."

"What's your name?" she asked.

He hesitated a couple of seconds before answering. "Walker Barnes."

"Uh huh," Mia said, raising her eyebrows skeptically. "Well, Walker Barnes, what you have here is a fake. If this thing was made before last week I'd be surprised."

"I think you're mistaken. Why don't you look again."

"You're the second person who's told me that in the last hour. It's as irritating now as it was then. I don't make mistakes. Look how new all the metal is. It's shiny as a copper penny. And thin. They don't make things the way they used to."

"Shit," he said, running his fingers through his hair. "Listen, I'm in a bind here. I really need to find a box just like this one that's real. Do you have one?"

Mia arched a brow. Now things were getting interesting. The cops were looking for the same music box as the biker. The question was why.

"Yeah, because I always keep identical merchandise sitting in my storeroom just for occasions such as this."

"No need to be a bitch about it."

"You're wasting my time. One of us needs to get back

to work. And in case you were wondering, that would be me."

"Look, my girlfriend really loves this music box, but I don't want her to find out it was a fake. Where can I get a real one?" he asked, taking a different approach.

"Your girlfriend likes it so much you decided to come in and sell it?"

Barnes flushed red. "No, I was just thinking if it was worth something I could trade it in to get her something a little nicer. She likes jewelry too."

"Can't help you. Ten bucks. That's my offer."

"Listen, I had a friend who said you can get all kinds of stuff. That you've got connections all over the place."

"What friend would that be?" she asked.

Barnes smirked. "He likes to stay under the radar. But he assures me that you can 'get' things for people."

"I get what I know I can sell or what interests me. You have nothing I want to sell and you don't interest me. So feel free to buy something or leave."

"So is it true?" he continued. "I might have a few things I want you to look for that went missing. I know a couple people who could help retrieve them if you can find them. Maybe we can work out a deal."

Mia was done with the charade, and her blood was boiling at the thought that they'd come in and try to...*test* her. That was the only way she could really describe how it felt. As if she were auditioning for a job she didn't know she was asking for. And what really pissed her off was that she was good at reading between the lines. He wanted to know if she was dirty. How far she'd go and if she could be bought. He was lucky she didn't take that music box and shove it up his ass.

"Let me make this easy for you because you don't seem too bright," Mia said. "I'm guessing you're working with the local task force, and I hope to God this is the first and only job they've ever sent you on because you're the worst operative I've ever seen. And believe me, I've see some bad ones."

Barnes stiffened. "Hey—"

"I'm not finished. You're either here for one of two

reasons," she said. "You're trying to set me up and get me to agree to buy stolen goods, which seems pretty stupid considering I know there are a lot bigger fish to fry in this neck of the woods."

"I'm getting pretty tired of you calling me stupid," he said between gritted teeth.

She ignored him. "The second option is you're trying to see if you can use me for something for your own gain. You need my expertise or maybe even my shop for a setup. You're wasting your time and mine. If you'd wanted my help all you would've had to do is ask. I like cops—with the exception of you. I run a clean place with clean merchandise. I enter all my inventory into LEADS just like everyone else."

LEADS was a database where pawnshop owners entered the pieces people sold them. The first place cops looked if there were stolen items was in the LEADS database. "And I don't know what you're fishing for, but you're not going to find it here. Don't let the door hit you on the way out."

Mia moved back to the items she'd been cataloguing, but it was impossible to focus.

He tried smiling and lifting his hands like he was innocent. "Maybe we got off on the wrong foot, but you got it all wrong. I ain't no cop, and I don't know what you're talking about as far as working out any deals. I just thought we could do each other a favor or two."

"Don't they have you on a leash? I would've thought for sure one of the big dogs would've come to rescue you already. You're drowning."

His eyes narrowed to hard, mean slits, and she realized maybe he was a little older than she'd originally thought. But she hadn't been wrong about his personality. A hothead. And he was about ready to explode.

"You're a real bitch, you know that?"

"You don't say?" she said, wide-eyed. "I've never heard that before." Mia watched as he tossed the music box back into the cardboard box. She tried to even her temper and she took a couple deep breaths.

"Listen," she said, calmer. "I don't know who your commanding officer is, but let me give you some advice. I spotted you as a cop the second you got out of your truck. Go back to patrol. Undercover work is going to get you killed. You're terrible at it, Walker Barnes."

He gave her a middle finger and said, "Fuck off."

"I'm all full of fuck offs for the day, but thanks for caring. I'm a pain in the ass. I'm sure your recon on me and this shop told you that up front. Unless you didn't bother to do recon and came in blind on your superior's say-so. And if that's the case, I'm going to call you stupid again."

He grabbed her wrist and squeezed, his anger calling the shots now instead of common sense. Bingo. She knew that temper was going to get him. Now maybe she could find out what the hell he really wanted.

"I said I'm tired of you calling me stupid."

"You're going to want to let me go. Right now."

"You think you're so smart? I got news for you. You're going to help us whether you want to or not. Or we'll make sure this cesspool you love so much belongs to the government by the time we're done."

"Have you ever heard the saying, *Don't Write A Check That Your Mouth Can't Cash?*" she asked sweetly. Then she brought her free hand up and hit him under the chin with the back of her wrist. His teeth snapped together and his head jerked back. She grabbed him by the hair and slammed his face against the counter. And then she leaned over and whispered in his ear.

"Fuck you and everything you don't stand for, Walker Barnes. Or whatever your name is. You're a disgrace to the uniform and the badge, and I'm saying this here and now where everyone who's listening in can hear me. You can take your empty threats and shove them straight up your ass."

She saw a black Bronco skid to a stop in the parking lot out of the corner of her eye. Mia wasn't about to be intimidated by anyone. And she knew Sheriff MacKenzie wouldn't allow it either, even if it meant he'd have to go against another cop. Cooper MacKenzie was the real deal. And he'd always do what was right. Mia wasn't without connections of her own. She'd been a cop for ten years.

The buzzer at the door rang over and over again, and she let go of Barnes's hair so he could stand up straight. He stumbled back and looked confused. She released the switch to allow entry and slowed her breathing so the red haze of anger could fade.

The door opened and boots scraped across the hardwood floor. Something in the atmosphere changed—an electric current that was all too familiar. It heated her from the inside out, but chills pebbled across her skin. Her nipples spiked right along with her temper. It had always been that way.

Zeke McBride looked better than she remembered—though he was harder and had more of an edge. He'd always kept his dark hair shaved close to the scalp, but she could see the threads of silver sneaking in, especially around the temples. He'd always had facial hair for as long as she'd known him, but he'd let it grow to full scruff, and there was plenty of silver in that too. The age looked good on him.

His eyes were a dark forest green with flecks of gold, and he had impossibly long lashes for a man. She'd always been jealous. Those eyes never missed anything. One of his eyebrows had a scar running through it. That was new since she'd seen him last.

Zeke had always been big—several inches over six feet and muscled like a bodybuilder. The sleeves of his black shirt fit tight around his tattooed biceps and he wore jeans and a pair of steel-toed black boots. He was one-hundred percent badass, and if she still wasn't so mad at him she'd have pounced and claimed what was hers.

He'd always loved the undercover life. In his mind it was the ultimate battle of good versus evil. It was a way to feed the adrenaline rush, play within the shades of gray, and ultimately put away the bad guys.

Memories assaulted her—love and fear and chaos and danger and arguments—lots of arguments—and she was suddenly back in the place she'd been seven years before. Hurt and scared and not willing to sacrifice anything more than she already had. And he hadn't been willing to sacrifice anything at all. Or it least it had seemed that way to her. But she'd been unbending—they both had—so she'd walked away.

"Well, fuck," she said.

"It's good to see you too, Mia."

Chapter Two

Zeke McBride was a gambling man. As any self-respecting, second generation, Irish-American should be.

He'd dealt his own hand. And maybe he'd dealt from the bottom of the deck, but sometimes a man had to go to extremes when the stakes were high. And when it came to Mia, the stakes were as high as it got.

He'd used agency resources, his men, and had made damned sure their mission territory had included Surrender, Montana. He was the commanding officer of a DEA taskforce, and no one questioned the orders he gave. They'd been stuck in the middle of nowhere for three years, building covers and gaining trust within different drug running communities. They were the good guys, but sometimes the lines blurred. They were a law unto themselves, forgotten by their brothers in blue who clocked in with regular shift work—unless someone got killed.

It was Zeke's job to make sure the men remembered that there was a law and not to blur it too much. And it was his job to make sure everyone under his watch stayed alive.

His men would laugh like loons if they knew part of the reason for this mission was because of a woman. They'd call him pussy-whipped and any other names they could think of as they rolled their eyes. And then he'd have to knock some heads together just out of principal. Which was why his men were never going to find out.

Sometimes situations were so complicated and pasts so entwined that it was hard to know where to begin to start separating the threads. And honestly, this was the only thing he could come up with.

But he hadn't been prepared for the jolt that had hit him square in the chest the second he saw her again. She'd occupied his dreams for almost seven years. He'd tried dating other women—Mia was the one who'd left him after all—but he found himself searching for women that reminded him of her. The only problem was Mia had always been unique. There was *no one* like her.

Her appearance had changed, but by the steely look in her eyes, her temper had stayed very much the same. That temper had been making him go rock hard since the moment he'd met her. She could no longer pass for the role of the high school kid she'd played when she'd worked undercover. She was all woman, and a slow scan of her body did nothing to help relieve the throbbing pressure behind his zipper.

She'd always been petite, topping just a couple inches over five feet. Her Italian heritage was strong, with clear olive skin and dark eyes fringed with thick lashes that reminded him of a gypsy that could bewitch with just a look. Her brows were thick and delicately arched, and she had a mane of dark hair that made him long to feel it across his skin once more.

Her hair was longer than it had been the last time he'd seen her. And gone were the waves that had been the bane of her existence. It was thick and straight, and streaks of royal purple peaked between the black. He liked it. A lot. And high on his priority list was getting his hands in it.

She wore a plain black tank top. Her arm was covered from shoulder to wrist with an intricate sleeve tattoo, and he could see she'd added to it since the last time he'd seen her. That arm told an entire story, and he wondered if she'd added him anywhere, or if he'd even mattered enough.

Her breasts were full and filled out the tank nicely. In fact, she'd filled out everywhere nicely. Gone was the girlish figure she'd had for most of her twenties. The way her ass filled out those jeans made his mouth water, and he remembered what it felt like to cup each round globe in his hands.

"Well, fuck," she said.

Her words pulled him back to the present. "It's good to see you too, Mia." His voice was husky and he cleared his throat. "I thought you told me you were getting as far away from this hell as you could? Looks like you didn't make it very far."

She smiled and a lesser man would've felt his balls shrivel. "No," she said politely. "I told you I was getting as far away from *you* as I could and to rot in hell."

He shrugged, unoffended. "An easy mix-up to make." He matched her smile with one of his own, and for the first time in too long he felt the embers of excitement starting to flame into anticipation.

That was the danger with working undercover. He'd been doing it for fifteen years. The fear wasn't as strong as it had once been. He had to pay closer attention to the little signs and signals that his gut used to be better at picking up on. He'd known for a couple of years it was time to get out of the game. Before he ended up getting killed or getting one of his men killed. It had taken him forty years on earth to understand what was really important in life. And she was standing right in front of him. Now he just had to prove it to her. And it looked like it was going to be a hell of a job.

Zeke looked at "Walker Barnes" and debated whether or not to rearrange his face for putting his hands on Mia. Or for just being an asshole in general. Whether he put a fist in his face or not, he could make the guy's life miserable.

"Take it back to headquarters, Baldwin. We'll talk when I get back. You're on unpaid leave until I can figure out what to do with you."

"What the hell? She just fucking tried to break my jaw."

"Every word she said is true. You pushed your way in here using intimidation and just being a dick. Your orders were simple. You're the one who chose to take them in a different direction. I didn't want you on my team to begin with, but didn't figure you'd be this stupid if I actually let you out in public. You're a disgrace to every cop that puts his life on the line. So you've got about three seconds before I don't ask you to go so nicely," Zeke said. "And if you ever touch her again you'll get to see what it's like to be someone's bitch behind bars."

Zeke almost wished Baldwin would do something stupid. He could see it in the other man's face. He had a quick temper, he wasn't a team player, and Zeke had never trusted him. He didn't deserve to carry a badge, but sometimes it was better to keep those people close where you could keep an eye on them. But Baldwin had lived out his usefulness and it was time for him to go.

The other man shifted his feet so he was in a fighting stance, and Zeke just grinned. Maybe he'd get to punch the son of a bitch after all.

"Baldwin," Mia said, before tempers could ignite any more than they already had. "Take my advice and don't be stupid. Have you ever seen Zeke fight? One punch and your skinny ass will be out cold. Leave with all your teeth intact and some of your dignity."

"Fuck you," Baldwin said. "What makes a pawnshop cunt a cop expert? Unless you just fuck so many your pussy's got radar."

"This pussy would tear you to shreds, little boy. I'm supreme cop bitch." She took a step closer and looked Baldwin up and down from head to toe. "Let me guess. You're a couple years out of the academy. Big city cop. But you're impatient. Wanted the brass without the years or the work. Why does a big city cop run away with his tail tucked between his legs and end up in Nowhere, Montana?"

Zeke was guessing Baldwin was too shocked by her accurate rundown to answer.

"I might not be working the streets anymore," she said, all serious now, "but some things never leave you. You'll never be half the cop I was or that your commander is. And if you ever touch me again you won't have to worry about being someone's bitch in prison. You'll be someone's bitch in hell. *Capisce?*"

Baldwin stared at her about two seconds before turning and walking out of the shop. He never made eye contact with Zeke. The chicken shit.

"Christ, no one gives better parting lines than you," he said, shaking his head. "You always had a mouth on you. And it always got you into trouble."

"And always got you out of trouble, if I remember right. What the hell are you doing here, Zeke? And what do you want from me?"

It was a hell of a question. One that didn't necessarily have just one answer. He made a decision and hoped it was the right one. They could deal with the other later.

"You want to know why I came here?" he asked.

Her eyes widened as he moved in and his hands went to the denim at her hips as he pushed her back against the counter. The pulse in her neck fluttered and he wanted to sink his teeth there. He wanted to sink into her every way he could.

His lips stopped a hairsbreadth from her own and he could feel the warmth of her breath. "You can give me another one of those famous parting lines later," he said. "But I'm going to do this first."

"This is a mistake, Zeke," she whispered. Her lips parted and her hands came up to grasp at his shoulders.

He whispered back, "Shut up and kiss me, Mia."

His lips covered hers—slanted over them, parted and invaded them. It was like coming home, and his body, mind, and soul recognized her as his. She'd *always* been his. Then the kiss turned from remembering and sweetness into something a little darker—a little edgier. It became more forceful, and he groaned as he felt the nip of her teeth against his bottom lip. She'd always been his match. In bed and out.

Within seconds he was lifting her by the hips so her ass rested against the counter. Her legs wrapped around his waist, and even through the denim he could feel the heat of her and knew she'd be soaking wet and ready to take him. His cock was past the point of hard and he rocked against her, drinking in her mewling cries of pleasure.

And then he did what he'd been wanting to since the minute he walked through her door. He grabbed the length of her hair and twisted it around his hand. He pulled her head back and she gasped in excitement as her throat was exposed to him. She'd always loved having her hair pulled.

"God. This is such a bad idea. Pull it harder."

He grinned and his mouth roamed just below her ear. And then he did as she asked. She was a demanding woman. And damned if he wasn't always happy to give her what she asked for.

"It's better than I remember," he said against the flesh of her neck. "Hotter—wilder."

"We never had issues in this area," she panted.

"How about we take a trip down memory lane?" He pressed against her and he thought she might orgasm just from that small touch. Her nails bit into his shoulders and he looked around quickly, trying to decide where to take her. He finally decided right where they were on the counter was good enough for him. To hell with customers or the fact that it was broad daylight. They were both so close it wouldn't last more than a few seconds anyway.

His hand went to the button of her jeans just as the buzzer rang. He swore and dropped his head down on her shoulder, his breath heaving in his chest. It took her a few seconds to realize why he'd stopped, and he smiled at the dazed look on her face. The buzzer rang again and she nudged at his shoulder for him to move back. He was surprised to find his legs weren't quite as steady as they should've been.

"It's probably for the best," she said, moving back behind the counter and pulling her hair over her shoulder so the red marks on her neck didn't show. "Eventually we'd have to get out of bed and talk. And I know that's never been one of your favorite things."

"That's where you're wrong, Mia. I've got a whole lot

to talk about. We can fuck and talk as much as you'd like. Seven years is long enough to run."

She looked at him somberly and Zeke felt something go cold in his chest. "Like you said earlier, I never ran very far. Which is why I asked what you're doing here. Because if you'd really wanted me you'd have found me a long time ago."

He wanted to argue with her. To say all the things he'd said over and over again in his mind since the last time they'd seen each other. But it wasn't the time.

"I've always wanted you," he said, gruffly. "But I've got my pride too. Maybe too much of it. You said you couldn't stay and watch me die. Well guess what, sweetheart, it's seven years later and I'm still here. Look at all the time you wasted."

He turned to walk to the exit but she stopped him. "Don't forget your music box," she said. "I'm assuming you'll eventually tell me why you're really here and why Barnes wanted the authentic piece so badly."

"Maybe he was just laying it on thick."

"Nope, that part he was genuine about. Never let that kid play poker. He's got so many tells I could've filled up a book. It's a good fake, by the way."

Zeke sighed knowingly and took the box. The buzzer rang again. "Riley MacKenzie's wife works at the museum. She has a contact that can recreate certain pieces."

"Handy. Now if I only knew why you need the piece so much and why you think it's going to show up at my shop."

The corner of his lip curled up in a smile and he changed the subject. "I should probably mention that Cooper MacKenzie has loaned me the use of the apartment above the Sheriff's Office while we're working this case."

"It's nice to have friends in high places," she said. "But it's good to know you've proved my point."

"What point is that?"

Her gaze went back to his and he saw so many things there—hurt, confusion, anger. "You didn't come here for me. You've always been incredible at undercover work. I'm a job just like any other. It's all you know. All you've ever known.

Don't forget that I'm the one person who can see past the man you pretend to be. "

"Not this time. I'm not the man I used to be."

"You look the same to me. Same deceptions. Same games. Same techniques when it comes to getting me in bed. If you're that hard up for sex just say so. No need for the lies. I can be accommodating. It's been a while for me too."

"I'm not finished with you, Mia. Not by a long shot."

Mia hit the buzzer and two little old ladies shuffled through the door with a large box. Zeke passed them on the way out and reminded himself that sometimes things had to get worse before they could get better.

Chapter Three

Mia waited until dark to close the shop and head home. And she wasn't afraid to admit it was out of sheer cowardice just to stay out of Zeke's path a little longer. She needed the time to think. To try and remember all the things they'd fought about. To bring back that feeling of why she'd left to begin with. But all she could remember was how much she'd missed him. And how much she'd loved him.

She'd had nonstop customers from the moment Zeke had left, and she hadn't gotten the opportunity to take a closer look at the music box. There had to be some reason both bikers and cops would be looking for it. And no one was telling the truth. So she'd wrapped it with packing material and put it in her backpack. She had less chance of being interrupted at home.

The moon was only a sliver in the sky and heavy clouds blocked the minimal light it gave. The wind cut through her thin jacket the moment she stepped out the back door and locked up, and she realized fall was coming to a close and winter was right behind it. It was pitch black and there were no sounds or car lights from the road. There were hardly any travelers along her stretch of road after dark anyway. It had never bothered her before. But tonight her senses were tingling.

She carried her weapon down at her side and her backpack slung over her shoulder as she unlocked her 4x4 and got inside. Thoughts of the biker coming back with his brothers had never left her mind, and she sure as hell didn't want to face them unarmed. Though in reality she'd be better off using the gun on herself rather than being passed between them.

The drive into Surrender was quick and easy. The town was locked up tight for the most part. All the shops downtown were dark except for the gaslights that flickered along the walkways. There were lights coming from some of the apartments above the shops, including hers, but it looked like most of the action was happening down at Duffey's Pub at the far end of Main Street.

She rolled her window down and could hear the beat of the music from the live band. Cars littered the parking lot and every light imaginable was on, inside and out. Duffey's wasn't her scene, but still she was tempted to take a detour and head that direction. Drink a couple of beers, dance with a couple of ranch hands, and keep her mind off Zeke.

But instead, she pulled into her parking space behind the building and climbed the stairs to the second floor. If she could get a cold beer and a shower then all would be right with the world. The only issue was the man sitting in her rocking chair.

"I didn't figure you'd want me going inside without you," he said, his smile easy. As if nothing more than a simple conversation had passed between them earlier. It was one of the things that had always driven her crazy about him. When he was over something, he was over it, and he moved on. Her emotions weren't quite as settled.

"You figured right," she said. "I would've shot first and asked questions later."

"I thought that temper of yours would've settled over the years."

"Nope, I'm mean as a snake."

"That's not what the ladies at the bakery downstairs said. Those are amazing cinnamon rolls, by the way."

"I know. Why are you here again? I figure if I keep

asking you'll eventually tell me."

"Don't you want to know what the ladies had to say about you?"

If she stood there looking at him too much longer she'd end up straddling his lap and throwing caution to the wind. He sent her body into overdrive—it didn't matter that it had been seven years. Hell, when they'd been together it hadn't mattered if he'd just taken her and she was still lying limp and sweaty beneath him. He always made her want him.

He lounged back in the chair like a big jungle cat, and his eyes were predatory. If she let him inside she knew where they'd end up. Even from where she stood she could feel the arcs of electricity between them. Her nipples were hard and her skin tingled. And the rigid length of his cock was visible beneath his jeans. He wasn't the least embarrassed to let her take her fill. He was a beautiful specimen of the male species. And he knew it.

"What do you say, sweetheart? Are you going to invite me in or do you want to stay out here for everyone to see? Unless you want to try that again."

Her body flushed hot and she remembered very clearly a time when they'd been on a balcony in a hotel in Mexico. The sun was brutal and small beads of sweat snaked down the hollow between her breasts, but the cool, salty breeze tickled her skin and pebbled her flesh. Waves crashed onto shore and then ebbed back in a hypnotic dance, and couples lay out on the sand in languid splendor.

And all the while, she'd been holding on to the balcony for dear life while Zeke fucked her from behind, the triangles of her bikini top pulled to the sides so her breasts were plumped and exposed. He hadn't even bothered to remove her bathing suit bottom. He'd just pushed it aside and buried himself deep.

She'd been mesmerized by all the people below. They were so close, and she'd been standing three stories above them, biting her bottom lip to keep from crying out and calling attention to herself. If they'd only looked up they'd have seen what he was doing to her, and it was that fear of getting caught that had pushed her to new limits. It had been one of the biggest rushes—the biggest turn-ons she'd ever experienced. And Zeke had held his hand over her mouth as she'd screamed through one of the most powerful orgasms she'd ever had.

Heat flushed her face as she saw the echoes of memory in his own eyes. "Come on in," she finally said, her voice husky.

She unlocked the door and went inside, leaving it open behind her. She heard the door close and the click of the deadbolt as he turned it.

"You didn't answer my question," he said.

"Well, you haven't answered any of mine." She shrugged and tossed her keys in the little bowl on the table and sat her backpack on the floor. The music box was a fleeting thought. There was no point trying to do anything with it while Zeke was there.

"Cooper and I spent the afternoon catching up over cinnamon rolls and coffee."

"I didn't realize you and Cooper knew each other that well. I just met him when I moved here."

Zeke's grin was easy to interpret. "You could say Coop and I spent some very memorable summers here when we were in college. The people in this town are still as curious as they were back then. They all remembered me. And then they started talking about you. Don't you want to know what they had to say?"

"Not really."

"I don't believe you. You're nosy as hell. I bet you know everything about each and every one of the people who work in these shops."

"Of course I do," she said over her shoulder. "Because I listen. You should try it some time."

"I've heard everything you've said since I laid eyes on you again a few hours ago."

"Yet here you are in my apartment, not answering my questions."

He grinned unrepentantly. "Listening and obeying are two different things. I'll show you the difference as soon as I get your clothes off."

She arched a brow. "Cocky bastard."

"Don't pretend you don't know where this is going, Mia. If we hadn't been interrupted today I'd have already felt that sweet pussy around me and had you screaming. And then I'd have done it again. And probably again, just for good measure."

"I find it hard to believe that you needed sex so bad you had to come all this way to get it."

"I need sex with you that bad. I've given you your space. It's time to stop running."

"I've been right here for seven years. Where have you been?" She took off her hip holster and hung it on the wall next to her bedroom door. "Oh, right. The job was more important than we were. I remember now."

"We were a team, Mia. We'd still be a team if you hadn't left. We could've had both."

"You're the only one that wanted both. I just wanted you. I guess I'm just different from you, Zeke. The body and mind can only withstand so much torture, and I watched enough friends die to last a lifetime. There comes a time when you have to evaluate your priorities and decide what's really important. What we had—what we could've had— was never important enough to you. I'm going to take a shower. You can stay or leave. It's your choice."

Mia went into her bedroom and peeled out of the jeans and tank she'd worked in all day. She'd loved being a cop. But watching her best friend executed in front of her eyes had been the last straw. It was part of the job—putting your life on the line every day—but knowing it could happen and seeing it happen were two very different things.

She'd carved out a good life for herself. It had been a risk taking her entire pension and putting it into *Pawn to Queen*. But she'd made it work, and she'd been turning a nice profit for several years. Her life as a cop was in the past. She'd left everything behind to start a new life where the nightmares weren't constantly screaming in her head. Zeke was part of that past, and she had no desire to make it her future. The lie wasn't sitting as easily as it once had.

What she needed was a shower, some hot and sweaty sex, and a good night's sleep. She just needed a little more time to prepare mentally. Zeke had been the love of her life. And she'd worked very hard over the last seven years to cauterize that wound in her heart. He wouldn't stay. He couldn't. Too many lives and operations depended on him. So all she had to do was enjoy the ride and keep her heart out of it.

"To hell with it," she said, shaking her head. She never used to be so indecisive.

Her bedroom was white. White walls, white furniture, white rug, and white bedspread. But she'd added color with bold paintings on the walls—pieces she'd loved enough that she'd decided not to sell in the shop. Gem-hued pillows sat on the bed, varied in size and shape, and the throw across the chair in the corner was emerald green. She liked pretty things. Had learned to appreciate them, as well as having the personal satisfaction of being able to choose each piece because she'd worked hard.

She grabbed a pair of thin, gray drawstring pants from the drawer and a loose black long-sleeve T-shirt, and then went into the bathroom and locked the door behind her. Not that a lock would keep him out, but she wasn't going to make it easy for him.

She found herself lingering beneath the hot spray, the scent of lemons from the soap she used permeating the air. And it wasn't long before she realized she wasn't stalling and giving herself the extra time to think. She'd already made up her mind. She was waiting for him to join her—to slip in behind her—his hands slicking over her skin and cupping her breasts and his cock pressing against her back.

Her senses were heightened, her clit throbbing and her pulse pounding. She was tempted to slide her fingers down between the folds of her sex just to take the edge off. She listened for the click of the lock on the door, but he never came. By the time she turned the water off, the anticipation had turned into disappointment and her body thrummed with sexual frustration.

Mia toweled off quickly and put on her clothes. She knew what he was doing. She expected him to come corner her in the shower—to move things to the next level and assert his dominance—and so he did the opposite and stayed back on purpose. Just to drive her crazy. Their life had been one constant chess game of the mind after the other. It was exhilarating and exhausting all at the same time. It wasn't often a person found that kind of challenge in someone they loved.

When she came out of the bedroom she was even more surprised to find him stretched out on her sofa, his eyes closed and his breathing even.

"I'm not asleep," he said.

"Whatever you say. Are you going to tell me why you're really here?"

"Fucking you isn't a good enough reason?" he asked, arching an eyebrow.

"It's a byproduct. You wouldn't have come all this way just for that. It's a waste of work hours and manpower. You want something else too."

"If I tell you will you feed me dinner?" he asked.

"No."

"It's been a while since we've had a date," he said, ignoring her refusal.

"I don't think we ever dated. I'm pretty sure we fell into bed and then went from there."

"An oversight on both our parts. We should have a date."

"Seven years too late. But I can put a frozen pizza in the oven. Mrs. Baker downstairs gives me things to put in the freezer because she's afraid I'll starve."

"If she made it, I'll eat it," he said.

Mia kept her hands busy by putting the pizza in the oven and grabbing two bottles of beer from the fridge. She tossed him one and he snatched it out of the air with a quick flick of his wrist.

He unscrewed the bottle top and took a long pull, and then surprised her by saying, "They love you, by the way," and then he shrugged. "I know you're curious."

"No, I'm not. You just want to tell me what they had to say because cops gossip as much as the women downstairs."

"What I want is for you to stop arguing with me, you hardheaded woman. Christ knows why I find that such a turn-on."

"You always were a perverse creature."

"You'd know better than anyone. Do you have a beer to go with the pizza?"

They'd been so much more than lovers. They'd been partners. And when you combined both of those things, there were no words to describe that kind of bond. The saying of being someone's other half was true. You had to know every part of their personality—their quirks and habits—their sorrows and joy. Partners were often closer than spouses ever could be. And then when you added the sex on top of that level of personal intimacy, it was as if you didn't belong to yourself anymore.

They'd had that, once upon a time. And then she'd severed the connection like she would a limb from the body. To protect herself. He'd refused to meet her halfway. She hadn't been able to face undercover work again. Not after what had happened. And he hadn't been able to leave it behind. The job had always come first.

"Mrs. Baker said that she likes that you slip her cat treats when you think no one is looking. And there was another lady in there, she looked a little bit like a female Milton Berle—"

"That's Ginny Goodwin," Mia said, knowing exactly who he was talking about from the description.

"Well, she said that sometimes you secretly pick up the check for people over at the diner. Especially the older folks that live on social security."

"So what?" she said, feeling uncomfortable all of a sudden.

"Don't get defensive. You've made your mark here. The way you work too hard and need to take better care of yourself. Their words, not mine," he said, holding up his hands when she started to snarl. "The way you pitch in on city cleanup days or sneak into the back pew at church on Sunday mornings."

"You've got a problem with church now?"

"I don't have a problem with anything. Other than you being a big phony. Mean as a snake, my ass," he said with a grin. "You've made a home here. Become part of the community. They don't see you as an outsider. You're one of them. And one of the older ladies said she was thinking about getting some tattoos like yours and some colored streaks in her hair. She said you looked hot and she could use a little hot in her life."

Mia snorted out a laugh. The timer dinged on the oven and she pulled out Mrs. Baker's pizza. It smelled so good she had the fleeting thought that it might be best to eat it all herself.

"It'll go straight to your hips," Zeke said.

"Stay out of my head."

"Didn't have to go in there for that one. I could read the intent on your face."

He got plates and found the pizza cutter in the drawer next to the stove. She narrowed her eyes and wondered if he'd come in and looked around while she'd been hiding at work, or if her patterns of where she kept things were so regimented that he knew right where to look.

They sat at the little bar in the kitchen and ate pizza and drank beer, and Mia decided to wait him out. Zeke had never liked silence between them. He'd start talking eventually.

"I know what you're doing," he said.

She stared at him blankly and took another bite of pizza.

He finally sighed and said, "I'm retiring from

undercover work."

None of the scenarios Mia had played through her mind had been that one, and she choked on her beer. She pounded at her chest and coughed a couple of times and then stared at him in complete and utter shock.

"Your mouth is hanging open," he said.

"I think I passed out for a second. I'm sorry, what did you say?"

"I should've done it years ago," he said and shrugged, ignoring her question. "I'm forty years old and it's a younger man's game. But I think sometimes it just takes men longer to realize when they've hit their limits. Our egos are fragile, I'm told."

"Are you sick or something?" she asked, only half joking. She got up and went to grab another beer. The news was a shock. And she was surprised by the violent rearing of her temper. She wanted to throw something. To ask what was so important now that he was able to put the work behind him. But she didn't. She took a long sip of beer and waited him out.

"I'm not sick. It's just time. I was offered the chief's job over in Carson. Normal hours and weekends off sounds better and better the older I get. It'd be nice to see what it's like to have a normal life."

"Wow—Carson." She still couldn't wrap her brain around it. It was like he was speaking another language and she wasn't able to process any of his words. It was a good job. Carson was the closest large city and he'd be running a full department of hundreds, not a twenty- or thirty-man task force.

"You're angry," he said, surprised.

"Nope," she denied. "Just trying to process."

"I thought you'd be happy. I thought it's what you wanted."

She debated on whether or not to throw the bottle at his head, but decided it'd be a perfectly good waste of beer. "It's what I wanted. *Past* tense. You are un-fucking-believable. What kind of ego does a man have to have to think that a woman would be waiting on him for seven years while he sowed his oats and finished up his career? And then what, Zeke? Did you think I'd run into your arms and everything would be okay?"

His cheeks flushed as his own temper rose and satisfaction crept comfortably through her.

"What makes you think that I'm not completely happy in my life as it is right now?" she asked. "Or that you'd assume I'm not involved with someone who does know the meaning of the word compromise."

"That's fucking bullshit, Mia," he said, scraping back his chair as he stood. "You gave me an ultimatum. And when I didn't cave like a whipped puppy you walked away like a spoiled brat."

"The only thing I ever asked of you was for you to love me enough. To put us first before the job for once. It was about priorities. You think I wanted to see you executed like I saw The Vaqueros do to Rachel?"

The Vaqueros were an outlaw motorcycle gang that spread from Montana and North Dakota up into parts of Canada. They ran drugs and guns and they were very good at what they did. They were one of the most violent gangs in the country.

"To stare into your eyes and see the knowledge that you were going to die just before they pulled the trigger?" she yelled. "You know as well as I do that if we hadn't busted them and caught the dirty cop giving away our identities and locations that you would be dead. Because they already had you in their sights."

"But we did catch them and we did bring them down. At least that cell. And you gave away your own identity by taking a bullet for me. Which still pisses me off."

"Because I blew my cover or because I loved you enough to try and protect you?"

"Because you almost fucking died, Mia."

"Everything that happened in that warehouse that day was a sign telling us it was time to get out. Your cover was blown, my cover was blown, and we lost three good cops. But what the hell do you do?" She was yelling and she didn't care. "You made sure yours was the first face I saw when I woke up. I was finally able to fight my way through the pain meds, and it felt like cinder blocks were sitting on top of my chest. Every breath felt like knives were stabbing me.

"And the first thing out of your mouth is that you've created a new identity and regrouped the task force to go after another Vaquero cell in a different territory. You were pissed you were going to have to lay low for a while and reestablish a new cover.

"Not once did you ever mention our relationship or that you loved me or even the fact that you were glad I was alive. All you could talk about was getting back to the job. And all I wanted was to get as far away from undercover work as I could."

She held the beer bottle to her cheek. The cool glass felt good against her heated skin. "Rachel was dead, and I felt like I should've been. Do you know how much therapy and how many years of nightmares I went through before I stopped seeing her die in my head? I needed out. That was the last straw. I couldn't function and I couldn't be a good cop. What I needed was you."

"Six weeks, Mia. Six weeks was how long it took for you to open your eyes and look at me. I was there every goddamned day and night with you. I lived and breathed you. For six weeks I'd had time to process and reassess and make decisions. I'd already said the things you wanted to hear. I begged and pleaded with you to wake up. Said prayers I hadn't remembered I'd known that you'd survive. I told you every chance I got that I loved you. But you didn't hear because your stubborn ass jumped in front of a bullet."

"And I would do it again. That bullet would've killed you. I needed you," she said again.

"And I needed to get back out there and wreak vengeance on the ones we didn't get for putting you in that hospital bed. What I needed was for you to understand."

She sighed, defeated. "There's no point in this, Zeke. The past is the past, and maybe we were just never meant to be. It was incredible while it lasted. But you and I both know cops don't make good life partners."

Mia tossed her beer bottle in the trash and moved to clear the dishes.

"I think that's bullshit. We know plenty of cops that have been able to make it work. But maybe we were both too selfish to realize what we had and how hard we had to fight for it. Maybe you're standing there now, scared to death, because you realize you didn't move on like you wanted to. Because you still love me."

Chapter Four

"You're out of your mind," she said, the words rushing out.

Zeke knew he was pushing. And he didn't care. He moved closer, boxing her in until her back pressed against the refrigerator.

"I don't think so, baby. And it's time for both of us to stop running and face the facts. We both failed each other."

The last seven years had haunted him. The mistakes they'd both made. The angry words and demands. And when it came down to it, the biggest issue was that they were both too stubborn and had too much pride. When she'd told him she was done with undercover work and that she wanted them both to move to a different area of law enforcement since it had become too dangerous, his ego had immediately reared its head.

Somewhere deep down he knew she'd been right. That getting back in the game was something he might not come out the winner of. And that was the thing—he'd wanted to win at everything—the argument, the job—and his own stubbornness had made them both losers.

The realization of what they both had to gain just by giving in a little made the tension creep from his shoulders. His body was still on high alert—how could it not be with her standing there looking flushed and angry and fuckable?

Her face was scrubbed clean, but she had a natural beauty that had no need of makeup. Her hair was pinned up in a messy knot and strands had come loose so it framed her face. The clothes she'd put on weren't meant to entice. Just lounge pants and a long-sleeve T-shirt, but he could see how hard her nipples were beneath the cloth and he wanted nothing more than to peel her out of the layers and rediscover her body.

"You always did have an oversized ego," she sneered.

The corner of his mouth curled up in a smile. "That's not the only thing that's oversized right now. Have I mentioned how much I love a good argument with you? How wet are you, Mia? Should I take you fast and hard so we can work out the frustration, or keep you on that edge and make you beg for it?"

Her eyes dilated and her lips parted as arousal flushed her cheeks. His head dipped down and his lips hovered just above hers, giving her the chance to protest. But her dark eyes widened and stayed steady on his, and then her hands came up and rested on his chest. He thought at first she was going to push him away, but then her fingers trailed down—slowly, slowly—until they rested just above the button of his jeans.

Bombs exploded in his head and fire rushed through his nervous system. Her touch could take him places he'd never been before, and he couldn't remember ever wanting anything as badly as he wanted Mia in that moment.

His arms circled her waist and his lips moved over hers, their tongues clashing and colliding in a familiar dance. A moan escaped her throat, and her fingers jerked at the button of his jeans. He grabbed her hands.

"Too fast, baby. I'll never make it if you touch me right now."

She tasted of beer and woman, and he drank her in like a man who'd found an oasis after being lost in the desert. He pulled her closer. He wanted to consume her, surround her, until his body was part of hers. She went to his head like a drug, and a barely leashed hunger raged inside him.

"Zeke, please. Enough waiting." Her head fell back as his teeth nipped at her neck. "I can't take it anymore."

"Oh, you're going to take it, baby," he whispered.

"Over and over again."

His hands moved over her, memorizing the shape of her. From her full breasts, down to her waist, and then farther down to the flare of her hips. *His.* The claiming was unmistakable.

He untied the drawstring at her waist and let the lounge pants fall to the floor. And then his hands roamed around to her ass.

"Jesus, Mia," he groaned, feeling bare skin where he'd been expecting the lace of her panties to be. He lifted her, the hard length of his cock notching against her clit. He could feel her heat, even through the denim that separated them.

Her nails bit into his shoulders and she cried out as he pressed against her. He slid a finger down her backside, over the tight bud of her anus to the creamy folds of her pussy. And then he slid a finger inside and felt her unravel in his arms.

* * * *

Every nerve in her body was screaming for more—for him to fill her completely. But even that small touch was enough to give her some relief from the glorious pleasure that had been building inside her all day. It had been too long since she'd felt Zeke hot and hard against her.

She'd always been a sexual creature, needing release like some needed food. But she'd long since grown tired of the toys she kept in her nightstand drawer or her own fingers. There was nothing quite like the feel of a hard body pressing you into a mattress.

Heat infused her and a startled cry escaped from her lips as a small orgasm ripped through her body. Her clit was swollen and rubbed against him, and she moved her hips, hoping to draw it out. But the quick release trailed off before it had barely begun and left her wanting more.

"God, Zeke. More. I'm going to go crazy if I don't have all of you."

Her hands grasped at his shirt, pulling at it until it was

over his head and tossed on the floor. She wanted to feel him flesh to flesh—the hard contour of muscles beneath her fingers. He was always so fun to touch—to look at. The shadows cast his face in a savage light, the dark scruff of his beard a contrast to his chiseled cheekbones and square jaw. He was, quite simply, beautiful.

His hands tightened on her ass and her legs wrapped like a vise around him, looking for another quick thrill before they got down to serious business. No one could command her body like he could—a maestro of touch, building crescendo after crescendo until she screamed at the pinnacle of pleasure.

He moved quickly toward the bedroom and jerked back her comforter, laying her down on the cool white sheets. He discarded her shirt and looked his fill. His finger touched the scar just above her breast and his face darkened. If that scar was just a hair to the left she wouldn't be here. And she realized it was the first time he'd seen her naked since she'd gotten it.

She felt exposed, even though he'd seen her laid out before him a thousand times before, but that thought quickly passed as his eyes darkened with desire and his breathing grew heavy. His finger trailed from the scar down to the rosy tip of her breast and she felt powerless beneath his touch. And then she remembered that she wasn't without her own brand of power.

"Mmm, you're bigger than I remember," she said, eyeing his broad chest with appreciation.

"Working out becomes an obsession when you don't have a personal life."

Her hands skimmed up her stomach slowly and his eyes followed, until she was cupping her breasts. They were full and heavy and ached with the need for his mouth. She tweaked her nipples between her thumb and forefinger and moaned as frissons of pleasure went straight to her clit.

"Christ, Mia. You'll make me come before I can get inside of you."

"Better hurry and get inside of me then," she dared.

"Witch." He loomed over her, the muscles in his arms bulging as he supported himself. And then he lowered his head and his tongue flicked a rigid nipple before taking it in his mouth completely. Her back arched as she pressed against him, her hands holding the back of his head so he'd never leave her.

He blew a cool stream of air across her nipple and she shivered in response. "I once could make you come just by touching you here," he said. "They're so sensitive. I've never seen anything like it."

"I'd rather feel you inside me," she panted as his teeth clamped down on a nipple. The sizzle rippled through her nervous system, and her clit throbbed with the pounding beat of her heart. She shivered and convulsed as he bit a little harder, just so there was a slight edge of pain, and then he suckled her, massaging her other breast at the same time. The suckling grew more intense, until she could feel each tug between her thighs. And then stars exploded behind her closed eyelids and she was crying out as wave after wave of pleasure consumed her.

She felt the bed shift and his weight lift as he discarded his jeans, but she was too relaxed to open her eyes and watch. She could've curled up like a cat and gone to sleep.

"Oh, no you don't," Zeke said.

She could hear the smile in his voice and her eyelids fluttered half open as he crawled back on the bed. And then her eyes widened and she cried out as he slid inside of her straight to the hilt. Her breath caught in her throat and her hips arched against him. She was wet, but the tissue inside her vagina was swollen from the small orgasms she'd had and his fit was more than snug.

It was like coming home after a long journey. Foreign and familiar all at once. The feel of his skin against hers, the way his chest hair abraded her nipples. She couldn't deny it. He'd always held her heart.

"God, Zeke. Love me."

She regretted the words instantly, and then had the hopes that maybe he hadn't heard her after all. His chest rumbled and an animalistic growl escaped from his throat. His dick went impossibly hard and grew in size as he came closer and closer to his own orgasm. He continued to pummel inside her relentlessly and she held on, her mouth open in a silent scream as the head of his cock touched somewhere deep inside of her—to a place that made the world go dark and explosions detonate from her womb and spread through her limbs until the muscles went rigid and the beginnings of an intense pleasure spiraled from the inside out.

She wasn't sure she could survive it, and knew he'd branded her like he never had before. Sensations built inside her until a deep, pulsing starburst of pleasure erupted through her core, coursing through her body. Her muscles spasmed, her limbs stiffened, and she cried out his name as he called out hers. Hot jets of his semen filled her and she tightened around him, wanting to take him all.

And then there was nothing but darkness as sleep consumed her.

* * * *

Zeke had never dreamed with such clarity before. Where his senses were primed so every sound was magnified and the slightest touch could send his body soaring. He had to be dreaming because nothing outside of dreams could feel like this.

His eyelids felt weighted down and he barely had the energy to grasp at the sheets beneath him as the liquid heat of Mia's mouth clamped around his cock. Her tongue swirled around the sensitive skin of his head before swallowing him whole. And she repeated the pattern over and over until his hips arched and he was fucking her mouth in earnest. And then she stopped and pulled away, and he groaned in protest.

"It's my turn," she whispered. "You'll lie there and take it."

And then he realized maybe he wasn't dreaming after all. He forced his eyes open and looked down the length of his body to see her between his thighs, his cock hard and sticking straight up and wet from her mouth, the veins bulging.

A small amount of light seeped in through the blinds from the porch light she'd left on. Her eyes were dark and seductive and her smile was wicked. She was in a playful mood.

"I thought I was dreaming," he said.

Her brow arched and her tongue flicked out, making his cock jerk. "Reality is always better."

"So I've discovered." He gritted his teeth as her hot little fist wrapped around the base of his cock and her tongue continued to wreak havoc on his system.

"I've always loved the way you feel. The way my mouth and tongue have learned the shape of you. Every ridge. The way you swell in my mouth just before you're going to come and the taste of you as I drink every drop."

"Jesus, Mia," he panted, his hands going to her head, his fingers tangling in her hair.

"Mmm," she moaned, swallowing him whole once more.

Her head moved up and down between his thighs and her mouth clamped tighter around him, milking him with every stroke. His balls were tight and he'd be done for in a couple more strokes if she didn't slow down.

"Enough," he begged. "I don't want to come yet." His gaze met hers as she looked up from the object of her focus. And the sight of his cock in her mouth while she stared at him out of those gypsy eyes was one of the sexiest fucking things he'd ever seen.

"Are you giving me orders?" she purred sweetly, licking him once more, like a cat, from base to tip.

"Has it ever done any good outside of an undercover op?"

"No," she said, smiling cheekily. And then she released him and sat up on her knees, steadying herself on his muscled thighs.

She looked like a goddess rising over him—powerful and wicked and just a little bit dangerous. Dark hair fell over her shoulders, covering one of her breasts completely and leaving the other exposed. Her muscles were toned—years of discipline and exercise keeping her fit even after she left the job—and his eyes were immediately drawn to the silver bar piercing at her belly button.

"I meant to tell you earlier that I like the piercing, but I was too busy fucking you."

Her lips quirked and her hand left his thigh to skim across her stomach, tracing the bar with her finger. "Yes, you were. Now it's my turn to fuck you."

His cock jerked as she said it. He'd always loved when she talked dirty. And then he lost his train of thought as she straddled his hips and sank down all the way to the hilt. She fit him like a fucking glove and his jaw clenched and his hands went to her hips as he struggled for control. His body was an inferno and he was surprised it was physically possible to withstand that kind of heat.

Her muscles contracted around him and then she threw her head back and rode him with abandon, her hips undulating and her vaginal muscles squeezing him in perfect time. Until he thought he'd lose his mind with the pleasure.

Then he felt the liquid heat of her surround his cock, the ripple of contractions and her screams of pleasure as her orgasm ripped through her. And he was helpless to stop himself from following after her.

Chapter Five

The shrill scream of the alarm coming from her phone jerked her out of a deep sleep. Three loud raps at the door followed soon after.

"What the hell?" Zeke asked, rolling out of bed in a fluid motion and grabbing his duty weapon.

"That's the alert for my shop alarm system," she said, turning off the phone.

Mia grabbed the gun she had in her nightstand and moved in a crouched motion to the chair in the corner where a gray pair of sweats were folded. She dressed quickly, but Zeke had already pulled on his jeans and was heading to the front door.

"Wait, dammit," she hissed. "It's my house."

"It's Cooper," Zeke said. "I looked through the blinds in the bedroom." He moved to the side and let her answer the door.

"My shop?" she said to Cooper, by way of greeting.

Cooper nodded. "There's been an attempted break-in. I don't know how bad or if they breached the inside. I was just on my way into the office this morning when the alarm company called through. The deputy on duty called me and I figured it was faster to stop here first."

She could smell the soap from Cooper's morning shower and his black hair was still damp at the tips. He was dressed for work—a chambray button down shirt with the

Surrender Sheriff's Office logo embroidered over the pocket and a pair of jeans and boots. He wore a shoulder holster and his badge was pinned on the left side of his shirt.

"I'll meet you there," he said.

"Thanks, we'll be right behind you."

Mia headed back to the bedroom in a daze. She heard the mumble of Zeke and Cooper's words as they talked, but everything was buzzing in her head and all she could think about was her shop and what that small piece of land and the building that sat on it meant—it was the symbol of her new life, of her independence. And now someone had violated that. It didn't go unnoticed that the breach and the appearance of Zeke had happened all in the same twenty-four-hour time period. That was something to think about later.

She looked at the clock and hadn't realized it was just past five. It was still dark outside and the air was bitter with the chill. It wouldn't be long before the first frost hit. Clothes were easy—a pair of jeans, a sweatshirt, and her boots. She pulled her hair back in a ponytail and topped it with a baseball cap. And then she grabbed her holster from the hook she'd hung it from the night before and strapped it on.

It didn't go past her notice that she and Zeke had fallen into a familiar routine. They'd lived together for a couple of years on and off, depending on if she had to live with a family to give the illusion that she was a student. They knew where to move and which order to do things in to be the most efficient so they could get where they needed to go.

By the time she grabbed her car keys and backpack, he was holding the front door open for her. They were both cautious as they approached her 4x4, scanning the area for signs of a threat. But all was clear and she got behind the wheel. He always hated it when she drove. It was funny how those memories came back now, when she'd forgotten the little details of their relationship during their time apart.

"Anything you want to tell me before we get there?" Mia asked.

She drove down Main Street—the lights were on in the

bakery and early birds were coming in for breakfast. Lights were on or flickering on in a few of the other shops, but she barely glanced at them. They were all looking at her as she drove by, however. There was no doubt the word had already started to spread about her shop. At least ten people she knew of had police scanners and kept everyone informed of any misdoings in the community.

She drove past Charlie's Automotive and then climbed the hill that led out of Surrender. Fiery fingers of the blazing morning sun crept over the landscape as she peaked the hill and then began the descent down the other side.

All in all, it wasn't a long drive. Maybe fifteen minutes. But it had felt like an eternity.

Zeke went still and quiet beside her. She recognized the blank look on his face. It was the same one he'd always had whenever he was trying to keep something from her.

"Let's just check it out and see if any damage was done," he finally said. "Maybe it was someone looking for some fast cash."

"This is my life, Zeke. Don't try to fuck me over. And don't try to feed me lines about you retiring from undercover work. All of a sudden seven years seems like an eternity. I don't know you anymore. And there's no reason to trust you."

"You have every reason to trust me. I love you, and as soon as this job is over I'm done. I just need to gather some facts before I start talking about things that might not have anything to do with you and everything to do with keeping other people alive."

Mia stayed quiet, not sure how to respond to his declaration of love. He'd never been one to say it often, but when he did she treasured those moments. And she hated that she couldn't be sure he meant it this time. Time had passed. Things had changed. And there was always an agenda.

She parked next to Cooper's Tahoe in the back of the parking lot. There was another truck she didn't recognize parked next to him, and three men stood in front of it. A fire truck with flashing lights was parked to the side of the building, but far enough away not to damage the scene. She tried not to despair at the sight of her missing front door. Other than that, on the outside, it looked untouched.

At least the building was standing. Anything else she could deal with. As if reading her mind, Zeke squeezed her shoulder as they walked over to the others, but she shrugged him off. Sympathy wasn't what she needed at that moment. Not if she wanted to keep it together. What she really needed was a cup of coffee.

"The alarm company silenced the alarms," Cooper said. "You'll need to call them to set things back up once you're ready to roll."

"Definitely not someone passing by looking for a quick buck," Zeke said, hands on hips as he surveyed the scene.

"Not by a long shot. They came prepared and knew what they were doing. Deputy Greyson was first on scene. The fire department pulled in right after him."

Mia knew Lane Greyson well. His wife, Naya, was one of her closest friends. Naya was a bounty hunter, and they'd hit it off immediately.

"Sorry about this, Mia," Lane said. "I know what this place means to you."

"Is the inside as bad as I think it's going to be?" she asked him.

His lips pinched together. "I brought you a to-go cup of coffee. It's in the cab of my truck."

"That bad, huh," she said, her stomach tied in knots. She went to the cab of the truck and opened the door, grabbing the thermal coffee mug from the middle console. Zeke introduced himself to Lane and they shook hands, and then he shook hands with Riley MacKenzie and slapped him on the shoulder. Mia was guessing he knew all the MacKenzie brothers as well as he did Cooper.

"What dragged you out of bed before noon?" Zeke asked Riley.

Where Cooper was dark-haired and blue-eyed, Riley was his polar opposite with blond hair and brown eyes. They had the same square jaw and eye shape, but at first glance it was hard to tell they were brothers. And then she looked closer and noticed they were very much cut from the same cloth, with broad builds and fighting man's hands. Neither of them looked as if they'd ever backed away from a fight. No wonder Zeke got along so well with them. He carried himself the same way.

"A crying baby," Riley answered. "It was my shift for middle of the night duty, so I was wide awake when Cooper texted. Of course, by the time I left the house the baby was sleeping again and the whole house was quiet. I figured it'd be better to tag along than to get my hopes up by lying down and trying to go to sleep."

"Sounds like fun," Zeke said. "I'm thinking of having kids in the next forty years or so."

"Hey, Picasso did it. It's good to have goals, man."

"Has there been time to secure the scene?" Mia asked. She knew the drill. Knew they were standing out in the parking lot for a reason. But God, she wanted to get in there and see what they'd destroyed.

"We walked the perimeter when we arrived," Cooper said. "Anyone who was here was long gone, but you'll see the marks on the sidewalk. I put the word out for who we're looking for."

Mia followed them toward the front of the shop, her boots crunching over gravel. She didn't see what Cooper was talking about until she was almost on top of it.

"Skid marks," she said. And one of the motorcycles who'd left it had ridden up her stairs and left them on the porch as well.

"Any reason why a group of bikers would pay you a visit, Mia?" Zeke asked.

Unlike the rookie who'd been standing in her shop yesterday, she knew how to lie. Years of practice made it as easy as breathing. There were techniques they'd been taught at specials ops classes that helped with the art of lying—body language, facial expressions, and making sure the lies were close enough to the truth that you didn't forget and stumble somewhere along the way.

"Not that I can think of," she answered. The music box was still in her backpack in the car. She knew she'd have to tell Zeke about the biker and the music box, but now wasn't the time or the place. If the details were part of whatever op he was running then Cooper and the others wouldn't know what was going on. And anything they found out could endanger a life.

She looked at Zeke and asked, "Any coincidence as to why bikers would show up and do this the same day you roll back into my life?"

"Not that I can think of," he said, parroting her.

"We didn't find any other breached areas," Cooper said, heading up the short stairs to her porch. "They knew the entry point they wanted and knew how to enter. This is a reinforced steel door and at night you pull down the cage behind it for added security."

"Yeah, but nothing is infallible," she said. "Obviously. But it's a time-consuming job. They had to cut through the hinges and remove the door completely. The alarm would've been sounding, but guys like that wouldn't care. And they'd have the right tools on hand to be able to get in. They'd use the same blade on the pull-down cage and then walk in. There are at least eight or ten skid marks and grooves dug into the gravel of the parking lot."

"Ballsy to draw such attention to themselves," Lane said.

"No one is ever on this stretch of road after midnight."

Zeke walked off toward the road and she could tell he was trying to get a better feel for how many there were, which direction they'd entered from, and hopefully, which direction they'd exited.

"They'd know Surrender would be the closest responding department," Mia said.

"And that we only have one on-duty officer working the night shift," Cooper finished for her, his look grim. "Proof of the liabilities of being a small town and working with a limited budget."

"This isn't your fault." She wanted to make sure he knew that. "It's location and timing. I'm pretty far outside of town. By design. And even though I'm technically part of Surrender, you and I both know that if I were on the other side of that hill with the other businesses, this never would've happened. But I'm not and there's no easy way for emergency personnel to get here. They knew they had at least twenty minutes to get the job done."

Zeke walked back to their group and said, "They split off in each direction. Pretty typical behavior. We can assume this is the work of The Vaqueros since this is their territory. And they're known to converge on a location, wreak havoc, and then separate so they can lay low for a while. They're well organized and they run an intelligent operation. I've watched the way they work from the inside. It's why they've been so successful running drugs these past years. They're like ghosts."

"We can try and pull identities from the security cameras," she said, "but knowing who they are won't help us on how to find them. Identifying them and plastering their faces on the news is like a badge of honor."

"Which brings us back to the question," Riley said. "Why here and why you?"

Cooper looked at her and said, "Have you had any run-ins with The Vaqueros?"

"I threatened to shoot one yesterday," she said. "I suppose he could've taken it personally."

All four men stared at her with varying degrees of surprise on their faces. "What? You know I'm always armed and I don't put up with bullshit in my place."

"Or maybe you could've mentioned it?" Zeke said.

"When would've been a good time? When you popped up in my shop asking for the same item the biker was, or maybe when you showed up at my apartment to get me into bed? You're right, Zeke. I should've confessed the second you showed up. My bad."

Riley coughed to cover a laugh and Cooper looked

down at his boots, but she could see his smile. Lane never showed much expression at all, but she knew him well enough to see that he wanted to smile.

Zeke's jaw was clenched hard and all he said was, "Mia," in that tone of voice that didn't bode well.

She arched a brow and narrowed her eyes. Now wasn't the time for him to try any macho bullshit.

"Might as well check out the inside," Cooper said. "You can see if anything is missing."

They stepped through the gaping hole where her front door had once been, and Mia had to stifle a gasp. Her heart thudded in her chest and a red haze clouded her vision. Everything was destroyed. The shelves were knocked down, the floor littered with broken glass. They'd not gotten the more expensive pieces locked behind the counter, though she could see the scratches on the bulletproof glass.

"What was the biker looking for?" Cooper asked.

Mia stepped over glass and an electric guitar that was broken in half. "He asked for a music box. Was very specific about what kind he wanted. He said that he'd been told someone had come in and sold it to me. He offered to double my money." She could hear the hollowness of her own voice.

"I told him he was mistaken and that I didn't have a piece like that. He got close and told me I'd better rethink my answer, so I cocked the sawed off I've got stashed under the counter. He decided to leave after that."

"He make any threats?"

She sighed. "Yeah, he said he'd come back for a visit with his brothers."

"Jesus, Mia," Zeke said. "Why wouldn't you report something like that?"

"Because I can take care of myself," she said, whirling on Zeke. "I was a cop, remember? How would reporting it have changed anything? There's not enough manpower to put out a protection detail."

"And now you've got a target on your back."

"They did what they came to do," she said. "They

destroyed and still didn't find what they were looking for. There's no reason for them to come back here. But they might target other pawnshops in the area if their intel tells them that's where the music box ended up."

"We'll put an alert out to all the surrounding areas," Cooper said. "We'll get in and out of here quickly so you can get the insurance company in and start going through your inventory."

"What's left of it," she said, looking around at the shambles of a room.

"I'll grab Thomas and Dane and we'll come back and put in a makeshift door with a sturdy deadbolt," Riley said, speaking of his other two brothers. "At least it'll deter anyone wanting to snoop or help themselves to what's available."

"I'd appreciate it. This is definitely going to put a dent in my new parking lot fund."

"I can call in a couple of favors," Zeke said. "I've got men at the DEA office that are twiddling their thumbs, waiting for a big case to drop. They can set up a patrol in the area and keep an eye out to make sure you don't get another visit."

"We'll coordinate with the surrounding departments and set up checkpoints and hot spots. The problem with The Vaqueros is their clubhouses are in the mountains. We might not see them for weeks. Or until they need supplies. And if we get a snowfall during that time it could be even longer."

"Lovely," Mia said. "Well, there's no use wasting time when there's work to be done. How soon do you think I can call insurance and we can start cleanup?"

"Should be ready for insurance this evening if he's available. You can probably start cleanup tomorrow."

She nodded and glanced at Zeke. He was staring at a painting that had fallen off the wall like it held the secret of life. It was a contemporary oil with bright colors, and she'd briefly thought about taking it home and hanging it in her dining room.

She thought about the music box tucked safely in her bag. She needed to get rid of Zeke so she could go through it in private. He'd been too secretive since his arrival the day before, and no matter what he said about still loving her, seven years was a long time. And people changed. Especially people who'd lived that underground life and spent their days and nights lying to people. She wasn't about to get caught in the middle of something that might ruin the life she'd built for herself.

As if reading her mind, Zeke turned his head and looked at her intently. "I'm bunking with you," he said. "And don't even think about arguing. I'll sleep on the couch if I have to, but it's too dangerous. You need someone to watch your back."

Or he needed to be right in the thick of things and she was the easiest access point, she thought.

Chapter Six

A week later, the first frost glittered across the top of the ground like tiny diamonds. And to Mia's surprise and supreme gratitude, her shop was cleaned up, the door repaired, and she'd managed to restock some of her inventory.

She'd never expected the outpouring of support from the community, and she never would've thought to ask for it. But almost as soon as she'd gotten back into town people were stopping her on the street, asking what they could do to help. And then the next morning, a group of people showed up at her shop unannounced with brooms and vacuums and cleaning supplies, and they all got to work.

She still didn't know how to respond. A thank you seemed inadequate. In her line of work she'd never expected the best from people, so their generosity astounded her. People donated items they were getting rid of, so by the end of the week everything looked almost as it had before, though the shelves were still a little bare.

Zeke had been true to his word and had stayed at her place. She hated to admit it, but having him there did ease her mind a bit. She'd been annoyed at his high-handedness and had given him an extra pillow and a blanket for the couch that first night after the break-in. He'd taken it with a smirk and a wicked glint in his eyes.

And then she'd been woken up sometime in the middle of the night, her shirt pushed up around her waist and his head between her thighs. She'd been dreaming of him, and then she'd woken to find her dream a reality. He hadn't slept on the couch since, and her muscles were sore in all the right places. Zeke had always been a thorough and athletic lover.

They also hadn't spoken of the past or his work. He still hadn't told her why he'd really come. But he'd continued to say he was retiring from undercover work, to the point that she wanted to believe him. He had to give the mayor an answer about the chief's job in Carson by the end of the month, and she'd be lying if it hadn't sneaked into her mind that Carson wasn't all that far of a commute from Surrender.

She'd forgotten how comfortable they'd always been with each other—the easy conversations, the things they had in common, the sports teams they argued over. Remembering the arguments had been the easiest thing to do. But there'd been more good times than bad.

They'd fallen into an easy rhythm. He'd leave sometime after midnight and go into work, or he'd disappear for an hour or so at random times throughout the day. Then he'd show up randomly at her shop, pitch in to help, and leave again. She remembered how it was. The erratic schedules. The missed sleep, anniversaries, holidays, and birthdays. The only difference was he no longer talked to her about work. It was the albatross in the room.

"You ready to call it a night?" he asked as she looked over the shop one final time to make sure everything was in place. She'd be back open for business on Monday.

"More than ready. I need a hot bath and pizza. Maybe a pizza while sitting in the hot bath."

"How about a trip to Duffey's instead? We can play a game of pool, eat hot wings, and drink half-price beer."

"Well, hell, that sounds way better than soaking my aching feet."

He grinned and tossed an arm around her shoulder, pulling her close. "I'll spot you a couple of balls since you're so tired."

"The hell you will," she said, her spine straightening.

He chuckled and they headed to Duffey's. It was the after-work crowd for the most part, but a lot of them had already thinned out to head home for dinner. The live music didn't start until ten o'clock, so they still had time to play and be able to hear themselves.

Duffey's didn't cater to the tourist crowd. It was a local bar with sawdust on the floors, scarred tables, and draft beer and a small selection of wine. There were no mixed drinks or cocktails. Trophy antlers hung on all the walls and she was pretty sure they'd never seen a dust rag.

Zeke went to the bar to order drinks and chatted with Duffey while he was waiting. She'd learned over the last several years that Duffey never smiled. He'd owned the bar for close to fifty years, and from the pictures hanging on the wall, he hadn't changed a bit in those fifty years. He always wore a white undershirt and trousers with a larger white butcher apron tied several times around his scrawny waist. The tuft of gray hair circling the bald patch on the top of his hair was coarse and wiry, and round, wire-framed glasses sat perched at the end of his nose. His lips were thin and he always looked like he'd just swallowed something sour.

Mia had learned early on that the best course of action was to stay off his radar, so she headed toward the back room where the pool tables were located. She passed Jana Metcalfe along the way. Jana had been a waitress at Duffey's since long before Mia had moved there. She was pleasantly plump and somewhere in her mid to late thirties, and she always had a wide and infectious smile.

"Is the pool table taken?" Mia asked her.

"A group just cleared out. It's all yours." She gathered empties from a table, balancing the tray and making it look effortless. "It's good to see Zeke back in town," she said, conversationally. "Almost didn't recognize him. He looks a lot different than he did at nineteen." She winked and chuckled. "He spent a lot of summers here. Lord, he and those MacKenzies got into some trouble. I'm surprised Duffey even lets any of them in the door."

"He must not be too mad," Mia said. "They're talking to each other."

"That's because Duffey is still trying to get Zeke to pay for some damages. Duffey just likes to complain. He'll overcharge Zeke for the beers and then he'll feel like he's gotten away with something. Let me give you a tip. When you're ready to order anything else, come find me. I'll make sure your ticket is right."

Mia shook her head and smiled. "Thanks, I appreciate it."

"Hey, you guys have had a rough week. Duffey should be giving you the beer." Jana stretched her neck out to the side to look around the corner toward Duffey. "Don't tell him I said that. That man's never given away a thing in his life."

"Why do you work for him?"

"I'm his granddaughter." Jana winked and smiled again, and then hefted the tray onto her shoulder and headed toward the kitchen.

Mia already felt the tension draining from her shoulders. Zeke had been right. It was nice to get out. They'd been cooped up at the shop or her apartment all week. It had been nothing but work and worry.

She headed to the far back of the restaurant and took the little hallway to the left. It was a private room they sometimes used for bachelor parties, but it was the only area big enough for the pool table. She tossed her leather jacket over a chair and went to check the cues. And then she racked the balls and waited for Zeke to arrive. *Spot her a couple balls her ass.*

* * * *

Zeke came in with a pitcher of beer and two frosted mugs, and it was a damned good thing he'd had a good grip on them. Mia was his every fantasy, and the sight of her leaning on her cue stick in worn jeans and a stretchy white top made his cock hard enough to drive nails. She'd let the natural curl in her hair reign free and it flowed down her back, tempting him.

The thought crossed his mind that he might be better off tossing her over his shoulder and heading back home, but then another idea came to mind. He kicked the door shut with the heel of his foot and brought the beer over to one of the little round tables, pouring them each a glass.

"Did you order dinner?" he asked.

"Not yet." She took a sip of beer and licked her lips, and he swore he felt her tongue straight down his dick. "I figured we could eat after I beat you a couple of times."

He arched a brow and grinned. "Now you're talking my language. What do you say we make it interesting."

"Irish boy," she said with a smile. "Everything's a bet."

"Life's a bet. So?" he asked. "You in?"

"What are the rules?"

"Winner takes two out of three games. Straight pool." He answered.

"And what do I get when I win?" she asked, arching a brow.

He laughed and felt the adrenaline surge through him. "Winner gets to be on top. And the loser has to do whatever the winner demands."

"Ahh, so laundry and doing the dishes. Sounds like a deal to me."

"Be careful, Mia. I haven't forgotten how to spank you."

"Mmm," she said. "You'd have to win to try it."

"Challenge accepted. Rack 'em."

Mia set her cue against the wall and went to the opposite end of the table, leaning over and pressing the balls tight in the triangular rack. Then she lifted it carefully. He could see right down the vee of her shirt to the soft mounds of her breasts and the lacy white bra that barely covered them. His cock had been hard from the second he'd imagined her stretched across that pool table, and he hoped he could concentrate enough to put his money where his mouth was. She was a temptress, and he wanted to be tempted.

As soon as the cue stick was in his hand, his competitive streak took hold. This wasn't a game he wanted to lose. He broke and the clack of balls hitting was like music to his ears. They'd spent a lot of time in pool halls over the years, watching drug deals go down or just becoming known in the community.

By the end of the second game, he was starting to worry that he might be doing laundry and dishes after all. He'd won the first game. Barely. And she'd taken the second game that had been equally as close as the first.

"You want to quit?" she asked.

"Are you forfeiting? Because if you forfeit that means I win." He waggled his eyebrows and said, "And I've been seeing my handprints on your ass in my head ever since I mentioned it."

"You're a sadistic bastard, McBride."

"You never used to complain, baby."

"Your break. Unless *you* want to forfeit. I've got a pretty amazing fantasy going through my head too. I'll let you wear my apron while you're doing the dishes."

"I'm just adding a tally of strokes that are going to show red on that sweet ass of yours. Keep talking, sweetheart. My hand is itching."

The corner of her mouth curled up in a smile and he recognized the look in her eyes. It was the look she had just before he usually found himself flat on his back with her hot mouth around his cock.

The game went quickly. He ran the table and then just missed getting the eight ball in the side pocket. He was sweating bullets as Mia had her own run of luck. She lined up her final shot, and he held his breath as she pulled back the cue stick. And then he watched in disbelief as her cue shifted just slightly out of alignment as she made the shot. The eight ball went in the corner pocket. But the cue ball didn't stop like it should have. It spun back and went in the side pocket on the opposite side of the table.

Zeke's eyes met hers as she looked up at him over her

cue stick.

"Looks like I missed," she said.

"Looks like you did."

He didn't remember how he got to the other side of the table where she was standing so quickly. He only knew she was there and his mouth was on hers—hot and wet—devouring. He couldn't stop. Wouldn't stop.

His tongue caressed hers and he shuddered as her fingers curled around his shoulders, her nails biting into them.

"God, Mia. You drive me crazy." His hands skimmed down her sides and he grabbed her hips, pulling her against him so she could feel the rigid length of his cock. His teeth nipped at her lips and he drank in her gasp.

"Let's go," she panted. "I want you inside me." Her head was arched back so her neck was exposed and her eyes were half closed, her lips swollen from his kiss.

"I won, baby. My rules. My demands. I'm going to fuck you right here." He felt her shiver against him and knew the idea of being caught was always a sexual high for her.

She shook her head. "No, Zeke. We'll be caught."

"Not if you don't scream," he whispered against her ear. "I'm going to fuck you. And you're going to feel the heat of my hand against your ass."

His arm wrapped around her waist and he spun and lifted her so she sat on the edge of the pool table. There wasn't a lock on the door, and they could both hear the rumble of voices and the clank of glasses from the bar. Their time was limited, so he knew he had no choice but to give them what they both needed fast and hard. He could take his time later, once they'd gotten home.

* * * *

Mia gasped as he lifted her onto the pool table. His mouth found her lips and then his teeth nipped playfully. His mouth moved down her neck and the rasp of his beard scraped against her jaw. She arched into him and felt the hard ridge of his cock press against her clit.

He always pushed her sexually. To discover what she liked, what she feared, and what turned her on. Sometimes the discoveries intertwined.

"God, Zeke. Hurry."

His hands came up and grabbed at the vee of her T-shirt, and then he ripped it right down the middle, exposing her bra. Her nipples tightened and her eyes widened with excitement. Her heart pounded in her chest and liquid pooled between her thighs. Her clit throbbed, and she knew it would take very little to plummet her over the edge.

"You are so fucking beautiful." His voice was rough and raspy and she shivered against him. And then his fingers flicked at the front clasp of her bra and her breasts were exposed to him.

"And you're making me crazy," she panted. "I said hurry."

"Baby, you know it never does any good to give me orders. I'm contrary like that. And I won. I'm issuing the orders here."

"You won because I threw the game. I decided getting fucked sounded a hell of a lot better than watching you do my laundry."

His fingers went to the button of her jeans and flicked them open. She lifted her hips so he could pull her jeans and underwear down to her ankles. Her boots were in the way and she growled in frustration at not being able to get her legs wrapped around him.

"Let me tell you a secret," he whispered. "Even if you'd won you'd still be sitting here on this table with your jeans around your ankles and your tits exposed to the world. You're too tempting, baby."

His fingers were rough and trailed over her hip to the slick flesh of her pussy. She was swollen and sensitive, and she hissed as he rubbed against her opening, sending pleasure straight to the taut bud of her clit. She was so close to coming her body tensed and her legs shook with anticipation.

"Anyone could walk in at any time," he said, continuing to stroke her. "Do you know what they'd see?"

"Zeke," she groaned, trying to move her hips against his fingers, but he had her anchored to the pool table with his arm.

"They'd walk in and see a woman so fucking sexy they'd be seeing you in their wet dreams from now on. A body that makes a man want to sit up and beg." He squeezed the hard muscles of her bicep and then brought his hand down so it cupped her breast gently. "You're hard and soft, all at the same time." His hand trailed down farther until he cupped her pussy again. "And then they'd see this—bare and pink and wet—just waiting to be fucked."

"Why don't you put your money where your mouth is, hotshot? Or in this case, why don't you put your dick in my pussy and we'll call it even."

"Fuck, that mouth of yours, Mia. Always getting you into trouble."

"If by trouble, you mean fucked, then thank God for my mouth."

She gasped and then laughed as Zeke pulled her to a standing position, turned her around, and then pressed his hand against her back so her breasts rasped against the felt of the pool table.

Anticipation soared through her as she heard the rattle of his belt being undone and the rasp of his zipper. And then she felt the thick head of his cock push between her thighs. He teased her, rubbing his dick through her wetness, and then she felt the burning and stretching of her pussy as he slid inside of her.

"Ohmigod," she moaned, her head arching back as her breath caught. She couldn't spread her legs because of the binding around her ankles, so the fit was tighter and she felt every inch of him as he invaded her. And then he was embedded to the hilt and she felt his testicles slap against the lips of her cunt.

He pulled back slowly and she felt every stretch of

tissue before he rammed home again. Her mouth opened on a silent scream as pleasure unlike anything she'd ever experienced arced through her body. Her muscles tightened around him and liquid honey coated his cock, and then he settled into a pounding rhythm that sent sensations tearing through her.

"Fuck, you're so tight. I'm not going to last long, baby. Let me feel that sweet pussy squeeze me tight while you come."

She heard the strain in his voice and felt his cock swell the closer he got to orgasm. The head of his cock pressed against her G-spot every time he thrust inside her and her fingers scraped at the felt of the table, trying to find something to anchor her during the storm that had taken over her body.

"Come on, baby. Come on," he panted.

And then she felt it. He pushed against her G-spot one more time and held there. Waves of sensation stole her breath. Her pussy clenched around him, spasming as the orgasm took her by surprise with its intensity. Her eyes rolled back in her head and she was vaguely aware that his hand clamped over her mouth as she began to scream out her release. She didn't care. A hundred people could've rushed through the door at that moment and her orgasm wouldn't have stopped. She was powerless against it—against the debilitating pleasure that devastated her system.

Ecstasy roared through her and Zeke grew harder and bigger inside of her. And then he leaned over her, his hand still over her mouth, and he bit into her shoulder to silence his own cries as he exploded inside of her. She felt the powerful jets of semen against her inner walls, and it triggered another small orgasm that left her gasping for air.

Seconds, or minutes, or hours passed. She had no idea how long they lay there like that—him covering her body, his cock still semi-hard inside of her. She'd be sore. Eventually. But at the moment she could barely form a coherent thought in her head and her body was numb.

He kissed her shoulder—a sweet gesture considering

the feralness of their lovemaking. And then he said something that would've made her laugh if she'd had the energy.

"If we hurry home we can do this again."

"As long as I don't have to do anything but lie there," she murmured, slurring her words like a drunk.

He slapped her ass and she gasped as he pulled out of her, the muscles of her vagina swollen and not wanting to release him. "And that's different how? You just laid there this time."

"If I had the energy I'd punch you for that."

"If you've got enough energy to punch me then you've got enough energy to be on top next time. Now pull your pants up and let's go or I'll throw you over my shoulder like you are and carry you out."

She wouldn't have put it past him, so she did as he asked.

Chapter Seven

Mia was half asleep as they parked the 4x4 in her spot, but movement near the stairs of her apartment caught her eye. Cooper was just coming down the stairs.

"I thought I'd take the chance y'all would be home," he said once they'd gotten out of the car.

Mia pulled her jacket tighter around her ripped shirt and wondered if she looked like she felt—like she'd been completely and satisfactorily fucked.

"What's up?" Zeke asked. "Come on in. We went to Duffey's for a couple beers."

To her surprise, Mia felt heat rise to her cheeks, and she was grateful it was dark.

"I'm surprised he even let you in the door," Cooper said, smiling. "Man, those were the days."

"I know. Whoever thought either of us would end up on the side of law and order?"

"Not Duffey, that's for damned sure."

Mia unlocked the door and shivered as a blast of cold

wind wrapped around her porch, and then they all stepped inside into the warmth.

"I won't stay long," Cooper said. "I wanted to let you know a couple of fishermen found a body out where they were casting. She'd been in the water a couple days, but the coroner was able to ID her from her prints. She's identified as Tina Wolfe and has a record. Prostitution and petty theft for the most part. And she's associated with The Vaqueros. She was a house mouse for a while and then moved up to old lady status. She belonged to Wild Bill Jones."

"What was cause of death?" Zeke asked.

There was something in the tone of his voice that made her turn and look at him. And then everything started to fall into place and she knew.

"Her tongue was cut out and her hands were both cut off. And they branded her on the inside of her thigh. They're obviously sending a message. She ratted them out somehow." Cooper looked at Zeke with some kind of silent communication and she remembered Cooper wasn't a fool. He'd done his time in the military and a stint or two undercover as well. "Cause of death was a single gunshot wound to the head. Execution style. Just like The Vaqueros like. Just thought you might like to know."

"Yeah," Zeke said, nodding. "Thanks."

Cooper left and she closed and locked the door behind him. And then she turned around to face Zeke. "Tina Wolfe was your informant?" she asked.

He nodded and then paced to the wall and back, running his hands over the top of his head in frustration. "Son of a bitch."

The waves of his anger were palpable, and she knew if he had something to punch he would have. He'd take responsibility for Tina's death. Blame himself. That part hadn't changed. He'd always felt a personal responsibility—whether it was to the lowest kind of informant or one of his undercover officers. Everyone was *his*. He cared. Too deeply sometimes, and that's why he'd had such a hard time walking away from the job.

"She came in the shop last week," Mia said. She understood now. Knew why he'd been holding things back from her. He was working an op and he'd been using Tina to gather intel.

"I know," he said. "Just like I know you've got the music box. I snooped through your bag the other night while you were asleep."

Her lips pressed together, but she couldn't be mad. She'd have done the same thing if their positions had been reversed.

"I knew I could trust you with the information that's hidden in that music box. So I told Tina to be patient and wait, and then to take it from Wild Bill when she could. He's the club president and she was given a certain amount of freedom that the other women didn't have. She waited until they were gone to a club meeting and then took the music box. She told the other girls she was heading out to get her nails done. And she never looked back once she hit the road.

"She contacted me immediately. We told her we'd bring her in for protection if she brought us the box, but she didn't trust cops. Some habits die hard, and she felt she'd be safer on her own. So we had to come up with another plan. I gave her the address for your shop and told her to sell it to you and only you. She was determined to escape, despite the danger she knew she was in."

"That's a brave thing for a twenty-six-year-old woman to do. Especially one that's been trained to that kind of lifestyle, where she's taught early on that she has no independence or choices. The club's will is her will," Mia said.

"She was different," Zeke agreed. "Had backbone. And plans. She'd known from the start she'd work her way up, get some cash here and there on the side, and then move on. Neither of us saw it ending like this. She never made it to the checkpoint site. I knew that meant she was dead. I just didn't want to face it."

"I'm sorry, Zeke. I know it never gets easier."

"You almost get numb to it. And that's a dangerous thing."

"How'd you know I'd keep it?" she asked. "That's a hell of a risk to take on a hunch."

"I've always known you, Mia. Better than you know yourself. I knew you'd want it for your own. You had a collection of antique jewelry boxes in our apartment. And if all else failed, I knew you'd never sell it back to the biker just out of principle. It's that intrinsic sense of justice you have. If you hadn't taken it for yourself, you would've saved it for some kid or some older woman who needed a special birthday gift for her granddaughter but didn't have a lot of budget."

"I don't like being pegged so easily," she said.

"You're a big softy, Mia Russo. And everybody knows it. It's why I'm glad you left the job when you did. It would've eventually broken you completely. You're not able to cut off your emotions and compartmentalize as well as some of us."

She frowned, thinking it was a criticism.

"That's a good thing, babe. It's what made you so good at your job. But it's what tore you up too. We can't save everyone."

"Would it help if I told you that about Tina?" she asked.

His smile was pensive. "No, I guess not. That's part of the job too. We think we can save everyone. And when we can't it's a hard dose of reality not easily accepted."

"You've gotten very philosophical in your old age."

"I think you just learn to appreciate what's important in life the older you get."

The way he looked at her made her feel like he was looking at her through a microscope. Like he could see her wants and fears and dreams. And that she loved him still. It was a distinctly uncomfortable feeling so she turned away and tried to find something to do with her hands.

Her gaze caught on her backpack that was still propped on the floor, and she went over to it and pulled out the wrapped box. She hadn't had the chance to look at it herself.

Zeke had ears like a fox, and if she'd tried to wake up in the middle of the night to look at it, he'd have heard her. She took it to the table and unwrapped it, and then set it on the table gently.

"What was in it?" she asked.

"It was a recipe for a new amphetamine. It's not controlled by the USFDA and it's not considered an illegal substance. You heard about the raids down in Wyoming?" he asked.

"As much as anyone. I try not to watch the news anymore."

"Consider yourself lucky. The Vaqueros opened fire on a restaurant on a Friday night after work. All in all, twenty-eight people were killed and a man name Joaquin Rivera was kidnapped. He was a scientist for the Del Fuego cartel before they were disbanded, and then one of the other cartels bought him because he's a very brilliant man with a twisted mind. He just happened to be in the United States visiting his sister, and The Vaqueros took full advantage of his visit. They tortured the recipe from him, shot him in the head, and brought it back to their territory here for their own cooks to experiment with."

"It would be worth millions on the open market."

"I know. But now we have it, thanks to Tina. And thanks to you. As far as we know this is the only copy."

"So that's the real reason you came to Surrender," she said. "Why didn't you just tell me the truth? I would've helped had I known."

"Because that's not the main reason I came to Surrender. It would've been much more convenient to set her up with a pawnshop a hundred miles away where our office is located. I came for you. Because I was tired of living without you. And anger and hurt can only carry a person so far before there's nothing left but emptiness.

"We made our mistakes, Mia. Both of us. I was too driven and you were afraid. And the timing wasn't right. But that doesn't mean we weren't right. My feelings for you have never changed. I went through phases where I wanted to blame you—hate you—but I couldn't because that would be like blaming myself—hating myself. And I didn't have the guts to live with that. Because you were the very best part of me."

She stared at him, her eyes pooling with tears, but they never fell. Panic enveloped him as she stayed silent and wrapped her arms around herself protectively. Couldn't she see she was holding his heart? He was giving her everything he had. And the promise of the man he wanted to be for her.

"What will it take, Mia? I don't have to take the job in Carson. I've been offered several administrative positions. Hell, I was even offered the chance to teach criminal justice classes at Declan College. Riley MacKenzie recommended me to the Dean. I don't have to be a cop. I love it. But it doesn't define me. All I know is that I'll do whatever it takes to be with you. What do you say? Can we give this a shot for real this time?"

* * * *

Mia felt numb on the inside—paralyzed by his words. For the first time in as long as she could remember the right thing to say wasn't waiting to roll off her tongue. Her vocal cords were frozen and she didn't seem to have any control over her emotions because she could've sworn she felt a tear slide down her cheek.

"Baby, you're killing me," he said. "Is the thought of spending your life with me that repulsive? I've never seen you speechless." He tried to smile but she could see he didn't quite have the ability to make it believable. He was serious. And she was terrified.

She opened her mouth to speak but nothing came out. Frustrated, she swiped the tear away from her cheek and wiped her hand on her jeans.

"Listen, we can take things slow," he said, rushing to speak to fill the silence. "I was going to buy a place here in Surrender. I like it here and it's an easy commute no matter where I decide to take a job. I was hoping it would be our home together, but we can live apart. You said we missed the dating stage. Now's our chance to make up for all that."

She wiped another tear away and laughed. The sound was rough and foreign, but at least she'd gotten something out. "Seven years too late," she said and watched his face fall into that empty mask he adopted whenever he didn't want someone to know if he was hurt.

And then she moved into him, wrapping her arms around him and crushing her mouth against his. He lifted her and she wrapped her legs around him, and then she leaned back and looked into his eyes.

"We're long past the dating stage," she said, rubbing her thumb along the edge of his beard. "Don't make me wait any longer for you. I've wanted you for an eternity." Her lips twitched and she said, "Maybe we can be grownups this time and have a serious relationship." She kissed him again and let her legs drop to the ground.

"Jesus, you scared the hell out of me."

"You took me by surprise. A part of me still thought you might leave."

He squeezed her tight and she could feel him shaking his head. "Such little faith. Don't worry, I'm sure I'll figure out some way to punish you."

"I can only imagine," she said, shivering against him at the thought of what was to come.

She looked him in the eyes, wanting him to know she spoke the truth. "Zeke, if you love being a cop then I want you to be a cop. Why would I ever ask you to do something you don't love? I love you too much to not want that for you. Whether you're back working patrol or you're sitting behind a desk. Make the choice. I'll love you any way."

The relief on his face told her she'd said the right thing. And she'd meant it. His happiness was as important as anything else. This time around they were going to put each other first and learn the value of compromise.

"If you don't like the house maybe we could keep living above the bakery for a while," he said. "I could get used to the smell of cinnamon rolls in the morning."

Mia moved in close so her breasts rubbed against him, and she nipped at his chest. "I could get used to having my way with you in the mornings."

His hands tangled in her hair and she leaned her head back so his lips could seek hers. "That's even better than cinnamon rolls," he whispered.

They were both laughing as he kissed her.

The End

* * * *

Also from 1001 Dark Nights and Liliana Hart, discover Captured in Surrender, Trouble Maker, and Sweet Surrender.

If you enjoyed reading The Promise of Surrender, I would appreciate it if you would help others enjoy this book, too.

Lend it. This e-book is lending-enabled, so please, share it with a friend.

Recommend it. Please help other readers find this book by recommending it to friends, readers' groups and discussion boards.

Review it. Please tell other readers why you liked this book by reviewing it. Or visit me at http://www.lilianahart.com.

Join the Liliana Hart Newsletter!

WIN $100!

Beginning in April, I'll be giving away a $100 gift card* on the 15th of the month, and every month after, to one newsletter subscriber. The winner will be announced inside the newsletter, so you'll have to actually open it to see who won :-) So if you're not a newsletter subscriber, go do it. This will also be open to international readers.

*Must be deliverable online

About Liliana Hart

Liliana Hart is a *New York Times*, *USA Today*, and Publisher's Weekly Bestselling Author of more than 40 titles. After starting her first novel her freshman year of college, she immediately became addicted to writing and knew she'd found what she was meant to do with her life. She has no idea why she majored in music.

Since self-publishing in June of 2011, Liliana has sold more than 4 million ebooks and been translated into eight languages. She's appeared at #1 on lists all over the world and all three of her series have appeared on the New York Times list. Liliana is a sought after speaker and she's given keynote speeches and self-publishing workshops to standing-room-only crowds from California to New York to London.

Liliana can almost always be found at her computer writing or on the road giving workshops for SilverHart International, a company she founded with her partner, Scott Silverii, where they provide law enforcement, military, and fire resources for writers so they can write it right. Liliana is a recent transplant to Southern Louisiana, where she's getting used to the humidity and hurricane season, and plotting murders (for her books, of course).

Connect with me online:
http://twitter.com/Liliana_Hart
http://facebook.com/LilianaHart
My Website: http://www.lilianahart.com

Also From Liliana Hart

THE MACKENZIE SERIES
Dane
A Christmas Wish: Dane
Thomas
To Catch A Cupid: Thomas
Riley
Fireworks: Riley
Cooper
A MacKenzie Christmas
MacKenzie Box Set
Cade
Shadows and Silk
Secrets and Satin
Sins and Scarlet Lace
The MacKenzie Security Series *(Includes the 3 books listed above)*
1001 Dark Nights: Captured in Surrender
Sizzle
Crave

THE COLLECTIVE SERIES
Kill Shot

THE RENA DRAKE SERIES
Breath of Fire

ADDISON HOLMES MYSTERIES
Whiskey Rebellion
Whiskey Sour
Whiskey For Breakfast
Whiskey, You're The Devil

JJ GRAVES MYSTERIES
Dirty Little Secrets
A Dirty Shame

Dirty Rotten Scoundrel
Down and Dirty

STANDALONE NOVELS/NOVELLAS
All About Eve
Paradise Disguised
Catch Me If You Can
Who's Riding Red?
Goldilocks and the Three Behrs
Strangers in the Night
Naughty or Nice

Captured in Surrender
A MacKenzie Family Novella
By Liliana Hart
Now Available

Bounty Hunter Naya Blade never thought she'd step foot in Surrender, Montana again. Especially since there was a warrant out for her arrest. But when her skip ends up in the normally peaceful town, she has no choice but to go after him to claim her reward. Even at the cost of running into the cop that makes her blood run hot and her sense of self-preservation run cold.

Deputy Lane Greyson wants to see Naya in handcuffs, but he'd much prefer them attached to his bed instead of in a cold jail cell. She drove him crazy once before and then drove right out of town, leaving havoc in her wake. He's determined to help her hunt down the bad guy so he can claim his own bounty—her.

* * * *

Lane knew the moment Naya had stepped back into his town. There was something about her that called to him, like she was a siren song and he couldn't help but answer.

It had been just over a year since he'd seen her last. Since she'd ridden into town on that wicked bike looking for her brother. Colton Blade had been in the military with Cooper MacKenzie, and he'd always told his sister that if he ever got into trouble, then Cooper was who he'd go to for help.

But Colt turned out to be a bad seed—alcohol, drugs, assault charges, bar fights…and attempted murder. Colt Blade was more trouble than he was worth in Lane's opinion—someone who'd been given too many second chances and pissed them all away. Naya knew it too. But she'd still come after him, hoping he'd listen to her when she asked him to go back and face trial.

Naya had found Cooper, hoping he'd seen or heard from her brother, but Cooper hadn't been in touch with Colt for more than a decade. Lane had just come in from lunch to see her standing there in the office, and despite her brave front, he'd seen the despair etched on her face.

The sight of her had been like a punch to the solar plexus. Her face was a study. It shouldn't have been beautiful—not if you looked at her features individually. Her face was angular and her cheekbones flat, attributing her Native American heritage. Her nose was long and straight and her chin slightly pointed. But her eyes were what made a man lose his mind—exotic in shape and the color of dark chocolate, fringed with full black lashes. Thick brows winged above them, giving her a perpetual look of challenge.

She was tall—close to six feet—and her jeans had hugged her curves in all the right places. The belly-baring top she'd worn had shown a pierced navel, and the muscles in her arms were sinewy and lean.

He'd been struck speechless at the sight of her, his cock going rock hard in an instant and the wild lust of need surging through his body like it never had before. He'd have done anything to keep her around longer, just to satisfy his curiosity and see if her lips were as soft as he imagined they were. To see if she felt the connection the same as he did. He'd seen the way her nipples had hardened when she turned her dark gaze on him.

It had been a no-brainer to volunteer to help her search for her brother. He'd done it as much for himself as for her.

He'd never believed in love at first sight, but the moment he'd met Naya, those beliefs had been reevaluated. Their chemistry had been palpable—a living, breathing thing. And the heat that sizzled between them was hot enough to singe anyone who got too close. He'd had no control over his body in that instant, and that's something that had never happened to him before.

It looked like things hadn't changed much. His dick was hard enough to hammer nails and the feel of her against him, the challenge in her eyes daring him to do something about it, made him want to bend her over the bike, strip off those skin-tight jeans, and slide right between the creamy folds of her pussy.

"You're under arrest," he said instead, taking a step back so she couldn't feel his arousal. He didn't recognize the sound of his voice, the low rasp of desire.

"Oh, come on now, Deputy." Her lips quirked as if they were sharing a private joke. "That fight wasn't my fault, and I am hardly to blame for all the damage that was done. If you remember, I believe I was otherwise—" she took a step closer to him so her breasts rubbed against his arm, and she whispered the words so he felt them blow across his lips, "—occupied when the fight started."

She'd definitely been occupied. They'd been in one of the back rooms at Duffey's Bar. They'd started out doing body shots of tequila, getting more daring with each one. A lick of salt across the top of her breast before the shot was thrown back, burning the whole way down. Another lick low on his belly, so her cheek pressed against his hardness as she swiped with her tongue.

It hadn't taken long until she'd borrowed his handcuffs and latched him to the gold bar that rimmed the pool table. And then she'd knelt in front of him and taken every inch of his cock like it was her last meal.

He remembered the bite of her nails on his thighs and the way she stared up at him with those dark bedroom eyes—dreamed about it for the past year until his body was so hot and his cock so hard that he'd had no choice but to stroke himself to completion just so he could get some damn sleep.

Sweet Surrender

A MacKenzie Family Novella
By Liliana Hart
Coming December 13, 2016

It's been twelve years since Liza Carmichael stepped foot in Surrender, but after her great aunt's death she has no choice but to return and settle her estate. Which includes the corner bakery that's been a staple in Surrender for more than fifty years.

After twenty-five years on the job, Lieutenant Grant Boone finds himself at loose ends now that he's retired. He's gotten a number of job offers—one from MacKenzie Security—but he's burned out and jaded, and the last thing he wants to do is carry the burden of another badge and weapon. He almost turns down the invitation from his good friend Cooper MacKenzie to stay as their guest for a few weeks while he's deciding what to do with the rest of his life. But he packs his bag and heads to Surrender anyway.

The only thing Boone knows is that his future plans don't include Liza Carmichael. She's bossy, temperamental, and the confections she bakes are sweet enough to tempt a saint. Thank God he's never pretended to be one. But after he gets one taste of Liza and things start heating up in the kitchen, he realizes how delicious new beginnings can be.

MacKenzie Family World

Dear Readers,

I'm thrilled to be able to introduce the MacKenzie Family World to you. I asked five of my favorite authors to create their own characters and put them into the world you all know and love. These amazing authors revisited Surrender, Montana, and through their imagination you'll get to meet new characters, while reuniting with some of your favorites.

These stories are hot, hot, hot—exactly what you'd expect from a MacKenzie story—and it was pure pleasure for me to read each and every one of them and see my world through someone else's eyes. They definitely did the series justice, and I hope you discover five new authors to put on your auto-buy list.

Make sure you check out *Troublemaker,* a brand new, full-length MacKenzie novel written by me. And yes, you'll get to see more glimpses of Shane before his book comes out next year.

So grab a glass of wine, pour a bubble bath, and prepare to Surrender.

Love Always,

Liliana Hart

Now Available!

Desire & Ice by Christopher Rice
Bullet Proof by Avery Flynn
Deep Trouble by Kimberly Kincaid
Delta Rescue by Cristin Harber
Rush by Robin Covington
Trouble Maker by Liliana Hart

SAVAGED SURRENDER
By Jennifer Lyon

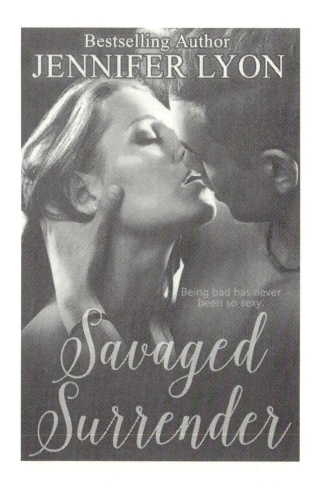

Acknowledgements

A huge thank you to Liz Berry and M.J. Rose for including me in the 1,001 Dark Nights Discovery Authors! It's truly an honor and pleasure to work with such a dynamic and successful group.

And a special shout out Rebecca Zanetti! This wouldn't have happened without you. Thank you, my friend.

Chapter 1

For a few hours Ethan Hunt was living the dream by cooking in the kitchen of Stilts, the newest upscale restaurant that stretched out on pilings over the bay in San Diego, California. Surrounded by gleaming stainless-steel worktables, industrial stoves, wicked-sharp knives and the drone of voices yelling out directions, he got to work with the one thing he loved most in the world—food. All under the watchful eye of Chef Zane.

The frenetic yet focused energy in the kitchen was similar to being in the gym back when he'd trained to be a mixed martial arts fighter. That was before he'd fucked up so royally that he destroyed his reputation, his ability to fight professionally ever again, damn near ruined his health and earned a pile of debt as deep as the sea.

"How's this?" His assistant for the day held up a pan.

He glanced over and couldn't bite back his grin. Ana Kendall was a mess. Her dark-rimmed super-cool glasses were askew on her face, dark-blond hair scraped back into a ponytail, and her white apron was covered in…hell, what was that? She must have spilled virtually every sauce in the kitchen on herself. Knowing her, she'd managed to taste all of them in the process. But she proudly held up the pan of crusty rolls he'd had her hollow out to toast for his goat cheese bruschetta.

"Perfect." He'd fix the uneven rolls when she got distracted by something else.

Chef Zane snorted behind them.

Ana shot him a look over her shoulder. "Still want that premium suite at Petco Park?"

The man's judgmental scowl morphed into a contrite expression. "Best work I've ever seen."

She nodded. "Thought so."

Ethan narrowed his eyes. "You offered him your dad's suite at Petco Park?" In trade for Ethan's chance to cook with Zane? Her dad had passed away suddenly less than two months ago. The shock and grief had rocked her, although in typical Ana fashion she was bouncing back quickly. But this? Her dad, a former professional baseball player, had prepaid for a suite at Petco Park baseball stadium for several of the Padres' home games. She was giving that away? "Ana—"

She cut him off with, "I need to change clothes."

Right, not the time to bring it up. Whatever she'd done to get Ethan this chance to cook with one of the best chefs in San Diego, he couldn't alter it now. Nor did he want to upset her in front of Zane and the staff by talking about her dad. He focused on her comment. "Why change? It's just us." He was cooking dinner for the two of them, and he didn't care if she wore shorts and a T-shirt. "Take your apron off and you'll be fine. Oh, and you might want to wash off the..." he reached up, rubbing his thumb over the smudge on her smooth cheek, "...soy sauce?"

Her brown eyes sparked, and a grin curved her mouth. "Chocolate. While you made the potatoes, Zane let me taste some desserts."

Figures. Ana's genuine friendliness and curiosity attracted people, and Zane was no different. Of course he wanted to show off his kitchen to the pretty girl. "You're supposed to be my assistant, little traitor."

God, he was going to miss her. Over the last few months, she'd become his closest friend. He could talk to her about anything. Well, almost anything; some subjects were off-limits. She didn't see the ugliness in him, and he wanted to keep it that way.

Ana sighed. "I'll make it up to you by eating the food you cook." Raising her eyebrows, she added, "Even if it tastes awful."

Her smart mouth amused the hell out of him. He leaned down, his face close to hers. "You'll eat it and love every mouthful." She always tasted every single dish he attempted. Ana was pretty fearless when it came to food and anything athletic.

Challenge gleamed in her eyes. "Or what?"

"No dessert."

Outrage yanked up her shoulders and puffed out her chest. "You can't do that. I have connections." She looked at Zane for help.

Ethan stepped in front of the man, cutting off her view. He easily had a foot in height and a hundred pounds on the little fireball. Not that he could intimidate her; she'd figured out quickly he'd never hurt her.

"I'm the chef tonight. I decide if you get dessert." Oh yeah, he loved taunting her.

"Is that right?" Ana's mouth quirked. "FYI, Chef Ego, I have frosted sugar cookies at home. I was going to be nice and send them with you to eat on your flight tomorrow. But you continue irritating me, and I'm going to keep them for myself." She turned and flounced out, her hips twitching in her shorts.

Ethan yanked his gaze away from her ass. Nope, not looking. *Friends.* They were friends. Ana wasn't some chick he'd bang and never think about again.

"Damn, she's cute."

Ice slid into his veins at Zane's comment. The man had to be a decade older than Ethan's twenty-two years. "Get your eyes off her ass. She's too young for you. Still in college." He didn't care if Zane was the toast of San Diego's culinary culture and becoming a cooking celebrity, he wasn't good enough for Ana.

The man rolled his eyes in his signature dramatic fashion. "I wasn't the one staring at her ass."

A guilty flush steamed his skin and irritated his conscience. *Off limits. Ana is off limits.*

"Are you two dating?" Zane asked.

"We're friends. I'm leaving town tomorrow."

"Right, she mentioned that. But..." Zane's attention drifted to the door, and his brows drew together. "She went to a lot of trouble to make a special evening for the two of you. I don't normally allow anyone in here to cook other than my staff, but she swore you have some cooking skills and won't annoy the shit out of me."

An odd sensation raced down Ethan's spine. Ana had given him friendship when most people avoided him after the news exploded that the up-and-coming MMA fighter had had a heart attack from steroid use at twenty-one years old. Called him a cheater, an ungrateful thug, a loser, a dangerous jerk...

And he was all those things. Every one of them. But sweet and sassy Ana Kendall befriended him and stubbornly defended him.

She was his sunshine. He'd been in a pit of black despair before she'd decided they'd be friends. And tonight she'd given him an opportunity to experience what it'd be like to achieve his dream of becoming a chef someday.

Zane went on, "That girl believes in you, man. It's more than friendship for her."

"It's not like that between Ana and me." He and Ana had agreed they were just friends. Ethan left tomorrow to join the protection and security team for the rock band Savaged Illusions's yearlong world tour. He wasn't sure he'd ever come back.

Probably not. His notoriety here in San Diego was another stain on him.

"Zane, got a problem," one of the other cooks called out.

"Be right there." The chef shot a look at Ethan. "Never seen any girl go to so much trouble for a *friend*. Might want to make sure you're both on the same page before you leave tomorrow. Because that girl? Special." He stalked off.

Special. Exactly. That was the reason he refused to feel anything more for her. He wouldn't be able bear the look in her eyes if she found out about his past. Sure, she knew he'd been a runaway living on the streets. But she didn't know what he'd done to eat. The old shame slithered and mocked, the taunting female words echoing in his memory. *"Once a whore, always a whore."*

He squeezed his eyes shut and breathed to control the rage that had once driven him. He knew what he was—dirty. No decent woman would want him to touch her. Not in public, anyway. And most definitely not Ana. The girl was too damned good for him. He'd known it the second he'd seen her in Sugar Dancer Bakery where she worked helping customers, taking extra time with the lonely older folks, making kids smile and just being Ana.

Then she'd turned all that sweet attention on him, and he'd been like everyone else who came into contact with Ana—helpless to resist her. So he'd compromised and walked the line. Friends. He wouldn't cross it.

They were fine. And tonight, he was cooking the best meal ever so they could enjoy their last night of companionship before he moved on to his new job. With renewed determination, he set about finishing the meal. He poured all his passion into the task, plating the crusted ahi and grilled sliced steak, potato and bacon au gratin, caramelized Brussels sprouts and the goat cheese bruschetta.

He took it all to a table against the glass wall of the open-air deck, surrounded by the bay glistening from the setting sun. It had to be perfect. His original idea was to bring Ana here for dinner, but she'd hijacked his plan, arranging for him to cook with Chef Zane. Now he wanted to give her the most delicious meal he'd ever prepared.

Something she'd remember when she thought of him, of their friendsh—

"Ethan."

Ah, there she was. After arranging the plates, he turned and froze.

Holy shit. Ana's hair fell in sultry waves around her face, and an electric-blue dress wrapped around her lithe curves. The hem ended midthigh, leaving too damned much of her tanned and toned legs bare, right down to her silver strappy heels.

His breath locked in his chest, and a buzzing filled his head. *Look away. Stop ogling her.*

But he couldn't stop. His control was taking a hell of a beat down. It wasn't just the dress—Ana was hot no matter what she wore. Nope, what blew his restraint out of the water was that Ana had taken off her glasses.

Her black-framed spectacles shouted *good girl* to him, and were a visual reminder that she was smart, sexy and way out of his league.

Unable to help it, he demanded, "Where the hell are your glasses?"

* * * *

Okay, that growling reaction wasn't exactly what Ana had hoped for. "I'm wearing my contacts." Zane had let her use his office and private bathroom to clean up and change. She'd meant to dazzle Ethan into yanking her out of the friend zone and into his arms.

He didn't appear dazzled. The light from the sinking sun caught the golden hues in Ethan's blond hair and highlighted the harsh lines of his strong cheekbones and rigid jaw. His blue eyes darkened as he glared at her. Backed up by powerful muscles packed into his six-foot-five frame, his stare alone was usually enough to stop huge men in their tracks.

But Ana wasn't a man, and she was damned tired of waiting for Ethan to pull his head out of his ass. He thought he was ignoring the attraction between them for her own good.

Screw that.

She wanted him to get on that plane in the morning and go do the job. How could she not support his goals? Of course she did. The same way he supported her goal to earn her degree and even teased her that one day she wouldn't just work for Sugar Dancer Bakery, but she'd be part owner with her boss and friend, Kat. He wasn't wrong. She'd make herself so indispensable to her boss, Kat would beg her to be a bigger part of the company. That was how Ana did everything, full-on and making herself too valuable to ignore.

But before he left, she wanted to show him he had a reason to come back—her. Once the band's world tour ended and Ana had her degree, they could give a relationship between them a chance.

"Why?"

His sharp question cut into her spinning thoughts. "Why what?"

Ethan regarded her for a beat, then grabbed a chair and pulled it out. "Sit."

Ana strolled over and settled into the seat. She carefully spread the napkin over her lap, aware of Ethan standing at her right shoulder.

Dropping his hand on the table by her filled plate, he leaned down, caging her in. "Why are you wearing contacts?" His gaze tracked over her bare throat and shoulders before his jaw tightened. "And that dress?"

She tilted her chin up. "To remind you I'm a grown woman." Oh look, he doubled down on his glare by adding a squint that made him appear even more lethal and totally terrifying. Or it would be if she didn't know for a fact that he'd never hurt her. She pulled out her perkiest smile. "Is it working?"

"This isn't a date." His jaw worked as he enunciated each word. "Just in case you're confused."

Heat rolled off him, along with the scent of food and pure, clean male. She loved Ethan's competitiveness, his fierce determination to pay off his debts and make his own way in the world. His quick humor and patience also appealed to her. But it was the slightly dangerous glint in his eyes that sparked erotic shivers in her belly, and a heated desire to challenge him. It was the sexualized version of the same drive that had her trying to beat him on their bikes and playing video games.

"Well then, since you picked me up and drove me here—" because Ethan was insanely protective and had insisted, going so far as to borrow a car since he'd sold his, "—should I get a ride home with someone else? I could ask Chef Zane." She worked some real evil into her grin. "Then we can be sure it's not a date."

His mouth twitched. "Smartass." He took his seat across from her, then poured some wine in their glasses.

"In a hot blue dress," she added, and sampled a small sip of her wine. She was still acquiring the taste, but she didn't think her beloved orange soda would really pair well with dinner. "You could be a little threatened that I might pick up another man."

Setting his glass down, he lowered his chin. "Try it and I'll toss your ass in the car and take you home. Now."

His words hung there, tempting the hell out of her. What was wrong with her tonight? But she knew—she couldn't bear the idea of losing Ethan. It just really hadn't hit home until the last few days that he was leaving. "That's kidnapping."

"And? Think there's a law I wouldn't break to make sure you're safe? Zane's a good chef, but that doesn't make him good enough for you, sunshine."

Her pulse skittered up, and flutters winged around her belly. Part of her wanted to surge up and run toward the kitchen just to test him on that. But since she wasn't two years old, she controlled the impulse and teased him instead. "However will I protect myself once you're gone? I'll be bored and probably date all kinds of nefarious bad boys." She broke off a small piece of bruschetta and popped it into her mouth. The warm bite of bread topped with bright tomatoes, spices and a crumble of goat cheese made her moan.

He reached for his water glass. "Have you lost your mind? You're not dating bad boys."

She fought a laugh at the ridiculous order and dug into her ahi. So good, it practically melted on her tongue. "You're right, maybe it's better to skip dating and just hook up."

Ethan choked on his drink and slapped the glass down. "Hell, I deserved that. I can't tell you who to date, I just..."

She leaned toward him, desperate to hear his answer. Did he feel that sick sting she did when she thought of him with other women? "What?"

His jaw tightened. "Let's talk about something else. How's your dinner?"

She wasn't giving up but let him change the subject for now. Focusing on the food, she enjoyed the flavors and textures but most of all, she swore she could taste Ethan's passion for cooking in each bite. "Amazing. I love it."

He set his fork down. "Thank you, Ana. I wanted to bring you here for dinner, but this..." He lifted his hand. "When you told me to come over early because you had a surprise, I never thought it'd be a chance to cook with a master chef."

Hot pleasure warmed her. She loved making him happy. "Today was fun for me too. Some of my best memories are of us cooking together."

"*Us* cooking?" He squeezed her hand.

"Watch it, dude. I've chopped a lot of onions for you. When you're famous someday, I could probably claim a percentage of your income."

He rubbed his thumb over her wrist. "My cooking helped you study and will ultimately lead to your success. I could claim a percentage of your future income. And I saved your life when you were dying of strep throat."

"Oh, now I was dying?" God he made her laugh. Ethen had shown up at her house to check on her, didn't like how dog sick she was and hauled her to urgent care. "I was fine in a couple days." After antibiotics and a lot of sleep.

"Pretty sure the doctor said you only had minutes to live."

Ana rolled her eyes. He'd make a totally exaggerated boast like that, but whenever Ana brought up the day he'd helped rescue her boss from a madman with a knife, he shrugged it off.

"But heroics aside," Ethan said. "I'll never forget this chance to cook with Chef Zane. Or you."

Do it now. I have to tell him how I feel. Her heart thumped. "I can't ever forget you." All her practiced words fled as a knot of desperation lodged in her chest. But she didn't want to lose this moment, and forced herself to go on. "I—"

"I've brought dessert and coffee." A smiling server carried a tray over. "Key lime pie and molten chocolate cake."

Ana resisted the urge to snap at the woman for interrupting them. The server was doing her job. Besides, the thing that kept them from crossing the line to lovers was that Ethan believed her too good for him. Talking wasn't going to convince him otherwise.

She had to show him she had a bad side too. For that, Ana needed privacy.

An hour later, he parked the borrowed Mercedes in one of her guest spaces, and they headed inside her condo. She loved her little home, but right now it felt too small and tight, like her skin. Her nerves pulled taut.

"Cookies are on the counter if you're still hungry." She gestured to the pastry box and headed to the fridge. Snagging two cold bottles of water, she inhaled a breath of cool air. When she turned around, Ethan was right there, looming only feet from her. She heard the soft whoosh of the refrigerator automatically closing behind her.

"I don't want cookies." He dragged his hand through his hair, his shirt pulling against his chest. Finally he dropped his arm. "You're my hardest goodbye, Ana. I'm not sure I'd have made it through these last months without you. You're my one good thing."

As she stood there with a bottle of cold water in each hand, her throat swelled. For seven years, she had done everything she could to make her dad and stepmom proud and never regret all they'd done to get Ana out of a bad situation and have her come live with them. Since that day, she'd been the ultimate good girl, always in control. It was exhausting, but with Ethan, she'd been able to let go a little bit. Yet the times when Ethan had almost kissed her and stopped, Ana hadn't pushed. Nope, she'd been the good girl, letting the man decided.

Either she took the risk of showing him how much she desired him, or she lost him because she really was exactly what he thought—too good of a girl to take a risk.

Setting the waters down, she hopped up on the counter in the place she'd sat many times while Ethan cooked. "This isn't goodbye."

Ethan settled his hands on either side of her hips, caging her with the force of his sharp attention. "Then what is it?"

Her mouth dried, and blood pounded in her ears. All the muscles in Ethan's arms bunched and strained. Power, restraint and a vibrant hunger pulsed into the air around them. He hadn't even touched her and her body hummed. A bright and fiery need throbbed low in her belly, making her want to break his rigid control and free them both.

Swallowing, she lifted her hands to his face. "This." She kissed him.

Ethan sucked in a breath and went utterly still.

Oh God, what if he rejected her? What if he hated that she threw herself at him? *No, don't give up.* She feathered her lips over his, pouring her caring and longing into each touch. All the days, weeks and months of yearning for his kiss flooded her system.

Ethan's control shattered on a groan. He sank the fingers of one hand into her hair, and plunged his tongue into her mouth. His palm slid down her back, gripping her ass and pinning her in place.

Yes. Her blood raced, heating her entire body. Sexy chills skated over her skin, and everywhere he touched left a blazing trail. Driven by a fierce urgency, she thrust her tongue against his, the wet slide sparking a fierce hunger.

Or was it the way he held her trapped where he wanted her? Not recoiling at her aggressiveness, but meeting it with his own? Wanting to get closer, she wrapped her arms around his neck. Her nipples ached, warmth swamped her belly, and deep between her thighs, insistent need pulsed.

His palm on her ass dragged her forward, shoving her skirt up and pressing her center flush to the thick ridge of his cock trapped in his jeans. The hard pulse against her panties tore a moan from her throat. Ana gripped his shoulders, rubbing along his shaft, desperation pitching up too fast and brutal.

"I knew you'd be like this." He skated his lips down her throat. "One taste of you and I'd lose my fucking mind."

His words and the warm, wet trail of his mouth sent more shivers from her nipples to her clit. She tunneled her hands beneath his shirt to feel his fevered skin over granite muscles.

With a low growl, his fingers on her hip tightened as he rocked his length along her cleft. Every thrust pushed her higher and she could feel his cock growing thicker, longer and more demanding. A reserve that had ridden her for years melted away, leaving her free to go after what she wanted.

Getting a hold of his hair, she angled his head up to kiss him again. She tasted their shared dinner and Ethan, the deeply male flavor that made her crazed for more. "Touch me. I can't bear it."

He wrapped his hand around her hair, restraining her. His eyes burned like a blue flame as he scraped his fingers up her thigh. "You have no idea the ways I can make you scream in pleasure."

She tilted her hips up, desperate to find out. When he didn't move fast enough, she caught his thick wrist, pulling his hand where she craved it.

The rough glide of his fingers over her swollen bud sent shocks of pleasure arcing.

"Ethan." Her cry ripped out. This was everything she'd dreamed. The ache ramped up to unbearable. She couldn't survive without him doing that again, harder and longer. She rubbed against his hand, chasing that rising desire with a wantonness. Only with Ethan could she be this free and wild. "Please. No one makes me feel like you do."

He jerked back, eyes nearly feral, cheeks flushed. "Goddammit." Fury swelled his shoulders. He clenched and unclenched his fists.

Her hands fell to the granite, and her stomach plummeted, all her hope crashing down into a pile of twisted pain. "What did I do wrong?"

She hated the weakness, the tiny part of her still desperate to just be enough. A little voice in her head said, *What did you expect? You're a pathetic little attention seeker, begging for it. He didn't really want you. You just imagined it.*

Stop it. This wasn't the same thing. Needing reassurance, she forced herself to look at Ethan.

Ruthless determination and regret dug into his face, making him appear older and harder. "Nothing. I'm the one who doesn't do relationships. Ever. I fuck, leave and never think about the chick again. Go find yourself a man who's good enough. I'm not that guy."

He snatched his keys out of his pocket and strode to the door. Opening it, he looked back for a breath of time.

Then he left, closing the door and breaking her heart.

Chapter 2

As part of the protection team surrounding the band Savaged Illusions, Ethan Hunt took the lead, walking in front. The group headed down the hallway of the concert venue to a private elevator.

"Did you see the packed house? The audience was sick! We were on fire!" Lynx, the drummer, high-fived the bassist, River.

"Hell yeah," River agreed.

Ethan tuned out their talk as the car shot up. When the elevator doors opened, he and Hank exited first, scanning the Skylight Lounge located at the very top of the concert venue. Floor-to-ceiling windows revealed the Tampa skyline lit up against the night. About fifty people, all with VIP passes, lounged in plush gray couches and chairs grouped around a sleek black bar draped in soft lavender lighting. Once they heard the elevator arrive, every eye turned to them.

Ethan focused on the lead bodyguard in the VIP section. At his nod that everyone in the upscale bar had been cleared, Ethan stepped aside.

Instant pandemonium erupted as the crowd surged toward the band. Cameras flashed, people laughed and yelled. He recognized two well-known actresses and a football player. A few familiar groupies, including the head of their fan club. Two men in suits and—

No way. Whipping his gaze back, he homed in on the small, pretty woman staring at him. His entire body vibrated with surprise.

Ana Kendall. The spitfire of a girl who'd haunted his dreams and invaded his days. No matter how many women he'd hooked up with or how far he traveled, she was there in his mind.

What the hell was she doing in Florida at a VIP afterparty for Savaged Illusions? He hadn't seen her in eleven months.

An uncertain smile wavered on her lips before fading.

For a second, everything around him was drowned out by a crash of memories and regrets. His muscles twitched with the urge to go to her, touch and tease her until she smiled and laughed the way she used to with him.

Ana looked away, breaking eye contact to talk to another person.

Ethan automatically took note of her two friends, Franci and Chelle, hovering by her.

Ana was here. He couldn't get his brain around that fact. But he didn't have time to dwell on it as the band headed straight for the bar. Snapping out of his shock, Ethan moved with them, taking up a stance at the edge of the bar to keep watch.

The others in security settled around the room at their assigned posts. With the band's fame skyrocketing, the security team took zero chances. After Ethan checked the position of all five members of the band, another man caught his attention. Young twenties; longish, dark hair; blue eyes; thin build in an expensive V-neck shirt; tight black pants and high-end suede sneakers all screamed money. But the way he stared at Justice set off Ethan's internal alarms.

If there was going to be trouble, this nervous kid would be it. He hovered at the edges of the crowd around the band, barely blinking, his eyes following Justice's every move.

Otherwise, everything appeared to be under control. The servers were all cleared and familiar with working VIP parties, and the guests were behaving. Ethan did another room scan, keeping his focus on the job.

Not on Ana in that pretty green dress, ordering a drink.

A current of awareness sizzled through him. Ana was watching him. Damn, she looked sweet and sexy. Her dress dipped between her small breasts, fit her waist and flared out around her thighs. He couldn't figure out why she was here. The need to talk to her formed an internal push. He ignored it to do his job and visually swept the room.

Unable to resist, he stole another look at Ana.

But she'd slipped away to talk to her friends.

A half hour later, his neck muscles were cramped from the effort of keeping his focus on his job, not Ana.

Justice lifted his hand in a signal to Ethan and headed to a private hallway. Damn it, the man knew to wait for him. Ethan strode after him, and noted the nervous kid following Justice. Getting between the possible trouble and the lead singer, he keyed the mic on his headset. "Hank, escorting Justice to bathroom. Possible shadow." He described the kid.

"See it. Stay with Justice. I'll find out what the shadow's up to."

"Right." He keyed off and said to Justice. "Go straight into the private hallway." This wasn't the time to get waylaid by fans.

The lead singer glanced over his shoulder. "Trouble?"

"You had a shadow." Ethan shot a quick look back to see Hank had stopped the kid. A heated conversation broke out.

Justice nodded, used to security controlling his life. Even things like taking a piss became an ordeal. Ethan nodded to the security guard watching the hallway to keep fans and staff out.

Once in the hallway, Ethan went into the bathroom with Justice to make sure the room was clear then headed for the door to wait in the hall.

"Ethan," Justice said.

"Yeah?"

"Give me a few minutes."

He got it. Sometimes it was a phone call one of the band members wanted to make, or even just a few minutes of no one pulling at them. "No problem." Ethan stepped out to the hallway and stopped in surprise at the girl talking to the other security guard.

"This is a restricted area." Josh told her.

Unable to resist, he crossed to them. "What's going on?"

Ana shifted her gaze to him. "Ethan, I, uh, wanted to say hi. I know you're working so maybe later."

He couldn't let her walk away and touched Josh's shoulder. "It's okay, she's with me."

The other guard nodded and Ethan led her deeper into the hallway where he could keep an eye on the bathroom door and Ana. "I can't believe you're here. What brings you to Florida?"

"Vacation with Franci and Chelle. We're staying at the Tradewinds Resort in St. Pete's." She licked her lips and shifted uneasily. "You look well."

The dress pulled tight against her breasts, and damn it, he didn't want to notice that. Or think of that last night when Ana had kissed him and he'd lost his mind. Two more minutes and he'd have had her panties on the floor and been balls-deep inside her.

Answer her. "Thanks, you too." She looked so damned good he had to dig his fingers into his palms to keep from touching her, and remember he was on the job.

"Franci and Chelle surprised me with the tickets to the concert and the VIP passes. I almost didn't come."

Because of him and the way they'd last parted? "What changed your mind?"

A grin touched her lips. "Franci and Chelle went to a lot of trouble to get the tickets and VIP passes, and I didn't want to ruin that for them."

How could he feel that pinch of disappointment when he was the one who'd pushed her away? What did he want, for Ana to have been sad all these months? God he was a selfish bastard. "How are you, Ana? The way I left—"

"I'm fine," she cut him off. "I graduated, and Kat promoted me at the bakery to the publicity director."

She seemed tenser, edgier than he remembered. Was it unease from seeing him again and the awkwardness stretching between them? Or something else? But the part about her finishing her degree and getting a promotion pulled a smile from him.

"Congratulations. You're a college graduate." While all he had was he GED, a certificate from culinary school, and his colossal failure as an MMA fighter. "I'm proud of you, sunshine." His old nickname for her slipped out before he could think better of it.

"Thanks. I'd love to hear about how you're doing. " She swallowed and blurted out, "I was hoping if you have time, we could grab some coffee or lunch? I'm here all week. I don't know how long you're staying."

She wanted to meet? Before he could formulate an answer, his earpiece crackled. "Ethan, threat has been neutralized. Stay with Justice until he's back in view."

So either Hank had determined the boy wasn't a threat or had removed him altogether. Ethan touched the mic and answered, "Got it." He gestured to his headset. "Sorry, work."

"Right, you're busy. Well, you know my cell number, if you're around. Nice seeing you." She started to turn.

Unable to help it, he touched her shoulder. Her soft, warm skin beneath his palm sent a zap of heat straight to his dick. Memories pressed in and woke up the ache in his chest. Damn it, he'd missed her.

"Ana, wait." He dropped his hand.

Her shoulders tensed, but she faced him.

He didn't know what to say. Did he want to see her?

Hell yeah.

But should he? "I'm here all week too. The band's taking a break after the show tomorrow night."

"Really?"

The spark of hope in her gaze made him pause. "Yes." He wanted to see her, but that last night in San Diego had made it clear—their attraction was so damned strong that with enough time together, they'd end up in bed. "But nothing's changed with me. I'm still not a relationship guy."

A flush crawled up her throat as she rocked on her heels. "I got that eleven months ago, loud and clear."

He'd embarrassed her. What was it about her that made him stupid?

"But things have changed with me."

Her words punched right into his chest and brought out his protectiveness. Changed, how? Ana didn't need to alter anything about herself. She was sweet, caring, ambitious and funny as hell. Why would she change? "What do you mean?"

She lifted her shoulders, every line of her small frame vibrating with resolution. "I grew up. I've been working hard to be what everyone else needs me to be. And that's okay, that's what I do. But right now, this is my vacation, and for a week, I'm looking for a chance to let loose and be a little bad with no strings attached."

Stunned, he struggled to think. "You want to be bad." With him? Jesus. No strings attached? Was this a prank? Or was this some kind of revenge? "Are you propositioning me?"

She compressed her lips. "God I suck at this."

He'd feel sorry for her if he had any idea what was actually going on. "At what?"

Sighing, she fiddled with the small purse hanging from her shoulder. "I wanted to meet and catch up, and if we still have an attraction, then yeah, I guess I'm propositioning you. But this time I'm not looking for anything more than a sexy fling and we go our separate ways."

He couldn't formulate an answer. Thankfully Justice was still in the bathroom, and no other band members had come into the hallway. "I don't know what to say."

"Right, okay." She forced a small smile. "If you decide you're interested, let me know." She turned and walked out of the hallway.

Did that just happen? With Ana? He got propositioned by groupies all the time. Sometimes he indulged and forgot them.

But Ana?

His muscles twitched with the need to go after her, drag her someplace private and find out what the hell she was thinking. But he couldn't; he had to stay outside the bathroom door and wait.

Frustration screamed in his brain, and hot need pulsed in his gut.

What was he going to do?

* * * *

Ana could feel Ethan's scrutiny searing her spine as she walked away. *Don't look back.* Her heart pounded from seeing him and the way she'd mangled that conversation. What was wrong with her, just blurting things out like that? She'd thought she'd been prepared to see him. But when all six feet five inches of him stepped off that elevator, it had been a punch straight to her heart. She'd missed him so much.

But she meant what she'd told Ethan, she'd grown up. She'd been out of line that night by trying to naively pull her friend into a relationship he didn't want.

Yet Ana had kissed him.

That humiliation still stung. And the way they parted—him walking out in anger and disgust was an ache that wouldn't quite heal. What if they could do it over? Recapture some of their friendship and all of that sizzling attraction? But this time Ana wouldn't push for a lasting romantic relationship. Instead, Ana and Ethan would both walk away with good memories. All she had to do was convince Ethan that she truly was ready to be bad while on vacation. But she'd handled that reunion with him almost as terribly as she'd handled that last night in San Diego. Clumsy and coming on too strong.

Franci approached her as soon as she got a few feet from the hallway. "Did you talk to him?"

"Yep." She'd rarely seen Ethan so shocked. Or maybe he'd just been struggling with how to turn her down.

"Well? Did you guys make plans? The band is on a break after tomorrow's show and staying in Florida for a week. It says so on their website."

"Stalker," she teased. Both Franci and Chelle had gone to a lot of trouble for tonight. Planning this trip to coincide with Ethan's schedule, buying the tickets and securing the passes to this afterparty. Their plot was a bit insane, but their hearts were in the right place.

"Hijacker. We had the perfect plan to help you. But no, you stole it."

Amused, she said, "I'm a hijacker?"

Franci nodded, her brown eyes full of alcohol-fueled sincerity. "You illegally seized control of our plan, which is hijacking. And you stole the keys to the rental car out of my purse. So you hijacked the plan and stole my keys."

Unable to help it, she tilted her head and said, "Are you sure I didn't illegally seize control of the rental vehicle, thereby hijacking it too?"

Franci chewed her lip. "The argument could be made… Hey. You're distracting me."

"'Cause I'm beautiful?" She was probably going to hell for toying with her somewhat inebriated friend. It was only fair since Ana had assumed the role of designated driver by swiping the car keys. Everyone knew the DD got teasing privileges.

"Funny. Our plan would have worked if you weren't a control freak who had to butt in and take over."

Ana laughed, even if there was an uncomfortable grain of

truth in that statement. "Or maybe I came up with a better plan of being honest."

Franci raised her eyebrows. "Okay, so you took over. How'd that work out for you?"

Ana forced a brilliant smile. "Great. He's going to call me." Maybe. Okay probably not. Heading for the bar, she added, "Come on, let's have some fun." She'd tried, and Ethan would either call or he wouldn't. Either way, she'd handle it and be fine.

Franci joined her, ordered a vodka and cranberry, and then shot her a smug look. "Bet you're regretting your hijacking ways now. If you'd stuck to the plan, I'd be the DD."

Ana ordered an orange soda. "I'll be glad when I don't have a hangover tomorrow."

While they waited for their drinks, she watched as Ethan returned and took up the same post at the end of the bar she'd seen him at earlier. He stood with his legs spread, arms crossed and giving off an alert-and-ready-for-any-trouble vibe. She couldn't tear her attention from him. In eleven months, she'd never tried to contact him—not even in her most terrified moments. Oh she'd thought about it, and in a strange way that comforted her. Telling herself that if she truly needed him, he would come.

She wouldn't ever have called though. It was only a fantasy to get her through the nights of worrying.

Now she just wanted a chance to break out and, well, be bad. Safely. For so long, she'd done everything right, struggled to be perfect.

Would Ethan be interested? Could he see her as more than that college girl he'd known?

His gaze slid to hers, and her stomach flipped at the sheer intensity.

"Do you know Ethan?"

The voice startled her. Ana forced herself to turn to a woman with long blond hair flowing around her sculpted face and memorable brown eyes. "You look familiar... Oh! You're Chef Siena Draco." Ana loved her show on the Food Network.

"Guilty. I noticed you talking to Ethan earlier. So you know him?"

It seemed odd that anyone paid attention. Curious, she said,

"He's an old friend. Do you know him?" What if they were lovers? She hadn't asked Ethan if he was involved with someone. The thought hurt way more than it should.

"Yep, we met at one of my restaurants."

"Wow." A celebrity chef was familiar with Ethan?

"Ana!" Chelle caught her arm, her blue eyes dancing with excitement. "Come meet the band. I just talked to them, they're awesome. I told them you know Ethan, and they want to hear all about it."

Siena laughed. "Apparently, I'm not the only nosey one."

As she was swept away, Ana looked back at Ethan.

He was watching them, his mouth flat. She could almost feel the heat of his gaze sizzle over her skin. *Possessive.* Her stomach fluttered again. Was it just his old protectiveness? Or was the attraction still there between them?

Would he call her?

* * * *

It'd been an hour since Ana's bombshell proposition that left Ethan buzzing with conflict and struggling to stay focused on his job. And lust, but that wasn't a surprise. He'd been attracted to her since the first time he'd seen her.

It was that good-girl thing.

And tonight? She'd just upped that to girl good wants to be bad. With him.

Seeing his boss striding toward him, he asked, "What's up?"

"Everything's quiet. A few people getting shitfaced, but no trouble. Go take a break before the band leaves. I'll cover your post."

Hank was a stickler for security getting a chance to stretch their legs, grab something to eat and let down their hypervigilance for a few minutes. Normally Ethan would snag a water and go outside.

But tonight, he had another goal and headed straight for the woman dominating his thoughts. Weaving through people clawing for the band's attention, he wrapped his hand around Ana's arm. "I'm on break, can we talk?"

She turned, her eyes wide. "Uh, sure."

He led Ana across the room to a high table tucked in a corner by the floor-to-ceiling windows. Holding her chair, he tried to ignore the enticing way her dress slid up her thigh. Why did he remember exactly what her skin felt like, and her shivers as he kissed her, his fingers trailing higher on her leg? The way she'd gotten demanding, needy, triggering a fierce urge to give her everything she wanted.

"You can say whatever you wanted to tell me," Ana said. "If you're not interested in seeing me, I'll accept that."

He clenched his jaw at the uncertainty swimming in her brown eyes. What had it cost her to come here tonight, face him and make the proposition of a no-strings-attached fling?

"I think about that kiss," he admitted.

Her mouth parted, and her tongue darted out to touch the tip to her plump bottom lip. "You do?"

"Yes. And I think about you." He ran a hand over his head. Did she have to look so damned beautiful and sleek? By most standards, Ana was cute, with her heart-shaped face and tiny stature. But to him, she was gorgeous and untouchable. "But the reality is, I'm still bad for you."

Her chin notched up. "Bad is what I'm searching for right now. Short-term bad."

Heat blazed over his skin at the idea of Ana, his sweet girl, wanting to be bad. "Why?"

"I'm tired of being good, of always trying so hard, and worrying that I'm falling short. I'm ready for some fun, but I don't…" She looked away.

She'd been honest with him right up until now, so why was this hard? Or did she fear him rejecting and hurting her again? Catching her chin, he turned her face to see her expression. "Don't what?"

Her eyes shimmered with a need that nearly undid him. "I can't seem to find the guy I want to be bad with. Except for you."

Hell. He stroked his thumb along her cheek. "Ana. You don't even know what you do to me." He'd struggled every damned day they'd spent together battling their growing attraction. Now she was offering herself to him, with no strings and no guilt. How could he resist that?

Tugging his hand away, he searched for a distraction before

his control could snap and he kissed her.

Not here. Not now.

He focused on her empty glass. "Can I get you something from the bar?" That would give him a minute to get his head on right.

She wrinkled her nose. "Nope. I'm DD tonight, so just sticking to orange soda or water, and I've had my fill of both." Shifting her attention on a point past him, she waved at a group. "They keep toasting me with their shots."

He followed her gesture to see Franci and Chelle laughing around Lynx, River and their entourage of the usual party chicks. They raised their glasses of whatever they were chasing the shots with, and made kissing faces at him and Ana.

"How did you end up DD, and why are they taunting you if it lets them have fun?" The Ana he remembered didn't drink much, especially for a college-aged girl, but he was curious.

"I foiled one of their insane plots." She shrugged. "This is their payback. But we'll see who's laughing in the morning. I'm so setting my phone to blast music at six a.m."

A chuckle rumbled up his chest at her gleeful voice. "I'll have one of the limos drive you back to the resort if you want a drink."

Surprise registered on her face. "You can do that? What about our rental car?"

"We have extra limos on hand tonight, it's not a big deal." He'd check, but if it wasn't being used, his boss Hank and the guys in the band wouldn't care. There were perks to the job. "I'll drive your rental to the manor where we're staying and bring it to you at the resort tomorrow." Ethan usually rode in the limo with the guys, but someone else could do it tonight.

"All the way to St. Pete's? It's a half hour to forty minutes from here."

Ethan leaned his arm on the table, enjoying being this close to her. "It'll give us a chance to catch up with each other. And talk about you wanting to be bad. With me."

"You're interested?"

He couldn't lie to himself or her. "I walked away once, and it only made me hungrier for you. But there's no future, Ana, not for you and me. That will never change."

"I know."

Her simple acceptance nagged at him. Why did she want this? Fast and hard sex and nothing more? For him, it was all he knew. But Ana...shouldn't she look for a real relationship? He started to ask her if everything was okay, but stopped himself. Once she'd have trusted him enough to tell him if something more was going on.

But now? After he'd left so abruptly that night, and then hadn't talked to her in nearly a year?

Yeah, time to ease up and give them both a little space. Instead he asked, "Want that drink now?"

"I think... Oh hell." Ana shoved off the high barstool.

Ethan shot up, automatically on alert. "What?" But he instantly saw the problem. Franci and Chelle were stripping off their tops.

Ana rushed over, pushing through the people gathering around. "Hey! Stop it!" She grabbed Franci's shirt, which was tangled around her neck, and forced it back down.

Ethan quickly caught the edges of Chelle's opened shirt and began rebuttoning it.

"No. We're shashing clothes."

He squinted, trying to make out the slurred words. "What?"

Furious, Chelle twisted in his hold, damn near ripping her shirt. "Ex-shash-ing."

It took him a second to work it out "Exchanging? Like trading clothes?"

"Yes! What I said."

"No," Ana said. "You can't exchange clothes with Franci."

"But we have a plan." Chelle stuck her bottom lip out.

Ana glared at him. "Don't you dare laugh."

"Too late." He couldn't help it. He saw this shit all the time. Ordinarily it was annoying, but Franci and Chelle weren't doing the usual dancing naked, swimming naked, trying to get screwed naked, or his least favorite, the dramatic female meltdown or temper tantrum. These two were original—they wanted to change outfits. Ana's friends were funny drunk or sober.

"Need a hand?" Hank asked Ethan, while two more security guards urged people away from the scene.

"I'm sorry," Ana said. "We'll leave. I didn't realize they'd had so much to drink."

Ethan stopped laughing at Ana's obvious distress. "Hey, no one's mad. They didn't hurt anything."

She nodded. "I'll get them back to the resort. Thanks for helping."

He caught her arm. "Take a limo. You can't handle them both while driving the car, and the driver can help you get them in the room." Chances were good the girls were going to pass out in the limo at some point.

Gratefulness filled her eyes. "Are you sure it's okay?"

Hank cut in. "It's perfectly okay, and Ethan's right. It's better you're not trying to drive and handle double trouble here." A smile twitched the man's mouth. "And don't look so distressed. These two were having fun. I've been watching them since they began doing shots. They had some plan for a fashion show…" He gave in and laughed.

Ana flushed again. "Thank you, uh…"

"Hank."

She straightened, obviously regaining her poise. "Hank. I'm Ana, and I appreciate your understanding."

He smiled at her, then said, "Ethan, help Ana get her friends packed up and on the road. Use Barb's limo. She can manage any problems."

"Limo!" Franci shouted.

Ethan nodded at his boss. "Got it." Together, he and Ana herded the girls down to the car. After coaxing them inside, he took Ana's arm. It was early morning, around one a.m., and the moonlight cascaded over her. "Text me when you're safely in the room and the details to bring the car back tomorrow."

"We'll be fine tonight, but I'll text you."

God he wanted to pull her against him and kiss her. But he was still on the job, and past experience warned him that a kiss with her could get out of control in seconds. "Ana."

"What?"

"Let me take you to lunch tomorrow. We'll talk and catch up, then if it's really what you want, we can move on to discussing the ways you can be bad."

Her eyes glinted with something. Curiosity? Mischief? "We can eat at the resort." She leaned toward him when noise from inside the car cut into the moment.

Franci and Chelle pressed their lips to the window, making exaggerated kissing gestures. Ana sighed. "It's going to be a long drive. They apparently aren't too drunk to remember Operation Kiss 2.0."

"Say what?" She'd lost him with that comment.

Ana caught his expression and laughed. "That's the name for their insane plot I mentioned earlier. They got the tickets to the concert and party, then planned to sneak off and leave me here so you'd have to take me back to the resort."

"They'd do that?" The idea of Ana stranded infuriated him. "That's dangerous as hell."

"They were going to tell you on their way out they had an emergency and ask you to get me back to the resort. They thought if we spent time together, we'd recreate the kiss of our last night together in San Diego."

She couldn't be serious. "The one where I walked out on you?" Ana and her friends teased each other, made hysterical bets with one another, but they'd rip apart anyone who dared to hurt one of them.

Ana's face flushed. "They don't know that part. I told them it was a hot kiss but we both decided the timing wasn't right since you were leaving."

"Why?" He didn't get it.

"Because they would have tried to find a way to get revenge on you if they thought you'd hurt me. This was simpler, better. Except now the tour will be over in a month and they assume you're coming back to San Diego."

Ethan glanced over at the two drunks now licking the window in a distorted parody of French kissing. Her meaning sank in. "Oh shit. They're matchmaking."

Ana nodded. "Yep. But it's fine. If we do have a fling, I'll tell them it just fizzled out. And if we don't, I'll tell them the chemistry died. See? Easy." Banging on the window had her sighing again. "I'd better get them back to the hotel."

Pulling open the door, he held it while she shooed Franci and Chelle back and climbed in. Ethan closed it and stepped aside as the limo slid away.

Why did he think letting her go a second time was going to be anything but easy?

Chapter 3

"You guys going to be okay?" Ana snagged a bottle of Gatorade from the fridge in the kitchenette of their fourth-floor suite. The sun streamed in through the opened slider, along with the sound of the beach just steps away.

"Are you laughing?" Franci demanded. Both of them were sprawled on the couch, dressed in shorts and T-shirts, still looking pale with dark circles under their eyes.

"Not since six a.m." Ana held up her hand. "Swear."

"Bitch," Chelle snarled. "That was evil."

She poured the drink into two glasses. "It was funny as hell." She really had set her cellphone for one of Savaged Illusions hard rock songs. It blared out at the stroke of six. The girls had begged her to make it stop. "I can show you, I videoed it." She handed each of them a glass of the sports drink.

Franci shot her a glare. "I have footage on my phone from your birthday."

Okay, that was low. One look at that recording of her attempting to sing at a karaoke bar had cured her dream of stardom. "Fine. Truce?"

"For now," Franci agreed. "But you owe us. Our plan worked. Operation Kiss 2.0 was a masterful plan. Right, Chelle?"

"Hell yeah." She dropped her head to the back of the couch. "God I am never looking at tequila again."

Ana had coaxed them into drinking some water and Gatorade in the limo, and dosed them with Advil too. Overall she didn't think their hangover was that bad. They'd be raising hell in a few hours. "Wrong. I'm seeing him because I hijacked your plot and did the cleverest thing of all by asking him if he wanted to get together and catch up."

Chelle got up and crossed the room to touch Ana's shoulder. "We're trying to help you. We weren't there for you when you found that lump. You went through a lot in the last weeks, and..." She looked away, her eyes wide with regret.

"I'm fine. I've told you guys that. I showed you the lab report."

Crossing her arms, Chelle pointed out, "You didn't show me, I found it in your bedroom. We wouldn't have even known you had a biopsy."

Ana took a breath, hating the cold loneliness that made her feel like the outsider. She'd tried to tell them, but Ana didn't get to have problems. She had to be perfect, the girl who solved everyone else's crises. *That's not fair, and you know it. People can't help if they don't know.*

She fought down her misplaced anger and tried to soothe Chelle with, "I would have told you guys if they found something. There's no cancer, I'm fine. And damned lucky." Too many people in the world got the bad news. Ana had been very fortunate and had no right to the little pity party trying to suck her in. She was on vacation to celebrate her good health.

Chelle softened a bit. "I just feel awful. I know you tried to tell me, and I was so panicked over work and—"

A knock on the door cut her off.

"Chelle, stop." She and Franci had been alternating between guilt and anger at Ana for not making them listen. "It's over, okay?" She didn't want to dwell on it. "That's probably Ethan now." She narrowed her eyes. "Be good, and don't bring up the biopsy." Ethan wasn't there to listen to her problems. This was for fun, nothing else. She wanted to feel like a desirable woman and push her boundaries a little bit.

She went to the door and opened it.

"Hey." Ethan took off his sunglasses and did a slow study of her print silk shift dress in island colors, legs bare all the way down to her flats. "Now that was worth the drive."

A flush warmed her against the room's air-conditioning. She looped her purse over her shoulder and called out, "We're leaving."

Franci rushed up to them. "Hi, Ethan. Thanks for saving Ana from us last night."

"No problem." He tossed her the keys. "Here's the car back."

Franci caught them, then frowned. "How are you returning to your hotel?"

Oh crap. Ana hadn't even thought of that. "I could drive you."

He waved it off. "I had a rental car meet me here. I'm good. Come on, let's get something to eat." He held out his hand.

Franci bumped her from behind. "Two words," she whispered. "Vacation sex. Chelle and I are going shopping. You can have the room all to yourself."

One look at the grin on Ethan's face told Ana he'd heard. She put her hand in his and hurried out the door. It was either that or slam the door so she didn't have to face his teasing.

Ethan squeezed her hand. "It seems Operation Kiss 2.0 has been upgraded."

Once inside the elevator, she went for bluntness. "Despite Franci and Chelle's shenanigans, you're perfectly safe with me. If you decide this isn't what you want, we'll both walk away."

He stepped into her space, raising their joined hands over her head. "What if it's you who's not safe with me?"

Her breath caught as Ethan loomed above her in the glass elevator. There was nothing threatening in him though, it was...protective. "In what way? You'd never hurt me."

"I walked away eleven months ago because you were still in college, your father had passed weeks before that, and you were too damned vulnerable. But my restraint just ran out. Understand that once our time here in Florida is over, I will leave again. Don't mistake me for a good guy. We both know I'm not. So the question is, can you handle that?"

The elevator lurched slightly as it stopped. Ana stood perfectly still, relishing in the feel of Ethan's hand bracing hers against the elevator glass, and his eyes eating her up. Could she handle it? Damn right she could. It might hurt—okay it *would* hurt—but she understood that she wasn't going to come first with Ethan. He'd made that clear.

Tilting her head back, she arched a brow. "Now that you've done your grand speech, can we have lunch?"

The edges of his eyes crinkled. "You always were impatient to eat." He tugged her out of the elevator. "You have someplace in mind?"

Regaining her wits after that display of caveman sexiness, she answered, "I'm taking you to the Flying Bridge. It's a dock out over the Gulf. It's too pretty a day to stay inside."

People wandered around in bathing suit cover-ups, shorts and sundresses, a few playing miniature gulf, splashing in the pool, some kids chasing each other and laughing. Once they got their seat on the dock and ordered, she let her curiosity surface. "Do you like doing security for the band?"

"I'm good at it. We've had some crazy stuff. Stalkers, psychos, one guy starting fires, and the women." He rolled his eyes. "I'd rather deal with a knife-wielding crazed man than a woman bent on trapping a rock star. They are devious little shits. The stunts they've pulled are insane."

"Wait, have you dealt with a knife-wielding crazy?"

"It's rare." He paused while the server set down Ana's Mediterranean vegetable wrap and Ethan's Philly special. After topping off their drinks, she left. Ethan took a bite. "This is good."

Worry for Ethan blared in her head. "But there have been knife attacks?" She knew his job had a dangerous element to it, but she hadn't dwelled on it.

"Had a guy with a knife go after Gray. We were hanging out in a hotel bar, but it was over in seconds. I saw the guy before he got close, shoved Gray down into a booth and disarmed the attacker. No one was hurt." He flashed a grin. "Okay, that's a lie. I caught Gray by surprise, and he smacked his face on the table. Had a bloody nose. Dude was pissed about that."

Oh God. "You weren't hurt?"

He gave her a look. "One guy with a knife, Ana. I saw him coming. If I'd been hurt, I'd have deserved it."

"I know." Ethan was capable and strong. He'd worked hard to shift his MMA experience into becoming the best security possible, including intensive weapons training. She was confident in his skills, but he was still her Ethan, and she couldn't help worrying. To distract herself, she picked up her wrap and took a bite.

Ethan stole one of her fries. "Stop fretting. The guy wasn't trained, just a nut. He believed that every time Gray chose to play the piano instead of keyboard, he was summoning the devil. Which is pretty funny because of the five of them, Gray's the most civilized."

"Civilized how?"

"He usually doesn't get into fights, trash hotel rooms, leave groupies suicidal or enraged the morning after, that kind of thing. Dude's not perfect though. He's our ghost."

Fascinated, she swallowed another bite and asked, "Ghost?"

"Disappears and we have no idea where the fuck he is. All of us on the team have lost Gray at one time or another. A knife-wielding psycho isn't as likely to take me down as Gray disappearing on my watch." He rubbed his chest. "That damn near gave me another heart attack."

She tried to keep a wince off her face at the mention of his heart attack. He'd been physically cleared to work on the security detail. "You look good. Strong and healthy." More than healthy. Unable to help it, she eyed his thick, muscular arms in his T-shirt. He'd worn shorts, revealing his powerful thighs and calves. She'd seen women eyeing Ethan as they walked to the Flying Bridge.

"You checking me out, sunshine?"

Ana lifted her chin. "Just making sure you haven't gotten fat without me around to motivate you." Ethan was as competitive as her. She missed trying to keep up with him on the bike or kicking his ass on rollerblades. She could beat him in the batting cages, too, but anything else he'd leave her in his dust and laugh. She'd loved that too. Ethan never held back in competition with her. Nor did he get pissed when he lost.

His mouth curved. "I'm doing double duty as a trainer for the band. I work out with them as a group and individually around my bodyguard duties. It keeps me in shape. And since four of them have some skills in martial arts, we spar. It's fun."

"You do all that?" She had to admit she was impressed.

"Yep. It's helped me to pay off my debts faster, and I like it." He stole another fry. "Now it's your turn. Tell me how it's going for you."

She set down the second half of her wrap. "You ordered fruit instead of fries, eat it." She reached her fork over and speared a juicy chunk of melon. "I told you I graduated and that Kat offered me a promotion. She expanded from her original San Diego bakery to open branches in San Francisco and Los Angeles, and I was in on all that. Developing and implementing marketing plans for each one is a challenge." Excitement bubbled just talking about it. "I travel more and more now. Plus we're working on a Sugar Dancer product line of bake-at-home products, so I've been meeting with reps of various retail stores, pitching the idea, talking about possible deals. I'm learning so much." She cut herself off. "Anyway, that's my life."

Ethan snagged yet another of her fries. "You love it."

"I do. It's gotten even crazier with Kat and Sloane's wedding only a month away." Her boss was marrying Sloane Michaels, the man who'd found Ethan living on the streets as a kid and took him in. While officially Sloane, a former UFC heavyweight champion, had done it as part of the Fighters to Mentors program, the reality was Sloane had finished raising Ethan and was more of a brother than mentor. She asked, "You're coming to the wedding, right?"

Ethan set his iced tea down. "Yes. But I'll probably be leaving soon after that."

"But isn't Savaged Illusions's tour done then?" It took everything she had not to cringe with embarrassment. "I wasn't hinting that we could go together or anything like that. You're close to Sloane and I know he wants you there, that's all I was thinking. I wasn't suggesting anything more." She got it, they weren't dating. Ana had learned an important lesson that night when Ethan walked out—she had no right to use sex as a way to make someone want to be with her.

"I didn't think that, and yes the tour will be over. But I have a shot at an apprenticeship with Chef Siena. You met her at the party last night, right?"

That gorgeous, funny woman? He'd be working with her? Ana's food suddenly tasted like dry sand, but she managed to nod.

"I haven't signed the contract yet, but it's a fantastic opportunity. I'd get to work in several of her restaurants, travel with her and appear on some of her shows."

"Oh, Ethan, that's wonderful." It really was, even if she had a pang at the thought of Ethan spending so much time with the beautiful chef. "Where did you meet her?"

"A big party at her restaurant in New York. I was there as security for the band, and that night the band had me sitting with them because they know I like to cook. Siena came out of the kitchen to meet the band, and we started talking. She showed me her kitchen, and one thing led to another."

Incredible. Even she'd never imagined such a huge opportunity for Ethan. "You're going to be a real chef someday." Unable to help herself, she added, "Do you think you'll ever come back to San Diego? Maybe open a restaurant? You know Sloane would invest in you."

He leaned in close to her. "I screwed up, Ana. I let down a hell of a lot of people who believed in me, spent money and time on me, who were invested in my success as an MMA fighter. It wasn't just Sloane, but all my trainers…" He trailed off, clenching his jaw so tight it bulged at the joint. "I'll pay off every goddamned cent I owe, and I'm not taking another penny from Sloane. There are others out there who deserve his help. I had my chance."

The blazing cold anger at himself ringing in his voice made the fine hairs on her arms prickle. It killed her that he couldn't see how amazing he was for the very fact that he owned his blunder and was trying to make amends. "It was a mistake."

"Don't do that. A mistake is choosing the chicken when you crave a hamburger. Injecting steroids on a concise schedule is a choice to cheat. Don't make excuses for what I did." He looked out to the Gulf, his eyes hard. Unforgiving.

Ana couldn't bear his self-recrimination. Yes, he had screwed up, but he'd paid the price. He'd cooperated with the police in every way, and he'd been working to pay off his debts. How could she not respect that?

Ana laid her hand over his fist clenched on the table. "What I know is that you made a bad choice, and when it blew up in your face, you could have been an asshole. Instead, you took complete responsibility down to working your ass off to pay Sloane back when we both know he didn't ask it of you." Kat had told Ana that, but Sloane was extremely proud of Ethan for doing it.

His brutal gaze softened. "You always see the good in people, stubborn girl." He rubbed his thumb over her skin.

Wrong. But Ana didn't want to get into old crap. "How long before you have to leave today?"

"Couple hours."

Smiling, she asked, "How do you feel about paddleboarding?"

Ethan hit her with an inquisitive stare, then seemed to make a decision and leaned in. "Does it involve you in a bikini?"

He'd never seen her in one, had he? "One way to find out. We'll stop by the resort shops and buy you a pair of boardshorts."

He leaned closer, his face inches from hers. "I want to see your bikini."

Her mouth dried. He was so close she could see the faint scar beneath his left cheekbone. His hand covered hers, his thumb stroking her wrist. His touch ignited the warm desire already pooling in her stomach.

This was her chance to experience Ethan. To indulge her fantasies of the one man she wanted.

Short term. This fantasy had an expiration date, and then she'd be alone again.

* * * *

Ana was taunting him as they took their paddleboards around the Gulf. Her hair blew around her shoulders and face, and her skin glowed from the sun and lotion she'd spread all over to prevent a burn. Her sapphire-blue bikini top formed enticing triangles over her breasts, then bared more skin down her belly to her tiny boardshorts. Long, lithe legs braced apart to balance on the board as she paddled near the shore.

He really needed to think about something else besides how hot Ana was. "How's your stepmom?"

Ana smiled. "Linda's good. She turned forty this year. To celebrate, she and her sister are in Italy. It's a special trip for her. Honestly I think it's the first time she's truly enjoyed herself since my dad died."

Her dad's unexpected death had been hard on her. "How are you doing?"

She glanced over. "I miss him, but it's tougher on Linda. I had moved out, had my own life, and getting back to my routine helped. But Linda...well it took a while. Anyway, she's loving Italy." Her smile was sad. "Dad would be happy to see her living again."

She meant that. Cared that much about her stepmom. He'd asked her about their closeness after her dad's funeral. She'd said that Linda saved her when she was a teenager, but hadn't explained. He debated asking now, but let it go and instead said, "The band played a couple concerts in Italy. Beautiful country, and the food is incredible. Of course we went to Taste of Siena too. If your stepmother is in the Tuscany area, she should try it." He couldn't help but add, "I was invited to cook with Siena there."

"What was that like?"

"Amazing. She's bigger than life in the kitchen, a lot like you see on TV. Passionate, charismatic and very sensual. We both have the same love for food, for creating an experience that feeds more than just the stomach." How could he tell this girl what it was like to feel empty and unloved, and then discover that feeding yourself and others filled a void? "Creating a meal is an expression. Like fighting or sex. When a mother loves a child, she feeds him. When a man romances a woman, he feeds her. At every major celebration, food is central. Being in Italy, cooking in her kitchen, it felt...like home." He clamped his mouth shut. What was he doing going off on a tangent about his obsession with food or what it meant to him?

Her silence stretched before she turned and gave him a brittle smile. "I'm happy for you. You're going to be famous, and you're doing what you love."

Yet her strained smile didn't match her warm words. What was going on with her? "I'll stop talking about cooking. I'm boring you."

"No, don't stop." Her smile grew into a real one. "I want to hear it. I guess I'm a little jealous."

"Of what? You said you love your job."

She nodded. "It's silly, but some of my favorite memories are all the times you used to cook in my kitchen. Now you have these amazing experiences that trump those. In a few years, you won't even remember me at all. I'll be that girl claiming that I used to know you and you cooked in my kitchen and everyone will roll their eyes and beg me to stop talking about it."

The memories assaulted him. He'd show up with groceries, Ana would dig through the bags, excited to figure out what he was going to try making. She never shied away from tasting. Or if he forgot an ingredient, she'd run to the store, sometimes several stores.

And by the end of their meal, as they cleaned up, the scent of the food he'd cooked would cling to her skin. Marking her. Making him crave a taste of Ana, to kiss and lick her. Consume her. "I'm not going to forget that, or you. I had fantasies about you. I could smell my food on your skin, and it made me hungry for you."

Ana's eyes widened, the blazing sun brightening the brown to gold. "What kind of fantasies?"

He debated for a second. His fantasies were a tad rough. But that night when she'd kissed him and he'd taken control—okay lost control—she had responded. "I wanted to push you over the counter and hold you down. Ask you if you got off on teasing me."

Ana blinked, her mouth parting slightly with a huff.

Ethan waited, giving her a chance to see if she liked the idea. Her sexual experience had been fairly limited from what he could tell, maybe two intimate boyfriends before she and Ethan had become friends. She might not be comfortable with rougher sex. Except she'd said she wanted to let go and quit worrying. He could give that to her.

A challenge glittered in her eyes. "I was a good girl, remember?"

"What I remember is how goddamned sexy you were without even trying. And today? Look at you." He tracked his attention down her, taking in the tiny swimsuit over golden skin all the way to her toes with the blue polish. He lowered his head a fraction to lock stares with her. "You're not being good now, are you, Ana? You're purposely taunting me, getting me hard."

Her smug smile answered him.

He loved that she didn't hide it. Why should she? "Is that your fantasy? Driving me out of my mind?"

"Is it working?"

Ana deserved to have a fling as much as anyone else. And as

long as it was with him, he'd make damn sure she was safe and satisfied. "You keep this up in the room when we're alone, and I'll show you what happens to bad girls who tease me."

"What?" Her fingers tightened on her paddle. "Tell me."

"Think hard, sunshine, because if I get you in that room and you taunt me, I'm pushing you up against a wall and those bottoms are coming down to your knees. If I touch your pussy and you're wet, I'm not waiting for permission. I'm going to bury my cock inside you. Hard, Ana. And you'll take it, all of it, and I'll make you come, over and over. Or maybe I won't…until you apologize for making me so goddamned hard for you day after day and burn for you every damned night." He heard the rough frustration in his voice, the truth of it. Even after he'd left, traveled the world and had plenty of women, it was Ana he wanted. Craved.

She shuddered.

Ethan searched her eyes, looking for fear. Nope, he didn't see it.

"What if I won't apologize? Maybe I'm not sorry."

He froze, going so still he could hear his own heart thumping in his ears. "Provoking me, sunshine? You don't want an orgasm?"

Her chin went up. "I know how to make myself come."

Christ. The very thought of her touching herself, showing him she didn't need him, inflamed his lust. But the defiance in her eyes intrigued him more. There was some need he couldn't define. Not yet.

"Hard to do if I have your hands pinned behind your back, fucking you slowly, keeping you right on the edge. Whispering in your ear to give in, just surrender and I'll let you come." He wanted that, forcing her to give him everything. The one girl he couldn't have, and he'd damn well have her.

Temporarily. That harsh reminder did nothing to dampen his lust, it just added a layer of desperation to it.

"You still want to taunt me?" Jesus, what was he doing here? The more he let loose on the reins of his control with her, the more his desires for Ana surfaced.

Her eyes glowed with a blatant dare. "Two things."

"What?"

"I'm on birth control, but I want to use condoms. I'm not risking an accidental pregnancy."

He'd never take her bare. Ever. Ethan knew what he was—an ex-whore who didn't deserve to touch her. But since he was going down this path, he'd sure as hell protect her. "All of us in the band and security have routine blood tests. I'm clean. And I always use condoms, no exceptions."

"Oh, I—" The first sign of doubt clouded her expression. "I haven't had sex in a couple years."

Two years? And he thought he was going to take her hard? Hell no. He'd still give her the experience, but he was damned glad she'd told him that. It didn't change how much he wanted her; if anything it made him want her more. It just meant he was going to enjoy getting her ready. Driving her to the brink with his fingers…

Enough. He had to get them in the room before he was too hard to walk. "You said two things. We discussed birth control. What's the other thing?"

"Yes." She put her paddle into the water and pushed off, heading for the shore.

Confused, he called out, "Yes what?"

She glanced back over her shoulder, a sexy smirk riding her mouth. "I still want to taunt you."

Oh her ass was his now. Temporarily. He couldn't forget that. A few days, and he was gone and out of her life. He'd never risk his past rising up to hurt and humiliate her. Nor would he be able to bear that look of disgust toward him in Ana's eyes.

Chapter 4

Ana slipped into the room just ahead of Ethan and rushed past the two queen beds, through the dressing and bathroom area into the living space.

She grabbed a plastic container from the fridge, snatched up a fork, and hopped up on the counter by the small sink.

Her heart thumped, and chills broke out on her skin as Ethan strode into the room. He didn't look at her, but walked straight to the huge slider and pulled it open. He stayed there, hands hanging loose at his sides as he focused on something outside.

What was he thinking? If he dared to change his mind now, she might just push him off that railing outside the sliding door. Ana wasn't up for another rejection. But she had an idea of how to regain his attention. After popping open the plastic lid, she dug her fork into the rich pie that just happened to be Ethan's favorite.

He spun around. "What are you doing?"

"Eating." She shrugged, trying to appear casual. "I got hungry."

He stalked toward her. "Is that key lime pie?"

Ha, she had him now. "What, this?" She stuck the fork in, gathering a creamy piece along with a bit of whipped cream and crust, and held it up between them. "Why yes, it is. I always heard Florida has the best, so I thought I'd try it."

"Right now? While I was standing there at the window, trying to keep from ripping off your suit and fucking you blind, telling myself to slow down because you haven't had sex in a couple years and might need a little tenderness...you got hungry?"

Did he just growl that last part? The realization that she hadn't lost his attention, but rather he'd been struggling for some control, sent a wave of triumph through her. And affection that he'd thought he had to slow things because of her dry spell.

"Yep." She slid the small chunk into her mouth. It really was excellent pie.

His eyes heated to pure blue, like the center of a gas flame. He slapped his hands on the counter, bracketing her hips. "Are you going to share?"

"Nope." She scooped up another bite and got it halfway up, when he caught her wrist and tugged it to his mouth.

Damn he moved fast. Before she could recover, his lips closed over the forkful. A low sound of pleasure vibrated in his throat.

Ana couldn't tear her gaze from him as he slowly savored the morsel. Heat radiated from the pit of her belly. "That was mine."

He dipped his finger into the whipped topping and spread cool, sweet cream over her mouth. "And this is mine." He swiped his tongue over her lips, lapping the treat.

The warm, wet licks sucked the air from her lungs.

Ethan tangled his fingers in her hair, holding her still as he cleaned off the whipped topping with an intensity that shivered through her. Not enough, it wasn't nearly enough. After dropping the pie on the counter, she sank her fingers into his thick hair and darted her tongue out to meet his.

Ethan groaned and deepened the kiss. Sliding his hand to her jaw, he tilted her head back and demanded she give him full access to her mouth. Wild need surged, and she couldn't get enough of his taste or the feel of his skin still hot from the sun.

She wrapped her arms around his neck, almost climbing up him.

His chest heaving, Ethan gripped her sides, pushing her back onto the counter. Breaking the kiss, he glared down at her. "No you don't. You're done teasing. I'm barely holding on to any restraint. We're doing this slow."

"I don't want slow." She wanted to just lose control and wipe out her ability to think or worry.

"Tough." He settled his hands on her bare thighs and skimmed his palms up. "I'll give you what you want if you tell me you're sorry for teasing and promise to be good."

The bastard was goading her. Paying her back. Given his massive hard-on, she knew she could push him over the edge of control. Reaching behind her back, she released her strap and yanked her top off.

Her freed breasts tingled from the cool air and Ethan's heated stare.

"Or, I could do this." She sank a finger into more of the whipped cream. She'd never done this kind of thing. But now? She had nothing to lose and could be as bad as she wanted. There were no emotional consequences. It didn't matter if he secretly thought she was asking for it. Hell she *was* begging for it.

And it was amazingly freeing.

Ana painted the dollop of cream over her nipple, making it pebble and her belly tighten.

Ethan grabbed her hand and closed his mouth over her finger to lick it clean. A second later he had both wrists pinned behind her hips, forcing her into an arch. "You're so going to be pay for that. I'm going to make you beg me to fuck you."

The helpless feel of his fingers locked around her wrists caused an excited rush straight to her core. She squirmed as her entire body pulsed with anticipation. She'd never been this needy before. But Ana loved it.

Ethan latched on to her nipple and sucked, his tongue lashing the sensitive tip.

Ana bowed at the sensation, struggling to free her hands. But it was useless, he was too strong. That thought made her clit swell and ache. She squeezed her thighs around him, desperate for relief.

After releasing her nipple, Ethan took her mouth, tangling their tongues in a frantic dance. His free hand clamped on her hip, dragging her to his hard cock and rocking against her.

"Let go." She wiggled, attempting to free her hands so she could touch him. Maybe push those boardshorts down and—

His dark chuckle sent shivers along her spine. "Nope. Not unless you really want me to release you, and we both know you don't." A smile curved his mouth, and his tone gentled. "You're beautiful, Ana. You always were, but like this? Hair wild, your skin glowing from the sun and desire. Nipples wet and puckered from my mouth…"

The tenderness in his voice breeched her defenses, causing something thick and scary to grip her throat. His gaze on her was too much. Too intimate. She tried to twist out of his hold. "Ethan."

Catching her chin, he kissed her then said, "Are you going to be good? Let me take you slowly? Lay you down, pull off those bottoms and make you come? As many times as it takes, to get you ready for my cock?"

A voice in her head tried to tell her to say yes. Stop this wildness. But she didn't want to back down. She wanted to drive them both higher. "Not a chance. If you can't handle it, then you know where the door is."

His fingers tightened around her wrists. "Bad Ana." Kissing a path along her jaw, he said, "Ask me to fuck you." He slicked his tongue along the shell of her ear. "Nicely."

Who knew Ethan could be so evil? She liked it. But she wasn't surrendering that easily. Instead she sank her teeth into his shoulder.

When he jerked, she laughed. "I don't surrend—" Before she could finish, his mouth was on hers, fierce, demanding.

She dropped her head back as he licked down the curve of her neck.

A noise echoed in the room. With her heart slamming in her chest, her body humming and needy, Ana struggled to focus. "What's that?"

"My phone. I have to check it. I'm technically on duty." Letting go of her hands, he strode to the table, snatched up the device and read something. "I need to go back."

The cold air chilled her overheated skin. Ana slid off the counter, found her top and retied it. Disappointment weighed her down. "Okay." What else could she say? Work came first. Looking around the room, she realized she hadn't planned this very well anyway. Franci and Chelle could return at any time.

"Ana."

He stood right in front of her. She'd been so fixated on the thoughts, she hadn't heard him move. Steeling her spine, she got over her frustration and smiled. "Operation Kiss 2.0 is thwarted again. Some things just aren't meant to be."

"It doesn't have to be over." He leaned closer. "I'm not ready to call it quits. Come with me."

"With you? Where? To the venue?"

"Back to where I'm staying at Bayside Manor. Come to the show with me tonight. I'll get you VIP tickets again, and then after the show, we'll go back to the manor. Spend the night with me." He laid his hand on her cheek. "We'll have more privacy in my room there. And more time to explore this need of yours to be my bad Ana."

The enormity of the invitation left her spinning. He was giving her more than she'd even hoped for. They'd actually spend real time together.

But was this smart? What if she couldn't really handle having sex and sleeping with him?

Really? Ethan's giving you what you wanted, and now you're getting cold feet? What did she think would be better? Have sex, then him walk out? That wasn't what she wanted either. Yeah, she accepted that they weren't going to have a future romantically. But if she truly wanted to be bad with Ethan and make some memories for both of them, why not take this opportunity and enjoy it to the fullest?

She could do this, and more importantly, she wanted to. Ethan was making a sincere effort for her.

"I'd like that." The logistics of the plan took shape in her mind. "I need to tell Franci and Chelle where I am. Are you sure it's okay if I stay? Is it a hotel?"

"Private manor we rented. Let me check with Hank, but I'm pretty sure Franci and Chelle can stay at the manor too. That way you won't be alone at the concert, and you'll have more fun with them around."

A million thoughts skidded through her head, but one stood out. "I'm not sure we can afford the cost. The tickets, the rooms at the manor…maybe we should just—"

"There's no cost. I can get you the tickets free, and the manor's already rented." He leaned down, brushing his mouth over hers. Raising his head, he said, "Say yes. The place is huge, right on the bay with a boat and watercrafts. There's a big home theater, a game room, walking trails, you guys will love it. You don't have to rush back here. We can have some fun."

The fact that he actually desired to spend time with her

stirred something that had gone cold and sad the day she'd sat alone in her doctor's office, waiting to hear whether or not she was sick. For the first time in a while, Ana felt wanted.

But it was only temporary. She couldn't forget that as she had no intention of getting her heart broken.

Again.

* * * *

She hadn't been sure what to bring, but finally she and Ethan were out the door and heading down in the elevator. Franci and Chelle had returned right after she texted them, and they'd all been running around the room, changing and packing. The two girls would drive the rental car to the manor once they were all set to go.

Ethan's voice cut in to her thoughts. "Is it always like that?"

She glanced over at him. "What?"

"That…chaos?"

Chuckling, she said, "Three women trying to pack and get ready in one contained space? Yep, that's usually how it goes. I'm guessing you don't have any sisters?"

"Nope."

Ana peered at him as the elevator stopped and opened to a courtyard. "Do you have any siblings?" All he'd ever told her was that before Sloane found him, he'd run away from home, lived on the streets and sometimes did underground fighting to survive. But he'd shut her down if she asked anything else.

"No." He laid his hand on her back as they walked, hauling her suitcase behind him.

There he was, quiet Ethan. She could feel the second he pulled away from her. When he withdrew like that, it burned. Worse, she could sense the pain that he held onto with an iron fist. It tugged at her need to fix things.

Despite his hard jaw and straight-ahead stare, she asked softly, "What happened to—?"

"Ana!" a male voice called out.

Surprised and confused, she spotted a dark-haired man dressed in tan slacks and a polo shirt striding up to them. He shot a quick look at Ethan then settled his brown eyes on her.

It was so unexpected, it took Ana a second to place who he was. It clicked finally, and despite the slightly humid air, goose bumps rose on her arms. "Gregory? What are you doing here?" She barely knew him, and she really wanted to keep it that way.

A grin tilted his mouth. "I'm as surprised as you are. In fact I wasn't even sure it was you when I called out your name. I'm here on a business trip and staying at the Guy Harvey Outpost. What are you doing here?"

Business trip? And why was he practically bouncing on his toes like a two-year-old waiting for a cupcake?

Because he was waiting for you.

Ana rubbed her arms, suddenly cold despite the blazing sun. What were the chances that the man she'd been trying to avoid for the last two weeks had shown up in another state the exact same time she did?

"You knew I was coming here. You were in the bakery the day I booked the flight." She remembered it because Gregory had overheard her on the phone and commented on her trip. *You can use the plane ride to Florida to read my book.*

Gregory waved a hand. "Oh, right, you're on vacation. Actually that's a lucky break then. You'll have time to discuss my mom's book and a contract to write your dad's biography. Why don't we meet for drinks and—?"

"Ana doesn't have time. She's with me."

She stiffened at Ethan's ice-cold voice. Shooting him a glare, she said, "Quiet." It was bad enough she hadn't handled things with Gregory as well as she should have. Okay, she'd been avoiding the problem. But she didn't need Ethan taking over. She'd fix it.

"Who are you?" Gregory asked.

"Her date."

Gregory eyed the suitcase, then shifted to Ethan. "Ana and I are friends, and we're working together on a project." He returned his focus to her. "You've read the book, right? And my proposal? We should get started right away on your dad's story. I know I can get a big publisher to pay attention to a story about Roger Kendall, the home run king."

Unbelievable. It was like Gregory had rewritten reality into a version he liked. Time for her to be absolutely clear. "We're not working together. I told you no, and I meant it. I'm not going to read the book you wrote or hire you to write my dad's biography." She didn't know how to be more specific than that.

He stopped bouncing. "But you said you would. This is my big chance. Publishers wouldn't even read my mom's biography, but they'll fight for your dad's. This will get me in the door. You have to—"

"Stop." She'd had enough. "The answer is no. It's not changing, and you need to leave me alone. Don't email, call, text or wait for me in the bakery." Frustrated, ticked and a little frightened that Gregory had actually arranged to show up where she was on vacation, she stomped away.

"Listen to her, or you're dealing with me," Ethan added.

Ana struggled to calm down and think. She'd talked to Gregory twice before he sent her his book through email. That was the moment she'd realized that he'd mistaken her casual chatter as something more. She'd told him she wasn't interested and avoided him after that. Ignoring him hadn't worked, so what should she do next? Should she call her dad's lawyer that had helped Ana and Linda settle his estate? Absolutely, she'd do that today. What about notifying the police? But Gregory hadn't made any threat, so...

"Who is that?"

Ethan's sharp question slowed her spinning thoughts. "Gregory Yates. He calls himself a sports biographer, but I think the only thing he's written is a book on his mother, who was a professional tennis player before he was born."

"So this guy's been bugging you, and you didn't say anything? What the hell, Ana?"

Like she wasn't concerned enough? Yeah she'd seen that Gregory continued to hang around the bakery, trying to talk to her. But Ana had been sidetracked and a tad more worried about the lump in her breast than a customer who didn't understand boundaries. She didn't need Ethan in her face about it now.

She walked faster, her irritation ramping up. "Why would I tell you? And what was that back there with you acting all caveman proprietary? '*She's my date. She's with me.*' You don't get to lay some claim on me when it's convenient but ignore me when I need..." Her eyes started to sting. *Shut up. Just shut up.* He hadn't even known, so she didn't get to lay that on him.

And jeez, get over it already. She'd had a little scare. Big fucking deal. People out there had real problems. Right now, she needed to focus on her more pressing issue of Gregory, not her self-pity because she'd faced a tiny ordeal alone.

"That wasn't a coincidence back there," Ethan nearly shouted back. "He was waiting for you to walk by. I saw him before he called out to you. He was watching, Ana. Are you hearing me?"

She'd already figured that out for herself, but he didn't give her a chance to answer.

"A man followed you from San Diego to Florida, and I'm supposed to stand there and let him believe you're unprotected? I don't think so. I need to figure out if he's dangerous. Hell, what am I saying, he fucking followed you. He's a stalker. Jesus, how did you get involved with him?"

"I didn't get *involved*. I talked to him in the bakery because he looked lonely. His mom died, my dad had died, and we talked about it. He told me he'd written a book. It was two conversations and suddenly he emails me a book and a proposal to write my dad's biography."

He pinched the bridge of his nose. "You gave him your email address?"

The aggravation in his voice snapped the last of her patience. "It's on my business card." She stopped walking, realizing they were already in the parking area. "I'm not explaining myself to you. I didn't do a damn thing I should have to defend, but even if I did, it's none of your business. Either you want a few days of fun, or we call it quits right now."

His hard face softened. "How about a two-for-one deal? A few days of sexy fun and a friend who's concerned. Because that shit that just happened with Gregory has stalker written all over it. The guy followed you on your vacation. Let that sink in. Followed you from California to Florida, checked into the hotel right next to you and hung around until he saw you."

A chill rippled down her spine. "It's creepy."

He wrapped an arm around her, pulling her against him. "Stay at the manor for a few days. He should get the message. And if he calls or texts, ignore him. Don't feed whatever delusion he has going on."

That was very sound advice. "All right. Thanks. I'll call my dad's lawyer once I'm settled in. He'll know the best way to handle this." Ignoring Gregory hadn't worked, so she had to get proactive. It sucked to deal with it on her vacation when she'd hoped to get away from responsibility for a week.

Ethan opened his mouth, but Ana cut him off, done with Gregory. "I'll take care of it. Up to now, he's been annoying, but he crossed a line today. I'll give everything to my lawyer and handle it. Gregory will soon learn I'm no one's victim."

Nope. She'd lived through that once, and when she'd asked for help from her mom, all she got back was accusations. Yeah, her dad and stepmom rescued her, but at a high cost to them, one she wasn't really able to pay back.

So now? Ana rescued herself.

* * * *

Ethan glanced over at Ana in the passenger seat of the Jaguar convertible. With the top down, the wind blew her hair, and she was struggling to tame it into a ponytail.

A gust tore the band out of her hand.

As she reached into her purse, fishing out another one, Ana's laughter pealed out.

That sound went right to his dick. So much better than her earlier worry and the sudden harsh withdrawal from him when Gregory confronted her. Ethan had automatically stepped in, making it clear she was his to protect. He didn't care if this was temporary. Someone threatened Ana, they dealt with him. It was that simple, except to Ana. She'd shut him down hard. Yet she'd had no problem letting him touch, kiss and restrain her wrists. That thought unleashed another torrent of lust. He'd always been attracted to her, but this? Christ, she was hitting all his buttons, the ones he purposely ignored.

His fantasies about forced seduction weren't a bad thing, but he avoided the intimacy that kind of sex game would require. It'd take real trust for a woman to allow him to hold her down, force her to climax for him and then bury his cock in her, wringing more orgasms from her, proving she wanted him.

"Your knuckles are white."

Her soft voice dragged him out of his introspection, and he loosened his hold on the steering wheel. He was too worked up. When he'd gotten the text calling him into work, he'd had the urge to ignore it. Turn off his phone and focus on Ana. He couldn't walk away from her again, not like he had eleven months ago. When she'd agreed to come to the manor with him, it had been an instant relief to know they'd have more time together. But right now, he had to distract himself from thinking about getting her naked.

Casting around, he searched for another subject. "You don't wear your glasses anymore?"

"Nope, I got LASIK."

She'd been cute in her glasses, but he liked her either way. "So are you still living in the condo? Or did you use some of your inheritance to buy another place?"

She sighed. "I'm so tired of everyone thinking I'm suddenly rich. Everything went to Linda. It's her money, not mine. Why don't people get that?"

He'd assumed Ana had inherited at least a portion of her dad's estate. She was his daughter, after all. "Some people might resent their stepparent getting all the money. Does it bother you?"

"No. I wish he'd lived. That bothers me. But Linda was the love of his life and more of a mom to me than my biological mother. I knew what was in my dad's will. None of this is a surprise or feels wrong to me."

Ethan studied her in between watching the road. She tucked the flared skirt of her sundress—the same one she'd been wearing earlier—tighter beneath her thighs to keep the wind from catching it. A bit of sadness clung to her, the grief for her dad.

But she really didn't care about the money.

Something else nagged at him. "Who else is bugging you about the inheritance?"

Her face twisted. "After years of near silence, my mom's been calling and texting me."

He never quite understood what happened with her mom. He knew Ana'd lived with her until around fourteen, then went to live with her dad. "Your parents never married, right?"

"Nope. That part of my mom's plan failed. My dad wouldn't marry her when she got pregnant. So she went to plan B, soaking him for child support. He paid, getting only minimal visitation in the deal."

"You don't like your mom much, do you?" Something he understood all too well.

"She's a gold digger. She married another rich guy just before I turned fourteen and moved us to Washington, making it even harder for me to see my dad."

"Why's she contacting you now?"

"Because she thinks I'm suddenly wealthy. Her latest thing is pressuring me about going up there for her husband's fifty-fifth birthday party."

"You going?"

"No." She fisted her hand on the leather seat.

Hmm. "You don't like him?"

"I'm not getting within a hundred feet of him."

The hairs on the back of his neck rose. Ethan steered around a truck then turned to her. *I'm no one's victim.* She'd said that a few minutes ago in reference to Gregory, but had she been her stepfather's victim once? Rage simmered along his nerve endings. If that bastard had hurt her... "What did—?"

"I don't want to talk about my parents." She forcibly relaxed in her seat and raised an eyebrow at him. "Unless you want to tell me about yours?"

Hell no. He didn't ever want Ana to know about that. He shut up and drove.

Chapter 5

"This is Bayside Manor?" Ana blurted out in awe. The massive gates slid open, and they drove up a long, winding road through lush lands and passed a few buildings. "What are those?"

"Recording studio with offices, and three casitas are scattered around. This place is owned by a record label."

Wow. The scope of the life Ethan was living sank in. Finally they reached a huge, multistory, sand-colored mansion overlooking Tampa Bay. The building had curving lines that made her think of a gentle wave. "This beats the hell out of a hotel."

Inside the house was even more breathtaking, all done in whites, ocean blues and sea greens. "How big is this place?"

"Not sure. Big enough for ten bedroom suites."

She crossed the cool marble floor, barely noticing the pristine couches stacked with blue pillows, to the wall of sliding windows that had been opened, leading to an outdoor room complete with a kitchen, thick-cushioned couches and chairs, a pool, and beyond that the bay and dock.

Back inside the house, she eyed the spectacular gourmet kitchen boasting two sinks, double ovens and even a pot-filler faucet mounted over a six-burner stove.

"Ethan," a new voice said. "I saw you come in on the security cameras. I have the tickets for Ana and her friends set aside for tonight."

It only took Ana a second to recognize the man striding toward them as Hank from the VIP party last night

"Chelle and Franci are on their way." Ethan checked his watch. "Probably ten or fifteen minutes behind us."

"Sounds good." Hank smiled at her then returned his attention to Ethan. "Preshow meeting in an hour at the Hyatt. The threat called into the venue has been checked out. No validity, but they brought in bomb-sniffing dogs anyway. You and I are going over there for a final update."

Ethan nodded. "Let me get Ana settled, grab a shower, and I'll meet you at the hotel." He guided Ana across the great room to an elevator.

"Why are you meeting at the Hyatt?" She had too many things she was curious about.

"The rest of the security team, staff and road crew are staying there. We'll go over everything for tonight's show."

The elevator doors parted to reveal another beautiful foyer.

"We're this way." He led her down a hallway and opened a door.

Ana walked into a living room with a TV, couch and a two-sided desk. She headed into the bedroom, taking in the huge king-sized bed covered in a thick white comforter. Her stomach fluttered. Going to the French doors that opened to a balcony overlooking the bay, she thought about all the effort Ethan had gone to for her, even inviting her friends. He was giving her everything she'd once dreamed of.

Ethan settled his hands on her shoulders. "Second thoughts?"

"None." She turned to face him. "Thank you for all this. You've gone to a lot of trouble. You didn't have to do this."

Surprise softened his face. "I'm happy to. That last night in San Diego, I wanted to do something nice for you, but you hijacked my plans and turned it into the most amazing night of my life by giving me a chance to cook with Chef Zane."

Part of her rejoiced, and the other part wanted to flinch in embarrassment at her stupidity later when she'd kissed him. But at least he had some good memories of that night too. It made her happy to believe she'd helped him see he had options. Back then, Ethan had been, well, depressed. If she'd helped him to heal and move on, that was good. "You're doing so well. Kat had told me you're happy, but I'm glad I have a chance to see it for myself."

He fingered a lock of her hair. "You worried about me?"

Every day and night. "Nope, I forgot all about you. Kat

would bring you up, and she's my boss, so I had to pretend to listen."

He smiled, and he tugged her against him. "I'm going to make damn sure you never forget me." He lowered his mouth to hers in a slow kiss. Tender. The word slid into her brain, and sparked a need to push away the vulnerability that came with it. She didn't need slow and tender, that was for people in love. She and Ethan were just old friends indulging in a fling. Wrapping her arms around him, she kissed Ethan back, capturing his tongue, and sucking.

Breaking the kiss, he caught her hair, his eyes intense. "When you fight me for control, I'll fight back. And I'll win."

The knot that had tightened after seeing Gregory loosened. She didn't have to hold back as much with Ethan as she did with everyone else. He was only interested in sex and fun. "Can't handle it?"

Moving fast, he spun her, wrapped an arm around her and pinned her back against his chest. "You don't learn, sunshine."

Ana squirmed, but he had her arms locked to her sides.

"Still want to tease me?"

Oh yeah. "Thought you had to go to work?"

He slid his hand up her thigh. "If I find you wet, baby, I'm going to take you right to the edge..." He kissed her ear.

Ana tilted her head, giving him access to the curve of her neck.

"...and leave you like that." He tunneled his fingers higher up her leg, his cock long and thick against her back.

The feel of him surrounding her fueled her lust. Part of her wanted to rip her panties off and beg him to touch her. But she wanted to prove she could make him more crazed.

Forcing a laugh, she said, "So? I told you, I know how to make myself come." Lowering her voice, she added, "Want me to describe it?"

"Fuck." His hot breath feathered over her neck, and his arm banded tighter. "Witch. You're going to plead for mercy." His fingers edged over her panties when her phone rang.

Ethan tugged his hand out and growled his frustration.

Ana couldn't believe this. "I hate technology right now." She snatched her purse off the mattress, fished out her phone and looked at the screen. "It's Chelle." Trying to calm the lust searing through her, she put the phone on speaker and struggled for a normal tone as she said, "Hi, Chelle."

"We're here at the gate. How do we get in?"

Ethan took out his phone. "I'll open the gate for you." He punched in some numbers.

Ana added, "I'll come downstairs. This place is awesome. See you in a bit." She hung up.

Ethan tugged her back into his arms. "After the concert, no more interruptions. The only thing that will stop me is you."

She shivered, liking this demanding side of him. "Do you see a stop sign on me anywhere?"

"I'll definitely do a thorough search tonight." He stepped back. "Go get your friends. I need to take a shower, get dressed and go over threat assessments. I might not be back for dinner. Will you guys be okay? The cook will make something. You can eat with the band or scrounge up what you like in the kitchen."

Ana cleared her brain of sex. He had a job to do, and he was serious about it. It hadn't escaped her notice that Ethan was part of the band's inner circle. That he could just bring her and two of her friends here said a lot.

"We'll be fine. Thanks." She headed for the door.

"Ana."

She looked back. Her mouth dried. He'd stripped off his shirt and untied his boardshorts.

"Sure you can find your way?" He slid them down. Slowly.

His cock popped out, fully erect, long, thick, the head nearly touching his stomach.

Dear God. Still clutching her phone, she took a step toward him. Ethan stood there, sunlight haloing him, hair spiky from the gulf water, wicked-ass grin on his face. Her nipples tightened, and air locked in her lungs. She'd never seen anyone so magnificent. So big…everywhere. Not perfect—he had scars that marked him as a man who'd survived things she couldn't even imagine.

But damn.

Finally she drew in a breath. "Uh…"

"Uh isn't an answer."

She forced her stare up to his face.

"You teased me by taking off your bikini top and doing

naughty things with the whipped cream. Thought I'd even the score." He wrapped his hand around the base of his cock. "Is it working?"

She wanted to touch every inch of him. Heat flooded her body, making her wet. So wet. He was showing her a side of him that enticed her mercilessly. She gripped the doorway between the two rooms. Erotically torturing each other was a game she'd discovered she liked. Ana upped the ante with, "Did I mention the dare?"

His hand slicked up to the head of his penis. Down. "No, I don't think you did."

"Last week, Franci and Chelle decided to get Brazilian waxes. They dared me to do it too."

He stopped jacking his dick, but he didn't let go. "Did you?" The words came out harsh.

"You'll have to find out for yourself. Later." It took everything she had to turn and walk away.

His dark groan followed her.

* * * *

Ana was still buzzing from the concert. She'd had as much or more fun than last night. But now she was thrilled to be alone with Ethan while the others went out clubbing.

Ethan unlocked the door to their room and stepped aside for Ana to enter.

She uttered a soft gasp. The coffee table in their room had a silver bucket, champagne and two flutes flanked by a tray of intricately designed chocolates and a second tray with chocolate-dipped strawberries. The candies were exquisitely crafted—one tiny square had a delicate lavender butterfly on the top of it. Another was white chocolate with dark chocolate latticework.

"You did this?"

Ethan closed and locked the door. He walked past her and called out from the bedroom, "I stopped by a chocolatier when I was out today and ordered this for you. Staff put it in here, along with the champagne."

His thoughtfulness touched her. She chose a dark chocolate topped with a swirl of white and red. She bit into it... Oh God.

Luscious chocolate with notes of amaretto and cherry gave it a decadence that had her closing her eyes to savor it.

"Good?"

Lifting her lids, she got an eyeful. Ethan had stripped off his clothes and was yanking on a pair of sweats. She assumed he'd wanted out of his work clothes.

"It's delicious. And romantic." As soon as the word left her mouth, she regretted it. This wasn't a romance.

He tugged the champagne out of the ice, wrapped it in a towel and opened it.

"You're pretty good at that." She indicated the champagne bottle he'd expertly uncorked. He'd developed a sheen of sophistication over the last few months, but that shouldn't really surprise her since he'd journeyed a lot of the world in that time.

After pouring out the golden liquid, he handed her a glass. "Practice. I've tried to learn as much as I can in our travels. This is an exclusive Krug champagne. I think you'll like it." He selected a strawberry coated in a white chocolate. He held the fruit out. "Open."

She parted her lips, the delicate shell giving way to sweet, tangy strawberry.

"Romance isn't my thing, but sharing things I enjoy with you is. That hasn't changed even if we're crossing the line from friends to lovers." Ethan brushed his thumb over her lip. "Watching you eat has always turned me on."

Her chest filled at the depth of his words. Not romantic? That was the most sensual thing anyone had ever said to her. "You realize I'm a sure thing, right?" She wasn't going to change her mind.

"I know. But I hurt you once, and I'm not doing it again. I don't mean sexually. You want it hard, I'll give you that. I mean when this is over in a few days or a week, you're going to know you were more than a girl I fucked then walked away and forgot about. Is that clear enough for you?"

The flutters turned into full-fledged wings beating in her belly. This was what she needed and why she came to him. But what killed her was the torment in his eyes, the belief that he really wasn't good enough for her.

You're not here to fix him, she reminded herself.

"Crystal clear. Your turn." She chose a dark chocolate berry and held it out to him.

He leaned forward, biting into the treat.

She took a sip of her champagne, enjoying the crisp bubbles with a hint of…hell, she didn't know. All she could think about was the man in front of her. He was what she wanted. Craved. The wine could be vinegar for all she cared. "Like the strawberry?"

He set his glass down and turned all his focus on her. "Good, but it's not you."

A buzz raced over her skin, and her nipples tightened. "You want to taste me?"

"Taste is too tame a word." Stepping closer to her, he slipped the flute from her fingers and set it aside. "I'm not tame, baby."

Something dangerous glinted in his eyes, like a wild arc of electricity that couldn't be captured, there and gone. It tugged deep inside her, igniting a need to chase it.

He framed her face in his hands. "You've taunted and teased me enough. You ready to behave?"

That question kicked her heart rate up. Going up on her toes, she kissed him, unleashing an aggressiveness that surprised her. Demanding access, she thrust into his mouth, appreciating the sweetness of the fruit she'd fed him.

It wasn't enough. She ran her hands over his shoulders and down his chest, eager to feel every dip and valley, to know him as no one else did. Her Ethan. *Hers.* Gliding her touch over the ridges of his abs, she relished the twitch of his muscles. She kept up the torment until her fingers brushed over the engorged head of his cock. Hot skin beaded with fluid.

Ana's pulse ramped up at the sight of his erection, so big and hard his cockhead had pushed out of the top of his sweats.

Unable to resist, she stroked the crown, spreading that bead of fluid and—

A hand clamped down on her wrist. "No."

Stabs of pleasure shot out from his hold on her arm.

"My cock is off-limits until you show me." The growl in his tone stroked her internally, while his firm grip touched a secret yearning buried inside.

Ana tried to free her hand as a test. No give. He didn't hurt her, not even a twinge, just held her trapped. A wicked flash of heat snaked through her, tweaking her nipples and sparking a throb between her legs. How far could she push him? Raising her chin, she said, "Show you what?"

His mouth curved, and he tugged on her wrist, dragging her off balance. Before she could catch herself, Ethan snapped his arm around her waist and lifted her of her feet so they were face-to-face. "Ask me again. Do it."

The feel of him locking her against his powerful body had her panting in excitement. Why did it turn her on? Easy answer—she didn't have to hold back. "Show you what?"

His eyes darkened as his other hand wrapped in her hair, preventing her from moving. He leaned a fraction closer. "Your pussy. It's mine tonight, Ana. You're mine." He slanted his mouth over hers, kissing her with a torrid fierceness.

Ana slapped hands on his shoulders, unsure if she wanted to try to fight him or yank him closer. Fire spread until she rubbed against him, desperate to relieve the growing ache in her nipples. What was he doing to her?

Ana broke the kiss. "Put me down."

He did as she requested and stepped back. "More than you can handle?"

After tugging off her shirt, she tossed it aside. "You're a lot of talk. I'm more a girl of action." She undid her bra and slipped it down her arms. "See, I don't make all these dire threats then never follow through. *'I'm going to make you pay. Make you beg,'*" she mimicked him. "And yet here I am, still waiting."

His gaze traveled down her throat, fastening on her nipples. "Keep going. Find out what happens."

She undid her jeans, shimmied them down and stepped out, revealing her black lace string bikini panties.

For one heartbeat, his eyes flamed hot enough to make her belly tremble. This was what she craved, to be the center of that intense regard. Knowing that in this moment he truly wanted her fueled her courage.

She slid the panties down her thighs.

"Bare." He took a shuddering breath and moved in a blur, scooped her up in his arms and strode from one room to the other.

Startled, she asked, "What——?"

He dropped her on the soft bed, leaned over and kissed her, hard, his mouth no longer savoring hers, but owning. Tongue demanding. Once he conquered her mouth, he went to the spot on her neck just below her jaw that made her moan. He kept going, kissing and sucking her nipples until she writhed with madness, each pull of his lips arcing straight to her clit.

"Everything, Ana. Show me everything." Not giving her a chance to think or answer, he pushed her back and knelt on the floor. His large hands caught her knees and pried.

Ana instinctively fought, not from embarrassment, but need, an unsettling impulse to see how far he'd go if she resisted.

Ethan's eyes blazed a challenge. "No more warnings."

She firmed her muscles to provoke him.

In one fluid movement, he shoved his hands beneath her thighs, yanking her legs up and apart.

Her breath whooshed out of her at how easily he had her at his mercy.

He draped her limbs over his shoulders and pressed a hand to her abdomen, imprisoning her on the bed. Slowly, he lowered his attention to between her widespread legs. "Look at you, so bare, wet and pretty." He glided a finger through her folds. Shudders wracked her as he buried his face between her thighs, his tongue exploring while he eased a digit inside, stretching and pushing deeper.

It'd been so long, Ana couldn't fight the sudden buildup of clawing need. "Ethan, please!" With nothing else to hold on to, she clutched his hair. The tension mounted, her belly drawing tighter, all her muscles clenching. Sounds spilled out, and she arched her back.

He latched on to her throbbing bud.

Ana exploded, her climax slamming into her. Hot, wild pleasure gripped her.

When she regained her breath, Ethan loomed over her, his eyes wild, jaw clenched. Tendons stood out on his neck. "More, Ana. Can't stop." His naked shoulders bunched, the power in him tightly leashed. "Don't say no."

Say no? Her desperation matched his. Ana shoved his sweats down and wrapped her fingers around his cock. "Now. I want to feel you inside me." She guided him to her.

His cockhead pressed against her opening. Ana dug her fingers into his back.

He groaned and began to push in. "Damn, you're tight. And wet. Christ." His jaw bulged as he tunneled in another inch. Then two.

The stretch as he filled her, the soft burn of her flesh yielding, fired her nerves. She lifted her hips, trying to get more of him.

"Never felt this good, this— Oh fuck."

Ana froze at the snarl. "What?"

Chapter 6

What the hell was he doing? He yanked out of Ana's sweet pussy and fought to get his breath. He'd never been so damned stupid before. He didn't deserve to touch her bare, to experience her wet heat gloving him with no barrier.

"Ethan?" The uncertainty quivering in Ana's voice spurred him into action.

"Condom." He shoved up, kicked off his sweats and grabbed the packet off the bedside table. After quickly sheathing his cock, he touched her mouth. "You tasted so good I lost my mind for a second."

Slow down. He lined up and began pushing in. Ana was small, tight and so hot, he shuddered. Sweat broke out over his flesh, and need clamped his muscles.

"Now. Hurry." She gripped his butt, showing him how badly she wanted him. "I need to feel all of you."

Inhaling her scent shoved him over the edge of control. He surged inside, going balls-deep. "Mine, Ana. Right now, tonight, you're mine."

She hadn't bought him like those other women and didn't need anything from him but this—letting go together. With him, only him. The thought of anyone else having her, even touching her, ignited a torch of possession.

Her gorgeous eyes turned fierce. "I always wanted to be yours."

Oh fuck. That shredded him. Ethan had never had anyone for his own. Ever. Fire seared his belly, while lust singed his balls. "Then give it to me. Come again."

He gazed down her hot little body, her stomach straining as she rose to meet every thrust. He could feel the slick walls of her pussy clenching around him in vivid need for more release. So damned gorgeous. Dropping to his elbows, he changed his angle, forcing his pelvis against her clit.

Her eyes widened. "It's too much. Help me."

Just like that, she gave herself over to him. He thrust again and again. He slid his hand down to her ass, tilting her hips, and Ana's eyes rolled back.

"Yes. God." She came apart, her walls gripping him in spasms.

His fingers dug into her skin, pinning her to the mattress while he pounded into her. His climax raced down his spine, driving him deeper into her, then exploded. He came so hard, the world blurred.

Except for Ana.

* * * *

Ana jarred awake, startled by the feel of a huge, warm body behind her and an arm draped over her side. Ethan. Realizing he was there drained some of the tension from her nightmare.

"You okay? You were thrashing around in your sleep," Ethan said.

"Sorry." She blinked to clear the cobwebs from her brain. "What time is it?" The room had blackout drapes, so she couldn't tell. But they hadn't gone to sleep until after three.

"Eight. What were you dreaming about?"

She sank back against him. "My dad on the roof, then it turned into you. I kept yelling at you to get off, but you laughed and said you don't have to listen to me. I just knew something bad was going to happen. You started to slip, and I woke up."

He wrapped her snugly against him and kissed her hair. "Do you have that kind of dream about your dad often?"

She didn't need her psych classes to tell her she already dreaded Ethan leaving her again. "Hardly ever. Go back to sleep."

"Yeah, like that's going to happen when I have your naked ass pressed against my cock."

His voice slid down her back, warming her. "Well now—" She tried to turn, but he held her firm.

"Stay put."

Surprised, she craned her head around to see him in the soft gloom. "Why?"

"Because I like holding you. Not rushing. This isn't something I get to do."

She could just make out his eyes. But it was the tone of his voice that made her think a part of him longed for something— maybe a connection that went deeper than sex? "Wake up with women?"

"With you. I never wanted to wake up with another woman. Right now, you're mine."

Not just any woman, but her. How could she not feel special with him? He'd always made her feel like she mattered. The warm, contented feeling of his arms around her added to the sensation. The truth was she craved this comfort as much as she did the sex they'd shared.

"There's something I need to know," Ethan said.

"What?" She rarely hid anything from him. He just never asked a lot.

"Did your stepfather touch you?"

This time, the shiver that slid down her spine was anything but sexual. "No. And it's gross to talk about him while we're in bed." Or ever.

"I don't give a shit. We're talking about it. There's nothing you can tell me that will change how much I want you. But if he hurt you, I need to know."

"He didn't." Old anger simmered up. "I didn't give him a chance."

Ethan threaded their hands together by her belly. "What happened?"

"I was thirteen, almost fourteen when they married. I didn't like him much and just stayed out of his way. But he started watching me." This time she couldn't repress the quiver of distaste.

"I'm right here. No one is going to touch you but me." He tucked her closer.

The sensation of Ethan wrapping his huge, powerful body around hers made her feel safe. "He started *accidentally* walking in on me taking showers or while I was getting dressed. He'd come into my room, shut the door, and when I'd be outraged, he'd say, '*It's no big deal, we're family now.*'"

Would Ethan believe her or think she'd asked for it? And why wouldn't he? Hadn't Ana all but begged him to screw her? Sick anxiety ballooned in her chest, making it hard to breathe. Why had she told him?

"He's a predator. That's a form of grooming a victim."

The words came out harsh, but the fact that he understood eased her fear. "You believe me."

He pushed up on his elbow and stared down at her. "I believe he tried it, and you refused to be his victim. I hope you kicked his balls into his throat."

His belief in her was so vivid, she blurted out the unvarnished truth. "I didn't fight. I felt trapped and scared, so I ran."

"Do you feel trapped now? The way I'm holding you?"

She didn't know how he could be this understanding. "I feel protected. Not trapped." It was so easy to talk to him she kept going. "One day he came home from work early when my mom was gone. He knew she was gone. I panicked and left. Went to my friend's house and called my dad."

"And?"

"He was traveling, and I couldn't reach him, so I called Linda instead. She told me to stay where I was until she got there. My cellphone started blowing up with calls from my stepdad and later my mom when she got back home. But I didn't answer. Linda flew to Washington and arrived at my friend's house. I told her everything. Then she took me home."

"With her?"

"No, back to my mom and Don's, where Linda confronted my mom. Don was out, supposedly looking for me. Anyway, my mom denied it and said I was trying to get attention."

"Bitch."

"Yeah." Ana knew exactly what her mom was. "Linda didn't

back down. She believed me and told my mom that I was going home with her. Of course my mom said no."

"Child support."

"Yep, she still had four more years to collect. So Linda pulled out her phone, accessed her bank account, and said, "How much for Ana to go home with me? You'll relinquish custody and can have visitation in San Diego. But never with Don, or we'll make public accusations that he's a creep intending to molest a teenage girl. I'll destroy both your lives. That's the deal. How much? I'll make the transfer.""

Ethan shifted slightly behind her. "That's why you love your stepmom so much. I always wondered how you formed that bond with her."

Ana would give Linda a kidney in a heartbeat. "I had no idea she'd even help me, but what she did—no hesitation. She left work that day, got on a plane and came to my rescue. So yeah, I love her, and I'll do anything for her."

"So why pay your mom? Why not just threaten to expose the bastard?"

"Because Linda and my dad didn't have custody or any legal standing. They could have fought, of course, but the system is slow, and there wasn't any real proof. It was my word against my stepdad's that he was coming on to me."

He squeezed her hand. "Got it. So how much?"

"Almost a million. Linda made the first payment that day but obviously couldn't move all of it in one transaction. But it was enough to get me out of there. The thing is, my dad had money, but not enough to toss away almost a million dollars." She turned her head back to see him. "Do you see why I didn't want his money when he died? He was my hero when I needed him—both he and Linda. Why would I want more?"

Ethan studied her for a beat. "Some would. But not you."

"I don't. I was happy with them. And I tried to be a daughter they'd be proud of." She'd worked so hard to be perfect, to never ask them or anyone for help again. Deep down she'd feared that one day her dad and Linda would come to resent her, to think that maybe she'd been looking for attention as her mom said. Or…

She shut it down. Going over old stuff was a waste when she was here with Ethan for only a short time.

"Let's talk about something else." She lifted their joined hands, and a patch of rough skin on his palm stirred another memory. Tracing the scar with her thumb, she said, "Remember the time you tried to cook roast duck?" They'd almost kissed that night, but her smoke alarm had gone off, jarring them out of the moment.

He buried his face in her hair, chuckling. "I deserved to burn the fuck out of my hand that night. I was so close to kissing you, I didn't even smell the smoke or realize the bird was burning."

"It's funnier now than it was then." She didn't care about the duck or her oven, but she'd been devastated that they'd lost the moment. Then once he burned his hand trying to get the sizzling pan out, she'd been worried about Ethan and hated his pain. Ana had insisted on taking him to the emergency room. "It's a pretty deep scar." She traced it along his palm, wishing she'd stopped him from grabbing the pan without a potholder.

"Battle wound, but I can cook a duck now. My sour orange duck is exquisite."

She laughed, leaning back against him. "You really do still love cooking, don't you?"

He was quiet for a minute, then said, "I told you I lived on the streets before Sloane found me."

Her stomach clenched, hoping he'd tell her more. "Yeah."

"I was hungry a lot. I'd hang out by dumpsters in the back of restaurants sometimes. They'd give me, or any of us hanging around, food. But anytime they opened the door, I would catch the scent. It was the sweetest torture. These amazing smells of roasting meats, herbs, citrus. I became addicted to them. Once I had real access to food, I wanted to recreate those smells. Only this time, I could eat it."

It killed her to think of him like that. She had to swallow against the pain. Food held such power for him. When he cooked, it brought out the youth in him, a joy. But how had he ended up starving and so desperate? "Why, Ethan? Where was your family?"

His fingers tensed around hers. "No family. Just my mother."

Ana stilled, barely breathing. That was the most he'd ever told her, always shutting down if she asked how he ended up a runaway. "What happened? What made you take off by yourself?"

"I ran away. Leave it alone."

The bitter ice in his voice chilled her, a stark contrast to his warm body and the soft bed. "You demanded to know my ugly stories but won't share yours." Despite his being right there with her, loneliness closed in.

"Shit." He took his hand away, rolled off the bed and went to the window, shoving open the draperies.

Light flooded in around Ethan. He stood there naked, his huge shoulders flexed, muscles standing out along his back down to his tight, round ass and powerful legs.

And yet, for all his strength, a thick desolation surrounded him.

After throwing off the sheet, she crossed to him. Regret and shame pressed down on her. She was trying to force something from him he didn't want to give her. Ana edged up next to him and laid her hand on his back. "I won't ask anymore. It's okay."

He turned his head, his eyes seeking hers. "My past won't stay there. People know. I haven't really kept it a secret, I just never wanted it to touch you."

Her breath caught at the turmoil churning in his eyes. What haunted him so? "Why not me?"

"Because you're my one good thing. When you look at me, you don't see that I came from a cesspool. My mother was a high-class call girl who eventually lost her earning power. But she noticed women taking an interest in me."

Horror seeped into her blood. "How old were you?"

He turned away, looking out to the water. "Twelve."

Nausea hit her belly. "She didn't."

"Oh she did. She created a whole market. She'd rent me out as a boy toy. Soon I became really popular among the rich and bored. They fucking owned me for however long they booked me for. My mother didn't care what they did."

Ana'd had no idea...none. His mother forced him to have sex with other women? At twelve? "She should be in prison. Tell me she's in prison!" Fury ate at her.

"She's dead. Overdose a year or so after I ran away."

"Good."

"Doesn't matter if she's gone." Ethan stared out the window into the blindingly bright sun. "I'm still a whore just like her."

"You're not! You got out of it." Her heart pounded at the

quiet agony in him. "Ethan, it was abuse and not your fault." Didn't he see that?

He turned then. "I ran. Then I got hungry, really fucking hungry. And guess what I did to eat? I tried underground fighting and roughly half the time got my ass beaten. Mostly because I couldn't control my fury at being so powerless. And those damned sex vultures loved it when I came slithering back, begging to let me be their little fuck toy." He rocked, as if trying to escape a memory. "I can still hear them. '*Once a whore, always a whore.*'"

His shoulders swelled, and color stained his face. His body vibrated with anger. A rage he'd controlled ruthlessly around her, and now she was seeing it. Seeing more of the real Ethan.

She didn't know what to say to him, how to help. Yet everything in her wanted to take the pain away. "It's not who you are now. Look at you, Ethan. You're protecting the most famous rock band in the universe and on your way to being a chef." Now she understood his drive, the need to gain power in a world that abused him when he'd been powerless. "You're the man I admire and want."

He stalked her to the wall. "It's exactly who I am. It always will be. It's why all I can offer you is to be your dirty fantasy for a few days." He smiled sadly. "Just like you've been my fantasy of what I wish I could have."

"You can." Didn't he get this?

He shook his head. "I won't do that, ever. People knew what my mother was. No other moms would let their kids play with me. When I was still in school and ran into a woman who'd bought me, she was horrified that I was in the same school as her two kids and told me to never talk them, ever. I shouldn't be there at all. That school was for decent folks, not trash."

"She paid for sex with a child and judged you?" Outrage exploded, making her head throb. "That bitch should be in prison, and a woman who loved you would stand by you. You're not trash, and there's nothing dirty about you."

"Wrong. I was born dirty. The kid of a whore and a man who paid her. I ran away to escape that, thinking I was better than her, and ended up selling my services just to eat. Don't you see? I repeated the pattern. Then later when I got a chance at becoming a MMA fighter, I cheated with steroids, making me a whole different kind of dirty."

Anger and self-disgust hardened his voice, and turmoil churned in his eyes. "I'm breaking the cycle, here and now. I'm going to make something of myself, something that's not about using and degrading people or taking shortcuts. Once I've redeemed myself, then if I run into someone who knows my past, it won't matter so much. I'll have proved I'm better than just a whore and cheater."

The irony was so bitter, she almost wanted to laugh. This was the very thing she loved about Ethan, he had the integrity to own his mistakes like using steroids and fix them. But that same integrity kept him from letting her close to his heart.

Or more likely, while he cared about Ana, he just didn't care enough. One day he might find a woman he loved enough to take the risk of finding out if she'd stand by him.

All Ana could do now was be his friend and support him. Touching his arm, she said, "You're going to make it as a kick-ass chef. And one day you'll see yourself as I do. A man I respect, care about and trust enough to ask him to help me be bad for a while."

He opened his mouth—

"Wait. If there's anything I can do to help, Ethan, all you have to do is call me. I meet a lot of people in the food industry in my job. I even see Chef Zane, who was very impressed with you. If you need connections or anything like that, call me. Keep in mind, I've gotten Kat on baking shows and other opportunities. I'm pretty good at what I do." She added a smile. "No strings attached. I know our little sexcapade is a one-time thing."

Sexcapade—the word was so stupid and shallow, not even close to what Ana felt with Ethan.

Cupping her cheek, he tilted her face up. "There's my good girl, always trying to help."

Not good enough. No matter how hard she tried, she always seemed to end up alone. But that was her problem, not his. She'd be fine, she always was. "I'm not here to be good now."

"No you're not. Lucky for you, I'm excellent at being bad." Gathering her hands in his, he raised them over her head and kissed her. Once he had her breathless, he leaned back, studying her. "Tell me how you want to be bad. Specifically."

She had nothing to lose by revealing the truth. "I like making you work for it. And I love making you lose control."

His fingers twined with hers tightened. His cock brushed her belly, hot, long and thick. "You do that. Last night, when you showed me your bare pussy, all I could think about was I had to taste you." His voice dropped to a growl. "Then you fought me. Refused to open your legs. Teasing me."

The memory of the way he'd taken what he wanted made her excited. Wet. "You know that feeling when you and I used to race on roller blades or bikes? You wouldn't give in, and neither would I? We fought all the way to the finish line."

"Adrenaline rush." His eyes darkened, and his cock branded her belly. "Is that what you felt when I forced you to give me what I wanted, then made you like it?"

Need splashed so hard, she trembled. "Yes. When you do that, I stop thinking and just feel. And part of me wants to go further."

Ethan pinned her hands firmer against the wall. "How far?"

"I don't know, but I want to find out."

Lowering his mouth, he kissed her again then picked her up and laid her on the bed. "We're both too raw for that right now. I'm going to be gentle with you. I need to show you that side of me, before I show you just how far and bad I can be—if it's what you really want."

"I do."

"Then give me this. Last night I told you that I need you to know you weren't a woman I'd fuck and forget. I need the same thing back from you—to know I'm more than just your dirty fantasy. Let me show you tenderness and pleasure, and then we'll explore any fantasies we both have."

Her stomach liquefied with desire and more. He'd been badly used and yet he cared enough to want to share with her a side of him he hadn't shown anyone else. She tugged Ethan into her arms.

And too damned much of her heart.

Chapter 7

"Hold on," Ethan shouted, taking the watercraft into a tight turn that sprayed up a wave right at Franci and Simon. The lead guitarist of Savaged Illusions coughed out a mouthful of water, totally making Ethan's day. Bastard had already showered them twice.

Behind him, Ana's laughter pealed out. His cock jumped. He'd missed her competitiveness and the way she threw herself into everything. Having her body pressed against his back, arms wrapped snugly around him, wasn't a bad way to spend an afternoon.

The sound of an engine to his left jerked his attention from Ana and his dick. A second later a wall of water slammed into them.

"Ha! Payback!" Chelle shouted. Lynx sat behind her on the machine, laughing his ass off.

Ethan chased them down, the wind whipping around, water spraying, the guys trash-talking while the girls plotted shenanigans and revenge. He couldn't remember the last time he'd had so much fun.

Getting low on fuel, he gestured to the others that he was going back to the dock. Once there, he secured the craft and gave Ana a hand to help her up. He kept hold of her hand as they walked back toward the house.

He wanted to keep going, get her in their room, strip those bottoms off her and bury his cock in her.

Again.

Being with her, hearing her laugh, her hand in his made him

feel clean. But he wasn't. He'd never outrun his past, and he refused to let that shame taint Ana. He'd done the right thing telling her. Now she'd understand why this couldn't last more than a week.

Ana dried off. "I'm going in to use the bathroom and check my phone."

Concerned, he asked, "Have you heard from Gregory?"

"No. Stop worrying, I told you my lawyer notified Gregory that any further contact with me must go through the law office. And security at the resort also talked to him. They took my concern seriously, and informed Gregory that if he bothered me again, he'd be removed and banned."

Although impressed that Ana wasn't messing around after that confrontation with Gregory, Ethan still worried. "He could escalate. Stalkers tend to get pissed when they can't get to their target."

"He can't reach me here. The whole place is gated and guarded."

True, which meant he had to keep her here with him. "Don't go back there. You guys can stay here until you need to go home."

She rolled her eyes. "I'll stay while we're having fun, but I'm not here to be a burden. If you and I call an end to this between us, I'll have security escort me, Franci and Chelle to our room, pack and we'll move hotels. I've got this handled."

She kept saying that, and it was getting on his nerves. Couldn't she just let him take care of her a little bit? Right. Like the time she was sick and told everyone it was just a sore throat? By the time he got to her condo to check on her, she'd been burning with fever and scared the fuck out of him. He'd been damned closed to calling nine-one-one. After he'd dragged her to urgent care, he'd spent that night on her couch, not giving a shit that she insisted she'd be fine.

Fine his ass.

But arguing wouldn't do anything but make her more stubborn. "I need to check the duck."

She shot him a grin. "You just had to prove your duck dominance, didn't you?"

Ethan lifted an eyebrow as they walked in the house together. "You dare to question my duck dominance? You'll be eating those words, sunshine, when you taste my culinary delight."

"I tasted one of your delights this morning."

The image of Ana kissing down his chest and stomach to lavish attention on his cock seared his brain. His blood heated, and his dick engorged with a throb. She'd taken her sweet time torturing him, learning what he liked... He had to stop thinking about it.

Yanking her off her feet and up against his body, he fisted her hair, careful not to hurt her. "Making me think about you sucking my cock was evil, little witch." He pressed his hard-on into her belly.

Challenge gleamed in her eyes. "Don't burn your duck."

"Right now, I don't care if the whole house catches on fire." Not when he held Ana. Sweet and sassy as hell, and so giving it made his chest ache. "You keep it up, I'm going to drag you to the nearest private space, rip those shorts off and make you come."

"Tell you what. If your duck is as good as you claim, then I'll let you have your way with me. Anything you want."

Raw lust lashed through him. After she'd told him this morning she liked the adrenaline rush of a little force, he'd been thinking about it. "Careful with those promises, baby. I used to daydream about you in the bakery. I'd ask you out, and you'd tell me no. There are customers and your boss around, so I have no choice, I leave."

"That's a daydream? I think I've had sneezes more interesting."

He tightened his hand in her hair. "That's not the interesting part."

"What is?"

"I come back later, when the shop is closed, and it's just you in there all alone. No one to save you. Then I dare you to tell me no again."

The skin across her cheeks warmed to a golden color, and challenge sparked in her stare. "Maybe I'll make promises and change my mind. Once you're all hot and ready, I'll say no."

A shudder went through him. What was it about her? Before Ana, sex had been a cold itch to scratch. Emotionless. He never treated a woman badly, ever. He made sure they both got what they wanted and walked away satisfied. With Ana, it was a hot, fiery ache. "Think you can stop me? You taunt me enough, and I'll take you and make you like it."

Ana caught a handful of his hair. "Maybe I'm looking for payback. Eleven months ago, you left me after telling me I was too good for you. But do you know what I felt? Huh? Not good enough. I'm tougher than you think, and I might just lock myself in a bathroom and tell you to go fuck yourself."

He vibrated with the impact of her honesty and courage. She was a powerful combination of sexy vulnerability that captured his attention and wouldn't let go. It also fueled his need to make her forget her pain and scream his name in pleasure. Ethan nearly shuddered beneath the power of his desire for her. Would it ever recede? Or just get stronger?

One thing he knew for sure, if she wanted this, he'd give it to her. "I'm going to get us one of the casitas to spend the night in. It's secluded enough no one will see or hear us, so you won't have to worry if you want to scream, or even run out the door." He leaned closer. "Later tonight, you'll go there first. Then I'm coming for you, sunshine." He lowered his head, holding her tighter in his arms. His cock surged against her, but what mattered was Ana. They could surrender to what they wanted...as long as they both wanted it. He set her down before he lost the last shred of his control. "It's up to you if you want to yell at me or surrender."

She flashed him her megawatt smile. "If you want me to be in that casita tonight, your duck better rock my world, Chef Sexy." She spun and hurried off, her ass swaying in her tiny excuse for boardshorts.

Witch. Yet as he headed into the kitchen, trying to will his cock into submission, Ethan grinned. Ana needed him to want her so badly that he took what he craved from her.

The girl was turning him into a sap, making him wish he could be good enough for her.

* * * *

Everyone gathered around the big table, diving into dinner and chattering.

Ana took a bite of the duck nestled in a crepe. Her mouth

sent up a *hold the phone* signal. Her taste buds danced with excitement. She barely swallowed before taking a second bite. The rich duck meat married to the bright citrus embedded in a savory crepe ranked high on her best-thing-she'd-ever-tasted scale.

On her right, Ethan leaned close to her ear. "How's the duck?"

Tingles raced down her body from his sexy whisper. Swallowing, she faced him. "It's not the worst I've ever had."

His mouth curved with blazing confidence. "No?"

He knew how good he was, damn it. "But it's definitely the best. You've proved your duck dominance." Just saying it made her shiver more. "You win the prize."

His gaze burned with hunger. "I have the casita. The key—"

His cellphone went off.

Ethan frowned, leaning back to drag the device out of his pocket. Surprise registered on his face. "Siena is at the front gate. I see her on the cameras."

"The chef?"

"Yeah. Hang on." He put the phone to his ear. "Siena, what's up?"

Ana resisted the urge to lean closer. She could hear a voice but not make out any words.

"I see. I'll let you in." He fiddled with the screen then set the phone down.

"What's going on?"

"She came to work on the cookbook." He shifted uncomfortably. "We had a loose arrangement to do some work while I'm here, but I had no idea she'd just show up."

Disappointment settled hard, but she realized he was in a tricky position. "Thought you hadn't signed the contract yet?"

"I haven't. My lawyer's looking it over, and we've gone back and forth on a few issues. One sticking point is if I'm helping develop and refine recipes for the cookbook, then my name goes on it. So…"

"You're between a rock and a hard place." Oh she got it. If he wanted a guarantee of his name on the cookbook in the contract, he'd better damn well be ready to work when Siena called. She forced a smile. "I understand."

"I'll grab another place setting." Ethan got up and headed

into the kitchen.

River shoved back a length of the long dark hair the band's bassist was known for. "He and Siena talked about it at the VIP party after you left. But I don't think he knew then that you'd be here."

Ana nodded. "Should we leave?"

"No," Lynx said. "Hang out here. It's not a big deal. I rented an indoor climbing facility tomorrow. You don't want to miss that. It has a trampoline room too."

Ethan laid out a new place setting just as a bell rang. "That's Siena. I'll let her in. You all keep eating."

Ana watched him walk away, a sinking sensation in her stomach.

Ethan returned with the beautiful blonde next to him. Ana hated the wave of insecurity that passed over her. She'd quickly showered, leaving her hair to air-dry and skipping makeup. She wore shorts and a cute top, while Siena had her long hair clipped over one shoulder in a sleek style, polished makeup and a gorgeous shirt paired with white pants.

Siena smiled. "I didn't realize I'd caught you at dinner."

"No problem." Ethan led her to a chair. Once she sat, he filled her wineglass.

"Ethan, did you cook this?" Siena asked. "Duck and crepes?"

He held up the serving plate for her. "Yep. I made it for Ana."

She flushed with pleasure.

"Really?" Siena smiled at her. "Do you cook, Ana?"

"Only enough to stay alive, and I can bake if I'm following a recipe." She couldn't resist adding, "Ethan made the duck tonight to prove to me he could. The first time he tried to cook duck at my condo, he nearly burned the place down."

The entire table laughed.

"It's funnier now than it was then. He burned his hand pretty bad."

"Ah. That explains the scar on your palm." Siena took a bite of the duck wrapped in the crepe.

Ana tried not to feel a twinge of jealousy. Of course Siena'd seen the scar, it was right there on Ethan's palm.

"The two of you have been friends for a long time. And

now…?" She raised her eyebrows.

"Operation Kiss 2.0 is a success." Chelle lifted her glass and tapped Franci's.

"That's right. They're more than friends these days," Franci said. "If my law career and your graphics design business don't work out, we should opening a dating service, Chelle."

Ana wavered between embarrassment and exasperation. "I don't think Chef Siena—" she used the woman's title, trying to convey to her two friends that the woman was important to Ethan's career hopes, "—wants to hear about my and Ethan's friendship."

"Really?" Chelle ask. "Then I probably shouldn't have tagged Ethan's Facebook page with the posts of the two of you kissing out on the dock today. My bad."

Ana knew exactly when that had happened. She'd raced him to the Jet Ski—first one there getting to drive—and he'd caught her on the docks. Swinging her up and twisting her in his arms, he'd kissed her, hard and long. "You didn't!"

"Oh she did," Ethan said.

Pivoting around to Ethan, she muttered, "Sorry. You deleted it right?" Ethan used his Facebook page to showcase his cooking.

"Nope." He rubbed her back and grinned. "You're the one who told my potential employer I burned my first attempt at cooking duck."

Crap. She had done that.

Siena's laughter rang out. "True. She's probably not who you want to put down as a reference."

Her embarrassment deepened. Before she could think of a way to redeem herself, Siena said, "This duck is very good." The woman leaned toward Ethan, touching his arm. "Tell me your recipe. What method did you use to render the fat? And your orange sauce, there's an extra tang to it. What is it?"

Ethan explained, and the two of them launched into a detailed discussion.

Ana picked at her food as everyone else around the table talked about the rock-climbing outing tomorrow. She tried to focus on the topic and not on Ethan and Siena huddled together talking. Finally dinner was over, and staff magically appeared to start clearing.

Siena rose. "I'm going to go get my notes and computer out of the car. Is there a place we can work? We'll get it all sorted tonight and plan a time to test the recipes."

Despite the staff going in and out, Ana stood, scooping up her plate and walking into the kitchen. It was huge, with an industrial fridge, two ovens, wraparound counters and a big island, all overlooking the deck, pool and bay. The view did nothing to tame her disappointment over her and Ethan's cancelled plans.

"I'm sorry. I'm going to try to wrap it up soon. Just an hour or two, and I'll be all yours." Ethan stood so behind her, she could feel the heat of him spreading over her.

She turned. "Would it be better if I left? Franci, Chelle and I can go back to the Tradewinds and give you some space to work."

"Hell no. You're not going back there, remember? Not with Gregory around."

He was right, but that wasn't his problem. "We can find another place to stay." She couldn't bear the idea of being in the way.

Misery clouded his eyes. "Don't go." He leaned down, kissing her. "Please. I'll get away as soon as I can. We'll save our casita plans for another night, but we can go for a walk or hang out in the hot tub, even go down to the game room. Anything you want."

He was trying, and that meant a lot to her. "Okay. Chelle wants to check out the theater room. I'll watch movies with her and Franci."

Relief curved his mouth. "Perfect. There's a selection of prerelease movies in there. A fully stocked wet bar, candy counter and popcorn machine. I'll come find you when we're done here."

A naughty thought crossed her mind. "Any porn down there?"

Grabbing her waist, he pressed her against the counter. "What are you suggesting?"

"I haven't seen much porn. Maybe once you're done, I'll throw my friends out, then you and I can research the racy movies. And if we get warm in there…"

He dropped his forehead against hers. "You're making me hot. And you know it."

"Okay here's my… Oh sorry." Siena walked into the kitchen,

carrying a computer bag.

Feeling much better, Ana grinned. "Work fast." She strolled out with the sensation of Ethan's heated stare following her.

* * * *

It was after midnight when Ethan finally broke away from Siena. They'd done some good work, but he got a real sense of how demanding she would be. Which wasn't bad—she was going to pay him well, and a lot of doors would open for him after a year as Chef Siena's assistant. He'd be legitimate. The stain of his past as a whore and a fuckup would lessen.

Right now, he just wanted Ana. He headed to the theater, anticipation quickening his pace. The wall sconces cast low light in the large room. Ethan walked down the aisle between the sets of oversized recliners and spotted her.

Sound asleep.

He couldn't help but grin. Ana lay curled on her side, one hand tucked beneath her cheek. An empty bottle of Merlot and boxes of candy—including Ana's favorite Milk Duds—told him the girls had had a little party.

He assumed Franci and Chelle had gone to bed.

But Ana had stayed, waiting for him. Regret stabbed him that he'd let her down. Leaning over, he scooped her up.

"Ethan? What are you doing?"

"Taking you to bed."

"But I waited."

More regret piled on. "I know, baby. I'm sorry, I got tied up."

She rested her head against his shoulder. "I can walk."

"I've got you." He didn't mind. Up in their room, he laid her down, stripped her to her panties and grabbed some ibuprofen and water. She didn't seem that drunk, but he didn't want her waking with a headache. Once she'd taken the tablets and drank most of the water, he turned off the lights and climbed into bed. Gathering her against him, he stroked her back.

She went completely limp. Asleep.

Despite his aching cock, warmth spread in him. He liked taking care of Ana, liked that she curved against his chest, soft and trusting.

For eleven long months, there'd been an empty place inside him. Then she showed up, and it was like someone turned on the lights. He called her sunshine for that reason. He'd been in a dark place when she swept into his life, bringing a ray of light and a thin strand of hope.

This time next week, he'd be alone again.

He tugged her tighter against him, not wanting to let go.

But he had to. One day, his story would come out. Professionally, he'd handle it. Hell, in the culture they lived in these days, he'd probably be more successful.

But personally? It would hurt Ana or any woman. The stain of his past would mark them in the eyes of the world.

He wouldn't let that happen. Especially not to Ana.

His one good thing.

* * * *

Ana woke up alone and blinked the haze from her brain. After sitting up, she glanced around and spotted a note.

Went running, back soon with croissants. Be naked.

Still lethargic from the wine and candy, which upon reflection was not an ideal pairing, she got out of bed and stumbled into the bathroom, where she brushed her teeth and took a shower. The multiple jets blasting her skin chased off her sluggishness. Feeling much better, Ana wrapped in a towel and went back in the room to look for clothes.

Her phone vibrated on the nightstand. Picking it up, she frowned at a text from Gregory.

Why is your lawyer threatening me? I don't understand, you and I are friends, and we're going to be business partners. Oh wait, it's that guy that was with you, isn't it? I bet he's jealous of our friendship, so you had to act like it was no big deal. Look, I don't care about him, but you know how important this is to me. Those agents and publishers won't take me seriously, but they will now! And don't worry, I'll give you credit in the book too. We just need to get this deal finalized ASAP. I'm emailing you another copy of the proposal for your dad's biography, and a simple contract. We'll meet to sign the agreement and talk about the book. Call me soon.

Her stomach knotted, and she had to sink down on the bed. How had she not realized that Gregory and reality weren't well acquainted? Her palms were slick as she checked her email server. A new one from Gregory with attachments.

"Ana."

She jumped at Ethan's voice. He filled the doorway between the bedroom and sitting room. His white T-shirt was flung over a shoulder, leaving him in only running shorts and shoes. She tracked down his sweat-sheened chest, over his ripped abs, then caught sight of the white pastry bag in his hand. "Oh hi."

"You didn't hear me come in the room." Setting the bag and shirt down, he dropped onto the bed next to her. "What's up?"

She showed him Gregory's text. "I'll forward it to my lawyer, but you heard me, I told him no."

His loose mood iced as he read the message. "He's delusional and dangerous. He was really fixated on you in the conversation at Tradewinds. We'll go to the police here and tell them you've asked this guy to stop contacting you. Then once you're back in San Diego, if he contacts you again, you have some groundwork to hopefully have him charged with stalking."

How did it get this far? "I thought I was being nice. I felt sorry for him." That was the only reason she'd talked to him, and now she had a stalker who'd followed her to Florida. She forwarded the messages from Gregory to her lawyer.

Ethan rubbed the bridge of his nose. "Let's eat, and I'll grab a shower, then we'll go to the police station. After that, we can enjoy the rest of the day."

Right. Enough of her problems. Getting to her feet, she shook off her mood. "I'll make some coffee."

Ethan caught her hand and tugged her onto his lap. "I want to help you solve this before you go home. I need you safe. You get that, right?"

Warmth chased out her worry. This was exactly what she'd needed—to just feel important to someone for a little while.

Chapter 8

"After we go to the police station, we can meet everyone at the rock-climbing gym if you want to," Ethan said.

Ana pushed the elevator button. They'd had croissants and coffee out on their little balcony and now were on their way down to the first floor to see what everyone else was up to. "It would be fun, unless you have a better offer?"

"If you want to go, we'll go. Or—" He cut off when the doors slid open.

"Or what?"

He tugged her inside and pressed her to the wall. "While they're all gone, we'll use one of the casitas."

Her heart jumped a beat. "Casita." The idea intoxicated her more than the wine she drank last night. "I want that. With you."

He sucked in a breath. "You're making me hard again. I swear I can't get enough of you." The doors slid open, he took her hand and they walked into the great room.

Ana couldn't wipe the grin off her face. She loved that he wanted her, that she was exciting him as much as—

"There you are. We need to get going."

Ana stilled, her smile freezing. "Siena? When did you get

here?"

"Good morning, Ana." The woman nodded at her. "I stayed in a casita last night. Didn't Ethan tell you?"

She blinked, turning to look at him.

Ethan ran a hand over his hair. "She said she wanted to work on the descriptions for the recipes and review what we wrote together yesterday, so I offered her a casita." Shifting his attention to Siena, he asked, "Go where?"

"I had this fabulous idea. The kitchen here is quite adequate, so why not test our recipes? Let's hurry, though. We need the absolute freshest produce and seafood. By the time everyone returns from rock climbing, we'll have several dishes ready, and they can test them for us."

Ana couldn't believe it. "Now?" She ignored Siena to concentration on Ethan. "I thought we had plans."

"We do," he assured her, and said to Siena, "Let's do this tomorrow. I didn't realize you were coming last night, but I made time. I promised to spend today with Ana. We have some important things we need to take care of."

The woman's face tightened slightly. "I only have a few weeks to get this cookbook finalized and in to the publisher. One of the recipes I want to test is yours. If you want your name on the book, we need to focus on it." She turned to Ana. "Wouldn't you agree?"

Ethan's hand stiffened in hers.

Ana could feel the tension bleeding off him from the implied demand in Siena's tone and comments.

With a pained expression, he said, "We could shift our plans to tonight."

Part of her wanted to say no, but she was being childish. "Sure."

"Wait, we need to make that report." Ethan eyed Siena. "I have to take Ana to—"

"No." She didn't want Siena knowing her business, nor did she need Ethan going with her. "I'll take care of it." Releasing his hand, she said, "I'll go find Franci and Chelle and have them come with me." She headed for the doors to the deck and stepped out into the balmy air.

Chelle sat on a padded lounge chair, her hand moving in

graceful sweeps as she drew something in her sketchbook. "Where's Ethan?"

Dropping onto another lounge, Ana tried to swallow her disappointment. "Going shopping for the freshest produce and seafood."

Chelle's charcoal pencil stopped moving. "Is he making you a special dinner? That duck last night was good."

"No. He's cooking with Chef Pain in My Ass." Oh yeah, that didn't sound bitter at all.

"Seriously? I saw her skulking around the kitchen this morning. Thought she left last night?"

"Me too. We have a change of plans." She told Chelle about Gregory's text, that Ethan thought she should file a police report, and her lawyer had agreed when he texted her back.

Chelle shut her sketchbook. "I'll get ready, but back to Siena. Ethan didn't tell you that she spent the night?"

"No." This morning, Ana truly had felt like they were getting closer, then they'd come downstairs to reality.

Why hadn't Ethan told her Siena was staying at the manor?

* * * *

A day later, Ana, Franci and Chelle explored the game room and got into a heated battle playing a virtual reality dance game until Franci won.

"Pay up, girls," Franci taunted as she held up her phone.

Sighing, Ana looked at Chelle. "We may have been a tad overconfident."

"You think?" Chelle turned back to the camera and held up her sign that read, *This is my Loser Face*, then made a sad face.

Ana did the same.

Franci laughed and took the picture. "Posting to Facebook now." Looking up, she gave them her sweetest smile. "I'm tagging you both, of course. I wouldn't leave you out."

Chelle tossed her sign and pulled out her phone.

"No deleting," Franci said. "That was in the bet."

"We deserve it for making a bet with a law student," Ana muttered as she got out her phone and accessed her page. When the picture appeared, she couldn't help her laugh. "God, we look pathetic." She headed to the big sitting area.

"Oh, dolphin watching."

Confused by the abrupt shift in topic, Ana looked up at Franci. "What?"

"I have it on my agenda on my phone. I forgot about it with all the excitement, but I'd like to go. How about this afternoon? It's not too expensive."

Ana was torn. "Let me talk to Ethan when he gets back."

"Humph." Chelle sat on the arm of the leather couch. "That barracuda has her claws in Ethan—you'll be lucky to get him back in one piece. She's downright possessive."

Ana's stomach tensed. Siena was gorgeous, but even more importantly, she and Ethan shared the same passion—cooking.

"I have to agree with Chelle," Franci said. "You saw her at the wine tasting. She kept Ethan's attention focused on her."

Last night at dinner—which she almost hated to admit had been a spectacular array of Italian dishes Ethan and Siena had prepared—Chef Barracuda had announced that she'd arranged a private tasting with a wine broker to go over some pairings. Then she'd graciously invited Ana, Franci and Chelle along for the tasting. It'd been fun, but Siena had done exactly as her friends said, hovering over Ethan like a dog guarding its bone. They'd gotten home late, and Siena had insisted she and Ethan get all their notes together for the cookbook.

Ana'd ended up going to bed by herself.

This morning, Siena had snagged Ethan for a Skype meeting with their lawyers to work out the language of adding Ethan onto her cookbook.

Ana was really starting to hate that cookbook.

She stared at her phone when she noticed a new comment on the photo Franci had just posted. "Gregory."

"What?" Chelle said.

She shook her head in frustration. "He commented below the pic Franci just posted on our pages. 'Ana, as the daughter of a star athlete, you should know the three traits of a winner: Hard Work, Discipline and Ruthlessness. I outlined those in my mother's biography. She lived by those, and so do I. And now you will too. You'll see, you'll be much happier and productive, and I'll help you. Call me, we'll get the contract signed and start work.'" She shuddered, a sensation of being watched creeping up her back. "He's not giving up."

"Who's not?" Ethan strode into the massive game room.

"Gregory." One look at Ethan, and her crawling-skin sensation calmed. Ana stood and walked to him. "He commented on a picture on my Facebook. I should have unfriended him, but he never contacted me through Facebook or even liked my posts, so I didn't think about it." She held out her phone.

Ethan tensed as he read it, his eyes cold and pissed. "Where's that book he sent you?"

"I deleted it." Had that been a mistake? At the time, she thought he'd go away. And really, she'd had other things on her mind.

"Screenshot this, add it to your file. Have the police talked to him?"

"Yes, but he told them it's a misunderstanding, a coincidence that he's there at the resort at the same time as I am."

His eyes narrowed in concern. "Maybe it's time I go see him."

Ana laid a hand on his arm. "No. That'll only complicate things, and he could file some kind of harassment report. The police said no contact except through my lawyer for legal matters."

Anger flickered in his gaze. "What if he doesn't give up when you return to San Diego?"

It wouldn't be Ethan's problem, that's what. The emptiness loomed like a wave rising up, ready to consume her. *Get a grip, I'll figure it out.* "My lawyer is getting the request for a restraining order ready. He says the fact that I'm Roger Kendall's daughter will help with that." Before Ethan could form arguments, she went on, "But right now, I'm here. Franci, Chelle and I were talking about going dolphin watching." Ana wanted to spend time alone with Ethan, but she also didn't want to abandon her friends.

His jaw hardened. "I can't. Siena is insisting we go to her restaurant to tape some test videos to see how I do on camera."

"Well, that's a no then." She refused to look at her friends, not wanting to see their anger or pity.

"I came to ask you if you want to come. We'll have a late lunch or early dinner there."

"Just you, me and Siena?" Huh, good to know her sarcasm

was in perfect working order.

Tense silence hung between them before he said, "I'll try to get her to leave us to eat alone."

He looked harried and tired, but enough was enough. "She won't. And I'm not going to be a third wheel." Again. Nor was she going to sit here and sulk. "Franci, Chelle and I are going dolphin watching. It's a couple hours' tour. Will that be enough time for you to get the video shoot done?"

His forehead creased. "Yes, and this should be it. I think Siena's leaving tonight." He pulled her in for a kiss. "I know this isn't ideal, but hang in there, I'll get rid of her soon."

Ana wasn't so sure about that.

* * * *

Ana came downstairs freshly showered after their dolphin-watching expedition, and caught sight of Ethan in the great room. She stopped, absolutely stunned. He was dressed in a tailored suit that set off his shoulders while emphasizing his narrow waist and hips. He suddenly looked older, sophisticated.

The strain on his face melted into pleasure when he saw her. "Hey, did you see the dolphins?"

"Yep." But she wasn't interested in dolphins right now. "You look amazing." She'd never seen him dressed so sharply. He wore the suit with a naturalness that exuded power and confidence.

"We did some of the video test in chef whites and…" he glanced down, a wry twist to his lips, "…this."

"A formal suit? Is it new? Doesn't seem like something you'd have on hand as a bodyguard."

"Wrong. I often work close protection for formal events, and it's better if I blend in." He strode up to her. "Since Siena wanted formal, I figured this would work."

Oh it did. "You look awesome." Jealousy flickered. She wished she were dressed up and going out with him. "Maybe we should put that suit to good use. Go out to dinner?"

A real smile curved his mouth. "Anywhere you want. Even if they're booked up, I'll use Justice's name to get us a table. Have anything in mind?"

"Not really." A frown weighed down her face. "I don't think

I brought anything dressy enough to—"

"Ethan." Siena walked in on stilettos, wearing a black dress and her hair done up in a lovely twist. "Oh hi, Ana." She turned to Ethan. "My lawyers have the revised draft of the contract. They've sent it to your lawyers, and we have a meeting at the law office in an hour." She glanced at her watch. "We need to get going soon before the rush hour traffic. Hopefully we can get it finalized and have that done."

Oh come on! Ana stared at Siena's oh-so-serious face, then Ethan's tight one. She already knew how this was going to play out because, hello, anyone else seeing the pattern here? She almost opened her mouth, but clamped it shut instead. If she forced a choice, she knew how that would end. She was the girl he was screwing for a few days, while Chef Schemes-A-Lot held the keys to his future.

"No," Ethan said. "First, I haven't talked to my lawyers or seen the revision. I'm not signing it without a thorough review."

"I would hope not," Siena responded. "But it's the exact changes we discussed. Your lawyers are reviewing it, and a representative from their Tampa office will be there. The others will join us via Skype. You can go over it yourself in the car. I'll drive."

"Second," Ethan ignored her and went on, "I've promised to take Ana out, and that's what I'm doing. She's put up with enough interruptions. I already told you that in the car."

Surprised pleasure that he was choosing to spend time with her soothed Ana's irritation.

Siena straightened, and iron determination radiated from her. "Business comes first. The publisher wants an answer from me about the names on the cover, and I can't give it to them until we have a signed contract."

Ethan turned to Ana, his jaw rigid. "I'll be back as soon as I can."

Disappointment crashed into her chest. "You're actually going."

His mouth flattened. "It's business."

Indeed. "All right." She headed toward the elevator. The tightness in her throat made her mad.

"Wait, Ana," Siena called.

The click of the woman's heels on the floor pounded in Ana's head. She had loved Siena on TV, really enjoyed her fiery personality and flare. Watching her show, it was like she cooked with her entire soul.

Much like Ethan.

Now Ana'd definitely soured on Chef Siena Draco.

"Ana, please."

Fine. She fought to get the bitterness and jealousy out of her expression as she turned. But one look at Siena and Ethan brought home a harsh reality. The two of them were wearing beautiful, sophisticated clothes, while Ana'd put on shorts and a tank after her shower, her hair scraped back into a simple ponytail.

Which one of the three of them didn't belong in this picture?

Siena touched Ana's arm, and the scent of jasmine washed over her. "Ethan told me in the car that he was devoting his whole evening to you. Believe it or not I feel bad about this, and I know I've monopolized Ethan. To make up for it, I've made reservations for two at Nadine's Steak and Seafood. It's right on the bay. The food is amazing. It's on me as a thank-you. The two of you will have the entire night to yourself, I promise. No more interfering. But I just need Ethan for another couple hours, including the drive time."

Startled by the kind sincerity in the offer, Ana tamped down her earlier frustration. "That's very generous of you."

"Not really. I want Ethan happy working for me. And you seem to be a big part of his happiness. Anyway, the reservations aren't until seven. There's plenty of time if you'd like to go shopping for a new dress or get your hair done, whatever you like." She flashed her charming TV smile. "Forgive me for my workaholic ways? And forgive Ethan too? I'm not really giving him a choice here."

Before Ana could answer, Siena faced Ethan. "There? See, I'm not a total dictator. Now you can finish business without feeling torn and enjoy your evening. I'll wait in the car." She sailed out.

Ana stood there, still fighting the sting she didn't want to feel, hurt at always coming in behind another priority. Even her dad and stepmom put each other first, before Ana. Not in a cruel way, but the reality was there. However her baggage wasn't Ethan's fault. "Okay, well, I'll see you later."

He strode to her, pulling her into his arms. "I swear I'll get rid of her this time. We're going to have our night. Dinner out first." His eyes darkened. "But I'm paying for it. I'm not taking you out on my future boss's dime. And then we'll come back here to our own private casita. I'll be back here at six thirty on the dot to pick you up."

Relief soothed away the sting, and anticipation bubbled beneath her breastbone. But she wanted to make a point. "Don't let me down this time."

Ethan slid his hand down to wrap around her hip. His thumb dipped beneath her shirt to skate over bare skin. "I'll be here and all yours." He kissed her and left.

She desperately wanted to believe him, but Siena really did have her claws in him, and how could Ana fight that?

She couldn't.

* * * *

Ethan refused to be bullied. "No. I own my recipes." The contract put his name on the cookbook as promised, but added a clause that Ethan couldn't prepare the recipe outside of Siena's restaurants or shows, unless he gave credit to Siena in perpetuity.

"Ethan," Siena said, her eyes flat. "You're getting exactly what you asked for, your name on the cover and credit for the recipes in the book. But I own them, that's how this works."

He leaned back in his chair. "Fine. Buy the rights from me or split the royalties on the book. My lawyers will draw up the contract." He'd expected hardball and silently thanked his mentor for teaching him how to play. Yeah, he risked the whole deal, but while he was willing to pretty much sell his soul for a year, he wouldn't give up his rights to his recipes. "You already have my agreement not to republish the recipes for profit for a term of seven years." That he deemed fair.

Two hours later, he won the battle, with the language hammered out. When he checked his watch, it was six fifteen.

Fuck. Ana. He'd sworn to be to be at the manor at six thirty to pick her up. No way could he make it now. He stood, grabbed his coat off the chair and looked at Siena. "I'm late, we need to leave."

She raised her eyebrows. "We're nearly finished. They'll hold your reservation. Text her, tell her to wait."

His patience snapped. Ana had waited, over and over. For two days, he'd put business and his ambitions first. Not completely unreasonable if she was just some girl he was screwing, but Ana was more. A woman who'd been there for him when his world went dark. Now he was stringing her along like some meaningless hookup.

On top of that, Siena was fucking with him, manipulating to get between him and Ana. He'd begun realizing it yesterday but had wanted to let it play out to see how far she'd go. Pretty far. That meant she saw Ana as a threat to Ethan signing the contract, and she was willing to fight dirty. But Ethan hadn't intended to let Ana down again tonight, and guilt stabbed him.

"I'm done now. You have my terms. Meet them or the deal is off." He yanked open the door.

"Ethan, you can't leave. We came together in my car. You don't have a ride."

He refused to answer and left. Once he made his way out to the front of the building, he called for an Uber, then dialed Ana.

She answered with, "Are you going to be late or canceling?"

Another guilt-blade dug in. He'd make it right. "I'm leaving now. An Uber is on the way to pick me up."

"Why an Uber?"

"Because I just walked out, and an Uber car is close by. Can you meet me at the restaurant?"

"You really walked out?"

"Yes. This is our night, Ana." Low panic burned in his guts, and his neck muscles ached with the fear that she was done and would leave.

"I'll meet you at the restaurant."

Relief untangled his biting tension. "Perfect, my ride should be here any minute."

"Okay, but if you need something to entertain yourself while waiting, check out my Facebook page." She hung up.

Ethan pulled the phone away from his ear and loaded her Facebook page. A stunning image formed of her dark blonde hair, straight and sleek around her face, long neck and shoulders bared in a shimmering metallic gold dress that molded to her body and exposed her legs down to killer heels.

The second picture showed her back bared to her waist except for the straps riding over her shoulders and meeting in a twist at the center. That pretty dress cupped her ass, ending with a tantalizing slit. Ana looked back over her shoulder with a sexy grin that made his cock twitch and thicken.

Jesus, he couldn't breathe. All his ambition coiled into a knot of need, low in his belly, for only one thing:

Ana.

Chapter 9

Ana arrived at the restaurant before Ethan. The steak and seafood house had a huge wall of fish tanks with brightly colored creatures swimming lazily, creating a soothing atmosphere. Soft music played in the background, and white tablecloths with gleaming silver added to the ambiance. Ana settled into booth. She pulled out her phone.

Would Ethan show up, or would Chef-Cock-Block find a way to stop him?

Her answer arrived one minute later when Ethan strode toward her. He tugged off his suit jacket, the shirt clinging to his shoulders and arms as he tossed the garment on the opposite seat then slid into the booth next to her. His huge body took up three quarters of the seat, while his scent—warm and spicy—made her want to lean in to him.

Wrapping a hand around her nape, he tugged her to him. Heat simmered in his blue eyes. "Those pictures were hot, but you're more stunning in person."

Another first for her as she never posted sexy pictures. "You liked them?"

"So much that I've been walking around with an aching cock."

"Would you like to start with a cocktail or glass of wine?" Their server appeared tableside.

Ana repressed a laugh. Had the woman heard? She didn't look outraged if she had, so no harm done.

"They have an excellent Wagyu steak cooked on hot stones. Or did you have something else in mind?" Ethan dragged his thumb over her jaw, apparently unfazed. "Anything you want."

"The steak sounds good. Can they cook mine closer to medium?"

He gave the order, and once the waitress left, he said, "Tell me about dolphin watching earlier. I need to think about something else besides kissing you and how good you look in that dress."

Ana told him stories, showing him pictures of dolphins through the appetizer course. After a couple sips of the smooth Malbec, she got up the courage to say, "So, what happened in your meeting with the lawyers?"

He told her about the sneaky clause giving Siena ownership of his recipes.

"You stood your ground."

"On my rights? Hell yeah." He poured a bit more wine in her glass. "Then I looked at the time and realized how late it was."

"I thought you were cancelling."

His fingers clenched around his wineglass. "I was furious at myself. I got caught up in the fight and didn't watch the time. When Siena pulled her crap, she meant for me to let you down again. I was done."

Concern edged into her. "Will she rescind the offer?" Ana didn't intend to come between him and the job he wanted so badly.

His jaw tightened.

The server returned, bringing their stone-cooked steaks, the aroma wafting into the booth. "Is there anything else I can get you?"

"We're good, thank you," Ethan answered.

Ana stared at her meat sliced on a bed of greens, surrounded by baby potatoes and broccoli. It looked delicious, but Ethan's earlier silence left her uneasy.

"She overplayed her hand."

"Siena?"

He nodded. "The last two days, yeah. All the games to keep you and me apart. Obviously she saw you as a threat. Then the changes in the contract today trying to tie me to her indefinitely by owning my recipes. That tells me how important I am to her." Cold, brutal ambition hardened his voice and made his eyes flat, icy.

Ana leaned back. "How can I be a threat to you signing the contract? We're not even together. I mean not really. Not after this week."

He raised his eyebrows. "She doesn't know that. Once I sign, I'll be traveling all over with her, and most girlfriends would object to that."

Doubt crawled in, and she didn't like it. "Why does it feel like I'm a convenient pawn in your contract negotiations?" *Really?* She knew Ethan better than that. Okay he might use a situation to his advantage, but then, so would she when working to get deals for Sugar Dancer Bakery.

The chill in his gaze cracked as surprise and regret took over. "No. Jesus, Ana. It's a coincidence that you and Siena are at the manor at the same time. It just worked out this way and gave me an opportunity to see that she is serious about signing me." He frowned. "You knew this was my goal."

The words hit her like a reality slap. She didn't have any right to feel hurt or possessive. She was the one who'd approached him with this temporary fling proposition. If it came down to a choice between Ana or his job with Siena, his choice was clear.

"Forget business." Ethan stroked her face. "Right now I'm only interested in pleasure. Our pleasure." He cut a piece of her steak and held it out. "Try some meat."

Ana took a bite, consciously letting go of her insecurities to enjoy the food. Their time together was about sex and fun. The tense moment melted as they talked and ate. Finally she said, "I need to use the restroom."

Ethan slid out. "I'll pay the check."

Ana stood and hesitated. "I—"

He kissed her before she could speak. "I have it, Ana. I want to buy dinner. You're not a pawn to me. You're my lover and friend."

The sincerity riding his low voice reassured her. They were getting a second chance to redo the past and give each other good memories of their friendship.

You're such a liar. You're more in love with him now than a year ago.

Don't think about that, she told herself. *Not now.* Smiling, she said, "Thank you. It means a lot to me."

Rushing away, she remembered a small detail and glanced

back at him. "I have the key to one of the casitas. Hank gave it to me."

It didn't take her long to locate the hallway that led to the ladies' room. Once she was finished, she paused in the small foyer that separated the bathroom from the door, and surveyed herself in the mirror.

Ana saw a deep fatigue in her eyes. She desperately wanted to just let go for a little while. She'd been holding on so tight, trying to make herself useful enough to the people she cared about so they wouldn't leave her.

Ethan *would* leave. There was a freedom in knowing that right up front. No matter what she did, he wasn't going to care enough to stay, so she could just be herself. For tonight, he was hers. Anticipation simmered in her belly.

Feeling a bit lighter, she stepped away from the mirror and opened the door.

A hand slammed into her chest and shoved her back.

Ana stumbled, her heels sliding on the slick floor. Shock confused her. What was happening? Struggling to catch her balance, she grabbed the wall dividing the bathroom area from the foyer. She jerked upright in time to see Gregory turning the lock on the door.

"What the hell are you doing?" She couldn't believe this.

He spun around, latched onto her arm and dragged her toward the three stalls. He kicked every door until he determined they were alone.

Ana regained her wits enough to yank on her arm. "Let go of me."

His fingers bit into her skin. "I thought you were so nice when I met you. And now I see you have a discipline problem."

Discipline? At six feet tall, Gregory was long and strong. He didn't have Ethan's muscle, but he was solid enough to overpower her. "You're hurting me."

He bounced the same way he had when she saw him at the resort. "I don't want to. When I first met you, I didn't think I'd have to. Your father's a star athlete, I thought you understood." He yanked open the handicapped stall door.

Oh hell no, she wasn't going in there. She clutched the edge of the stall.

Gregory reached his arm out to the right.

Ana started to turn to figure out what he was doing when a force hit the back of her hand. Oh God, pain exploded out. A scream tore from her throat.

His palm clapped over her mouth. "Shut up. There's no crying or screaming in discipline. You'll learn. Work comes first, not partying and goofing off. Work. Now sign the contract."

What contract? What is happening? She pressed her throbbing limb against her belly. It took her a second to figure it out—he'd slammed the stall door on her hand.

He dragged her to the counter. After releasing her mouth, he slapped a piece of paper down, then a pen. "Sign. Now."

Ana stared at the black ballpoint lying on a typewritten sheet of paper that had fold marks in it. In the mirror, she eyed the reflection of her injury. Carefully she moved the fingers. The pain had lessened but it still hurt.

Gregory jerked her arm. "Do it, pick up that pen."

She reached out with her good hand and fisted the pen. She had one chance—

A loud pounding sounded. "Ana?" Ethan called out. "You okay?"

Gregory grabbed her sore hand and tightened his fingers in a threat of more agony. "Say yes. Get rid of him."

Like hell. Ana bent her elbow, then snapped her fist down hard, jamming the pen into the lunatic's thigh. At the same time, she yanked her arm free and screamed, "No! Gregory's in here!"

Run. Don't look back. She hauled ass for the exit.

"Stay back. I'm coming in," Ethan yelled.

Ana skidded to a stop at the exact second the door flew open, banging against the wall.

Ethan stormed in, menace on his face. He didn't slow, but leapt into a flying tackle, hit Gregory and both of them slammed onto the tile floor.

Before Ana could blink, Gregory lay facedown. Ethan had one knee on the man's back and his arms pinned behind him. "You move, I'll rip your arm out of the socket."

"My leg. She stabbed me."

Ethan glanced at the bloody pen on the floor, then her. "You okay?"

She was still trying to take in how fast Ethan had moved. And the door... "You kicked it open. It was deadbolted."

"Look at me."

The gentle command pierced the wild pounding of her heart and buzzing in her ears. She focused on Ethan. Even in a half crouch over Gregory, strength exuded from him.

"Good. Now tell me if you're hurt. Where did he touch you?"

"My arm." She looked down at the angry red fingerprints. That would leave a bruise. "Slammed my hand in a stall door." She held up her arm and eyed it. No blood, but it was swelling and throbbed.

"Ana."

She blinked and returned her attention to Ethan. Shock, she wasn't focusing. "Sorry, I'm okay." She glanced at the doorway filling with people gawking at them.

A woman pushed through wearing a uniform. "Police. What's going on here?"

A cop already? "That was fast."

"I was in the area when a call came in. What happened?"

Ana filled in the police officer while the efficient woman checked Gregory for weapons and cuffed him.

"She stabbed me," Gregory whined. "Arrest her."

"You attacked me," Ana snapped.

Gregory glowered at her. "If you'd just read the book, you'd understand. Hard work, discipline and ruthlessness. I failed as a tennis player because I wasn't ruthless enough. Now I am. I won't fail, you'll see. You'll all see. When I write Roger Kendall's biography—"

"Not going to happen." Ana cut off his ranting. "Not now or ever."

Ethan wrapped his jacket around her shoulders, while keeping his scrutiny on Gregory. "How did you know where Ana would be?"

"It's on her Facebook. Bragging about her new dress for her date at Nadine's instead of working with me. I just had to wait for her to use the bathroom to get her alone."

Figured. Every time she tried to get a little bad, a little wicked, it bit her in the ass. "You need to get help, Gregory. And leave me alone."

* * * *

Ethan drove the car through the quiet streets with Ana in the passenger seat. She hadn't said much, but she had to be tired. It had taken a while to give their statements, then the hospital trip to X-ray her hand. Thankfully it was only bruised, not broken. Ethan regulated his breathing, keeping a lock on his emotions. He'd take her to the casita—not for their fantasy game—but so she could rest without a bunch of questions.

She could have been hurt worse. The sound of her voice yelling, "*No! Gregory's in here!*" beat over and over in his head. What if he hadn't realized something was wrong in the bathroom?

As he turned onto the street leading to the mansion, more anger leaked through his control. He tapped his thumb on the steering wheel. Ana had no idea how close he'd been to ripping that bastard's arm out of his socket for the pleasure of hearing him scream.

She belonged to Ethan. She'd belonged to him since the day he'd seen her in the bakery. *Mine.* He knew damn well he couldn't have her. The stain of his past was a black mold that would grow and fester in the dark corners of her mind. It'd eat away at her feelings for him until she had nothing left but an ugly disgust.

"How'd you know something was wrong when I was in the bathroom?"

Her voice pulled him out of the pit, and he glanced over. She sat still, with the cold pack resting on the back of her hand.

After stopping at the wrought iron gate to the manor, Ethan used his phone to open it, then drove through. "A woman tried the door and found it locked. I heard her telling the manager." The hairs on the back of his neck had stood up as all his instincts went hot. "I knew something was wrong."

"Oh. Well, thank you. I'm glad you were there."

"What if I hadn't been? You weren't going to make it to the door. That bastard was right behind you when I got in there." That anyone would hurt her enraged him. "He's crazy and completely fixated on you."

"I'll handle it."

His control cracked. "Really? Because you've been doing an

awesome job of it so far. Did you walk right by him in the restaurant and not even notice? He had to be by that bathroom watching for you. Oh and posting exactly where you were going to be at a specific time online? Genius. Fucking genius."

Silence spread between them, and Ethan clamped his mouth shut. He took the smaller road to the private casita then turned to Ana. She stared out the window at the two-story building in the glow of ground lights, her face pale, strained and remote.

He was an ass for yelling at her after she'd been accosted in the bathroom. He wasn't mad at her, he was worried and frustrated. "I'm sorry, that came out harsh. I have a lot going on. We're finalizing all the security on the last leg of the tour, I'm playing hardball on contract negotiations that can make or break my career." But what happened if Gregory got out of jail and returned to San Diego? Would he go after Ana? His aggravation at the situation built and shot out of his mouth. "The last thing I need is to worry about your safety."

"Then don't." Ana released her seat belt and faced him. "It's time to cut bait. This isn't working between us. I'll stay in the casita tonight, then fly home tomorrow and take care of myself. I always take care of myself."

Go home? She was leaving him? Panic closed in on his chest. Tonight, when he'd realized she was in trouble and a locked door stood between them, something had snapped in his brain. He'd have killed in a second to protect her. He didn't want to let her go. Struggling to breathe past the building pressure, the need to find a way to have her while proving himself to the whole damned world, he said, "Ana—"

She turned away from him and shoved open the door. "You'll be free to focus on the important stuff. Thank you again for dinner and helping me tonight. I told the restaurant to charge any damages, like the door, to me." She banged the car door and darted up the stone walkway.

Christ. He'd handled that like a champ. After ripping off his seat belt, he jetted out of the car and yelled, "Damn it, stop."

She spun around. "Go back to the house, Ethan. I'm done." She vanished inside, closing the door on him.

Who was the fucking genius now?

It took all his will to get in the car and drive away.

This was better for Ana. It didn't matter how much he loved her, it'd never work. His past would be exposed, people would gleefully dissect it, and Ana would feel the shame. He couldn't—

He hit the brakes so hard, the rear tires skidded, taking him into a spin. He gripped the steering wheel, hands sweaty, heart pounding and a crackling in his ears. His training kicked in, and he got the car under control.

Loved her? He'd always cared, but what did he know of love? Enough to love Ana, apparently.

After parking in front of the manor, he glanced in the rearview mirror and didn't like what he saw. A man who'd left the woman he loved alone, a woman who'd been hurt and terrorized tonight. But not before he'd made it clear that his job and his chance at an apprenticeship were more important than her.

No wonder she'd wanted to leave him. He was an asshole and clearly not good enough for her. He'd more than proved that this evening.

He should go in the house, tell her friends she needed them, and they'd go take care of her. If Gregory got out of jail, Ethan would do anything he had to in order to keep her safe, including break his contract with Savaged Illusions to protect her himself. Yeah, he'd be a fuck up professionally, but Ana would be safe.

That's what mattered.

Go inside. Yet, he couldn't. How much time had passed since he'd left Ana? Fifteen or twenty minutes?

The front door opened, and Chelle stormed down the steps toward their rental car when she spotted him. Pivoting, she jogged to the passenger side of Ethan's car, ripped open the door and dropped into the seat. "You're a jerk."

Ana must have called her friends, and Chelle had probably been on her way to the casita. "I know."

"I'm not done. I'm guessing Ana didn't tell you, or maybe she did but you're so busy with your new exciting life you don't care."

His guts clenched, and dread dug in. "Tell me what?"

The anger drained out of Chelle, leaving her pale. "Ana's fine. But for a couple weeks, she was scared to death that she had cancer. She went through it all alone." Chelle's eyes welled with tears. "We never knew. But the worst thing is she tried to tell us, but Franci and I were so busy dumping our problems on her, she never did. She went through finding a lump, the doctor's exam, mammogram, biopsy and getting the results by herself."

Jesus. He couldn't get his head around it. "I don't understand, how could she not tell anyone?"

Chelle looked away. "Because I'd gotten in way over my head with my graphic design business, and my boyfriend dumped me. Ana spent several nights working with me on QuickBooks so I could invoice customers correctly. She loaned me money to get me through. I'll pay her back. I swear it."

Guilt bore down on his chest, tightening it until he could barely breathe. Ana had been fucking scared, and no one had been there. But it made sense why she hadn't realized how much Gregory was fixating on her in San Diego. She'd been distracted.

"And Franci's dad found out her mom was cheating. Ana helped him find a good lawyer and stood by Franci as she was torn in two by her loyalties to both parents. Plus Franci's been worried about paying for law school."

Ana hadn't said a word to him. Nothing. But she had told him repeatedly that she took care of herself. Obviously she had. Another thought hit him. What if the doctors had found something and she wasn't telling them? "Are you sure she's okay?"

"Yes. I only found out about the whole thing because I was at her condo and saw the biopsy report. She's clear, no cancer." She scrubbed the palm of one hand on her thigh. "She had no one. Ana refused to tell Linda about her cancer scare for fear she'd cancel her trip to Italy."

Ethan closed his eyes, knowing exactly why she hadn't told Linda. In Ana's mind, she owed her stepmom for helping her when she needed it. She wouldn't burden her again. God. He rubbed his chest.

"And tonight you told her she was too much trouble. All she asked was for you to make her feel alive and wanted for a little while. Like maybe she didn't have to be so damned perfect all the time. Ana's done this for so long, she doesn't know how to let someone else take over and help her anymore."

Her words slammed into him. All this time, Ana'd been telling him that. Asking him to let her have this fantasy with him where they could both lose control for a while. But he'd been too busy struggling with his demons and going after his big dream to really hear her. She'd been asking him for help, and he'd let her down.

Just like everyone else.

Then tonight, he'd been scared, worried, and lashed out at her, basically telling her she was a burden. No wonder she told him to leave.

"I'm going to her now, while Franci packs the rest of our things. We're getting her out of here, away from you, tonight."

Chelle's words snapped him out of his thoughts. "No, wait. Give me another chance. Please, just let me go to her now."

She lifted her head, eyes blazing. "Finally pull your head out of your ass?"

He blinked. A lot of people mistook Chelle's creative flightiness for stupidity. That was a mistake. The girl was smart and caring. She'd seen through Ethan when even he couldn't admit the truth.

"You either get real here and figure out you love her, or you let her go. What's it going to be?"

He'd known it the second Ana'd called out to him behind the locked bathroom door. He loved Ana, but would she give him another chance?

Chapter 10

Ana sat on the couch in the pretty casita with her knees pulled up to her chin, scanning the airline flights for tomorrow on her phone.

She couldn't concentrate.

"The last thing I need is to worry about your safety."

Ethan's voice rang in her head. Her throat ached more than the throb in her arm and hand. She wanted to hate him, but instead it just hurt. It was worse than when her mom refused to listen to her about her stepfather. She'd always known she was nothing more than a pawn to her mom.

But Ethan…deep down she'd thought he cared. Idiot. Hadn't he made it clear eleven months ago that she wasn't important enough to keep? Pressure built behind her eyes. She wished she could cry, just break down and let go for a while. Get some release from the swelling pressure inside her.

But she couldn't. Not anymore.

She hadn't cried since that day she left her mom's house. She'd tried hard to be good, not a moody or difficult teenager. No dramatics, no sobbing over boys or arguments. She'd trained herself not to break down. Yet the pressure inside kept growing. It freaked her out.

Like she was cracking inside where no one could see.

She glanced at the door.

She'd told Franci and Chelle what happened, but then insisted she was fine and would sleep here.

But wouldn't they check on her?

You told them you're fine. Why would they?

There was really something wrong with her. She didn't know how to ask for help anymore.

Except with Ethan. That twisted inside her, pain so deep she squeezed her eyes shut. *Help me.* The words had come out when he'd been deep inside her, driving her to pleasure so intense, it was the flip side of the pain she felt now.

And she'd had that same sensation of not being able to let go. But he'd helped her.

Later, she'd told him about her stepfather, and he'd believed her.

Then tonight he'd saved her.

And decided she was too much of a burden.

A click echoed in the room. Ana jerked her head up. What—?

The front door opened. She shot off the couch, her skin prickling. The terror drained once she recognized who was coming in. "Ethan." She didn't understand; he'd left, she'd heard the car drive away. "What are you doing in here? How?"

He lifted a key. "Master." He tossed it on the table and prowled toward her. "I'm sorry for being an ass tonight." He settled his hands on her face. "No job is as important as you are. The truth is, when I realized you were in trouble in the bathroom and that door was locked, I freaked the hell out. Something in me broke—I'd have killed anything that got between you and me."

"I don't…" She backed up, backing away from his touch. This wasn't real. She'd learned that lesson twice with him, and it had finally sunk in. Trapped between the couch and coffee table, she had nowhere to go. "Don't do this because you feel sorry for me. I'm fine."

His jaw flexed. "No, you're not. You were attacked by a crazy bastard and I blamed you. Yelled at you for not seeing him in the restaurant. Which, by the way, I should beat my own ass for that. I'm trained to spot trouble, and I didn't see him."

She didn't know what was happening here. "Okay. But it doesn't change anything. I need to go home. I know it was supposed to be just sex, but there's something wrong with me." She didn't want to tell him she was breaking inside. That she loved him so much it hurt to breathe. She'd been a fool, lying to herself and him. "I can't do this. I can't." She fisted her hands, then winced at the pain in her left one.

Ethan caught her hand, gently caressing her fingers. "Aside from your injuries from tonight, there's not a goddamned thing wrong with you. You're the bravest person I know. I'm the coward here, so afraid to admit that I'm in love with you. I kept telling you I was protecting you from my past, but it was me that was afraid to take a risk. But you? I rejected and hurt you once, and yet you tried again. That's brave."

She'd been desperate, not brave. Like she was too close to the edge of a cliff and had no one to catch her before she fell over.

Ethan went on, "You're my one good thing, and I was too fucking stupid to hold on to it and fight to keep you. Please, just stay a few more days, and I'll prove it to you. I'll talk to Hank—"

His boss? "For what?"

"I'll leave the job and help you get through this ordeal with Gregory. You're going to have to fly back here for depositions and trial if it goes that far. Or if he gets off by some fluke, I'll be there to protect you."

"Ethan, no." He was upset and feeling responsible for her. "You're making promises you don't mean."

"Let me take care of you for a few days, will you give me that?"

Say no. Just go home. Stop this now. "I can't."

He looked down. "Okay. I'll make the arrangements for tomorrow afternoon. I'll fly with you on Savaged Illusions's jet, then meet with Sloane. He's going to make sure you're safe if Gregory is released and allowed to leave. Right now, let's get you to bed."

He was giving her up that easily? He really hadn't meant it. "I don't need you to stay."

"Too bad. I'll sleep on the couch, but I'm staying." Before she could form a protest, he got her up into the loft, helped her change, and tucked her into the soft sheets and thick comforter. Her head was spinning from the adrenaline crash, vulnerability and the pain pill he'd coaxed her into swallowing.

"I'll be right downstairs. No one can get in without going through me. Go to sleep." He kissed her forehead.

She didn't want to be alone. This was her last night with the man she loved. *You're not making sense. One moment you can't be near him anymore, and the next, you can't let him go.* But right now, he was all she had to hold on to. "Will you sleep with me?"

The harsh lines of his face softened. He climbed into bed and pulled her against him.

Ethan's warmth surrounded her as the drugs kicked in, pulling her under.

"I'm right here, I won't leave you. You're safe, Ana."

How was she going to face the rest of her life without him?

* * * *

Ana stumbled down the stairs toward Ethan's voice. Who was he talking to?

"I want to meet with you alone first." Ethan stood in the small kitchenette, his shoulders tense as he held his cellphone to his ear.

Who did he want to meet with? *Siena?* Pain stabbed her chest and she hated herself for it. She knew how important the apprenticeship was to Ethan, yet she was jealous and wishing she could be that significant to him. But she wasn't. Her nose clogged and tears she couldn't shed burned her eyes. Her head ached.

Ana had been going to the coffeemaker, but she changed direction and went to the couch where she found her cellphone. After sitting, she unlocked the screen and stared in surprised. She had a dozen missed calls and texts.

"What's wrong?" Ethan moved up to sit on the coffee table directly in front of her. He grabbed a throw pillow, slid it beneath her injured hand, and arranged a cold pack over it.

She hadn't heard him finish his call. Had he just hung up? "My stepmom tried calling several times."

"News broke overnight that Roger Kendall's daughter was attacked in a restaurant bathroom. She probably heard and is worried. You need to call her."

"I will." She didn't want Linda upset.

"How's your hand?"

Beneath the ice and ace bandage, she gently flexed her fingers. "Little sore. It'll heal." She made herself look at him. *Tell him goodbye.* "It sounds like you have a meeting. I'll call Franci and Chelle—"

"Franci will be here in a few minutes," he cut her off. "I

didn't want you alone while I'm gone."

Surprised, she blurted out, "You talked to them?"

"Chelle caught me last night as she was rushing to the car to get to you. I begged her to stay at the house and let me take care of you." He swallowed. "I'd hoped you'd change your mind and stay. Give me another chance."

Elation sprang up in her chest, but Ana shut it down. Hadn't she lied to herself enough? She was always going to come in second, and if she got in the way of his career, he'd resent her. It'd be like this week with Siena pulling him one way and Ana the other. And which way did he go each time? Siena. Ana wasn't enough. "I can't." Everything hurt at letting him go, but it'd be worse later when he finally realized he just didn't love her enough. "I'm sorry. I—"

"Don't apologize. You gave me two chances. I have to prove myself to you before you ever give me another."

Prove himself? She didn't know what he meant by that.

"We'll fly home this afternoon on the band jet. It's all arranged. I'll make sure you're safe in San Diego."

"Gregory's in jail here. You don't have to do that."

He smiled sadly, and leaned forward to push a strand of her hair back. "I want to. Please, Ana."

Then he'd be able to walk away with a clean conscience. Ana loved him because he was this man who would go to all this trouble. But then he'd go on and become Siena's apprentice. "Okay."

His eyes burned into hers. "One more thing. I'm sorry I wasn't there, that you didn't think you could call me and I would come. It doesn't matter what I say now, you won't be able to believe me."

"There for what?" She couldn't keep up.

"When you found the lump. For all of it. I can't believe you didn't tell anyone."

Stunned, she drew back. "You know?"

"Chelle told me last night right after she ripped me a new one for being a jerk."

Now it made sense. Why he was so upset and gentle last night. Between the attack and finding out she'd had the little tiny cancer concern, he'd felt sorry for her. *Tell him it's fine, that you're fine*. Instead she blurted out, "I almost called you. The night before the biopsy, I couldn't sleep and sat there holding the phone opened to your number." She slapped her good hand over her mouth. What was wrong with her? "I shouldn't have told you that," she whispered, her voice thick and raw. She was making him feel worse.

Ethan slid his hands beneath her and lifted her into his arms. "Ana." His chest rattled against her cheek as if he drew in a ragged breath. "I fucking hate that you were alone."

She had to fix this. Fisting his T-shirt, she raised her head. "I'm very lucky. Not everyone gets good results. But coming here to you, this was wrong, Ethan. I was using you, trying to heal something broken inside me. But you can't do that, only I can. And this—we're hurting each other. I know you care, but you have dreams." She loved him enough to want him to be happy. "Go after them and be successful. You have a meeting with Siena, right?"

Something fierce flickered in his gaze. "Yes."

She scooted off his lap and grabbed her phone and ice pack off the floor. "I'll call Linda and then get my stuff together."

Ethan rose and went to the small dining table. He scooped up his wallet, phone and keys then looked her. "I get why you can't trust me, why you didn't call me when you were scared. You were afraid I'd let you down."

She opened her mouth, but he went on.

"Hush. Give Linda a chance, Ana. She loves you. Think about how you'd feel if she kept something like a breast cancer scare or a stalker from you. What if she was in trouble and didn't tell you?"

The realization hit her dead center. "I'd be upset." She was beginning to realize just how much she'd hurt her friends too. She should have made them listen, and they would have. "I'll call Linda. And apologize to Franci and Chelle."

Relief eased a fraction of the tension in his jaw. "I'll be back."

She clenched her sore hand, the physical pain better than the ripping sensation in her heart. He was going after his dream exactly as she'd told him to. Every step he took toward the door cut deeper. She managed to say, "Good luck."

Ethan paused at the door, his gaze locking with hers. Then he nodded once and vanished.

Ana sank down on the couch and stared at the phone in her hand. Desperation clogged her throat. She needed help and reached out to the one person who'd rescued her in the past.

As soon as Linda answered, Ana spilled out everything from the moment she found the lump to now in a torrent of words.

"Honey, why didn't you tell me?" Linda asked. "I'd have cancelled my trip. Nothing is as important as you. You're my daughter."

She couldn't breathe past the swelling in her chest. "Linda. I—"

The door opened, spilling in Franci. Her friend's dark gaze swept over her, saw the phone in her hand and she waved an acknowledgement that Ana was on a call.

"Honey," Linda went on in her ear. "If you need me, I'll get on a plane and be there as quickly as I can."

Give Linda a chance. Half her instincts screamed to assure her stepmom that she was fine. But she wasn't. A man she barely knew attacked her, and Ethan…oh God…he'd told her loved her and she was terrified to believe him. A merciless fist in her chest squeezed her heart. "I don't know what I'm doing anymore. I love him too much."

"Ethan?"

"Yes. He said he loves me, but how can I know?" Unbearable agony swelled in her throat. "I really messed this whole thing up." The words clawed her throat. "He's feeling guilty or some responsibility and—"

"Wrong," Franci interrupted, striding up to stand over her.

Ana jerked her head up. "Linda, hold on, Franci's here and telling me something about Ethan." She faced her friend. "What do you mean?"

"He told me outside before he left—he's meeting with Chef Siena to turn down the apprenticeship."

"Wait, what?" Ana shot up to her feet, unable to believe it.

Franci touched her shoulder. "He's hoping it'll convince you he'd choose you over anything else. Even his shot at being a chef."

No. That's what Ethan had meant that he'd prove it to her. She'd refused to believe him when he told her he loved her, so he was giving up his dream for her. Sick agony pounded in her chest. She clutched the phone. The need to get to him gripped her. "Linda, I have to go save Ethan from a huge mistake."

"I heard. I love you honey. I'm booking a flight home, I'll call you later."

Ana stopped halfway up the stairs. "I love you too, Linda. I called you today because I needed my mom. That's you."

"Damn right, and don't ever forget it again."

That made her smile despite the urgency beating at her to get to Ethan. "I won't."

* * * *

He'd let another woman come between him and Ana. That ended now. Siena might be able to give him a career, but Ana owned his heart. He didn't know if he could ever heal the damage he'd done to her trust. He'd finish the tour and pay off his debts, then go home to San Diego. He'd find a job and work hard to win Ana back no matter how long it took.

After parking, he headed into the building and straight to the conference room.

Siena waited by the window. "Why did you insist on this private meeting before signing the contract?" She strode to the table and slapped her hands down. "I'm not accustomed to demands from my apprentice. Before we do sign, you need to be clear, I expect you to be one hundred percent dedicated and passionate about the job. No distractions."

He stayed at the other end of the table. "Like Ana?"

"Exactly. I don't care if you're screwing random women, as long as they don't interfere with the job." Straightening up, she added, "You ever walk out of a meeting as you did last night, I'll fire you on the spot."

He narrowed his eyes and stayed silent. From a business perspective she had a point. But she'd been the one to arrange the reservations for him and Ana, making a big deal of reassuring Ana he'd be done by then. "You set it up to make me late or cancel."

"Damn right I did. From the second I met Ana at the party, I knew that girl was messing with your head. You have a huge future in front of you. The video tests showed you're amazing on camera. Your cooking is very good, though you need more experience, but that's something I can give you. You have a fresh, creative flair I'm looking for. But I won't accept you being distracted or telling me you have other commitments. For one year, you're mine. Choose—the girl or your career."

The ultimatum hung in the air. A week ago, cold dread would have filled him at the idea of failing to secure this apprenticeship. And this morning? "Thank you for the opportunity. I'm choosing—"

The door burst open. "Don't do it!"

Whipping around, he blinked in surprise. Ana stood there, her face flushed, hair wild, and wearing the dress from last night.

She rushed up to him and gripped his arm with her uninjured hand. "Don't. Franci told me what you're doing. Please, this chance means everything to you."

She'd come down here to stop him?

"Listen to her," Siena interrupted. "I'll open doors for you all over the world."

Yeah, she probably would. Ignoring Siena, he smiled down at Ana. His one good thing. "I don't want it. I want you."

"I'll wait. If you really want me, it's only a year. I'll wait."

The impact of her words sank in. Ethan was afraid to believe it. "You'll give me another chance?"

"Yes, but you don't have to give up this apprenticeship."

He pulled her against his side and turned to Siena. "I'm choosing Ana."

Ana stiffened. "Ethan, no!"

"Yes." He kissed her forehead. "I don't want to be away from you for another year. I'll get a job, I swear. I'll put in a call to Chef Zane to see if I can get a job as one of his line cooks. Or I can work for Sloane's security team, or another place. I'm going back to San Diego once the band's tour is over. I'm going to prove to you—"

"Touching." Siena cut him off. "But I wonder? Does Ana know all about you? I do. I had you investigated."

Ethan stilled, a vile taste slicking his tongue as a low drone of fury rumbled like distant thunder. He'd signed papers for a background check. Taking his arm from Ana, he faced the woman he'd once admired. "The steroid scandal is public knowledge."

"Yes it is. But this…" Siena picked up a dark gray folder, "…is not." She slid the folder across the table.

He raised an eyebrow, refusing to show a reaction, while his mind blared, *"Once a whore, always a whore."* Were there pictures in there? The idea of Ana seeing him that way, a kid servicing women, exploded in his head, nearly making him vomit. All his instincts screamed to grab that folder and destroy it.

But he didn't move a muscle. To win Ana's trust, he had to give her his. And that meant trusting her with his worst moments and biggest regrets.

"Go ahead." Siena gestured to the file. "Show your girlfriend the investigator's report. You were a—"

"Child." Ana snatched up the folder, waving it in front of her as she stalked to Siena. "I know Ethan's truth. And I know this— if there's one picture, even one so-called testimony of someone who abused that boy, I'll have you arrested and charged with trafficking child pornography. I'll ruin you in ways you haven't even thought of. So tell me, Chef Siena, should I look in this folder?"

Siena's eyes rounded, and she stepped back. "Are you threatening me?"

Ana smiled. "Consider it an ironclad guarantee. You can't imagine the misery I'll rain down on you if you release this stuff. And I won't stop there. I'll rip your world apart until I find who took any pictures or told any stories of child abuse. Those women were all adults hiring a child. I'll destroy them too."

Ethan couldn't tear his gaze from Ana. She all but stole the words from his mouth, but coming from her? Defending him? It was a thing of beauty and filled his throat with so much love, he grabbed the back of the chair to keep upright.

"It's just a report," Siena blurted out. "No…no pictures. I—"

"Ethan, check." Ana held out the folder to him. "Let's see if we have the chef dragged out of here in cuffs today or not."

She didn't want to look for herself? He took the folder and flipped through the three pages. "No pictures. Only rumors and bullshit." He couldn't even be relieved, there was no room with so much love and amazement filling every one of his cells. It finally hit him—his past was just that, his past.

But Ana was his future.

"We'll take that copy as insurance." Ana turned from her stare down with Siena and walked out.

Ethan faced Siena. "You want to come after me, bring it. But you try to fuck with Ana in any way, I'll destroy you before she gets to you." He strode out and caught up with Ana in the parking lot.

She had her uninjured hand pressed against the side of the car, leaning over, panting.

He set his hand on her sweaty back. "You okay?"

She looked up, her eyes fierce. "I almost killed her. I could actually visualize myself doing it—leaping over that table, grabbing her throat and slamming her head onto the table. I was so mad. You were a child, and she tried to use that to hurt you. I hate her."

He kept rubbing her back. Her reaction wasn't surprising given her past. Ana had run, but she never got to face down her abuser. Today she'd faced down a woman that represented the ones who'd abused Ethan. "I've never seen anyone as amazing as you were in there."

Sucking in another breath, she stood up and touched his chest. "What about you? I'm so sorry. I know that was your worst nightmare."

The concern in her eyes reached into his heart. "I thought it would be. But seeing you go all Rambo on her ass, standing there defending me, no one's done that." How did he tell her what that meant? "For the first time in my life, I didn't feel dirty."

"I'll defend you. Every time."

He believed her. "I have to ask you something though. You handed the folder to me. Why didn't you look for yourself?"

"I don't need to. You told me what happened, and I didn't know what was in there. If there were pictures, why would I need to see those?"

This was what love felt like—this clean acceptance. He'd never known how freeing it was. He stared into the eyes of the woman who'd stood up for him. "I'm in love with you, Ana. You're my brave, beautiful and bad girl. If you need more time, I'll wait. I'll spend years proving myself to you if that's what it takes. I love you too much to give up."

Her eyes filled with tears. "I don't cry. I never cry. I can't—"

"Yes you can." He pulled her against him, stroking her hair. He didn't care that they were out in a public parking lot and people might see or hear. Ana was his, and she'd been too perfect and alone for too damned long. "You're mine now, sunshine. Let go, baby. You can always let go with me."

He held her close, the gift of Ana's love and trust seeping in to heal his heart. Once he was nothing more than a commodity to women, but to Ana?

He was the man she loved enough to defend, fight with, surrender to and trust with her most vulnerable moments.

Once Ana had been his one good thing, but now? She was his everything.

Chapter 11

One Month Later:

"Are you really okay with the plea deal?"

Ana shifted in the passenger seat of the car to look at Ethan. She'd returned to Florida to meet with the District Attorney's office regarding the case against Gregory. Refusing to let her handle this alone, Ethan had flown in first, picked her up from the airport and went with her to the meeting where they'd learned the DA was offering a plea deal to Gregory for probation and mandatory treatment to be served in California. "I'm glad it's over, so yeah. Gregory's family lives in Los Angeles. He'll be settling there, and that's three hours away from us, depending on traffic."

Us. Ethan had been on the road for the last few weeks, but she flew out for long weekends with him. Next week he'd be coming home for good.

"How about you? Are you excited to start working for Chef Zane at Stilts?" Zane had offered Ethan a position as his apprentice. It would be long hours and hard work, but Ana was delighted for him.

"I can't wait. I like this job, and it's taught me a lot. But cooking is what I love." He took her hand. "Not as much as I love you, though."

She knew that. True to his word, Ethan had flown home to San Diego with her after her vacation ended last month, stayed a couple nights until Linda got home from Italy and demanded Ana stay with her a few nights. Turns out the two of them had anticipated Ana would have some nightmares in reaction to her attack, and they were right. Franci and Chelle were there too, along with Kat and Sloane.

She opened her mouth to tell him how much she loved him when he pulled up to a gate. "Bayside Manor? But I made reservations at the Marriott."

"I cancelled them and changed our plans."

"But..." Why was she surprised? Ethan had powerful friends. He just so rarely used them, and when he did, well it was almost always for her.

Ethan guided the car through the gates. "No one else is here at the manor, no staff or security, just us for the night." He turned off the main road that led to the house.

Ana recognized where they were headed and her heart started to thump. Her pulse jumped. "We're going to the casita."

"Yep. I made you a promise of capturing you, holding you down and taking you so hard you'd never again doubt who you belong to. I didn't make good on it, and that's unacceptable. I don't break my promises to you, ever. So I hijacked your cute little romantic night of dinner and sex for this, Operation Savaged Surrender."

Ana took off her seat belt, went up on her knees and braced a hand on his shoulder. "You did this for me?"

"For us." His blue eyes burned with intense love, filling Ana. "When I promise you something, it will happen. You can count on that."

She realized that now. "Why Savaged Surrender?"

His mouth tilted up. "Because we're giving in to our savage sides and surrendering to each other. Totally surrendering, even me. What's the one thing you've been asking me for?"

Hot excitement shuddered between her legs. "Bare. I want your cock inside me without a condom." In the beginning, she'd wanted a condom in addition to her birth control as another layer of protection. In the last month, Ethan had shown her a love that was about true trust. If her birth control failed, the two of them would handle it together. But it went deeper for Ethan—taking her bare, especially in forced seduction, meant she accepted all of him, including his past.

"When I catch you tonight, you're mine. You're going to get all of me, sunshine, right down to my unsheathed cock."

His trust wrenched her heart and ignited her desire. Both of them were letting go on the deepest, most intimate levels. Ethan had feared his past while Ana had feared her inner bad girl. Tonight, they would truly surrender the last of their fears to an all-consuming love. Ana took his face in her hands. "I'll run and fight. You so sure you can catch and tame me?"

One of his hands curled around her hip. "I'll always catch you, but I never want to tame you. I love you exactly as you are."

Had anyone ever loved her this way? Before they lost themselves in this moment, she wanted to tell him how she felt. "For years, I got it in my head that people would leave me if I was bad."

Ethan closed his eyes for a second, then opened them with so much love it floored her. "You're not bad, sunshine."

"But I'm human. I just didn't realize people would love me even if I wasn't perfect. You gave me that. You showed me that I could relax and be myself, and you'd still love me."

"Every damned day." His fingers glided over her cheek in a reassuring touch, but one that sank into with her the knowledge that this was what love felt like. Safe and free to be herself.

"You're the strongest man I know. You survived a life I can't even bear to think about to become the man who is my friend and lover." She kissed him and added, "I love you."

"I love you too. So much." His jaw hardened, and a wicked gleam flashed in his eyes. "You have five seconds. Run."

A sense of freedom and joy exploded through her, propelling her out the car door and running full bore. It didn't matter how tonight played out.

She'd already won because she had Ethan.

About Jennifer Lyon

Jennifer Lyon is the pseudonym for USA Today Bestselling Author Jennifer Apodaca. Jen lives in Southern California where she continually plots ways to convince her husband that they should get a dog. After all, they met at the dog pound, fell in love, married and had three wonderful sons. So far, however, she has failed in her doggy endeavor. She consoles herself by pouring her passion into writing books. To date, Jen has published more than fifteen books and novellas, including a fun and sexy mystery series and a variety of contemporary romances under the name **Jennifer Apodaca**. As Jennifer Lyon she created a dark, sizzling paranormal series, and *The Plus Once Chronicles*, an emotionally sensual adult contemporary series. Jen's won numerous awards and had her books translated into multiple languages, but she still hasn't come up with a way to persuade her husband that they need a dog.

Find out more about her at http://jenniferlyonbooks.com/meet-jen/

Also from Jennifer Lyon

The Plus One Chronicles Trilogy
The Proposition (Book #1)
Possession (Book #2)
Obsession (Book #3)
The Plus One Chronicles Boxed Set

The Wing Slayer Hunter Series
Blood Magic (Book #1)
Soul Magic (Book #2)
Night Magic (Book #3)
Sinful Magic (Book #4)
Forbidden Magic (Book #4.5 a novella)
Caged Magic (Book #5)

Writing As Jennifer Apodaca

Once A Marine Series
The Baby Bargain (Book #1)
Her Temporary Hero (Book #2)
Exposing The Heiress (Book #3)

JUMPSTART
A Crossroads Novella
By Riley Hart

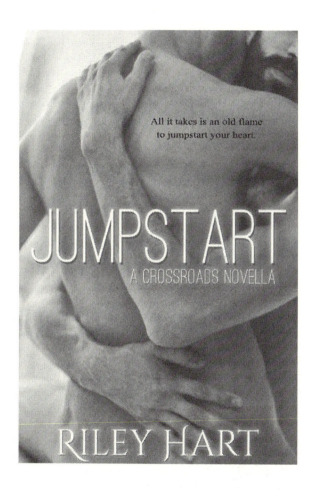

All it takes is an old flame
to jumpstart your heart.

JUMPSTART
A CROSSROADS NOVELLA

RILEY HART

Special Thanks

Special thanks to my husband for making me fall in love with motocross. I never thought I would enjoy it like I do. It's even more special since I get to share it with you. And hey, I made you a trainer!

Acknowledgements

First and foremost I want to thank my readers. Thank you for the support, for the love you have shown the Crossroads men, as well as all my other guys. I am thankful for you every day.

Thanks to Jessica and Hope from Flat Earth Editing. Also, to Judy's Proofreading. My books wouldn't be what they are without you.

I'd like to thank Christina Lee, Heather and Wendy for reading early versions of Beckett and Christian's story.

I'd like to thank everyone from 1001 Dark Nights for including Jumpstart in one of your bundles. I'm honored to be part of such an incredible, supportive program.

Last but not least, thank you to Riley's Rebels and The M/M Daily Grind. You guys make my days brighter.

Chapter One

"Supercross Champion Beckett Monroe is Gay!"

Beck looked at the news article from his phone and groaned. "I'm bi, you dickheads," he whispered softly.

"Excuse me?" the older woman in the first class seat beside him asked. She looked up at him sweetly like the grandmother from a fairy tale who was sugar and spice and everything nice, and here he was calling people dickheads.

"Nothing. Sorry." He didn't add anything else. He was no doubt a bear to be around and the woman didn't deserve his surly attitude, but he couldn't help it. He was pissed.

He'd known news would break today—known shit that shouldn't be headlines would be—but knowing ahead of time didn't edge his anger. Part of it was his own damn fault. He knew it was. If he'd been honest about himself from the start, there wouldn't be headlines right now.

Actually, that was just him lying to himself. There would have been headlines when he'd come out and headlines after. The world was shitty like that. He didn't believe anyone should *have* to declare their sexuality if they weren't straight, but the fact was, they did, he hadn't and now there was a shitstorm of publicity because god forbid a motocross star liked dick.

And he did. He liked dick a lot.

He'd also been ready to let the world know who he was because he was tired, so fucking tired of keeping that part of himself a secret. It's the reason he'd gone to the gay bar that night when everyone was in town for the race. It's why he'd given his name when people asked. It's why he'd let it slip in mixed-company what he was in town for. He hadn't given a shit anymore.

Still, it pissed him off that every major motocross magazine treated his sex life like it was important to anyone but himself and whoever he was with. The world had a whole hell of a lot more important things to talk about than who he happened to be fucking at the moment.

He glanced at the article again before exiting the screen and powering down his phone as he waited for the plane to take off.

As soon as they began taxiing down the runway he closed his eyes, hoping to take a nap and get his mind off everything. Not just the headline and his family's reaction but also his career that, despite his wins, hadn't felt right for a while now.

His eyes were only closed a moment when he felt a light tap on his shoulder. *Damn it.* He tried not to groan before opening his eyes to look at the woman beside him.

She gave him that sweet smile again, making it hard to be frustrated with her.

"I don't understand it." She shook her head before nodding at his phone, making his hackles immediately rise. Of course she'd seen what he'd been looking at, and of course she had to tell him her opinion about his life. Why should he believe otherwise? The universe obviously wasn't very happy with him right now.

"With all due respect, ma'am, there's nothing to understand. I'm not expected to understand why you're straight so why should you have to understand why I'm bisexual?" *With a heavy lean toward men.*

Her smile was different this time—full of mischief as her eyes sparkled. "Well, that's not very progressive of you. If straight shouldn't be the default, why do you assume I'm straight?"

Okay...well, she had him there. Who the hell was this lady? She had to be at least seventy-five years old. It showed in the wrinkles on her face and the tremor in her hands, but he had a feeling she could give anyone a run for their money. He had to bite back his smile. "You're right. I apologize. What don't you understand, then?"

"Why it matters. Why we have to have headlines like that. The world is a funny place, isn't it?"

"You can say that again." Beckett blew out a deep, frustrated breath.

"Margaret Edwards," she told him.

"Beckett Monroe, ma'am."

"So tell me about yourself, Mr. Beckett Monroe." As nice as she was, Beckett wasn't really in the mood to talk right now. He felt like that's all he'd done recently—talk to his parents on the phone, talk to his sponsors, his team. Right now, he just wanted to *be*.

The plane rocked, the familiar feel of turbulence shaking them. Margaret's trembling hand shot out and grabbed his wrist. She closed her eyes, took a couple deep breaths and when the turbulence stopped, she looked at him again. "Sorry about that. I hate flying. I lost the love of my life in a small plane crash."

His heart ached for her, and it made him wonder where the hell the rest of her family was. They shouldn't leave her to fly alone.

When the plane bounced again, Margaret clutched him a second time as the pilot spoke on the overhead about keeping seatbelts on and the ride being a bumpy one. Beckett opened his mouth and said, "Well...I'm a professional motocross racer, but I guess you know that already."

The distraction seemed to work. Margaret winked at him and said, "A *gay* motocross racer."

"Actually, I'm bisexual, but yes."

"And you have a broken heart," she whispered.

"Huh?" He shook his head. "I don't have a broken heart." He was angry, confused. Tired of talking about his sexuality, tired of explaining himself to his family and friends. Frustrated over the passion he'd felt in the dirt being dimmed the past year or so. Dirt bikes had always been his life. He didn't understand why the same adrenaline didn't pump through his veins when he rode or why flying over jumps didn't feel the same.

"Sure you do. People with broken hearts always recognize each other."

Her words slammed into his chest. Beckett looked at her, opened his mouth then closed it again, not sure what to say. He didn't have a broken heart—not after all these years. "I don't...I'm not..."

The plane bumped around in the air again, this time worse

than the other two. Margaret sucked in a sharp breath and it was Beckett who reached for Margaret's hand.

She squeezed his hand, closed her eyes, and he let her hold him. He tightened his grip and before he knew it, he found himself saying, "I don't have a broken heart." He didn't really have the right, considering it was his fault they weren't together—or at least his fault that they hadn't tried. "But there was someone…a long time ago. He was never really mine though, and I'm the one who ruined it." He shook his head, tightening his grip on Margaret's hand. "We haven't seen each other in years. It was over a long time ago."

He shifted, uncomfortable with the conversation.

"What does time have to do with anything?" she asked and Beckett didn't have an answer for her. But the truth was, he still thought about him. He still missed their friendship.

"What's his name?" Margaret asked.

"Christian."

"And what happened between you?"

"I hurt him," Beckett said truthfully. "I didn't stand by him the way I should have and then I cut contact with him."

He would always regret that. No matter what, they'd been friends and friends didn't treat people the way Beckett had treated Christian.

Beckett cleared his throat, sat up straighter. "What about you?"

Margaret rolled her eyes at him. "I'm boring. You're the bisexual dirt bike racer, let's talk about you."

He couldn't help but chuckle at that…and he also couldn't help but talk. He told her about riding, about getting his first used bike at four and falling in love. About everything his family had sacrificed for him to ride, for him to go pro. They hadn't had the money and his parents had worked hard for Beckett's dream to come true.

He even spoke a little about Christian—how they'd been best friends all their lives and all the trouble they used to get into together.

Before he knew it, the plane was landing in Norfolk, Virginia, where he would get his rental car and drive out of the city to where his friend Landon lived. They'd met in Florida. Landon was a motorcycle mechanic who had done some unofficial work on one of Beckett's bikes.

Landon had moved back to where he was raised when his sister got married. He worked in a shop and had gone and fallen in love with a man who ran an adult novelty store. Beckett hadn't met Landon's partner, but he knew his friend was happy. He couldn't wait to spend some time here and to unwind.

As they waited to deplane, Beckett couldn't help but watch Margaret. She had only her small purse with her. He wanted to know what she was doing here. If she was coming home or leaving.

Going off instinct, he grabbed a napkin and asked, "Do you have a pen?"

Margaret retrieved one from her purse. He took the pen, wrote his phone number on the napkin and handed both to her. "I know this is a little strange, but…I just want you to have this, in case you ever need anything. Please, don't hesitate to call."

Margaret's eyes became slightly watery. "Thank you." She took the napkin from him. As the people in front of them began to deplane, she added, "Being alone is no fun, Beckett Monroe. You fix that broken heart of yours, okay?"

He nodded and then Margaret stepped into the aisle and walked away. He wanted to. He really did. The only thing was, he didn't know how to fix it. He didn't know what was wrong with him or how to make himself feel whole again.

* * * *

"Supercross Champion Beckett Monroe is Gay!"

Christian Foster read the same headline three times. He tossed the magazine to the table and whispered, "He's bi, you dumb shits," before he immediately leaned forward and picked it up again. He had to check out the full article. There was no way he couldn't read the whole damn thing. Beck was the reason he had a fucking subscription to *Motocross Today* in the first place. He'd never been into bikes quite as much as Beck was. Sure, he'd enjoyed riding when they were kids. It was a rush in a lot of ways but in others he'd done it because that's what Beck was always doing and they'd been best friends their whole childhood. Where

Beck was, Christian wanted to be.

Or at least he used to always want to be where Beck was. That was a long time ago.

Christian read the article detailing Beckett's night at a gay bar, that and the blurry pictures of him kissing a man outside made his gut twist uncomfortably. Jesus, it read like a soap opera or something. It wasn't as though the magazine never ran personal stories about riders, just usually nothing like this.

No one else outside the moto world would know—or give a damn. This was a first for the community though, and as much as he didn't want to, he couldn't help but wonder how Beck was dealing with it…how his team and sponsors were dealing with it. Then he wanted to burn the fucking magazine because it shouldn't matter. There shouldn't *be* anything to deal with.

Beck's family was a different story. They loved him. There was no doubt about that. Christian didn't think they would do anything foolish…but Christian remembered how awkward things had been when he'd come out—or been dragged out—before he was ready by a stupid letter written in teenage angst about loving another boy. It had been a shock to his parents and Beck's as well. Since they were so close, the first question had of course been…is this about Beckett?

They'd assured their families that it wasn't even though it really fucking was *and* had been mutual. Beck had continued his career and left for training—Christian had come to California for college; he and Beckett had stopped speaking.

"Fuck." Christian dropped back against the couch and groaned. It had been a long time since he'd let Beck in his head like this and he didn't like it. He could always call his mom to ask if she'd spoken to Beck's parents…. "No. I'm out of my damn mind."

"Talking to yourself is one of the signs." Quinn walked out of Christian's room wearing nothing but a pair of underwear. "Are you coming back to bed?" he asked.

He probably should. He needed the rest, but he shook his head and held up the magazine. "He's out. I'm not sure how it really happened, but he's out." It wasn't as though most motocross riders were recognized on the streets like other sports stars—that's why he didn't understand how this had even happened.

Quinn sighed, walked over, and fell on the couch beside him. "Your teenage crush-slash-love of your life who likes to play in the dirt?"

Christian couldn't help but chuckle. "Yes." He sighed and dropped his head on Quinn's shoulder. He'd been Christian's first friend when he moved to California. They'd met in college and he helped Christian acclimate to life here. They were close. The only person Christian had ever been closer to was Beckett, but there had never been anything other than friendship between him and Quinn. Most people didn't believe that, but it was true.

"You sound sad, boo."

Christian rolled his eyes. He was going to fucking kill Quinn. "Don't call me boo."

"Would you prefer bae? I don't quite get that one but I'd be willing to use it for you."

He knew Quinn was just trying to make him laugh, but he couldn't. He felt ridiculous that after all these years, Beckett's life still had an effect on him. It wasn't that he was in love with Beck anymore but…"It's hard to explain. Until I was eighteen years old, every major event that happened in my life—hell, most of the minor ones too—involved him in some way. Then I realized I was gay and had feelings for him and I was scared out of my damn mind. I did everything I could to hide it from Beckett and everyone else."

"And then things changed between you and he was part of you accepting who you were and then he broke your heart. It makes sense that Beckett finally being public about who he is would make you think some thoughts."

Again, Christian chuckled. "Think some thoughts, huh?"

"You know what I mean. I'm tired. You and your damn insomnia."

Quinn was right. He just needed to go back to bed and quit thinking about Beckett Monroe. He'd done fine without him for ten years. "Come on. Let's go."

But Quinn didn't get up. He set a hand on Christian's thigh and squeezed it. "You know you can always call him. Or hell, go see him. It's not as if you can't take the time off. You deserve a vacation, as hard as you've been working, and it *is* understandable that he might be struggling a bit. If he wasn't ready to come out, then that article can't be a good thing. There's nothing wrong with being there for an old friend."

Again, Christian didn't understand it. How something like that could have happened. Still, what was he supposed to do? Track Beckett's phone number down through their parents? Beckett hadn't needed Christian in a long time and he sure as hell didn't need him now.

Chapter Two

Beckett had gotten into town late last night. He'd rented a car so he wouldn't have to depend on Landon to help him get around. He would no doubt be busy with his partner, Rod, and working at the motorcycle shop—which was where Beckett was headed now. They'd decided to meet there and then grab lunch together. He was excited to see his friend. It had been too long since they'd hung out.

Landon had always loved bikes the way Beckett did, and nestled deep inside him was the hope that spending time with him would remind Beckett why he'd always lived and breathed being on two wheels. It was different than talking shop with his trainer or his crew. Landon was a personal friend. They were both bisexual men. He knew Landon on a different level than the guys he rode with—even though he did love the hell out of them. It was just a different kind of love.

The GPS on his phone told him where to go as he made his way to the shop Landon worked at. It was about forty-five minutes from him.

When he pulled up in front of the white building with the stalls open and filled with bikes, he saw Landon standing outside. As he put the car into park and got out, Landon pushed off the wall. They met in front of the vehicle and he immediately pulled Landon into a hug. "It's good to see you, man," he said.

Landon squeezed him back. "I heard what happened. You okay?"

Beckett pulled away and nodded. "Yeah...yeah I am. We'll talk about it over lunch." Sure, things were awkward. He had a lot on his mind. He didn't know what the fuck he was doing. But he was okay.

"Let's get out of here then," Landon told him. "My buddy Bryce—he owns the shop—isn't in today. He's going to lose his mind that he missed you. He nearly had an orgasm when I told him I know you." Landon laughed as they climbed into the car.

Even after all these years it was a strange feeling to have someone excited to meet him. To have someone want his autograph. "It's so odd."

"I know. I told him you're probably the biggest dork I know, but he just mumbled Monster Energy Cup and Supercross champion."

Beckett playfully rolled his eyes. He was damn proud of everything he'd accomplished. He'd never expected it. He'd grown up dirt poor. His parents had sacrificed a lot for his career—taking him to races, extra hours at work to buy him bikes. He'd gone pro as a teenager and it hadn't been easy. To think about how far he'd come...it blew him away sometimes but then, why did he feel such emptiness inside? Why did it keep growing inside him like some kind of fucking cancer or something?

He didn't understand it.

"Eh, I'm nothing special, but I'd love to hang out with him sometime. I want to meet your friends and that man of yours. Holy fuck. I never thought I'd see the day you'd settle down."

"I never thought I'd see the day either. He snuck up on me, that's for sure. Rod's fucking crazy and I love it. He makes me laugh like no one I've ever known." Landon was still smiling to himself as he gave directions to the diner down the road.

Beckett could hear the love in Landon's voice and he felt a small twinge of jealousy in his chest. *Huh. That was odd.* "I'm happy for you."

He drove them to the diner. It was an old fashioned, yellow building that looked like it came from the fifties. He was comfortable in places like this because he'd grown up in a small town in Georgia that was full of them.

It was pretty slow inside. They were seated, had their sweet teas and ordered before Landon said, "You were tired of hiding, weren't you?"

He leaned back in the matching yellow booth and gave a

simple nod. It was more than that, though. Since he was bi, there was a part of him that had always told himself when he was ready to settle down, he'd eventually be able to do so with a woman he loved. But then the older he got, the less women he dated or slept with until he knew it would never happen. It hadn't been a conscious decision, he didn't think, or at least he just didn't want to admit it. Still, he'd never really seen himself coming out. The whole thing was just so fucking odd to him, having to declare to people who he found attractive and what he wanted.

"I'm not sure what's going on with me."

"You were tired of living a lie," Landon told him.

"True," but…"it's not only that. I just feel…off. I've never loved anything the way I love moto. You know that, Landon—and I still do. Jesus, there's nothing like being out there in the dirt but on the other hand, it's—fuck, I don't know." He ran a hand through his dark hair as he struggled to put into words something that he didn't understand. "I guess it feels lonely lately and I don't know why." Which he was aware sounded all sorts of fucked up. Motocross was a one-man sport but it had never made him feel alone before. That's why he hadn't ridden as well this Supercross season. It had to be. He'd won the championship last year. This year, he was third in points. It had just suddenly stopped feeling the same.

Landon opened his mouth to respond, just as the waitress brought their food over. They'd each gotten a burger and fries. She asked if they needed anything else and when they said no, she left them alone again.

"That's because there comes a time when it's not enough. Whether it's bikes, art, fucking cross-country skiing, I don't know. Whatever it is that you love, eventually you need *more*. That doesn't mean you don't love it. It just means you're ready to let yourself love more than just that thing. Congratulations Beckett Monroe, you're all grown up now."

Landon winked at him and Beckett couldn't help but let out a laugh.

Whatever it is that you love, eventually you need more. That doesn't mean you don't love it. It just means you're ready to let yourself love more than just that thing.

He had a feeling his friend was right.

* * * *

"Your cell is ringing," Quinn called from the living room. Christian stood at the bathroom sink, towel wrapped around his waist, shaving. Quinn didn't live with him, but he might as well with all the time he spent at Christian's place.

"Grab it for me and tell whoever it is I'll call back." He ran the blade down his jaw again before rinsing it and then tossing water on his face and wiping the shaving cream away.

It was less than half a minute later when Quinn rushed into the bathroom holding his phone out to him as though he'd just received a call that he won the lottery or something.

"Who is it?" Christian asked and turned off the water.

Quinn looked at him with soft brown eyes and somehow he knew, *fucking knew* that it was Beckett. That the man was calling him for the first time in ten years. He felt ridiculous when his pulse sped up. But then...this wasn't about him. If Beckett was calling, it was because something was wrong. Quinn had no doubt been right that Beck was struggling.

"*Fuck*," he cursed softly before taking the phone from his friend. Quinn winked at him before he walked out of the room, giving Christian privacy. "Hello?" he said into the phone as he made his way to his bed and sat down.

There was a pause. He heard Beck breathe and then..."Hey. Sorry. I didn't mean to interrupt. Jesus, this is fucking awkward and a really bad idea. I don't know what in the hell I'm doing."

"I heard," Christian said before he could hang up.

"Small town gossip back home? I'm sure the news made it through the grapevine and back to your family. They're definitely putting second thoughts into all those sleepovers we used to have when we were kids."

And there was Christian's stupid letter. He didn't bring that up, though.

"Nah, they've become surprisingly progressive since getting used to having a gay son. They don't pay attention to childish gossip. I have a subscription to Motocross Today," he admitted.

It surprised him that after all these years, he could notice the amusement in Beck's voice when he said, "Do you, now? That's interesting."

"I've always enjoyed the sport. If you remember, I used to ride with you quite often." There was an elephant on the line with them they were both obviously trying to ignore. They were doing a decent job until Beck spoke again.

"I remember, Chris. I remember everything."

Yeah...yeah, Christian remembered too.

"I don't know why I called," he confessed. "I thought maybe my mom had given me the wrong number when your boyfriend or whoever that was answered. She had to call your parents for the number. I suddenly feel like I'm in a romantic comedy. Or, you know, twelve or something."

Christian didn't correct the boyfriend comment. He gave a soft chuckle at what Beck had said and replied, "His name is Quinn. I was shaving and my phone was in the living room with him. It's fine that you called, though. How you doing, Beck?"

"I'm good."

Christian blew out a breath.

"No, I really am. It was time...past time, honestly. I have two weeks before the outdoor season starts. I'm in Virginia, of all places." He gave Christian the name of the town and then they both went silent. So he'd taken a break between Supercross and Motocross seasons. That made sense. Christian wasn't sure what else to say, and it was Beckett who continued the conversation. "Just getting some much needed R&R and thought—hell, I don't know what I thought. That maybe I should call my childhood best friend who I haven't spoken to in ten years, for absolutely no reason. That wouldn't be awkward at all."

Christian let out another laugh. Beck had always been good at making him smile.

"Now that I've made myself look like an idiot for shits and giggles, I should let you go."

"It's okay," Christian told him. "I'm pretty sure we've both looked like idiots around each other too many times to count. Ugh. Remember the first time I got drunk and I fell asleep in my own vomit? We'd snuck into my house and I got sick and my mom came in and saw me in the morning. You told her you'd gotten a stomach ache and thrown up on me. Why did you do that anyway? It would have been just as believable that I'd thrown up on myself."

"I choked! I just knew she was going to take one look at me, know I'd been drunk and call my parents."

They'd been ridiculous. That was one of many stories Christian remembered. "You never had a real good poker face, did you?" Beckett was a terrible liar. All it took was one look at him to know when he was being dishonest.

"Not about most things," he acknowledged. They both knew the one thing he had been really good at lying about. "I should let you go," he said again.

"Are you sure you're okay, Beck?" He couldn't keep himself from asking again; he knew to the marrow of his bones that something wasn't right.

"I'm good. I'm twenty-eight years old. It shouldn't have taken me this long."

But there was more, there was more and Christian knew it but he wouldn't push. It wasn't his place. "Call anytime, all right? It was good talking to you."

Beckett breathed into the line a couple moments before he said, "It was good talking to you too, Chris." He hung up the phone. Christian tossed his cell to the bed just as Quinn came in.

"It was good talking to you? That's all you had to say?"

Christian threw a pillow at his head, which Quinn dodged. "Nosy bastard."

"I like to call it being a good friend." He flopped down on the bed beside Christian. "That didn't go anything like it does in the movies."

"You're insane. And what movies are you watching? All LGBT movies end without a happily ever after." Not that he was looking for that with Beck. It had been too many years for that.

"You're right. That needs to change."

"Very true." Christian sighed. "That was odd. I never expected Beck to call. Never in a million years." He'd sounded...different. Not just because it had been ten years but as though there was too much weight on each of his words. As though he was tired.

"You're familiar to him. Sometimes we just need something or someone who makes us feel safe."

He rolled his eyes and pushed to his feet. "I am not what

Beckett Monroe needs. As long as he has a four-stroke bike and open space, he's okay."

"Can't talk to a bike."

"As long as he can ride, he's good."

"Then you're a two-fer! He can ride you *and* talk to you!"

He wished there was another pillow nearby that he could throw at Quinn. But the truth was, Quinn was right. He thought Beck did need something familiar. If not, he wouldn't have called.

Christian sighed. "Fuck. *Fuck, fuck, fuck, fuck, fuck.*"

"That's my boy." Quinn stood, knowing Christian all too well. "Go get dressed."

Without another word, Christian headed back to the bathroom to do just that.

Chapter Three

Beckett sat on the back deck of the house he'd rented. It was a small, two-bedroom cabin with a fireplace that was too warm to use, nestled between trees that kept the property shaded.

The humidity wasn't as bad as it was in Florida. He was used to it, having lived in humid environments most of his life. It was a plus when he raced this direction because not all riders did well in humid conditions.

He had his eyes closed as he relaxed into the porch chair. There was a cooler on the deck with him, a cold beer beside him and nothing but birds chirping and the sound of nature around him.

He needed this. He needed it badly.

When his cell rang on his lap, Beckett tensed. He wasn't even one beer in yet and didn't want to deal with anyone. It was likely his mom again...or one of his sponsors...or someone from his team....Jesus, he should just throw the fucking phone into the woods. But when it rang again he forced himself to open his eyes and pick it up. He frowned when he saw Christian's name on the screen. He'd saved his number when they spoke earlier that day.

His gut twisted as he remembered the completely ridiculous phone call. He'd felt like a sixteen-year-old calling his crush. Still, he swiped his finger across the screen and said with forced confidence, "Your turn to take a walk down memory lane?"

"Eh, more like my turn to embarrass myself because I have no fucking clue what I'm doing, why, or how you'll feel about it. I have a layover in Dallas. My plane lands in Norfolk at ten fifteen tonight. Can you pick me up?"

Beckett's pulse raced, that same feeling he got when his bike accelerated as he fought for the holeshot. He loved getting the strongest start, but the best finish was even more important. He leaned forward in the chair, thinking he must not have heard Christian right. "Excuse me?"

"You know what I said, Beck. Is this a good idea or a shitty one?"

Honestly...? "I don't know."

"Yeah...yeah, I feel the same," Christian replied.

"But I want to see you." His gut coiled tight at the thought—both nerves and excitement fueling him. It had been a long time since he saw Christian—too long.

Christian went quiet for a moment and Beckett wondered what he was thinking. Wondered why in the fuck he was coming. At the same time, he couldn't help being glad his old friend was visiting.

"Most people do," he finally replied, making a smile tug at Beckett's lips.

"Cocky motherfucker." He'd been the same way when they were kids, but playfully. He hadn't always been that way with Beckett though, because Christian had known he could be himself with him the same way Beckett didn't have to build himself up with bravado around Christian. They teasingly competed but it was all in fun between the two of them.

"I learned from the best."

"Pfft." Beckett rolled his eyes. "Don't blame me. That was all you."

The tight twist in his stomach began to unwind. It felt good talking to Christian. Even in just the few minutes they were on the line together he found himself wishing he hadn't lost this—hadn't lost his friend.

"Will you come?" Christian asked, some of the seriousness back in his hoarse voice.

"Yeah. Of course." He had to know that, right? Had to know that Beckett would want to see him and that Beckett would go get him...but then, maybe he didn't know. It wasn't as if he hadn't left Christian hanging once before, though he'd spent the last ten years regretting it.

After Christian told him the airline, they got off the phone. It wasn't until he leaned back in his chair again that he remembered the man who'd answered Christian's cell earlier. He wondered who they were to each other, if he had a right to have a say in Christian coming here or not, if he'd ever been serious about someone or if he was now. Did he like California? It was a whole hell of a lot different from where they'd grown up.

There were so many things he didn't know about his old friend and it was his own damn fault.

* * * *

Okay…so this might be a little weird. Jumping on a plane to go see a friend he hadn't spoken to in ten years, and who he'd had a not-so-pleasant last meeting with, wasn't something Christian did every day. For the hundredth time since Quinn dropped him off at LAX he wondered what he was doing. Yes, Beck sounded off-kilter during their first phone call and yes the thing that Beck had feared happening when they were kids had recently occurred in his life but the truth was, that had nothing to do with Christian. Not anymore. What did he expect? To come here and save the day? To show Beck that he might not be a Supercross champion but that he'd made a good life for himself? That he was happy? As much as he hated to admit it, that likely had something to do with it.

That, and the truth was, he'd likely always come if he thought Beck needed him. That's what friends did for each other, or at least that's the way Christian saw it. Despite the time that had passed, he couldn't turn off the part of him that considered Beck one of the most important people in his life. He wasn't sure if that made him a saint or someone who really needed to get over the past.

The Norfolk airport was rather small. Christian had to grab his checked bag, but it wasn't long until he stepped outside the glass doors just as a blue SUV pulled up. Before he saw the driver, he knew it was Beck.

A strange discomfort settled at the base of his spine, making him tense.

The passenger-side window rolled down. His dark hair was only a couple inches long. He had a matching beard that hid the jawline Christian had always enjoyed looking at. He gave Christian a smile but it didn't reach his eyes. Still, there were small wrinkles around them that hadn't been there before—smile lines from the years of laughs he'd had that Christian hadn't been a part of.

A melancholy sort of heaviness weighed him down because he'd never seen that happening between them. Yes, it had been ten years and he knew that but seeing Beck again in person made it all the more real.

As if he could sense something was wrong, he cocked his head slightly. Was he thinking the same thing? Did he have any regrets? Christian didn't really think he could. All of Beck's dreams had come true.

He fought to shake those thoughts from his head as he walked the short distance from where he stood to the vehicle. He opened the back door, tossed his bags in and then climbed into the front. "You look old," he teased and Beck barked out a rough laugh.

"Fuck you. I'm tired. It's been a long week." He eyed Christian up and down. Christian's light brown hair was shorter than it used to be. He was clean-shaven, wearing a polo shirt and jeans. *Did Beckett think he looked different?*

"You're very polished. Los Angeles took the *good ole boy* out of you, didn't it?"

"That shit was exorcised out of me a long time ago." It wasn't that he didn't love where he came from. He did. Christian hadn't had a bad childhood—he'd had a pretty fucking good one—but he'd also never felt like he fit in. "That likely started the first time I jacked off to a picture of a boy in a magazine, though."

He clicked his seatbelt into place, but Beckett didn't pull away from the curb. Christian knew he should turn and look at him. Knew they should say something important. There wasn't a part of him that doubted that Beck's eyes were on him right now. It wasn't until Beckett whispered a soft, "I can't believe you're here," almost as if he really didn't believe it, almost as if he thought Christian might disappear. That's what made him turn to look at him.

Christian fought the urge to tell Beck he wanted to make sure he was okay. Fought the urge to say it hadn't felt right not to come because why in the hell should it matter if he was here or not? Instead he just grinned and tried to play it off. "Where in the fuck is here, anyway? I mean, why Virginia? And you might not be so glad that I decided to come because I haven't even booked a room yet. I wasn't sure where you were staying. I thought it might make things easier if I got a room wherever you are."

"We're going to play it like that, are we?" Beckett asked.

Damn him for calling Christian out on his avoidance of the heavy stuff. "We are."

"Yeah," Beck replied. "Yeah, maybe that's smart. I'm not sure why I couldn't reel that in." He looked to make sure no cars were coming and then pulled out. "Here is...somewhere I've never been before. I have a buddy; his name is Landon. He's a mechanic I used to hire to do some private work for me when I didn't want to go through the factory. He moved here a while back. I needed to get away. He was the first person I thought to call, so here I am."

The words were like a jab to his heart. He'd come here because he thought Beck might need someone. Jesus, did he really think Beckett wouldn't have other friends to support him? He really was a cocky motherfucker. Christian hadn't been the person Beck went to when he needed a friend in a long time, just like Beck was no longer that person to him—speaking of, he pulled out his phone and shot a quick text to Quinn—I'm here—and then he shut his phone down, not wanting Quinn's answer right now.

"Fuck, I should have thought about that. It makes sense that you would come here to see someone." A thought slammed into him. "Jesus, did I cockblock you on a hookup?" But then...Beckett *had* called him.

"What? No. It's not like that. I mean, it *was* like that once but Landon is just a friend. Plus, he's crazy in love with his partner, Rod."

"Thank God." Christian let his head rest against the seat. "I was going to feel like the world's biggest asshole. So, hotel? Do you think they have vacancies?"

"No hotel," Beckett replied before making a left turn. "I'm staying in a rental. There's an extra room. You'll stay with me." He spoke as if that was law, as if there were no other options...and Christian didn't argue.

Chapter Four

Beckett couldn't keep his eyes to himself. Every couple minutes he found himself glancing Christian's way. He felt an unexpected calmness inside him, like he was in the eye of a hurricane where the chaos of all his recent thoughts—the way his love of motocross felt muted, coming out, his family adjusting, thoughts of his career, and the fact that he wasn't riding like himself—couldn't reach him. They were still there, twisting and turning around him but right here, right now, they were quieted by the fact that his oldest friend was here. That he'd thought Beckett might need him and he'd come.

They were silent most of the ride to the house. It was surprisingly a comfortable sort of quiet. He hadn't expected that after all this time. There was a whole lot of shit between them, things that needed to be discussed but it was as though they both managed to put that aside and it was only Christian and Beckett in the car right now. How many times had he heard that yelled over the years? *Christian and Beckett!* Most of the time, they were getting into some kind of trouble.

He let out an amused chuckle.

"What?" Christian asked as they pulled into the driveway of the cabin.

"Just thinking about all the trouble we used to get into. About how many times we heard our names getting yelled by someone frustrated with whatever antics we'd gotten up to that time."

"Oh God. Don't remind me. You were such a bad influence on me."

Beckett cocked a brow at him. "I'm pretty sure you have that the wrong way." But really, he just thought trouble came looking for them when they were together. He couldn't let Christian blame it on him without blaming it on Christian, though.

"I think you might have hit your head a few too many times during crashes." Christian stepped out of the car, then opened the back door. "I was a good boy. You were always the one saying, *'Let's take the bikes on this path, Chris. Who cares if it's private property? No one will catch us. Let's try this jump, Chris. Oh, we can steal some beers and drink them in that abandoned house, Chris.'* I just went along for the ride." He grabbed his bag and grinned at Beckett. Christ, this felt good.

"You have selective memory, but I'll let it slide for now. It's the least I can do after you came all this way." Once he was out of the car, they went for the steps that led onto the small front porch of the cabin. "Are you hungry?"

"No. I could use a drink though."

"Beer?" he asked as he unlocked the door.

"Perfect."

They made their way inside. "I'm staying in the room at the end of the hall. You can put your bag in the first room on the left and change or whatever. We can head to the back deck, watch some TV inside, or if you just want to take your drink and go to bed, I understand. You had a long day of traveling."

To Virginia to see him. He still couldn't believe that Christian was here with him now.

"Some fresh air sounds good," Christian replied, and then they stood there looking at each other without moving. His eyes looked bluer than Beckett remembered. They were like the ocean in a painting—bright and magical.

He had a small mole next to his eye. A fading scar on his chin from when he went off his bicycle on a ramp and hit the concrete. Memory after memory slammed into him, washed over him like waves in the same ocean he was just thinking matched Christian's eyes. Christian represented a part of him that was real and honest in ways Beckett never let himself be. Even when he'd meet a man on an app or at a club it wasn't honest. They didn't know each other or care about each other or keep each other's secrets. They hadn't laughed together or gotten scared together or even held each other while they cried.

That was only Christian.

Christian who broke their silence with, "Well, this is awkward. I think we just had a moment there. It's a little too soon for that. I'll put my bags away and be right back."

Damned if a warmth didn't spread through his chest and a smile tug at his lips, and if all those questions about his career and what would happen and where his passion was going didn't bury themselves a little deeper. Christian had always been good at making him forget things.

"I'll get the beer."

"You do that."

"I will," Beckett said and then he rolled his eyes. "I think we somehow went through a time portal and we might be sixteen-year-old kids again. Christ, you're making me act weird." Before they continued to play the staring game, Beckett turned and went for the fridge to get their beer. He heard Christian's footsteps get farther and farther away until he didn't hear them at all anymore. That's when he breathed.

* * * *

Christian tossed his bag onto the bed and rubbed a hand over his face. He'd expected the awkwardness to lie heavily upon them but it was different to know something than to experience it. They'd left a lot of things unsaid ten years ago. They were both different men—they had to be—but when he looked at Beck, he wanted to see his childhood friend. The person he'd gotten in trouble with and laughed with. The one who he'd thought would always be in his life. The boy he would have done anything for…the boy who hadn't been able to say the same about him.

Grow up, Chris. That was a long time ago.

The truth was, he might have come here for himself just as much as he'd come for Beck. This was a way to make peace with the past. A way to move on, and maybe become friends again.

Christian picked up the bag again and made a quick trip to the attached bathroom, where he changed into a t-shirt and a pair of basketball shorts so he'd be more comfortable. After cleaning up he forced himself to shove all the thoughts about Beck, their past and the tension between them to the back of his mind and made his way to the living room.

There was a sliding glass door off the back of the room decorated in earth tones. The glass was open, a screen between him and the outside where he saw Beck sitting on a reclining lounge chair. There was a table beside him and a matching chair on the other side of it. Circular lights hung from various beams around the deck giving off soft light. Beyond the deck, all he could see was darkness and the outlines of trees and nature in the distance.

"You're being very creepy standing behind me like that," Beck's voice drifted through the screen door.

Christian chuckled. "You think you're funny in your old age, do you?" He took the last few steps and then opened the door before going outside to take the other seat.

"Old? You say that again and I might have to kick your ass. You have no idea how much I get that at the track. I'm one of the old guys."

Young men often dominated the sport but, "You've won how many championships? You're in excellent shape. I don't think you have much to worry about. You're out there schooling those youngsters."

Beck turned his head, still letting it rest on the back of the chair and looked at him. "Thank you for defending my honor— and I'm in excellent shape, huh? I think I might need you to expand on that a little bit. Exactly what is it about my shape that's excellent? As many details as possible please." He rubbed his beard, no doubt hiding a smirk. That was the Beck he knew. Playful, flirty and a little cocky.

"I'm not making your head even bigger than it already is. Now where's the beer you promised me?"

Beck chuckled and then reached into a cooler on the other side of him. He pulled out a bottle of dark brew and handed it over to Christian. He opened it, took a long swallow, quenching his thirst before he set it on the table.

And then it was quiet as they looked out toward the pines. It sounded as though there was possibly a river there, too.

"It's nice out here. It always takes some getting used to when I head home for a visit, or hell, anywhere outside of the city. It's like the whole world is asleep."

He heard Beck let out a deep breath, then he took a drink of his beer. "Yeah, yeah it is." He took another drink. Christian watched his Adam's apple move as he did. "Tell me about your life. You're making games just like you always wanted."

He smiled at that, because he was. While Beck had always wanted to ride, Christian had always wanted to get lost in the world of video games. It was then that a thought steamrolled him and he couldn't help but get a kick out of it. "It's funny that we both just wanted to grow up and play."

"Is there any other way to live?" Beck asked, with amusement in his voice.

"Hell no."

"But it's hard work, too. Both of us…we work hard."

"We're lucky we get to do what we love," Christian countered. "Not everyone can say that."

He glanced Beck's way, waiting for a response, waiting for him to agree, for his eyes to light up and for his body to nearly glow with the passion for riding that he'd always shown. Christian loved a lot of things. He loved games and creating but he'd never had the passion for anything that could hold a match to the fervor that Beck had for riding.

One beat, then two and three. Seconds ticked by with no response. Beck finished his beer and then set the bottle down on the table, but still, nothing.

"What is it?" Christian asked, a heaviness in his gut. "Does this have something to do with being outted? Did it cause problems in your career?" Or hell, maybe the fact that after winning Supercross last year, it had been expected for him again this year, but hadn't happened.

"No, no." Beckett shook his head. "It's not that…and I'll admit something to you, Chris, I wasn't outted. Not really. Would anyone outside the MX world really know me well enough to take a picture of me like that?"

He'd wondered the same thing. But still, he didn't get why Beck didn't just come out, if that's what he'd wanted. "What'd you do?"

He shrugged. "I didn't do much of anything. I went out after a race, wanted to get laid. It wasn't something I put a lot of thought into I just…let go. I was tired, Chris, so fucking tired of sneaking around and being elusive. I met a guy, danced with him, he asked what I did and I told him I'd just won a race that night. I didn't get as many first place podiums this season as I'd wanted and needed to celebrate. It was like…" He went quiet for a moment. Christian watched him, waited, heard the wistfulness in his voice when he spoke again.

"It was like I could breathe. I know that sounds crazy and maybe a little childish, but it's true. It was like my anchor had been lifted. I hadn't realized how heavy it was, Chris. The guy I was with, he thought it was cool that I'd just won a race that night and he was talking to everyone about it. Each person we spoke to, I just kept getting lighter and lighter. That night, I felt better than I had in a long time."

He looked Christian's way, his brow furrowed. "Does that sound crazy?"

Christian wanted to know everything. If there was more to Beck not agreeing with him on loving their careers than whether he was out or not. If there was something he was holding back. But he didn't ask those questions. He just reached over and squeezed Beckett's hand. It was bigger than his own, slightly rough, with prominent veins. "No. Of course it doesn't sound crazy. It has to wear you down, keeping a part of yourself in chains your whole life." He couldn't imagine the feeling. When he'd first been accidentally outed, he'd been devastated. It wasn't long before he was thankful for it.

"I knew you'd understand," Beckett told him. The truth was, they might not have spoken in ten years but he still felt like he knew Beck. This moment on the deck was just as comfortable as it would have been when they were teens.

"I do. And don't think I forgot that you changed the subject about loving our jobs. I won't let that go for long."

"There's not a part of me that doubts that." Beck chuckled and then, "I love riding. I'll love riding until the day I die."

"There's not a part of me that doubts that," Christian returned his words back to him.

Beckett nodded, opened another beer and took a sip. "Remember when we used to sleep in your back yard on the trampoline all night?"

Christian smiled at the memory, saw it clear as day in his

mind. The dark sky, dancing with stars. They spent most of their summers sleeping outside. "I do. We used to stay up most of the night talking."

"With *wake-up flips* thrown in between."

A laugh formed in Christian's chest, and he let it out just as Beck did the same. They'd get up and do back flips and front flips on the hour to keep themselves awake. Otherwise…they'd just talk.

He thought maybe he wanted that again—minus the flipping part. He'd likely break his neck now. Christian had a feeling Beck wanted it too.

"What's your favorite track you've ridden?" he asked.

"Oh that's easy…" They went from tracks to trainers. From video games to dancing. From movies to clubs in LA. Friends and restaurants. Books and vacations. They let each other experience the last ten years of their lives. They relived them until the sun started to peek over the horizon in yellows, pinks and oranges.

When the sun finally made its grand appearance, they decided it was time to get some sleep. Beck stood, stretched. Christian took in the view as his t-shirt pulled up, showing a muscular stomach and a dark trail of hair that disappeared under his jeans.

He wanted to know what it tasted like. How his skin would taste and how Beck would smell. He wanted to experience those things they hadn't really done when they were younger. Back then it had been nothing but kissing and rubbing off on each other through their clothes.

Beck cleared his throat. Christian let his eyes lazily rise to meet Beck's, not hiding the fact that he appreciated the view.

"Thank you," Beckett said softly. "Thanks for coming…for talking. I missed you, Christian."

A knot formed in Christian's chest, one that was hard to speak around because even after all these years, he'd needed to hear that. Needed to know Beck had missed him the way he'd missed Beckett. Christian stood. "I missed you too."

He stepped forward, wrapped his hand around the back of Beckett's head and pulled him closer until he could press a kiss to Beckett's forehead. Then without another word, Christian headed into the house and went to bed.

Chapter Five

It was good to be home.

It had been eight months since he moved to Florida to live with his trainer. His parents had wanted to come but they couldn't afford it. They had their home in Georgia, one they couldn't sell, so as hard as it had been, they'd let him move, live in a different state and homeschool all in the name of motocross. It would be worth it in the end though. It would be worth their sacrifices— driving a car that often broke down so Beck could get a new bike and equipment. The distance, the hours worked, it would all be worth it. Just a few more amateur wins and he would be moved up to Supercross at eighteen years old. He would spend the rest of his life making sure their sacrifices weren't for nothing.

Their small house had been full of people all night—a welcome back and congratulatory party all in one. As awesome as it was, he really just wanted to spend time with Christian. They spoke on the phone or emailed almost every day but this was the first time he'd gotten to see his best friend in months.

Beck couldn't stop himself from watching him at the party— he danced and laughed. Made other people laugh. His pulse went crazy every time he looked at Christian.

He's beautiful, Beckett thought and then shook his head at the notion. It felt strange to think of Chris as beautiful, but really he was.

As always, Christian's parents were the last to leave. He tensed up when he felt Christian's hand rub his as he walked by and said, "Hey, Ma, can Beck come stay over like old times? We can sleep outside on the trampoline."

She gave him the evil eye that even scared Beckett. "Not if you think it's okay to say, Hey Ma, to me."

He knew Chris well enough to know it was a struggle for him not to roll his eyes right now.

"Yes, ma'am. Can Beck come over tonight?"

"That's better," his mom smiled and two hours later they were at Chris's house, in his enclosed back yard. It was at an angle where his parents couldn't see it from their bedroom. The house was already dark and had been for a good hour, as they lay there, looking up at the stars.

"You're really gonna do it, Beck. When we were kids, no matter how many races you won, it was like a dream. But you're really gonna do it. Your dreams are gonna come true," Christian said softly from beside him.

They were both on their backs, the netting on the trampoline providing them with what almost felt like a barrier to the outside world.

"Yeah...yeah I am. I can't fucking believe it."

"Are you scared?" Chris asked.

"Kind of...but really, I just want it. There's nothin' I've ever wanted more." The statement made his gut clench, though he couldn't say why.

The trampoline moved beneath him, and then Christian rolled over onto his side. He leaned on his elbow so he could look down at Beckett and damned if his stomach didn't start doing backflips. Looking at Christian always made his insides go haywire. Christian said looking at him did it to him as well. "I wish you could come with me. Maybe we could find a way—"

"I got accepted to USC. I'll be going to Southern California."

Surprise punched him in the gut. He didn't even know Chris had applied.

"Wow...that's...wow...." And then, "Why didn't you tell me?"

"I don't know," he answered simply. "Maybe because I never thought I'd get in. I'll be the first person in my family to go to a university. I can't wait around here for you, Beck. And I can't follow you around the country like a lost puppy dog or something. That's lame. I have dreams too."

Anger took the place of surprise, blazing a path of fire

through him. "What the fuck, dude? I would never ask you to wait for me." Still, he couldn't believe Christian had applied for college in California and not told him. Plus, it's not like he thought he and Chris would be together forever or something. They were just messing around. Beckett liked girls, too. He'd always planned to marry a woman one day.

But as sadness flooded him, as it took him over, made his breathing feel bumpy like he was riding on a track that was too rutty, he realized he wasn't ready for that yet. He didn't want to call off the secret make-out sessions he and Christian had. He wasn't ready to stop messing around with him and just go back to being friends again.

"Southern California has one of the biggest motocross scenes in the United States. I'll be out there all the time. My trainer has a facility in Riverside County. It's like two hours from LA, but we can still see each other. We can still keep doing...this if you want to."

And then he held his breath, waited and embarrassingly hoped like hell Chris would say yes.

"Secretly date Beckett Monroe, the next big name in motocross? Fuck yes!" Christian teased, making him laugh.

"It has to stay a secret though...I can't risk my career before it even happens. My parents have dedicated their whole lives to my career and—"

"I know, Beck. I just...I wanna be with you...however we do it..."

And then Christian leaned forward and kissed him. It was just like riding—wild and exciting...freeing. Everything he loved felt like it was wrapped in this moment. He and Christian could keep doing this. They could hide together and enjoy each other a little while longer.

Beckett's eyes jerked open from his dream, an incessant ringing in his ears. It took a second for him to make sense of where he was, for his eyes to adjust to the bright yellow light beaming in from the curtains he'd forgotten to close and for him to realize it was his cell going nuts on the bedside table.

He reached over and picked it up to see that it was just past eleven and Landon was calling.

He swiped his thumb across the screen and then almost

fumbled the phone as he put it to his ear. "Hello?" His voice was rough, his throat dry.

"Oh, shit. I didn't mean to wake you. I'm off today and tomorrow so I wanted to see about getting together. I'd like you to meet Rod."

Beckett really wanted that too, but then he thought about the man in the bedroom down the hall. The one who'd jumped on a plane to come and see him after Beckett called him for the first time in ten years. "Christian's here."

There was a pause and then, "We're talking about the Christian you told me about, right?"

"No, a Christian I picked up at church last night."

Landon was the only person he'd ever talked to about Chris. He was the only person besides Christian who'd known that Beck was attracted to men other than guys he picked up and then never saw again.

"Wow...okay then. I'll leave you to it today. My brother Justin invited us all over for a barbeque and swimming tomorrow. He and his partner Drew just got a new pool put in."

Justin and Landon were half-brothers. They hadn't known each other existed because Landon's father had cut all contact when he left Landon's mom. He'd had another family and when he was diagnosed with terminal cancer he'd come clean with Justin, before the two of them made the trek to Virginia to make peace with Landon and his sister. It had been hard on his friend. "Damn. I didn't realize there were this many out, gay or bi men in Small Town, Virginia."

Landon let out a stiff breath. "You can say that again. I guess we're just lucky. We don't let anyone steal our sparkle here."

They both laughed again and then Beckett told him he'd talk to Christian about tomorrow before they got off the phone. He wanted to go. He'd missed spending time with Landon and that had been the point of coming here, but then, he hadn't expected Chris to be here either.

Spending time with Christian last night had soothed a restlessness inside him that he hadn't known needed soothing. It was as though no time had passed. Like they could step right back into each other's lives and be friends the way they'd been so many years ago.

Or hell, maybe he just really fucking wanted that so badly that it clouded his vision. But he did want it. He wanted his friendship with Christian back.

He pushed out of bed and went straight for the bathroom. After taking a piss he washed his hands, brushed his teeth and then headed for the door. When he hit the hallway he realized the door was open to the room Christian was staying in.

"Up already, huh?" he peeked his head inside the room and saw Christian at the desk there, with his computer out and various equipment around him.

"Yeah, I don't sleep very well sometimes. I figured I'd take advantage and get some work done." He ran a hand through his dark-blond hair and looked Beckett's way.

"Sorry. I didn't mean to interrupt. I'll go make some coffee."

He turned to leave but Chris's voice stopped him. "No, it's fine. I've been at it a couple hours now. Coffee sounds almost as good as sex." He pushed to his feet, stretched, and then followed Beckett out of the room.

Chris sat at the cherry-wood table while Beckett put the coffee grounds and water into the machine. "So what are the plans today?" Christian asked. "Are we going to play tourist? What's there to do in Virginia?"

Beckett turned to face him, while leaning against the counter. Now that he thought about it…"I'm not sure. I didn't get that far."

Christian playfully rolled his eyes. "Well you sort of suck at vacations then, Beck."

A laugh jumped out of Beckett's mouth. Jesus, he'd missed this man. "In my defense, it wasn't supposed to be a real vacation. I just wanted to get away."

"Excuses, excuses."

"How long are you here?"

"It depends. I wasn't sure how it would go, honestly. I can't stay any more than five days though."

A cold ache settled into his chest. Five days. It wasn't as though Beckett had much longer, but it felt like it was only a blink of time.

"Speaking of home, I should probably call Quinn."

Beckett's eyes shot up at that. The ache in his chest spidered out, infiltrated his veins. It was a ridiculous reaction. He had no right. Plus, he'd only spent the last twelve hours with Chris in the past ten years. It shouldn't matter who Quinn was or wasn't to him, but somehow it did.

As Christian pulled out his phone, Beckett grabbed two mugs from the cabinet and filled them. He heard Christian behind him saying, "I can't believe you didn't answer. Unless you're pouting because I didn't talk to you last night. Knowing you, I'm sure that's it."

Christian had that familiar playfulness in his voice as he spoke to Quinn's voicemail. They were obviously close. Maybe dating. Another thing Beckett had denied himself. It wasn't very easy to date someone when no one could know. Sure, he'd seen a few women over the past ten years, maybe a part of him had even hoped it would turn into more than just dating, but it never had. He'd never felt that connection he couldn't deny. A connection he'd only ever felt with the man in the room with him right now.

Jesus, what's wrong with me? He was turning into a sap. "How do you take it?" He asked as he set a cup down in front of Christian.

"Bitter like my soul."

Beckett shook his head. "You're so weird."

"You like that about me."

And Beckett did. He doctored his own coffee while Christian drank his black. He joined Chris at the table a moment later, as the man sat there scrolling through the phone.

He held it out so Beckett could see too. "Come on. Let's find something for us to do today...oh look! There's fishing."

He couldn't tell if Christian was serious or not. He had a feeling Chris wasn't so sure himself. "I haven't been fishing since I was a kid."

"Me either," Christian replied and then, "I'm not letting you anywhere near a fishhook!"

The old memory came roaring back to him, like a summer storm in Florida. "Oh fuck. I forgot about that." They'd been planning a fishing trip when they were fourteen. Beckett had gotten new lures. He'd opened the packages, somehow dropped a treble hook in the floor, which Christian had stepped on with no shoes. Beckett had walked into the room to see the hook hanging off his toe, and they'd spent the morning at the emergency room getting it removed instead of fishing.

Hell, maybe he'd wanted to catch Christian even back then. "You know we have to go fishing, don't you?"

"I'm a city boy now. I don't fish."

Beckett nudged him with his arm. "Come on, Chris. For old times' sake. I swear I won't hook you."

Christian grinned, rolled his blue eyes and said, "Fine. You spoiled bastard. You always get your way."

When he looked at Chris, all he could think was, not always. Though that was likely his own damn fault.

Chapter Six

Christian was playing this all off like it was a lot easier than it really was. On the one hand, it was almost as though he and Beck fell flawlessly back into their friendship like nothing had happened. And maybe it should be that way because they'd been kids when Beckett had walked away from him. He'd been protecting himself, doing what he saw as protecting his family and Christian got that. Plus, who didn't fuck up when they were young? Christian still fucked up almost daily as a twenty-eight-year-old man, but he also had to admit that Beckett had hurt him. Regardless of the why of it or how old they'd been, he still felt like Beck left him on his own back then. He'd covered for himself, and let Christian deal with the rest.

He wasn't quite sure how he felt about those thoughts, so he tried to ignore them. He could handle that for a few days.

They'd both gotten ready quickly, before looking up a sports store and heading there for supplies. Afterward, they went grocery shopping and filled a Styrofoam cooler with food, drinks and ice before they made their way to the lake. He wasn't sure why they didn't go to the river behind the cabin but he just let Beck lead and he followed. The day was more than halfway over by the time they settled in at a quiet spot on the lake in cheap plastic chairs.

"It's hot. Why did we decide to do this again?" Christian teased, though he knew the answer. He'd always had a hard time saying no to Beckett Monroe.

"Because we haven't seen each other in ten years and the last time we tried to go fishing together, I left a fishhook on the floor that ended up in your toe. I'm making up for my mistake."

There was a sort of melancholy tone to Beck's voice. It made Christian wonder how hard the past ten years had been on him. No one would know it, not when they saw him tearing it up on the track. Not when they saw him hit the podium week after week as he racked up the wins. Even this last season. He knew third in points would feel like a disappointment to Beck, but it was still an amazing accomplishment. Christian wanted to know what was going on beyond the surface. If Beckett was somehow trying to make up for the past.

"How did your family take it?" He asked as he watched his bobber float in the water. There wasn't a part of him that thought either of them would catch a fish today, but he also didn't believe they were really out here for that.

Beck sighed. "They're doing okay. It's harder on Dad than Mom. She feels guilty...like she should have known. Especially after you. Every time I talk to her, I have to assure her it wasn't her fault I didn't say anything. That it was all me, all up here." He tapped his temple.

"You thought you were protecting them, in a way, Beck. You did it because you worried their hard work would be for nothing if it caused problems in your career." Regardless of why he'd done it, that hadn't meant he'd had to sever ties with Christian though. No matter what happened between them, he never should have done that.

"That was my excuse at sixteen, seventeen, eighteen, but what about later? Make no mistake, part of it was my own weakness and fear. There's no denying that."

"It's not always an easy thing to do—especially in the sports world."

Beckett glanced his way and gave him a sad smile. "You always used to do this."

"What?" he asked, really not knowing what Beckett meant.

"Make excuses for me. Cover for me. Do whatever you could to make me feel better. I'm a big boy now, Chris. I need to take responsibility for my own shit."

It was almost as though the whole world stopped around them as they looked at each other. Beckett was right. It was still a reflex for Christian to want to take care of him.

He nodded and turned back toward the lake, surrounded by

greenery he didn't often see in Los Angeles. "And your dad?"

"I'd be lying if I didn't admit he's a little uncomfortable. I hear it in the stilted way he speaks to me over the phone. It's going to take some getting used to, which is sad, but what can you do? Mostly he doesn't understand, I guess. He thinks the way I did when I was a kid…if I'm bi, I can just choose to settle down with a woman. I can choose to pretend I don't want men. It's hard to make him realize it doesn't work that way. Sure, if I fell in love with a woman, that would be different—I'd be committed to her. But I can't force myself to only seek out women—to pretend that side of me doesn't exist."

Christian didn't envy him, that was for sure.

They were quiet for a moment, as they pretended to care if they caught fish or not, when Beckett said, "I'm sorry."

There was no doubt in Christian's mind exactly what Beckett was apologizing for. Maybe he shouldn't, but after all these years of hurt, he'd needed to hear it. "It was a long time ago."

"So? That doesn't change the fact that I did it."

He closed his eyes, remembered what it felt like that day. It was when Beckett had come back for a visit from Florida. They'd had a party at Beck's house and then they'd gone to Christian's to sleep outside. He'd told Beck about getting accepted to USC and they'd decided to keep seeing each other. All teenage Christian had known was that he loved Beck and he would take him any way he could get him. That wasn't him anymore.

They'd gone riding the next day. He watched Beck fly as he went over jumps and corners perfectly. He had always been incredible in the dirt.

When they went back to Christian's house, Beck's parents had been there. They were sitting in the living room waiting to pounce. Christian's parents had found a letter Christian had written about being in love with a boy. A letter that was about Beckett but one he'd never been able to read.

"Is it you? Christ, Beckett, are you sneaking around with Christian? Do you know what this could do to your career? We put so much work into it! So much fucking work." Beck's dad paced the room and Christian thought he would throw up.

"Earl, calm down," Beck's mom told him.

Christian's mom cried. His dad wouldn't look at him.

"Is it you?" Earl yelled again and Beckett didn't respond. Their arms touched they stood so close to each other and Christian could feel him tremble.

"It's not him. He doesn't know...I never told him, I'm gay..." Christian looked toward the ground, waited for Beck to reply, waited for Beck to stick up for him, but the words never came.

And that was when Beckett Monroe cut contact with him. He'd sat quiet while Christian had to defend himself, and then he'd avoided Chris when he called, until he made a call of his own to Christian, just yesterday.

"I hated myself for a long time after that. I just fucking rode—trained harder than I'd ever trained. I think I believed if I did well, if I succeeded at motocross, it would have made the sacrifice worth it, it would have meant I did it for a reason." He paused, shook his head, and then continued.

"It didn't change anything though, Chris. Not a day has gone by in my life that I don't regret leaving you to handle that on your own that day. Not a day has gone by that I don't miss your friendship, or regret walking away from it. You were always my best friend—from the time I learned to speak until this moment right now—even if I didn't show it."

Christian let those words swim around his chest. Let them sink in because a part of him really needed to hear it.

When he didn't reply, Beck asked, "Can I admit something else to you?"

"Yeah."

"I've been getting to the point lately that I've lost the joy in it. I think that's why this last Supercross season went like it did. There's a part of me that knows it's in there—that passion I've always felt as I grip the handles and the dirt bike roars under me. That love is still in there, but it's been hard to find the past year or so and it keeps getting worse."

Beckett leaned forward, and let his elbows rest on his knees. "It's like the weight, the denial, all that shit just kept getting heavier and heavier to carry. The more I struggled with it, the harder it was just to feel pure fucking joy in anything anymore. I'm so damn scared of losing that joy, Chris. Who is Beckett Monroe if he's not the guy who loves motocross more than anything else in the world?"

There was the truth Christian had been looking for last

night—why Beck hadn't been able to say he loved what he did even though Christian knew he did.

"I don't know, man. That's what you have to figure out." But Christian did know—he was the man who loved riding, who wanted to take care of his family, who had a work ethic like no one Christian had ever known. He was Christian's best friend, the guy who made him laugh and shared so much of his past. He was a terrible fisher, and a bad liar. He hated TV unless it was MX related and never understood Christian's love of games. It was up to Beckett to discover himself, though.

"I'm trying to. That's why I did what I did. That's why I'm here. I think it's why I called you. I always knew who I was with you."

Christian closed his eyes. Tried not to curse. He didn't know if he was ready to hear things like that from Beckett again or if he ever would be. The thought of caring for Beck again scared the hell out of him, but on the other hand, it almost felt inevitable.

"You don't give yourself enough credit, Beck. You never did. I have no doubt you'll figure it out, and would have without me."

"Thank you," Beckett said softly...and then they were quiet again. A frog croaked in the background and Beck began to reel his line in.

Finally, Christian told him, "It was a long time ago. I forgive you."

He likely had the second he heard Beckett Monroe's voice on the phone, but to say it out loud released something inside of him that he'd held onto for too long.

Chapter Seven

They only spent a couple hours at the lake. They had dinner and then headed back to the rental house. Chris was a little quieter than he had been before. Beckett wished he hadn't had to bring up his behavior when they were younger but it was important to him to apologize. If they were going to have any kind of friendship from here on out, it was imperative.

Eventually things began to lighten up. The conversation was likely still on both their minds but they had a good night.

It was like old times, in a way. They drank a few beers out on the deck again. When they wanted a snack, they popped a frozen pizza into the oven.

They played cards and talked shit and just spent another night getting to know each other again. In a lot of ways, it felt like they'd never stopped knowing each other.

This time, they headed to bed around eleven. Beckett found himself wondering if Christian was able to sleep any better tonight than he had last night before he dozed himself.

The next day they lounged around part of the morning before showering, eating breakfast, and heading to Landon's brother's house.

"You don't know any of these people, right?" Chris asked as they drove.

"Not except Landon," Beckett shook his head. "I know Rod will be there. Rod's his partner. He said it's Justin's house and he lives with his partner too. I can't remember if he told me the guy's name and then there's Bryce. He owns the motorcycle repair shop that Landon works at. I don't know if there will be anyone else there."

Christian nodded and then looked out the window. "It's so damn green out here. It really is beautiful."

Justin lived outside of town. There'd been nothing but trees for miles as they weaved their way through the countryside. "You sound like you forgot what the country is like."

"Nah. I remember. And don't get me wrong, I love Los Angeles. I'm not sure I could live anywhere else permanently again but I do miss this sometimes."

Beckett thought about Florida, where he'd made his home for over ten years. He liked it there too, but he didn't feel the same passion for it that it sounded like Chris felt for LA. "You're really happy there."

"I am," the answer came immediately. "I found my tribe out there—friends from work, the apartment complex where I live, Quinn. Took me a little while to settle in and realize it was okay to be myself. Moving to California helped with that."

Beckett tried not to let the sadness weigh down his bones. He was happy for Christian…but he wanted that too. He should have had it ten years ago. He wished he could have experienced it with Christian when they were young, the way it should have been. Beckett wanted that *and* motocross.

He fought hard not to let himself focus on Christian's mention of Quinn. Fought not to let out a possessive growl, because Chris wasn't his. He'd given him up a long time ago.

"In five hundred feet, turn right," the GPS on his phone told him.

"Looks like we're there," he grunted as his jealousy of Quinn, of what Christian had, flooded his over-stimulated body. He'd gone through a hell of a lot of emotions in the past couple weeks.

"Looks like we are," he replied as they pulled into the driveway. "Jesus, his house is gorgeous." It was a large, colonial-style house with beautiful beams, and a wrap-around porch.

"Yeah, it is." They got out of the car and headed for the house. They'd stopped on their way to grab a pair of swimming trunks for each of them, since they hadn't brought any along. When they stepped up onto the massive porch, Beckett could hear music and laughter coming from the back yard. He raised his hand to knock just as the door was pulled open.

"I was instructed to keep an eye out for you," the dark-haired man in the doorway said. "I'm Justin, nice to meet you."

It was odd to see him. He looked a lot like Landon. Beckett couldn't imagine going through what their family had. "Beckett, nice to meet you." They shook hands. "This is my friend Christian. He came out from LA to spend some time with me."

It was then that another man walked in from the back of the house with what looked like a lab-mix by his side. As soon as the dog saw them, it came bounding for them, tail wagging and tongue sticking out.

"Ireland, come here, girl." The guy with the backward baseball hat called just as she jumped onto Christian, her front paws on his belly, demanding attention.

"Shit, sorry. She's a little spoiled," Justin told them.

"She's a sweet girl," Christian said, rubbing her head as she fought to lick him like crazy.

Beckett chuckled. "I get it, girl; I like him too." He reached over to pet the dog and Christian winked at him.

"Hey. We're glad you could come. I'm Drew," the newcomer announced. The guy was all muscle—wearing swimming trunks and no shirt. It was obvious he spent a lot of time working out, which Beckett could appreciate. He'd fallen in love with it through his own training.

They made their introductions before Justin and Drew led them into the house. Pieces of the puzzle began to click into place from previous conversations he'd had with Landon. He remembered Landon telling him that Justin had fallen in love while here before their dad passed and then packing up and moving in with Drew.

Ireland bounded beside them as they made their way through the house and toward the back door. He saw the pool, which was currently empty, a hot tub, a deck, and another dark-haired man he didn't recognize.

"Look who we found," Justin said as they stepped out. Beckett's eyes hit Landon first. He sat in a chair with who Beckett assumed was Rod, on his lap. He was smaller than Landon, younger, with short hair and dark eyeliner around his eyes.

Rod put his hands on his cheeks like the kid from Home Alone, jumped off Landon's lap and shouted, "Oh my God! It's Beckett Monroe!"

Beckett felt his face warm up. Landon shook his head and chuckled. From everything Landon had told him, Rod kept him on his toes and he could see that his friend hadn't exaggerated.

Rod grinned, "I'm kidding. I don't know shit about motocross. I just didn't want Bryce to feel alone if he nearly blows his load in your presence."

Landon couldn't control his laughter now, as he held his stomach and leaned forward in the chair. The man sitting beside him was cracking up too, as Beckett's eyes darted between all of them, not sure what to say or how to react. "Um…"

"Excuse us while I drown him and then hide the body." The man who'd been pacing swooped in and scooped Rod into his arms.

"How many times do I have to tell you? I'm not interested in you that way, Bryce! Before Landon, yes, but it's too late now," Rod told the man who apparently might be jerking off to thoughts of him later today and Landon laughed harder.

"We can't take you two anywhere," the man beside Landon said, before both of them stood up. "Put him down, Bryce."

"But I really want to drown him."

"Not with all these prying eyes," the man told him.

"Please, Nick? Please can I drown him?" he asked before setting Rod down and saying, "You never let me have any fun."

Landon reached him by then, his face red, Beckett assumed from laughter. "Sorry, my crew is crazy and Rod is the craziest of them all, especially when you get him and Bryce together. This is obviously Bryce who may or may not be a big fan of yours. He promised me there would be no jerking off, though."

"Everyone thinks they're a comedian," Bryce responded before holding out his hand. "They're clean. I'm really not as bad as they say."

"Eh, I get the allure," Beckett teased, wanting to play along. Landon introduced Nick next. He was the man who'd been sitting beside him. He and Bryce were together, and Nick was apparently a chef and had made some of their food for today.

"And this, of course, is Rod," Landon introduced him last.

Rod gave Beckett a smile as bright as the sun. "Sorry, I couldn't help myself. It's great to meet you, though. Landon has told me a lot about you."

"It's good to meet you too," and it really was. "This is Christian. He's…my oldest and dearest friend."

Everyone said hi to Christian and then Landon wrapped his arms around Rod from behind, and whispered something in his ear. Rod laughed. Drew pulled out a few more chairs and Justin and Nick were obviously ribbing Bryce.

He realized then that just like Christian, Landon had found his tribe, his crew. Beckett had that in the moto world, but not in his personal life. It wasn't the same…but he wanted it. He really fucking wanted it.

Chapter Eight

"I really need to get you to LA," Christian told Rod as they sat at an outside table. "You'll have a blast. One night in West Hollywood and you'll fall in love."

"He'll get you into trouble," Landon countered.

"That's not a bad thing." At least, not in Christian's mind. He really liked everyone here. It had been a couple hours since they'd arrived. He wasn't sure he'd ever laughed so hard in his life. Bryce and Rod's back and forth was hilarious. They always seemed to be trying to one-up each other. Apparently they met when Nick and Bryce went shopping for sex toys at an adult store he worked at. Christian was shocked to discover that being with each other, was Nick and Bryce's first time with another man. He could only imagine how that trip to the *romantic gift store* had gone.

Rod now had his own place called Rods-N-Ends.

There was a lot of motorcycle talk. Bryce and Landon were in love with being on two wheels the same way Beck was. They both mostly rode street bikes but enjoyed motocross too, which meant Beck was in heaven. Drew owned a gym, Justin was going back to school, and Nick obviously loved food and feeding people who were important to him. They were a mishmash group of people, but you could tell they all loved each other. They were a close group of friends.

Christian couldn't help but direct his eyes toward Beck. Did he have that? People he knew he could be himself with? People who would stand by his side, no matter what? Christian hoped he had that within the motocross community but the truth was, he just didn't know. He knew Beck's past. He even knew who Beck was. Ten years apart hadn't changed that but he didn't know Beck's day-to-day life.

The thought made him frown, put an ache in his chest. And when Beckett looked his way, he could see the questions there, in his dark, soulful eyes. Saw that Beck realized Christian was wrestling with something...and he was. Because he realized now that he couldn't lose Beckett Monroe again. He'd be the friend who Beck always had in his corner.

Christian reached out, and squeezed Beckett's thigh, and then he didn't pull his hand back. Beckett gave him what was almost a shy grin, then set his hand on Christian's before joining the conversation with his friends again.

* * * *

"The first race of the upcoming outdoor season is in Texas, right?" Bryce asked as they ate. They'd gone swimming for a little while, and then gotten out to finish cooking. Nick had taken care of a few things inside while Drew had the grill going for the ribs. They said Nick had marinated them in a homemade sauce. They nearly fell off the bone and had a sweet, tangy taste that Beck couldn't get enough of.

"Yeah. No rest for the wicked. We ended up with two weeks between Supercross and outdoors this year. I should be training right now but they gave me a few days considering everything that's going on." Which actually made him feel like shit. He shouldn't have to take a break. Especially with how he'd ridden during Supercross season.

"You're the fastest, most skilled rider there is right now. Taking a few days off won't hurt," Christian told him.

"I didn't get here by taking time off, though. I stay on top of my game because I'm the last guy to leave the track every day."

"I know." Christian eyed him, but Beckett couldn't read what his expression meant. The air around them did feel heavier though. "I remember. And that's a good thing, but there's more to life than motocross. Don't forget that." He didn't smile, didn't look away from Beckett and he could see the seriousness in Christian's stare. He now saw how much Christian wanted to make sure Beckett got the message. Christian wanted him to have a life outside of motocross.

"Wait. There is? I didn't know that," Bryce teased.

"Shh! They're having a moment," Rod teased and then Justin promptly started choking on his food. Drew hit him on the back as the table burst into laughter again.

"I guess we'll finish this conversation later," Beck winked at him.

"Sorry, we typically keep them locked away. They haven't acclimated to spending time with adult humans yet," Nick added. They were a riot—all of them. Beckett turned toward Christian, who grinned at him. He had a light dusting of dark, blond hair along his jaw, obviously having skipped out on shaving this morning. Beck wanted to feel it against his skin. The last time he'd kissed Christian, he had the smooth face of youth, as had Beck himself. He wondered if Christian would enjoy the feel of his beard against his flesh as well.

He cocked his head at Beck, and he couldn't help but wish Christian was having the same thoughts—which likely made him an asshole since there was a Quinn out there.

Beckett turned away from him just as Landon asked, "Do you have time to take a quick walk?"

"Yeah, sure." He turned toward Chris again. "I'll be right back."

Landon kissed Rod's forehead and then the two of them went down the stairs from the deck and toward the back of Justin and Drew's lush property.

"Now that you're here, I hope you plan to come back to visit," Landon told him.

There was no question he would. He felt like he fit in with Landon's friends in a way he desired in his life. "Absolutely…you're happy."

"I am. Are you?" he asked.

"I love what I do." And he did, regardless of the emptiness he'd felt lately.

"That wasn't my question."

"Fucker," he teased. Of course Landon wouldn't let him off easily. "I'm trying to be," is the reply he settled on.

"You also have feelings for Christian." He cocked a dark brow.

Beckett waved him off. "He's been back in my life for a couple days after not seeing him for ten years."

"So?" Landon asked. "People are so strange. We try to put rules and regulations on everything. You can't do that with feelings. There's no specific time it takes to fall for someone—or at least to want them." He grinned and Beckett couldn't help but remember when Margaret had said, *What does time have to do with anything?*

Landon continued, "Plus, you've likely always had feelings for him. I knew it when you told me about him years ago and I see it now when you look at him."

The truth was, Landon was likely right. He'd never gotten over Chris, he'd just tried really fucking hard to pretend he had. "I'm pretty sure he has someone."

Landon kicked a twig that was on the ground as they walked. "Well, that might complicate things a little. It's funny though…the way he looks at you? The way his eyes are always seeking you out and the way he smiles at you…it's not the look of a man who has someone else."

Beckett didn't respond. He wasn't sure how to. His life was slightly a mess right now. He wasn't sure how the outdoor season would go, how things would be with his team. Hell, he was scared to death he ran the risk of falling out of love with something that had always been his life because right now, he resented it. It wasn't until this moment that he realized that's what it was. He resented motocross because in it, he'd hidden part of himself.

"Sorry, it's not my place to butt into your life. But you're my friend, Beck. I just want you to be happy."

"I'm trying to be," he repeated, before his mind went right back to Christian again.

Chapter Nine

"I had fun today," Christian told him as they pulled back into the driveway of Beck's rental. He hoped Beck made it a point to come and see them more often. Christian thought it was good for him.

"Yeah, I did too. They're a good group of guys."

The door of the car squeaked when Christian opened it. He stepped out just as Beckett did.

"I want to try and make it out again. I miss seeing Landon."

A small twinge of jealousy itched at the middle of his chest. Forget that just a few seconds before he'd been hoping that Beck came to see his friend again and that Landon was obviously one hundred percent in love with Rod.

He didn't reply as they took the stairs leading to the cabin, as Beck unlocked and opened the door.

"He's always been a good, loyal friend to me even when we both kept each other at arm's length because of personal shit. I could use more of that."

He closed the door. The sound sort of echoed in Christian's head. The twinge of jealousy started to spread out, to rapidly grow, a disease taking over his body inch by inch.

He would have been that same thing for Beck if he'd been given the chance. He wanted it right now. Wanted more than that if he was being honest. Christian wanted to know if he still tasted the same—mint and spice. If he still smelled the same—like trees with the teasing scent of motor oil.

He wanted Beck to think about spending more time with him and desired to do all of the things to Beckett Monroe they were too scared to do as kids.

And this was his chance to do it.

"I was thinking we could—" Christian silenced him with his mouth. He'd taken Beck by surprise. It was obvious in the tightness of his lips and the way he held his hands up like he wasn't sure what to do.

But then? Then he was kissing Christian back. His hands were on Christian's shoulders, pulling him closer as Beckett's back hit the door.

He still tasted the same. It went straight to Christian's head, he still smelled the same and Christian wanted to inhale him. To engrain the scent even more fiercely into his memory. He felt the burn of Beck's beard against his face and the bite of Beck's blunt nails digging into his arms and *fuck yes* Christian wanted to devour him. To wrap himself up in Beck. To taste him everywhere. To bury his dick in Beck's ass and feel the sweet burn of Beckett doing the same to him.

His cock hurt it was so fucking hard, ached. He rubbed his hand over Beck's erection. Ate the moan Beck let go into his mouth as he hungered to feel Beck's prick there, while he took him all the way to the back of his throat.

So he started kissing his way down, licked the Adam's apple he'd just been admiring a few days before. "Wondered what that tasted like," he whispered against Beck's skin.

Beck groaned, dug his fingers into Christian's arms again. He shoved his hands under Beck's shirt, pushed it up, wanting to feel his heat against him, wanting to lick and suck and trace every one of his muscles with his tongue.

Beck lifted his arms, and Christian shoved his shirt off. He sucked Beck's neck into his mouth, began kissing his way down Beck's chest, while letting his fingers make a path to the other man's shorts.

"I've been wondering for more than ten years what it would be like to have your dick in my mouth." Christian rubbed his hand over Beck's thick erection again, watched as he dropped his head back against the door and closed his eyes.

"Chris…"

He was breathless and Christian loved it. "Feels like a nice fucking cock, Beck. I'll take good care of you. I love giving head and I'm telling you now, I'm really fucking good at deep throating."

Beckett trembled, let out a stream of curses, but just as Christian was about to fall to his knees, he whispered…"Wait," then grabbed the hand Christian had on his prick and said, "fuck, I hate saying this but wait…"

Christian tensed—surprise, confusion and a little bit of hurt all swimming together in his brain.

"What about Quinn?" he asked.

Christian felt his own face scrunch up. "Huh?"

"I want you. Jesus, I want you so fucking bad, I feel like I'm going to lose my damn mind, but what about Quinn? I can't do this if you're with someone else."

He smiled. His pulse went a little crazy. "Honorable Beckett Monroe. I always loved that about you. Quinn is my friend—nothing more and he will always be that. He helped me adjust to living in LA. He will always mean the world to me, but we're not that way. I forgot I let you believe that."

"Oh…I thought when he answered your phone…"

"I won't lie. He stays at my place often. When he does, he sleeps in my bed, but it's not about sex and it's not my story to share."

Beckett gave him a small nod. Grabbed ahold of Christian's hips, as he looked down on him. He was a good three or four inches taller than Christian was. His tongue snuck out and traced his lips, a familiar spark of mischief in his dark, brown eyes. "Then get on your knees for me, Chris. You have no fucking clue how many times I dreamt about taking that sweet mouth of yours. Show me what you can do with it."

Christian grinned. "You'll lose your motherfucking mind."

"Cocky."

Christian palmed Beckett's dick. "You're one to talk."

And then he did as both he and Beck wanted. Christian went down on his knees for him. He shoved Beck's shorts down, and he stepped out of them. His dick sprung free—tall and hard, the head purple and leaking. It was everything Chris wanted it to be.

He rubbed his finger in the pre-come at the slit.

"Fuck…" Beck groaned out as he put a hand on the back of Christian's head. "Please…please, Chris. Need to feel you."

"You will. This moment has been a long time coming; let me

play, Beck." He palmed Beck's balls. They were heavy, full but hung low. He didn't know why but he'd always had a thing for low hangers. He was full of thick, pulsing veins. The hair around his prick just as dark as the black hair on his head and covering his jaw.

Christian leaned in, nuzzled him. Breathed in Beck's scent. The hand on the back of his head gripped him harder, pushed him closer until Christian could breathe nothing except Beckett's scent.

He let his tongue sneak out, lashed it across Beckett's sac, before he sucked one of his balls into his mouth.

"Oh fuck, Christian. Jesus, I hope I don't embarrass myself."

Christian smiled into Beck's crotch before he pulled back far enough so that he could look up at Beck, who stared down on him, as he ran his tongue from the base of Beckett's shaft to the tip.

The other man let out a guttural cry as Christian took him deep, worked Beck as far into this throat as he could.

"Yes...Chris, you feel so goddamn good."

Christian savored the taste of him, the scent of him, the feel of Beck's heavy cock in his mouth. He pleasured him as best he could, like his fucking life depended on it—alternating between sucking, licking, and swallowing around the fat head of his dick.

He wanted to taste him, wanted to swallow him down. Beck's hungry sounds got louder and louder. He pumped his hips and Christian took it, let the other man have his way with his mouth. Just when he thought Beck was going to let loose, he jerked out of Christian's mouth, pulled him to his feet and then lifted him in his arms.

Christian let him, wrapped his legs around Beck's hips as he made his way toward the hall.

"I'm not ready to come yet. I want your dick, too." And then his mouth crashed down on Christian's. He kissed the hell out of him as he walked them to his room. It was messy and frantic, filled with ten years' worth of hunger.

In the back of Christian's mind, he wondered if this would be enough to sate him...if this would be enough to sate either of them.

* * * *

There is no Quinn....Well, there was a Quinn but there wasn't a Christian and Quinn. That pleased Beckett probably more than it should. Still, as he squeezed Chris tight, as he savored the feel of him writhing against him as he devoured his mouth, he realized there was nothing he'd ever been more thankful for.

Chris wasn't with someone else.

And he wanted Beckett, at least right now he did.

When they got to his room, he went straight for the bed, lay Christian on his back off the edge, and went down on top of him. He rubbed himself against Chris's shorts. Wanted them gone but wanted to keep his possession of Chris's mouth too.

He'd wanted this for so long, wanted Christian for so long.

He nearly came when Christian's hands went to his ass, as he squeezed the globes to pull Beckett closer.

He wanted that too, wanted Chris inside him, wanted Chris to drive him out of his mind as he fucked him.

Beckett pulled back. "As much as I want to keep kissing you all night, this might end before we get to the good stuff if we don't hurry."

Christian chuckled as Beckett slid down his body. As he went down to the floor between Chris's legs. "Ass up." He swatted Christian's leg. He lifted himself and Beck pulled his shorts down, had to maneuver himself out of the way so he could get them free. Chris pulled off his shirt next and then Beck was there, kneeling as Christian sat on the bed, with his legs hanging over the side, his prick right there for Beckett to take.

"You're beautiful." He wasn't embarrassed by the awe in his own voice. Chris wasn't quite as long as he was, but he was thick—thick and swollen. Clear pre-come dripped from the slit and down his cockhead. His pubes were trimmed in a way Beck's weren't, light brown in color. His balls were tight, swollen.

"No need for the compliment. You already got me into bed."

"Hey, I've waited a long time for this."

"Are you going to continue it?" Chris asked and he was, he so fucking was.

Beckett immediately began to suck him off. The carpet rubbed against his knees. Christian's dick jerked in his mouth. He worked him as best he could. He let his tongue circle Christian's cockhead before he took him deep again, bobbed his head up and down in Christian's lap, loving his place here.

He held Christian's slender waist, heard him growl above him and Beck knew he was close. He was stuck between wanting to finish him off and having Chris inside him. "Fuck me," Beck said when he pulled off him. "Wanna feel you inside. Wanna feel you let loose inside me."

He was jerked toward the bed then. He felt like his muscles had turned to mush as he fell to the bed.

He lay on his stomach and then Chris was there, between his legs and kissing his neck. "Condoms and lube?" he asked before his teeth gently bit into Beckett's right shoulder.

"Bag by the bed."

"Thank God, I don't have to go far," he teased and Beckett smiled.

Christian leaned over the side of the bed. Beckett heard him rummage around in the bag he was also thankful he left there. Just a few seconds later, he rested between Beckett's spread legs. He trembled when Christian ran his hands over his globes.

"This ass, Beck. It's so fucking sexy. I can't wait to take it." He ran his finger down the crack and on reflex, Beckett undulated his hips. Jesus, his dick hurt so bad, but the friction of rubbing it against the bed helped.

"You're hungry for it, aren't you?" Christian asked as his finger slipped between his cheeks.

"I've been starving for a taste of your dick for ten years, Chris."

He wasn't sure if it was an admission he should have made because Christian went rigid over him. His finger stopped moving for one beat, two, and then…"Yeah, yeah me too."

Beckett heard the condom wrapper rip. Heard the bottle of lube open. He looked back, over his shoulder and watched Christian wet his finger. His heart jackhammered. His dick leaked all over the bed. He spread his legs wider, as Christian slipped a slick finger between his cheeks. "Such a tight little hole, Beckett."

He rubbed Beckett's pucker. He couldn't stop himself from thrusting, from fucking the bed and then his bones melted when Christian pushed a finger inside. He'd always been one for ass play. He'd let Christian play back there all night if he wanted, all damn day tomorrow too, but he also really, really wanted Chris's cock.

"I'm good. Christ, that feels fucking incredible, but I want more. Give me more, Chris."

Beckett didn't have to ask twice. Christian squirted more lube into his hand, and stroked it up and down his sheathed erection.

And then he lay down on his side, beside Beckett. Pulled Beck so he was on his side too, his back against Christian's chest.

Christian hooked his arm around Beckett's top leg, holding it up, opening him up so he could get inside. It was awkward but he was able to use his other hand to guide his prick, and then he was there, pressing against Beckett's hole and slowly easing his way inside.

There was a slight burn, a stretch—but it just made Beckett's dick get harder, made the need to come ratchet up to new heights. "Do it, Chris. Fuck me."

Christian kept going, worked his way inside until his pelvis was flat against Beckett's ass, buried as deep as he could go.

They were breathing heavily, their breaths alternating as they adjusted to the sensations that were no doubt wreaking havoc on both of them. At least Beckett knew they were turning him inside out and he hoped they were doing the same to Chris.

Christian pulled nearly all the way out, and then slammed forward again. He worked himself into a groove. Each time he thrust in, his dick rubbed against Beckett's prostate just how he liked.

"Oh fuck, Beck. Wanted this for so damn long. I don't know if I can last."

He liked hearing that, liked knowing he was driving Christian as wild as Christian drove him. Beckett wrapped a hand around his prick, held tight and started to jerk himself off as Christian railed into him from behind.

The whole bed shook. Pleasure shot through him with every pump of Christian's hips. When he turned his head so he could look up at Chris, he smashed his mouth down on Beckett's. Pushed his tongue into his mouth the same way his dick owned his body.

Beckett's balls drew tight. He couldn't hold himself back anymore, and he gave into the pleasure. His body felt like it broke apart, shattered into a million pieces as he shot, as he came all over his hand.

Christian kept going, kept slamming into him until Beckett felt him surrender. Lost his mouth as Christian pulled back and came, a loud roar in Beckett's ear before he dropped Beckett's leg and his arm came down, a heavy weight over him and his face buried in the back of Beckett's neck.

That wasn't enough. That wasn't nearly enough. Now that he'd had Chris, he wasn't sure if he could ever get enough of him.

The way Christian held him, Beckett wondered if he could possibly feel the same.

Chapter Ten

They slept together in Beckett's bed. At one point in the middle of the night they'd woken up, Christian had sucked him to a climax, while jerking himself off, and then they'd eaten half a bag of chips before passing out again.

Beckett couldn't remember when he'd felt happier...when he'd felt more like himself. Sure, he felt happiness and contentment every time he was on a bike but there was still a part of himself that he'd held back, a part that made it feel tinged with dishonesty.

When they woke up in the morning, he knew exactly what he wanted to do—what he might need to do with Christian before he left the following day.

He didn't know what would happen between them after Chris left. Beckett would be heading to Florida to train and Christian home to California, but he tried not to focus on that. Right now he just wanted to be in this moment with Chris.

Beckett ran a hand over Christian's short, dark-blond hair as he slept. Christian didn't move, didn't seem to notice him. He touched his collarbone next, ran his finger across it. Brushed his thumb over one of Christian's nipples and then the other one. He had such a beautiful body—lithe, with tight muscles beneath his pale skin.

Beckett felt this relentless need inside him for Christian that he couldn't dim. It kept getting hotter and hotter, brighter and brighter, even as he logically told himself not to rush, that there was so much on his plate right now.

But still, he just wanted Chris.

He couldn't stop himself from leaning forward, letting his tongue rasp over one of his nipples. Christian shifted so Beckett did it again, and pulled away just as Christian's eyes fluttered open, their blue irises on him.

"Wake up, sleepyhead," Beckett told him.

"Here I had my best night's rest in weeks and you decide to wake me up."

Beckett frowned at him. "I'm sorry."

"I'm giving you shit. You're horny. There's no need to apologize for that."

"That's not why I woke up. I mean, I am horny and I'm down for whatever you want to do, but I also have a request. I want you to go riding with me today."

Christian's eyes widened at that. "As in on a dirt bike? The last time I did that I was with you and we were eighteen years old. I might kill myself."

Beckett chuckled. "You won't."

"You'll feel guilty if I do."

"But you won't," Beckett told him. He didn't know why, but he really needed to do this. "Please? I'll do whatever you want...I'll suck your dick again."

"Yeah, but you'll do that anyway."

Christian was right about that. "Come on, Chris. It'll be fun. It'll be like old times." That, he realized, was why he needed to do it. To feel like they could go back before it all went to hell. Where there was no time, or betrayal or anger between them. When they could forget there was a world outside the two of them and just have fun together.

Beckett thought Christian might see it, see his need because he nodded his head. "Yeah, of course, I'll go riding with you."

Beckett smiled, kept his promise and sucked Christian off, and then they were on their way.

* * * *

Beckett had brought gear with him, because of course he would take motocross gear with him everywhere he went. But then, Christian couldn't really blame him since he'd taken his computer with him, too.

Christian on the other hand, didn't even own gear, so they'd had to make a quick trip to the motosports store. They'd gotten everything Christian needed to ride, found out about a quiet riding trail that wasn't too far from them, and were lent bikes from a contact that Bryce had. It was amazing how quickly things could be put together when your name was Beckett Monroe.

Before he knew it, they were pulling the truck Bryce had loaned them off a dirt road next to a trail that lead off through the grass and brush.

"I can't believe you're making me do this," Christian told him as they changed into their gear by the truck. Really though, he was excited about it. He'd never been half as good as Beck was on a bike, but he'd always loved riding with him—the loud, *braaaaap* of their bikes together as they flew through the dirt.

"You used to love riding. I can't believe you don't do it at all anymore."

Christian hesitated for only a second before he gave Beck a dose of honesty he wasn't so sure either of them were ready for. "I used to love riding with *you*. It wasn't as much the riding as being a part of…" He thought and then just went for it—*balls to the wall*. "I guess a part of your heart. It's always been made up of a four-stroke engine."

Beckett looked up at him as he was tucking his blue jersey into his moto pants. He was fucking gorgeous in his gear. There was something sexy as hell about the rough, blue pants and matching jersey. "You've always had a part of my heart, Chris. Always. Even when I fucked up. Even when we weren't talking, you were always there."

The truth was, there wasn't a part of Christian that doubted that. Maybe he had in anger when he was younger, or hell, maybe even a week ago, but he believed Beck. Trusted him. He couldn't deny the connection that had always been between them. Still, he teased, "Aww, stop before you make me blush."

"I'm serious."

Christian gave him a simple nod. "I know you are. And you know it's the same for me."

They stared at each other for a moment, the past blending with the present, binding them together in a way they'd likely always been, a way they'd likely always be. They couldn't lose each other again. Christian wouldn't allow it, and somehow he knew Beck wouldn't either. He didn't know in what capacity their relationship would be, but they would have one.

And then, before they ended up rolling around in the brush together, riding each other instead of the bikes, Christian changed the subject. "I forgot how uncomfortable all the gear is." He wore knee braces, pants, boots, a chest protector, neck brace, his jersey and still needed to add his gloves, goggles and helmet.

"You get used to it," Beck told him.

"Yeah, I know. I'm going to have to get another suitcase to put all of this in to take it home with me."

Beckett cocked his head slightly. "Are you going to ride when you get home?"

Christian winked at him. "Maybe."

"I'll come to California and drag your ass out there. You live in one of the best states for motocross. It's a crime you're not on the track."

"I guess you'll have to come out and make sure I'm out there then." He pulled his gloves on.

"Guess so," Beck replied and then ran a hand over the bike. "She's not a Yamaha, but she'll do. Do you need a crash course, or are you good?"

"I almost want to kick the shit out of you for that question." Did Beck really think he'd forgotten how to ride?

Beckett held up his hands. "Hey, I'm just asking. You're the one who said you might die out here."

"That's because I was in bed with a sexy man, sleepy and horny. At the time I just wanted to fuck, nap, and then fuck some more."

"Why did we come out here again?"

See? Now Beck saw his logic. "That's what I was wondering." But then, he shrugged and added, "I really do want to ride with you. We can get to the sex again later." Then he pulled the helmet over his head. Beck did the same. Once they each added their goggles, Christian kick-started a bike for the first time in ten years, next to the man who had been his best friend and first love.

The man he likely had never stopped loving.

"Let's do this!" Beck shouted at him. Christian nodded as if to tell him to go first. Their bikes made the familiar *braaap* that

Christian had heard so much in his life, and then Beck was off. Christian twisted the throttle and raced behind him like he'd done so many times before.

The wind rushed around them. Leaves flew as they raced through the brush. Beck was going easy, Christian knew that. He would have already left Christian in the dust if he rode the way he did in a race. He allowed Christian to pull up beside him. He glanced Beck's way just as he did the same and Christian had no doubt he was smiling behind his helmet.

The bike vibrated beneath him. He got it when he was out here, understood Beck's love and the freedom he felt. The rush of adrenaline that flooded his system was euphoric and he didn't have half of the love for it that Beckett did.

In this moment, the only thing that mattered was the two of them and the bikes beneath them. Hell, it felt like they were the only people in the whole fucking world.

Beckett and Christian, the way it was always supposed to be.

Chapter Eleven

They rode for most of the day. They took breaks back at the truck but then were back on their bikes again. Beckett enjoyed watching Chris ride—the set of his body and the way he automatically remembered to keep his elbows out. It was almost as if he'd picked up exactly where he'd left off.

The passion Beckett had always felt for riding burned through him, a wildfire he couldn't control but one he didn't want contained. It jumpstarted some of the emotions that had felt dormant inside of him for too long.

He remembered what it was like to feel alive.

He wanted to hold onto that feeling with everything he had, everything he was.

They leaned against the truck after their last moto. They were both sweaty and dirty. Christian breathed a little heavier than Beckett did, since he wasn't used to riding anymore. "It feels different to ride with you," he admitted.

Christian's brows pulled together. "Different than it used to?"

"No. Different from riding with anyone else. I'm just Beck when I ride with you. I missed it."

Christian's eyes lit with understanding. He wrapped an arm around Beckett's shoulders, pulled him close, and kissed his forehead. "Yeah, I missed it too."

It was as though the reality of their situation suddenly bore down on both of them. This trip was about fantasy. They would be both leaving that fantasy tomorrow to head back to reality. It was there waiting, the fact that they'd been separated for ten years, that they lived on opposite sides of the country, that Beck had come here because he'd faced an upheaval in his life, even if it was of his own making, that he had to deal with. It was easy to forget all of those things when they were together.

"What are we going to do?" Beckett asked him. "After tomorrow?"

Chris sighed. "I don't know, Beck. We have to be realistic. We've spent four days together in the last ten years. Our lives are completely different. You have a lot to deal with right now— getting ready for the outdoor season, not just being Supercross champion Beckett Monroe anymore, but Gay Supercross champion Beckett Monroe, because as shitty as it is, we both know that's who you'll be, at least for a little while." Christian was right about that. His sexuality would be an identifier now—and even though he was bi, it would be gay. That's just how everyone would see it.

"I think you need to focus on that reality right now before anything else," Chris added. "You have a big season coming up. I know you and I know you're going to want to do well because you consider coming in third as a failure when it's not. Your mind needs to be on motocross and getting comfortable with yourself."

Beckett had spent too many years lying. He wouldn't do that anymore. But he also knew Christian was right. "I don't want to lose you. I need you in my life."

"Shucks, I'm touched," Christian teased. When Beckett didn't laugh he nudged his elbow. "You won't, Beck. I'll always be your friend. We'll figure out the rest of it later—let's get you through the twelve weeks of outdoor season. I'm not going anywhere. Plus, no matter how we feel right now, it's been ten years, Beck."

Fuck. Beckett was tired of waiting. Tired of just letting things go, but he thought Christian was right. At least they were on the same page this time. He nodded.

"Last race of the season is at Glen Helen. Will you come?" Glen Helen was in San Bernardino County in Southern California. It would be close to a two-hour drive for Christian from LA, but he hoped like hell he could make it. Hoped Chris would make that commitment to him.

Christian turned and faced Beckett so his side was against the truck. He crossed his arms. "I have a confession to make."

Worry stabbed at his insides. "Yeah?"

"I watch you ride every time you're in Southern California, Beck—San Diego, Anaheim, Glen Helen." A chill of shock and satisfaction went up Beckett's spine as Christian continued. "When you're local I'm there and if you're not within driving distance, I watch you on TV. I always watch. Quinn thinks I'm obsessed."

Beckett nearly growled at the mention of Quinn's name. They might only be friends, but Quinn had him all this time when Beckett didn't.

"It's because of him that I'm here."

Beckett smiled. "I like him." But then, "You really watch me race?"

"Always."

He realized it then, as his pulse sped up and his chest felt full—he was still crazy in love with Christian and he always would be.

* * * *

It had taken them quite a while to get back to the rental by the time they'd returned the bikes, the truck, and grabbed some dinner.

When they'd gotten back to the cabin, Christian showered while Beck made phone calls to his trainer and team owner. He had no idea what they'd said. Beckett had seemed like everything was fine when Christian came out of the bathroom. He wanted to believe it was, that there would be no problems for Beckett, but sadly, you just never knew.

Beckett had been in the bathroom for the last forty minutes now, while Christian lay on the bed in his room, wearing nothing but a towel.

The second Beckett had called him, a part of Christian knew they would end up here—twisted together in their emotions and their realities. When he'd gotten on the plane, he'd confirmed it. He might not have admitted it, even to himself, but there had never been another option for him as far as Beck was concerned, and he knew that.

A sound came from the other room and Christian realized Beckett must be finished showering. He turned, got off the bed and headed for Beck's room. When he rounded the corner, he saw Beckett sitting on the edge of the bed, a towel wrapped around his waist just as Christian had. His dark hair glistened with wetness. Water dripped down the side of his face. Beckett lifted his right hand, and rubbed the dark beard on his face and then said, "Come here."

Christian went easily. He stopped in front of Beckett, who flicked at Christian's towel, making it open and fall to the floor.

Christian was already half hard, and Beckett wrapped his arms around Christian's waist, pulled him close. He leaned his head against Christian's stomach. Christian ran his fingers through Beck's hair. "Did everything go okay?" he asked.

"In the shower or on the phone?"

He rolled his eyes. "On the phone, smart-ass."

"It went fine. They assured me they don't give a fuck who I sleep with. We're a team and they need me to be a part of it. Yada yada. They said the same thing from the get-go. In reality, I know they mean it, but it's also just words. I should have been training this week. Everyone knows it. I think they're worried about my state of mind, but it's fine."

Christian hissed when he felt the warmth of Beck's hand cup his sac. His tongue darted out and licked the head of Christian's erection that had grown to full mast. "I'm not thinking about my team or even motocross right now. I'm thinking about you. Come here."

Beckett leaned back slightly. When he did his towel opened, revealing his prick, thick and long against his stomach. He still sat up as Christian did as he was asked. He straddled Beck's lap, wrapped his arms around Beckett's shoulders just as a pair of strong arms wrapped around him.

They moved, causing their cocks to rub against each other. Christian looked down; pre-come leaked from both of them—a beautiful fucking sight. He curled his hand around their swollen pricks and jerked them both, loving the feel of them together.

"Fuck," Beckett groaned into the space between Christian's neck and shoulder. "You drive me crazy, outta my fucking mind with how much I want you."

Then, they were kissing—teeth clanking, tongues gnashing, urgent, hungry, kissing.

Christian thrust against him as Beckett devoured his mouth. Both their dicks fucked into his hand but it wasn't enough. He wanted inside of Beckett or Beck inside of him. He pulled back, licked at Beck's mouth and asked, "What do you want?"

He rubbed a hand up Christian's back, grabbed onto his shoulder from behind. "You. Want you to fuck me until I can't move, until I can't see straight."

Christian trembled. His dick jerked, very much liking that idea. "Such a greedy little bottom. Who knew?"

It was then he realized a bottle of lube and a condom already sat on the bedside table. "I like a man who comes prepared."

"Then stop wasting time and get in me," Beck said before he swatted Christian's ass.

He laughed and then climbed off Beckett's lap. As Christian went for the bottle and the condom, Beck leaned back against the pillows, legs spread wide. "I could get used to this—your thick, muscular legs spread wide for me." He climbed between them and kneeled there.

"Don't think I won't want your ass too," Beck threw back at him and Christian's lust exploded to new heights.

"I'm counting on it...but for now"—he squirted lube onto his finger and then rubbed Beckett's rim—"such a sexy, fucking hole. I want inside it." He pushed his finger in, past the ring of muscle and watched Beckett's eyes roll back, as he arched up toward him.

Fuck, yes. He loved driving Beckett Monroe out of his damn mind.

Christian pushed his finger in deeper, rubbed Beck's prostate as he leaned forward and licked Beckett's nipples the way he'd done to Christian just that morning.

"Oh fuck, Chris. Yeah, right there."

He smiled around Beckett's small nipple. Thrust his prick against Beck's as he kept fingering his ass. "I'm going to want to stay in here all night, Beck—my finger, my cock, my tongue. Such a nice, fucking ass. I'm gonna live right here as long as I can."

He thrust his finger deeper. Beckett let out a guttural groan. "Let's get started with the dick, first. Jesus, I want you."

"Bossy motherfucker," Christian teased him even though he wanted that too. His cock ached, throbbed with the need to feel

Beck from the inside again. "Don't move." He pulled off of him.

"Who's the bossy motherfucker now?"

"Both of us," Christian winked at him. He ripped open the packet and rolled the condom down his prick, before lubing it up. He pushed Beck's hairy thighs toward him, making sure he was open. He was still in the same position, on his knees, between Beckett's legs, but he scooted closer, so the top of his thighs touched the back of Beck's.

He squirted lube onto Beckett's swollen erection, and Beck immediately started stroking it as Christian slowly worked his way inside Beck's hole. "Oh fuck," he shuddered. The head of Christian's dick was inside him, Beck's ass squeezing him, milking him. "Jesus, it's so goddamned tight inside of you. So fucking hot and tight." Yeah, he definitely wanted to spend his night here, playing with Beck's ass for as long as he could.

"Fuck me, Chris. Christ, get in me." He let go of his own cock to grab Christian's ass and pull him forward and then Christian was there, buried balls deep. They both breathed heavily. Christian pulled almost all the way out, before thrusting forward again.

"So good," Beckett rasped out. "So fucking good."

Christian pushed Beck's legs farther up, opened him more and held them there as he leaned forward and took Beck's mouth. His tongue made love to it the same way his dick made love to Beckett's body.

Beck held his ass. His fingers were calloused, rough pads against his skin.

He gave Beckett everything he had. Sweat ran down his forehead and onto Beck. Christian slid his hand between them, stroking Beckett's dick as he continued to make love to him.

He rolled their bodies, managing to keep himself inside of Beck as the other man ended up on top of him. From his position on his back, Christian grabbed Beckett's ass as Beck rode him. He moved expertly, rising up before lowering himself onto Christian's cock...the cock that was damn close to shooting.

"This has always been my fantasy," he admitted and Beck smiled down at him, obviously knowing exactly what he meant.

"To be taken for a ride by Beckett Monroe."

"No," Christian shook his head. "Just by Beck."

There was a spark in Beck's dark eyes telling him that was the right thing to say. Christian wrapped his hand around Beck's prick again, knowing that his own balls would let loose at any second. He jerked Beck three times before his hole clenched around Christian's dick and his cock spurted once, twice, two thick jets of come landing on Christian's stomach and running down his fingers as he continued to work Beckett's erection.

Then he felt his own balls draw up, felt them give into the pleasure as his hoarse voice called out in an orgasm of his own.

Beckett fell on top of him. Christian wrapped his arms around him, their bodies slick with sweat.

It took them a few minutes to catch their breaths and when they did, it was Beckett who spoke first. "You're mine now, Chris. Maybe we have to take things slow for a while, feel things out and figure out how we're going to do this, but we are going to do this. You're mine," he said again and Christian didn't argue.

Chapter Twelve

Beckett looked up at the sign his trainer held as he sped around the track. He was two seconds faster this round than he had been earlier today.

He wanted to be faster.

He leaned the bike into the turn, put his leg out as he took it and then twisted the throttle on the straightaway. His bike flew through the air at the jump.

His pulse went faster than his bike. His body felt amped up, but his mind was also at ease.

Beck felt a fire burning through him, one that hadn't fully ignited in years. He fed off of it, it pushed him, made him completely focus as his bike bounced over the whoops—he'd always loved racing over the small hills—and then he took up the speed again.

The passion he used to ride with reignited within him. Everything he loved about riding was intensified, an explosion inside of him. When he finished the last lap, and pulled up to his trainer, team and team owner as they watched on, he felt invincible.

As invincible as he felt, he knew there was a reason the Rush Racing team owner was here. The truth was, he couldn't find it in himself to worry. Not anymore. He was a Supercross champion. He was the fastest guy on his team, even if he hadn't ridden like it last season...and he was bisexual, and hoped to be in a relationship with a man. They would have to accept that.

"Christ, you're smoking out there, Monroe. You can tell you're really feeling it. That's the Beckett we know! Where was he hiding?" Bill, the team owner said as Beckett pulled his helmet off.

"Thank you. I feel better than I have in a long time, if I'm being honest. But I can be faster. I know it."

"If you were doing what you were doing while not feeling good," Bill said, "I sure as hell can't wait to see what you can do now."

The men all laughed, but Beckett just waited for him to get on with it. He wanted Bill to say whatever he'd come all the way out here to say.

As if he sensed that Beckett didn't want to beat around the bush forever, he said, "Listen, I just want you to know, you'll always have a place with Rush Racing. I know we said it before, but I want to reiterate. You're part of the team…of the family. That's all that matters, Beck. We take care of our own at Rush, and you're one of us."

"Agreed," his trainer, Dom, told him.

The three other members of the Rush Racing team chimed in around him.

Just like that, any residue of worry melted off of him. "Thank you. I appreciate it."

"It's sad that in this day and age, we even have to say that. Not quite sure how any of it has to do with how you race, but sports are funny like that." Bill shook his head. Unfortunately, it wasn't only sports where people felt that way.

"Thanks, man," Beckett said again. He probably should have realized he'd still been worried about it but he was likely in denial. He wasn't worried anymore.

Bill nodded. "I'll let you boys get back at it." And then he was gone and Beck wanted back out on his bike. Wanted to beat his last time, work out, and then head home so he could call Chris and tell him how his day had gone.

He wished like hell he could tell him in person.

* * * *

"Did he win yet?" Quinn asked Christian from the other side of the couch. Christian sat with his ass at the edge, leaning forward, his leg bouncing up and down.

"You look like you're going to try and jump through the TV.

Don't try and jump through the TV, please."

Christian looked over and rolled his eyes at his friend. "He crashed. Beck never crashes. That knocked him down to tenth place."

"But he's in sixth place now."

"I know he's in sixth! That's why I'm losing my fucking mind. Oh fuck! He just passed Edwards!" Christian shot off the couch as though that would help. "He just passed Edwards," he said again. "Now he's in fifth."

Christian kept his eyes glued to the television. His heart threatened to burst through his chest, it beat so damn hard. Beck would be devastated if he didn't at least get a podium today. He'd won the first three races of the season. He was the points leader. While not taking the first race today wouldn't be the end of the world, he would see it that way.

"Jesus, you're really in love with this guy."

Christian didn't turn away from the television when he said, "No shit."

"I knew it. I always have. It's just good to see you at peace with it."

And he was. He really was. They spoke every day. He felt like he was in a romance novel every time he saw Beck's name light up on his phone. It was ridiculous really, but he didn't care. It was as though he found a piece of himself he hadn't realized he'd needed so damn badly. He'd always known he missed Beck, that he cared for him, but having him in his life again felt like he'd been put back together when he hadn't known he'd been broken.

Not that he would tell Quinn all of that...but he also knew he had to tell Quinn something or the man wouldn't leave him alone.

"Being at peace with something or knowing it's true still isn't a guarantee, Quinn. You and I both know life doesn't always work that way. I want him. There's not a doubt in my mind he wants me."

"Cocky."

"Confident for good reason." He grinned at Quinn. "We have a lot to figure out. It's been pretty much an unspoken agreement that we don't make any decisions until after this season." It wasn't something they brought up when they talked, but that truth was always there on the line with them. "Now can we stop with the mushy shit? I'm trying to watch the race."

Quinn dropped against the back of the couch and laughed. "Sorry. Me man. Must watch race. Is that how I'm supposed to sound?"

He rolled his eyes and couldn't help but chuckle too.

"Oh shit. You're laughing. That means I need to work on being *masc*, right? Should I lower my voice?"

Christian sat back down onto the couch with his friend. He wanted Beck to meet him so badly. He was lucky to have both of them in his life. "No," Christian told him. "You're good the way you are. Now watch the fucking race before I kick you out. Holy fuck, he's in third! See what you made me miss?"

And then the two of them were both on edge, both cheering on Beckett Monroe as he did what he did best, and pulled out a win.

Chapter Thirteen

Beckett hated when they raced in Colorado. The elevation really got to him. It affected most of the riders who didn't grow up riding where the air was so much thinner.

He felt like shit. He'd taken second in the first race today and first place in the next one. He was still the man everyone was racing to catch, with a small points lead over Meyers. He felt like his old self out there and he loved it…but it was a long season, too. They were on their eighth race out of twelve. Eight weeks out of twelve and even though he'd gone ten years without seeing Christian, the last two months had felt like the longest of his life. It didn't matter that they talked every day. He needed to see him. To hold him. To claim him.

Those five days in Virginia had changed his life, but it was that logic that told him he needed to slow the hell down and not jump the gun. Five days. They'd spent five days together in ten years. They lived on opposite coasts.

Neither of those things seemed to matter when it came to Chris.

He rolled over in the hotel bed, and reached for his cell. The second he did, the damn thing rang like it could read his mind. Unfortunately, it wasn't Christian's name that showed up on the screen.

"Hey, Ma," Beckett said into his cell.

"How's your breathing? Was it bothering you up there today? Dad said he could tell you were struggling a little bit."

"Don't tell him that, Nansi!" his dad said in the background and Beckett smiled.

"Pick up the phone, Earl," she called back to him and he waited while they bickered—his mom wanting them both to talk and his dad making excuses why they shouldn't. His dad had never been a fan of them both being on the line at the same time but he usually did it. Beckett couldn't help but wonder if he wouldn't now because he still wasn't sure how to talk to him. As if he thought Beckett was suddenly a different man.

"Tell him I said to pick up," he told his mom. She paused for a moment, likely surprised, but then did as he asked.

"Beckett wants to speak to you, Earl."

There was a pause. The sound of a hand over the phone. And all he could do was close his eyes and shake his head. He'd always been close to his dad. He knew his dad loved him. It shouldn't be hard for him to speak to Beckett now.

A moment later, he heard the clatter of the other phone being picked up. They were the only people he knew who regularly used landlines outside of work. His dad was pretty anti-cell phone. He only had one because Beckett and his mom had forced it on him.

"So you could tell through the television that I was struggling, or what, old man?" Beckett teased, trying to break the ice. He wouldn't let things be awkward between them. He wanted to make sure his dad knew nothing had changed.

"Who you callin' old man?" his dad replied. "And I just know ya. That's all. You kept riding and you pulled out the win, though. That's all that matters."

"Agreed," Beckett told him and his mom gasped before speaking.

"That and the fact that he could breathe! Geez, I don't know how I made it raising you for twenty-eight years. You're going to give me a heart attack one of these days."

"What did I do?" Beckett asked and the three of them laughed. No matter what had happened in the past they were good parents and Beckett knew they loved him.

They spoke a little bit about the season so far. It felt like it used to when he talked to them—like his parents still felt like they knew who their son was and he didn't feel like his father was carefully navigating what he said so he could avoid the topic of Beckett's newly outed sexuality.

The league had been better than he'd expected when it came

to labeling him any time they spoke about his racing or standings. He didn't give a shit who knew anymore, he just didn't think it had anything to do with motocross.

But this? Talking to his family was different. He'd hidden Christian from them before and he didn't plan on doing it again. He always flew his parents out for the last race of every season and this year it would be in California. This year, Chris would be there with him.

"Christian is going to come to the final race at Glen Helen."

The line went quiet—the kind of quiet that slithered down his spine. It was of course, his mom who recovered first. "That's good. I'm glad to hear the two of you are talking again. His parents will be glad to hear it, too. It's a shame you boys got too busy to keep up your friendship. You know I've always liked Christian. Isn't that good, Earl?"

His dad cleared his throat. "Yes...yes, that's good. Are you sure it's a good idea for him to go to the final race? It won't distract you? Meyers is awfully close to you in points."

He could hear the change in tone of the conversation. Even through the line he felt the heaviness of it. "It'll be fine. He won't distract me. I want him there. I need him there. And we didn't lose touch with one another because we were too busy. I think both of you know that."

"What's between you and Christian is between you and Christian. You don't need to tell us about it," his dad blustered.

"Would you say that if I were talking to you about a woman?" Beckett asked. The silence on the line was the only reply he needed. "I'm not going to go into detail about my relationship or lack thereof with Chris...but it's important to me that you know I care about him...that I'd like to have a relationship with him. You're my parents and I love you. You both sacrificed so damn much for me. You would have given anything for me to have my dream. There's nothing I can do to repay you for that, but I'm asking you for something else too...I'd like your support in this. Not having it won't change who I am or what I do, but I love you, and I plan on being with Christian. I want your support."

And then, Beckett waited. He heard his mom's soft cries in the background, but it was his father who spoke first. "We will always support you in anything you do, Beck. I'm sorry if I led you to believe otherwise. All we've ever wanted is for you to be happy and if Christian makes you happy then you go for it, you make it happen like you've done with everything else in your life."

Those words were like salve to his heart. "Thank you," he whispered.

The truth was, Beckett wanted Christian, wanted him more than he'd ever wanted anything, more than motocross. It didn't matter where they lived or how they made it work, all he knew was one way or another, he would be with Christian.

Chapter Fourteen

"Christ, there are a lot of pretty boys here. Why didn't you tell me so many pretty boys like to play in the dirt?" Quinn asked Christian as they made their way through the pit. There were factory tents, signings, and other activities going on before the first races began.

The air was stifling hot as they were so far inland. It was dusty and barren with the constant buzz of bikes and people in the background. Christian had to admit, he loved it.

"Because you're obsessed with pretty boys," Christian told him. "And that always gets you into trouble."

"Pretty boys are obsessed with me. That's not my fault. And you're obsessed too. At least with one pretty boy."

He didn't bother to respond to that.

Christian had made sure they weren't around when Beckett was signing. He wanted to give him his space before the race, even though it had been twelve weeks since he'd seen him and it was killing him. He figured it might already be awkward for Beck with him here and he didn't want to make that worse. He probably shouldn't have taken Quinn with him because he had a habit of sticking his foot in his mouth but it was too late now.

"If we see Beck, don't piss me off."

"Come on, Christian. You know me better than that—oh shit. There's a fucking jersey with his name on it. Your boyfriend has a goddamn jersey with his name on it. I'm buying it."

"Oh fuck. I knew I shouldn't have brought you. The first race for the 250 class is about to start. Let's go watch."

They headed toward the area Beckett told him to go watch.

The bikes with 250 and 450cc engines had two, thirty-minute races each—plus two or three laps, depending on when the winner crossed the finish line. It might not seem like it but that was a long time when you were out there holding onto a bike that was bumping through a rutty track.

When they made it to where Beck told him to go, Christian realized a few things at once: The fucking podium was right there, as was the finish line, and the area was roped off. Security guards were at each of the four corners. He had no doubt the people behind that rope were friends and family of the racers.

All those things hit him before he saw Beckett's parents behind that very rope.

He stopped dead in his tracks, Quinn running into him from behind. "Oh fuck," Christian whispered. He didn't know why he was surprised, but he was. This was…this was a big fucking deal for Beck to have done. His chest immediately felt full while his stomach tied into knots.

"He's making it official, Christian."

"No shit."

"This is big."

"You think?" Christian asked.

"I do," he replied and Christian wanted to fucking kill him.

He also wasn't going to stand here all day. He wasn't sure exactly what Beck might have told them but it was obvious the people behind that rope had to be expecting him or Beckett wouldn't have told him to come over here. He knew Beckett's parents must know he was coming, even though he hadn't known about them. He might have to kill Beckett for that later. "Let's go," he said and then they made their way toward the roped off area.

When they got to the right corner where there was an opening and one of the security guards stood, he said, "My name is Christian Foster. Beckett Monroe told me to come over here to watch the race."

The man uncrossed his arms, looked at a clipboard in his hand and said, "Two?"

"That's me," Quinn piped up from beside him. The guard nodded, and unlatched the hook so they could pass. "Are your in-laws here?" Quinn whispered.

"They're not my in-laws, you bastard, but yes, they're here."

The announcer went on in the background as they made their way toward Nansi and Earl. There were oversized screens not only here but all throughout the track so they could see the whole course.

Just as he made it to them, Earl turned his way. Christian paused, but then the older man smiled. "Christian, you made it just in time. It's good to see you."

His overfilled lungs finally deflated.

"You didn't expect us?" Nansi said before pulling him into a hug. He should have. It made sense they would be here.

"No, I didn't…but it's good to see you."

She squeezed his hand. "It's good to see you too, Christian. I was so glad to hear you and Beckett reconnected."

Earl cleared his throat before saying, "We were both glad."

That was their blessing. It filled his chest to capacity. They knew he wanted to be with Beck, and they were okay with it. "Thank you."

He introduced them to Quinn before they settled in beside them.

People screamed and cheered. Drank beer and talked riders and the season, Beck's name popping up more than once.

It was surreal being on this side of it, being here as Beck's guest, when for years he'd watched from the outside.

Christian wanted nothing more than to see him race tonight. Wanted nothing more than to see Beck be the first man to cross the finish line, and win the motocross championship, because he knew that would happen. They'd dreamed about this when they were kids. Sure, this was nothing new for Beckett, but for Christian it was because now he felt a part of it. Now, it was the way they had always said it would be.

"Hey," Quinn nudged his elbow. "You good?" he asked softly.

"Yeah," Christian told him. "Yeah, I am." He felt incredible.

* * * *

"He got the holeshot. He got the fucking holeshot!" Christian threw a fist in the air and cheered. Quinn watched intensely beside him.

"That means he has the strongest start, right?" Quinn asked and Christian only nodded, unable to take his eyes away from Beck. He was out front, but Meyers was right behind him. He was second in points for the season and too close for comfort. Outdoors were Meyers's thing. He'd won the past few years because he excelled at it more than he did Supercross, but this year, this year was Beck's and Christian knew it.

His chest felt like it would burst open each time his heart pounded against it. He could hardly stay still as he watched Beck's bike bounce over the whoops. "I fucking hate those. It's hard as hell to hold onto the bike. Watch Beck though. He's fucking great at them," he told Quinn as Beckett sped over them like they were nothing, all fluid movement like he was one with the bike. He gained a few tenths of a second on Meyers.

His bike leaned as he cut a corner, making Christian hold his breath. He took a straight away before owning a double for his first trip around the track.

Meyers tried to get around him, tried to cut him off, but Beck held him off. "He wants Beck's line," he said to Quinn without looking his way. "Come on, come on, come on," he whispered as though Beck could hear him. "Keep your line, Monroe."

And Beck did. Over thirty minutes later, Beckett Monroe flew over the finish line, his bike and arms in the air as he took the first race of the day and everyone around them jumped and cheered.

Finally, Christian could breathe.

* * * *

Beckett sat in the tent, elbows on his thighs, looking down at the ground.

People moved all around him. His trainer went on and on about trying to get the inside line. He and Meyers were neck and neck. Beckett was ahead but just hardly. He had to finish better than Meyers to win.

"Beck. You hearing me?" Dom thumped him on the head.

"Yeah. Fuck. I'm concentrating."

"I know you are, but I need you to listen to me. The track is rutty as hell. It's gotten torn up since your lost moto. The whoops are a mess. How are your hands doing?"

"Fine," he shook off the question. He was lucky. He didn't have a problem with his hands like a lot of riders got.

"Good. All right, you gotta get your ass out there. Your head in it?" he asked.

"Fuck yeah." It was. The title was fucking his. He would make sure of it.

Beckett pushed to his feet and made his way to his bike and threw his leg over it to sit down. It was already running. They would have just started it for him so it could warm up.

He pulled his helmet on, then his goggles. Dom handed him his gloves and he pulled those on too, before making his way to the starting gate.

He felt like there was an earthquake going off inside of him—a constant shake that wouldn't go away. Having won the last race meant he'd gotten to pick his starting spot first, so he sat in his sweet spot, the bike vibrating beneath him as he waited for the gate to drop.

His eyes found their way to where Christian would be watching with his parents. He'd wished he'd been able to see him before the race. It likely would have calmed his nerves. He probably should have told Christian what he was doing but he'd wanted to keep it to himself. Hopefully, he enjoyed the surprise.

He made his eyes look to the front again. There was so much energy inside him he felt like he could burst open at the seams. This felt different than any other championship race he'd ever ridden in. Like the stakes were higher, like this was just the beginning to the next chapter of his life and he knew that had to do with Christian.

The gate dropped and Beckett twisted the throttle. *Holeshot. Just have to get the holeshot.*

He always saw a race in sections and not a whole. He had one race to win, then he'd move to the next.

His pulse jumped when he hit the corner first and started to pull out in front of the pack. The crowd cheered, then *ooohed* and he knew there was a crash behind him. After a while he'd learned to read the crowd. Some guys tuned them out, but for Beckett they were not only fuel, but extra eyes on the track.

His brains rattled when he went over the section of whoops. His bike jerked, shook as he sped over the rutty track. It wouldn't deter him though. He wouldn't let it.

As he stuck his leg out and leaned the bike to make a turn, he tossed a quick glance over his shoulder. Meyers was right on his ass and he wasn't surprised.

Just keep going. One lap down, now time for the next.

Beckett's tire hit a deep rut. He almost lost control of the bike but managed to keep it steady. It was just the mistake Meyers needed to pull in front of him.

Motherfucker.

Come on, come on, come on. Just get around him. Get around him and I'm good. That was the only race he was in right now, getting around Meyers. Once he accomplished that, he'd be going for the title again.

Meyers pulled farther ahead. As he made a turn, he glanced at the board held up for him. *One second. I got this. He's only one second ahead.*

Beckett twisted the throttle more. Leaned with the bike, stood as he went over a jump. Found the line he wanted as he passed a lapper, who rightfully moved out of his way.

He didn't ride the same line through the whoops this time.

He was closer to Meyers than he had been before. Mud shot onto his goggles and Beckett ripped one of the peel-aways off to clear his vision again.

He watched Meyers at the track. Studied them both. He stayed behind Meyers for three laps before the other rider changed his line. It was the mistake Beckett needed to shoot around him on a corner and then pull ahead.

Don't fuck up, don't fuck up, don't fuck up.

All it would take was one slip-up for Meyers to be in front of him again.

The longer the race went, the lighter Beckett's body felt until it was almost like he was part of the bike. They moved together, worked together as he saw a sign that told him he was now a little over a second ahead of Meyers.

The other rider didn't let up. He gave Beckett competition until the end. He could have lost it at any second. His brain told him that over and over again until he took that last jump, flew through the air and over the finish line.

Yes! He'd done it. He'd fucking done it.

He couldn't wait to share it with Chris.

The second his bike pulled to a stop, his trainer nearly tackled him. His owner cheered. People grabbed at him, hugged him, screamed for him until he felt dizzy.

Where was Christian? He just wanted to share this moment with Christian.

He was suddenly off his bike, but he didn't know how or when it had happened. His helmet was off too. The crew tossed an energy drink at him—one he was supposed to hold when he went to the podium.

People were pulling on him, leading him to the podium while his eyes frantically darted around.

The second he was pulled onto the stage there was a woman and a microphone in his face. His owner was right beside the stage, his trainer too, the whole fucking crew. His mom was there. She was crying and so was his dad. Still, he kept scanning the crowd. Where was Christian? He had to have come. He wouldn't have left Beck like this.

"How does it feel to be the AMA champion?" the woman holding the microphone asked him.

Beckett opened his mouth, not sure what he would say until the words came out. "Good, I think. Right now...right now I just really want to know where my boyfriend is."

The reporter chuckled, with a friendly smile on her face. It was the first time he'd acknowledged his relationship status—the first time he'd confirmed that he was indeed attracted to men on camera. "Well, I'm sure he's going to be happy to hear that the first words out of your mouth after winning the championship were about him!"

It was all about him. This moment was more real because of him. His whole fucking life was.

That's when Beckett saw him. Chris stepped up beside Beckett's parents, the sun glinting off his too-blue eyes. He smiled at Beckett and it damn near stole his breath. Jesus, he loved this man. Wanted to spend every moment of the rest of his life loving him. A grin split Beckett's face.

Christian nodded as if to tell him to continue.

"I just…I want to thank my team—Rush Racing. My trainer, Dom. Everyone who's stuck by me. My mom and dad, friends, the fans I…" He made eye contact with Christian again, Chris's eyes firmly on him, just as Beckett was handed the flag. He couldn't believe he was standing here with Christian in front of him. "And Chris…thank you for giving me a second chance. Thank you for loving me. For giving me the jumpstart I needed, without even realizing you were doing it." He'd won titles before and while they all meant something to him, none of them meant what this one did. Motocross was his dream, his career, his passion, one of his loves, but he hadn't been fully living, not before he was honest about who he was, not before he had Christian back.

"Thank you," Beckett told the reporter. "Thank you all," and then he stepped down from the stage and went straight for Chris. He wrapped his arms around Christian's waist, pulled him into his arms, as Christian's went just as tightly around him.

"We did it. We fucking did it, Chris," he whispered into the other man's ear.

"I'm pretty sure you did it," he replied, but Beckett knew Christian got what he really meant.

"I thought these twelve weeks would kill me." He kissed Christian's forehead. Rubbed his face into Christian's neck. "I'm so fucking in love with you. I don't want to be without you anymore. I don't care where we live or how we make it work, just promise me we're going to make it work, Christian."

"Yeah, you know we will. We'll make it work. I love you too, Beck. You know I've always loved you."

He let out a sigh of relief, just having needed to hear the words.

The space around them got tighter and tighter. More people filled around—laughing, talking, congratulating until they had no choice but to pull apart. When they did, Beckett saw his parents standing there…and it was his dad who hugged him first.

"I'm so damn proud of you, Beckett."

There was no question in his mind that his dad wasn't talking about the championship, but Christian.

"Thank you, Dad."

His mom pulled him into a hug next. "I love you," she said

through her tears. He consoled her, told her he loved her too.

From there it was interviews and more congratulations. He got to meet the infamous Quinn, who made them all laugh, and also happened to be wearing a Monroe jersey.

Beckett soaked every moment of it in, lived it, breathed it, the way life was supposed to be, the moment made even sweeter because he had the man he loved by his side.

Epilogue

Beckett set the last tray of dip on the table before the doorbell rang.

"I got it," Chris called from the other room. It was a cool November day in Virginia and they were expecting their friends to come over to see their place. They'd decided to get a small house in Virginia. It wasn't where they would live most of the year. It just wasn't feasible. Christian loved California and worked there. It made the most sense to spend the majority of their time in California since Beck could train there as well. Still, they'd wanted somewhere else that could be theirs. A place to go in the off season, for vacation, or just for much needed rest and relaxation and this seemed like the best spot.

He only had a year left on his contract and who knew what would happen after that? Maybe he would sign another one. Maybe he'd stop racing and take up training, which honestly was the most likely answer. He could help another kid who loved racing as much as he did. The only thing he did know was whatever he did, he would do it with Chris by his side. Nothing would ever come between them again.

Beckett looked over as Chris opened the door. On the small porch stood Landon, Rod, Drew, Justin, Nick and Bryce. Their friends.

"Hey, thanks for having us," Landon told Chris as he walked inside, followed by a trail of men behind him. He was pretty sure they might be in the gayest town in Virginia and he fucking loved it.

"I brought some food." Nick held up a pan, the light

reflecting off the gold engagement band on his finger. Bryce had proposed to him a few weeks before. Landon had said it was pretty incredible. Beckett and Christian hadn't been back yet so they'd missed it.

"Thanks." Beckett walked over and took the dish from Nick. He wanted his ring on Christian's hand as well, and it would be one day. There was no doubt about that. Right now they were just living, though. Enjoying life and loving each other. The rest would come.

"Am I going to see you tomorrow?" Drew asked Beckett.

"Absolutely." He was going to teach Drew some of the workouts he used while training. The man was always looking for something new to do.

"Are you coming with him?" he asked Chris, who shook his head.

"No. I have a conference call with Quinn and I need to get some work done." He was only working part time with Quinn at the moment but he was also able to do some other contracted work. The spare room was set up as an office so Chris could still work when he was away from LA.

Their lives would be hectic for a while, filled with a whole hell of a lot of traveling, but they'd make it work.

They had a great evening with their friends. Beckett couldn't remember ever laughing as much as he did with this crew together. How could you not with Bryce and Rod in one place? They talked about Rod's store which was thriving and Justin's plans after graduation. Nick's hopeful remodel of the restaurant, and an upcoming weekend spent with his nieces and nephews.

He realized the people in this room were all a family, and they'd invited him and Christian into it.

He was happier than he'd ever been. Despite how hectic their lives were, he was more stable than he'd ever been too.

This was the life he'd always wanted. He had his dream, yes, but he had more than that. He had a world outside of motocross, which was what he'd been lacking before he made the call that had brought Chris into his life again.

They had a good visit with their friends for a few hours, before everyone started packing up to head home.

He and Chris cleaned up and then headed to bed for the

evening. The next day, he spent a few hours at the gym with Drew, before he stopped off at the store because Christian called him asking for eggnog. He hated the shit but he remembered back from when he and Chris were kids, he'd always drank it around this time of the year.

As he browsed the aisles for his spoiled boyfriend's treat, he heard, "If it isn't Beckett Monroe," come from behind him. At first he froze up. It wasn't often that he was recognized, but then the voice struck a chord with him from a day on a plane when his life had been so fucking up in the air.

"Margaret." He turned to look at the older woman. He'd wondered about her more than once over the months. Had wished he'd gotten her phone number rather than just giving her his.

He'd wanted to check on her, wanted to make sure she was okay...but he'd also wanted her to know—"You fixed your broken heart," she told him without Beckett having to say it.

"I did."

"I saw it on the TV." She smiled at him. "But even if I hadn't, all it would have taken was one look at you to know it. Congratulations."

"Thank you," he told her, pulling her in for a hug. She returned it, her shaky arms going around him. "Do you live around here?" he asked her. "I wondered about you."

She pulled away, a sadness in her eyes. "No. My Lizzy is buried in town, though. I come to see her often...the way I should have done when she was alive."

He closed his eyes. He'd always wondered if that was the case. If she'd lost the woman she loved...if she had regrets the same way he used to have when it came to Chris.

"It was a long time ago. I married. Had kids. Lived a happy life. It's hard to have regrets about her, when so many of the things I have now wouldn't be in my life if I'd been able to keep her."

He understood that. He didn't know if his life would have been any different if he'd admitted to his family he loved Chris when he was eighteen. Maybe he wouldn't have had his dreams come true. Maybe he would have. Or maybe he and Christian would have just accomplished different dreams together. All he knew was he felt damn lucky to have him now, and he wished there had been a way Margaret could have had everything she did now, and still have Lizzy.

"You can have everything in the world and still have a broken heart. You can still be happy and have your dreams but still wonder, *What if*...I'm glad you don't have to wonder *What if* anymore, Beckett Monroe. I wasn't brave enough to go for mine while Lizzy was still alive and now it's too late. I'm doing my best to make it up to her now."

He couldn't help but pull her into another hug. He held her too long, too tight. When they parted, he invited her for dinner, but she declined. He asked her to please keep in touch, but he didn't know if she would.

He thought about her the whole way back home to Christian. When he got there, he filled a glass of eggnog and took it to Chris in his office.

"What's wrong?" Christian asked the second he laid eyes on him.

So he told him—told him about Margaret and their flight. How she told him to fix his broken heart and he had. He then told Christian about seeing her tonight, and about Lizzy.

As soon as he finished his story, Chris pushed to his feet and walked over to him. "You and that big, fucking heart of yours." And then he kissed him. It was a slow kiss, full of love, of life, of possibilities and their future.

"I love you," Beckett told him, so fucking thankful to have Chris in his life again.

"I love you too."

"Hey...I always wanted to ask you, what was in that letter back then? The one you wrote when we were kids?"

Christian's eyes darted away, and he actually looked embarrassed. "This...I just talked about this...having you. Being with you one day. Knowing you would always be mine. Wanting to spend my life with you. All that sappy shit."

Beckett would never get tired of hearing things like that. "You're stuck with me now. You're never getting rid of me."

"Don't want to." He nodded toward the door. "Come on. I kind of want to fuck you now."

Beck couldn't help but laugh. "What about your eggnog? I

went all the way to the store to get it for you."

Christian took a sip of the drink. "I know. Now it's my turn to thank you for it." He winked at Beckett and then it was Beckett dragging Christian to their room, and Beckett who worshiped Chris's body, the way he planned to do every day for the rest of his life.

THE END

About the Author:

Riley Hart is the girl who wears her heart on her sleeve. She's a hopeless romantic. A lover of sexy stories, passionate men, and writing about all the trouble they can get into together. If she's not writing, you'll probably find her reading.

Riley lives in California with her awesome family, who she is thankful for every day.

Other books by Riley Hart:

Weight of the World

Crossroads Series:
Crossroads
Shifting Gears
Test Drive

Rock Solid Construction series:
Rock Solid

Broken Pieces series:
Broken Pieces
Full Circle
Losing Control

Blackcreek series:
Collide
Stay
Pretend
Return to Blackcreek

Sign up for the 1001 Dark Nights Newsletter
and be entered to win a Tiffany Key necklace.

There's a contest every month!

Go to www.1001DarkNights.com to subscribe.

As a bonus, all subscribers will receive a free
1001 Dark Nights story
The First Night
by Lexi Blake & M.J. Rose

Turn the page for a full list of the
1001 Dark Nights fabulous novellas...

Discover 1001 Dark Nights Collection One

FOREVER WICKED by Shayla Black
CRIMSON TWILIGHT by Heather Graham
CAPTURED IN SURRENDER by Liliana Hart
SILENT BITE: A SCANGUARDS WEDDING by Tina Folsom
DUNGEON GAMES by Lexi Blake
AZAGOTH by Larissa Ione
NEED YOU NOW by Lisa Renee Jones
SHOW ME, BABY by Cherise Sinclair
ROPED IN by Lorelei James
TEMPTED BY MIDNIGHT by Lara Adrian
THE FLAME by Christopher Rice
CARESS OF DARKNESS by Julie Kenner

Also from 1001 Dark Nights

TAME ME by J. Kenner

For more information, visit www.1001DarkNights.com.

Discover 1001 Dark Nights Collection Two

WICKED WOLF by Carrie Ann Ryan
WHEN IRISH EYES ARE HAUNTING by Heather Graham
EASY WITH YOU by Kristen Proby
MASTER OF FREEDOM by Cherise Sinclair
CARESS OF PLEASURE by Julie Kenner
ADORED by Lexi Blake
HADES by Larissa Ione
RAVAGED by Elisabeth Naughton
DREAM OF YOU by Jennifer L. Armentrout
STRIPPED DOWN by Lorelei James
RAGE/KILLIAN by Alexandra Ivy/Laura Wright
DRAGON KING by Donna Grant
PURE WICKED by Shayla Black
HARD AS STEEL by Laura Kaye
STROKE OF MIDNIGHT by Lara Adrian
ALL HALLOWS EVE by Heather Graham
KISS THE FLAME by Christopher Rice
DARING HER LOVE by Melissa Foster
TEASED by Rebecca Zanetti
THE PROMISE OF SURRENDER by Liliana Hart

Also from 1001 Dark Nights

THE SURRENDER GATE By Christopher Rice
SERVICING THE TARGET By Cherise Sinclair

For more information, visit www.1001DarkNights.com.

Discover 1001 Dark Nights Collection Three

HIDDEN INK by Carrie Ann Ryan
A Montgomery Ink Novella

BLOOD ON THE BAYOU by Heather Graham
A Cafferty & Quinn Novella

SEARCHING FOR MINE by Jennifer Probst
A Searching For Novella

DANCE OF DESIRE by Christopher Rice

ROUGH RHYTHM by Tessa Bailey
A Made In Jersey Novella

DEVOTED by Lexi Blake
A Masters and Mercenaries Novella

Z by Larissa Ione
A Demonica Underworld Novella

FALLING UNDER YOU by Laurelin Paige
A Fixed Trilogy Novella

EASY FOR KEEPS by Kristen Proby
A Boudreaux Novella

UNCHAINED by Elisabeth Naughton
An Eternal Guardians Novella

HARD TO SERVE by Laura Kaye
A Hard Ink Novella

DRAGON FEVER by Donna Grant
A Dark Kings Novella

KAYDEN/SIMON by Alexandra Ivy/Laura Wright
A Bayou Heat Novella

STRUNG UP by Lorelei James
A Blacktop Cowboys® Novella

MIDNIGHT UNTAMED by Lara Adrian
A Midnight Breed Novella

TRICKED by Rebecca Zanetti
A Dark Protectors Novella

DIRTY WICKED by Shayla Black
A Wicked Lovers Novella

THE ONLY ONE by Lauren Blakely
A One Love Novella

SWEET SURRENDER by Liliana Hart
A MacKenzie Family Novella

For more information, visit www.1001DarkNights.com.

On behalf of 1001 Dark Nights,

Liz Berry and M.J. Rose would like to thank ~

Steve Berry
Doug Scofield
Kim Guidroz
Jillian Stein
InkSlinger PR
Dan Slater
Asha Hossain
Chris Graham
Pamela Jamison
Jessica Johns
Dylan Stockton
Richard Blake
BookTrib After Dark
The Dinner Party Show
and Simon Lipskar

86031478R00421

Made in the USA
Columbia, SC
23 December 2017